# MAFIOSO

---

### BOOKS ONE TO THREE IN THE ITALIAN CARTEL

### SHANDI BOYES

# COPYRIGHT

Copyright © 2021 by Shandi Boyes

Model: Jonny James
Photographer: Kruse Images & Photography
Cover: SSB Covers and Design
Editing: Nicky @ Swish Editing and Design
Beta: Carolyn Wallace
Proof Reading: Kaylene @ Swish Editing and Design
Writing: Shandi Boyes

# WANT TO STAY IN TOUCH?

Facebook: facebook.com/authorshandi

Instagram: instagram.com/authorshandi

Email: authorshandi@gmail.com

Reader's Group: bit.ly/ShandiBookBabes

Website: authorshandi.com

Newsletter: https://www.subscribepage.com/AuthorShandi

# ALSO BY SHANDI BOYES

### Perception Series

Saving Noah (Noah & Emily)

Fighting Jacob (Jacob & Lola)

Taming Nick (Nick & Jenni)

Redeeming Slater (Slater and Kylie)

Saving Emily (Noah & Emily - Novella)

Wrapped Up with Rise Up (Perception Novella - should be read after the Bound Series)

### Enigma

Enigma (Isaac & Isabelle #1)

Unraveling an Enigma (Isaac & Isabelle #2)

Enigma The Mystery Unmasked (Isaac & Isabelle #3)

Enigma: The Final Chapter (Isaac & Isabelle #4)

Beneath The Secrets (Hugo & Ava #1)

Beneath The Sheets(Hugo & Ava #2)

Spy Thy Neighbor (Hunter & Paige) **Standalone**

The Opposite Effect (Brax & Clara) **Standalone**

I Married a Mob Boss(Rico & Blaire) **Standalone**

Second Shot(Hawke & Gemma) **Standalone**

The Way We Are(Ryan & Savannah #1)

The Way We Were(Ryan & Savannah #2)

Sugar and Spice (Cormack & Harlow) **Standalone**

Lady In Waiting (Regan & Alex #1)

Man in Queue (Regan & Alex #2)

Couple on Hold(Regan & Alex #3)

Enigma: The Wedding (Isaac and Isabelle)

Silent Vigilante (Brandon and Melody #1)

Hushed Guardian (Brandon & Melody #2)

Quiet Protector (Brandon & Melody #3)

## Bound Series

Chains (Marcus & Cleo #1)

Links(Marcus & Cleo #2)

Bound(Marcus & Cleo #3)

Restrain(Marcus & Cleo #4)

Psycho (Dexter & ??)

## Russian Mob Chronicles

Nikolai: A Mafia Prince Romance (Nikolai & Justine #1)

Nikolai: Taking Back What's Mine (Nikolai & Justine #2)

Nikolai: What's Left of Me(Nikolai & Justine #3)

Nikolai: Mine to Protect(Nikolai & Justine #4)

Asher: My Russian Revenge (Asher & Zariah)

Nikolai: Through the Devil's Eyes(Nikolai & Justine #5)

Trey (Trey & K)

K: A Trey Sequel

## The Italian Cartel

Dimitri

Roxanne

Reign

Mafia Ties (Novella)

Maddox

Demi

Ox

Rocco

Clover

Smith

CJ

## RomCom Standalones

Just Playin' (Elvis & Willow)

Ain't Happenin' (Lorenzo & Skylar)

The Drop Zone (Colby & Jamie)

Very Unlikely (Brand New Couple)

## Short Stories

Christmas Trio (Wesley, Andrew & Mallory -- short story)

Falling For A Stranger (Short Story)

## Coming Soon

Skitzo

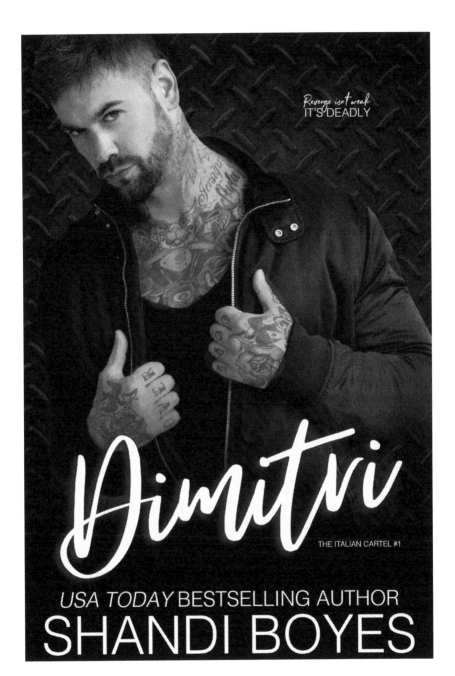

Revenge isn't weak
IT'S DEADLY

# Dimitri

THE ITALIAN CARTEL #1

USA TODAY BESTSELLING AUTHOR
# SHANDI BOYES

*There's a moment in fighting when strength of muscle ain't everything because the enemy has already given you enough energy to gain the victory.*

— *Toba Beta*

# PROLOGUE

## DIMITRI

While cracking my knuckles, I peer out a window spanning one wall of my suite. Cabs honk, commuters pepper the sidewalks clouded by ominous skyscrapers blocking out the sun, and pompous pricks in Tom Ford suits weave in and out of buildings similar to the one I'm stationed in, unaware their existence doesn't depend on the digits in their bank accounts or the nine-to-five investment banking job their daddies secured them straight out of college. It's wholly dependent on the men who built this city from the ground up.

I don't care what you say, New York was built by the Cartel. The Italians, the Greeks, hell, even the Albanians had a hand in making this what it is. Blood, sweat, and tears went into every skyscraper—literally. More bodies are buried under the buildings surrounding my hotel than my hotel caters for guests each night.

Before the assassination of the boss of all bosses in 1973, every inch of this godforsaken town was the territory of the Italian Cartel. If you worked here, we ran your union. If you lived here, you were living in an apartment built by my ancestors.

If you ran drugs here without permission, you were a dead man.

Nothing happened here without the Lucianos, Gambinos, and Petrettis knowing about it. They were the governors of this realm and feared more than they were respected. It was the golden era to be a member of a criminal association, a time I'd give anything to go back to.

Alas, all good things must come to an end.

If that ending had been because of criminal prosecution, I would have a different viewpoint of my family's demise. Regretfully, that isn't close to the truth. The three families mentioned above operated as one unit. The Lucianos controlled Queens, Staten Island, Brooklyn, and Long Island. The Gambinos influenced the Bronx, New Jersey, and Connecticut regions, and the Petrettis had a stronghold on Manhattan, New York City, Westchester County, and parts of Florida.

Between 1889 and 1953, these sanctions were untouchable. Law couldn't catch them, rivals couldn't compete with them, and money, drugs, and guns were in abundance.

It all went downhill when Bria Petretti and Eleonora Gambino birthed sons only a month apart.

If they had followed in their fathers' footsteps by forging a mutually respected relationship, my grandfather, Giulio Petretti, III, and his best mate, Benito Gambino, were set to become the next boss of all bosses. They worked hard for their greater families, and the Lucianos didn't have a suitable candidate, so originating a dual-leadership was the fairest option.

However, as I said earlier, all good things must come to an end.

My father, Col, and Benito's son, Matteo, didn't have the comradery their fathers had. They hated each other. Women, wayward drug shipments, even the sizes of their cocks were constantly bickered about. They didn't want to be the boss of the bosses. They wanted to be *the* boss—point-blank. And that's precisely what happened when one of my father's coked-up friends decided he needed some extra coin he wasn't willing to work for.

Theft never ends well in this industry. If you cross the Cartel, you die. Can't explain it any simpler than that. Regardless, your family, friends, and children are supposed to go unharmed.

My father couldn't let bygones be bygones. He was only sixteen when Leone was taken out to The Hole, a grisly dumping ground regularly used back in the day, but he massacred the people he believed responsible for his death like the repercussions of his actions wouldn't have blow on effects for decades to come.

He should have been dead. The penalty for killing a son of a prominent family member always results in the death of both the person responsible and the hierarchy of his realm. However, my grandfather fell on the knife on the agreement his son would be spared.

His negotiations were unheard of at the time. I doubt they would have been considered if it weren't for the friendship he had with Giulio. My father forgot centuries-long relations in an instant. Giulio couldn't. He didn't want to kill his best friend, but he had no choice. He had lost a son. His death needed to be avenged.

The story of my family's demise grows weary from that point. Some say my father was removed from all Cartel activities and left to fend for himself. Others say he was gifted the Florida chapter with the hopes he'd eventually straighten his life out and resurrect our family name from the grave.

I say they should have killed him instead of my grandfather. That would mean I wouldn't be here, but then I also wouldn't be twiddling my thumbs in a hotel room, waiting for word on if the ransom I paid for my pregnant wife has been received. My family name is tainted with so much disrespect, my rivals think I'm a schmuck to be messed with.

That is also far from the truth.

Rimi Castro, leader of a subsidiary criminal entity that branched off the Gambinos two decades ago, was smart when he requested a third-party drop off the 3.8 million-dollar ransom he demanded for the safe return of Audrey. I would have tortured him until he told me where she is, then I would have killed every member of his crew to show him I'm nothing like my father.

You don't mess with me and expect to live. I have all the markings of my father. I'm a merciless, heartless motherfucker who kills before thinking. Audrey chipped away some of the decay the past ten months, but it will never be entirely gone. You can untwist the ugliest wreck, however no amount of straightening will smother scars hidden deep within. They're more hideous than the ones our bodies wear and take longer than a lifetime to fix.

I learned that the hard way almost a decade ago.

Rimi will learn it tonight.

I still can't understand how he got the upper hand on me. I'm cautious about everything I do, untrusting of anyone, most notably those who share my lineage. My marriage is unknown, the baby growing in my wife's stomach hasn't been publicly acknowledged even with our daughter being due in a little over four weeks. I don't even live in the same state as my wife for fuck's sake, yet, she still got snared by a life someone as pure as her should have never been invited into.

I'll be sure to fix the injustice once she and our daughter are returned safely. It won't be just the Castros feeling the sting of my wrath, though. It'll be the industry as a whole. An unspoken rule was broken earlier this week.

*Famiglia prima di tutto.* Family first of all.

Audrey may be excluded from that motto, but our daughter

most certainly isn't. She's mafia royalty and will be protected accordingly.

When the beep of an electronic lock sounds through my ears, I spin to face the entryway of my room. The knot in my gut takes on a new meaning when Clover enters the opulent space with the ransom bag he left with. It's noticeably slimmer, but still, why wouldn't Rimi's men take it with them?

I scoff when Clover pushes out, "They checked the bundles for bugs." His voice is rough with an Arabian accent. He isn't called Clover because he shines luck down on anyone who locates him in a patch of weeds, it's because you'll be wishing for a lucky charm when he enters your life. The chances of escaping him are similar odds to finding a four-leaf clover in a patch of an over-worked field. Basically nonexistent. If he doesn't kill you before you spot the clover tattoo on his cheek, you'll beg for a weapon to kill yourself.

Mercy isn't something Clover often gives. It's why I sent him to do the drop. If I couldn't do it, he was the next best choice. Clover is a hired hitman. He has worked for my family on many occasions, and usually gets the job done without the slightest bow to his brow.

He isn't giving me that vibe today. He looks a little undone, like his wish to kill isn't as strong as mine. I get he's a killer in every sense of the word, but we have to play the game as Rimi is requesting.

Once Audrey is returned, all bets will be off.

My decision has nothing to do with money. Despite my father's many fuck-ups, I have plenty of it. The wholesale price in the industry is ten percent of its street value. There's money to be made if you're willing to get your hands dirty, but that isn't what this is about. It's the principle. If I let Rimi play me for a fool, I'll take it up the ass from my competitors even more than my father has the past fifty-plus years.

My family name might not be what it once was, but it will take more than a weasel of a man like Rimi Castro to have me cowering from a fight. The older generation started the war, but it's the younger generation fighting their battles.

I don't mind. I was born to fight, and fight I will.

I battle to keep my anger on the down-low but fail when Clover places the ransom bag onto the entryway table. It's brimming with the bundles of cash I withdrew at multiple locations earlier this week. I know federal agents are watching every deposit and withdrawal from my account, so I kept the transactions below ten thousand to ward off suspicion.

"Where's Audrey?" Nothing but desperation is heard in my voice. Clover follows orders. He's paid to do precisely that, so why the fuck did he go off script today? His facial expression reveals he drew blood, his itch to kill has been satisfied. That can only mean one thing—he went against direct orders. "You were to hand over the money, get Audrey out, *then* we were to make our move."

"Plans changed when they handed me this." He tosses a USB stick onto the round table housing a vase of Audrey's favorite flowers. India, Audrey's neighbor/best friend, thought they'd lessen Audrey's anxiety once she was freed from captivity. She's been at the mercy of a rogue crew for five days. If a hundred-dollar bunch of flowers would weaken the clutch they had on her, I was open to the suggestion.

"It was supposed to tell me Audrey's location." Clover locks his eyes with mine. They're deadlier than ever. "It was nothing but a snuff film. Those fuckers are playing games, so I played back."

I'm not surprised to spot a number of dismembered fingers when he yanks open the ransom bag. Clover's proof of deaths always arrives with some sort of body part. "I got a majority of your money back, but a few bundles fell through the cracks."

Falling through the cracks means he used the money to find marks. It isn't a negotiation tactic he often uses, so the fact he needed it tonight exposes how dire things are.

After finding the object he's seeking in the bag, Clover hands it to me. He doesn't speak any words, he doesn't need to. I recognize the ring on the mutilated index finger in my hand. It's the same one in the bottom right-hand corner of the photo couriered to my office last week. That's how we unearthed Audrey's kidnappers' identity. All Castro 'family' members wear the same trademark.

"Was there any indication Audrey was there?" I know Clover didn't find her. If he had, we wouldn't be having this conversation. Clover would be holed up with some hookers and the best cocaine money can't buy, celebrating his victory, and I'd be at the hospital with my wife, having her and our daughter checked over.

My jaw works through a hard grind when Clover shakes his head. "She *had* been there, though. The room the ransom photo was taken in was at the back of the compound, and I got DNA proof by the bucketloads."

"What type of DNA?" I'm shocked I can talk. I'm so fucking angry, I am five seconds from blowing my top. If Clover's switch-up of the rules has fucked me over, *he* will be fucked over. No fear.

"Blood," Clover answers nonchalantly like his life isn't in danger. "Lots of it."

My blood boils over when he digs his cell phone out of his pocket to show me the photographs he took at the scene. Bodies litter almost every inch of the floor space, but my focus is on one thing and one thing only—the dingy, dirty mattress they had Audrey sit on when they snapped her picture for the ransom request.

Although she's missing from Clover's images, I can still see her ashen face and cracked lips with precise clearness. She has always been the quiet one. Softly spoken and happy for everyone else to steal the attention.

The last image I have of her isn't close to any of those things. It's one of pure fret. Like she didn't believe I could get her out of this in one piece.

If the horrifying thoughts bombarding me now are anything to go by, she had reason to fret. The mattress is covered in blood. It isn't formed how you'd expect from someone being fatally wounded by a knife or gun. There's an outline of a body—a slim, you-wouldn't-know-she's-eight-months-along-if-you-were-looking-at-her-from-behind outline.

I snap my eyes shut, hopeful it will suffocate my wish to kill Clover when he announces, "Preacher did a quick swab of the mattress. Amniotic fluid was present."

Confident I'm hearing him wrong, I shake my head before reopening my eyes. "She isn't due for another four weeks. It's too early—"

"Scalpel was also found..." He scrubs at his jaw before he pushes out, "And fetal matter."

"Fetal matter? What the fuck do you mean fetal matter?" As my eyes bounce between his, horrifying notion after horrifying notion smack into me. "My daughter..." The rest of my question lodges in my throat when despair darts through Clover's eyes. He doesn't show emotion, not ever, but there's no denying the sympathy in his eyes now.

Those fuckers didn't just kidnap my wife.

They've taken my daughter.

Before he knows what's hit him, I pin Clover to the entryway door of my suite, then press my gun against his temple. He's almost three inches taller than me and nearly double my width, but that doesn't mean shit since my fury is fueled by blackened hate.

"You killed her. You fucking killed her!" The spit off my roar sizzles on his cheeks. "If you had followed the plan, they would have let Audrey go, and my daughter would be safe."

Some of my anger turns to vengeance when Clover shakes his head. "The fluid was almost dry to touch. This shit ain't on me. Rimi has you played."

The confidence in his tone should lower my agitation.

It doesn't.

I'm seconds from ending his life as he had tried to do mine years earlier.

Arabian oil tycoons weren't happy when they didn't get what they paid for from my father. I've been making it up to them ever since.

Don't feel sorry for me. They're the reason *all* my bank accounts are in the eight-figure range. Whores, crack, guns, and unlimited entertainment are readily available in Bahrain, but you don't enjoy it as much with your family breathing down your neck.

Rich dignitaries from the twenty-two Arab nations are invited into my home to discuss oil exchanges, money laundering, and weaponry distribution all 'families' are associated with. The above-mentioned is the icing on the cake, and the only reason I'm not fish food.

Only a fool would turn down a proposal worth eighty-three million dollars a year.

Clover isn't one of them.

With that in mind, I suck in a big breath before lowering my gun. Killing Clover won't get my wife and daughter back. If anything, it will delay their return.

"What was on the USB drive?" Rimi's men wouldn't have given this to Clover for no reason. His family's legacy is as bad as my mine, but instead of rising it above the ashes, he's tainting it with more controversy.

My lips purse when Clover mutters, "Sick, twisted shit." He has an ironclad stomach, nothing ruffles him, so for him to say the video is fucked up, it most certainly is. "I wouldn't recommend watching—"

I cut off his words with a slice of my hand. My relationship with Audrey isn't close to traditional. She fell pregnant within weeks of us hooking up, we got married to ensure she could stay in the country to birth my child, and we have more things out of common than agreed upon, but she's my wife and the mother of my child.

Our daughter makes her my family, and family comes first of all.

My heart thumps against my ribs when I crack open my laptop. Details of the ransom drop are still displayed on the screen. A team of cyber specialists have been working on it since it was received. They've yet to find a single snip of evidence to identify where it was sent from. For all we know, Audrey may not even be in the country.

"*Cazzo...*" I push out with a growl when the video commences playing on a woman being held down on the stained mattress. I can only see the lower half of her body, but her strength is undeniable. Even with four goons pinning her to the filthy bedding, she thrashes and kicks, her will to live seen without a single word being spoken.

Her stomach is gleaming from how far it's extended, but its redness tapers when a scalpel is dragged across a section of skin usually hidden by a panty line. Although the video has no sound, I can imagine how blood-curdling her screams are. They're removing her child from her stomach without anesthetics, acting like ruthless barbarians with callous rules.

My skyrocketing blood pressure gets a boost when one of the goons moves to the right of the frame, exposing the tiniest birthmark on the lower left side of the victim's stomach. It's the shape of a mulberry leaf and unearths the victim's identity in an instant.

"It's Audrey," I mutter out while dragging a hand over my almost black hair. "It's my fucking wife."

While Clover commences putting actions into place to respond to Rimi's break of the rules, I continue watching the video. The footage is horrifying, but I have no choice but to watch every sickening second. The simplest thing in the background could be the *only* clue to Audrey's whereabouts. I can't miss seeing it because my stomach is twisted up in knots.

On instinct, my thumb caresses the screen of my laptop when a bloody and white film-coated baby is pulled from Audrey's stomach. Aware I'm most likely watching, a man concealing his face with a balaclava holds my daughter by her feet like he's showcasing a prize-winning catch before he shifts to face the camera.

I freeze the image when the cuff of his sleeve rises half an inch. His tattoo is the typical flame design most bottom-dwellers have. I stare at it until it's burned into my retina before hitting the play button. He just signed his death certificate, and I'm the Grim Reaper coming to collect his soul.

When the body of my child is dangled an inch from the camera, my eyes whizz over every inch of her upside-down face and grubby body, seeking any signs that she's breathing. Her chest is as flat as mine, her nostrils un-flaring. She's as still as a statue, her legs as frozen as her mother's in the background.

"Come on, Fien," I beg under my breath after taking in an identical mulberry leaf birthmark on her stomach. "Fight like your mother did when choosing your name." I didn't hate the name Audrey had picked, but I wasn't a fan of it either. I wanted our daughter to have a traditional Italian name. Fien is of Dutch heritage, just like her mother. It's short for Jozefien which is Audrey's mother's name. Fien's grandmother.

My eyes shoot to the left of the screen when a pair of tiny hands enter the frame. This person's wrists are slimmer than the man's clutching my daughter's feet and nowhere near as hairy, making me confident she's female.

Just as the unseen woman removes Fien from the goon's clutch, a white sheet is draped over Aubrey's lifeless form, then the video ends. As I struggle to keep a rational head, I wring the screen of my laptop as if it's Rimi Castro's neck. I would wholly destroy it if the USB stick would come out of the carnage unharmed.

That horrifying video is the only proof I have that I have a daughter. No one knew she existed. No one *knows* she exists, but if I have it my way, those who now know will die to ensure my revenge lives.

*Famiglia prima di tutto.*

Vengeance is a very close second.

# 1

## Dimitri

**Nine long months later...**

Ignoring India's concerning glance, I scream for the driver to stop. It's pissing down rain, and we're running late to a function with a mafioso seeking a new realm in a town he isn't wanted, but the redhead standing under the awning of a Publix supermarket has too many similarities with Audrey to ignore. Same svelte frame, fiery red hair, and enticing curves I'm certain won't alter no matter how many kids she rears.

"Dimitri... it isn't her—" I lodge the remainder of India's words into the back of her throat with a stern glare. She may very well be Audrey's neighbor/friend, but she has no right to speak to me in such a manner.

Until Audrey and Fien are found, my search won't end. I thought India understood this. If she doesn't, she should leave now, because my belief that she understood my quest is the sole reason I've kept her around this long. She has a face that encourages visitors to our side of the pond, but her beauty is a dime a dozen—easily replaceable.

It will do her best to remember that.

While raking a shaky hand through my hair, I growl out, "I'll never stop looking for her."

"I know that."

India scoots closer to my side of the bench seat. We've put bells and whistles on tonight's festivities. A stretch limousine, whores by the bucketloads, and a woman who will never eye him as she forever eyes me. In a way, India should consider herself lucky Audrey classed her as a friend, or her unwanted sideways glances the past nine months would have caused her demise. She's trying to profit from her friend's downfall, or worse, use me as part of her grief process.

If I were to believe rumors, India's husband has been presumed dead as long as Audrey has been missing. Although I feel sorry for India, I will *not* tolerate her suggestion that two broken hearts can meld into one.

Alas, I have to keep my cards close to my chest until it's my turn to show my hand.

"But I also know the redhead isn't her, Dimitri. Audrey only cut her hair the week she..." my tightened jaw slackens when tears well in India's eyes, "... went missing."

Just like me, she refuses to say Audrey is dead. Her legs were as still as Fien's when she was torn from her stomach, but that doesn't mean anything. I'm granted confirmation on the third of every month that my daughter is alive, so who's to say Audrey didn't find the same strength?

Despite having the weaponry and capital for a century-long war, and a crew of blood-thirsty men, Rimi has yet to man up.

Although it frustrates me to no end, I can't say I don't understand his tactic. Why risk a net profit of 1.8 million dollars annually when all they have to do is provide proof my daughter is alive?

My grandfather would roll in his grave if he knew how cartels were being run these days. In his era, it was about infrastructure, drugs, and weapons. Now nothing but profit is on the mind, and innocents like my daughter get caught up in the bullshit.

Although pissed, I'll find Fien, and when I do, there will be hell to pay.

The old saying, 'Before you embark on revenge, you should dig two graves.' I'll need more than two. At last count, the Castros were sitting at eighty-nine men. That will take my quota to over ninety because despite what my father says, the Castros aren't acting alone. Rimi isn't smart enough to pull off a stunt like this without help. His family has only been in this industry for the past twenty years. Exploits like this require decades of experience. If it were simple, my father would have dabbled in it years ago.

He learned nothing from our family's downfall and is forever looking for a way to make a quick profit. I could challenge his leadership, however my bend of the rules wouldn't have the same outcome my father achieved. He didn't kill the leader of the allied crew. If he had, he would have been dead no matter what.

After laboring my jaw side to side, I get back to the task at hand. "I'm not saying she's Audrey, but there's no harm in checking."

Before India can issue a single worry I see in her eyes, I snatch up an umbrella from the storage in the door, then slide out the back seat of the limousine. With rain making it seem as if winter arrived early, I tug up the collar of my coat, hiding both my neck tattoos and goosebumps that have nothing to do with the winds whipping in from the east.

Nothing says gangbanger like a set of neck tattoos.

"Audrey..." I won't lie, my heart stops beating when the redhead commences pivoting my way. India is right, her hair is a little longer than Audrey's, and more an orange-red than a sapphire coloring, but their similarities are uncanny.

"Dimitri, hi," greets a woman I swear I've seen before.

It takes me a few seconds to click on to who she is, but when I do, I am shocked. I'm not just chasing ghosts of my past anymore. I've caught up to them. "Justine." She appears stunned I remember who she is. I don't know why. We were born in the same hospital and attended the same school. I've just had my head up my ass too long for immediate recognition. "What are you doing out this way? I didn't think the Walsh's would ever leave Ravenshoe."

When she smiles, I discover how well she grew into her buck teeth. She's always been beautiful, but her legs were miles too long for her body, and her front teeth seemed to have a mind of their own. I can't say I fared much better during the awkward preteen years, but my family name stopped it from being mentioned—as did my fists.

I stop smirking about times bygone when Justine discloses, "They still live in Ravenshoe. I'm heading home for Thanksgiving weekend. Thought I better grab some supplies first. As my mother always says, an empty hand is an unwelcoming one."

"Do you live around here?" Shock echoes in my tone. Justine has four brothers. That's the equivalent of living in a convent when you're both the youngest *and* the only girl in your family. Why do you think it took me so long to realize she's grown into her rabbit teeth? I wasn't sure getting through her brothers would be worth the effort. Despite the heavy knot in my stomach advising me differently, I'm slapping myself up the back of the head right now.

Locks of red lava fall onto Justine's shoulders when she

notches her chin to our right. "I'm a sophomore at Eastwood State. It's—"

"An easy hour drive to Ravenshoe," I interrupt, unsurprised. Her brothers would never let her lead get too long.

Justine smiles again like she heard my inner monologue. "Yeah." After a nervy swallow, she asks, "How about you? Last I heard, you were in New York."

Is she keeping tabs on me? If so, I don't mind. Our unexpected reunion has the first rays of sunshine breaking through the murky cloud that's been hanging above my head the past nine months. I even feel capable of sucking in an entire breath. It's been a long time since I've felt this way.

When Justine coughs, prompting me that I've failed to answer her question, I say, "I've been floating in and out of states. I'm about to head home for a couple of days this weekend as well." Her unique aquamarine-colored eyes widen when I unexpectedly add, "We should catch up?"

"Umm... sure. That's sounds good."

She doesn't sound eager, but I pretend not to notice. "Do you have your phone on you?" Nodding, she pulls her cell out of her clutch purse before handing it to me. I'm not surprised to discover she doesn't have a lock code. She's lived a sheltered, naïve life.

When she drinks in my tattooed hand as I punch my details in her contacts, I gabble out, "My nonna warned me to keep my body art to an area only the privileged get to see." With a hidden smirk, I mutter, "It's the *only* region on my body not inked." The way I say 'it's' leaves no doubt about what I'm referencing. Excluding my cock, I have tattoos from my ankles to my jawline.

Like all teens craving a rebellion, I did the opposite of what I was told. I didn't keep my mutiny to a tiny bicep tattoo on my eighteenth, I had my entire back done. My artwork has grown substantially since then.

I wait for Justine's cheeks to flame to their full potential before muttering, "Do they bother you?" I'm not surprised when she shakes her head. Even hundreds of miles from my hometown, I heard rumors she was getting around with a tattoo artist during summer break. "Do you have any?"

Her nod switches to a shake. "I've not yet built the courage. I'm not a fan of needles." Her cheeks whiten as a tiny shudder racks through her body. "Or blood. Brax tells me I have nothing to worry about, but how can I be sure he isn't giving me the line he gives all his clients?"

That's the name I've heard thrown around with the rumor —Brax.

"Is Brax your boyfriend?" That came out way more possessive than intended, and I'm not the only one noticing.

While accepting her phone, Justine does a nervous twist on the spot. "No. It's not like that." She sounds like she's trying to convince herself more than me. "We're... *friends.*"

My lips furl at the way she stammers out friends. With how low her tone dipped, she should have said fuck buddies.

Although I have no intention of calling her out on her 'arrangement' with Brax, I can't help but move forward with a plan that suddenly popped into my head. Knowing she isn't as innocent as her brothers make out will progress things along nicely.

After popping open the umbrella I grabbed to act chivalrous, I commence guiding Justine to the car I'm certain is hers. It's the only decent one in a lot full of shit boxes, and even then, it would be an effort to fetch a few thousand for it at auction.

My intuition is proven spot on when Justine stuffs a wonky key into an outdated lock a few seconds later. Once the latch pops up, I open her door for her. She's surprised by my chivalry but also pleased about it.

I wait for her to place her bag of groceries onto the passenger side seat before saying, "We should do dinner."

"Dinner?" She swallows her spit before she chokes on it, then wrings her sweater with her hands, torn on if she should act excited or play hard to get. We're doing dinner either way, so she can act however she likes. "Umm..."

"Come on, J. A girl has got to eat." Her brother's infamous nickname will get me over the line long before my wolfish grin. Maddox is the only one who calls her J, and he's the apple of her eye. Reminding her that we are 'friends' will do me more good than harm. "I heard the Petrettis signature dish is still to die for."

"It is. Maddox and I were there only last month," she replies, her smile matching mine. After sliding into the driver's seat of her bomb, she raises her eyes to mine. "Maddox and Demi have a casual thing going on. We could always do a double date with them?"

"That might be a bit awkward." When confusion blasts through her eyes, I mutter, "Trust me, Maddox won't enjoy his meal if he's forced to watch his sister exchange spit with his *friend*." I air quote my last word like a pompous, no-dick prick. My dealings with Maddox extend further than friendship, but its best to keep that between us for now. "I never did when riding shotgun with Ophelia's dates."

The lust firing through Justine's eyes shifts to sorrow. "I heard about her accident. I'm sorry for your loss."

"Prove it. Share a meal with me *without* a tagalong." Using my dead sister to get a date is wrong, but if it gives me a chance to get back my daughter sooner rather than later, I'm willing to go there.

Although shocked about my eagerness, Justine falls for my ruse. "I only have Thursday and Monday free."

"Thursday works. I'll arrange for a car to collect you at seven."

As domineering as I am cocky, I close her car's door, spin on my heels, then walk away, stealing her chance to reply.

I can't have her driving to our date in her car. Not only will it weaken the authenticity of my ruse, but her shoddy engine gives her an excuse to back out of our date. I've heard all the lines before—*I have to wash my hair, my car broke down, I'm engaged to another man*—and every one of them came from Audrey.

# 2

**Roxanne**

As I drag my mouth away from my boyfriend's kiss-swollen lips, goosebumps break across my skin. It's cooler today than usual for this time of the year, but the drizzly weather isn't to blame for the icy chill shuddering through me. Not even Eddie's hand tracing the seam of my panties can be held accountable. There's a weird sensation in the air, like more than an inappropriate hook-up location is set to cause trouble.

Eddie and I have been dating for two months. Even being in my second year of college won't see my nanna bending the rules when it comes to boyfriends. Until we're in a 'solid' relationship for six months straight, I can't bring boys home. Hence the reason Eddie and I are getting frisky in the alleyway between the movie complex and our local grocer. It isn't the ideal location, and a mattress would be more comfortable than a brick wall, but beggars can't be choosers.

When the prickling of the hairs on my arms grows to a point I can't ignore, I shift my head to the side. Since it's late in the day and stormy, I can't see out of the alleyway as clearly as normal, but there's enough light to unearth the reason for my body's odd response.

A man is making his way to a stretch limousine idling in the lower section of the parking lot. Despite the fact he's clutching an umbrella, his trench coat is the only protection his pricy suit has from the downpour. He has an arrogant walk, similar to the one a quarterback does when running onto the field during State Championship weekend. It's more teasingly paced, though, and mesmerizing.

I'm paying more attention to his cocky strut than the sneaky slip of Eddie's hand. Instead of caressing the lace edging of my panties, his hand is now burrowed deep inside the inexpensive material.

Although this is the furthest we've gone, and we could be busted at any moment, for the life of me, I can't get the word 'stop' to fall out of my mouth. My jaw is hanging too low from my eyes briefly colliding with the stranger's to follow the prompts of my brain.

He's spotted my gawk, but instead of calling for security, he slants his head to the side and rakes his eyes down my body. He drinks it all in—my black mid-thigh boots, my miniskirt and skin-tight shirt, and my bleached to within-an-inch-of-death hair.

He even takes in Eddie's fumbling hand as he strives to find my clit.

The last part he finds more amusing than arousing. His smirk tells me this, much less the humor blazing through his expressive eyes when he returns them to my face. I expect him to wink, then walk away, too cultured to watch two teens fumble their way to third base, but he surprises me for the second time this afternoon by sticking around to watch the show.

His scrutiny should have me clamping around Eddie's fingers in disgust, but it seems to have the opposite effect. Instead of announcing to Eddie that we have an audience, I adjust the span of my thighs to ensure he can notch the rest of his finger inside of me before breathing heavily into his neck, encouraging his pursuit.

The stranger's dark, rain-flopped hair hides most of his face, only the tiniest snippet of blue pops out of the flattened mess, but I'm confident in saying he's gorgeous. You don't have the suffocating aura he does with a cat's bunghole for a face. His whole persona screams of wealth and superiority, albeit a little blackened by haunted memories.

I guarantee he's brutally beautiful, and the thought of unearthing his dark side has me acting wildly reckless.

A grunted moan leaves Eddie's lips when he finally locates my clit. He thinks I'm giving myself to him, when in reality, that's far from the truth. I'm not imagining his thumb circling the bundle of nerves between my legs. My focus isn't on him in the slightest. I have nothing but the piercing blue eyes of a stranger on my mind, and they have me even wetter than the downpour that's drenching the handsome stranger.

"You're so responsive to my touch," Eddie mutters into my ear a short time later while flicking my clit like he knows what he's doing. He doesn't, but my body is wired so tight from the dark-haired man's watch, it's happy to pretend he does. "I knew you'd be explosive. All blondes are—"

I clamp my hand over Eddie's mouth, shutting him up. "Shh, you'll get us busted." I'm not really worried, his words are barely whispers, but I can't hear him and the stranger's shallow breaths at the same time.

Even the way the dark-haired man breathes is sexy, all rugged and unhinged. I imagine his heated breaths fanning my skin when he places feather-like kisses from my ankle to my inner thigh. Just the thought of his mouth floating over my aching sex has zaps sparking through me. I bet he gives good head, and he'd smell divine while doing it—like expensive cologne and over-priced whiskey. He wouldn't wear shop-bought deodorant just like he wouldn't drink bottom-shelf whiskey. He's too refined for that, too sophisticated, so wickedly evil he'll watch a woman be brought to ecstasy on a lazy Friday afternoon like it's the most natural thing in the world to do.

"Yes, Roxie," Eddie moans on a growl when the sinfulness of what I'm doing unexpectedly slams into me. He's barely touching me, but I swan dive over a cliff, shuddering, moaning, and coming wholly undone. I've always been a little edgier than my friends. I don't shy away when challenged and am willing to give anything a try once, but this, this is new even for someone with as little morals as me. "Give me the sweet nectar of your loins."

I cringe through the remainder of my climax instead of relishing it.

*Sweet nectar of my loins? Who says that?*

I'm not the only one shocked by Eddie's lack of class. I can't hear the stranger's laughter, but I most certainly can see it. His chest is rising and falling as rapidly as mine. He isn't sucking in much-needed breaths like me, though. He's struggling to hold in the laughter rumbling in his chest—laughter he loses the ability to harness when a security guard arrives out of nowhere.

"Hey, you, you can't do *that* there!"

When the guard sprints down the alleyway, Eddie dumps me onto my feet so quickly, my backside is subjected to a nasty graze compliments to the brickwork he had me hoisted against. I'm horrified for the second time in under three seconds when he pivots on his heels and darts in the direction opposite the one the guard is coming from, leaving me defenseless to the angry, weapon-wielding man.

I just climaxed. I can't run, and I'm not going to mention how my legs can't pump in the stupid boots I bought specifically to woo him. Furthermore, the security officer isn't a standard old overweight, balding man. He's so fit-looking, he'd be able to chase me down even if I hadn't orgasmed.

"Eddie, come back!"

When he continues hightailing it, I realize it's me against the world—*as it always is.* My wit is the only currency I have, and its rarity doesn't make it priceless.

After flashing a quick glance to the stranger, I dash in the direction Eddie went. I'm on a scholarship to college. If I get arrested, my plans will go up in smoke like this godforsaken shithole did a decade ago. The community was supposed to rebuild. Instead, half the townsfolks packed up and left, leaving nothing but a wasteland of desecration.

I'm partway down the alleyway when the bang of a gun booms into my ears. While freezing like a statue, I survey the area. The guard's boots no longer thud against the road surface. I can't even hear his frantic breaths. If I didn't know any better, I'd swear I was the only person in the alleyway.

With my heart in my throat, I crank my neck back to add images to the theories running through my hazy head. The euphoria pumping through me seconds ago shifts to despair when I spot the security officer slumped on the ground. Blood is seeping through the back of his uniform, and his arms are pinned beneath him like he was struck down midstride.

When I stray my eyes to the end of the alleyway, my heart thumps out a jazzy melody. My wide-with-terror eyes make the dark-haired stranger hard to see, but I don't need 20/20 vision to recognize the black object in his hand. He has a gun, and its barrel is pointed my way.

I blink several times in a row when the bang of a gun being fired for the second time ricochets down the alleyway. While my stomach braces for impact, my pathetically-short life flashes before my eyes. The video montage is over in less than two seconds, but disappointed is the only pain I'm experiencing. Even with the cruel sound of a bullet shredding through a hard surface echoing in my ears, I somehow remain uninjured.

Certain my mind is playing tricks on me, I pivot around to investigate where the crunching sound originated from. I grow untrusting of my legs to keep me upright when I take in remnants of a security camera hanging messily from the corner of a Publix supermarket chain. Its exposed wires reveal it's a hardwired device, however it won't be recording anything but brickwork right now.

Although lost on what the hell is happening, I can't help but shift my focus back to the unnamed man at the end of the alley. I should be in fear for my life, but for some reason, I'm not. He gunned down a guard for me, I'm certain of it.

My lungs take stock of their oxygen levels when he winks at me as I anticipated earlier before he spins on his heels and enters an idling stretch limousine, leaving me alone with a dead man and no alibi.

Crap.

# 3

**Dimitri**

Smith's dark eyes lift to mine when I slide into the back seat of our shared limousine. "Remove all footage from before the guard commenced undoing his belt."

Smith is my tech guy. If I want something permanently deleted from the World Wide Web, he gets it done within minutes. I want this deleted. I don't give a fuck someone may view the footage and think I'm a perverted bastard who gets his rocks off watching a teen get fingered in an alleyway. I'm more worried I showed weakness by gunning down a man because he liked what he saw as much as me.

The security officer wasn't approaching the blonde to make a citizen's arrest for performing a lewd act in a public place. He wanted in on the action, and from the way he grabbed at his belt while sprinting after her, he was going to join in even if she said no.

I hate fuckers like that.

The Petrettis have been meddling in the prostitution conglomerate for as long as I've been born, so you can trust me when I say not all hookers cater for high-end johns. Some are willing to break a twenty depending on what you're seeking. You don't need to force a girl to do a sex act on you if you're down on your luck. Go see my father, he'll negotiate with a homeless man if it benefits him in some way.

Smith jerks up his chin, understanding where I'm going before he pulls his laptop out of his bag. He's never without a bunch of equipment. It's as vital to him as the blood in his veins. "And the girl?"

I drag the towel Rocco, my number two, handed me over my wet head before replying, "Listen for chatter. If they don't rule this as self-defense, I'll put other measures in play."

Rocco twists his lips, shocked. Usually, I don't give a fuck about anyone but myself. This time around is different. Not only am I forging ahead with plans to get my daughter back sooner rather than later, but I'm also the hardest I've ever been. It wasn't watching what the punk-faced weasel did to the blonde that caused my cock to press against the zipper in my trousers, it was the way she stared at me while he touched her.

It takes a lot of gall to get off when the person you're fantasizing about isn't touching you. Imagine how quick she'll explode if I were to touch her? The thought should disgust me. I was only in the rain chasing the ghost of my wife, but for some reason, it doesn't. What can I say? I was raised by a mongrel of a man. Mental stability isn't my favorable trait, and neither is chivalry —*usually.*

"And you?" Smith asks, shocked I left myself out of the equation. That's as rare as my father doing something ethical because it would do more good than harm.

"I doubt the footage of me is more than a blur of black." I

know this as I strained my eyes while striving to take in the blonde's features. "If it's more, let them have it. The Feds haven't done me any favors the past nine months, so I'm not inclined to cooperate with them either."

Against my better judgment, I sort help from a contact my family had many years ago when Audrey's ransom note arrived at my office. Although he doesn't follow the book to the letter of the law like his pompous counterparts, he still has too many rules and protocols for me to follow. He wants to get Fien back without bloodshed.

I'd rather endure a bloodbath than endure another long nine months pass without seeing my daughter in the flesh. Our opposing opinions don't meld well, and they often find us placed on different teams. I guess that's expected when one side of the duo works in law enforcement, and the other is well-known for his criminal ties.

"Call Joshua." India hands a business card to Smith like he's her personal assistant. "He'll have the slug removed from the guard's body before the coroner and will keep an eye on proceedings." With her jaw as set as mine, she slumps low into her seat before twisting her torso to face me. "What was that about?"

I arch a brow, wordlessly suggesting she check her tone. I don't know who the fuck she thinks she is, but she's neither my wife nor my mother, so she has no right to badger me. If I want to watch a truckload of women being pleasured by men incapable of the task on a rainy Friday afternoon, so be it.

I can do whatever the fuck I like.

That's the joy of being me.

Either stupid or hoping to die, India disregards my stern glare. "You can't replace Audrey and Fien. It isn't possible."

"I know that." I lean so close to her, her hot breaths take care of the droplets of rain on my face the towel missed. She isn't worried.

She's excited she forced a response out of me. I rarely give her the time of day. This afternoon won't be any different. "But that doesn't mean Rimi Castro won't believe that. Look at you, all rattled and upset thinking I'm moving on. Who's to say he won't reach the same conclusion?"

Because she's fighting to keep a calm head, India's accent comes out more pronounced than normal. I'm not exactly sure of her ancestry. I just know she's foreign like Audrey. "I'm upset for Audrey, Dimi." Calling me Dimi puts her in my shit book, only my friends are allowed to call me that, much less what she says next, "She doesn't deserve to be replaced with a cheap, knock-off version of herself."

"Shh." I push her platinum blonde hair out of her eye before tucking it behind her ear. "No more lies. We both know you're praying Audrey is never found." When a flare of deceit fires through her eyes, I speak faster, "Just like you'll forever wish we didn't bump into her when we fumbled into your apartment after our date." I track my thumb over her ruby-painted lips and across her jaw before stopping it at the throb in her throat. "It must have stung having her steal my attention the way she did."

"She wasn't supposed to be there," India mutters before she can stop herself.

"But she was, and you were discarded... *again*."

I take a second to suck in the fear slicking her skin before inching back with a smirk. India plays the role of a widower well, however her husband is only 'presumed dead' by her. From what Smith unearthed earlier this month, India's husband is a foreign aristocrat with a fascination for little blonde playthings. Rumors are he tossed his wife aside with the hope his favorite whore will become the queen of his realm.

"Is that why Audrey was taken, India? Because you once again had your crown stolen?"

"Not at all," she immediately fires back. She's a damn good actor. Even someone trained to seek deceit would have trouble spotting hers. "I attended your wedding. I'm the one who encouraged you to get married so Audrey wouldn't be deported—"

"And you were the last person to see her alive!" I'm back up in her face in an instant, my hand around her throat, my lips an inch from hers. "You told her to meet you at the restaurant."

"Because I was hosting a surprise baby shower for her. I had no clue there were men there waiting for her. You didn't even see them when you walked her to the door." Her words are breathy and weak, strangled by the fierce clutch I have on her neck. I'm not just furious at her, I'm angry at myself. I glanced away for barely a second, and *poof*, Audrey was gone. "I would have never hurt her, Dimitri. She was my best friend... my *only* friend."

I don't want to believe her. I want to hang her out to dry as I've desired many times over the past nine months, but there's too much truth in her eyes for me to ignore. Women like India and Audrey don't make friends. They're ridiculed for their beauty like they should be punished God gifted them with enticing features, and we won't mention the fact they're foreigners living in a country known for its disrespect of women. In my motherland, women are treated like goddesses. It's one of the reasons my father rarely visits Italy.

After a few big breaths, I weaken my grip on India's throat. Once I've worked my anger down a few notches, I sink back to my side of the bench seat before straightening the disheveled collar of my trench coat.

My clothes are drenched through, but you wouldn't know it from the fiery heat teeming out of me. It's so blistering hot, I'm confident I'll be bone-dry in seconds.

Certain I've got everything in order, I stray my eyes to Smith's side of the cabin. "Once you cleared the footage, commence implementing the ruse we discussed last week. Any chatter regarding me moving on is to come directly through me."

"Understood." Smith gets straight to work like he's already cleared away the footage of the unknown blonde getting fingered in the alleyway and was dying for another task. He likes to keep busy. "Do you want the compound included in the catchment zone?"

India doesn't move her head, but I can feel her eyes on me when I dip my chin. "Word got out about my marriage. It was a guarded secret, so either someone in this car is a snitch, or we have eyes and ears in unknown locations." It sucks to admit you can't trust your own blood, but this isn't the first time I've felt this way. Why do you think I kept my relationship with Audrey a secret?

"And tonight's plans?" India asks, jumping back into the conversation like she wasn't almost choked to within an inch of her life.

I don't look at her. I can't. If I do, I'll want to finish what I started. "Will continue as planned." While tapping out a quick message to my father, telling him we'll be delayed a couple of minutes since I stopped for some lighthearted entertainment, I add, "While you convince Miceli your husband's claims about you disliking oral sex are fraudulent, Clover, Smith, Rocco, and I will convince his crew they'd rather settle anywhere but Hopeton."

By convince, I mean we'll get heavy. New York was run by three separate entities of the Italian Cartel, however Hopeton most certainly isn't.

*Famiglia prima di tutto...* until it isn't.

# 4

**Dimitri**

Ignoring my cracked and bleeding knuckles, I raise a recently printed photograph of my daughter off a dust-coated desk. Unlike last month's shotty and blurred image, this one shows every inch of Fien's chubby cheeks, toothy grin, and birthmark-blemished stomach with precise clearness.

The figure attached to her picture speaks a thousand words. My ruse is working. I've been requested to deposit one hundred fifty thousand dollars into a foreign account on the third of each month without fail the past nine months. This month's demand only cites one hundred thousand dollars.

Her kidnappers didn't lessen the amount of her ransom because her upkeep this month is less than the previous nine. They've lowered it because they're worried I'm weeks from forgetting her. Why pay out of the eye to keep someone safe when you can replace them within months? It seems demoralizing and cruel to even consider, but it's exactly the way men in my industry operate. They wouldn't pay to keep their blood safe, especially if that blood has female hormones running through it.

My father loved my mother, yet, he profited from her death instead of mourning it. If he'd known how beneficial her death would have been, he would have put plans into play years earlier. Guaranteed.

My mother was killed during a joint FBI and CIA sting many years ago. Her death sparked controversy across the globe. The outrage ensured my father would never be prosecuted for his crimes. The uproar about the loss of an innocent was louder than the calls for my father to serve time. If he were put away, his many children would become wards of the state. No one wanted that, not even the men who had spent years hunting him.

Once the heat settled down, my father sued the state for an undisclosed record-setting amount. He won. My mother was a good woman. She was the only person capable of getting through to my father. Our family dynamic drastically changed when she was killed.

For years, I blamed authorities for the hell I was raised in. If the large, balding Russian standing in front of me hadn't convinced me otherwise, I'd still be avenging her death. A bullet from an agent's gun killed my mother, but that was only because my father pulled her in front of himself as a shield.

Why believe the Bureau over my own flesh and blood, you ask? Tobias had footage no amount of manipulation could alter. It was as gory and as terrifying as the video on a USB drive stored in my safe.

When I place Fien's photograph on my desk, Tobias continues with the conversation we were holding before her ransom note arrived. "I have strong intel on a new Castro compound popping up in the New Mexico region. A crew was deployed there last week."

"Where exactly in New Mexico?" The land there is rugged and spread out. I'm sure Smith would eventually unearth Rimi's location since he can't demand money without using some form of electronic communication, but I'd rather Tobias spell out the details for me. It will be quicker this way, although it could also be a heap bloodier.

Rimi isn't keeping Fien in one location. He's bouncing her around the country, constantly altering her location, so I can't get a solid lead for longer than a day, two at most.

"I can't tell you that."

The stiffness of my jaw is heard in my reply. "Then what can you tell me?" Although I'm asking a question, I don't wait for Tobias to respond. "Your department has been sitting on their hands for months. I've shared intel with you, trade fucking secrets, and what have I been given in return for it? Nothing. Not a single fucking thing."

Tobias doesn't rattle easily. "I placed men on your date to ensure she doesn't get snared by the same trap as Audrey."

I slouch low into my chair before making a teepee with my index fingers. Since my beard is thicker than I usually wear it, my jaw's tick isn't as obvious. "Don't act like you did that for me, Tobias. Your wish to keep Justine out of harm's way has nothing to do with me, and you know it."

There it is, the brutal pulse a vein in his neck gets any time I'm on the money. I don't know who fucked Tobias over, or how well he was fucked, but I guarantee you he doesn't look at Justine with the same set of eyes as me. I doubt he even views her how her brothers do. He sees a person, not an asset.

"Whether it's downright sinister or ingenuously brilliant, my plan is working. I received Fien's proof of life earlier this month, and the ransom is lower. Rimi is growing worried, which means he'll get sloppy."

Tobias breathes heavily out of his nose before slumping into the chair opposite to mine. Since our meetings need to be kept on the down-low, dust kicks up around him in protest to his large frame squeezing the last bit of air out of the chair's cushioning. "I agree. Impatience is one of Rimi's biggest downfalls. I just have a bad feeling about this one. The New Mexico region is the Castros' stomping ground. Rimi would only go there for one reason."

"To end things?"

When Tobias jerks up his chin, I take a moment to deliberate. Tobias's extensive knowledge on how the Cartel works is the sole reason I've continued to keep him updated on Audrey and Fien's case. He knows how these guys tick because he's been undercover in their organizations longer than some of the main hitters have been helming their reigns. If anything is about to go down, Tobias generally knows before it occurs. He tried to talk my father out of his failed takeover bid on the family now running New York. He didn't listen to him as I am tempted to do this time around.

"I can't let this go. The evidence is too overwhelming to discount."

"I agree," he says again. "But I also think you need to tread cautiously. Castro reacts stupidly when scared."

I shouldn't smile at the thought of Rimi quaking in his boots, but I do. What can I say? I like knowing he doesn't have one up on me. Tell me one air-breathing man who wouldn't? He's had my daughter for nearly ten months. Most men would have cracked by now.

Confident all is said and done, Tobias stands to his feet. "I'll try and get word to you before we make a move. In the meantime, stay out of Erkinsvale. Even with the security guard being shot in the back, his death has murky cartel smears all over it."

I slant my head to hide my smile. I shot the guard in the back to weaken the Feds' suspicions. I should have realized that wouldn't work with Tobias. He has an uncanny knack for knowing when his targets are coming out to play.

When Tobias's silence gets the better of me, I mutter, "He was going to rape that girl."

He shifts on his feet to face me. Even with him being close to sixty, his swagger is highly noticeable. "I know. Why do you think my cuffs are still shackled to my belt?" He waits for my gut to absorb his first hit before he whacks me with another. "Was he one of your johns?"

"Hypothetically speaking?"

His smirk matches mine. He isn't impressed with my negotiating skills, but he's aware we won't talk without them. "When aren't things hypothetical with you, Dimi?"

As my smile doubles, I shrug. "Hypothetically speaking, his kink was rape. He liked them un-bled and young—"

"Younger than the girl you left to clean up your mess?"

I shrug again. "Depends. How young is she?"

I'm seeking answers from the wrong person, but I can't fucking help myself. Even with my week being tied up dating Justine and praying Rimi is as stupid as he looks, the bleach blonde's sullied green eyes barely left my mind. I swear I've seen them before, but for the life of me, I can't remember where.

With his smirk as edgy as his mood, Tobias replies, "Young enough I shouldn't need to tell you to stay away, but I will. She doesn't belong in this life any more than Fien." Confident I'll adhere to his warning, he leaves the warehouse cloaked by a moonless sky, sidestepping Maddox Walsh on his way out.

Maddox's fists are balled tighter than they were when I approached him at an underground college fight months ago, and fiery ambers are blazing through his icy gaze. I want to say the scum who tried to rip him off of five thousand cool ones last week is the reason for his anger, but I doubt that's the case. Rumors about me moving on aren't just reaching Rimi's ears. Justine's brothers have heard them too.

Although I know the reason for Maddox's visit, I try and downplay it. I've got a third date with his sister to organize. I don't have time to babysit men big enough to crawl out of their own shit. "The funds from last month's fights will be deposited into your account by the end of business Friday. I don't have any intel on the fighters being brought forward for next month."

"I'm not here about our arrangement." His voice is gruff like he's taken one too many jabs to the throat. I guess it's part and parcel of being an illegal street fighter. His skills are good enough not to get hit, but he knows the more strikes he takes, the bigger his prize will be. Even if it's rigged, idiots pay top dollar to watch two men come to blows for longer than a couple of minutes.

After planting his ass in the seat Tobias just freed up, Maddox locks his blue eyes with mine. "Is it true you're using my sister as bait?"

That wasn't close to what I was anticipating for him to say, but I keep a cool head. "Whatever do you mean?"

"Don't play the dumb card with me, Dimitri. You might have all the stupid fuckers around here believing you've got the hots for my sister, but I know there's more to it than you're letting on. You paid the dessert menu more attention last week than you did Justine, yet you're trying to organize another date. Why?"

I'll give it to him. It takes gall to call a man out as a liar on his turf. His valor sees me issuing him some leniency—just. I inconspicuously aim my gun at his stomach instead of straight-up pressing it to his temple like I usually do.

"She's not in any danger—"

"That wasn't what I asked." He winks, then leans forward, aware I have my gun on him but uncaring. If I gunned him down now, Tobias would be on my ass in an instant, and Maddox knows it.

Tobias isn't my friend. Only a fool would believe otherwise. We work together because we must, not because we want to.

"You're willing to die for your sister?" When confirmation flares through Maddox's eyes, I switch tactics. "How does Demi feel about that?"

Justine hinted that Demi and Maddox were going casual last week. I know it's more than that. Maddox isn't just fascinated with my cousin, he's wholly fucking taken by her. Enough for me to be confident in saying, "If Demi were taken by your enemies, how far would you go to get her back?"

I see the answer in his eyes—there's no line he wouldn't cross —but it doesn't mean he'll go easy on me, though.

Fortunately for me, I have another card up my sleeve.

"And what about that kid of yours growing in her stomach? The one you don't know about because you're ignoring all the signs. What if he or she were ripped away from you? How far would you go to keep her safe?" He's taken back by my suggestion his girlfriend is pregnant, but he doesn't deny my assumption, confirming he has an inkling that everything I'm saying is true. "My daughter was cut out of my wife's stomach. They butchered her like a piece of worthless meat. I don't care who I have to trample, I won't stop until they're forced to pay for their mistakes."

Maddox stands from his chair so quickly, he topples it over. "Justine is my sister. I won't have her used like this."

"And she's my daughter!" I thrust Fien's photograph onto his side of the desk before lining up my pistol with the crinkle between his brows. "She ranks higher than anyone."

I discover the Walsh's don't just fight with their fists when Maddox draws a gun on me. It's clear it is one he picked up from a gangbanger in a back alley, but the quality of the weapon shouldn't enter the equation when calculating how much time you have left. The skill of its user is the only sum needed.

Do I think Maddox has the guts to kill me? Probably not. But he won't hesitate to maim me if it increases the odds of keeping me away from Justine.

If only the heat didn't get too hot for Tobias, then we would have found out. He interrupts our conversation long before I get the chance to prove nothing will ever come between Fien and me.

Not a woman.

Not the law.

No one.

"Lower your guns." When we remain standing firm, Tobias's voice rises as readily as his anger. "Don't make me repeat myself. I'll shoot you both before leaving you here to rot. Trust me when I say two less criminals in a sea of many won't be missed."

Unsurprisingly, Maddox lowers his gun first. He has the instincts of a killer, he just needs to hone his skills. I'd be happy to teach him if he weren't glaring at me like he wants my insides hanging out of my belly button.

"Stay away from my sister."

Stealing my chance to reply that I wouldn't be the only one licking wounds if I did that, he dumps his gun onto my desk, spins on his heels, then walks away.

You have no idea how satisfying it is when Tobias strays his eyes to mine to seek permission for Maddox to leave. Some would say it's because Maddox entered my premises with a loaded weapon, so Tobias is simply following the law. I know it's more than that. Tobias cares for me in his own twisted way. I guess that can be expected since he killed my mother.

Guilt does weird things to people.

As does vengeance.

I know that better than anyone.

# 5

## Roxanne

"Come on, Roxie, don't be like that. You were into it last time."

While rolling my eyes at Eddie's highly inaccurate statement, I continue down a dark alleyway. I can't believe I was so stupid to fall for his sob act. He doesn't care that my scholarship floated precariously in the wind for three months after the security guard was murdered, or that I sat at a police station for fourteen hours giving testimony about an incident I'm still struggling to comprehend.

Even the officer taking my statement was wary about my recollection of events, and I was as honest as Mother Mary. I even told him about the stranger watching Eddie notch his finger inside of me, aware that it could get me in trouble, but hopeful it would see me skipping a murder conviction.

It worked, however my life hasn't been the same since. My nanna is still angry at me, the dean at my school won't stop eyeing me like a freak since our emergency meeting to save my ass, and all my friends bar one up and vanished.

You'd think that would keep me on the straight and narrow, but no, I'm clearly a weirdo who gets off on danger. Why do you think I agreed with Eddie's suggestion for us to camp out in a dark alleyway on a rainy Friday night? It isn't the same alleyway as three months ago—Eddie was smart enough to pick one two towns over from the crime scene of our last farce—but I'm still striving to relive an event I should give anything to forget.

*Someone call the mental hospital. A new patient is at the ready.*

"Roxanne..." The clomp of Eddie's flip-flops on the wet ground irks my last nerve. "I wanted tonight to be special. Why do you think I bought you flowers?"

By special, he means he wants to slide to the home plate by doing something as simple as purchasing a bunch of gas station flowers. *If* he purchased them. I wouldn't put it past him to steal them. That's how cheap he is.

Too angry to let his bad taste slide, I say, "You left the price tag on the flowers, Ed. For future reference, $3.99 won't get you close to home plate." I let out a soundless whine before spinning around to face him. "Even if you did pay for them, which I'm highly skeptical about, I forked out fifteen dollars for *your* movie ticket, so if we're counting merit points, *I'm* coming out of this date shortchanged, not you."

"I tried to even the score." He slants his head so the moonlight can catch the speckles of yellow in his brown eyes. I'm a sucker for the uniqueness of his golden eyes. "But you weren't into it like you were last time."

If I were an honest, upstanding member of society, I'd tell him my lack of interest isn't his fault, it's the fact the mysterious stranger's watchful gawk was missing, but sadly, I'm not just a horrible person. I'm beginning to wonder if there's more wrong with me than an inclination for getting freaky in public.

"This isn't working, Eddie. I need…" *A guy who doesn't wear flip-flops and holey jeans on a date. Someone with hair darker than yours and eyes full of trouble. I need anyone but you.* "… to concentrate on my studies. If I lose my scholarship, I'll be stuck in our horrid town along with all the other geriatrics for the rest of my life."

Proof he doesn't know me at all shines through when Eddie replies, "That wouldn't be so bad, would it? Our families have lived in this region for decades—"

"Yet I haven't seen my parents in years. This isn't the life I want, Eddie. I want—"

"A stranger's gawk so you can come?"

I don't breathe for a good eight seconds. I had no clue he spotted the dark-haired man's stare three months ago.

None whatsoever.

"I don't need anyone to watch. I just—" I stop talking, having no plausible way to say I only want *one* man's gawk without making it seem as if I'm certifiably insane. I could barely see the stranger's face, yet here I am, basing all my hopes and dreams on him. "Can you please take me home? We'll talk more about this tomorrow, I promise. I'm just tired and hormonal, that's all."

"All right, I'll take you home." Eddie digs his keys out of his dirty jeans to authenticate his pledge. "After you answer one question." Although I can see in his eyes it will be a doozy, I dip my chin, agreeing to his request. "Did you orgasm because of what I was doing or because *he* was watching?"

My heart sinks as quickly as my mood. "Eddie—"

He cuts me off with a stern glare, reading me better than he should considering he doesn't know me at all. "As I thought. You're nothing but a gutter rat."

"Excuse me?" I snap back in shock. "You're expecting to hook up in an alleyway. If that makes anyone ratty, that'll be you, Mr. Cheapskate."

After rolling his eyes with an immaturity you'd expect from a man with no class, he cranks open the driver's side door of his car, then slides inside.

My brows stitch when I attempt to mimic his movements. The passenger side door is locked, and he isn't leaning over to undo the latch.

"Eddie..." my words trail off for the second time when he plants his foot on the gas pedal. "Are you kidding me? It's late, and we're miles from home!"

When he continues rocketing toward the lot's only exit, I pick up the first thing I see and peg it at his car. My throat works hard to swallow when my swing is better than expected. The can of soup I thought was empty doesn't just smack into the rear window of his outdated ride, it smashes right through it.

It must have been as jam-packed as my anger.

I block the blinding rays of Eddie's headlights with my hand when he dangerously executes a U-turn. When he revs his engine like a deranged man, a normal person would run into the safety of the alleyway. My efforts three months ago reveal I'm nothing close to ordinary. I watch his approach with wide, terrified eyes, only blinking when the bumper of his car buckles my legs out from underneath me.

My body's grotesque impact with the front window of his car causes as much damage as the can of soup did to the rear window. It cracks into a million pieces, sprinkling both mine and Eddie's hair with shards of glass.

I think the worst is over—I can't feel the lower half of my body, so how much worse can it get—but realize things are never easy for me.

With his narrowed eyes revealing how worthless he thinks I am, Eddie throws his gearshift into reverse before he whizzes back at a speed too quick for me to remain on his hood.

I fall to the ground with a thud, breaking more than my pride.

I also crack my head.

# 6

**Dimitri**

Justine's eyes float up to mine when I order our meal in my native tongue. Although displeased I didn't ask what she'd like to eat or drink as I did our previous two dates, she's too shocked about me requesting a bottle of the most expensive wine to announce her annoyance.

I had wondered if she understood Italian when I took a call during our drive from her dormitory to this restaurant but played it off as inquisitiveness. I know better now. If the clipped tone I used on the waiter was a test, Justine just nose-bombed the finals.

Things are tense between us tonight. I guess that can be expected. Most of the women I bedded before Audrey had a three-date rule. Although it took me longer to convince Justine to discount her brothers' multiple warnings to stay away from me, tonight is technically our third date. It doesn't mean anything, though. I'm not looking to hook up. I just want my rivals to *think* I am.

While handing our menus to the waiter, confident Justine won't have the gall to go against me, I say in Italian, "I can order you something else if you'd prefer?"

Under normal circumstances, my pigheadedness would occur in private. Regretfully for Justine, I need it to be as apparent as possible. A bursting-at-the-seams restaurant in her hometown would have been ideal, but since I'm testing both Maddox's loyalty and those who share my blood, I altered our plans last minute. My family's restaurant will still have the effect I'm aiming for, just minus the glaring heat of Justine's brothers from across the room.

Usually, the fervor wouldn't bother me, however the past three months have been some of the longest in my life. The strain is prominent on both my face and my demeanor.

After Maddox left my warehouse minus a bullet wound, I was hit by one shitstorm after another. The gap in my dating schedule with Justine saw Fien's ransom requests returned to their original amounts. My father's wish to keep Miceli out of his realm resulted in four Arabian tycoons canceling their 'work' trips to my side of the globe this quarter, and Tobias's unusual quiet had nothing to do with him being forced to intervene on my 'conversation' with Maddox. It was because he was killed during a rogue operation two and a half months ago. The same operation he assured me would see Fien freed from captivity.

Tobias's death was the proof I've been seeking the past eleven months. Rimi isn't working alone. He doesn't have the means nor the ability to pull off the sting he did almost three months ago. He's getting help, and if the inkling in my gut is anything to go by, it isn't just from our side of the law.

The only reprieve I was given the past three months was news that despite her hankering for public hookups, the teen in the alleyway skipped prosecution. It probably helped that Smith erased the surveillance footage from the security company's servers faster than Erkinsvale detectives drool their way through a box of glazed donuts.

Although Smith works at a lightning-fast pace, the quality of his work is never diminished. The fact he works fast *and* clean is the main reason he's on my team. Trust is a very close second.

My intuition about Justine understanding Italian is proven spot on when she mutters, *"Sono contento di quello che hai ordinato."*

"Ah, so you do speak Italian?"

The genuine surprise in my tone awards me my first smile of the night. "Amongst other languages," Justine replies as her smile picks up.

Her eyes shine as brightly as the diamond drop necklace I gifted her at the commencement of our date when I scoot to her half of our booth so I can lay her napkin across her lap. I'm bringing out all the charm tonight, hopeful the glitz will hide my wolfish insides well enough, she'll be convinced her brothers' worries the past three months were nothing more than them being overprotective ogres like all good siblings should be.

I can't say I don't understand their approach. I had a similar neurosis with my siblings before all but one of them perished. Roberto has been missing for a little over four years. Ophelia was killed in a traffic accident years ago, and CJ would rather live as a recluse than endure another two decades under our father's command. He says he's happy in his log cabin miles from the closest town.

Until Fien is returned, I'll never discover if he's telling the truth. My daughter is the only reason I've remained in this godforsaken town. Just like she was the very reason I strived so hard to leave it a year ago.

Part of me wonders if that was why Audrey was taken. Did rumbles of my wish to cut ties with my family reach my enemies' ears that they were left with no choice but to respond before they lost the chance? Or did the rumors only reach my father's ear, and he did everything in his power to ensure his legacy lived on?

I don't want to believe the latter is true, but until I'm proven otherwise, I'm looking at everyone with the same tainted set of eyes—blood included. It wouldn't be the first time my father has gone against his children. I doubt it'll be the last.

My thoughts shift back to friendly territory when Justine runs her hand down my arm. "Are you okay?" She keeps her tone low, aware there are more than just her eyes on me. My family's reputation isn't what it once was, but that doesn't mean it isn't notable.

Fear is often more respected than gallantry.

"I'm fine." Needing to ease the tension strain creasing her forehead, I add, "I was just wondering whether we should eat dessert here or order it to go."

Although Justine shrugs like a nightcap isn't on the agenda right now, I know that's far from the truth. Her eyes aren't twinkling from the waiter setting down our scrumptious-looking hors d'oeuvres. Interest is responsible for some of their gleam.

* * *

While laughing at something wittingly intelligent I said, Justine dabs at her saucy lips with her napkin. Petretti's isn't as elaborate as the first two restaurants we dined at, but the quality of its meals and service is undeniable. If Justine wasn't seated across from me, I'd be convinced I was in Cefalù, a coastal city in northern Sicily. It's the only place I run to when I've had enough of life. I've not been back there since Audrey was taken.

Some days it seems as if I'll never get back there.

My moping isn't saved by Justine this time around. The waiter who's working super hard for an impressive tip has returned to our table to offer us the dessert menu. Although my earlier comment about us taking dessert home to eat was in jest, the slightest smell of Justine's heated skin has me reconsidering my objectives.

In my industry, the smell of a woman in need is sampled as regularly as a fresh brew of coffee. It's never had this edge before, though. Justine has a pure, unaltered smell, and although she isn't fawning for my attention, her interests are undeniable.

I slant my head to hide my devious smirk before asking, "Have you decided what you'd like?"

If she replies with one of the many options on the menu she's perusing, I'll continue portraying the gentleman I've been feigning the past three months. However, if her reply is anything close to the vulgar ones running through my head, all bets are off. Women have practically thrown themselves at me the past year. I've yet to accept a single offer. I want any exchanges to be on my terms, when I'm ready, and not because my father is convinced a woman's cunt wrapped around your cock is the answer for everything.

My mother's body wasn't even cold before he moved on. I'm not solely talking about sex, either. He married his favorite whore a month after my mother's death. Wife number three lasted exactly thirty-eight days. She no longer occupies my father's bed, but the rose garden at the front of my family's compound is well-fertilized.

I peer at Justine beneath lowered lashes when she mumbles, "Umm... I'm not sure what I want." I won't lie, when she returns my glance, my cock twitches. It isn't the same full-blown throbbing erection I got while watching the blonde get fingered in the alleyway three months ago, but it most certainly wouldn't have any issues getting the job done. Justine is beautiful, and although I can't replace Audrey, I can forget her for a night *or lose myself in someone with almost identical features.*

After handing my dessert menu to the waiter, I request him to place our meals on my tab. He almost shits himself when I suggest he add a hundred-dollar tip to the tally. His excitement is as high as Justine's when I scoot out of the booth before offering to help her out.

She accepts it, albeit hesitantly.

Little Red Riding Hood knows she's being stalked by the Big Bad Wolf.

While guiding Justine to the car I requested the valet keep close by, I silence my cousin, Demi's, third call of the night. She's most likely calling to gripe about the fight she had with Maddox earlier tonight—a fight I instigated with the hope it would keep Maddox off Justine's tail long enough for me to slip her away for a secret rendezvous.

Did it work?

Justine is being guided to my car, isn't she?

Once I've assisted Justine into my low-riding car, I jog around to the driver's side door a second valet is holding open for me. I gunned down a man in cold blood only a week ago, yet my heart rages more when I slip behind the steering wheel than it did back then.

Monogamy has never been my strong point, but it feels different this time around. My woman isn't holed up at home waiting for me in a toasty chiropractor-approved bed. She's most likely buried in an unmarked grave, her stomach still open and barren.

Since anger is surging out of me in hidden waves, I shut my door with more force than needed. Justine was supposed to be a ruse, a way to get my daughter back. My cock shouldn't be leading our exchange. Yes, it's been over a year since I've had a woman quiver beneath me, but that's part of my penance, isn't it?

I took my eyes off my wife to admire another woman, fascinated at how she could exude such beauty while thick black tears rolled down her face. She was more Gothically dressed that I would have liked, and far too young, but I couldn't take my eyes off her. She was too ravishing to deserve a half-scrutinized glance.

For over a year, I've failed to understand how Rimi got the better of me. Only now am I realizing he didn't blindside me. It was the unknown redhead on the corner of 29th and James street. She was so tiny, my body would have blanketed hers in an instant. The thought on how she'd respond to my big, brooding frame had me so mesmerized, I didn't realize Audrey had torn away from me until it was too late. My enemies had captured her.

She was carrying my daughter, my flesh and blood, yet, my wandering eye sees my daughter paying the price for my stupidity. I'd turn the knife on myself if it wouldn't make me as selfish as my father. For years, I craved his approval. I thought becoming his shadow would return our family's name to the stature it deserves.

Alas, he only taught me one thing. *Famiglia prima di tutto.* Fien is my family, she's all I have, so she comes before anyone —even me.

My focus returns to the road in just enough time to spot an overloaded truck heading my way. The driver flashes his lights, warning me the weight he's hauling is too heavy for him to stop our collision, leaving the task up to me.

I won't lie, my heart races more now with adrenaline than unease. The thrill zapping down my spine is maddening and addictive at the same time. I'm pissed I've gotten myself into a situation that could leave Fien to defend for herself, but I haven't had a surge of energy like this in months. It makes me feel alive like I'll can overtake the arrogant prick whose speedo has probably never been over thirty and make it back into my lane with a few seconds to spare.

"Dimitri..." Justine forces out through the panic clutching her throat when I flatten my foot on the gas pedal instead of the brake.

My car is a prototype designed to respond on demand, and I'm determined to see if its guarantees stack up. The needle on the speedo goes from thirty to seventy in one blurring second. The horsepower behind its motor glues me to my seat while the vibrations of the steering wheel mimic the spasms a woman's cunt does when I tease her clit with my tongue.

When we whizz past a brand-spanking-new Buick, the windows of my Hennessey Venom F5 rattle. My brutal speed isn't solely responsible for their shudders. Most of their tremors are compliments to the truck whipping past us a nanosecond after I slot into the minute space between the Buick and a chunky-tired Chevrolet.

Like a recently admitted mental patient, I commence laughing. I'm not talking a little, hey-that-was-fun laugh, I'm talking full-blown, cackling like a hyena who ate an entire dish of hash brownies. I had no idea how dead I felt on the inside until now. The adrenaline hit will wear off as quickly as it arrived, but the reminder that I'm alive will keep the blood in my veins hot for a few weeks to come.

Once my laughter dies down, I stray my eyes to Justine, shocked by the silence on her side of the cab. During our many hourly 'chats' the past three months, I couldn't shut her up, so her quiet is just unusual. It's a little unnerving.

Justine's back is one with her seat like mine and her eyes are wide. I can't tell if she's excited or scared. It could be a combination of both. She isn't asking me to pull over like Audrey did anytime my foot got friendly with the gas pedal, but is that because fear is clutching her throat too fiercely for her to talk? Or does she love the adrenaline hit as much as me?

If I were half the man I used to be, I'd ask her. Since I'm not, I slackened my pressure on the gas pedal before returning my eyes to the road.

For the rest of our fifteen-mile trip, I maintain the law. I blinker before turning, stay within five miles of the designated speed limits, and stop at pedestrian crossings.

It's the most mundane trip of my life.

Who buys a limited-edition sports car to drive it like a senior citizen in bad need of a bus pass?

The only good that comes from my slower pace is my ability to pay attention to other things besides how well my tires grip the wet asphalt.

We have a tail.

The lowness of my tailgater's ride assures me it isn't the Feds or a member of the local law enforcement, much less the heat of their glare. I should have known Demi wouldn't have called until *after* her fight with Maddox. Who stops an argument to make a call mid-crisis? Not any female I know.

With one plan out the window, I commence another. "Dammit, I forgot my place was being fumigated tonight. Do you mind if we swing by my father's house instead?"

As her jaw unhinges, Justine's still wide-with-terror eyes drift my way. "You want to go to your *dad's* house?" She cringes out 'dad' like most men do when their side dish brings up marriage during their first hookup.

"He's away for the weekend. Won't be back until Monday."

The width of her pupils double. I understand her shock. I pretty much just hinted that we should spend the weekend fucking at my dad's house. I don't have a cunt, but even I can comprehend how that would make most women want to close their legs instead of opening them.

"Other people will be there."

"Oh..." Justine's throat works through a hard swallow before she asks, "Like who?"

"Ah..." *Fuck, when did I lose the ability to lie on the spot?* "Friends and family."

"Oh." This one is much more approachable than her previous one. "That sounds nice."

Nice isn't a word I'd use to describe anyone in my father's crew, but with Maddox riding my ass, I've got no other option but to take his sister back to my family's compound. It has the means to keep Maddox out long enough that gossip will circulate to my enemies that I took Justine to meet the family.

In this industry, that's the equivalent of knocking a woman up with your kid.

With my foot once again becoming friendly with the gas pedal, I enter my family's fortified mansion approximately thirty seconds before Maddox. The window isn't wide, but it's long enough for me to request for the goon on the gate to commence full lock-down. That means no one comes or goes without my permission —not even the authorities.

After pulling up to the side of the mansion-like building, I switch off the ignition. "Things are usually pretty rowdy in the main quarters, so we'll head to the ones in the lower half. It'll be quieter down there."

"Okay," Justine says, hesitantly nodding.

Once I've assisted her out of my car, I commence guiding her inside. I can tell she's uneased about the ruckus we hear more than we see, but I pretend not to notice. She has four older brothers. I'm sure she's accustomed to the 'situations' most men find themselves in late on a Friday night. Even someone as mind-fucked as me prefers the cries of a woman in ecstasy over a wounded soldier being slain.

With my hand on the small of her back, I direct Justine past the den filled with drunken men and half-dressed whores until we reach the hallway that leads to the lower living quarters of the compound. If she was unaware of the lifestyle I was raised in, she isn't anymore. Men in this industry have no shame. If they want to fuck a whore, they do it wherever they please—including the very hallway we're walking down.

"Third door on the right," I tell Justine as my cell phone commences vibrating in my pocket.

My hand is only just hovering above her skin, but I feel the spike in her pulse when we enter my room. It's a large loft-type space with a separate seating area, mock-up kitchen, and grand bathroom, but the first thing everyone's eyes zoom in on is the four-poster bed. Although it was purchased as a joke, it's very much like me—designed for fucking. The handcuff grooves in the thick posts reveal this without a doubt, much less the leather straps that pull out from beneath the mattress.

Although I can drop the gentleman act since we're behind closed doors, I ask Justine if I can take her coat. I've never seen my daughter in the flesh, but that doesn't make me any less of a father. If Fien is ever allowed to date, I can sure as hell tell you her prospective partner better ask to take her coat. If he doesn't, he'll lose more than his fingers.

Justine's denial blasts through her eyes before she articulates. She's freaked, although if her scent is anything to go by, she's more uneased about where she is than *who* she's with.

I shouldn't like the thought, but I do.

With Justine looking for any excuse to leave, I stop ignoring my buzzing cell phone. "While I take this call, why don't you wash up?"

Not waiting for her to respond, I nudge my head to the bathroom door on our right before sliding my phone out of my pocket and dragging my finger across the screen. Since I'm anticipating my caller to be Demi, I don't bother peering at the screen to check who's calling. I just growl down the line, "This better be good."

The voice that responds is much too gruff and manly to belong to Demi. "Where are you? I have current surveillance on the package."

"Fien?" I ask at the same time Justine whispers, "I think I should head off." She points to the door like it will magically zip her back to her dormitory that's almost an hour and a half from here.

"It's late, and I've got to..." Her words trail off when the sound of someone being pounded into submission overtakes her whispered words. It's clear the people in the room next to us are fucking. The droning "more, more, more" chant bellowing through the paper-thin walls is indicating enough, much less the sound of a headboard rocking and rolling with every thrust.

I'd tell them to keep it the fuck down if Smith didn't grunt out an agreeing hum. Now nothing but my daughter is on my mind. "How current are we speaking?"

When Justine attempts to interrupt me again, I hold my index finger in the air, rudely asking her to shut up for just a minute. Unless I've paid for the privilege, I haven't had a spotting of Fien since she was born. I can't sidestep this to walk Justine though a bout of unease because a couple is having a good time in the room next to us. I'm not asking her to join them, I simply need her to be quiet for a second.

My heart thuds in my ears when Smith says, "I'm looking at her now. It's a live feed."

"You can see her?" Even though I'm asking a question, I don't wait for him to reply. "Send me a link."

When a whoosh sounds through my phone, I drag it away from my ear. Like magic, footage automatically commences playing on the screen. I don't breathe while taking in the face I'd recognize no matter how grainy the image. I don't do anything for a good three or so seconds. I just absorb all the tiny features of my daughter's adorable face as she snuggles into the chest of an unknown blonde. She looks tired, and she's sucking her thumb like I have witnessed many times in her ransom photos the past twelve months.

"I'm backtracking the surveillance camera's footprints. I should have a location in thirty or so seconds..." Anything Smith says next is drowned out by the frantic thump of my pulse. Rimi doesn't have Fien out in the open for no reason. They're moving her. How do I know this? She's being carried on a large commercial-size private jet. Rimi would only order that size jet for one reason—he's going on a long-haul trip.

"I need to know her location, Smith, and I need to know it now!"

A keyboard being punished by tattooed fingers booms down the line along with Smith's accented voice. "I'm working on it. The fuckers are throwing up a ton of firewalls. I've never faced a security system this hard to crack..." His words are replaced with a groan. "I'll call you straight back." Not giving me the chance to tell him I'll kill him if he hangs up on me, he disconnects our call.

Since our connection is lost, my screen returns to its normal setting, losing me the image of Fien's sleepy face. I grip my phone to near death, both frustrated and as angry as fuck. It's good we have a lock on Fien, but how far and few between will that be if she's taken out of the country?

With my anger at a pinnacle, I forget Justine is in the room with me until she whispers, "I'm going to go," like it's impolite for her to depart without announcing she's leaving.

Believing it's best for all involved for her to do precisely that, I nod before digging my keys out of my pocket. "You'll have to take my car. I can't leave."

My cell works anywhere, but I don't have access to a state-of-the-art weaponry room in any old town. This compound isn't called The Artillery for no reason. Every weapon combination you can think of is here, and I've used them all at one stage in my life.

"Oh… umm, that's okay. I can call a taxi?" Justine suggests like it's perfectly normal to find your way home after a failed hookup.

Under different circumstances, I would organize her a ride with one of my crew, but since the rumblings of battle are vibrating under my feet, I jerk up my chin like a soft cock for the second time tonight. "I'll organize a cab while walking you out."

Relief crosses Justine's features. It's quickly chased by worry. Instead of her heart rate pelting my hand as it did during our walk to my room, mine thuds against her back when I guide her out of my room. My heart rate is so sky-high, I feel seconds from coronary failure.

Partway to the front entrance, my cell phone rings again. I'm so eager to dig it out of my pocket, I almost drop it. I inwardly curse, annoyed by both my fumbling hands and discovering how badly I work under pressure. I didn't need to fetch a cab for Justine. Her brother is being held up by the goons at the gate. The numerous texts they sent me requesting permission for Maddox to enter the compound assures me of this, much less the quickest peek of his Pontiac parked at the side gate.

Maddox can drive Justine home, allowing me to shift my guilt to a person it shouldn't have left for even a minute.

After sliding my finger across the screen of my phone, I squash it to my ear. "Are you in?" When Smith whistles out an agreeing noise, I cup the speaker of my phone, then lock my eyes with Justine's. "Will you be all right from here?"

We're mere feet from the gate. Even a recently bled virgin would make it out of a house full of vampires unscathed in the distance she has left to travel.

Justine's chin barely dips an inch when I spin on my heels and race away from her as if she has cooties. It's a jerk-hat move, but as I've said before, Fien comes before anyone.

"Where is she?"

I stop dead in my tracks when Smith replies, "She's been under our nose the entire fucking time. She's in Ravenshoe."

# 7

## Dimitri

As I race for the weaponry room to stock up on supplies, Smith advises why he had trouble tracking Fien's location. "You know the hold Isaac Holt has on Ravenshoe. His security personnel was never going to let me in without groveling." He scrubs at his hair-less chin while disclosing, "I'm down a dozen favors, and he wouldn't even let me piggyback his trace. Fucker."

I'm not surprised. Isaac and I have met before. Let's just say things aren't amicable between us, so I don't see him letting his hacker work for me even if I offered to pay. "Did you ask him to cancel the flight?"

My jaw tightens when Smith's hum this time around isn't agreeing. "Tried. The airstrip is privately owned. Hunter agreed to throw up some server blockers to delay their departure. It'll give us thirty, forty minutes tops."

Thirty minutes works. I can get to Ravenshoe easily within thirty minutes. "Clover—"

"On his way with Preacher. He's taking the tank."

Smith's reply frustrates me to no end. "We can't go in heavy. Fien could get hurt." While weaponing up with my arsenal of choice, I take a moment to deliberate. "Tell Clover to wait. He's not to make a move until I've arrived."

I inwardly curse again, panicked I'm doing the wrong thing but also aware of how Clover works. He's a killing machine who craves a massacre no matter the cost. His passion for a bloodbath could get Fien killed. I'd rather lose sight of her for another year than lose her altogether.

"Monitor the situation with Hunter, if circumstances change, patch it through to the Range Rover feed. I'll take Rocco with me."

Confident he'll follow my orders to the T, I disconnect our call, stuff a second colt down the back of my trousers, then hotfoot it in the direction I last saw Rocco. He was the one getting frisky in the hallway when I guided Justine down it.

Rocco drives like a madman, has done two stints in prison, and has a murder count nearly as high as mine, and it was all achieved before his twenty-fifth birthday. His impressive stats aren't the reason I'm pulling him into this, though. It's because he achieved all of the above while under my watch.

I needed someone deep in the prison system for future plans. Dirty guards are always handy to have up your sleeve, but they've got nothing on true gangbangers. Despite what the warden tells you, he isn't in charge of anything that happens in the yard. He doesn't even have a hold on the cells. They've always been run by the Cartel.

The sweet smell of sweat-slicked skin streams into my nose when I enter the hallway where my room is located. Rocco is still going at it. I'm not surprised. He only has one whore on the go. He usually has two or three. "I need to get to Ravenshoe in under thirty minutes. We'll take the Range Rover most of the way."

To the disgrace of the brunette he's balls deep inside of, Rocco immediately withdraws, yanks his jeans up his stout thighs, then tucks away his cock. After winking at his whining counterpart to ensure her he'll be back to finish what he started later, he follows me toward a hidden bunker at the side of the compound.

My brutal speed slows a few seconds later when the quickest flash of galaxy black paint gleaming in the moonlight captures my attention. Maddox's pride and joy is still parked by the side gate. He's seated behind the steering wheel.

*What the fuck?* I thought he would have been long gone by now.

My brain is still striving to work out two plus two when India arrives out of nowhere. Her visits have been few and far between the past three months. I don't know if my almost choking scared her away or the fact Miceli likes smacking his girl around while she gives him head. She would have needed more than a stick of concealer by the time Miceli was done with her.

I shouldn't relish the thought, however I do.

Something about India rubs me the wrong way. She's supposed to be an innocent like Audrey, but her eyes reveal she's nothing close to that. They're as evil as mine, and it isn't just a hankering for danger firing them.

"Dimitri, quick. It's Justine." To a stranger, she sounds worried. In reality, she's just out of breath. The only exercise she does is running her mouth. She can't even tick sex off as strenuous activity. I haven't bedded her—much to her disappointment—but I've heard rumors. "Your father caught her on the way out. He isn't happy."

"Col is back?" Nothing but shock highlights my tone. I wasn't lying when I told Justine he was out of town. I would have never brought her here if I had an inkling he was returning early. That's just asking for trouble. He has issues with anyone coming between him and his foot soldiers. It's one of the reasons I focused my search for the culprits of Audrey's kidnapping closer to home the past few months. There are too many missing pieces of the puzzle for me to believe the Castros are acting alone. They've had help, and I'm just really fucking praying it isn't someone within these walls. If it is, my family name will be tarnished more than it's ever been.

My gut twists when India nods her head. "He's sending her to the Gauntlet."

I curse out loud this time around. The Gauntlet is where my father sends people to die in the most inhumane way possible. Torture. Gang rape. The dismemberment of multiple parts of your body. He chooses his punishment on a whim. There's no rhyme or reason to his process other than undeniable proof that he's a madman.

India's eyes bounce between mine and Rocco's while asking, "Are you coming? I doubt she has long."

I jerk up my chin, commencing my lie in a nonverbal way. "Head down. I'll be right behind you."

She doesn't believe a word I'm speaking, but she's aware she'll take Justine's place if she dares to go against my direct order. "I'll do everything I can to delay things."

I wait for India to disappear in the compound before racing into the bunker to yank off a dusty tarp from an old minecart. It was stolen decades ago when Bronte's Peak was blasted into a cliff edge partway between Ravenshoe and Erkinsvale. We call it the Range Rover because it has the tags Clover swiped from my father's mint condition Range Rover last year.

Although the minecart is a rust bucket, it, along with the underground tunnel my father commenced drilling four decades ago, will get me to Ravenshoe in under twenty minutes.

I considered having my father's head examined when he

unveiled the finished project after too many glasses of port when I was sixteen. Now I'm glad I encouraged his madness. I've only used this tunnel a handful of times, mainly to skip prosecution when shit went down at the underground fights we regularly hold on the outskirts of Ravenshoe, but you can't put a price on having an unknown escape route.

I'll never use it to hide from my enemies, but you can be assured I won't hesitate using it to sneak up on them unaware. When you're storming a compound, the last place you foresee being attacked is from behind. It will leave my enemies clueless while helping my empire grow.

While Rocco fills the Rover's tank, I yank my phone out of my pocket and call the last person I expected to speak to tonight. Maddox answers two rings later, and even over the phone, I can tell he's fuming mad. "I swear to fucking God, Dimitri, if you don't bring my sister out here immediately, I'm going to wring your fucking neck."

"If you want your sister to get out of tonight alive, I suggest you shut your mouth and listen to me." My brutal tone immediately gets his attention. I doubt he's even breathing. That's how menacing my voice is. Although I'm not technically prioritizing Justine over Fien—it only takes one person to fill the gas tank, so I'm more utilizing my time wisely than fucking around—I still hate that I'm in this predicament to begin with. "Tell the goon manning the gate that you need to go to the Gauntlet, give him the passcode 'cannon.' When you arrive, fall to your knees and fucking beg. Say anything and everything Col wants to hear—"

"Dimitri..."I don't know whether he pauses to catch his breath or to plot one of the many ways he plans to kill me. Whatever it is, he's wasting time he can't afford. My father has no patience whatsoever. Once he's handed down a ruling, it is *immediately* executed.

If Justine isn't dead, she's walking straight toward it. "What the fuck is going on?"

When Rocco nudges up his chin, wordlessly announcing the Range Rover is good to go, I say down the line, "You said you'd die for your sister, right?"

I hear Maddox swallow before he pushes out, "Yeah."

While slipping into the makeshift seat in the minecart next to Rocco, I mutter, "Tonight is your chance to prove that. Your life for hers, Maddox. I don't see Col taking any less."

Stealing his chance to reply, I press the end button on the screen of my cell, stuff it into my pocket, then tap on the roof of the Range Rover telling Rocco to floor it.

I never wanted to be a hero until I looked into the eyes of my daughter.

Tonight is my chance to become one.

My lungs wheeze in protest to the stuffy conditions, and I'm covered in dust, but as predicted, we make it out the other side of the tunnel in just under twenty minutes.

"Leave it uncovered, we don't have time," I tell Rocco when he commences sheltering the mineshaft cart with the camouflage netting he pulled off a real-life Range Rover. "Smith sent logistics to the Range Rover's mainframe. The airstrip is eleven miles from here." I lift and lock my eyes with his so he can see the urgency in them. "I need to be here ASAP. The jet is fueled and ready to go."

"Give it to me." After sliding into the driver's seat, he snatches my phone out of my hand. His eyes zoom over the screen as he calculates the quickest route.

Once he's confident he has his bearings right, he jabs his finger into the ignition button, fires up the engine, throws the gearshift in reverse, then peers over his shoulder. There's nothing but scrub behind us, which he parts like the Red Sea two seconds later.

Spotting my shocked gawk, he mutters out, "Why go around when we can go over?"

He flashes me a wink that has me forgetting the direness of the situation for a few seconds before he whacks the gearshift into first to commence our trek over sandy plains.

We pop out onto one of the many freeways servicing Ravenshoe a couple of minutes later. Since it's late, traffic is practically nonexistent.

The frantic beat of my heart slackens when I realize how close to the blue dot we are. Rocco's shortcut shaved a good three to four minutes off our travel time.

"Take the next exit," I advise Rocco when a message from Smith pops up on my screen. He's hacked into my system to advise us of the most direct route to take.

The further we travel up the ramp, the more the headlights of the Range Rover bounce off a figure coming from the other end. Although the ground is wet from a recent sprinkling, all the clouds have moved on, exposing a full moon. It adds to the deathly halo shrouding the petite blonde.

"What the fuck is going on here?" Rocco mutters under his breath when the brightness dims enough, we spot the streams of blood gushing down the blonde's face. She's barely walking, her wobbly strides more stumbling steps than polished strides. Her dress and boots are ripped like most punks pay out the eye for when selecting designer jeans, and her blonde hair almost looks red from how much blood it's absorbed.

She's either been in a car accident or run over by one.

Their list of injuries are about the same.

"Someone fucked her over good," Rocco summarizes, stealing the words straight out of my mouth.

He glares at me like I'm insane when I demand him to keep going. Although he didn't place his foot on the brake, he did loosen his pressure on the gas pedal, slowing our pace.

"We don't have time. Fien's jet could taxi toward the runway at any moment." I can see the lights of a control tower just over the horizon. We're almost there. "I'll send someone back for her once Fien is safe."

"All right." Although he's agreeing with me, he isn't happy about my decision. He has a soft spot for battered women since his momma was one. His dad used to beat the living shit out of his mother. Discovering the reason for her many bruises saw him facing his first stint in juvy at fifteen. His second was for his father's murder. I loaded the gun and handed it to him. He took care of business how I should have done with my father years ago. Regretfully, my surname means there are rules I must follow. Back then, Rocco didn't face the same issue.

With Rocco's jaw as tight as mine, he increases his pressure on the accelerator. The paintwork on my door gets friendly with the railing on the side of the road when he takes a wide birth around the stumbling blonde. I don't pay any attention to the brutal grind. I can't take my eyes of the one green eye popping out from a mattered mess of unbrushed locks when we whizz by the blonde.

I've seen that eye before—more than once.

"Stop!"

Rocco locks up the brakes so quickly, I'm winded when my ribs collide with the glove compartment. It'll teach me for not wearing a seat belt. Ophelia was killed when she was flung out of the wind-shield of CJ's ride. If she had been wearing her seat belt, she may have survived their accident.

With my mouth refusing to relinquish my words, it takes me a good three seconds to garble out, "Go back."

"Back?" Rocco double checks, not willing to risk death if he heard me wrong.

Although certain I'm making a mistake, I scream, "Yes! Now! Go!"

Rocco thrashes the living hell out of the Range Rover's engine after tossing the gearshift into reverse. We arrive at the bottom of the ramp in an instant, but the blonde is nowhere to be seen.

"Where the fuck is she?" My eyes go wild, seeking the reflection of her stark white hair. "We're the only people out this way. She couldn't have just up and vanished."

My eyes stray to Rocco when he mumbles, "Why go around if you go over."

When he spots the confusion on my face, he points to a section of the railing a few spots up from where we are. Bright red blood gleams off the silver material.

"Fuck." I throw open my door and sprint three solid strides to the portion of the blood-stained railing. My lungs react as if they ran a marathon when I spot the battered blonde at the bottom of the ravine. She's breathing, but only just. "Bring me a rope."

Nodding, Rocco pops open the back of the Range Rover before sliding out of the driver's seat. While he does as requested, I remove my suit jacket before rolling up the sleeves of my dress shirt.

I have one sleeve in place when Rocco arrives at my side with a used length of rope. How do I know it's been used? It's soaked with blood. Guns, knives, and Molotov cocktails aren't the Cartel's only source of weaponry. Everyday instruments can be just as useful in the right hands.

"Secure it to the railing."

I don't need to tell Rocco what knot to use. He knows all the tricks of this life, so he's more than aware the last thing you want is for a rope to snap when your boss sentences a man to be hung.

"I'll go," Rocco suggests when I wrap the loose end of the rope around my wrist so it can support my scale down the gorge. I don't need it to keep me safe, but it will come in handy to hoist the blonde out of the ravine.

Although appreciative of Rocco's offer, I shake my head. "I want to do this." I don't know why, and I'm reasonably sure I'll regret it at some stage in the near future, but I want to do this.

Rocco nods for the second time before he steps back, so I can swing my leg over the railing. It's slippery because of the recent rainfall, but I make it down the gorge relatively fast.

"Bring the car back around to the freeway. It'll be quicker to walk her out than pull her out," I shout after surveying the area. "I can see the interstate from here. It's about the same distance as the height of the gorge."

I wait for the lights of the Range Rover to disappear from above before kneeling at the blonde's side. A massive crack splits her head from the top of her skull to the middle of her forehead, she has a number of bruises and scrapes on her arms and torso, and her legs are all types of fucked up. The only part of her that looks untouched is her midsection, so that's what I toss onto my shoulder before hot-footing it in the direction I requested Rocco to meet me at.

The blonde grunts and groans with every step I thump, but it's better than her being silent. Silent would mean she's dead. Although she'd probably wish for that to be the case if I lose my daughter for the second time.

Rocco cranks open the back passenger side door. "Is she alive?"

"Just." I place her onto the back seat of the Range Rover as gently as possible before slipping in next to her.

When Rocco slides behind the steering wheel, I scream for him to go. I'm in two minds, torn between wanting to assess the blonde for injuries and causing her more harm.

Because I acted on impulse instead of the cruelness I was raised by, I wasted precious minutes I don't have—minutes that could have Fien torn away from me forever.

As Rocco races us back up the exit ramp, he strays his eyes to the rearview mirror. "Wrap your belt around her thigh. If the blood squirting out of her wound is a femoral artery, she'll bleed out in minutes. Trust me when I say no amount of scrubbing will remove her blood from your interior if you let that happen."

Under different circumstances, his murderous gleam would be entertaining.

Tonight, it's anything but.

While yanking my belt through the loopholes of my trousers, I hear my phone buzz. Naturally, I search my pockets.

It isn't there.

It's nowhere to be found.

I return Rocco's uneased gaze when he tosses my phone into my lap. "You left it in your suit jacket." I haven't been without my phone for a second over the past twelve months. Not once. It's my only form of contact with the people holding my daughter captive. I don't do anything without it being on me. Not a single fucking thing—*except this.*

Pissed at the fool I'm portraying tonight, I cinch my belt around the blonde's leg with more force than needed. Blood stops oozing out of the gash in her thigh, but she barely rouses. From experience, I can tell you her chances of surviving are low. When you stop feeling pain, you soon stop feeling anything.

Guilt for hurting her leaves when I read the message Smith sent. Fien's jet is taxiing toward the runway. My daughter is about to leave the state if not the country.

"Hurry the fuck up, Rocco."

Hearing the desperation in my voice, he mounts the curb edging the entrance of the private airstrip and drives through the steel security fence instead of going around it. While he creates his own path over rugged, sandy plains, I signal for Clover to move. It's fucked I have to warn him what will happen if he kills my daughter, but I'd rather him be cautious than go in bombs blazing like he usually does.

The scene replicates a stunt movie when our bumpy ride switches to a smooth one. We're at the far end of the runway. The jet is heading straight for us.

If playing chicken with twelve thousand pounds of metal isn't adventurous enough for you, you could always join Clover on the wheel of the jet. He's hanging on like a real-life action figure, unconcerned about the speed the jet picks up the further it careens down the runway.

"What's he placing on the jet?" I scream down comms when the placement of a metal box on the underbelly of the twelve-seater plane is quickly chased by Clover's huge ass rolling across the asphalt. This is usually when I'd plug my ears in preparation for a massive blast. He's a detonation expert as much as he is an assassin.

My heart stops punishing my ribcage when Smith's gruff tone barrels out of my phone's speaker. "Tracking device. Depending on the length of travel Rimi is planning to do, it may hold on."

Even though he can't see me, I jerk up my chin, understanding his objective.

Although I'd give anything to be handed a few minutes to deliberate, things are progressing too quickly for that. I have to once again act on impulse.

Fingers crossed it works in Fien's favor as it did the blonde's.

"What will happen if I shoot out the window of the jet?"

Fingers fly over a keyboard before Smith replies, "On the ground, nothing much. No guarantees on her staying in the air if she takes off, though. All aircraft have holes in them, and the pressurized system is capable of taking an additional one or two, but if you blow out the window..."

When his words trail off, I fill in the gap, "I could kill Fien?"

"Possibly." He sucks in a big breath before continuing, "It's like all aspects of life, Dimitri, you either take a risk and hope you don't fail or sit back and let someone else control your life." Even aware his comment was more a personal reflection on his life than our current situation, it still hits me square in the stomach. First, I let my father puppeteer my life, and now I'm letting a weasel of a man like Rimi Castro get the better of me.

This needs to stop.

"Pull over."

Proof Rocco was born for this life is exposed when he yanks up the parking brake before he tugs on the steering wheel. He brings the Range Rover to a dead stop parallel with the jet still whizzing down the runway.

After grabbing an M16 stuffed behind the seat, I throw open my door, then climb onto the roof of the Range Rover. I'm not surprised when my glare down the scope has me stumbling on Rimi Castro in the pilot seat. He doesn't trust anyone, not even a qualified pilot. That's why he does everything himself.

I'm kind of the same, not that I'd ever admit that to anyone, especially not my enemy.

My target is locked and loaded, my finger is hovering over the trigger, but no matter how much my brain screams for me to fire, I can't. Firing at a moving target takes skill and precision. I have both of those, but what if Rimi pulls Fien into the line of fire a nanosecond after I take my shot? What if I kill her like my father killed my mother? He may not have fired at her, but he did use her as a shield. He *is* the reason she's dead.

"Five," Rocco commences counting down a short time later,

warning me that the jet will be in the air by the time he reaches zero.

"Four..."

I recheck my scope before wetting my lips, my mouth suddenly bone-dry.

"Three..."

While inching back the trigger until the clip is close to releasing a bullet, I suck in a final breath. It could very well be my last if my shot shatters the cockpit's window, and Rimi still takes off. He's stupid like that. He'd rather die in a fiery wreck than give in.

"Two..."

The vibrations of the jet's engines overtake the shrill of my pulse in my ears.

"One..."

I take my shot.

My bullet perforates through the cockpit's windshield exactly where aimed, but I fail to hit my target. Rimi slanted his head with barely a second to spare. His life was saved by less than a millimeter, and I'm too late to take a second shot. The plane's wheels are no longer on the runway. They're zooming past my head.

When the jet disappears into the moonlit sky, I discharge the remainder of the bullets from the M16 into the tarmac. Several of them lodge deep into the blistering surface, however a handful ping off the rigid material, coating both my car and face with shrapnel.

The one that skims my cheek enough to scold my skin all but obliterates my last nerve. I'm fuming with anger and willing to take it out on anyone I deem responsible for the loss of my daughter for the second time in my life.

Seemingly having a sixth sense to my inner psyche, Rocco places himself between the back passenger door of the Range

Rover and me when I leap down from the roof. "This isn't her fault."

"How is this not her fault? If we didn't stop to pick her up, Fien would be here!"

It's clear he has no desire to live when he replies, "Carrying her out of the gulley took about the same amount of time for you to line up your shot. If you want to shift the blame here, Dimi, you're gonna need to look in the mirror."

He smiles like a sadistic fuck when I dig the barrel of the colt under his ribs. I slant my gun upward, so it's facing his heart before getting to within an inch of his face.

Most men would piss their pants by now. Rocco isn't my number two for no reason. "You gonna shoot me, Dimi? You gonna gun down the only man whose *always* had your back?" He brings his face even closer to mine. "Who stood at your side when you buried Ophelia? Who helped you search for Roberto when he disappeared? Who has offered time and time again to pop bullets into your father's stomach because you can't?" The disappointment flaring through his eyes is as obvious as mine. "That was all me, D. Every fucking one of them was me. But if you want to kill me, go ahead because you ain't touching that girl."

"I need to kill." I can't put it simpler than I just did. The urge is so white-hot, it's burning me up on the inside even more than the truth of Rocco's statement. If I don't kill someone, I'll turn the gun on myself. That wouldn't just end things badly for me, it would leave Fien defenseless. The only time women in the industry are seen as valuable is when their womb is ripe with the next leader of the Cartel. Fien is years away from that age. If I die, she dies. There are no guarantees in my life *but* that.

"You can't have Rimi yet, so why not go after the next best thing?" My brows inch together when Rocco takes a step to the right, unblocking the visual of the almost unconscious blonde.

Even with the roar of a private jet's engines barreling over her head and the discharge of a semi-automatic weapon, she's still out cold. "She didn't get banged up like that for no reason. Whoever did that to her is the person you should be taking your anger out on. She wouldn't have needed rescuing if someone hadn't fucked her over."

As my lips itch into a callous smirk, I snag my cell phone out of the Range Rover. "Smith..." Adrenaline thickens my veins when he hums a second later. "Do you have a spare laptop at the ready?"

The crack of a laptop screen being pried open sounds down the line before Smith asks, "What do you need?"

Rocco's grin matches mine when I say, "It's time to go on a scavenger hunt," but it sags when I add, "*After* we've dumped her far from here."

What I said earlier is true. Women are worthless in this industry, so I wouldn't do myself any favors adding another one into the mix. If the reports blowing up my phone are a true indication of how Justine encountered the Gauntlet, the nicest thing I could ever do for this unknown blonde is wipe the slate clean for her so she can start afresh.

If that means I have to remove *everyone* from her life, so be it. I'll do that. I'll do anything to ease the guilt tearing me up from the inside out.

# 8

**Roxanne**

My stomach swirls as violently as my temples thump my skull when I attempt to open my eyes. I don't know how long I've been out for, but if the dryness of my throat is anything to go by, I haven't had a drink in a thousand years. My mouth is bone-dry. I can't even conjure up the slightest bit of spit to moisten the burn of my swallows.

"Eddie..." That's the last thing I remember—paying for tickets to a stupid action flick Eddie wanted to see. If the price tag on the flowers wasn't a jarring enough reminder that we have hardly anything in common, his choice in movies should have been the icing on the cake.

Alas, I'm a sucker for his sweetly intense brown eyes.

Did I fall asleep during the movie? That could explain why my body is aching so much. The new theater complexes aren't as spacious as the out-of-date one in our hometown, and I couldn't afford premium tickets, so perhaps I'm kinked up because of the rigidness of the chairs in the theaters?

"Or not," I mutter to myself when I attempt to ease the throbbing of my temples with a quick swirl of my fingertips. My wrist is cuffed to a steel railing. I'm shackled to a bed like a convict at the start of the movie we watched.

"They said you murdered someone," whispers a shy, frail voice next to me. "That you cut him up into little pieces because he hurt you." After switching on the light hanging over her bed, a petite brunette with sunken, blood-stained cheeks and black eyes rolls over to face me. "Is it true? Did you kill him because he did that?"

"Did what?" I ask, truly confused.

My heart pains for her when she leans over to open a drawer next to her hospital bed. Her face isn't the only thing beaten up, so are her arms and torso.

"Who hurt you?" I ask when she hands me a compact mirror.

She tugs her nightwear in close to her body to hide her many bruises before lowering her eyes to her shoeless feet. "No one. I'm very clumsy. I often fall."

I want to reply, *headfirst into a fist by the looks of it*, but I keep my mouth shut. I'm not one to judge. I look just as bad as her, except my cuts and bruises can't be hidden with makeup. I'd need to grind out the stitches and staples running down my forehead first, and even then, I doubt the world's highest-rated concealer would help.

The only good to come from my battered and bloody appearance is the knowledge I can stop bleaching my hair. Its natural red coloring doesn't seem as bad as it did when I was a child. It gives me a unique edge not many women have.

*It also may be the only way I can take the focus off the scar running down my forehead.*

While licking my lips to soothe their deep cracks, I toss the compact back to the brunette's side of our room. I'd walk it over to her like she did me, but since I'm cuffed to my bed, I can't.

With that in mind, I ask, "If I'm so dangerous, why do I have a roommate?"

Her blue eyes widen to the size of saucers. "Umm..."

When she forcefully swallows, the truth smacks into me hard and fast. "We're not in a standard hospital room, are we?"

She only shakes her head for a second, but it's long enough for me to deserve the title of a mental patient. I scream like I'm in the process of being murdered while thrashing against the cuffs like I'll have the strength to break out of them. I don't. I'm too weak and pathetic for that, but my many pledges that I'm not insane does allow some clarity to form.

"We're not in a mental hospital," the brunette assures, pacing back to my side of the room. "We're in a special wing of a hospital. A *guarded* wing." Her next set of words take her nearly ten seconds to articulate. "It's where they put criminals awaiting trial."

"I'm not a criminal..." I stop talking when the first part of our conversation replays in my ears.

*'They said you murdered someone.'*

*'That you cut him up into little pieces because he hurt you.'*

"Who died?" I'm shocked I can talk with how hard fear is clutching my throat. Surely, I'm dreaming. This can't be real.

The brunette rushes a spew bag to my side of our room when her reply makes me heave. She didn't say any random old name. She said my boyfriend's name—his *full* name. Eduardo Emanuel Cordova.

"I didn't kill Eddie. I'd *never* hurt him," I blubber out through violent sobs. "I loved him..." My words fall short when the deceit in my tone reaches my ears. I cared for Eddie, but it was nothing close to love.

I raise my watering eyes to the mystery brunette. "What

happened?" When she drags over a chair, preparing to settle in for the long haul, I ask a second almost just as important question, "And why am I the only one cuffed?"

# 9

**Roxanne**

Who knew straight-up murder rates higher than a measly manslaughter charge? My ex-roommate drove her car headfirst into a cypress tree with her abusive boyfriend in the passenger seat, however she only faced a manslaughter charge. I was 'allegedly' rundown by my boyfriend before being run over by him. Then, miraculously, I somehow got myself to his apartment two towns over from where I was left to die to, I quote, "Torture the complainant over a six-hour period." End quote.

Six. Hours.

That was the hole in my defense that had me transferred from the criminal wing of Erkinsvale Private Hospital to a standard ward. I was found in an ambulance bay by a medic going out to have a cigarette a little after one in the morning. Surveillance footage from my assault proves it occurred just after dusk. Despite wishing I was able to torture Eddie for six hours, it wasn't possible for me to be in two places at once, hence the reason my charges were dropped.

Do I feel bad about what happened to Eddie? Yeah, in a way. I'm more remorseful for his family than him. They have nothing going for them and will most likely never get off welfare, but they didn't deserve to lose their son the way they did.

I reached out to them a couple of weeks ago to offer my sympathies. When I got an automated message saying their number is no longer in service, I sent them a letter instead. Having their services cut is nothing out of the ordinary for the Cordovas.

"Are you ready?"

Ignoring the apprehension swishing in my stomach, I raise my eyes to my rock the past three months. My best friend, Estelle, grew up in the housing estate next to my nanna's ranch. With my grandparents refusing to sell no matter how elaborate the offer, housing developments popped up all around them. Now they have the only ten-acre block left in this area of Erkinsvale.

The executor in charge of my grandparents' will said I could make an impressive profit if I were willing to sell their decades of hard work. Sadly for him and his commission-seeking cousin, I missed my nanna's funeral because I was in a coma, so the last thing I'll ever do is see her legacy bulldozed.

She loved and took care of me when no one else would. Then she died alone.

I can't forgive myself for that.

The injuries that placed me in a coma for a month weren't my fault, but I do blame them for my nanna's death. She had told me time and time again that Eddie was no good. If I had listened, she wouldn't have been out searching for me when I failed to make curfew, and then she wouldn't have been knocked down a ravine by a drunk driver.

Mistaking my remorseful face as sympathy for Eddie, Estelle

says, "Don't look so glum, Roxie. You survived for a reason." I roll my eyes when she chuckles out, "We just need to find out why that is." That's just like her. Even when we should be blowing snot bubbles out of our nose while in the throes of despair, she finds humor in every situation.

When I take a right out of the hospital room I've called my home the past three months, Estelle wraps her arm around my shoulders. "Nu-uh. Claudia isn't there anymore, remember?"

My sigh is soundless, but Estelle still hears it. My ex-roommate wasn't as lucky as me. Even with numerous witnesses saying they saw Claudia's boyfriend's hand on the steering wheel in the lead up to their crash, prosecutors pushed forward with their case. Claudia will give birth to her son in prison since she was served three years for involuntary manslaughter last week.

"We could visit her next weekend?"

I raise my eyes to my best friend, loving that she can read me like no one else. "Yeah?"

She bumps me with her hip, causing me to smile. "Yeah. You know me, always open for a three-hour drive to a maximum-security women's prison."

"How could you not when you say it like that?"

Laughing, she breaks away from my side to open the passenger side door of her beat-up Honda for me. Her car is a total write-off, but she loves it as much as she loves me. Nothing screams freedom like your own set of wheels. I'm hoping to scrounge up enough money for my own sometime this year.

"Your chariot awaits, m'lady," she says, all pompous like.

Giggling about my immature tongue poke, Estelle races around to the driver's side door. Because I forever admire her animalist grace, my eyes follow her trek partway around. My stare is incomplete because I'm looking at a pimped-out Range Rover parked across from the passenger loading bay. It's not often you see flashy cars like that in Erkinsvale, and very rarely is there a pair of piercing green eyes glancing out of the crack in the driver's side window.

"Roxie..." Estelle stammers out in confusion when I hotfoot it across the street without checking for traffic.

I almost get wiped out by a car traveling in the opposite direction. The whoosh of its outdated metal whizzing past my face is strong enough to add an extra hobble to my shaking strides, but it isn't to slow me down.

"Hey." I race faster when the engine of the Range Rover fires up. "Wait!"

It darts out of its parking space so quickly, the smell of burning rubber lingers in my nostrils long after it rockets out of the hospital's parking lot.

"Who the hell was that?" Estelle asks, out of breath. She isn't gasping because she followed my sprint. She runs miles every single day. She's as breathless about the eerie unease ridding the air of oxygen as me.

There's only one time I've felt this restless. It was when I was in the alleyway with Eddie. Not the time he ran me over, but three months earlier, when he brought me to ecstasy under the watchful stare of a pair of vividly beautiful blue eyes.

The pair that just rocketed away were nowhere near as entrancing as the ones that stared at me almost seven months ago today, but they were most certainly just as dangerous.

The knowledge shouldn't excite me, but for some reason, it does.

# 10

**Dimitri**

When Rocco places down his phone to make a quick getaway, I drag the timer on his live feed back a couple of seconds. I don't want the image of Roxanne Juniper Grace when she spotted Rocco's gawk half a block down from her apartment building, I want her reflection in the side mirror of the Range Rover Rocco's manning at my command when she chases him down like she did outside the hospital three months ago. The second in time when her big green eyes are wide and unconcealed.

Restless edginess thickens my cock when I find the footage I'm seeking, which is utterly ridiculous considering I'm in a boardroom with thirty of my father's closest confidants. He believes I'm in Sicily strengthening foreign ties. I'm here because it's the last confirmed place the tracker on Rimi's private jet was pinged. The Castros are either here, holed up at an unknown location, waiting for the heat to die down after their operation killed thirteen FBI agents and two CIA officers, or they took a secondary jet to another location.

Rimi's crew has been silent for over six months now—double the length of time Roxanne was an inpatient at Erkinsvale Private Hospital. I don't fucking like it. A ransom payment for Fien hasn't been requested in months. That makes me edgy because if I'm not paying to keep her safe, how can I be assured she is?

Although I understand the reasoning for the silence—Rimi now has both sides of the law chasing him—usually nothing stops business from progressing in this industry. Not even having my wife kidnapped and my daughter forcefully removed from her stomach saw me awarded any leeway. I work or die. I don't have any other option, so why isn't it the same for Rimi?

After grinding my jaw side to side, frustrated by the world I was born in, I restart the live feed just as Rocco's face fills the screen of my phone. "Satisfied?" he asks, sounding anything but.

Even with the eyes of thirty men on me, impatiently awaiting my verdict, I jerk up my chin. I don't know why I needed to see Roxanne move into a tiny one-bedroom apartment in the middle of Erkinsvale anymore than I needed to watch her walk out of the hospital three months ago, but for some reason, the urge wouldn't pass no matter how hard I fought it, so I gave in and let fate play its hand for once.

Will my indecisiveness see me scolded for the third time in my life?

Only time will tell.

"What now?" Rocco mutters, aware one task never ends without another one taking its place.

Hummed whispers bounce around the room when I reply, "Organize the jet to collect me. It's time for me to return home."

The sternness of my jaw doubles when Rocco mutters, "For your girl?"

His smile tells me his comment had nothing to do with my daughter, but I act stupid. "If you're referencing Fien, yes."

"What?" He pushes out a few seconds later, incapable of ignoring the wrath of my glare for a second longer. I've always been a temperamental prick with a short fuse, but it's grown substantially worse over the past six months. "You've had me stalking that girl for months. Justine's recovery didn't even get this much heat, and you take the blame for what happened to her."

I didn't think my mood could get any worse, however it just did. My father's verdict for Justine's 'supposed' disrespect was an hour in a room with a dog trained to kill. Maddox moved fast after I called him, but he was still minutes too late. Justine was torn to shreds.

I asked Rocco to keep me updated on the progress of her recovery. That surveillance wasn't as easy for him to conduct as it was Roxanne's because Justine has an army of people propping her up. Roxanne has no one. From what Smith tells me, her parents are alive, but she hasn't seen them in years. Her grandfather passed away a year before her grandmother, and she has no known siblings.

Do I feel sorry for her? Not. At. All. There are far worst things she could have faced than being forced to live with her grandparents. Her daddy could have sold her to his friends for the night like he has her mother multiple times when his drug supplies get low.

If a man pays to fuck you, he'll take it with or without your permission. Nearly every man around this table has done so in the past. The sex slave industry is rife at the moment. It's right up there with baby-making factories.

That's what my meeting today is about. A new baby-making facility is hoping to place footholds in the Sicily region. They want to take sex slaves, impregnate them, then sell their babies to the highest bidder.

Although this scheme isn't close to my predicament, I can't help but source similarities from it. Fien wasn't sold to the highest bidder, but is that because I can afford to keep her safe? What would happen if that changed? Would she be passed on to the next candidate? Or killed like her mother?

Just the thought has my mood souring to the lowest it's been. "Organize a meeting with my father within hours of my return," I say down the line after standing to my feet, hopeful the table's height will hide the raging pulse of my cock not even a bad mood could slacken. "I have some questions I'd like to ask him."

Rocco scrubs at the stubble on his chin. "I don't think it's wise to mingle with him right now, Dimi. He's knee-deep in some murky shit."

"Murkier than this?" His silence speaks volumes. The only time Rocco is ever quiet is when I'm right. If I'm wrong, he shouts it from the rooftops. "Although the journey to my takeover is miles away, at one stage, I must take the first step. That time is now, Rocco."

Since all is said and done, I disconnect our video chat, shut down my phone, then slide it into the pocket of my trousers. Despite the brief intermission, today is all about business, so I'm dressed to the nines—expensive suit, designer tie, diamond-encrusted cufflinks. If you didn't know any better, you could confuse me with a legitimate businessman. It's just the crooked people I'm forced to deal with day in and day out that would have you thinking differently.

"I gave your business proposal my utmost devotion the past week. The figures cited are impressive considering the lack of capital needed, and it appears as if you have infrastructure and clientele at the ready." The faces of the men seated around me gleam with hope, optimistic I'm about to approve their baby-making facility. "But..." I wait to ensure they have plenty of time to absorb the snip of annoyance in my tone before continuing, "Operations like this don't sit well with me. I want to drag my family's name out of the mud, not smear it with more dirt."

"But Dimitri, your father—"

"Lost the ability to make decisions for this sanction many moons ago," I interrupt, equally frustrated and shocked someone had the gall to speak against me. The day you lose respect in this industry is the day you retire.

I don't mean to an old folks home. I mean *eternal* retirement.

When my eyes stray to my contester, the reasoning behind his boldness becomes apparent. Cristo is one of my father's longest-known associates. He practically ran this chapter of Italy before I arrived. He didn't like handing over the reins, but he didn't have much choice. Names open doors in this industry, not decades of service.

"I said no—"

My nostrils flare to suck in a quick breath when Cristo defies me for the second time. "Your father approved our tender. Today's meeting is merely to tie up loose ends..." His arrogant words are gobbled up by a big swallow when I nudge my head an inch to the right, wordlessly demanding for Clover to move to his side of the room. Clover won't kill him. He'll just linger nearby in case he needs to muzzle his mouth. I'd hate for his throaty gargles to frighten his employees.

More times than not, a bullet to the head instantly kills you, but there are a handful of occasions where the bullet doesn't traverse through the midsection of the brain, leaving the victim gurgling on their blood for a good three or so minutes. It's rare but possible to survive a bullet wound to the head. I've seen it twice in my lifetime.

My lips twist when Cristo goes down without the slightest snivel. I wouldn't have minded hearing him sob. He was an arrogant prick who should have been taken out with the trash decades ago.

With my gun still hot from being recently fired, I place it on the tabletop along with my palms before roaming my eyes over the group of men staring at me with an equal amount of fear and respect. "This chapter is being placed into involuntary administration. You either let it die quietly or take the exit Cristo just took. The choice is yours."

Almost all of them hum out a collective agreement that I've made the right choice, but a handful aren't as eager as the rest. They're the ones I mentally jot down for execution, unforgiving that they could have wives and children relying on their 'income' to keep them feed.

Someone will hand their wives a few thousand at their funerals for food and expenses. By the time the money runs out, they'll have a new 'man' taking care of them. That's how fast things move in this industry.

"Luca, Davis, Porter, and Michel, you're free to go. The rest of you, place dinner orders with Gia. You're in for a long night." A ghost of a smile touches my lips when I drift my eyes to Clover. "Perhaps you can show our unneeded guests the way out?"

The deadly gleam in Clover's eyes reveals he understands what I'm asking—none of the four men named above will be breathing by the end of tonight—so I don't need to mention the hearty swallow they do when Clover opens the boardroom door for them. A paid killer only opens the door for you when he's planning to knife you in the back.

With Clover's mood appearing as tense as mine, I don't see the men's deaths being handled quickly. If that's the case, I might join him later. Excluding Cristo's quick, unsatisfied kill mere seconds ago, I haven't witnessed the weakening of a man's pulse since I sentenced Eduardo Emanuel Cordova to death for his crimes.

Rocco and I took our time with Eduardo. His murder was more satisfying than Cristo's, especially when he cried while begging for his life to be spared, but it could have been better. He could have pleaded for forgiveness for what he had done to Roxanne instead of begging for his own pathetic life. We might have gone a little easier on him if he had shown an ounce of remorse. Alas, even bottom-dwellers think their lives are worth more than their female counterparts.

That's why my daughter was taken and my wife was killed, and it is the very reason I'm not leaving this boardroom until I find out exactly how deep my father's ties are with already established baby-making facilities.

I've wondered for months if my family had anything to do with Audrey's disappearance. Tonight I will find out. You can put your money on it.

# 11

**Roxanne**

My race into the living room of the one-bedroom apartment I share with Estelle slows when I spot how she's celebrating Thanksgiving holiday weekend with her new beau. Braydon has her pushed up against a wall our tiny television doesn't come close to filling. Estelle's dress is wrapped around her midsection, and Braydon's hands are hidden in an area I'm going to act like I never saw.

They're creating their own things to be grateful for, and I'm insanely jealous.

Who doesn't want a hot, brooding man to pin them to the wall like they're not slumming it in an apartment that would only look more authentic if it were in the Bronx? A mattress would make things better, but since the only one in this apartment belongs to me, I'd rather they keep their hip-thrusting to the living room. I can sterilize a wall with a little disinfectant. I can't afford to steam clean an entire mattress.

"Wish me luck?"

When Estelle's lips drag away from Braydon's, mine pucker into an air kiss. I can't get mad about her getting freaky in our living room. She lost the only room in our dingy apartment in a rigged game of rock paper scissors—she always picks rock, by the way—and although I would have the means to rent something fancier if I were willing to sell my grandparents' ranch, Estelle has never once given me grief about that. As far as I'm concerned, that means Braydon could go down on her right now, and I wouldn't bat an eyelid. Our friendship is solid, and I don't see anything ever coming between it.

Despite Estelle being my rock, I've been in somewhat of a rut the last twelve months. I was the only witness to a murder, run over by my boyfriend, and accused of his murder. To say it's been shit is an understatement, but that is all set to change today. I have a job interview—finally!

A year of online courses and many *many* hours of free labor has been reduced to this. A permanent part-time position at a company I've never heard about in a town forty miles from here.

It could be worse. I could have been shortlisted for the position at the old folks' home. Even someone without a college degree knows that's a last resort for any twenty-year-old. I understand if you can't wipe your bottom anymore, someone has to do it for you. I'd just rather that someone not be me.

Estelle smiles a blistering grin when I whine, "I really hope Dimitri isn't as old as dirt. Momma needs some new pretties, but graveyard ready isn't the vibe I'm aiming for."

"Even if he's as fugly as Mr. Mugly, you're gonna get down on your knees and peer up at him with your pretty green eyes out in full force. This is the opportunity you've been waiting for, and it's offering thirty-five dollars an hour." Estelle exhales with a pompous flare. "I'd fiddle with a shriveled-up chunk of shrimp for thirty-five dollars an hour!" After winking off Braydon's stink-eye like it doesn't hold any steam, she meets her eyes with mine. The humor glistening in them exposes her dramatic performance was more to ruffle Braydon's feathers than mine, but it does little to hide her worry. "Are you sure you don't want me to come with you? I can sell ice to an Eskimo, so a college dropout with a partial credit for a double business diploma will be a walk in the park."

Although she can sell meat to a vegetarian, and I wholeheartedly appreciate her offer, I shake my head. "My interview is in Hopeton, and you're rostered on to work a double tonight. Our schedules are a no-go."

"Hold up, go back," Braydon interrupts, talking through his kiss-swollen lips. "You're going to Hopeton for an interview with a man named Dimitri?"

Nodding, I snag my purse off the kitchen counter before joining them in the living room. Our apartment isn't a loft. It just feels like one since it's so tiny. "Have you heard of him?"

"Have I heard of him! My God, Roxie, did your mama drop you on your head?" He grunts like his words jab his heart instead of mine. Even if every word he speaks is true, being truly, madly, and deeply in love won't stop Estelle from punishing him for talking down to me. Dropping me on my head would have been a kind thing for my mother to do to me. Estelle knows that, and now, so does Braydon.

After issuing his apologies to Estelle with only his eyes, Braydon shifts them to me. They're riddled with unwarranted guilt. "I'll come with you."

"No, Braydon, it's fine. You've got... *Estelle* to take care of." That was close. I almost reminded him he has nothing but a substantial inheritance to worry about. That wouldn't have been very nice considering he's not once shoved his money into my face.

I've reminded myself time and time again the past few months that he isn't one of the rich snobs I tussled with when trying to have my scholarship reinstated after my 'accident.' He's down-to-earth and kind, and on more than one occasion, he's offered for me to be his personal assistant even with him having nothing for me to do.

If life were about money, I'd accept his offer in an instant. Alas, I wasn't born fighting for no reason.

"Estelle has a double shift tonight, so I'd rather you ensure she gets home safely than worry about me. Hopeton is dangerous, but it's safer than here."

Confident I have Braydon's worry honing in on another target, I snatch up my house key before hightailing it to the door.

"We'll talk about this more tomorrow," Estelle shouts through our rapidly closing front door.

By 'this,' she means me plopping her in the deep end without a life raft. It was deplorable for me to do, but what can I say? If an opportunity presents to shift the focus away from me, I'm happy to take it.

---

"The agreed price was forty-dollars." I thrust my iPhone toward the Uber driver's side of his car to show him our agreement. "We're still miles from Hopeton."

He shrugs like it isn't a big deal he's asking me to exit his car three miles out of town while wearing heels. It's chilly, and since his heating is as shitty as his personality, my toes are on the verge of snapping off.

"I didn't anticipate the traffic in Ravenshoe to be so thick."

"How is that my fault?" I argue back, beyond annoyed.

I didn't factor in traffic either since I've never driven through the town that was nothing but cornfields when I was a child. If I had, I would have scheduled for him to arrive an hour earlier. Not only am I late for my interview, if I'm forced to walk, the business I'm being interviewed at will be closed by the time I get there. The sun is already setting.

I fan the bangs I had cut specifically to hide the horrid scare on my forehead before issuing one final plea. "Please, Mr. Kind Driver Man. I'll do anything you want if you'll take me to my requested destination. I've got a few nickels in the bottom of my purse." I yank out the Starbucks voucher I got for my birthday last year. "This gift card still has eight dollars on it. That'll get you're a super frothy mocha latte. And..." I search my almost empty purse for something more appetizing than year-old mints and lint balls. When I fail to find anything, I say, "We could grab that latte together? If you want?"

I instantly regret my decision when lust flares through the stranger's dark eyes. I don't know where he grew up—which I'm guessing took place over five decades ago with how gray his ear hairs are—but inviting someone for coffee means you're *only* inviting them for coffee. This isn't Vegas.

While throwing open his back passenger door with a grunt, I snarl, "Say goodbye to your five-star rating, Mister. I'm going to one star your ass all the way to Uber headquarters."

I don't know what he replies. I can barely hear anything over the skid of his tires when his foot gets friendly with the gas pedal not even two seconds after I stepped out onto the road surface.

"And to think I was going to share my nanna's mints with you!"

I add a handful of expletives to my squeal before I commence my trek to Hopeton. I'll never make it in time for my interview, but Hopeton's bus station is closer than Ravenshoe's. My nickels might not have been on the Uber driver's radar, but I don't see a bus driver being as fussy. If he's lucky, I might even arrive on the scene with a super frothy latte for him.

Three painstaking miles later, I'm on the verge of deliriousness. My legs are quaking like they *never* have under any of my college boyfriends, and my mouth is bone-dry, but I've made it to my destination. Shockingly, the establishment my interview was to be conducted at is still open. It probably helps that it's an Italian restaurant bursting at the seams with clientele eager to get something more than overcooked turkey in their bellies, and it has the same last name as the man seeking a personal assistant. *Perfect!*

After twisting the Celtic ring on my thumb, so it faces the front, I throw open the door of Petretti's Italian Restaurant and make a beeline for the dining hostess. "Hi, my name is Roxanne Grace, and I'm here to see—"

"Booth or regular seating?"

I stray my eyes over the blonde's teeny tiny uniform and popping blue eyes before replying, "Excuse me?"

"Booth or regular seating?" she says again while dragging her eyes down my body in the same manner I just did hers. "Even if you're eating alone, I'd still suggest the booth. It'll save the clientele getting depressed when they see you eating by yourself on Thanksgiving weekend."

*Ouch.*

"I'm not here to eat."

She cocks a faultless brow. "Then why are you here? This is a restaurant."

Her pitied glare doubles my annoyance. "I'm aware it's a restaurant. I can read." *Unlike you.* "I'm here for an interview." I dig out the piece of paper I jotted my interview details on this morning before thrusting it the blonde's way. "I'm supposed to ask for Dimitri."

"You're here for Dimitri?" When I nod, her humored gaze

extends to her collagen-filled lips. "Trust me, honey, excluding your hair coloring, you're not his type. One sideways glance, and he'll kick you to the curb. Save the bruise, leave now." She ushers me away from her podium with a wave of her hand like I'm worthless.

I'm not backing down this time. It's been a hard and long twelve months for me, and this blonde is about to be hit with the brunt of my annoyance. "I don't care if I'm not Dimitri's type." I air quote my last word an inch from her face, issuing her the same *snap-snap* dismissal her nails did when she waved me off. "I'm here to be interviewed for a position on his team, so I'm not leaving until Dimitri himself tells me to leave."

I fold my arms in front of my chest to hide the shake of my hands when the blonde says, "Okay." I hadn't expected her to give in so easily. "Dimitri's office is at the back of the restaurant. You need to go down the side alley and take the third door on the left."

"Side alley, third door on the left?" I repeat like I'm suddenly stupid.

When she purses her lips with an agreeing nod, I say, "Okay. Thank you."

I won't lie, I strut like Catwoman under Batman's watch while following the restaurant hostess's directions. I'll never be picked as the demurest woman in a room, but for how many times my ass has been kicked the past year, I'm taking tonight's triumph as a win. Even if I don't get the job, I'll feed off the adrenaline of my victory for weeks to come.

The quickest flashback of a pair of golden-brown eyes flashes before my eyes when I'm partway down the dark alleyway. The food scraps on the ground make it obvious the restaurant receives most of its deliveries here, but because of the late hour and the early closure of businesses due to Thanksgiving, it seems shadier and more obsolete.

"Third door on the right," I mumble to myself when I stop in front of one that has 'Distribution' etched on the door.

Believing there will be a less-shady entrance past the graffiti-coated door, I push it open with only the slightest creak. The décor isn't any more inviting on the inside. There's nothing but scary shadows dancing across the faces of four middle-aged men.

The scene grows more confronting when I notice who their attention is fixed on. They're honing in on a smaller, more timid-looking man huddled against an outer wall. His face is bleeding, and his hands are held out in front of himself in a non-defensive manner. He's clearly scared.

My throat dries when a lone soldier breaks away from the pack of hungry wolves. He speaks to the frightened man in a heavy accent, his tone both demoralizing and angry. "The service you ordered was delivered as specified, so not only am I refusing your request for a refund, I'm anticipating a subsequent payment for your insolence."

Even with my business diploma unfinished, I'm not so stupid to believe this is a distribution disagreement. I've heard rumors about a mob mentality in Hopeton, but I've previously brushed them off as hearsay. I can't do that this time around. My potential employer is getting fleeced—fleeced of money that could possibly come from my thirty-five dollar an hour salary.

With my veins still hot with adrenaline from my clash with the restaurant hostess, I conjure up a ruse that will see both Mr. Petretti and me leave this room uninjured. I should be scared, but seriously, what's the worst that could happen? The men I'm about to confront are pushing sixty, if not seventy. I survived being run over by a car, so I can most certainly handle a mobility scooter.

Confident I've got what it takes to divert disaster, I blurt out, "I've called the police. They'll be here at any moment." I didn't call anyone. My cell battery died 1.8 miles from Hopeton. I just want them as scared as Mr. Petretti. "If you don't want to be arrested, I suggest you leave right now."

My gall takes a step back when the man in the center of the group pulls a large black gun out of the back of his pants. I was prepared to face a handful of bruises from the whack of a walking cane, not a maiming bullet from a semi-automatic weapon. "Or perhaps I'll just take care of business now instead of later."

The minute snippet of air in my lungs races out with a scream when he cocks back the hammer on his gun before he squeezes the trigger. He doesn't just gun down the man he was in the process of shaking down. He blows off his entire face.

Certain I'm next on the maniac's hit list, I mumble out, "Never mind," before pivoting on my heels and darting away.

I make it three steps before a bullet whizzing past my ear stops me in my tracks. "The next one I'll aim at your head." Confident he has me scared enough I will do anything he asks, the lone soldier requests that I spin around. "I want to see your pretty face one final time before I blow it away."

After forcefully swallowing the bile racing up my throat, I do as requested. My knees weaken halfway around. The elderly gentlemen circling the now-faceless man aren't the only men in the room. There are another four in the far corner of the dark space. They're all wearing black and have guns much larger and more capable of hindering facial recognition in their hands.

They appear bored until the only man seated rises to his feet. Unlike his mean-looking counterparts, he starts his assessment of my body from my snap-frozen toes to my whitened face. He takes his time, seemingly storing every little detail for future use.

I wonder if he does that to all his victims, or am I special in some sick, twisted way?

My hand unintentionally moves to flatten my frizzed hair when the stranger's narrowed gaze shifts from my eyes to my hair. It's longer than I normally wear it, and back to its natural red color. Waking up in a hospital room cuffed to a bed changed me. I'm not as straight as an arrow, but I'm most certainly trying to improve myself.

Being 'me' was the very first step.

I drop my hand like it's a bomb when the dark-haired man pushes off his feet to cross the room. He has an arrogant walk full of cockiness and self-assuredness. It matches his persona, which is almost as suffocating as my lungs' inability to suck in air when he stops to stand in front of me.

Goosebumps rise across my skin when he raises his hand to my face. I'm anticipating for him to wipe away the blobs of wetness rolling down my cheeks, so you can imagine my shock when he merely brushes away the bangs I had cut to cover a scar no amount of concealer can hide.

The room is cloaked by darkness—in more ways than one— but I can tell the exact moment the ugliest of my past rears its horrid head. The dark-haired man's discovery of my two-inch scar screws up the face of the elderly man behind him. He looks sickened like I'm suddenly as ugly as I feel.

I'd rather his disgust over the gleam his eyes held when they first landed on my face. Even someone with the purity of a saint couldn't have mistaken the longing in his heavy-hooded gaze.

I glance over the stranger's shoulder when the man behind him says, "You seem to have caught the eye of my son. I'm not surprised. He has quite the fascination for redheads." The man I'm guessing to be mid-sixties places himself between his son and me. His strut is as vile as the amused smirk on his face. "Is she one of yours, son? A little plaything for the night?"

My throat aches to release a frustrated scream when the man whose eyes seem oddly familiar mutters, "I forgot I ordered her.

What can I say? The schedule of women coming and going from my life every week often gets confusing."

Everyone laughs except me. I know he's lying, but I can't tell if that's a good or bad thing. He's a little hard for me to read. He seems to be protecting me, but there's an undeniable amount of anger radiating from him. It's as if he's torn between wanting to soothe my panic or double it.

I stop seeking answers in his beautifully tormented eyes when the man with the gun points it at my head. "Unfortunately, you'll have to find another plaything for the night. This one knows too much."

I shake my head, assuring him I know nothing. "I won't tell anyone what I saw." I shakily cross my heart. "I swear to God."

"God can't help you now." He smiles a grin you should only ever see in hell. "But be sure to tell him I said hello."

I don't breathe for a second when he curls his finger around the trigger for the second time. His expression is so impassive. He shows no emotion whatsoever.

I can't cite the same thing.

The lady at the makeup stand lied earlier today. The mascara I paid twenty-two dollars for isn't waterproof. I can't see my cheeks, but I can feel the big black smears rolling down them. They're mixed with the saltiness of my tears, but the chunkiness that comes from applying three generous coats of mascara is highly obvious.

I stormed in here feeling as brave as a soldier.

Now I'm on the verge of peeing my pants.

That makes me ashamed of myself.

"Do it. Kill me." I step up to the man until the barrel of his gun digs into a dress too thin for this time of year. It makes the shudders reeking with my body more apparent, but has me proud I won't die a coward. "Put me out of my misery once and for all."

"Do you want to die, little girl?" asks the man with a thick Italian accent.

"No," I answer with a shake of my head. "But I'm not going to beg for my life to be spared. That would have me dying a coward. I'd rather die than be seen as weak." My words are strong, however my composure is anything but. I'm shaking so much, the black blobs rolling down my face quiver in the panted breaths when they cling to my top lip.

"You should be happy you made it this far. Usually, I would have shot you in the back." He shrugs like killing is something he does every day before he raises his gun to my head. "A change-up is as good as a holiday. I can see your eyes now."

I'm at a loss as to what he means, but his son has no issues understanding him. He grabs the barrel of his gun in an instant, shocking me so much my eyes bulge. "Let me." His voice is extra deep like his cock is hard just from the thought of killing me. I'm not surprised. He seems like a man who gets off on danger. "It's my fault she's here, so it's my responsibility to clean up the mess." When his father hesitates, the stranger adds more authenticity to his assurance. "Then I can get my money's worth during our trip to the woods. I paid good money for her, so I plan to find out if she was worth her price tag."

His father smiles a wickedly evil grin that has my stomach flipping even with him weakening his clutch on the trigger of his gun. "I understand your interest. She has such a feisty spark." My chest labors through a challenging breath when he angles his torso to face his son. He isn't peering at him in a loving manner. It's as if their family has as many issues as mine. "She reminds me a lot of your wife." He assesses his son's face for a response. Like he's hopeful his words will hurt him. "Is that what has you so fascinated, son? Or are you looking for a cunt to keep your dick warm for the night? Or a replacement spouse?"

"A man has needs." Even not knowing the dark-haired man, I'm confident in saying he's exuding mammoth self-restraint. His dipping tone is indicating enough, much less how white his knuckles are. His hands are balled so tight, even if his father were to yank back the trigger, the bullet wouldn't make it through the barrel. That's how fierce his grip is. "I had them long before I married, and I still have them now." His eyes are deadly, tainted with hate. "Do you have an issue with that?"

The tension in the room turns roasting. It hisses and crackles in the air even more than the energy that teems through me when the gray-haired man lowers his gun two heart-thrashing seconds later. "Fine. Do with her what you may, but be sure to have it done by sun-up."

Vomit scorches my throat when he fills the gap his gun no longer takes up. I never understood the term 'skin-crawling' until now. My skin does precisely that when he runs the back of his hand down my mascara-stained cheeks. If there weren't so much evil in his eyes, I could have mistaken his gesture as kindness. It's almost gentle, in a psychotic, mass-murderer type of way.

"Just don't be too gentle with her. I want to hear all about her screams." He waits for his son to dip his chin before he sidesteps me and exits the gloomy room.

I think I'm clear of danger.

It was silly of me to ever believe.

The door has barely banged closed when a white cloth is pressed over my mouth and nose. The scent vaping off it bombards me with horrendous nausea in less than a nanosecond, and even quicker than that, I black out.

# 12

## Dimitri

I hold my finger in the air, cutting off the scorn I see in Rocco's eyes before he can deliver. My mood is teetering on the edge of a very steep cliff. I'm the most unhinged I've ever been. Now is *not* the time for him to lecture me. I know what I saw, I know who Roxanne is, and I plan to make sure she takes responsibility for the death of my wife.

I knew I had seen her mesmerizing green eyes before. The change in her hair coloring and the maturity of her looks threw me off the scent for over a year, but there's no denying them now.

Her mascara stained-face is undeniable.

When she stood across from me minutes ago, riling my father like he wouldn't gut her where she stood, it felt as if I had stepped back in time. I was once again entrapped by her beauty, stunned she could emanate such appeal on her darkest day.

Roxanne was the woman standing on the corner of the restaurant Audrey was kidnapped from. The woman I gawked at for so long, I didn't see my enemies creeping up on me until it was too late. She's the reason Audrey is dead and the cause of me not laying eyes on my daughter in person since she was born. Now she must pay the penance for her stupidity.

I just need my cock to get the memo first.

It's as hard now as it was when I watched her being fingered in the alleyway almost a year ago today, pulsating with an equal amount of desire and adrenaline. Its response can't be helped. Roxanne's paper-thin dress is pushed an inch above her tiny lace panties, and her thigh gap allows an uninterrupted view of a cunt I'm sure tastes delicious.

Although her eyes are shut due to the strength of the chloroform Clover used to subdue her, I don't need them to be open to know they're the same emerald green color of her dress. I've studied them multiple times the past nine months in the many surveillance images Rocco took of her. I know every speckle and every flaw.

I also know them well enough to know they'll never be the same once I'm done with her.

I can't believe it took me this long to place all the pieces of the puzzle together. She's always been there in the background of every scene. At the restaurant Audrey was taken from, in the alleyway when I instigated my ruse to make it appear as if I were moving on, and on the very ramp that led to the airstrip that ripped my daughter away from me for another nine long months. I just stupidly saw it as fate instead of the intricate ruse it is.

My father left Roxanne's punishment to me. He never does that. If he has the opportunity of watching the light in someone's eyes be snuffed, he's there with bells on.

This time around, he walked away.

That can only mean one thing. He doesn't believe I have what it takes to kill her.

I'm more than happy to prove him wrong.

# 13

**Roxanne**

I wake with a groan, the punishing pound of my temples as notice-able as it was when I woke up in a hospital room with life-threat-ening injuries several months ago. Although my eyes have yet to follow the prompts of my brain, I am aware I'm in the backseat of an expensive ride and that my hands are bound behind my back with a thick, scratchy twine. The coolness of leather upholstery caressing the back assures me of this, much less the sickening drone of four tires rolling over asphalt. They churn over the road surface as intensely as my stomach wishes to expel the contents weighing it down.

I don't recall ever feeling this ill, and I've had some horrific hangovers. That's why I rarely drink anymore. I'm not one of the lucky ones who wake up the next day feeling fine. For every drink I have, it takes me four hours to recover. That wasn't a schedule I encouraged while endeavoring to keep my scholarship afloat.

Sadly, I haven't had to worry about that the past nine months, meaning I should have had more than my share of drunken benders.

I couldn't be 'me' if I were a drunk like my father.

My eyes sluggishly open in just enough time to see the shadows of a city on the horizon. We're surrounded by sandy plains and overgrown bushes—an ideal spot to dump a body.

As my throat dries with worry, I divert my focus to the vehicle churning out the miles despite the bad conditions. Instead of the middle row of seats in the large SUV facing forward, they've been fixed to a privacy partition shielding the driver from the main section of the cab.

The configuration of the cab ensures I have no trouble locking eyes with the dark-haired stranger when I raise them front and center. He sits across from me with a tight smile and balled fists. He doesn't need to tell me where we're going. I can reach my own conclusion. I told them I had called the police, so it makes sense they'd move my murder away from their business premise. No one will find me out here.

Well, except the vultures, and that's only if they make my grave shallow.

If my death is anything like Eddie's, there probably won't be much of me to bury.

I stop praying for a quick, painless death when an accented voice ripples through the air. "You shouldn't waste your breath on him. He didn't mention you at all." When confusion crosses my features, the man with the evil, yet somehow appealing blue eyes says, "Eddie." He smiles at the widening of my pupils, loving my unease. "Or Eduardo Emanuel Cordova as he was known to us." When he says 'us,' he nudges his head to the men seated each side of me. Their shoulders are butted against mine like I'm the princess of their realm, and they swore an oath to protect me. "He didn't mention you once. He merely groveled for his own pathetic life, so why are you wasting your last words on him?"

Tears prick my eyes. I don't know if they're for Eddie or because the man glaring at me as if I am gum under a park bench just admitted I'm moments from my death. Eddie got what was coming to him, but still, the stranger's confession is a hard pill to swallow.

"I wasn't praying for Eddie," I force out through the sob sitting in the back of my throat. "I was praying for my death not to be as painful as his."

Humor flickers through the stranger's eyes like ambers in a fire. "Who said his death was painful? There's no body, so how would anyone know that?"

My nanna always said my mouth would get me in trouble, which it does precisely two seconds later. "They said he was cut up into little pieces. That he was tortured for hours." I lick my quivering lips before asking, "Is that true?"

He nods without shame, angering me further. "Why? What did he ever do to you?"

"He took my daughter away from me." The expression on his face turns menacing when he spits out, "As did you."

I balk, suddenly sickened. "I did *no* such thing. I don't even know who you are, much less know you had a daughter."

"Have. I *have* a daughter!"

Since my hands are bound behind my back, I have to use my legs to kick him away when he suddenly lurches to my side of the cabin.

Although I give it my all, his hand curls around my throat a mere second before his hot breaths batter my neck. "And if it weren't for you, she'd be snuggled in her bed. Instead, she's been bounced state to state, or worse, country to country."

When a dangerous gleam darts through his eyes, the reason

behind their familiarity smacks into me. He's the stranger who stood outside the alleyway, the man who toppled me into ecstasy even faster than Eddie's hand. It was rainy, and my mind was blitzing about what we were doing, but I am confident he's the same man.

The already tight squeeze he's clutching my throat with doubles when a horrid thought enters my mind. Did my stunt that night prompt the kidnapping of his daughter? He was watching me as intensely as I was watching him, so there was plenty of time for his enemies to undertake a well-planned attack. It takes less than a second for evil to launch.

*Oh, God, I feel sick.*

"I didn't mean any harm. I was just fooling around. I had no clue about the controversy it would cause." He firms his grip around my throat for every word I speak. His hold is so fierce, I feel seconds from blacking out, but I push on, determined to make peace with my guilt before my life expires. "I liked you watching me, but I wouldn't have done it if I knew what would happen to your daughter. I'm sorry. So very, *very* sorry."

My apology seems to anger him more. His face goes red as the candor in his eyes fades to black pits of pure rage. "My wife is dead because of you. My daughter is missing. I should kill you now."

With my brain shut down due to a lack of oxygen, I ask, "Then why haven't you? It's been almost a year."

He must have a weird fascination for toying with his victims longer than necessary because I anticipated my question to increase the pressure he has on my neck, not weaken it. "My daughter has been gone longer than a year." Although his hand remains curled around my throat, slithers of air still manage to make their way to my lungs. It's only just enough to keep me conscious, but it's better than being dead. "She was cut out of my wife's stomach five days *after* she was kidnapped from the foyer of the Slice of Salt restaurant in New York." When my pupils unwillingly dilate, the furious pulse shooting through his palm turns rampant. "Have you heard of that establishment before?"

Even aware I'm adding a nail to my coffin, I nod my head, the pain in his eyes too intense to ignore. My honesty awards me the ability to once again breathe. I gasp in hurried breaths to pacify the scream of my lungs before straying my eyes to the pained ones still glaring at me.

"I met my father in a watering hole next door to that restaurant once. It was after my grandfather passed away. I thought he wanted to get to know me a little better." A flare I've never seen before darts through his eyes when I stammer out, "All he wanted to know was how much inheritance he was set to get from his father-in-law's death. He didn't care about me at all." Disbelieving of fate, and stupidly curious, I ask, "What date was your wife taken?"

The air I've only just gulped down rushes back out when the blue-eyed man replies, "February twelve."

"February twelve, last year?"

My throat works through a tough swallow when his twitching lips deliver his confirmation. He's placed his puzzle together the wrong way. I'm not to blame for what happened to his wife. I was near the restaurant he mentioned to meet with my father. Agreeing to his request was the only stupid thing I did that day.

When I say that to the dark-haired stranger, the furl of his lips turns nasty. "You don't have to whack someone across the temple with the butt of a gun to take part in their kidnapping."

He adds evidence to his comment by splaying his hands across his body. I'm bound in his car, at his complete mercy, however if you exclude him testing the heartiness of my pulse, he hasn't laid a hand on me.

"People can be manipulated in many ways. Take a pretty

redhead on a corner with thick black tears streaming down her face. All it takes is for a man to glance her way for a second, and *poof*, his entire existence is snatched out from beneath him."

The men seated beside me appear as shocked by his confession as me. They either didn't know the part he played in his wife's disappearance or they're damn good actors. It may be a combination of both.

Desperate not to be punished for something I didn't do, I mutter, "Just because you glanced my way that day doesn't make me responsible for what happened." I'd take the blame for what happened if his daughter was kidnapped while he watched my deplorable act in the alleyway, but this isn't my fault. "I've done nothing wrong."

"Yes, you have." His voice rises as rapidly as his anger. "You distracted me, you caught me off guard long enough for my enemies to get the better of me. That makes you responsible for Audrey's disappearance."

My retaliation is as loud as his, my determination just as robust. "I was merely in the wrong place at the wrong time. I am *not* to blame."

His hot breaths hit my lips when he snarls, "Confessing your lack of judgment is the only way I'll offer you *any* type of leniency. It'll do you best to remember that."

The anger surging through causes my usual levelheadedness to go askew. "Leniency for a crime I didn't commit, for a kidnapping I had nothing to do with. How can you expect me to confess to something I didn't do?"

"You distracted me—"

"Because you couldn't keep your eyes on your wife. That isn't my fault!"

He recoils like my words slapped him hard across the face. It's clear he feels guilt about his wife's kidnapping, but that doesn't mean he'll go easy on me. I'll have to work for every leniency I want him to give me.

"If I hadn't looked at you, my wife wouldn't be dead. If I hadn't stopped to find you, my daughter would be here. You're responsible for *everything* that has happened." His voice cools to that of a madman before he adds, "And I'm done playing nice."

"Dimitri..."

I don't get the chance to register the shock of learning my attacker's name. I'm too busy staring into Dimitri's soulless eyes, wordlessly begging for him not to shoot me with the gun he butts up against my temple.

I'm not a parent, so I'll never fully understand what he's going through, but I've often wondered what it would feel like to have a father who'd protect me no matter what. In my eyes, Dimitri's daughter is lucky, but she won't be if Dimitri doesn't learn to focus his anger on those deserving of his wrath.

When I say that to Dimitri, he cocks back the hammer on his gun. I'm about to die, and the man who brought me to ecstasy more times in my dreams than any man in real life is my executioner.

# 14

### Dimitri

My back molars crunch together when Rocco fists my dress shirt so firmly, two of its buttons pop. I have a gun in my hand, and the itch to kill is skating through my veins. He's a fool to fuck with me now. Someone is about to die, and it's a very close call on who the departed will be.

"Listen," Rocco demands my devotion with an authority I didn't realize he held. "She's telling the truth." He squashes my cell phone under my ear like I'm hard of hearing before requesting for Smith to repeat what he said.

"You're right. Roxanne was near the Slice of Salt the day Audrey was taken." The sheen in Roxanne's eyes doubles when he adds, "She paid the tab for the whiskeys her father had in an establishment next door before she arrived on an almost maxed-out credit card."

Even not knowing Roxanne any better than a hooker on a

corner, I'm aware Smith is telling the truth. Shame was the first thing that darted through Roxanne's eyes when Smith's words reached her ears. It was quickly chased by regret.

"But she left minutes *before* Audrey was spotted on surveillance being guided out the back entrance. She hasn't been back there since, and there's no chatter of any kind on her social media accounts or messenger apps. It truly seems as if she was in the wrong place at the wrong time."

Even though Smith can't see me, I shake my head. "There are too many incidents to discount." My gun is directed at Roxanne's head, but I act as if she's invisible. It annoys her more than anything. "She's popped up too many times for *any* of this to be a coincidence."

With my anger at a point it can't be contained, I push Rocco off me before sinking back into my seat opposite Roxanne's. The barrel of my gun is still aimed her way, but I'll have to pop a bullet through my second-in-charge if I want to take her down.

Rocco is protecting her like he failed to do his mother.

The fact I contemplate the carry-on effect Rocco's death would cause my empire reveals how badly I'm spiraling. Tell me one man who wouldn't get a little fucked in the head right now? I haven't had confirmation of Fien's well-being for almost nine months, then, suddenly tonight, a mere three hours before Roxanne shows up out of nowhere, a request for ransom drops into my inbox. Her proof-of-life video was grainy, and it was only four seconds long, but there's no doubt in my mind it was Fien.

Not in a million years would I forget her face.

After working my jaw side to side, I breathe out, "She didn't turn up tonight for no reason. Roxanne *is* a part of this."

"I'm not," she denies with a shake of her head at the same time Rocco spits out, "Yeah, that's probably true. But is it via her choice? Or is she being forced into a fight she doesn't belong in?"

When confusion darts through my eyes, Rocco gets smug. "You're always racing ahead, Dimi, leaving nothing but a trail of destruction in your wake."

He said a similar thing when I told him I was marrying Audrey in a civil ceremony hours after she told me she was pregnant. He wanted me to hold off for a few months, citing there was no need to rush since Fien wasn't due for another eight months. I could have listened to him, but as he said, I'm always racing ahead.

"He could be onto something." Clover shifts the bulk of his heavy frame to the edge of his seat before he hands me a ripped piece of paper. "I found this in her purse when I rummaged through her things."

After gauging Roxanne's reaction to her privacy being invaded, which I'm shocked to say barely altered, I drop my eyes to a set of handwritten instructions on what looks to be part of a university letterhead. The word 'interview' scribble at the top has been underlined three times, revealing the person jotting down the details was excited they'd been granted one.

My anger shifts to confusion when my eyes skim the interviewer's name. It reveals I was supposed to interview Roxanne at my family's restaurant at the exact time Fien's ransom request landed in my inbox.

I drift my eyes back to Roxanne's watering ones. She's scared— there's no doubt about that—but she's also curious, and if I'm not mistaken, angry. Her emotions appear as uncontrolled as mine. "Who sent you this?"

The bangs I pushed aside when I was certain I was dreaming fall back into place when Roxanne shakes her head with a shrug. "An employment agency?"

Her blasé response agitates me to no end. The last time I took the focus off Fien for this long, I lost sight of her for nine months.

I won't let that happen again.

"You didn't think to ask who they were?"

Unsure where my fury stems from, Roxanne shakes her head. "I'm so desperate for a job, I don't ask questions. I just accept any interview offered."

Even with the rattle of her vocal cords chopping up her words, I'm confident she's telling the truth.

People are more honest when they're in fear of their life.

"Smith—"

"Already on it," he says down the line, his thick voice vibrating through my phone's speakers. "I'll have every number that's called her cell for the past year in five... four... three... two—"

My eyes snap to the side when Rocco blurts out, "It was me. I organized her interview."

Just as quickly as my eyes rocket to Rocco, they dart to Roxanne. She appears as shocked by his confession as me, meaning I can shift the focus of my gun to Rocco's head despite my gut begging for me to reconsider.

"*You're* playing *me*? *I* made you who you are. *I've* given you everything you have, but now *you* fuck *me* over."

Red hot anger scorches through me when I consider exactly how long he's playing me for a fool. We've been friends for over two decades. We skipped school together in the eighth grade. Was he a traitor back then? Or only when the gleam of money became too bright for him to ignore?

"Did you take my daughter, Rocco? Did you cut her from my wife's stomach!"

A numbed expression crosses his face. "No, Dimi, fuck! I organized Roxanne's interview so you could see Fien again, so you'd have the chance to get her back."

Nothing he's saying makes any sense. How could forcing Roxanne back into my life help me get Fien back? She's the reason I lost everything to begin with.

I stare at Rocco like he's disturbed when he mutters out a name I never anticipated hearing right now. "Justine." Nothing but remorse is seen on his face when he adds, "Your ruse was working, Dimi. When you had Justine on the go, Fien's ransoms arrived like clockwork. They were *never* late, and you were given undeniable proof that she was safe every single month." He works his jaw side to side, his anger as noticeable as mine. "That hasn't happened in nine months, D. You haven't had a single ransom request—"

"I got one earlier today."

The truth smacks into me like a wayward missile a mere second before Rocco spells it out for me. "Because I organized Roxie's interview at your favorite hook-up location two weeks *after* placing a photo of you together on your social media accounts."

"Jesus Christ, Rocco, you didn't tell me it was for this," Smith says down the line at the same time Clover pinches his gun to Rocco's temple, aware he's more of a threat right now than Roxanne.

"I'm just going for my phone," Rocco assures Clover, frustrated and fighting the urge to retaliate. For the most part, they get along, but it hasn't always been that way. Clover is a member of my crew because he's paid for the privilege. Rocco is here of his own free will. He was here before the money came, and if I don't kill him for his deceit, he'd be here even if we lost it all. "See."

He swivels his phone around to face me. It has a photo of me carrying Roxanne out of the ravine. Because it was taken at an angle, it appears as if we're fooling around instead of Roxanne being on the brink of death. You can't see her blood-stained face or body, just the grip I have on her ass to keep her on my shoulder while sprinting out of the scrub.

My brows pinch when Rocco demands that I check my email. "What?" He smiles, clearly blind to how precariously his life is floating in the wind. "I want to see how fast they react. I bet your numerous requests for a better proof of life for Fien tonight has been answered now. My latest upload to the Dimitri and Roxie show has been in the wild the past ten minutes."

He shows me a second image. Just like the first one, the angle is badly deceiving. It looks like I'm about to kiss Roxanne instead of strangling her like I almost did ten minutes ago. "What's the bet an email dropped into your inbox within the last eight minutes."

Too curious to discount, I hit the email app on the screen of my phone. I know what I'm going to find before I discover it. Smith's silence is telling enough, much less the brutal drum of my heart against my ribs.

Rocco was right. My three requests for a better proof of life were answered precisely seven minutes ago. The footage is double the length of the last one, and it's crystal clear. It even has sound this time around.

I'm not going to lie. I was raised in a cruel, hard world that's only grown crueler the longer I've sucked the life from its veins, but my daughter's tired giggles are enough to bring the strongest man to his knees. It's perfectly balanced like she isn't being raised by a group of dead men walking amongst the living.

Although I could stare at Fien's smiling face for a lifetime, hearing her laugh for the first time doesn't dampen my wish to find her. If anything, it triples my determination. "Smith—"

"On it. I'll pass on any findings ASAP." Eager to get to work, he disconnects our call before remotely logging into my phone.

I take a few minutes to gather my bearings before locking my eyes with Clover's. Roxanne's sigh of relief is more audible than Rocco's when I wordlessly instruct Clover to lower his weapon. He isn't happy about my request, but he does as he is told.

All hired hitman do.

Once Rocco has slipped back into his spot next to Roxanne, I ask a question no amount of anger could have me setting aside, "How did you know they'd respond so fast?"

Rocco's lips twitch in preparation to respond, but before he can, Roxanne gabbles out, "Because your daughter's captor is a woman."

# 15

**Roxanne**

Dimitri stares straight at me. Even in the shadows of a near moon-less night, I can't miss the tight clench of his fists and jaw. His aura is unnerving, but since his menace isn't directly focused on me this time around, it doesn't make me quiver like it did earlier. The shudder of my thighs is now more a positive shake than a negative one. He's watching me like he did in the alleyway a year ago, appearing as if he wants to join in but never will.

At least now I understand the reasoning behind his withdrawn demeanor. He isn't just dark and dangerous, he's fighting not to be as cruel as the people holding his daughter hostage. I doubt he'd hold back the urge if she were safe and in his arms. He wants to maim the people responsible for the scars no number of good looks will hide, and in all honesty, I can't blame him. After hearing his daughter's giggles, I want to do the exact same thing, and I haven't even seen her yet.

"How do you know her captor is a woman?" Dimitri asks while staring at me as if I'm the only person seated across from him.

"She's jealous and acting out. All traits of a scorned woman." I wet my dry lips before asking a question I guarantee he's never been asked before. "Did you cheat on your wife?"

"This isn't a custody dispute." His words are fired out of his mouth like bullets. "I saw Fien removed from Audrey's stomach in a dirty, unsterile room. No amount of money would have a mother putting her child in danger like that."

Although I agree with him, his skirting of my question won't get us anywhere. "I didn't ask if the kidnapper was your wife. I asked if you cheated on her."

He's pissed about my line of questioning, but since the safe return of his daughter is more important than anything, he lets it slide. "Yes, I cheated on her. Multiple times."

"Did she know?"

I have no clue why I asked that question. It will make no difference to my assumption whatsoever. I'm just curious to discover if he's a man who cheats and lies about it, or does he parade it around for the world to see.

Dimitri adjusts the expensive-looking cuffs on his sleeves, something he seems to do when frustrated, before muttering, "It wasn't something we openly discussed, but she was aware of my inability to keep my dick in my pants."

"And the woman you cheated with? Did they know?" This set of questions has a direct correlation with the theory I'm running. If any of the women he slept with while married experienced half the jealousy I'm being bombarded with now, they could have gone as far as kidnapping his wife and taking his daughter. I want to stab a bitch, and Dimitri isn't even mine.

"Know what, exactly?" His voice is so menacing, I peer down at his gun, anticipating for him to curl his finger around the trigger at any moment.

When that fails to happen, I answer, "That you were married and expecting a child. Some women are very possessive. They may not have taken the news well."

I'm talking from experience more than assumptions. My high school boyfriend's strut was never the same when I caught him kissing Belinda McCotter in the bleachers during the homecoming week game.

I begin to wonder how many women Dimitri has slept with when he pauses to consider a response. I can't see the women he's mentally ticking off, but I can see the flicker of his eyes as he scrolls through his little black book of bed companions. It makes me insanely jealous.

"Most were aware, but some were not," he answers a short time later.

"Do you think any of them would be capable of doing something like this?"

His lips furl at the corners. "I don't know. I wasn't with them to conduct a psych exam." His eyes snap to Rocco's so quickly, he misses my scoff. "I thought you said she was a double business major."

Rocco's scrub of his jaw to hide his grin is pointless when I mumble, "I can be anything you want for the right amount of coin."

With his eyes back on me, Dimitri arches his brow. "You want me to pay for your help?" When I nod, he slouches low in his chair before shaking his head. "Why would I do that?" I'm about to sell myself in a way that would make Estelle proud, but he continues talking, foiling my attempt. "I don't need to pay you to do anything. I can just *force* you to do it."

"It wouldn't be authentic." I take a mental note to have my

head examined after this. I just witnessed a murder, and I'm reasonably sure the timer above my head is minutes from expiring, yet here I am, negotiating with a mobster. I've been in such a rut I'd do anything for an adrenaline high, but still, this is ridiculous. "It would be more believable if I were there via my own choice."

"*Where* of your own choice?" Dimitri asks, humoring me with fake interest.

He isn't laughing on the outside, but I can see the chuckles he's struggling to hold in his rising and falling chest. It's heaving the same way it did when Eddie 'milked my loins of their nectar.'

Usually, any type of laughter would have me backtracking on every decision I've ever made. I can't do that this time around. We're still heading toward the woods. My life is on the line, so I either sell my soul to the devil or relinquish it for nothing.

I don't know about you, but I'd rather go out fighting.

"On your arm. By your side." I swallow the brick lodged in my throat before muttering, "In your bed."

My lungs fail to follow the prompts of my brain when Dimitri scoots to the edge of his seat. He moves so close to me, even if I wanted to press my thighs together from his hot, heated stare, I wouldn't be able to. His knee is wedged between them. "Once again, why would I pay you to do that when I could make you do it for free?"

My ability to reply is lost by the thick, accented voice of the heavily tattooed man sitting next to me. I haven't caught his name yet, but he has a tattoo of a clover on his cheek. "It's the curse of the golden pussy, boss. All girls think they have one." As he sucks his bottom lip into his mouth, he drags his eyes down my body in a slow and dedicated sweep. "It's rare to find one who does, but she might have one. Her smell is sweet enough." He releases his lip with a pop before straying his eyes to Dimitri. "Maybe you should give her to the boys for a few rounds, see if they think her pussy is worth paying for."

I don't breathe while snapping my eyes back to Dimitri's. He wouldn't do that, would he? He wouldn't risk his daughter's safety because I insinuated I'd only sleep with him if he paid me. Only an insane man would let his pride get in the way of his daughter's well-being. Dimitri isn't one of them.

My eyes pop open when the truth smacks into me. He watched me come via the hand of another man before he murdered the security guard who interrupted his show, then he tortured my boyfriend for six hours straight. Those events could have seen him facing thirty years to life in a maximum-security prison. He's far from sane.

"I'll do it for free!" My eyes dance between Dimitri's frozen ones when I join him in sitting on the edge of my seat. "On the agreement you let me go once your daughter is found."

I doubt I'm getting through to him, but am denied the opportunity of hoping when our negotiation is interrupted for the second time. This time it isn't from the large brute on my right. It comes from the front of the car, from the driver. "We've got a tail. They're a few spots back, but they've been with us the last two miles."

"Fuck," Dimitri curses under his breath after cranking his neck back. The moon is barely a slither in the sky, meaning even someone with poor eyesight would have no trouble seeing the curved headlights of a sedan in an almost pitch-black night. "Pull over here."

I watch nervously when our break is closely mimicked by the car tailing us. They're close enough for their presence to be felt but far enough away, they won't see the sweat that beads on my temples when Dimitri throws open the back passenger door and slides out. He doesn't approach the vehicle three hundred yards back. He heads straight for the trunk where he removes two shovels and a tarp.

*Oh my God. I'm about to be buried where I'll never be found.*

"Please," I beg when Dimitri dips the lower half of his body into the cab so he can pull me out a few seconds later. "I can help get your daughter back. Rocco proved I'm worthwhile. You just need to give me a chance."

Since my arms are bound behind my back, it takes Dimitri no effort at all to pluck me from my seat and drag me to the front of his sleek ride. Not even digging my heels into the rugged terrain slows him down. In a matter of seconds, I'm kneeling on the tarp he laid out, and his gun is aimed at the petrified crinkle between my brows.

"Please," I plead to the man who stood in the rain to watch me climax instead of the maniac standing in front of me. "I'll do anything you ask. I can cook," I groan about my inability to lie, "Not very well, but it's edible... for the most part. I'll clean, wash your clothes. I'll do anything you want as long as you don't kill me. I don't want to die." The dusty conditions make the tears welling in my eyes feel like sawdust. They scratch my eyeballs as well as a sudden urge to live warms my veins. "I've barely lived. Please, Dimitri. I'll do anything you ask."

"You're the reason my wife is dead."

His words are barely heard over the drumming of my heart, but I cling to them as if they're a life raft, and I'm in the middle of the Indian Ocean. "I know, and I'm sorry. I'd take it all back in an instant if I could." When my words appear to break through Dimitri's cold, hard exterior, I keep blubbering. "We'll be good together. I saw the way you looked at me in the alleyway. You liked what you saw." I pause to see if truth registers on his face before continuing, "If we had that much spark from a distance, imagine what we'll have when we're close together. Your enemies won't doubt our connection. They'll truly believe you're moving on."

I'm not one hundred percent sure what Rocco meant when he said Justine's ruse worked, but I'm so desperate to live, I'm willing to give anything a shot. "If you want your daughter back, you need me. You can be angry at me, you can hate me, but you still *need* me." I bounce my drenched eyes between his. "I'm no good to you dead, Dimitri. I'm worth more to you alive than dead. I can be what you want me to be. I can be *anything* you need."

After running the back of his hands down my mascara-stained cheek, he smiles as if I flashed him my tits. I didn't, but it was pretty damn close. I offered myself to him, wholly and without constraint. I'll be his *if* he doesn't kill me.

"Please, Dimitri. I'm begging you for mercy."

His smirk shifts to a full teeth-bearing grin, full of angst and confusion. I understand things drastically changed for him from the last time we stood across from each other, and that he's most likely only holding on by a very thin thread, but his anger shouldn't be projected at me. It should be rained down on the people holding his daughter captive, and the ones responsible for his wife's death.

When I say that to Dimitri, the muscles in his neck bunch. "Why do you think you're here, kneeling before me?"

With his lips arched at one side and his eyes locked on mine, he curls his finger around the trigger and takes his shot.

# 16

### Dimitri

As the scent of my recently fired gun lingers in my nostrils, I stray my eyes to the black sedan idling a few spots back. The brightness of the Audi's high beams ensures I'll never see the occupants inside, however my gut has no issues identifying him.

My father doesn't trust anyone. He is who I got my neurosis from. He's so distrusting, I'm surprised he didn't request to helm our trip to the woods.

I'd be lying if I said I didn't understand his concern. Roxanne saw him murder Old Man V for a measly ten-thousand-dollar dint in his profit margin. That's an instant one-way ticket to a graveyard. I'm seeing things differently now, though.

Although Roxanne was a witness to one of my father's many mistakes the past three months, unfortunately for him, she wasn't his *only* witness. He's made an incalculable number of costly blunders during his reign, but tonight's was by far his most senseless.

He showed his hand way too early, and now this wolf is primed with anticipation.

I've been seeking answers for months, and it came in a way I never predicted. Because my father was as distracted by Roxanne's tear-stained face as I was on that night almost twenty months ago, he fucked up in a way he can never come back from. He ruined his legacy with one little word.

He said, 'wife.'

Not plaything.

Not whore.

Not a cunt to keep me warm throughout the winter as he called Audrey many times the seven months of our marriage.

He said wife plain and clear for all to hear.

I failed to join the dots together until Roxanne peered up at me with mascara smeared down her cheeks mere seconds ago. She once again had me trapped, blinded to everything happening around me that didn't include her. I was so caught up by her beauty and determination to live in spite of her horrid upbringing, I played her re-entrance into my life on repeat until the clog in my mind spilled away.

Roxanne *is* to blame for my wife's disappearance. She *is* the reason I haven't laid my eyes on Fien in over nine months. But she *is* also responsible for my father's slip up. If it wasn't for her, I'd still be trying to push a four-pronged puzzle piece into a three-pronged spot. She freed my mind from the torment, and she did it all the while offering herself to me.

I catch sight of my unforgiving smirk in the fender of my modi-fied Range Rover when the headlights of my father's chauffeur-driven Audi shift to the right. This is a one-way track, so his driver, Mario, either executes a three-point turn in atrocious conditions or squeezes by the minute snippet of space my Range Rover isn't taking up.

My father would never allow the latter to happen. He'd rather risk being bogged than show weakness. It's another unwanted trait I inherited from him. We're more alike than I'll ever admit, but there's one difference between us—I'm willing to show weakness if it's for the greater good.

This is for the greater good.

Roxanne's eyes lift to mine when the taillights of my father's car disappear into the black abyss of an almost moonless night. They're wide and terrified and have my cock tapping at the zipper in my trousers like it did when she placed herself onto the table during our unrequired negotiations.

They were unrequired because if I wanted to fuck her, she'd be splayed across the hood of my Range Rover now, being thoroughly pounded as my cock has begged to do since I spotted her in the alley. However, that isn't what this is about. For once in my life, my libido isn't part of the equation. This is about placing my daughter before anyone—even me.

"You will do what I say *precisely* when I tell you to do it, or we'll come back here and settle the score. Do you understand?"

She has nothing to fight with except her looks, which she uses to her advantage when she dips her chin. It isn't the rake of her teeth over her plump bottom lip I'm paying attention to, it's the fat, salty blob rolling down her cheek. It's stained with blackness and has me recalling the color of the blood that runs through my veins.

It wasn't always that way. Before my heart was scolded beyond repair, my blood used to run red. Now it's stained with the murkiness of my dark, bleak existence—an existence Roxanne is now a part of.

# 17

**Roxanne**

Rocco's hand falls from my face when the gravelly voice of Dimitri rolls across the cabin of his car. "Let it be. It's just a graze." He locks his eyes with mine. They're as tormented and beautiful as they were when he took his shot. He fired at me as predicted, but instead of the bullet burrowing deep into my skull, it skimmed past my right cheek, leaving a slither of a burn. "The more you pick at it, the more it will scab. If you don't want another scar, leave it alone."

The heat from the graze on my cheek is barely noticeable until he returns his eyes to the scenery whizzing by his window. He's been detached since our negotiations were finalized during the first forty minutes of our trip like his mind is far from here.

I discover that's the case when he tugs his cell phone out of his pocket. Although he doesn't dial a number, he speaks down the line as if he did. "I need my father's schedule synced with mine as soon as possible." The man he's speaking to attempts to interrupt him, but Dimitri continues spraying out orders, faulting his effort. "His movements the past three months are to be on my desk before dawn, and any upcoming functions over the next two weeks should be forwarded with them."

"On it," says a man with a uniquely distinctive accent. It's either British or Australian. It could even be a combination of both. "Anything else?"

"One last thing." My pulse twangs in my neck when Dimitri shifts his eyes to me. They're as hot as ever, even with them being the color of ice. "Call Alice. I want to see her tonight. Offer her double for the late hour."

It's deplorable to comment on the jealousy roaring through me, so I won't. We're not friends or lovers. I am his property until he says otherwise. His stipulations during our one-sided talk were as clear as glass. I'm to do what he says, when he says, for exactly how long he says. If I do that, I'll come out of the exchange with my life intact. If I don't, I won't want to know the consequences of my stupidity.

His threat would frighten me if I had more family than I do. If it weren't for Estelle, I may have let him kill me.

My eyes float up from my clenched fists when the man on the other end of the line says, "Consider it done."

Dimitri's eyes remain on me even with his focus being devoted to his caller. "Tell her I want the works." When my eyes unwillingly roll, his lips do their favored half-smirk. "No holds barred."

I imagine the gleam in Smith's eyes matches Dimitri's when he replies, "Alice knows what you like, so she won't let you down."

Their call ends just as the Range Rover pulls onto the curb across from my building. You'd think the embarrassment I felt begging for my life would keep my annoyance on the down-low. Regretfully, my hair isn't red for no reason.

It matches my fiery personality.

I slip out the back of Dimitri's car so fast, even if he wants to follow me, the brutal slam of his door in his face won't allow it. I'm not running. I know the terms we agreed upon during the first half of our trip. My ass is Dimitri's until his daughter is returned without a scratch. But that doesn't mean I have to continue displaying the weak, pathetic woman I did in the woods an hour and a half ago.

I hate that I begged at Dimitri's feet. I've only ever pleaded for one thing in my life, and that teary wish was never answered. I want a redo of my last conversation with my nanna. If I knew how things were going to end, I would have hugged her fiercely instead of storming off in a huff the way I did. I was angry she was still treating me like a child, having no clue she was only treating me that way because I was acting like a child.

My eyes snap to the door of the outdated elevator in my building when a tattooed hand shoots out to stop it from closing. I'm anticipating for Rocco to join me inside, although quiet, he seemed more on my side than Dimitri's during our negotiations, so you can imagine my shock when Dimitri enters the confined space in his place.

After pulling across the rickety gate that's meant to keep us safe in this death trap, he jabs his finger into the 'close door' button multiple times in a row, obviously impatient.

Once the elevator shudders into action, he shifts on his feet to face me. He looks set to remind me of our agreement, but instead, steers our conversation in a direction I never saw coming. "Stay away from Rocco." His gruff tone gobbles up my scoff. "He has a soft spot for battered women, but that isn't what *this* is about." While saying 'this,' he shifts his hand between us. "If you want to fuck him after this is over, that's your choice, but I won't allow it to occur under my watch. I won't be made to look like a fool."

"Like your wife was?" I snap out before I can stop myself.

Mercifully, the elevator car arrives at my floor a nanosecond later, saving me from being scolded by the wrath of his anger in a tight confinement. I barely survived it in his car the past hour and a half, so I don't see me faring well in a much tighter space.

Incapable of breathing through the sternness of his glare, I mutter out, "I understand your request. I'll keep my mitts to myself."

I break into the hallway before he can see my mouth's arched response to the hesitation firing through his eyes. He was satisfied with my response until he realized that means my hands won't go anywhere near him, either.

It's as if he yanks out the electrical cord responsible for my snippy attitude when he says, "I wasn't lying about Eduardo. He didn't murmur your name once. You weren't on his mind at all when I punished him for hurting you."

Aware he only said his comment to return my serve, and a little unsure how to react to his confession he killed Eddie because he hurt me, I stab my house key into the rusty lock on my apartment's front door before pushing open the water-damaged wood.

"We're behind on the electric bill. There's a torch on the kitchen counter," I advise Dimitri when his multiple flicks of the light switch fail to illuminate the room.

It's the fight of my life not to let my laughter be heard when he crashes into the entry table I purposely forgot to warn him about. He can't bitch-slap my attitude back to next week because he didn't look where he was going.

After lighting a candle on the dresser in my room, I head for my overflowing closet. One of the benefits of stunted growth is the ability to wear clothes from my teen days. My height hasn't altered since I got my learner's permit, and despite my budget only affording me the privilege of grease-laden food, my waist is around the same size as well.

I sense Dimitri's presence before I hear him rummage through the bag I've just commenced packing. With Estelle at work, it isn't hard to miss the disapproving huff of someone hating my sense of style.

"You won't need any of this." He upends my bag onto my bed before he drags his narrowed gaze over my candlelit room. The further his eyes travel, the more disgust crosses his features. "You won't need *any* of this."

I sound like a whiny brat when I snap out, "You said I could pack my things."

"Yeah, things you need. Not *this* junk."

Heat creeps up my neck when I struggle to hold in a blood-curdling scream. "These are *things* I need. They're all I have."

My anger shifts to confusion when he replies, "Then we'll get you new *things*." He slants his head to the side and arches a brow. "Better *things*."

I thought begging for my life was embarrassing, but this is ten times worse. "I can't afford new *things*. That's why I have these *things*."

"Sorry. Let me rephrase." Think of the most arrogant man you've ever seen in your life. His attitude wouldn't be one-third of Dimitri's right now. "*I* will get you new *things*."

"Fine." He's shocked by how quickly I cave, but I'm done arguing for today. I'm cold, hungry, and hormonal. If anyone should be in fear of their life, it shouldn't be me. "But I'm taking this."

I snag the most hideous-looking dressing gown you could imagine in your life off the end of my bed. It's a replica of the one Fran Drescher wore on *The Nanny*, one of my all-time favorite sitcoms.

"And them."

I snatch a pair of panties out of Dimitri's hand that I only ever wear when I'm worried about exploding tampons.

"And this."

My voice is nowhere near as punchy as it was when I snag my nanna's photograph off my nightstand. Even with her death still not feeling real to me, I miss her so much.

"Is that it?" My brashness isn't the only thing taking a back seat, so is Dimitri's bossy demeanor. He doesn't know who the lady in the frame is, but the wetness filling my eyes makes it obvious that she was important to me.

My head bobs up and down two times before it switches to a shake. "One last thing."

After blowing out the candle, so we don't start a fire, Dimitri follows my walk to an ancient tape recorder on the entryway table, taking a wide birth to ensure his crotch doesn't once again become friendly with its poky edges.

Once I've exhaled to clear my voice of nerves, I push record on the device before lifting it to my mouth. Dimitri almost jumps out of his skin when I scream at the top of my lungs. "I got the job! Thirty-five smoking big ones an hour for the next four weeks minimum." I have to be over-the-top dramatic, or Estelle will never believe my ruse. "The thing is, the ridiculous amount is because it's a live-in position. Mr. Petretti is graveyard ready." I drift my eyes to Dimitri when I feel the heat of his rising blood pressure. "He's old, like hideously archaic. He has wrinkles and gray hair. I doubt even Viagra can help him now." After hitting Dimitri with a frisky wink, hopeful it won't see me murdered where I stand, I get back to the task at hand. "Anyhoo, I just wanted to let you know why I'm AWOL... because I'm wiping an old dude's ass like we always knew I would. Ciao, chica. I'll see you in a few weeks."

With a hard swallow, I hit the stop button before placing the recorder back into its rightful place. Even with me seemingly exuding a ton of confidence, my hands shake when I tie a red ribbon around the recorder's overused exterior. It's our equivalent of a blinking red light on the answering machine we can't afford.

I want to believe Dimitri will uphold his side of our agreement once his daughter is returned, but a part of me is worried he's never been taught the principle of honesty. He said it himself, he cheated on his wife multiple times, so why would he be honorable to a woman he hardly knows?

I'm snapped from my dreary mood by Dimitri's curt tone. "Let's go." He nudges his head to my partially cracked open door as he's over the depressing environment I call home as much as me.

After a final glance at the dim and dreary space, I shadow his walk to the elevator cart, my steps slow and lethargic. This place might be a dump, but it's the only true home I've ever had.

We ride the elevator in silence. I wouldn't necessarily say it's uncomfortable, it's more foreign than anything. Silence isn't something I often crave. I did it many times before my parents dropped me off to live with my grandparents. Even something as simple as breathing too loudly got me in trouble when Mother woke up angry. That was more often than not when I was a child.

I safeguard my grandmother's picture under my dressing gown when our trek through the foyer of my building reveals the heavens have opened up. It isn't pouring rain like it was the night I first crossed paths with Dimitri, but it has the possibility of wrecking the only photograph I have of her.

I'm just about to dart through two parked cars when my arm is jerked out of its socket. I'm about to give Dimitri an ear full, but the brutal roar of an SUV whizzing past my face stuffs my words into the back of my throat.

"Jesus Christ, Roxanne! You almost got yourself killed." My eyes bounce between Dimitri's when he pins me to the back of an outdated minivan with shaky, splayed hands. "You need to start paying attention to your surroundings, or one day, it won't be a close call." My dress is soaked through, but I don't feel the cold. There's too much fury radiating out of Dimitri for me to feel the slightest chill. "Did your near-miss at the hospital teach you nothing?"

"That was you?" Shock highlights my tone. The eyes peering at me through the crack in the window all those months ago were undeniably dangerous, but they didn't have the risqué edge Dimitri's have, so I was confident it wasn't him. "You were outside the hospital when I was discharged?"

My confusion augments when Dimitri shakes his head. "It wasn't me."

He sounds honest, but I'm done acting as if I have air for brains. "Then how do you know what happened? I didn't tell anyone, and I doubt Estelle shares her friend's stupidity with the customers at her work."

Before he can answer me, I spot some truth in his eyes.

"You had someone following me?" Another flare darts through his eyes before the cut line of his jaw turns fascinating. "I told Estelle I wasn't making things up. She thought I was going crazy, that I needed my head examined." I laugh like I'm in desperate need of a psych workup. "But that wasn't it at all. I was being followed... by you."

Dimitri's anger picks up right along with his clutch on my arm. "It wasn't me."

The way he speaks down to me doesn't deter me in the slightest. "But it was someone *you* ordered to watch me. Why were you watching me?"

"I don't know."

My eye roll matches my maturity level. "You know why, you just don't want to tell me."

"I said I don't know!" He pushes me back with enough strength to crack the rear shield of the van before he hightails it to his sleek ride. "Get your ass in the car before your promise of being away for a month won't see your roommate sleeping in your bed." He peers back at me for the quickest second. His eyes are deadly and black. "Not even reformed Goths like sleeping on their friend's blood-sodden mattress."

He's hoping his underhanded threat will have my knees knocking together. That might have been the case if I hadn't spotted the tiniest flicker of light beaming out of my apartment in his narrowed gaze. It isn't the shimmer of a recently lit candle. It's too bright and breath-stealing for that. It's a beacon of hope that the man I sold my soul to isn't as malevolent as he wants me to believe.

Besides Estelle and me, Dimitri is the only person who knows we've fallen behind on our bills. Braydon only visits during the day, and Estelle keeps his thoughts far from the fact our television's standby light is never on or that our microwave's clock has been on the blink for months on end.

Furthermore, despite his impressive bank balance, I doubt Braydon has access to a computer genius who can find a credit card transaction I fought tooth and nail to have reversed from my card in less than a second—my father didn't say goodbye to me, so there's no way I wanted to pay his bar tab—but Dimitri sure as hell does.

Are Smith's skills impressive enough to have electricity reconnected to a property in under five minutes? If you had asked me that very question two hours ago, I would have said no. Now, I'm confident it was him. Dimitri's phone's screen wasn't lit up when I joined him in the elevator to ride it to the lobby, but that doesn't mean anything. He used it to communicate with Smith earlier tonight without touching a button. Who's to say he didn't do the same thing this time around?

My clue hunt ends when my name snaps out of Dimitri's mouth in a thick, accented roar. He's standing at the side of his vehicle, holding open the back passenger door for me. Although his expression is as impassive as it was when he held his gun to my head, something in his eyes has changed. He's either shocked how quickly Smith works, or he's hoping I missed his handiwork.

I'm leaning more toward the latter.

He'd hate for me to think I have more power than he deems necessary because even mobsters know there's no greater strength than a woman determined to prove a man wrong.

# 18

**Dimitri**

The *click-clack, click-clack* of Roxanne's inexpensive shoes tap along the marble floors in the foyer of my home when she shadows my walk into the quiet space. Her heels aren't the only disturbance. Her hot breaths as she takes in empty room after empty room are just as meddling. They hit my neck as they did my face when she slid past me to enter the backseat of my Range Rover idling at the front of her apartment building.

I had hoped she wouldn't notice the illumination of her living room since it was eight floors above. Regretfully, she's as nosy as she is attractive. I should have instructed Smith to wait until we had left Erkinsvale before remotely connecting Roxanne's electricity. Alas, I hadn't anticipated a near-fatal to occur within seconds of exiting Roxanne's apartment.

That woman should be dead. She's a klutz who speaks without thinking and leaps in front of cars without a single consideration for her safety.

The hate that's bred in me since I was born usually craves a bloodbath. If it had been anyone but Roxanne, my hand wouldn't have darted out to clutch her arm. I would have watched the carnage, smirked, then moved on.

Things are starkly different this time around. I'm not seeking a cape, nor do I want the title of hero. I merely want my daughter back, and as much as this kills me to admit, I believe Roxanne can help me achieve that faster than planned.

She was right when she said our spark is undeniable. It was blistering when we went toe to toe in the elevator, and it didn't dampen when I insulted her idea of style. It will make my ruse more authentic this time around, and if I keep her off my father's radar, everyone will come out of this agreement in one piece— including Fien.

"Take off your shoes. Their clicking is driving me bonkers."

I don't give a shit about the noise Roxanne's shoes make while we walk. I just need to notch up my asshole radar a few decibels until the sly grin she's been wearing since we left her apartment is gone.

She isn't here as my guest.

She's here as my slave and will be treated so accordingly.

After tugging off her shoes in a manner that reveals she knows they're worthless, Roxanne follows my trek up a long curving stairwell. I purchased this property the month Audrey was kidnapped. It wasn't to be our family home but more a means to ensure our family would forever live in comfort.

This property is where I host my foreign dignitaries. The events here range from one-on-one meetings with the clients' favorite prostitutes to all-in orgy fests. Tomorrow night's festivities will be milder than previous guests' level of kink, but it will be the perfect place to commence plans I've had in the works for months. My father will be in attendance along with hundreds of men we class as both competitors and allies. It's ideal and has me hopeful I'll see Fien in person sooner than I'm hoping.

"This time tomorrow, these rooms will be filled with important members of my association. You're to treat them with respect and to be courteous at all times."

When the sweet smell of Roxanne's heated skin streams into my nose, I half the length of my strides. The fear her body coats itself in is so intoxicating, I'm tempted to throw her to the wolves just to see how engrossing it can be.

Regrettably, if I want my enemies to believe my ploy that I'm moving on, I need to be the jealous, neurotic prick I was when Audrey's beauty caught the eye of an admirer.

I cheated on my wife, but if someone so much as looked at her in the wrong manner, they would have lost an eye at the very least.

"The event is black tie. Hors d'oeuvres will be served in the parlor at seven. Main festivities will commence at nine."

My pace slows even more when Roxanne garbles out, "At night?" When my brow props high into my hairline, she nods. "Night. Right."

"I'll meet you in the foyer at six forty-five sharp."

"Okay." Her eyes flicker like she's mentally jotting down everything I'm telling her. "Will we be doing dress shopping before or after noon? I want to know whether I should hit the carbs at lunch or breakfast."

She's joking. However, I'm not amused.

Now is not the time for jokes.

"Sorry," she apologizes for the umpteenth time tonight. "I blubber when I'm nervous."

I want to say she's nervous because we're alone in a very big house, but alas, that would be a lie. For some absurd reason, she isn't afraid of me. She knows I could end her life in an instant, and that she's under my control until my daughter is returned, but fear isn't the sole emotion that passes through her eyes when she spots my inconspicuous glances. Desire is there as well.

She fought for her life not because she believes it's worth fighting for, but because of what she hopes it could be.

That's the exact reason I've fought so hard for Fien. Her video earlier tonight showed she's a happy, well-adjusted toddler, but that doesn't mean her life couldn't be better. I can give her more than she's ever had because only I can give her a father's love.

With my mood teetering toward the negative, I push down on the handle of the master suite's door with more aggression than needed. Roxanne's deep exhale fans my nape like Justine's did when I opened the door of my room in my family's compound, except her exhale is more in exhilaration than fret.

A similar-size four-poster bed sits in the middle of the back wall, a private seating area/reading nook is on its left, and an office/library is on its right. With my room used more for business adventures than sexual conquests, my desk looks more original to the space than my rarely used mattress. I'm one of those people who catches sleep on the fly. Little power naps here and there keep me going well into the wee hours of the morning where I usually crash on the couch or in my office chair.

I'm about to give Roxanne the standard old you-can-wear-one-of-my-shirts routine, but the lowering of my eyes to the hideous sleeping ensemble she's clutching for dear life stops me. At first, I was shocked she'd pack something so warm, our nighttime temperatures never get close to freezing, but when I sent Clover and Rocco home, it made sense. We're not in winter, but the iciness of untouched waters is always a little cool.

Roxanne's emotions don't know which way to swing when I say, "While you shower and change, I'll conduct my meeting with Alice before grabbing you something to eat." She's excited about washing up and being fed, but her eagerness waivered during the middle portion of my sentence.

Good. That's exactly how my competitors should see her. Wide-eyed about everything I do, terrified she could lose me at any moment, and seemingly under my thumb—the perfect Cartel wife combination.

"In you go," I say with a smirk, praying a smile will hide the yearning roaring through my veins. I'm not thickening below the belt because she appears to have the makings of a mafia kingpin's wife, it's from the way her pupils widen when she spotted Alice standing at the top of the stairs waiting for me. She's being hit with the same crass feelings that swamped me when the dweeb she called her 'boyfriend' located her clit. I didn't want him touching her, but for the life of me, I couldn't stop him. It was like seeing a family sedan stuck on the tracks as a train barrels toward them. I shouldn't have watched, but I did, and I devoured every second of it.

As I do again now.

The tint Roxanne's eyes get when she's jealous is even more intoxicating than when she comes. It makes them a murkier green like they're too tainted for me to corrupt.

The thought alone has me the hardest I've ever been. If Alice wasn't at the end of the hall staring at me as Roxanne is staring at her, I may not have been able to set aside a craving so strong it has me wanting to fall to my knees.

Mercifully, Alice doesn't just have impeccable timing, she's a sure-fire knockout. Big brown eyes, glossy blonde hair, and an hourglass figure that could turn over revenue like seconds on a clock if she had the gall to sell herself to more than one client a night. She's a perfect ten out of ten, and I'm not the only one noticing.

Roxanne could only be greener with envy if she were forced to watch us fuck.

"Don't make me ask again, Roxanne. I do *not* like repeating myself." There's an urge in my voice I can't contain. It's thick and hot and as potent as the blood surging to my cock. It has me listening to the head between my legs instead of the one on my shoulders.

With the grunt of a man with holes in his heart, I shove Roxanne into my room. When she falls onto her knees, the situation goes from bad to worse. She's in the perfect position to take my dick between her lips, to suck me down as I've dreamed about her doing more times than I should have the past twelve months.

I could order her to as threatened earlier tonight or remind her of the pledge she made to be on both my arm and in my bed, but I won't. She won't have the look needed to make my ruse authentic if I can't control myself around her within an hour of us being left alone.

Furthermore, she got one up on me when she noticed Smith had connected the electricity to her apartment. I can't let her get more leverage because despite what my cock thinks, she's enemy number one, and it will take more than a roll in the hay to change that.

# 19

**Roxanne**

I curse at the soap as if it's my stupid lust-fired brain when it slips from my grip for the second time the past five minutes. I'm scrubbing my skin like one of the many dangerous thoughts that flared through Dimitri's eyes when he shoved me into my room occurred instead of him locking me in the palace-like setting before he moseyed to his hookup for the night.

Well, I'm assuming it's a one-night-only fling. They had a familiarity with each other like they know each other's kinks. Alice didn't bat an eyelid when Dimitri shoved me into my room, nor did she flinch when he cockily strolled her way.

How do I know her response, you ask? I peered through the keyhole of my bedroom door like a freak who can't get her rocks off without watching another woman get hers.

There's nothing wrong with voyeurism until you realize you don't want to be the watcher, you prefer being watched.

When that tedious bit of information curdled my stomach, I

gathered myself up from the floor and drudged to the bathroom. My room is so opulent, it should have taken care of the massive knot in my stomach straight away. Regretfully, no amount of glamour can hide ugly truths. Estelle has hot water, electricity, and a bed to sleep in for the next God knows how long, but I have no way of contacting Estelle to tell her I'm safe, no way to check if she made it home from her double shift okay, and no way to tell her I miss her even though we've only been apart for hours.

The very first thing Dimitri confiscated when he let his goons off for the night was my phone. It occurred a mere second after he told Smith to disconnect all the home servers and landlines. He promised I would have a way of contacting Estelle during my stay, but I won't be given the privilege until I've proven myself worthy.

I'm not exactly sure what he wants me to do to prove my worth. I all but begged for him to answer one of the thoughts in his head when I toppled onto my knees, and I was still turned down.

Don't judge. Until you're in my predicament, you can't say how you'd react. I can't bribe Dimitri with money. By the looks of his house and the expensive cars I saw in the driveway, he has plenty of it. The cheap weed I've occasionally bought from my long-lost cousin wouldn't come close to the stack of foiled bricks I saw when shadowing Dimitri's walk through his home so that only leaves me one option. Sex.

If it were with his father or any of his gun-toting elderly friends, I'd cringe at the idea, but I'd be lying if I said the faintest trickle of hope didn't race through my veins when I considered how I could make Dimitri realize I'm worth my weight in gold.

When it dawns on me that scrubbing my skin raw won't stop my ears from working when I exit the bathroom, I shut off the faucet before stepping out of the steam-filled space. My nanna was a fan of letting your skin dry naturally, so I slip into my dressing gown instead of drying myself with the gold 'P' embossed towel on the heated towel rack.

While scrunching my hair to encourage natural waves, I use my spare hand to wipe away the condensation on the gold-framed mirror. The ring I inherited from my grandmother clinks against the foggy surface.

Once it's all cleared away, I take a step back to get a better overall picture. The girl peering back at me doesn't look as frightened as she should. I don't look like a slave of a notorious gangster. My eyes are a darker shade of green than they usually are, and my hair appears more a reddish-brown since it's dripping wet, but my lips are extra plump from the number of times I've dragged my teeth over them, and the smears of mascara my shower didn't remove give my eyes a smoky look. For the most part, I look okay, somewhat desirable.

*Just not enough to save myself without praying for a miracle.*

I want Rocco's plan to work. If it does, Dimitri's daughter will be safe, and I'll get to go home to my one-bedroom flat, in a town I hate, to the endless job applications at old folks homes where men like Dimitri's father can't wipe their own bottoms.

Can you understand why I'm so conflicted? My edges have always been more frayed than my friends. I'm as daring as I am stupid, but shouldn't I be seeking my cheap thrills anywhere *but* here? Dimitri has almost killed me twice. He tortured my boyfriend before killing him, threatened to harm those I love if I don't comply to his every request, then tossed me out with the bathwater when his late-night party favor arrived as scheduled, yet, I'm more jealous than I am angry.

That proves how insane I am—no evaluation is needed.

My lunacy can't be helped. Every time I look at Dimitri, I remember what I experienced when he watched me in the alleyway. It's the most alive I've ever felt, and it has me willing to take heedless risks to see if I can recreate it.

With a grumbling stomach and still soaking wet hair, I enter the main part of my room preparing to settle in for the night. I'm not a diva. I shower within the four-minute water restriction guidelines brought in years ago when droughts occurred miles and miles from here, so I'm confident I have a good thirty or more minutes before Dimitri returns with the food he promised.

Since my annoyance is higher than my wish to sleep, I'm startled to within an inch of my life when the entrance to my room has me stumbling onto Dimitri standing just inside the bedroom door. He's still dressed in his powerhouse-ready suit, but his jacket and tie have been removed, and the sleeves of his dress shirt are rolled to his elbows.

"Back so soon?" I say before I can reprimand myself for being petty. I'm not upset he has returned early. I'm too gleaming with happiness to feel any type of disappointment. "I thought you'd be gone for hours."

My smugness gets snuffed when he drops his eyes to my dressing gown as he grunts out, "Remove it."

"W-w-what?" Don't ask if I'm stuttering in fear or excitement as I wouldn't be able to answer you.

Once I'm confident my voice will resemble some sort of normalcy, I ask, "Why? Didn't you get your kicks from Alice?"

My heart thrashes against my ribs when Dimitri pushes off his feet to stalk my way. His walk matches the one I've dreamed about time and time again the past year. His hands just aren't moving for the belt of his jeans as my fucked-up head recalls the security guard doing. I hardly took my eyes off Dimitri, so why do flashes of the guard's hands moving for his belt constantly pop into my head when I'm daydreaming?

I'm drawn from my thoughts when Dimitri asks, "What was our agreement, Roxanne?"

"You can call me Roxie. All my friends do..."

My offer to fake niceties fades to silence when the gritting of his teeth overtakes the shrill of my pulse in my ears. "What was our agreement, Rox-*anne*?" He overemphasis my name to prove a point.

"That I am to do what you want, when you want, for how long you want," I chirp out like an obedient little bird.

Dimitri slants his head as his eyes flare with an unknown glimmer. "And what did I ask you to do?"

"You asked me to remove my dressing gown." Knowing this is a test, I unknot the cord around my waist, toss open my dressing gown as if I'm wearing a onesie underneath, then let the material fall to the floor. I don't care if this is a credit for my double business diploma or a sick, warped mind-fuck, I refuse to have another 'F' marked against my name.

The fluffy, static-loving material descended to the floor with a whoosh. Its breathy drop has nothing on the air that whistles through Dimitri's teeth when he takes in my naked form for the first time. He can deny me all he likes and have his staff tell me I'm not his type, but the crotch of his pants isn't so lucky. It's fatter in an instant, and I'm not the only one noticing.

After adjusting his footing so his erection isn't as prominent, Dimitri cranks his neck to the side of the room. When I follow the direction of his gaze, my mouth falls open. We're not alone. The owner of the woman's name I spat out as if it was vomit is seated in a leather chair behind a bulky desk. She's taking in my naked backside as eagerly as Dimitri did.

"Leave it," Dimitri shouts when I bob down to gather my dressing gown off the floor.

I freeze like a statue, aware of the repercussions if I ignore his direct order. Rocco barely survived Dimitri's wrath when he demanded he switch places with the driver partway back to Hopeton. It ended with a gun being drawn and Rocco grumbling that Dimitri is a surly bastard who couldn't see a good thing if it slapped him in the face.

Even with the heat of two beady eyes on me, I keep my hands balled at my sides and my eyes planted on the floor. I'm adventurous, but I am not comfortable with this. Estelle hasn't seen me naked, and she's been my friend for a hundred years.

"What do you think?" This question came from Dimitri, but it wasn't directed at me. It's for his gawking, bug-eyed friend.

"She's a little skinny, and her hair could use a trim, but I don't see any issues. Her body has a nice symmetry between her hips and breasts, and she's very attractive. She'll turn heads no matter the notoriety of your guests." Alice has an accent like nearly every other person in Dimitri's crew. It isn't as strong as the others but still noticeable.

My eyes float up to Dimitri when he asks, "And her scar?"

In the corner of my eye, I spot Alice making her way across the room. She either sees naked women regularly, or she isn't interested in anything I'm offering. Her eyes never leave mine—not once. She saw what she needed of my body, and now her focus is elsewhere.

Through twisted lips, Alice asks Dimitri, "You don't want to keep her bangs?"

"No, it hides her face. It's one of her best assets. I don't want it hidden." His reply is almost a compliment until he adds, "I just need to get rid of her scar."

I inconspicuously drape my arms in front of my breasts when Alice stops in front of me to brush my bangs off my forehead. She doesn't cringe when she takes in the scar I got from hitting the ground headfirst. She hums out a moan. "I agree with your assessment. Even pinning her bangs back will give her face more appeal. And her eyes..." There she goes with her inappropriate moaning again. "They're perfect." After dropping her hand from my face, she shifts on her feet to face Dimitri. "Are you sure you don't want her to become an asset? The men will love her."

"I'm not interested in selling her." When relief darts through my eyes, Dimitri is quick to shut it down. "Yet." Leering at my pout, he nudges his head at me like he hasn't been ogling the shadows between my legs the past five minutes. "Get your measurements. I need outfits by morning."

Alice's smile matches Dimitri's hidden one when she replies, "No need. I have everything I need right here." She taps her faultlessly perfect nail on her even more faultless head. "Six or eight? I can't do seven because Lucy has a Skype session with her father. The warden would only agree to a morning session." A pfft vibrates her lips. "Anyone would think he was running the show around there."

Dimitri laughs. I don't know his laughs, but I'd register this one as being sixty percent fake, even with him seeming friendly with Alice. "We'll do six. Roxanne is about to head to bed, so she'll be well-rested." He commences walking Alice to the door. "And if you want me to talk to Ashton, let me know. He's new, so he still has a lot to learn."

"I've got it, but thanks for the offer." A stupid rush of jealousy scatters through my veins when she presses a kiss to Dimitri's mouth. She doesn't do the air kisses the rich folks do. She presses her mouth so firmly to his, even though I can't see Dimitri's lips, I know they're coated with lipstick. "Until tomorrow."

When she farewells me with a wiggle of her fingers, I snatch up my dressing gown from the floor. I have one arm in and the other just about to burst through the opening when Dimitri demands me to 'leave it' again.

I don't listen this time around, too mortified with embarrassment to care about being punished. Not only did he parade me in front of a woman who has more plastic than a Barbie doll, he made me feel hideously ugly while doing it.

"Why do that? Why agree to my help if I'm not up to your standards?" After tying the dressing gown's belt around my waist like it will take more than a set of hands to undo the knot, I air quote my last word.

"Tomorrow's guests are very important to my overall plan. They'd never believe my ruse if you showed up in a Ross Dress for Less dress."

I stare at Dimitri, wondering how the hell he knew my dress was from my favorite discount clothing chain.

He douses my curiosity in an instant. "Your dress tag had the infamous last season strike through it. It wasn't showcased at Fashion Week this season." He snickers in a way the men for *Queer Eye for a Straight Guy* would be proud of. "It probably wasn't featured in the last two decades."

My anger is lessening, but I still scoff, not over the jabs he hit my ego with just yet. "And your revulsion of my scar? What's your excuse for that?"

Air whizzes out of my nose when he has the audacity to laugh. I'm glad he's finding amusement in our exchange. I'm anything but humored. "I'll do what you ask. I will follow your plan. I'll even let your over-polished bozo make me look like a gleaming piece of plastic, but the next time you look in the mirror, ask yourself how you'd feel if your daughter ended up with a man like you."

Ignoring the furious heat bounding out of him, I drag down the bedspread on the king-size bed I'm standing next to, then slip between the sheets.

"You need to eat before sleeping." Dimitri's words are ground through clenched teeth and a pulsating jaw. Right here, right now, he wouldn't care if I starved to death. The only reason he's acting like he gives a shit is because he wants his daughter back, and Alice's visit filled him with hope that I could help him with that. "Roxanne—"

"I'm not hungry."

His roar nearly shudders my heart straight out of my chest. "I don't give a fuck if you're hungry or not. You heard what Alice said. You are far too skinny. You need to eat."

When a stretch of silence passes between us, he growls out my name again. Unfortunately for him, my hair coloring matches my personality.

Lately, I'm as stubborn as I am stupid.

"Fine. Don't fucking eat. You can starve for all I care." Although he sounds more frustrated than vindictive, his words still kick me in the gut. My ego hasn't gotten over his earlier battering. It didn't need another walloping.

My wallowing in a self-pity party is bookmarked for another date when the sound of someone getting undressed trickles into my ears a few minutes later. Too curious to discount the odd noise considering I'm in the room with a stranger, I slant my head to the left before glancing across the room.

My parched throat becomes a thing of the past when my eyes lock in on Dimitri's half-dressed form. His dress shirt has been removed, and he's in the process of yanking a wife beater over his head.

The number of tattoos on his hands, forearms, and neck should have clued me in on the fact he has an extensive collection, but I had no clue it was this vast. Black artwork covers almost every inch of his body—even the top of his thighs which I get a bird's-eye view of when he toes off his shoes before tugging down his trousers. It's a beautiful collection that grows more exquisite when you take in how they accentuate the cut groves of his body. I doubt he works out, but his body proves he doesn't leave the heavy lifting to his goons. He gets in on the action as often as possible.

"Sweet Mother of Jesus," I whisper on a moan when he leans across his desk to dump a set of cufflinks into a silver dish. His backside is divine, an ass worthy of a top-rated centerfold.

When Dimitri suddenly freezes, no doubt feeling the heat of my stare, I snap my eyes shut and pretend I'm sleeping. In less than a second, it dawns on me that my ruse is futile. Not only do I feel the heat of his eyes on me as I ogled him only moments ago, I hear his sock-covered feet indenting the thick carpet pile. He doesn't cross the room with his infamous cocky strut. He takes his time, moving slyly like a fox, forever on alert, yet somehow easily distracted.

"I had wondered if your refusal to eat was because your hunger had nothing to do with food." His voice is thicker than it usually is, twanged with his Italian heritage. "But since I always double-guess myself around you, I once again brushed it off. Silly me." He's at the side of my bed now, so close the fine hair on the tops of his legs brush the arm draped across my body. "Everything you want to see is right in front of you, so why don't you open your eyes, Roxanne?"

Either determined to prove he doesn't scare me or that I'm downright stupid, I pop open my eyes at Dimitri's request. The visual is ten times better than the one in my head. I don't know where to look first—at the thick rippling of muscles in his midsection or the sturdy thighs holding up the incredibly mouthwatering package. Perhaps I should start at his bulging biceps before finishing at a hardness more than a spark of attraction would be required to instigate?

His cock is thick and hard, meaning the stretchy material of his trunks is being put through the ultimate durability test. They're a quality brand, however they look seconds from fraying under the pressure of his pulsating rod of flesh.

My eyes slowly float up to Dimitri's face when he says, "All it takes is a few seconds of distraction and *poof*, your entire existence is over." I'm confused as to what he means until I attempt to stop him from uncinching the belt holding my dressing gown close to my body. My hands are bound above my head, secured by a set of cuffs that have been used often enough to leave notches in the bedposts.

"Let me go." Just the thought of any woman being cuffed to his bed has my voice the most unhinged it's ever been. It's fueled more by anger than fear, peeved as fuck that even when my life is in danger, jealousy is still my most paramount emotion.

I couldn't understand Eddie's anger about me climaxing over another man's watch, yet here I am getting blistering mad over a man I hardly know playing sex games on the bed I'm resting on.

I'm certifiably insane.

Dimitri's smile is as white-hot as the surge that bolts through me when he shakes his head. "Not until you say please."

With his eyes locked on mine, he undoes the knot in my dressing gown cord faster than I can snap my fingers. His chest rises and falls in rhythm to the throb in my throat when he pries open the material. He doesn't part the seams far enough that my nipples become exposed, but the heat from his hooded-gaze makes it seem as if he did.

The friction his meekest touch causes is unbelievable. It has heat blazing through me, and its fiery response grows in intensity when he glides his index finger through the galley between my breasts. He's barely touching me, but every inch of my body tightens, anticipating more. *Wanting* more.

When his hand stops near my chin, my head naturally slants

so I can nuzzle my cheek into his palm. It's as sticky as the mess between my legs, his body temperature too high to discount.

Dimitri's body isn't the only thing warming up. Heat burns at my cheeks, just not all of their redness can be blamed on desire. Some of it is shame. Shame he killed my boyfriend, and I don't feel the least bit bad about it. Shame his touch should revolt me when it doesn't. Shame that even after he made me feel as tiny as an ant, I'm on the verge of begging him to touch me.

"Say please, Roxanne," Dimitri grinds out through clenched teeth. "Say please before I remember you're the reason my wife is dead, and my daughter is missing. Say please before I remember for every hour of every day that *you* are responsible for everything that has happened." He locks his eyes with mine. They're dark and tormented, but oh so beautiful. "Say please before I remember no amount of pleading will *ever* see me sparing your life. Say please, Roxanne." He lowers his hand from my cheek to my neck. "Say it now before it's too late."

The last of the air in my lungs rushes out with a moan when he grips my throat with enough strength both my clit and my lungs award his aggression with their utmost devotion. They both scream with need, one is just slightly louder than the other.

"Please."

# 20

**Dimitri**

Although Roxanne's one word is as breathless as her lungs, and the itch to kill is skittering through my veins begging me to ignore her request, I tamp down the debilitating restlessness I was born with before weakening my grip on her throat.

Her gasps as she fights to fill her lungs with air excites me even more. It's a genuine need that spreads through me like a wildfire as hot and heavy as the blood feeding my cock. She has so much attitude, so much spit-fire—the very thing Audrey was missing.

My wife's attitude didn't live up to her brash hair coloring. She was always the quieter one in the room. She didn't raise her voice or fight for the top position in the room. As long as it kept her out of the spotlight, she was happy to let anyone take the lead. She could see another woman's lipstick on the collar of my shirt, smell her perfume on my skin, and she did nothing—not a single fucking thing.

Her inability to fight for me saw me fucking around on her

more. I wanted to see her cheeks inflamed with jealousy, for her to tell me she hated me before vowing to kill the woman who dared to slip between our matrimonial sheets.

I wanted to feel needed.

I *never* got that from Audrey.

Not once.

The same can't be said for Roxanne. She didn't ask me to stop because she's sickened at the idea of me touching her. She did it because she's angry at herself. Even the risk of dying isn't enough to offset her desire for me. I killed her boyfriend, threatened her family, and told her I'd bury her alive just to hear her screams suffocated by the dirt clogging her lungs, yet she still wants me to fuck her, lick her, kiss her, and claim every single inch of her.

She wants me like my wife never did, but in a way I'll never be able to fulfill.

I can learn from my past, however I can't forget it. Fien deserves more than to be set aside for a woman who infuriates me as much as she intrigues me. She's my daughter, my blood. She comes before anyone—even me.

With that in mind, I snatch my hand away from Roxanne like her scar revolts me as much as she believes before heading for the attached bathroom. The agony between my legs worsens when I flick on the faucet in the freestanding shower. Roxanne's scent is stronger in confined spaces. It's why I couldn't keep a cool head when her breast continually brushed Rocco's arm during our drive to Hopeton. I could have blamed the bumps in the road for their constant contact, but my fucked-up head refuses to play nice when it's spiraling out of control. One more brush and I would have popped a bullet between Rocco's eyes like he hasn't been my friend for the past two decades.

While waiting for the water pumping out of the showerhead to turn blistering hot, I shred off my all-black trunks before moving to stand in front of the mirror. I briefly consider returning to my room when I take in how red and angry my cock looks. He's throbbing with need, his thickness solely reliant on the woman handcuffed to my bed.

My lips curve to the side when I recall how easily I distracted Roxanne. Not even the clanging of the cuffs when I removed them from my bedside table shifted her eyes off my body. She dragged them over every inch of me, heating my skin with the same frantic buzz of a tattoo gun.

Her distraction should give my guilt some leeway. Unfortunately, that's far from the truth. I stopped seeking excuses months ago. I fucked up, I looked away, and now I'm paying for the consequences of my actions.

When I step into the steam-filled space, my hand stirs to drop to my engorged cock. I want to squeeze it a little to release some of the tension causing its agony, but since I refuse to let the fiery little wildcat mere feet away know the hold she has over me, I lean into the scorching hot water, praying it will scold her touch from my skin as effectively as it will drain the blood from my cock.

Usually, my cock reacts to burning heat the same way it would if I plunged it into an ice bath. It isn't having the same effect today. I like the passion that comes from a fiery response. Whether the death of an insolent man or the slap of a scorned woman, there's an emotion attached to every response, a thrill you can't get from wrapping your hand around your cock and batting one out. It requires a woman's touch. Her heated breaths on my neck. Her silky-smooth skin under my hand. Her cunt wrapped around my cock.

*Jesus.* I should have taken Alice up on her offer. Wanting Roxanne to experience the inane stupidity that pumped through me from Rocco's protectiveness, I overexerted my words when requesting Smith to organize a late-night appointment with Alice.

He must have conveyed my request to Alice in the same manner. She came over ready to suck my dick. Her logic that penetration isn't cheating always sees her ready to get on her knees.

I told her no. I walked away.

I'm regretting it more than ever right now.

*Perhaps I can be quiet? Maybe Roxanne is already asleep?*

*No!* I release my cock from my hand before grabbing a bar of soap from the soap dish. I scrub my skin until it's raw, then attack it with the same amount of intensity with a towel.

By the time I walk back into my room, my anger is as high as my dick rests against my stomach. My fury hasn't weakened its pulse in the slightest. Its hardness is fed by the same gall firing in Roxanne's eyes when she spots my naked stalk across the room. She doesn't speak, she just raises her brow that exposes her red hair color is natural while silently stalking me.

"You should be sleeping. Alice is *never* tardy." She learned what happens to slackers the hard way seven years ago. "She will be here at precisely six."

Roxanne waits for me to pull on a pair of sleeping pants before she raises her eyes to my face. Although her hooded-gaze is brimming with lust, they reveal she's still scared. "I can't sleep." She chews on the corner of her plump lips before halfheartedly shrugging. "I'm kinda hungry."

Air whizzes out of my nose as I fight not to roll my eyes. "Of course you are."

I gather up a plain white tee before marching to her side of the room. I pretend not to notice the blistering of goosebumps racing across her skin when I adjust the angle of her head so I can see if my earlier anger left a mark. Her neck is a little red where I gripped her, but for the most part, she's relatively uninjured.

Mistaking the annoyance in my eyes as sorrow, Roxanne frees her lip from her menacing teeth before saying, "It's more frustrating than sore." She jangles the cuffs circulating her wrists. "Kind of like these." As she bounces her pretty eyes between mine, she asks, "Can you please take them off?"

Her cutesy act gets side-swiped when I shake my head.

She's back to her feisty self in no time.

"Why not?"

Although I don't appreciate being interrogated, this line of questioning doesn't bother me. "Because that's only something that will occur *once* you've gained my trust."

"How can I gain your trust while cuffed to a bed..." Her words trail off as her throat works hard to swallow. She noticed how thick I was when I re-entered the room, so her thoughts immediately deviate toward wicked territory.

So do mine, but I pretend otherwise. "You can start by answering some questions for me."

When she hesitantly nods, unsure how she could possibly have any information I need, I gather a manila folder from my desk and the chair from underneath it. While I set up a makeshift command center on Roxanne's half of the room, she maneuvers herself into a half-seated position. It's no easy feat considering she's cuffed to the headboard, but she makes it appear easy.

"Ready?"

Ignoring the dangerous drape of her dressing gown, she dips her chin.

Feigning the same level of calmness, I drop my eyes to the stack of paperwork Smith delivered during our commute from Erkinsvale to here. For the most part, it's my father's movement sheets for the next several months, but there are also snippets of the information he shared about Roxanne's movements the day Audrey was kidnapped.

"Do you recognize any of these men?" I show her a photograph

Smith pulled from the FBI's database several years ago. It's the last known group shot of the Castro crew.

"Look longer," I demand when Roxanne shakes her head within a few seconds of drinking in the group shot. There are over thirty men pictured. It isn't possible for her to have scanned all of their faces in that short amount of time.

When I say that, Roxanne scoffs. "I don't need a longer look. They all have dark, ethnic appearances. I grew up in Erkinsvale, so you can trust me when I say we've never crossed paths."

"What about when you met with your father in New York, did you see them, then?"

Her cheeks whiten when reality dawns. "Are these the men who took your wife?" When I nod, she scoots as close to me as her cuffs will allow. "Can you hold it a little closer? I don't have the best vision."

Unappreciative of the humor in her voice, I hold it to within an inch of her face.

After a period long enough to ensure me she scanned each face with precise detail, she inches back before once again shaking her head. "I'm sorry, none of them ring a bell." The anger making my skin sticky eases when she adds, "But I've seen him before."

When her eyes drop to a surveillance image of my father, my breath comes out in a rush. "He killed Old Man V earlier tonight. You don't get any credit for that."

My brows fetter in confusion when she replies, "Not tonight. At the bar next to the restaurant your wife was taken from. I swear he was seated at the end of the bar, although he looked a lot younger back then than he does now." She lifts her eyes to mine, even though confusion is clouding them, I can tell she's being honest. She has truthful, wholesome eyes. "His hair was darker, and his stomach was a little rounder, but I remember him because he was wearing a St. Jude pendant, but instead of it being on his necklace—"

"He wore it on a leather bracelet on his left wrist?"

When her pupils dilate in confirmation, I feel like I've been punched in the gut.

"Was it him?" I ask after gathering a photo frame from my desk and clearing away the dust coating it. It's a photograph of me with three of my siblings—Roberto, Ophelia, and CJ. It was taken by Rocco at my twenty-first birthday, a mere month before everything went downhill for my family.

"Yeah," Roxanna answers with an unsure nod. "But he had put on some weight and aged by almost a decade. Who is he?"

"He's my brother," I answer, too shocked to think up a lie. "My brother, who's been missing for almost five years."

Roxanne raises her eyes to mine. Worry, I think she's leading me astray, is seen all over her face. "Maybe it was your father, then? My head was all types of muddled that day. I was eighteen and in the big city alone for the first time. I could be mistaken."

I know she's lying, and so does she. She either saw Roberto or his biological twin. Either way, I need to know *exactly* who he is because there's no way my missing brother being at the same restaurant my wife was kidnapped from could be classed as a coincidence.

"Smith..."

Forever on alert, Smith's voice comes through the speaker of my cell phone two seconds later. "Yeah?"

Roxanne arches a brow when I ask, "Are you still friends with the composite sketch artist at Ravenshoe PD?"

"Yeah, but I don't see her coming out at this hour." His snickers out a laugh before continuing, "She might if you were willing to offer her some kind of incentive."

By incentive, he doesn't mean money. The male counterparts

of Ravenshoe PD are all about favors, money, and uncut blow. The female half are all about the D. You can have anything you want around these parts if you're willing to toss a few orgasms at the depraved women running this place. Even the chief of police's daughter shared trade secrets when I was balls deep inside of her.

I'm about to tell Smith to get her here no matter the cost, but the faintest trickle of a whisper stops me. "I can draw." When my eyes stray to Roxanne's, hers roll at the shocked expression on my face. "If you don't believe me, tell Smith to take a look at my Instagram page."

"She's telling the truth," Smith chimes in as image after image pops up on the screen of my phone.

I hear Roxanne's throat work through a hearty swallow when I move to gather my phone off my desk. Although her confidence is hot enough to blister my skin, she's nervous about what my response will be to her drawings.

She has no reason to fret. She has an immense amount of talent.

"You drew these?" The drawings range from portraits of dogs and cats with their tongues hanging out to couples in various stages of erotic content. The detail is undeniable. Even with the sketches being black and white, I can see the texture of the dog's shiny coat, and I'm not going to mention the realistic veins in one of her model's cocks, or he'll have a bounty on his head by the end of tonight.

"The animals were commissioned pieces on Fiverr. People emailed me photos of their animals, and I turned them into sketches for five dollars a pop." She drags her tongue over her plump lips. "And the people are from the images in my head." Shame burns on her cheeks when she mutters, "If I dream about them, they end up in the pages of my sketchbook."

I'm torn between wanting to explore the shame in her eyes and getting back to the task at hand, so instead of picking, I do both. "Send someone out to purchase a sketchpad and pencils." When Smith hums an agreeing noise, I send him a quick message about a request I can't articulate in front of Roxanne before devoting all my attention to her. "Do you think you can sketch the man you saw that night?"

A current I haven't experienced in years trickles into my veins when she once again dips her chin.

# 21

**Dimitri**

His face is rounder than I remember, and his stomach is almost double in size, but there's no denying the man Roxanne saw at the Slice of Salt is my brother, Roberto. His eyes are the same wintry blue coloring as mine, his bushy brows hang heavily over his eyes, and the faintest of scars from where I accidentally jabbed my stick-sword into his right cheek is present in Roxanne's sketch.

It's Roberto. I'm one hundred percent confident of this. The only thing I can't work out is why. Audrey was taken less than two years ago. Roberto has been missing for almost five years. The math doesn't add up. Roberto, along with Ophelia, CJ, and I wanted to leave the family behind, but we were meant to do it together. We were a team, a unit, and we pledged never to leave the other behind, so why did he? And does his reasoning have anything to do with Audrey's kidnapping and Fien's disappearance?

There's only one way to find out. "Pack everything up. We leave in an hour."

Roxanne's eyes dart up to mine, seeking answers, but I'm out the door before a single syllable can be fired from her mouth.

"What do you make of this?" I ask Rocco, who leaps up to his feet since my unwarranted jealously saw me stationing him outside of Roxanne's room instead of inside of it.

When I thrust Roxanne's drawing into his chest, his lips purse. "What does Roberto have to do with this?"

"That's exactly what I'm trying to work out." He follows my fast pace down the hall. "Roxanne saw him around Slice of Salt the night Audrey was kidnapped."

"Shit." Rocco drags a hand across tired eyes before pushing out a set of words I never anticipated for him to speak—especially when it comes to Roxanne. "Are you sure we can trust her? Maybe you should hold back for a moment and take a good look at the evidence."

I freeze partway down the hallway before glaring at him with steely, annoyed eyes. He forced Roxanne into my life believing she could help me get Fien back, and now he's asking me to tug on the reins just as things get interesting. Is he brain dead?

"I'm not saying she's untrustworthy. I just need you to be cautious." When his roundabout excuse fails to hit its mark, he tries straight-up honesty instead. "Smith sent me to collect Roxanne's sketchpad from her apartment as per your request." That was what I texted Smith about earlier. I didn't want Roxanne knowing how fascinated I was to see if I had featured in her dreams, so I didn't vocalize my needs. I sent them via a text message. "There was more than one sketchpad. They went back years. This one is from when she was in primary school." He thrusts a cheap, flip notepad into my chest. "From the dates, I'm guessing she was around eight or nine."

The already brisk cantor of my heart jumps up a notch when I flick through the extensive collection of drawings. Although Roxanne's talent isn't at the level it is now, there's no denying she was a skilled artist even back then. But the thing is, the sketches are too graphic for a child, far too erotic. The images only adults should see, and even then, they'd be paying top dollar to see them. I know this because my empire was built on this type of filth.

After handing the notepad back to Rocco, I ask, "Roxanne said her drawings are based on dreams. Could that have been the case back then?" My question is a woeful waste of time. I've never seen Fien in the flesh, but even I know this type of behavior isn't normal for a child.

Rocco shifts from foot to foot while nervously breathing out of his nose. "Smith said her mother dropped her off to live with her parents when she was only a child." He lowers his eyes to the notepad holding graphic images of couples in various stages of raunchy sex. "Could this be the reason?"

I shrug, truly unsure. The information Smith unearthed about Roxanne's family months ago reveals her parents are fucked in the head, but come on, this is beyond that. You can be dependent on drugs, but that doesn't stop you knowing the difference between right and wrong. A parent is supposed to protect their child, they're supposed to love them like no one else can. They are *not* supposed to make them a mental case like my father did me.

Although my jaw is tight and the wish to kill is doubling the width of my veins, I can't let this slide. "What if she isn't wrong, Rocco? What if she did see Roberto that night? If I ignore that, and it turns out she was telling the truth, I'll never forgive myself. I need to know if she saw Roberto. I need to know if he's a part of this." I bounce my eyes between Rocco's. I'm incapable of recognizing the man glancing back at me but I know one day he will eventually expose himself. "Then once I know, I'll deal with *this*. I'll make *this* right." The way I say 'this' reveals who I am speaking about. "Just not until Fien is home. She has to come first, Rocco. She should have always come first."

"All right," he agrees with a frantic bob of his head. "Tell me what you need and where you need it, and I'll get it there for you."

I slap his shoulder, grateful for his understanding. "I need the jet fueled and ready to go. It's time to head back to New York."

---

I halt flicking through one of Roxanne's many sketchpads when Rocco enters the plane without her. Although something isn't sitting right with my stomach, the longer I peruse Roxanne's collection of artwork, the more my curiosity is piqued. There are no faces on the people she sketched during her childhood, no identifiable marks or features that would help Smith track them down. There are just arms, torsos, legs, and pelvises in various stages of movement. The detail of each piece is so vivid, I can imagine the positions each couple made during their intricate tryst.

If I were unaware the sketches were drawn by a child, I'd purchase every one of them like a crazed collector, aware the artist would be big one day. But since I know that isn't the case, I'm tempted to burn them all until they're nothing but chunks of charcoal Roxanne could use to start all over again.

With my emotions not knowing which way to swing, I place the overloaded notepad into my suitcase before raising my eyes to Rocco. "Where's Roxanne?"

My head slants to hide the tick of my jaw when he answers, "She isn't coming."

"What do you mean she isn't coming? She doesn't have a choice." I drift my eyes to the Range Rover parked at the side of the plane. I know Roxanne is sitting inside of it because not only did I buckle her into the seat in more ways than one before our thirty-mile trip, the lights illuminating the hangar are shining into the back seat, lighting up Roxanne's already bright hair.

My eyes rocket back to Rocco when he mutters, "She said she'd rather be buried in a shallow ditch than forced into a sex trafficking circuit." When shock crosses my features, he chuckles out a breathy laugh. "Think about it, Dimi. She has a point. How is nearly every white American female lured into the trade these days? Fancy mansion, top-of-the-line Range Rover, and a private jet, then, before you know it, *boom-shaka-laka*, you're eating porridge from a dog bowl in a cage. If I were a chick, I'd be gripping the door handle as hard as she is now. You wouldn't get me in here for shit."

Neither amused by his humor nor having the time for it, I snap out, "You don't *ask* her to join us, you *force* her to join us."

He holds his hand out in front of himself like I ordered for him to suck my dick. "You know that isn't me, Dimi. I don't do that shit." My foul mood worsens when he adds, "Especially not to Roxie. I ain't got no beef with her."

Needing to leave before I pop a bullet between his quirked brows, I unlatch my seat belt, clamber down the stairs of a private jet, then throw open the door opposite to the one Roxanne is clutching in fear for her life.

"Don't you want to come to New York with us?" It's the fight of my life to keep the surprise off my face. I'm stunned by how calm and collective my question came out considering my veins are being obliterated with blackened rage.

Roxanne takes a beat to consider my question before she timidly shakes her head.

"All right. Then off you go."

The shock I'm struggling to keep off my face jumps onto Roxanne's. "I'm free to go?"

Her 'duh' face is cuter than I care to admit. "Uh-huh. You did as asked. You gave me information I needed to identify Fien's kidnappers."

"But I said her captor was a woman. Roberto isn't a woman." She pauses to reprimand herself for trying to talk herself out of going. "I guess he could be working with one?"

"Perhaps, but I won't find out here. I need to go to New York."

"Okay." Her constant licking of her lips shouldn't be sexy, but it is. "Then go. I can find my way home from here."

I almost smile at her cunningness. "When I leave, this vehicle, along with my possessions inside of it, will return to the Petretti compound. If anything is removed from it without my permission, it'll be classed as theft. Theft is a big no-no in this industry, Roxanne. Do you know what happens to people who steal from me?"

Her pupils don't dilate in the slightest when she answers, "They die."

"Uh-huh. Is that what you want to happen to Maio?"

Her eyes lock with Maio's in the rearview mirror for the quickest second before she shakes her head.

"Then, you need to leave this airstrip before me."

A smirk begs to notch my lips higher when she once again shakes her head. I should have known she's too smart to fall for my tricks. She might only be twenty, but she's lived a harsh life that matured her at double the rate of her peers. It's the same for me. I'm barely notching twenty-six, but it feels like I'll be seeking an assisted living facility within the next year or two. That isn't surprising considering hardly anyone in this industry lives past thirty.

When Roxanne's knuckles remain white from her death-clutch on the door handle I cuffed her to for our trip, my bad mood gets the better of me. "All right. Then, I guess I may as well shoot Maio now."

Before Roxanne can blink, I blow Maio's brains out. He slumps forward, the honk of the horn announcing to the rest of my crew that the trash has been taken out. I didn't just kill him to scare Roxanne out of my car. His sneaky hands were stirring one too many pots, and don't get me started on the comments I heard him whispering to my men when I guided Roxanne to his car, or I'll discharge my entire clip into the space of air his brain should have been taking up.

Respect for Roxanne's determination whizzes out my nose when she throws open the door she's been clutching the past ten minutes, slips out, then hightails it away from me. She doesn't look back my way once, her focus solely on escaping.

I could threaten to shoot her if she doesn't stop, or chase her down, but why exhaust myself if I don't need to? She's running straight toward the marshlands Clover hid in while waiting for us to leave so he could take care of Maio.

She isn't going anywhere but to New York with me.

After dumping my gun onto the floor of the Range Rover so Clover can clean up my mess—the Petretti run on the 'no bodies, no time for our crimes' theory—I return to the private jet.

Rocco eyes me with confusion slashed across his features, shocked I returned without the package I went to collect. His bewilderment is alleviated two seconds later when a kicking and screaming Roxanne is walked into the plane over Clover's shoulder. She's fighting him with everything she has, which only doubles the amusement on Clover's face. He's so big, I doubt he's feeling the slightest twinge of pain from her fists whacking him in the back.

"Did someone order a redhead with a slice of feisty?" Clover asks with a chuckle.

As the men around him laugh, my jaw tightens. There are too many hungry eyes watching Roxanne's every move. It has me itching to kill even more than Maio's attempt to bite the hand that fed him.

Rocco's eyes snap to mine as quickly as Roxanne stops pounding the shit out of Clover's back when I say, "Take her to the bedroom."

Knowing better than to double-guess my direct order, Clover immediately commences moving Roxanne to the lower half of the jet.

Rocco doesn't follow his obedient lead. "Dimi—"

I shut him up with a stern sideways glare. "Tell the pilot I want wheels up in no less than five minutes. We're already behind schedule."

Too tired to answer the many questions his narrowed eyes are throwing my way, I sidestep him before shadowing Clover's walk.

I've only just entered the compact yet luxurious sleeping quarters at the back of the jet when Roxanne lands on the bed with a thud. She springs back onto her feet in under a second, but my stern grumble telling her to sit stops her bounce off the springy mattress.

"We had an agreement. You have not yet fulfilled your side of our agreement, so you're not free to go."

"This was *never* part of our agreement." She peers past my shoulder to the men I feel watching her. There's no doubt they're interested, but since they'd have to get through me to touch her, she has nothing to worry about.

The pounding of my heart matches the vein working overtime in Roxanne's neck when I request for Clover to disembark the jet. She watches his exit, her eyes only returning to mine after I've fastened the latch on the only bit of safety between her and my thirsty crew.

"If you think I brought you here to fuck you, you're wrong." My next set of words are hard to articulate when the late hour has me confusing the flare darting through her eyes as a disappointed one. "If I wanted to fuck you, you'd already be fucked. If I wanted them to fuck you..." I nudge my head to the door I just locked, "... they'd be lining up for round two. But that isn't what this is about. *None* of this is about you. It's about Fien, my daughter. I'm trying to protect her as your daddy should have protected you. I'm trying to keep her safe."

For the first time tonight, the wetness in Roxanne's eyes isn't from fear. She's remorseful, although it has nothing on my guilt when I ask, "Did your father fuck with your head or his druggo friends?"

This isn't a conversation we should be having now. I doubt it's even one we should have in the near future, but for the life of me, I can't hold back my interrogation. The knot in my gut won't lessen until Roxanne gives me the answers I'm seeking, and even then, I'm certain it'll take more than words to fully smooth it out.

"What?" I can see how badly she wants to deny my claim, but with her mouth refusing to relinquish another lie, she could only get one word out.

"You have the markings of an abused child, a fascination with the man who watched you get off in an alleyway." I didn't just feature in her latest drawings. My rain-soaked, cloaked-by-darkness form is the *only* thing she has sketched the past year. "The sexual maturity of someone much older and wiser." I lock my eyes with her watering ones. "And your nipples bud every time you feel threatened or scared." She can deny my accusations all she likes, but the straining of her nipples against the thick material of her dressing gown is undeniable. "So that leads me to believe your daddy either fiddled with you, or he sold you to his drug-fucked buddies like he did your mother."

Roxanne's hands ball as tightly as mine when she shakes her head, denying my accusations. "He never touched me."

"So, his friends did?"

"That isn't what I said." Her words are as icy as the color of my eyes and just as lifeless.

With anger clutching my throat, every word I speak is delivered with a gravelly growl. "You didn't deny it either, Roxanne. So what is it? Did they touch you? Or did your sweet ole Pa treat his daughter like a dirty little whore?"

"It was neither of those things!"

When she attempts to race by me, I grab the tops of her arms and drag her to within an inch of my face. "Then... What. Was. It?" My voice is as loud as hers, my anger just as palpable. I'm not angry at her. I'm fighting the urge not to track down her father and slit his pedophile throat.

This kills me to admit, even more so since Ophelia's life was cut short right around the age Roxanne is now, but Roxanne's eyes hold the same dark, gleaming secrets Ophelia's did any time our father returned home after a long stint of absence. They were badly stained, but not enough to have you believing they were wholly broken. They could be fixed if the right person was willing to put in the hard yards.

I thought Isaac Holt was that person for Ophelia. I was wrong then just like I could be now, but I can't stop pushing. I need to know who hurt Roxanne. I need to know more than my lungs need their next breath.

"Did he touch you, Roxanne? Is that why you were sent to live with your grandparents? Did your mother try to protect you *after* your father already fucking hurt you?"

"No," she denies again, even with her eyes screaming the opposite. "He didn't touch me!"

"Then what did he do? Why do you act as if he doesn't exist?" I crowd her against the door of the private jet just as its engines roar to life. "Why do you hate him so much that just the thought of saying his name has you wanting to vomit."

"He made me watch!" she shouts before she can stop herself. "He made me watch what they did to my mother." Tears roll down her ashen face unchecked as she repeats, "He made me watch."

I want to kill, I want to go on a rampage, but instead of doing either of those things, I do the last thing anyone would ever expect. I pull Roxanne into my chest, hopeful her tears will cool the rage burning me up inside.

If they don't, I'm sure I can find another means to dispel my anger.

Torturing her father will be a good start.

# 22

**Roxanne**

Sighing, I rest my cheek onto the top of my knees. The meal a member of Dimitri's staff is placing on the bedside table smells as divine as the previous three, but no number of excited rumblings from my stomach will pull me out of the slump I'm in.

I cried in the chest of a man who'd rather kill me than bed me.

If that isn't bad enough, it seems as if that was the beginning of my punishment.

I've been shunted from activities. Left out in the cold like the naughty child I am.

The confession Dimitri forced out of me three nights ago on his private jet isn't to blame for my disturbing ways. I was barely a child when my father found humor in my pink cheeks and wide eyes. He wanted to embarrass me, where in reality, he sparked a sinister curiosity for sex.

I didn't see the men sleeping with my mother—I didn't even see her—all I saw was two bodies becoming one, the gripping of flesh, and harmonic sounds I'd never heard before. I saw how the simplest movements could change the light in someone's eyes in an instant.

I saw beauty when all I should have seen was darkness.

When my grandparents discovered the reason for my almost erotic drawings in grade five, my grandfather contacted the first shrink he found. He was mortified like Dimitri, confident there was something horrendously wrong with me.

Mercifully, my grandmother saw past my chipped exterior and overstimulated curiosity. She understood my vividly graphic drawings weren't to recreate acts I should have never seen. I wanted to recapture a unique beauty I hadn't seen since I went to live with my grandparents, not live in wickedly naughty thoughts.

My nanna was light years ahead of her time. She taught me it was okay to be sexually inquisitive as long as I wasn't being forced against my will to explore it nor encouraging others to experiment in ways they weren't comfortable. She slackened my lead with things like reading novels not recommended for my age but retightened it when she believed my curiosity couldn't be curbed in a non-physical manner.

Her system was faultless until that night in the alleyway a year ago. There was no beauty in my previous exchanges with Eddie, no crackles in the air, or breathy, wordless moans. There was nothing but lackluster, lifeless exchanges that had me wondering if the memories of my childhood were as jaded as my devilishly immoral compass.

Then he arrived out of nowhere as dark and dangerous as ever. When I spotted Dimitri, the faintest trickle of desire floating through my veins switched to a full-blown pandemic of heated rushes and core-clenching tingles. Every inch of my body tightened in anticipation. I was trapped, mesmerized, and finally free from the chains that had held me down for years.

It wasn't just him watching me that heightened my senses to beyond belief. It was wondering what he'd do to me if he weren't a spectator, how I'd react if his hand were to replace Eddie's. Would the light in my eyes change like they did for my mother, or would they fill with tears like hers did every time my father's friends left?

Although the thought of discovering the truth should have haunted me more than it did, my nanna's constant reminder that I'm a perfectly balanced and normal person kept it on the back burner.

I'm an adult now, so it's perfectly okay to be fascinated with sex. I just had to find the right person to spark a response out of me.

Dimitri does that. He just wishes it wasn't true.

He hasn't looked at me the same since Thursday night. Other than ordering for my hair to be peroxided back to the blonde coloring it had been in the alleyway over a year ago, he enters our shared room well after the noise in this fortress-like bunker dies down and exits long before a member of his staff enters with my breakfast.

It feels as if I could stand in front of him naked, and he wouldn't notice me. He hasn't even checked to see if the chemical peel a well-known dermatologist placed on my scar worked, and he paid out the ass for an emergency appointment.

I guess his rejection should be expected. If someone repulses you, the last thing you'd ever feel for them is desire.

With another sigh, I shift my eyes to watch a middle-aged European woman exit my room. The brittle beat of my pulse notches up a little when I fail to hear the lock latching into place before her shadow disappears from underneath my door. I'm usually confined to my room, the order to keep me under lock and key handed down from above. No one here would ever do anything to defy Dimitri because they fear him as much as I do.

There's just one difference. Their fear is that he will kill them. Mine is that he'll never look at me like he did in the alleyway over a year ago.

Forever curious, and somewhat willing to break the rules with the hope of forcing a response out of Dimitri, I throw my legs off the bed I'm sitting on before tiptoeing across the room.

My heart rate jumps into a cantor when the lowering of the door handle isn't hindered by a reinforced latch. I'm uncuffed, and my door isn't fastened by prison-like bolts.

After a quick breather to ensure I don't collapse from a lack of oxygen to my brain, I carefully peel open the door. This could be a test, however failing has never scared me. As long as you get back up, you can fall as many times as you'd like.

The party-like atmosphere I've heard through the floor of my room the past three nights booms into my ears the more I move down the corridor. The ambiance gives off an elegant, ritzy feeling compared to the grittiness of a nightclub. It probably helps that this fortress is more suitable for a king than rough-and-ready mafia men. The drapes are thick and expensive, and all the fittings are top-of-the-line. So much detail has been placed in every inch of this hallway, I'm confident in saying it's better fitted than my apartment building and ten times more expensive.

Although I'm not dressed as flashy as the people milling around, they let me slip by with only the quickest glance. There's too much beauty to drink in to worry about little ole me ruining the glamourous atmosphere.

"Hello," I murmur to a couple getting friendly against the wall leading to the curved stairwell.

Who am I to judge their hookup location? At least they're under the privacy of someone's residence.

When I leap off the final stair, I take an urgent step back. Dimitri is in a formal sitting area to the right of the stairwell. He's swirling an amber-colored liquid around a whiskey glass while talking to a group of men. Although the closest women to him are several feet away, an intense rage of jealousy blasts through my veins. All the women are topless, and their pleated miniskirts leave *nothing* to the imagination. I'm not going to mention how they can't take their eyes off Dimitri, or I might do something more stupid than cry into the chest of a cartel kingpin.

Certain I'll be booted from festivities the instant Dimitri spots me, I head in the direction opposite to the room he's seated in. Even with most of Dimitri's 'guests' not speaking English, it appears as if they're having a good time. The gaming area is over-flowing with men placing bets at a line of craps tables while smoking cigars. Unlike the room Dimitri is in, the topless women in this part of the compound are either seated on the men's laps or accepting their bets.

The further I travel, the more excitement slicks my skin. This is unlike any party I've ever been to, but it doesn't make it any less exhilarating. Think of the dirtiest, riskiest, most all-out naughtiest event you've ever wished to attend. Now double it. That'll give you an idea of the 'festivities' Dimitri and his guests are being wooed with.

It's as if Vegas and Times Square had a baby. Everything you could possibly want is in the one space—scantily dressed women dancing in crystal birdcages, acrobatic gymnasts daringly floating above your head, bloody men fighting bare-knuckled in a UFC-authentic cage, and gambling is in abundance.

There's even sex if you enter the right room.

Hot, raunchy, sweat-producing sex.

I hesitate for a beat before entering the square box with only one solid wall. Although the couple going for it in clear-view for all to see are too engrossed with each other to pay me any atten-tion, I can't help but wonder if I'm walking headfirst into a trap.

With how much sexually stimulating content this party is pumping out, I'm not surprised a viewing area I've only ever read about is empty. I'm more disappointed than anything. The priciest artwork can't compete with the beauty of two bodies intimately joining.

After wetting my dry lips, I enter the sex-scented space, willing to take a risk even if it kills me. With three out of four walls being floor-to-ceiling glass, I'm soon awarded an unimpeded view of three couples in various stages of undress. The cube on my right has a topless blonde on her knees about to suck the cock of a man whose mask is shielding half his attractive face.

The couple directly in front of me is ticking off every office romance novel checklist. A brunette with lace-topped stockings and black-rimmed glasses has her thong-covered backside planted on a desk covered in papers while an almost still fully clothed dark-haired man in a fiercely cut suit pounds into her. She calls him 'boss' on repeat while he refers to her as his 'naughty little secretary.'

Although the two exchanges I just told you about are appealing to the eye, the couple on my left is far more interesting. They're not just producing a feast for the eyes with needy grabs and fluidly precise rocks of their hips, they have my ears satisfied as well. They're the most vocal of the group, and if the way the orange-haired man has his partner bent over the couch is anything to go by, this isn't the first time they've fucked. They move together so well, I'm mesmerized by them in under a minute. It's a beautiful scene of pounding flesh, light-altering eyes, and moans I've only heard leave my mouth once before.

If I had a sketchpad and a chunk of charcoal at the ready, I'd be in my ideal fantasy. I don't care that they're fucking or that I'm sneakily witnessing them at their most venerable. It's the raw magnificence of the exchange I'm paying attention to. The way sweat rolls down the blonde's temples every time the man plunges his veiny penis inside her, how the light above their heads enhances the wetness on his thick shaft, and then there's their undeniable connection. It's so blistering hot, my skin perspires as if I have just ran a marathon.

The heat bouncing off them has my temperature rising as rapidly as my panic when the only shroud of light lighting up the room is suddenly blanketed by a large, brooding frame. The poor condition means I can barely see an inch of my approacher's face, however I don't need to see his features to know who he is. His aura is telling enough.

"I kept your name off the guest list to ensure you didn't end up in this room, and where do you venture to the instant you're freed from captivity?" I can't see Dimitri's face, but I can imagine his scold when he answers his question on my behalf. "In the very room you have no right to be in."

When he enters the space now feeling ten times smaller, the sound of skin slapping skin fades into the background. I can't hear anything but my raging pulse. Dimitri's eyes are holding the same murderous gleam they had when Eddie found my clit, and his jaw is so firm, I'm afraid it's about to crack.

I discover the reason for his fury when he slants his head to the side and growls, "Get out."

Sickness rolls through my stomach when a man I hadn't noticed in the corner of the black space stands from a chair. Even with conditions being poor, my eyes have adjusted enough to the dark to understand his intentions. The crotch of his trousers is extended past the length of his zipper, and his belt is undone and hanging loosely in front of his stout thighs.

Although he's as tall as Dimitri and almost as wide, he appears the size of a dwarf when he commences shimmying past Dimitri's ominous frame. Dimitri could take a step to the side to give him a clear passage, but he won't. He won't do anything that will risk him taking his scorning eyes off me. He's pissed the stranger witnessed my immorality, and he's more than happy to make sure I'm aware of that.

His scorn makes me all types of hot. It also tells me why he's arrived out of the blue. I disobeyed him. As far as he's concerned, that's cause for punishment.

I'm tempted to follow the stranger's flee when he squeezes through the minute portion of air Dimitri's menacing frame isn't taking up, but lose the chance when Dimitri takes another step. My feet root into the floor, both mesmerized by the fury radiating out of him and scared. I don't think he will hurt me, but in a way, that's as scary as the thought of him never touching me.

"Do you know what this room is, Roxanne?" His voice is low and husky in the quiet of my wickedly dreary thoughts. It demands my attention even more than the couples fucking around me. I don't pay them an ounce of attention. My focus is entirely gobbled up by the brute of a man in front of me.

When I nod, Dimitri *tsks* me like I'm a child. Determined to prove I'm not as stupid as he thinks, I fold my arms in front of my chest to hide the rattle of my hands before mumbling, "It's a viewing chamber. They're usually found in BDSM clubs or fetish dungeons. They're for people who enjoy watching others have sex."

"Close." He takes another step my way, trapping my perception as well as smarts. My clit is buzzing more now than it was when the ginger-haired man bent his date over the two-seater sofa to take her from behind. "This is a play space for people who like being watched." The dark, shiny locks framing his face fall away when he peers up at the ceiling. "The voyeurs are up there."

Like magic, the black ceiling that appears to be made out of glass turns transparent. It unveils a group of thirty to forty people glancing down at us with hungry, wanton eyes.

*Shit.*

"They..." Dimitri's eyes are still on the people watching our every move, "... pay good money to watch people have sex." Once his eyes are back on my face, he drags his teeth over his lower lip. "However, you can hire these pods for other *things*." The ceiling shifts back to its original setting when he takes another step closer to me. "You can suck your brother-in-law's dick without guilt, fuck your secretary without your wife knowing. You can even celebrate your fifth wedding anniversary if that's your kink." His eyes shift to each couple he's referencing before he returns them to me. "You can even be punished here when you don't do as you're told."

The coolness of a wooden desk brushes my backside when Dimitri's next step sees me taking a giant one back. I'm not scared of the menace in his tone. I need something to balance on to ensure my legs remain upright. That's how smoking hot his voice is when its fueled by undeniable anger.

"What did I tell you to do tonight, Roxanne?" he asks after taking in the faintest press of my thighs.

"You said—"

"Louder."

I swallow the saliva threatening to pool in the corner of my mouth before trying again. "You said I was to stay in my room until you returned."

He smiles like my submissiveness is hardening his cock.

If the bulge in his trousers is anything to go by, it is.

"Is this your room, Roxanne?"

When I shake my head, he arches a thick brow, demanding a voiced response.

*Bossy bastard.*

"No. This isn't my room."

Another step is closely followed by another squeeze of my thighs. "Then why are you here?"

With this the simplest question to answer, I reply, "I wanted to join in—"

"Louder."

"I wanted to join in," I almost shout. "I don't like that you're excluding me."

His smirk would have you convinced I said what I really wanted to say. That the more he ignores me, the more I crave his attention. I'm like a disobedient child who doesn't understand good attention far exceeds bad attention. I want it in any way I can get it.

I guess that's why my father's endeavors to embarrass me didn't work?

With my mood not as chipper as it once was, I attempt to side-step Dimitri. "I'll go back to my room."

He grips the top of my arm before I'm halfway to the door. It isn't a painful hold, but it's most certainly a domineering one. "If you want to be included, Roxanne, I'm more than happy to include you."

I don't know whether to gleam with shock or horror when he requests me to lean over the desk and raise my ass high in the air.

"W-w-what?"

I realize the spectators can hear us as clearly as we can hear them when Dimitri repeats, "Lean over the desk and stick your ass in the air." They're as turned on by his domineering command as me, they just vocalize their excitement, whereas I remain as quiet as a church mouse. "Don't make me repeat myself, Roxanne. I am not a patient man."

I'm torn. I don't want to agitate him more than I already have, and I'm super curious to see where he's going with this, but only now am I realizing I don't want to be fucked in front of spectators.

I don't want anyone but the person I'm sleeping with to see if the light in my eyes changes. It isn't something I want to share.

With that in mind, I shake my head. "No."

Dimitri balks like I slapped him. "What did you say?"

"I said no." I run a shaky hand across my cheeks to ensure they're still dry before adding, "I want to be a part of the festivities, not fucked like a whore."

He lowers his head until we meet eye to eye. "Who said I was going to fuck you?" He cages me to the desk by bracing his tattooed hands on each side of my hips and leaning in really close. The strong smell of whiskey bounds from his mouth when he whispers in my ear, "These rooms are only rented for an hour." He locks his eyes with mine. They're as blistering as ever. "I'd need a lot longer than that to work out all your kinks." I don't know if he's sucking in the scent of my arousal or fear when his nostrils flare during his next statement. Either way, it doubles the width of his pupils. "But your punishment for entering this room with another man won't take an hour. I'll have your ass as red as your cheeks in not even five minutes."

I respond to the jealousy in his tone as if it's legitimate. "I didn't know he was sitting there. I would have never entered if I knew he was there."

"These rooms are for fucking, Roxanne. You only enter them to be fucked or to fuck someone." When he takes a step back, the mask he was wearing when he entered the room slips back over his face. My closeness didn't calm his agitation. It made it worse. "Mitis thought you were here for him, and he was prepared to make you his no matter how many times you begged him not to." The expression on his face reveals he isn't lying. This isn't a room where 'no' is acknowledged. "That alone deserves punishment for both of you."

I have a feeling I'll leave this exchange less scarred than Mitis.

The vicious glint in Dimitri's eyes assures me of this, much less the murderous smirk etched on his face when his eyes shifted to the door Mitis snuck through only moments ago.

My eyes snap to Dimitri's when he growls out, "If I'm forced to repeat myself, you won't leave this room until your ass is dribbling blood like the bullet hole between Mitis's brows." He shifts on his feet to face the only solid surface in the room. "Chest flat on the desk, ass high in the air. I won't ask you again."

Ignoring the tremble of my thighs—which I'm confident are shuddering with an equal amount of excitement and worry—I spin around to face the desk. Spit seethes through Dimitri's teeth when I curl over the sturdy material. The high rise of my dress is already indecent, but my stretch to reach the other side of the desk makes it outright immoral.

My butt cheeks are showing, but no matter how hard I try, I can't force my hands to tug at the hem. I could use the excuse that Dimitri is towering over me, so even the spectators who paid top-dollar for a prime spot will leave tonight grumbling about bad seats, but what excuse do I have for the wetness between my legs?

Unexpected hotness races through my veins when Dimitri lifts the hem of my dress, so it sits on the lower half of my back. He doesn't take the time to notice the only underwear Alice supplied me with for the next four weeks are lace thongs, he just takes a step back, breathes noisily out of his nose, then spanks my right butt cheek.

The brutal crack his palm makes with my backside verifies he didn't hold back with his hit. It doubles the heat teeming between us and has me torn on whether I should sob or curve my knees inward.

I've never been spanked before, but I'd be lying if I said it was more painful than enjoyable. It's an odd feeling that rapidly explains why people crave it along with hairpulling. It's naughty but oh so good.

"Grind your pelvis against the desk, Roxanne. I don't want to miss." Dimitri's voice has me wondering if he's enjoying this as much as me. It's hot and edgy and has me so eager to reacquaint his hand with my ass. I stretch my toes to the max, seeking the hand he's pulling back in preparation for his next smack.

I call out when his second hit has perfect aim. It doesn't just add to the fiery burn racing across my butt cheeks, the tips of his fingers encroach an area thudding as fast as my heart rate.

By his third spank, I've forgotten we have an audience.

By his fourth spank, the fact this is supposed to be a punishment has slipped from my mind.

By his fifth spank, I'm grinding against the desk as per his earlier request, needing something to take the edge off the tension in my clit. It's buzzing like crazy, verifying my madness. I'm being used as a gimmick like my mother was, showcased as if I'm a dirty whore, yet, I feel the most alive I've ever felt.

I'll do anything for this to continue, anything at all.

I will even beg.

"Again. Please."

My words are separated by big, needy breaths, but Dimitri has no issues hearing them. He spanks me again, his hit so exquisite, an orgasm crests at the peak of my core, threatening to topple at any moment. I just need one more spanking, one more brief touch of his fingers on my drenched panties, or better yet, the quickest flick of his thumb against my clit, and I'll be done.

But instead of doing any of those things, Dimitri lowers the hem of my dress, demands for me to immediately return to my room before he pivots on his heels and exits the sex chamber without so much as a backward glance.

# 23

## Dimitri

Damn Smith and his ability to reach me at any time.

Damn foreign dignitaries who prefer to watch instead of participating.

Damn my whiskey-soaked veins that had me refusing to listen to a rational thing my brain has to say.

And damn Roxanne and her delectably fine ass.

When she begged for me to spank her again, my cock sat so snugly against the zipper in my trousers, it took everything I had not to whip it out and plunge it inside her drenched cunt. She was so wet, every spank had evidence of her arousal glistening on the top of my fingertips. Even smacking her ass six times didn't see its redness overtake the wanton heat on her cheeks. She wasn't embarrassed I was punishing her in a room full of spectators, she was too turned on to care we had an audience.

Roxanne's non-existent morals had me wanting to forget my objectives. I almost took her right on the desk, as destitute of standards as her greedy cunt. If Smith's desolate tone hadn't snapped me from my trance, I guarantee my cock would be coated in her juices right now. I only went into the sex pod because of the urgency in his tone, just like I left it for the exact same reason.

He doesn't interrupt me unless it's urgent. Saving Roxanne from a man who'd cut her up like an animal was urgent. It better be the same case this time around as my patience is stretched as thin as the thread struggling to hold my cock's reaction to Roxanne's moans.

My fucking God, my cock twitches just recalling how delicious they sounded. They're as delectable as the scent of her skin mingled with mine, and the very reason I need to put more distance between us than I have the past three days.

Pulling Roxanne into my chest four days ago was one of the stupidest things I've done. Ever since then, instead of my focus remaining on freeing Fien from her nightmare, it continuously shifts to ways I can eradicate Roxanne's. I'm not prioritizing my time on the right person, and the injustice is both souring my mood and worsening my daughter's chance of survival.

That's why I stepped into the room with guns blazing. I was mid-conversation with a man who knows the whereabouts of every gangbanger in the country when Smith updated me on Roxanne's location. I tried to tell myself she's a big girl who can get herself out of the riskiest exchange, but the longer the movie on how that would go down rolled through my head, the higher my blood pressure spiked.

It was within danger territory, only two stomps away from the man who could possibly know Roberto's location, and it wasn't going to settle until I took my annoyance out on the person responsible for its incline.

A public spanking seemed like the ideal punishment.

Roxanne's multiple sketchpads should have told me differently.

If I was being honest, I'd say a part of me knew how she'd reply to my arrogance. Her willingness to please would usually stop my eagerness in its tracks. However, there have been a handful of times my cock has overruled my head. Roxanne has been in the picture for every one of those days, so who's to say it wouldn't have been the same this time around?

"Roxie was right—"

I hold my finger in the air, halting Smith's update midsentence before shifting my eyes to Rocco. He's standing in the corner of the command center. His fists are clenched at his sides, and his jaw is tight, wrongly believing I used Roxanne's fucked-up childhood against her. He's all for fucking, has been from the age of thirteen, but if it involves marking a woman's body with anything but his cum, it's a no-go for him.

He wasn't up in the viewing chambers watching Roxanne's punishment firsthand, but Smith has eyes and ears over every inch of this compound, meaning he didn't need to be in the room with me to get a bird's-eye view of Roxanne's punishment. He just needed to hack into the camera in the button of my shirt.

The tightness of Rocco's jaw slackens when I say, "Make sure Roxanne gets to her room in one piece. I'll be up to check on her in a bit." I don't know why I added the last half of my statement. Most likely as a warning to Rocco that he won't have time to nurture her like he's hoping.

It won't stop him from ribbing me about the possibility, though. "Want me to rub some cream into her welts for you, too?" He doesn't wait for my growl to work its way up my chest. He just smirks, gives me a one-finger salute, then exits the room with a pompous flare I usually relish more than hate.

It doesn't have the same effect tonight. I'm hard, pissed as fuck, and fighting not to shake off my funk with a few lines of coke and an endless number of whores. Returning to the drug-fucked idiot I was before I became a father won't help anyone, but some days, I wonder if it would make life a little easier to take.

Do you have any idea how gutting it is to know your enemies have been fucking you in the ass for almost two years? Weak. Pathetic. An incapable man. There are a few words I'd use to describe myself when the negativity enters my mind with a refusal to leave until I've killed a man. Considering it's almost daily lately, you can imagine how high my death count now sits. Trying my hardest not to become the monster my father wanted me to be, sees me becoming exactly that.

After working my jaw side to side, I shift my focus back to Smith—for the most part. "Put Roxanne's room up onto the main feed." It's playing on a smaller monitor on my left as it has been the past three nights, but I want to avoid eyestrain while stalking her to see if goosebumps prickle her skin when Rocco is within sniffing distance. They've become close the past three days, and I don't fucking like it. It agitates me to no end, much like my continuously deviating mind.

"What was Roxanne right about?" My clipped tone warns Smith I'm at the end of my teether. If his findings tonight aren't associated with Fien, we will exchange blows. No fear.

My attitude gets sliced in half when Smith replies, "Roberto. He was at Joops like Roxie said." He twists his laptop screen around to face me. It has a still image of a much older and fatter Roberto on the screen. Just like Roxanne's composite drawing, I'm confident it's him. "As you know, we couldn't get anything off the restaurant's surveillance cameras. They were wiped before you realized Audrey had left your side." His comment isn't an underhanded swipe at my stupidity, he doesn't do anything underhandedly, he's merely relaying the facts as he sees them. "I worked credit card transactions for Joops. I didn't get anything significant, so I shifted my focus to cell phones."

"Which also came up blank?" I interrupt, pushing him along. We're having this conversation with my dick pressed up against the zipper in my trousers. The sooner it's over, the better it will be for all involved, and I'm not going to mention the jumping of my blood pressure from watching Roxanne's arrival to her room. Rocco doesn't drop her off and leave, he walks her inside like they're returning from an intimate date. It frustrates me more than it should, but there's no denying the obvious.

Even Smith has noticed a change in my temperament. He tugs at the collar of his shirt as if his temperature is rising as rapidly as mine before moving at a steadier pace. "Yeah, they didn't come back with anything either, but I was working off pings for pre-2010 circuit phones, assuming not even six-year-olds get around with flip phones these days. I should have realized the rules don't apply for some people." He tosses an outdated and cracked phone onto the desk between us before nudging his head to a bank of monitors on my right.

This kills me to admit, but it takes me a good three to four seconds to shift my eyes from the monitor broadcasting Roxanne's room to the one Smith wants me to look at. Roxanne and Rocco are moving toward the bathroom—the only room in this compound without a motion-activated camera.

When a bloody and bruised man bound to a rickety chair in a dungeon-like room confronts me, my annoyance deepens. Rocco wouldn't have roughed-up Roxanne's dad unless he has some sort of feelings for her. He gave me that exact same line when I ordered for Ian's whereabouts to be unearthed. This is what I meant when I said Roxanne is distracting me from what really matters. The absence of the two men I sent out to bring her father in was barely felt, but the time I put Smith on the case to discover his current location was most certainly noticeable. Every second he hunted the demon of Roxanne's past added a second to my daughter's captivity.

Can you understand now why I can't tell which way is up?

"What did you find on Ian's phone?"

With the smile of a man at the top of his game, Smith nudges his head to Roberto's photo. I'm about to ask for further information, but within two keystrokes, Roberto's blurred image zooms out until he's nothing but a speckle in the background, and Roxanne's big green eyes take up a majority of the screen. Because she cried off most of the gunk she had coating her lashes, the greenness of her eyes is mesmerizing.

"Who did he send that to?" The image is attached to an outgoing text message. I don't give a fuck who may have seen Roberto in the background of this image, it's the text attached I'm getting worked up about. He's offering his daughter for sale, asking how much he can get for her since she's reached prime breeding age. It appears as if Roxanne was only spared because his purchaser was too slow with his calculations. His offer of fifty thousand dollars was received two minutes after Roxanne's teary exit.

I feel as if our search is going in circles when Smith replies, "It was a burner phone, but its last ping was off a cell tower a few miles out of Ravenshoe."

"Did Ian receive a down payment for Roxanne? A contract? Anything we can seek similarities from?" The fact Ian said 'breeding age' has my interests immensely piqued. It could be a coincidence my wife was taken when she was eight months pregnant, but Roxanne's constant thrust into my life the past two years has me looking at any angle.

Smith slumps low into his chair. "Not a thing. He either had an attack of the conscience or..." His words trail off as aware as me that Roxanne's father would have only pulled out of negotiations if a better offer was placed on the table.

"Where's Roxanne's mother?"

Air hisses between Smith's teeth as he shrugs. "If she's still alive, she's clever at hiding her tracks."

"Or making tracks that don't require a credit card."

Smith jerks up his chin, agreeing with me.

After a beat, I shift the direction of his focus for the third time this week. Although it appears as if I've got him working on the ghosts of Roxanne's past, this will benefit Fien as much as it will Roxanne, so I'm okay with it. "Find Sailor's last movements. As much as we wish it were different, no one just disappears. Everyone leaves tracks. Center your focus around the time of Roxanne's meeting with her father. I don't care how much of a deadbeat she was, no mother would sit on the sidelines when her daughter pops up on the radar for the first time in almost a decade. She was either at that restaurant watching or fighting for the chance."

Smith twists his lips, shocked he hadn't considered that angle. I give his slip-up some leeway. He isn't a parent, so he shouldn't be expected to think like one.

"And him?" He once again nudges his head to Roxanne's father, Ian. "Rocco made him shit his pants. If we don't do something soon, the guests might start complaining. That's the last thing we want. They already have their knickers in a twist from having the location of their 'working holiday' changed last minute."

I take another moment to ponder. It does little to ease the tick of my jaw. "Send Clover down to pay him a visit. Tell him not to kill him. Just drive him to the brink of death. He hurt Roxanne, so, at the end of the day, it's up to her whether she wants him dead or not." I wasn't supposed to articulate my last sentence, but I'm glad

I couldn't hold back. It felt good passing the responsible baton to another person even if it was for only a second.

"Before you go," Smith says just before I dart through the door as fast as I barreled through it only minutes ago. Roxanne and Rocco are still in the bathroom. It has me super eager to leave, although not as eager as I am to pummel someone when Smith adds, "I know you want my focus on Roberto, but something in your father's schedule deserves mentioning."

I hadn't meant for my quest to find Roberto to diminish his inquiries on my father. His shadiness deserves more than a once-over.

When I lift my chin encouraging Smith to continue, he hands me a sheet of paper. "A credit card scanned at Slice of Salt the night Audrey was taken was used to buy a ticket to an event your father is hosting. I didn't think much of it until I noticed the recipient's address. She's originally from Ravenshoe."

"She? The purchaser is a female?"

When an agreeing hum vibrates his lips, I scan the name of the person attached to the credit card search. Usually, we immediately discount any women who come up in our searches. However, Roxanne's comment from days ago still rings in my ears. It's right up where her begging moans will now be. *"Because your daughter's captor is a woman."*

"Get me tickets to this event."

As his fingers tap on his keyboard, a smile tugs on Smith's lips. The reasoning behind his smirk smacks into me like a wayward missile when he asks, "The event is a couples-only event. Would you like me to put Roxanne's name down as your plus one?"

My eyes dart between the feed from Roxanne's room, the dingy one holding her father captive, and the last still image I have of Fien before I shake my head. "I'll call in a favor with a friend." I can't have Roxanne distracting me like she did tonight, so for that reason, and that reason alone, I have to pull back the reins of our ruse.

It could be my raging heart having me mishear Smith, but I swear he says, "It's your funeral," as I bolt out the door of his wired-up hot box.

My first thought is to race up to Roxanne's room to see what the fuck she and Rocco have been doing in the bathroom the past ten minutes, but my blood is too hot to give that thought proper consideration. I'm seeking answers, and since only one person can give them to me, I take a left at the base of the stairs instead of climbing them.

Smith wasn't lying when he said our guests would soon start complaining about the smell coming from the basement. The man bound to a chair in front of the boiler is in desperate need of a shower. He stinks like shit, piss, and vomit, and once I'm done with him, he'll also smell like death.

I've paid millions of dollars to keep my daughter safe.

He tried to sell his for fifty-thousand.

That means we can't be friends, and I'm more than happy to show him how I treat people I don't class as friends.

## 24

**Roxanne**

The zealous gleam in Rocco's eyes catches the dimmed lights above our heads when he slants his to the side to get a better look at the sketch I'm undertaking. The shy bob of his head would have you convinced his arms aren't double the width of an average man's nor covered with a range of interesting tattoos.

He has everything you could think of when it comes to art. Popeye with a can of spinach. A seahorse. He even has a half-naked gypsy with one of her eyes gouged out. His array of body art has had me scratching pencil to paper nonstop for the past hour. I usually only sketch nudes when I'm drawing the human form, but I've mixed things up tonight. It's nice focusing my attention on something other than the sting on my backside.

While drawing the top half of Rocco's body, I've barely had a minute to think about the bruise my ego got from Dimitri leaving me stranded in the middle of a sex-scented room on the brink of ecstasy. It was almost as painful as the spanking he gave my backside. I've channeled the energy into something more cathartic, purging it from my body in a way that won't get me killed.

Well, I hope it won't.

Dimitri's response to Mitis's stalk didn't end well, so I doubt he'd appreciate his second-in-charge sprawled on the bathroom floor of his room without his shirt on, and I won't mention how authentic the bumps in Rocco's midsection look on paper. Considering I'm using pencils designed to enhance my face, they've done a mighty fine job outlining all his good points. My drawing is so realistic, I'm fighting the urge to fill in the parts I can't see with my vivid imagination.

With my cheeks burning, I peer down at the eyeliners teetering between Rocco and me, seeking a better color to match his unique-colored eyes. When I find one with just the right amount of golden, Rocco's lips tuck in the corner. "What did I tell you? Just like shop-bought ones."

He grabs a green eyeliner from the pile of many before holding it up to my face like I did his. He's also drawing on the paper he stole from a cleaner during our silent journey to my room. He hasn't commented on my punishment, but I'm reasonably sure he witnessed it. His eyes are as telling as mine. I also think it's the reason he chose to host our art lesson in the bathroom. The cool tiles are a godsend to my burning backside, although the hardness isn't as welcoming.

I float my eyes up to Rocco's when he asks, "How did you get the spinach to sparkle like that?"

He's not happy with the grassy green coloring he's selected for my eyes, but since lime green went out of fashion many moons ago, he doesn't have a better option for my eye coloring. The makeup kit Alice shoved into his chest before our flight four days ago is massive, but it doesn't have the endless color palette artists generally work with.

"It's all about getting the right mix of colors." I pick up a gold eyeliner I wouldn't use in a hundred years before snagging a pair of eyelash curlers off the vanity sink. "A little bit of contrast will pick up the color you want."

With his skills a mix between novice and a first-grader, I shave the slightest bit of the gold pencil onto the circles of green in the middle of his picture, hopeful they're my eyes.

Rocco's laugh is a nice thing to hear in a dark and dreary place. "That was supposed to be your hands, but I guess it'll work."

"Sorry," I say with a grimace. "You have a Jackson Pollock vibe going on."

"Is that your way of saying my drawing is shit?"

His question is laced with humor, but I still shake my head, mortified he thinks I'd pick on him when he's been nothing but kind to me. "One day, people will pay good money for that."

"Of course they will." Because I'm leaning close to him, the faintest smell of toothpaste lingers in my nose when his tongue darts out to replenish his lips with spit. "It's a picture of you. That makes it priceless."

I stagger backward with a squeak when the rough and gravelly voice of Dimitri fills my ears. "Not as priceless as you'll be when I weigh you down with bricks before dumping you in the deepest ocean."

When Rocco's smile switches from a smirk to a full-blown grin, I stare at him like he's mental. Dimitri's voice didn't have an ounce of amusement behind it. He sounds really mad like he's on the verge of killing someone.

I realize that someone is more likely to be me when Rocco stands to his feet. "I guess we'll finish *this* later." His 'this' was much too throaty for my liking. He made it seem as if we've done more than drawing the past hour and a half.

With a wink of a man not in fear for his life, Rocco twists on his feet and stalks away from me. I try to keep my eyes on the mess next to my thigh, but I can't help but gawk when Dimitri halts Rocco's departure partway through the door. His clutch on his Rocco's arm makes his knuckles go white, but it doesn't dampen Rocco's grin in the slightest. Anyone would swear they're playing a game of chess, and Dimitri just fell straight into Rocco's well-thought-out game plan.

My eyes drift past a set of well-splayed thighs, a belt that's more haggard than new, a crisp, recently laundered dress shirt, and a stern set of lips when a pair of polished black shoes enter my peripheral vision a few seconds later.

After dragging his eyes over my semi-nude sketch of Rocco, Dimitri asks, "Have you showered?"

I shake my head, shocked. "No. That would be a little hard to do with Rocco babysitting me, wouldn't it?"

My breathing shortens when he asks, "I don't know, Roxanne, would it? You two seem very comfortable with each other."

When his jaw tightens after taking in Rocco's shirt dumped under the vanity sink, checkmate rings in my ears on repeat. I just unearthed Rocco's game plan, and for once in my life, I feel as if I'm on the winning team.

"I prefer sketching people au naturel. Wet hair doesn't allow that." Still salty about how he left me hanging after my spanking, I snatch up Rocco's drawing as if I can't bear to part with it before making my way into the main part of my room. "It's a pity you arrived back earlier tonight than the previous three. I can't finish my sketch now."

I realize exactly who I'm messing with when Dimitri's hand darts out to seize my wrist. His hold isn't close to nice, and it has my heart rate climbing as high as it did when he spanked me in front of an audience—even more so when I notice the splatters of blood on his hand. They're proof his shirt is new because there's no way he could have got that much blood on his hands and none on his shirt. He's changed since our exchange in the sex chamber, and for some reason, that annoys me more than the aggression of his hold.

"Let. Me. Go," I seethe through clenched teeth.

My show of jealousy doesn't faze him in the slightest. He's too bristling with his own idiosyncrasies to pay mine any attention. "You need to shower before going to bed. I can smell Rocco's after-shave all over you."

"That isn't aftershave. Just like the hairs on his chest, Rocco's smell is au naturel—" My last two words leave my body in a grunt when Dimitri pins me to the main wall of the bathroom with his heaving, he's-going-to-kill-someone form. I went one step too far, and he's more than happy to call me out on it.

He crowds into me so profoundly, I'm blanketed by his big, brooding frame in less than a second. The contrast of our heights is undeniable. He literally towers over me as he did in my dreams many times the past year, except now, I don't just feel his hot breaths on my neck, I also see his sexy, yet angry face.

"Shower. Now."

He stops the shake of my head by gripping my face in a deter-mined hold. It's an aggressive clutch that has me wondering if my childhood affected me more than I realized. Instead of being scared by his dominance, I'm turned on by it. His mouth is an inch from mine. I can smell the whiskey he was drinking earlier on his lips and feel the hardness my closeness is inspiring. This could only be better if we were kissing.

"I wasn't asking, Roxanne. Whether I hold you under freezing-cold water until you're drenched through or dump you into a scalding-hot bath, you will shower before you'll ever enter my bed smelling like another man."

He steals my chance to reply by gripping the front of my dress and shredding it off me with the strength of the Hulk. Buttons fly in all directions as an unexpected moan leaves my lips. That was fucked, but it was also exhilarating. It has me truly unsure how to respond.

I'm not wearing a bra, so there's no hiding how hard his aggressiveness made my nipples, but my hands are itching to slap him across the face. I've never felt such a conflicting array of emotions. I want to kiss and hurt him at the same time, and I'm not the only one noticing this.

Dimitri brings his lips so close to mine, I get drunk off the whiskey fumes in his breath as much as I do the knee he wedges between my legs. His closeness makes me dizzy. I'm panting, hot and on the brink of begging for him to kiss me.

I hate how weak he makes me, but it can't be helped. He's as brutally beautiful as I imagined in the alleyway all those months ago, and he has my head void of a single thought that doesn't include him.

Desire pulses through me when he shoves my head to the side so he can drag his nose down the throb in my throat. It has me all types of excited until he growls in my ear, "I should have killed you in the alleyway like I did the guard. Gunned you down like you thought I was going to. Then you wouldn't have me so fucking confused."

When I push him away from me, too angry to let his hurtful comments slide without protest, he crowds me even closer to the wall. "It would have been awfully convenient for me if your boyfriend achieved what he set out to do, then I wouldn't be wasting my time chasing ghosts, years too fucking late! Do you have any idea how much time I've wasted on you this week? How many hours you've added to my daughter's captivity? Even now, instead of working on pinpointing her location, I'm here, dealing with you... again."

"No one asked you to do that. I was perfectly fine with Rocco."

My shouted response agitates him the most. He doesn't speak a word, but I can see the last four ones I spoke filtering through his head on repeat. He works them over and over and over until the tension crackling between us turns dangerous.

Confusion draws my brows together when Dimitri takes a step back, unpinning me from the cool, tiled wall. For how worked up he is, I hadn't expected him to give in so easily.

I realize I still have a lot to learn about this man when he says, "I wonder how 'perfectly fine' Rocco will be when I remove his scent from your skin with more than water?"

Not giving me time to decipher his cryptic message, he yanks me forward by a rough tug on my wrist, throws an arm around my thighs, then hoists me onto his shoulder.

When he moves me in the opposite direction of the washing facilities, I fight him with everything I have. I slap, kick, and bite at him, aware he has a gun in his bedside table, a big scary gun I have no clue how to use, much less defend myself against.

When I'm dumped onto the bed with the same aggression Clover used only days ago, I spring onto my feet. I make a dash for the door, but Dimitri's grab-sweep-yank routine on my ankle sends me toppling on the mattress.

With one hand pinning me to the mattress, the other works on undoing the buckle on his well-worn belt. Instincts scream for me to protect my face when he drags the battered material out of the loops of his trousers, but its quick clatter to the floor halves my efforts, and I'm not going to mention the lowering of his zipper, or you'll accuse me of being mental.

This sucks to admit, but I'm more petrified I'll miss Dimitri's unexpected strip than worried he's going to beat me like my father did my mother any time her moans seemed too authentic for him.

He was happy to humiliate and degrade her, but at no time was she to get pleasure during his quest for happiness.

Twisted emotions spiral through me when Dimitri's painfully erect cock springs free from his trunks he yanks them down his thighs. He's thick and angry, hard to the fact I'm worried he's about to pass out.

*How is it possible to direct so much blood to one region of the body and not get dizzy?*

I suck in a quick, terrifying breath when the removal of his trousers is closely followed by him fisting my hair in a white-knuckled hold. He uses his leverage on my overbleached locks to drag my head toward his impressive cock he's strangling like he is angry at it.

I won't lie, I've dreamed about this very moment for over a year, but it wasn't like this. It wasn't against my will. In my dreams, I sucked the dangerous and mysterious stranger's dick because I couldn't wait a second longer to discover how delicious he tasted. He didn't force me. I did it willingly.

I realize I have the situation wrong when Dimitri's thick timbre breaks through the panicked breaths shrilling in my ears. "Look at me."

When my eyes immediately jump to the command in his tone, the flare of his nostrils mesmerizes me in under a second. He stares straight at me while frantically working his cock in and out of his clenched fist.

A gleam in his eyes reveals the mammoth restraint he's exuding, but for once, he's not harnessing his desire to kill me. He's fighting not to take what I'm unwilling to give, holding back the urge to finish what he started downstairs.

He's doing everything in his power not to make me his, even with his actions doing precisely that.

My eyes return to the angry, red beast rocking in and out of his fist an inch from my breasts in just enough time to witness the final two pumps needed to bring him to ecstasy.

He grunts when a stream of white cum jets out of his engorged knob.

I moan.

Watching him bring himself to climax is both thrilling and excruciating. Thrilling because it doubled the erotic tingles between my legs that haven't quit since he spanked my ass raw, but excruciating because the cruel curl of his lips tells me this is as far as our exchange will go.

This isn't about getting me off. Even with his hand strangling his still-erect cock to ensure every drop of his cum is expelled onto my breasts, this isn't even about Dimitri. He removed Rocco's smell from my skin by replacing it with his as a reminder that I'm his property. His gimmick. His toy to fuck with time and time again.

I am his, despite the fact he has no plans to fully claim me.

# 25

**Roxanne**

I pull away from my bedroom door with a groan, appreciative of Rocco's concern, but also mortified by it. I'll never play a damsel-in-distress skit well. "He didn't hurt me."

"Other than the occasional spanking, he won't physically hurt you. That isn't D's way. Up here, though." After joining me in my room, he taps on my temple still wet from a recent shower. I'm not usually a fan of showering late in the day, but Dimitri only granted me permission to wash off his cum twenty minutes ago. I thought it was so I could get ready to attend the fancy event he had a tuxedo delivered for late this afternoon. Silly me. He left our room within two minutes of me entering the bathroom, and my door remained locked until Rocco's unexpected arrival thirty seconds ago. "That's an entirely new ball game. You've got to play this game with wit, Roxie, or he'll never let you in from the cold."

Still frustrated about what happened last night, I take my

anger out on the wrong person. "Maybe I don't want him to let me in. Have you ever thought about that?"

With a laugh, Rocco flops onto my bed. It flashes up images of Dimitri doing the same to me last night, and for some crazy reason, it has my knees almost touching instead of my face screwing up.

What did I tell you? I'm certifiably insane.

"If that were true, you wouldn't have invited me into your room." After straying his eyes to the camera perched in the corner of the large space, Rocco asks, "Are you hoping my visit will have him ordering for his car to be turned around? Or are you praying for a re-run of last night?"

My throat grows scratchy. *He knows about last night?*

Upon spotting my shocked expression, Rocco hits me with a frisky wink before he props himself onto his elbows. "I don't know exactly what happened, Smith cut the feed..." I smile at the immature roll of his eyes, "... but I got the gist of it when Dimitri arrived at my room late last night with these."

Mortified heat blazes across my cheeks when he digs a teeny tiny thong out of the pocket of his black trousers. They're the pair I was wearing yesterday, the pair that were soaked through when Dimitri smeared his cum over my breasts, collarbone, neck, and lips with the same hand he used to stroke himself.

Once my torso was coated with the sticky substance, he tugged off my panties before he demanded me not to move until he returned. I thought he was taking a breather to regather his bearings. I had no clue he went to hand my soiled panties to the man responsible for his blood-thirsty rage.

I attempt to snatch my underwear out of Rocco's grasp while asking, "Why do you have them?" I say 'attempt' as my efforts are fruitless. Rocco is too quick for my weary head. I hardly slept a wink last night. Not only was the smell of Dimitri's cum keeping my heart rate high, once he returned to our room, his eyes burned a hole into the back of my head the entire night.

I give up on my endeavor to free my underwear from the now insanity of my life when Rocco says, "He used them as a deterrent. Said if I don't step back, then next time I see your panties, they'll be smeared with your blood."

As unease treks through my veins, my throat works hard to swallow. "Then why are you here?" After calculating how many steps it will take to barge him out of my room, I triple it, aware his large frame will require additional shoves. "If you leave now, maybe Dimitri will go easy on me. Tell him you were bringing tampons or something. I'm sure you can make something up on the fly."

My eyes snap back to Rocco when I spot him shaking his head in the corner of my eye. "I'm not leaving."

"Why not?" I want to punch myself in the gut for how whiny my voice is. It can't be helped, I like Rocco. Outside of this dark and demented world, I believe we could be friends, but I'm soon learning you can't take notions from outside these walls and use them here. This is a different world. Nothing is as it once was. The fact I almost came twice from two highly demoralizing activities is proof of this. "If you don't go, he will kill me, Rocco. Is that what you want?"

He shoos away my worry as if it's a fly. "He won't kill you."

"You just said he threatened you with panties smeared with my blood!"

I take a step back, horrified when he replies, "Your virginal blood. Not *blood* blood."

"What?" One word shouldn't be so breathy, but when your lungs are void of air, you work with what you have. "Who said I'm a virgin?"

The hits just won't stop coming. "Your daddy. He used it as a bargaining chip when Dimitri had him brought in. Don't worry. I worked him over so good, he won't use it again any time soon."

"You beat my dad because he used my 'supposed' virginity to bargain for his freedom?" Surprise is the last thing I feel when Rocco nods for the second time. If he has the chance of making money from it, nothing is off-limits for my father. "And Dimitri heard him?"

Rocco's head bob shifts to shake. "Nah, he was getting ready to spank your ass around that time."

The fact he talks so nonchalantly about certain subject matters should shock me, but for some reason, it doesn't. "So how does Dimitri know I'm a virgin?"

He rubs his hands together like a kid in a candy shop. "So, you *are* a virgin?"

"That isn't what I said."

His wink makes me hot even when it shouldn't. "It doesn't matter what you say. We both know it's true." When I fail to deny his accusation, he adds, "And so does, Dimi. He paid your old man a visit last night. Discovered he held off on your sale with the hope he'd fetch top-dollar for your virginity first. There is a heap of dirty old men willing to pay in the six figures to break in a tight cunt for the first time."

He bombards me with so many facts at once, I don't know which one to respond to first. I guess I should start at the most important point, although it doesn't feel like he should have the top rung on my worries. "Is my father alive?"

Rocco halfheartedly shrugs. "Kinda. Might not be if his theories don't stack up."

"Theories?" Although I'm asking a question, I don't wait for him to answer. "You can't believe anything he says, he's a pathological liar. He'll say anything if it helps him."

"Like saying you're a virgin?" I shoot him a wry look. It doubles the width of his toothy grin. "He had information about a baby-making ring near your hometown." His smile is completely obliterated when he mutters, "He told Dimitri the names of the playmakers he met when he tried to sign you up for their service." I haven't gotten over my first shock when he hits me with another. "His confession hit Dimi hard. That was too close to home for him to ignore." After dragging his eyes over my face, he says, "You remind him of his wife."

I groan before joining him on the bed. "That's the last thing I want to hear."

Dimitri spared my life on the belief I could help locate his daughter, but what has his focus been on the past four days? My fucked-up past.

The pain in my chest eases when Rocco barges me with his shoulder. "Not who she was, what she was missing. The spark. The feistiness. The desire so strong, even when you hate him, you'll still take his dick between your lips." He laughs when I scoff during the last half of his comment. "Deny it all your like, Princess P, you've been walking around the past four days with a doe-eyed look I haven't seen since a rainy afternoon in an alleyway many months ago."

After falling backward onto the mattress, I throw an arm over my eyes. "You saw the footage from the alleyway?"

Rocco drags my arm to my side while answering, "Nah. I saw Dimitri's face when he re-entered the limo." He boinks my nose. "He had the same doe-eyed look you have now. You fascinate him." He laughs like I'm an idiot when I roll my eyes about his highly inaccurate statement. "Why do you think he reacted the way he did last night?"

I make a 'duh' face. "Because he didn't want your aftershave embedded in his pillow?"

I slant my head, so I can peer at him beneath lowered lashes when he chuckles out, "Dimi isn't worried about me. You're not fucked-up enough for me. He's just struggling to understand why he wants you when he shouldn't."

"He isn't the only one struggling," I say before I can stop myself. "He killed my boyfriend, murdered men directly in front of me, and had my father brought in to be tortured—"

"To be tried for crimes we both know he committed," Rocco corrects.

I continue talking as if he never interrupted me, "Yet, I forget everything happening when he's standing across from me." My horrified expression grows. "My brain must have seeped out of my head when it cracked open."

Rocco laughs like I'm joking. I wish I were. Something drastically changed for me in that alleyway all those months ago. Unfortunately, I don't mean the night Eddie used his car as a weapon. My life hasn't been the same since my eyes locked on a dark, shadowy figure in the pouring rain. I was so convinced he'd award me the adventure I was seeking, it made everything since seem mundane.

After a prolonged stretch of silence, I roll onto my hip until I'm facing Rocco front-on. He's stretched out lazily, at ease with our friendship as me. "Can I see my father?"

Any humor left on his face evaporates before he shakes his head. When he sees the disappointment on my face, he says, "Dimitri won't kill him until you give him the go-ahead, but seeing him like that won't do you any favors."

He appears as shocked as me when I ask, "What if I don't want him to die? What if I want him to live?"

"Is that what you want?"

I shrug, truly unsure. My father isn't a kind man, but does the occasional whack of a belt across the back of my thighs warrant the loss of his life? I say no, but I also don't know the full extent of my so-called 'sale.'

"Will keeping him alive help get Dimitri's daughter back?"

Rocco waits a beat before halfheartedly jerking up his chin. "Possibly."

"Then I guess we have to keep him alive." I roll off the bed, straighten out my clothes, then walk to the door to open it for Rocco. "That's why I'm here, isn't it? To help Dimitri find his daughter?" It sounds as if I'm asking questions, but I am more summarizing my position in Dimitri's life than seeking answers from Rocco. "Forcing him to interact with me won't do that. It will only make matters worse."

As the creak of my bedroom door being opened sounds though my ears, Rocco slips off my bed. "There's no shame giving a man a reason to live, Roxie."

"That's what his daughter is for."

While shaking his head, he *tsks* me. "Some things you can't get from your blood." He tucks a strand of blonde hair behind my ear before trekking his finger down the throb in my throat. "You should know that better than anyone."

# 26

**Dimitri**

I clutch my phone in a death-tight grip when Rocco trails his index finger down the vein working overtime in Roxanne's neck. She's giving him no indication whatsoever she's interested in anything he's selling, but he still can't help but touch her.

I'd order for the valet to bring my car around immediately if I hadn't noticed Roxanne's panties in the middle of our bed. If Rocco truly wanted her, he wouldn't give up her panties for anything. He would have kept them as a trophy, paraded them in a way I tried to act unaffected by when I handed them to him. You only ever give something away like that when you're not interested, or you want people to believe you have no interest in them.

I'm in the latter field.

Do you have any idea the immense amount of control it took for me to end things where I did last night? My cum was smeared from Roxanne's collarbone to the rim of her teeny tiny panties, yet, it still wasn't enough. I wanted every inch of her smelling like me

—her tits, her ass, that delectable pussy that appears more ravishing the more times I see it. I just don't want my insatiable appetite to negatively impact my daughter as it has in the past.

Claiming Roxanne's virginity would do that. Her purity gives me a way into the world I'm petrified is holding my daughter captive. It's the key I've been seeking the past twenty months, and the very reason my gut is twisted up in knots.

A virgin—fuck. I still can't believe it. Roxanne has the spunk of five women, and the gall of a hundred, but she hasn't even unleashed her full potential yet. Imagine the power she'll yield when she realizes how some men can be controlled by their cocks? They move mountains for the right woman, break the rules.

They even feel sick at the thought of selling her purity to the highest bidder.

I don't want to do this, however I don't have a choice. If I want any chance of raising my daughter, I have to sell my soul to the devil, or at the very least, Roxanne's.

Fighting the urge not to demand Smith to send someone to Roxanne's room to forcefully remove Rocco, I shut down the live stream of her room, slip my phone into my pocket, then slide into the booth one of my father's most respected comrades just vacated.

My father's eyes reveal his shock at my arrival, but he plays it cool like he always does. "Son, what brings you to New York? I didn't think this was your scene."

While silently mocking me about my dislike of the wife-swapping caucuses that net the Petretti entity a tidy profit every year, he strays his eyes over the two-hundred plus attendees at the annual event. I understand most of the men's objectives in this room, fucking the same woman for the rest of your life could get tedious, but why shell out thousands of dollars to have another man's leftovers for the night? And don't get me started on the fact they're happy to loan their wives out. That isn't something I could ever do. If you touch what is mine, expect to pay dearly for it.

Rocco is about to learn that the hard way.

"I have a business proposal I'd like your opinion on before moving forward with plans. I heard whispering that you're in favor of this type of industry. Although I could have waited until you returned home, this is a time-sensitive matter."

After signaling for the topless waitress responsible for keeping my father's glass well-stocked to bring me a double shot of whiskey, I dig out the photo I had Smith print earlier today before sliding it to my father's side of the table. It's a still image of Roxanne after I left her in the sex chamber. Her eyes are wide and terrified, her cheeks are flushed, and the undeniable gleam of lust makes her pasty white skin look almost translucent. She puts forth the image of a woman in desperate need of a hard and rough fuck, but her innocence is undeniable.

I'm not surprised when my father tosses Roxanne's photo down without the slightest smidge of recognition forming in his eyes. When you've been in this industry as long as him, you don't recognize one blonde over another. It's why I had a member of my staff peroxide Roxanne's hair before booking an emergency dermatologist appointment to lighten her scar. Two simple changes immediately removed her from my father's radar.

I was hoping it would be the same for me. Alas, even knowing how much grief she's brought into my life hasn't altered my opinion of her. I'm as captivated by her as I was when she tried to hide her beauty with chunky boots and punk meal attire. I just can't react to my impulses this time around. Until Fien is safe, business must come first.

My dreary thoughts snap back to the present when my father says, "She'll fetch a few thousand a night. Call Mario, he'll put her straight to work."

He arches a bushy brow when I reply, "I want more than a few thousand for her. She's untouched. Pure. The wholly fucking grail of womanhood." My father tries to act disinterested, but I can smell the excitement slicking his skin. "She can cook. She had above-average grades in school and is obedient to a fault. I doubt it would take much to train her to her master's specifications, but I'm also curious to discover if there's a way I could profit off her more than once." My words aren't mine. I stole them from Roxanne's father.

My father stares at me for several heart-thrashing seconds before he lowers his hooded gaze to Roxanne's photo. "Has her purity been verified?"

"Yes," I lie. "I attended her appointment in person. Moses could barely slip his index finger inside of her."

When the waitress sets down my glass of whiskey, I raise it to my mouth, needing something to hide the clench of my jaw when the recognition I was seeking earlier darts through my father's eyes. I've never met Moses. I merely used a name Roxanne's father blurted out when I crucified his insolence one nail at a time.

He isn't bound to a chair with rope anymore.

He's nailed there.

My smirk slips when my father asks, "What were the results of her scan?"

I almost stumble, but the quickest memory of Ian blubbering about him not being able to afford a scan of Roxanne's ovaries and uterus for the delay in her sale keeps my ruse authentic. "They were clear. She's ready to breed."

"Hmm..." He slouches low into his chair before twisting his lips. He hates the idea of trusting me, but since I've never given him any reason not to, he does. *Thank fuck.* "She'd make a decent profit by selling her virginity then putting her in the trade, but I think you're right, the margin will be larger in another market."

Not willing to give away his trade secrets in front of people he considers lesser than him, he props his elbows onto the table wedged between us before leaning over to my half. "There are several ways you could do this. Where do your interests lie?"

"On whatever makes the most money."

He huffs out a proud chuckle. That's all my father cares about —money. "It does make the world go around." After another laugh that's more creepy than exciting, he asks, "Is she your only asset?"

"For now," I lie again. "I have others in the works, but I figured I'd tip my toes into the water with her first, get a sense of the market. I've grown bored of the prostitution conglomerate. I need something fresh and exciting." Don't ask why my mind strayed to Roxanne during my last sentence. It just did. "But I'm out of my league here, Pops. I need a big gun to show me the way." That fucking hurt to say. Every word was the equivalent of dragging a razor blade up my throat. It stung like a thousand bees, but it was extremely effective. I've never seen my father look as pompous as he does now.

"Let's talk somewhere private. We can't be sure our competition isn't listening in."

I down my whiskey in one hit before following his slide out of the booth. Its burn gives me an excuse for the heat on my cheeks when a ghost of my past flies back into my life on her witch's broom.

Theresa Veneto was once in charge of the narcotics division at Ravenshoe PD. She's also one of the female officers I mentioned who are willing to disregard drug distribution tips when she's flat on her back being fed my dick. We played nice when we needed to. When we didn't, things turned ugly.

I lost thirty thousand dollars in un-cut coke when she walked in on her deputy giving me head. That's a street value of over two hundred thousand dollars. I didn't take the hit in revenue well. If it weren't for Audrey calling to tell me she was pregnant with Fien, Theresa wouldn't have left Ravenshoe PD breathing.

Strands of long blonde hair fall onto Theresa's shoulder when she leans in to place a kiss on the edge of my father's mouth. "I thought we were dining alone tonight?"

A well brought up person would acknowledge her quiet tone as a wish to keep her conversation between my father and herself. I'm not close to normal. "Plans changed. You can see yourself out."

When I click my fingers two times, demanding for one of my father's goons to show Theresa the door, she locks her eyes with my father's. "Col?" Shock filters across her attractive face when he doesn't immediately jump to her defense. "We have business to discuss."

"Yes, yes, I'm aware of why you're here and what your nagging will entail." My father's snapped tone reveals he's less than impressed with her whine. "But this can't wait. Megan can."

After dismissing Theresa with a wave of his hand, he commences walking toward the exit. I shadow his stalk, albeit a little slower. I've heard the name Megan before. It's a common name, so that isn't surprising, but it isn't every day it's mentioned in front of a cop who put a man away for life for the murder of a woman with the same name.

My father agreed to spare Justine's life on the agreement Maddox would take the wrap for the murder of a local woman. Her name was Megan Shroud.

"Smith—"

"Cross-referencing all Megans who've had contact with your father and Theresa Veneto now. I'll come back to you as soon as I have anything significant," he says down the bead-size listening device in my ear.

Even though he can't see me, I jerk up my chin before increasing the length of my strides. I reach my father just as he breaks through a group of people milling on the sidewalk. Worry that he overheard my brief conversation with Smith smacks into me when he grumbles under his breath, "I should have known he'd be around. He's always meddling in business that has nothing to do with him."

I'm about to defend Smith but lose the chance when my father tears away from my side. I curse into the cold night air when I spot who he's making a beeline for. Isaac Holt is making his way out of a nightclub a few spots down from the venue my father's function was held at. He's clutching the hand of a pretty brunette with flushed cheeks and a wobbly stride.

I don't know what my father says to Isaac when he reaches him, but it changes the expression on Isaac's face in an instant. He's wearing the same haunted look he had the night Ophelia and I organized for him to fight at our father's underground fight circuit.

We rigged the fight schedule, knowing our father would never value Ophelia's life enough not to use it as a bargaining chip. We were right. He offered her up as if she was worthless. We just had no clue CJ was fighting that night until it was too late.

Isaac won their match as anticipated, but his victory came at a cost I never anticipated. Ophelia didn't handle his win well. She was so distraught seeing CJ lying bloody and lifeless on the boxing ring floor, she took her anger out on Isaac instead of our stupid ruse.

Her anguish was nothing on what I felt when Tobias arrived at our family compound only hours later. Ophelia and CJ were in a car accident. CJ was wearing a seat belt. Ophelia wasn't. She didn't survive her sail through the windshield, and our family has been in tatters ever since.

After signaling for my father's goon to follow me, I join my father on the curb in front of Club 57, a famous nightclub in the heart of New York, where he's undertaking a pissing contest with a man undeserving of his wrath.

I should have accepted Isaac's answer when I attempted to recruit him to my family's fighting circuit when he was still in college. If I had, perhaps my life would be starkly contradictory to what it is. Karma has a way of biting back, and she's been gnawing my ass nonstop the past seven years.

"What has it been?" my father asks, acting oblivious to the fury radiating out of Isaac's gray eyes. "Six years and I don't even get a greeting from you." He snarls like Isaac should be bowing at his feet, unaware the millions of dollars he lost after Ophelia's death wasn't solely Isaac's doing. I had a hand in his demise as well.

How do you think I funded CJ's retirement to a wood cabin in the middle of whoop whoop?

When my father's attention shifts to the brunette plastered to Isaac's side, Isaac pulls her behind him in a protective stance. It doubles the arrogance slicking my father's skin with sweat, whereas it triples my inquisitiveness. Isaac cared for Ophelia, he may have even loved her, but I never saw him act as possessive with her as he is with this unnamed brunette.

Before I can work through half my curiosity, several voices bark down my earpiece in one go. They're so loud, I almost want to rip the device out of my ear. The only reason I don't is because one voice is instantly recognizable. It too angelic to be wrangling two angry mobsters.

"She's not FBI, Smith. She's part of the Russian Mafia."

Although Roxie's voice is crystal clear, it's obvious she isn't talking to me. I don't even think she's aware I can hear her.

"She was featured in a crime documentary last year."

I slant my head to the side, inconspicuously cupping my ear with my shoulder to ensure I don't miss Smith's reply. "That documentary was filmed three decades ago. It isn't possible for her to be the same person."

I'm drawn from their debate when my father's beady eyes burn a hole in my temple. I raise my head immediately, lost as to what the fuck I missed. My father is glaring at me, Isaac looks smug, and Murph, my father's goon, looks relieved all the focus is on me.

"Go!"

My father's roar startles several partygoers mingling in the distance to watch a battle of mafia kingpins. I'm just as shocked, but instead of freezing to watch the charade unfold, my hand itches to slide into the back of my trousers to retrieve my gun.

I've been embarrassed by my father many times—chewed up, spat out, and used more times than I can count—but this is the first time he's disrespected me in front of an enemy.

His disregard will open a floodgate for many more incidences. If you're not respected by those in your realm, you're not respected by anyone. I can't explain it any simpler than that.

He broke the ultimate rule, and it's taking everything in me not to retaliate with the same amount of inanity. I wouldn't hold back if it weren't for Fien. As much as this pains me to admit, her survival rate is hinged on my father's immortality.

Roxanne's virginity is the key to unlocking my daughter's freedom.

My father owns the lock.

I can't do this without them.

With that in mind, I pivot on my heels and walk away as per my father's request. My anger is so stubborn, I grip my date's arm with more force than needed to guide her to my car I requested for the valet to keep close by. Leah doesn't seem to mind. She's as worked up as I am after witnessing my father's conversation with Isaac.

"He won't let bygones be bygones, will he?" Her guilt is as

palpable as mine. If she hadn't encouraged Ophelia to consider my ruse, her college roommate/best friend would still be here.

After sliding into the back seat of a rented SUV on Leah's heel, I rip the earpiece out of my ear, yank my cell phone out of my pocket, then dial Smith's number.

He answers two rings later. "I'm still cross-referencing—"

"What was that?"

The noise of his chair clicking into place sounds down the line before his confused hum. "What was what?"

"The argument between you and Roxanne."

A brief stretch of silence teems between us.

It agitates me to no end.

"Smith—"

"She must have accidentally hit the mic button."

Leah's pretty hazel eyes float from the scenery whizzing by her window to me when I snarl, "Why was she there to begin with? She should have been in her room." She's fine with women being traded as long as it's of their own free will. Only when you hold them captive, as I have Roxanne the past four days, does she have an issue.

I don't know if it's anger skating through my veins or worry when Smith replies, "She found my hub when looking for her father."

"You didn't think to lock the door?"

His laugh has me itching for a blood bath. "She didn't exactly sneak up on me, Dimi. I knew she was coming before she entered."

"Then you should have escorted her back to her room."

He scoffs like I'm being irrational. It's barely heard over Leah's disappointed sigh when I say, "I put a price on her virginity tonight. If she's wandering around unsupervised, someone might be tempted to claim it without paying for the privilege."

"Fuckin' hell, Dimitri." Smith's relapse to my full name exposes his annoyance. "You were supposed to use Ian's information to get *your* foot into the industry, not dump Roxanne knee-deep in it."

"I couldn't get my foot in the door without using Roxanne's virginity." When he remains quiet, I stack some reassurance onto my ploy. "She won't be touched under my watch. I won't let anyone hurt her."

"You wanna fucking hope so, D." This gravelly tone doesn't belong to Smith. It's the voice of an undeniably pissed Rocco. "Because if she gets hurt, you'll have to load your own bullets into the gun you want to kill your father with because I'll be done."

It takes everything I have not to smash my phone when Rocco ends our call by doing precisely that to Smith's cell. The only reason I don't is because Smith's face on the screen of my phone is quickly gobbled up by the symbol I use for my father—a reversed pentagram.

*Col: Meet me at Chasity's at midnight. Come alone. It's time to expand the family franchise.*

# 27

**Roxanne**

My eyes lift to the door when the creak of overworked hinges sounds through my ears. Relief engulfs my senses when Dimitri enters my room. I haven't laid my eyes on him in over twenty-four hours. He didn't return to our room after he snuck out yesterday afternoon, and none of his staff knew of his whereabouts when they brought in my meals. It was as if he vanished into thin air.

Even though I shouldn't have worn a hole in the rug fretting about him, I did. The last time we were together, he was a raging, neurotic caveman, but I still get a weird sense of comfort from sharing a bed with him. Seeing his bad points firsthand awards me the knowledge that he is able to protect me if needed. It arrives with a heap of possessive idiocies, but I'd rather those than to have him sit back and watch the carnage unfold like my father would.

The more my conversation with Rocco yesterday afternoon filtered through my head, the sturdier my disdain for my father became. He tried to sell my virginity—more than once. That burns. I've known for a very long time that possessions are more valuable to him than anything, but still, I'm his daughter, his flesh and blood. He isn't supposed to profit off me.

My thoughts snap back to the present when Dimitri crosses the room. When I drink in his features, the knot in my stomach tightens. He looks exhausted—that isn't unusual, he always looks exhausted, but it's more prominent this morning. Dark rings circle his eyes, a crinkle is burrowed between his brows, and he's wearing the same tuxedo he snuck out of the room with last night —but he also looks as sexy as hell. His scruffy beard has been replaced with an almost clean-shaven chin, and his dark hair has been slicked back off his face. With a teasing number of tattoos peeking out of his impressive-looking tuxedo, he's showcasing the ultimate bad-boy persona—brooding mood and all.

"Hey," I greet him when he stops at the end of my bed. I'm not a fan of his quietness. I'd rather he pin me to the bed and scream in my face than tackle the bad aura suffocating his usually viva-cious personality. "Are you just getting in?"

I loathe the jealousy my question was asked with, but it can't be helped. I know he didn't attend his function alone. I spotted a pretty redhead hovering in the wings of the surveillance footage Smith wasn't quick enough to shut down before I saw it last night. Before Dimitri left her alone to speak with his father, she was fawning all over him.

"Yeah. It was a long one." Eager to skip the awkwardness of a martial-like conversation when we're not close to being in a rela-tionship, Dimitri lowers his eyes to the stacks of drawings on the mattress. "What are these?"

His inquisitiveness is understandable. I usually only sketch erotic nudes or cute animals. The twenty-plus works of art I slaved over for hours last night are life-like portraits.

"These are the faces of the people I remember seeing at Joops the night your wife was kidnapped. I drew the ones I couldn't cross off from Smith's database." I copy the scan of his eyes. "Most are entire faces, but a handful are a mix of side profiles or the angle I saw them at. It isn't much, but something as simple as an odd-shaped nose or a risqué haircut could add a name to your list of suspects." I lean over to snap up a drawing of a woman's hand I finished just before he arrived. "Like this one. Her ring is a custom piece. Perhaps Smith could locate the designer who made it? Or this one..." I snatch up the picture of a man with a military squadron tattoo on his arm. "His tattoo is only for current or previous servicemen and women. An everyday civilian can't get it."

My eyes float up to Dimitri's face when he asks, "Why are they separated into two piles?"

"This pile..." I point to my left, "... are the people who left before you arrived with your wife. These ones..." I shift my hand to the stack on my right, "... were still at the restaurant after I left."

I grow worried I've overstepped my mark when a brief stint of silence stretches between us. I'm confident Dimitri is appreciative of my help, but I doubt he's ever been given it without a heap of stipulations attached.

The hammer hits the nail on the head when Dimitri asks a few seconds later, "Why are you doing this, Roxanne? Why now?"

I lick my dry lips, hoping a little bit of wetness will help ease out my next set of words. "This is why I'm here, isn't it? To help get your daughter back?" Although my presence doesn't eliminate the reason Dimitri had Rocco follow me for the nine months after my accident, my offer of assistance was the only chip I had during our negotiation. "You don't want my help in the way Rocco suggested, so I'm trying to find another way to be helpful."

"It isn't that I don't want your help. I just..."

When his words trail off to silence, I help him out. "Blame me for what happened?"

He shakes his head, but his eyes say differently.

When he realizes I've spotted the truth in his eyes, he rakes his fingers through his dark locks. "She was right there, Roxanne, right fucking there, but I stopped to find you, and I couldn't take back the time I'd lost."

Unease twists in my stomach. "You stopped for me?"

He doesn't need to nod, I can see the truth in his eyes, but he does, nonetheless. "You made it two miles from where you were run down." A *pfft* vibrates his lips. I don't know if it's a good or bad *pfft*. "Your effort that night should have been applauded, but all it did was create months of misery. I lost contact with my daughter for *nine* months. There were no demands for ransom. No proofs of life. She was gone, and I was convinced I'd never see her again." Although this hurts to hear, I'm loving his brutal honesty. "Then you showed up again... and so did Fien."

Reading between the lines, I say, "I didn't have anything to do with her disappearance or reappearance, Dimitri. You have to believe me."

Our conversation ends as quickly as it begins when he mutters, "Belief takes trust. I don't give that to anyone." His eyes bounce between mine for several heart-thrashing seconds before he adds, "And neither should you." He dumps the drawing of a petite blonde with big blue eyes onto the stack on my right before he heads for the bathroom. "I'm going to wash up before having a drink downstairs." I'm anticipating for him to announce he'll have his staff bring a nightcap to my room, so you can imagine my shock when he says, "You can join me if you'd like."

# 28

**Dimitri**

While exiting the bathroom I've shared with Roxanne the past five days, I dry my hair with more aggression than needed. Roxanne is stretched across the mattress, picking shards of pencil shavings out of the bedding. One of my shirts she's wearing as sleepwear is riding up high on her thighs. Since she isn't wearing any panties, inches upon inches of her delectable ass are on display. The exposed regions of her body reveal where her spanking marred her skin, however my handprints don't deter her sexiness.

A woman's virginity is supposed to automatically cloak them in innocence. They're usually seen as pure and unadulterated, the unsullied angels of a dark and twisted world.

Roxanne blows those theories out of the water.

She's ridiculously sexy, so much so, I'll have to tame down her looks for tonight's ruse to be effective. Important guests are arriving for festivities this evening. They're not the Arabian tycoons I usually cater for. They're just as rich, arrogant, and self-proclaimed, but instead of paying out the eye for a hooker for a night or three, they purchase wives specifically trained to their specifications.

I've had suspicions for months that my family was dabbling in this industry, but only last night did I receive official confirmation. For longer than I've been born, the Petrettis have been distributing mail-order brides, trained sex slaves, and the absolute kicker, babies.

Don't let your mind wander too far just yet. I almost killed my father where he stood when he disclosed how many children our family had sold over the past four decades. My mind instantly went to the gutter, aware if it brought in an income, it was to be explored—the pedophilia market included. It was only after inconspicuously passing on a handful of names to Smith did I learn otherwise. The purchasers of the newborn babies appear to be average, everyday Americans, although in the highly-craved two percent of the population. They had money—enough they could buy their way into parenthood.

Did the information lessen my agitation? Hardly. I'm still pissed, and it has me taking my anger out on the wrong person.

"Did you wear panties while lying on *our* bed with Rocco last night?" Think of the most possessive, disturbed prick you've ever met, then you'll have an indication on how bluntly I asked my question.

My foul mood can't be helped. Being an asshole sucks the life right out of me, so you can imagine how hard the fight becomes when the faintest whiff of the woman I should hate stirs my cock in a way no other woman has. Although Roxanne didn't hold the knife to Audrey's throat when she was marched out of Slice of Salt, nor to her stomach when she was forced through a dangerous caesarian, I can't help but still blame her.

It's ten times easier than shunting all the blame onto myself.

As Roxanne spins around to face me, she pulls down on the hem of her shirt. "I was wearing panties then. I took them off when I showered."

The honesty in her eyes does little to ease my annoyance. "Then why didn't you replace them when you got dressed?" Eighty percent of my staff are men, meaning the odds her meals today were delivered by a male is highly probable. The thought of them seeing her as I am now pisses me off. They were eager before her virginity was unannounced. Now they'll be blood-thirsty.

Roxanne's throat works hard to swallow. The liquor I guzzled down to keep my expression neutral while my father revealed his bag of tricks has me picturing her swallowing my cum while staring up at me with her pretty eyes out in full force. "The idea of drawing the people I saw smacked into me in the shower. I was so eager to start, I borrowed one of your shirts so I could get straight to work."

"Did you borrow my shirt or steal it?" I ask, looking for any excuse to punish her. Punishing her may be the only way I'll make it through tonight without killing everyone in attendance. That's how worked up I am.

Roxanne's reddish-blonde brows join as confusion crosses her features. "I didn't steal it, Dimitri. I'd never steal from you..."

Her words shift to a gasp when I interrupt, "Take it off."

"W-w-what?"

She heard what I said. She's just testing me as much as her big green eyes are testing the durability in the thread of the towel wrapped around my waist.

After jutting out my left leg to hide the crease my cock is causing to my towel, I growl out in a menacing tone, "Take. It. Off."

My switch-up in footing doesn't do me any favors. There could be a truck parked between us, and Roxanne would still spot my raging boner. I'm so fucking hard, my cock is seconds from uncinching the knot holding my towel to my waist. My thickness has nothing to do with Roxanne's hand inching toward the hem of my shirt, and everything to do with the little wildcat rising in her eyes. She's noticed my body's reaction to my request for her to get undressed, and she's milking it for all its worth.

Do you blame her?

I could tell her until I'm blue in the face that I don't want her, but my cock will always say otherwise.

Roxanne's breasts lift high on her chest when she pulls my shirt over her head. Alice was right, the symmetry of her breasts and hips are perfect. They're meaty enough to be appealing but small enough they won't be weighed down by gravity any time soon. Her nipples are more a reddish-brown than the bright pink natural redheads usually have, but there's no denying her heritage. The slightest slither of hair hidden by the shadows between her legs leaves no doubt the vibrancy of her hair days ago didn't come from a bottle.

"Leave it," I demand when the whoosh of my shirt to the floor is closely chased by her bobbing down to gather up the hideous dressing gown she uses to hide more than to keep warm. "You need to shower. You smell..." I almost say like Rocco, but I can't force the lie out of my mouth. She smells like I was balls deep inside of her when I released my load onto her chest instead of in her delicious-smelling cunt like I really wanted to.

Mistaking my delay as an insult, Roxanne rolls her eyes before she sidesteps me to head to the shower. I try to let her go, to act unaffected by both her closeness and her disappointment, but before I can stop myself, my hand darts out to seize her wrist.

She freezes in an instant, her chest falling and rising in rhythm to mine when the alcohol steeped through my veins speaks on my behalf, "You smell like me."

Goosebumps break across her skin when I drag my nose down

the throb in her throat. A growl rumbles in my chest when our intermingled scents linger in my nostrils. She smells so fucking intoxicating, it's taking everything I have not to double her scent.

Roxanne strains her eyes to look at me without moving her head when I say, "No one will ever believe you're a virgin if you smell like me. I'm tainted. Dirty. I smell of pure evil." I shift on my feet to face her front on. "If I want any chance of getting my daughter back, I need you to smell nothing like me."

Confusion is the first emotion to register in her eyes. It's quickly followed by determination. She doesn't know my plan, but she's willing to follow it.

Her silent pledge of assistance has me deviating my ruse in an instant.

As my cock flexes, I scrub my thumb over her ruddy lips. She wasn't lying when she said the tension between us is so blistering, no one could ever deny it. It crackles in the air, thickening my cock to the point it's painful.

Her needy breaths fan my lips with minty freshness when my hand lowers to the budded peaks on her chest. Her nipples are as erect as my cock, painfully strained with undeniable desire.

Unable to fight a battle I'm never going to win for a second longer, I brush the back of my hand down her budded nipple. When its tightness firms from my briefest touch, a growl rumbles in my chest. She's so responsive to my touch, even more than I've wondered too many times to count the past year.

When I brush my hand down her nipple for the second time, her thighs shudder like she's on the brink of ecstasy. One flick on her clit, and I'm certain she will be done.

As the heady scent of a hungry cunt clutches my senses, I return my eyes to Roxanne's face. She stares straight at me, soundlessly begging for me to loosen the restraints I've lived with the past almost two years.

After the shit twenty-four hours I've had, I'd give anything to forget my life for an hour. To push Roxanne onto the mattress and test the authenticity of her virginity. To taste her. To smell my skin against hers. To claim her like my fucked-up head tried to last night.

I want her in a way I've never wanted a woman, but in a way I can't have her.

At least not until Fien is home. Not until she's safe.

Roxanne's needy breaths switch to a groan when I glue my hands to my side. If she thinks this is easy for me, she has no fucking clue how I operate. Excluding my search for Fien, I've never fought so hard in my life.

Something so simple shouldn't cause such a catalyst of emotions, but the thought of never touching her feels worse than death. I've been drowning since the moment I studied Fien's lifeless, upside-down face, now I'm being strangled as well.

Upon hearing my unvoiced rejection, Roxanne scuttles into the shower as fast as her quivering legs can carry her. She has barely left my side for a second when the itch to kill skates through my veins. I'm angrier now than I was when I agreed for a handful of my father's clients to visit my compound unvetted. His request means I'm walking into tonight's festivities blind. I have a list of aliases and their favorite kinks, but no indication of how they fit into the industry I've been trying to get my foot in the door of. All I know is that they prefer them young and unbloodied—just like Roxanne.

While working my jaw side to side to weaken its strain, I head to the closet to get dressed. Tonight's festivities will run similarly to my previous event, but the women were hand-selected by my father. Roxanne was his first choice. The rest are a random variety of women. He didn't do that for no reason. He's testing the authenticity of my ruse, aware not every man will set aside lifelong dislikes for money. We're not all like him. Sometimes we value people more than possessions.

Partway to the walk-in closet, a stack of papers on my desk draws my focus. They're the sketches Roxanne showed me earlier. They are still separated into two piles. One stack is much higher than the other. They're the group of people still in attendance after Roxanne left with a flood of tears rolling down her cheeks.

Too curious to discount, I head to my desk instead of the closet. My mind was spiraling too much earlier to give Roxanne's drawings the consideration they deserved.

My cock hardens when I lift the first sketch off my desk. Roxanne's attention to detail is phenomenal. Just like her nudes, only the grain of the cheap pencils she used gives away the fact they're drawings. You could almost accuse her of tracing the images from photographs. I know she didn't, though, because none of these faces register as familiar, and I've scanned the images from that night over a dozen times the past twenty months.

"Smith, how long will it take to do a facial recognition scan for around two dozen people?"

"Photographs or sketches?" The fact he asks that tells me he's watching me. He better have logged into the feed after Roxanne entered the bathroom, or we'll have more than words.

I try to keep my annoyance on the down-low, but it still echoes in my tone when I say, "I need to know who these people are." I twist the sketch of a man with long-ass sideburns and a chipped front tooth around to face the camera in the corner of the room.

Even with the screen of my phone being as black as night, Smith's reply comes through the speakers with precise clearness. "Have someone bring them down. I'll get a start on them while waiting for the rest of Megan's info to come through."

*Fuck!* With everything going on, I completely forgot I sent him down that rabbit warren several hours ago.

While heading to the closet to get dressed in a pair of black trousers and a pinstriped dress shirt, I ask, "What have you unearthed so far?"

Smith's disappointed groan tightens my jaw. "Her case is a fucking mess. There's no body—"

"That's not unusual. There's *never* a body."

A smirk tugs at my lips when he replies, "You're preaching to the choir, but tell me one time a murder investigation is open and closed on the same day with no DNA, no witness, and no missing person report from a relative or friend?" He doesn't wait for me to reply. "Something is off with this case. Megan rarely used a credit card before her death." The way he spits out 'death' means he's as disbelieving of her homicide as I am. "But there were sprinklings of her in other electronic means... bus tickets, online music purchases, an annual subscription for *Rock Punk* magazine."

"Did she cancel her subscription?"

I can't see Smith, but I picture him shaking his head when a whoosh sounds down the line. "That's the thing. Her subscription was renewed last month."

"Last month?" I double-check, certain the blood rushing to my lower extremities has affected my hearing. "Megan has been dead for over a year."

"Mm-hmm. Don't you know all dead people keep their rock obsession current?"

After a beat, I say, "Keep me updated on anything that comes in, however I don't see us getting the answers we need from a computer. For now, shift your focus to the men arriving tonight and Roxanne's sketches."

"All right." His chair clicking into place sounds down the line. "I've got everything ready to go, but I must warn you, Dimi, this won't be as easy as you're hoping. Facial recognition isn't like it is in the movies. It takes time."

"I can be patient." When Smith's snicker rolls down the line, my hands ball into tight fists. "I can." His chuckles reveal he has no clue how much restraint I just exuded. It keeps him off my hit list —for the night. "I've waited this long for answers, so what are a couple more days?"

Before he can remind me that every second I'm away from my daughter feels like a year in hell, I toss my cell phone onto a stack of drawers next to the walk-in closet before slamming the door shut, blocking out anything he has to say.

# 29

**Dimitri**

"Fuck me."

For the first time tonight, Rocco isn't swearing at me. His focus isn't even on me. He's staring at someone across the room with an unhinged jaw and bulging eyes.

My jaw doesn't know which way to swing when I discover who has caught his attention. If it wants to tighten with fury, I'll need to collect it from the floor first.

Like Cinderella arriving at a mafia ball, Roxanne floats into the parlor at exactly eight. The modest hem of a pale blue dress swishes against her thighs when she twists to face the group of thirty or so men watching her every move. Although her bangs remain fanned across her forehead, the rest of her hair has been pulled back into a high ponytail. Her makeup is basically non-existent. Only the slightest sheen of lip gloss glistens on her mouth. She looks nothing like the sex-pot I left hungry and impish forty minutes ago, and everything like the naïve virgin my guests highly crave.

With my suspicion high, I drift my narrowed eyes to Rocco. "What did you tell her?"

When Rocco returns my watch, my blood pressure goes through the roof. His eyes are massively dilated, ensuring there's only one jaw about to swing—to the left when my fist lands on it with a crack. "I didn't tell her shit."

"Then why is she dressed like that? Why does she look like every dirty man's wet dream?" My interrogation ends when my exchange with Roxanne before she entered the bathroom rolls through my head. I told her to smell the opposite to me, to smell pure. If that wasn't a flashing red beacon warning her to the shit-storm I was about to thrust her in, I don't know how much more obvious I could have been.

If she knows my ruse, why is she here? Shouldn't she be responding to my attempt to sell her with the fury I instilled on her father when he tried to do the same? Or at the very least, be as mad as hell?

I take a staggering step back when the truth smacks me hard in the gut. She isn't parading her virginity for me or her. She's pimping herself out for a child she's never met—my child. She's doing it for Fien.

Before I can get over my shock that the lady responsible for my daughter's captivity is doing everything in her power to free her, Roxanne stops to stand next to me. Although she seems put together, her nerves are noticeable. The furious shake of her hands is indicative enough, much less the rattle of her vocal cords when she asks Rocco if the drink he's nursing has alcohol in it.

Rocco lifts his chin. "Vodka. Do you want—"

Roxanne cuts off his offer to fetch her a drink by stealing the one in his hand. She downs it as if getting smashed is something she does every weekend before requesting another.

When she throws down a second double nip like it's water, I remove the glass from her hand before placing it on the mantle-piece behind us. I understand she needs some liquid courage, but her life will never be the same if she ends up with one of these men in a room while she's drunk. They won't spank her and walk away. They take everything she has on offer—even the stuff she isn't willing to give.

The fact she's putting her life on the line for my daughter ensures I'd never let that happen. I'd massacre every man in this room before I'd let her be hurt under my watch. When you are on my side, you're on my side for life. Roxanne's efforts tonight expose whose team she's on.

"Point me in the right direction." It dawns on me that Roxanne isn't talking to me when her eyes float across the men gawking at her like she's a movie star. It isn't just the occasional nod she does that gives it away. It's overhearing Smith advising her which guests he's got hooks into that makes it obvious.

Once she has a rundown of the room, Roxanne locks her wide eyes with mine. "Anything identifiable, right?"

It takes everything I have to jerk up my chin, and even then, it's a soft, weaselly lift. Throwing her to the wolves and standing back to watch the show feels fucking wrong, but when you're desperate, you must take desperate measures.

"All right. Wish me luck." Not waiting for further instructions, she glides across the room with slow, wary strides. Her chin isn't held high like the women paid to keep the guests entertained. She tucks it into her chest while fiddling with the material of her dress.

Her shy act awards her even more attention than her beautiful face. Men are drawn to her like moths to a flame, their interest so notable, my father's underhanded comment that she'd fetch a record-breaking price seems logical. Her ruse is the ultimate display of how easily men can be manipulated. They're practically fighting to secure her attention, completely oblivious to the fact she's hoping to take them all down. Not even I feel safe from slaughter.

"Follow them," I say to Rocco when a man with slicked-back hair and a heavy set of wrinkles guides Roxanne toward the library at the side of the parlor for a one-on-one compatibility chat. From the whispers of the group tonight, he needs a new wife after his was strangled during a sex act. He thought she was holding back on how much she could take. He was proven wrong when his multiple attempts to resuscitate her were fruitless.

My pulse thuds in my chin when Rocco asks, "If he gets out of line?"

Deliberating the consequences of my actions usually takes longer than half a nanosecond. This time around, it doesn't. "Take him out."

I'll be out on my ass if I kill any of my father's wealthiest associates, but just the slimebag's hand on the small of Roxanne's back has me thirsty for a bloodbath. This isn't an itch I can scratch without someone dying. If that someone ends up being me, at least my daughter will have a reason to be proud.

Up until now, I haven't given her much to work with.

Although Rocco is still pissed I forced Roxanne's involvement in this industry, his annoyance isn't as noticeable when he enters the library on Roxanne's heel. He had no clue my ruse would pan out the way it did. In all honesty, neither did I. I wouldn't have hidden my plans from Roxanne if I had any inkling she'd go along with them.

I wait for Roxanne and Rocco to disappear from view before shifting on my feet to face a camera in the corner of the room. I don't say anything. I don't need to. Smith's squawks reveal he can feel my wrath. "She didn't want to go in blind. I should have told you she came to me—"

"Yes, you should have."

He continues talking as if I didn't interrupt him. "But she asked me not to."

"Who do you work for, Smith?" When a stretch of silence teems between, I ask my question again, with more fury this time around. "Who *the fuck* do you work for, Smith?"

He says the last name I expected to hear. "Fien. I'm here for Fien." He wets his lips before adding, "And so is Rocco, Clover, and Roxanne, so how about you appreciate the help instead of seeking reasons for it. I know you were raised to believe different, Dimi, but not everyone is out to play you." The heavy drone of him giving his keyboard a thrashing sounds down the line before he says, "Don't mind me, I've got sicko pedophile identities to unearth."

Stealing my chance to reply, not that I have anything to say, he disconnects our connection.

---

Even though I deserved Smith's anger hours ago, it cut deeper than I care to admit. It's been fucking with my psyche as much as seeing Roxanne work the crowd. She's been in and out of rooms all night, her suiters so eager to get her alone, some offered cash incentives just for five minutes of her time, others offered to pay her college tuition in full on top of their prospective bids.

Although I am as edgy as fuck, her one-on-one meetings have given Smith crystal clear images of the men's faces to run through the nationwide database. It's been a long, drawn-out process, and I'm feeling every second of it. Most of the men have been respectful of the rules they agreed to abide by when they arrived, however a handful have been testing the boundaries.

Take the man Roxanne is talking to now. If it were anyone but me watching Roxanne's every move, they wouldn't notice his sneaky touches of her elbow or his gentle strokes down her inner arm. He doesn't go for the obvious areas Rocco and Smith deem unacceptable. He's touching her like he intimately knows her, caressing her as no one ever has. He's being tender to the point of being a gentleman, and it's pissing me off to no end.

Even a novice in this industry knows there are rules you can't break. Touching something that doesn't belong to you is at the top of the list. As much as this dweeb wishes it weren't true, Roxanne isn't his, and I'm more than happy to remind him of that.

"Shutdown surveillance before requesting Rocco to take Roxanne to my downstairs' office." Smith isn't just shocked at my request, he's pleased with it. The profiles of tonight's guests would even make non-parents' stomachs swirl. We have every combination you can think of. Millionaire tech giants, schoolteachers, politicians, doctors, and the absolute kicker, an OBGYN who was so eager to place a bid on Roxanne, he didn't attempt to woo her with the coin he was willing to spend a night with her. He went straight to the hierarchies with an offer, the amount staggering.

My father would have accepted his offer in an instant. It was three times the amount the other bids received, and there were no added stipulations such as proof of her purity or that shipping costs be included in the sale of her virginity.

Dr. Bates' eagerness won't go over as easily with me. Nothing against Roxanne, she has the looks to set any man's pulse racing and a body of pure dynamite, but in this industry, you only pay over the asking price for one reason—you're not planning to follow the rules. Roxanne's sale was touted as a virginity-only trade. There were no long-term commitments or talks of marriage.

This was a one-night-only deal. So why the fuck is Dr. Bates offering a little over five hundred thousand dollars for the privilege?

His bid set alarms off in my head, but for once, instead of them ringing in warning, they're sounding in victory. For months, I've constantly felt one step behind my enemies, but tonight is the first time I feel like we've raced ahead. Although we've been working toward this for months, I truly don't believe it would have been achieved tonight without Roxanne's help. She has the bidders eating out of her palm so readily, they divulged information to her the sternest torture wouldn't have unearthed. She was handed business cards, blank checks, and keycards for permanently-booked suites in Manhattan. That's a treasure trove of information that makes our guests tonight easy to trace, and it was handed to Roxanne quicker than Smith could run their faces through the database.

The shocked excitement on Smith's face grows when I say, "Once I've shown our guests out, I don't want to be interrupted for the rest of the night unless it's urgent." I should have said morning considering it's well after two, alas, I am too tired to consider how stupid I'm acting.

I didn't sleep a wink last night, so I'm not just tired, the whiskey I've been guzzling to dampen the fire in my gut is hitting me harder than usual. I'm half fucking tanked, but alcohol isn't giving me the buzz I need. I need something more potent, more addictive. Something you can't get artificially.

I need blood and warfare, and perhaps the heat of a woman's cunt around my cock.

Aware Smith will follow my orders no matter how imprudent, I exit his computerized hub. While pacing through the party-like atmosphere which died remarkably quick since all the guests were chasing the same woman, I scan my eyes over the ones who barely got a once-over. My gaze usually sharpens on the redheads in the room, my favorable choice, but tonight, they seek a sultry blonde with a tiny waist and grassy green eyes that are more sinful than saintly.

When my eyes collide with a woman matching my requirements, she stumbles like she chugged down the fifth of whiskey warming my veins. Even with her focus seemingly on a man with ginger-red hair and a knockoff Tom Ford suit, she watches me cross the room. The heat of her watch is as stifling as it was before I joined Smith to assist with surveillance, and the exact reason I kept my distance the past six hours.

If I hadn't stepped back, our ruse would have never had the effect it did. Not even men who pay are willing to look past undeniable chemistry. They would have mourned the missed opportunity for a few seconds before moving onto their next target.

I owe it to Fien not to let that happen.

That's done and dusted now, though. Preferring to go home alone than with a woman not close to Roxanne's league, the high-priority guests lodged their bids and left. Although they'll still be scrutinized with the same fine-tooth comb as the more well-to-do guests, I don't believe the stragglers have the gall to pull off the scam Rimi has been running the past two years. Kingpins don't let their prospective playthings be wooed in front of them without incident. He'd control everything she does from the moment she registered on his radar, and perhaps mark her with his scent so every other man would get the hint to back the fuck up. He might even go as far as removing the fingers that touched her skin without his permission.

Roxanne's virginity may have been on offer tonight, but her sale came with a heap of rules, the main one, she wasn't to be touched. I don't appreciate my directive being ignored, and will have no trouble relaying my annoyance in both physical and non-physical manners.

I don't know which side of the coin Roxanne's punishment will be on yet. With my cock as tight as my jaw, it may end up being a combination of both.

Don't misconstrue. I'm not saying Roxanne should be punished because she was touched against her wishes. It's the way she leans into her prospective purchasers' side to keep her legs upright I'm frustrated about. Instead of letting her knees buckle out in response to the tension bristling between us, she accepts comfort from another man.

That is unacceptable.

Women like Roxanne don't want to be nurtured like children. They want to be claimed like we're still in the Stone Age, protected with the infamy of a madman, and fucked like possessiveness is the highest form of flattery.

They also want to be owned, and I'm about ready to stake my claim.

# 30

**Roxanne**

Nerves tap dance in my stomach when the handle of a door that was locked earlier tonight slowly lowers. A man with so many distinguishable features, Smith unearthed his true identity faster than I could snap my fingers and attempted to guide me into this room earlier tonight. Timothy Jamison—a primary-school teacher if you can believe it—was so desperate to talk to me in private, he acted as if he could sidestep Rocco's shadow as easily as Dimitri avoided my heated watch from across the room.

It was unfortunate for Timothy that Rocco didn't cave as easily as Dimitri. I was only onto suitor number three when Dimitri made a beeline for the exit with clenched fists and a firm jaw. He raced out the room like his ass was on fire, and if you exclude him offering to show my final suitor the way out an hour ago, I hadn't seen hide nor hair of him since.

I won't lie. When the full extent of Dimitri's ruse smacked into me while I was showering, I was fuming mad. I couldn't believe he was undervaluing me as my father always had. Then I thought about it a little longer. For years, I wanted what every little girl wants—the love of her father. I did everything and anything to get it. I was the good girl who didn't speak when told to be quiet, spoke politely when given a chance, and I always remembered my manners.

When common courtesies didn't work, I gave the opposite a shot. I lashed out and got angry. I screamed at the top of my lungs. I became an exact replica of my father. And do you know what? It still didn't work. No matter what I did, he didn't give me the love I was seeking.

Even with the crazy world still being new to me, I'm confident in saying Dimitri's daughter will never face the same issue. He hasn't seen her in the flesh, yet he loves her so much, he constantly sets aside his needs for her. I doubt one thing he's done the past two years has been for him. Every decision he makes is based on how it will affect Fien. He wouldn't even breathe if it had a chance of negatively impacting her. That's how much he loves her.

My decision to forgo tonight's event was already teetering, but when I exited the bathroom, they fully imploded. The sketches I had worked on for hours on end weren't where I left them. They were gone, replaced with an art lover's vault of pencils, paints, sketchpads, and charcoals. The items covering every inch of the desk in Dimitri's room couldn't have been gathered on the fly. Some of them can't be picked up at any store. Whoever purchased them for me went out of their way to do so.

My gut wanted to believe Rocco is as generous as he is stirring, but my heart refused to consider it for even a moment. It knew my gifts were from Dimitri, just like he knew I was going to participate in his ruse even if it came with a risk I wouldn't come out of it unscathed. Fien deserves the chance to experience a father's love as I never have. If I help her achieve that, perhaps my own failure won't feel so horrific.

I jump up from the couch like an obedient lapdog when Dimitri enters the large office in the lower half of his compound. Although the well-decorated space is shrouded in blackness, I know who he is. Not only have my eyes adjusted to the dark, his scent is highly distinguishable as is his suffocating aura.

It chokes the air of oxygen even more when he barks out, "You did good tonight, Roxanne. The bidders' eagerness to woo you had them spilling secrets left, right, and center." Air whizzes out of his nose. "But you also did bad. What was the first rule Smith told you tonight?"

The nerves twisting in my stomach are heard in my reply, "That I wasn't to touch anyone." I'm not worried I broke the rules. Just remembering the men were here to buy my virginity assured my hands wouldn't get close to them. I'm petrified I haven't given Dimitri a reason to punish me. His punishment would have been far more pleasurable than painful.

When Dimitri slants his head, the light outside the hall unshadows half his ridiculously handsome face. "And what did you do?" I'm about to answer, *kept my hands to myself*, but he continues talking, foiling my chance. "You touched."

I almost shake my head until I realize it isn't anger pumping out of Dimitri. It's jealousy.

A one-way ticket to hell drops into my inbox when I mumble, "I didn't mean to. I find it hard to communicate without my hands."

I anticipate for him to call me out as the liar I am, so you can imagine my shock when he commences pacing to a big wooden desk in the corner of the room. His arrogant walk wasn't dissuaded from the seediness of tonight's undertakings. It's as cocky as ever, and it has my pulse racing.

Once Dimitri has the starchy material of his dress shirt rolled up to his elbows, he strays his eyes to mine. They are as brutally beautiful as ever. "Remove your dress and bra. You can keep your panties..." His lips curve to his infamous half-smirk before he adds, "... for now."

I almost double back, stunned he's gone straight for my jugular. I'm not comfortable being naked, but the collision of our eyes alters the direction of my course in an instant. Just like when he commanded me to remove his shirt earlier tonight, his steely blue eyes expose this is another test.

Although I hate that he's forever testing me, only days ago, I decided that failure will no longer be associated with my name. So, with that in mind, I raise my shaky hands to the neckline of my dress to undo the first button.

The first four buttons come away without too much drama. The same can't be said for the final few. The heat teeming out of Dimitri is too much. It has me torn between wanting to fall to my knees and beg forgiveness for my lie and marching across the room to soak up every blister of his scold. I'd rather he not be angry, but I also prefer his jealous fury over no emotional response whatsoever.

Once my bra is sitting on top of my dress, I raise my eyes to Dimitri's. Not even the dark can take away from their allure. They're icy pools of seduction.

My already brisk heart rate breaks into a canter when he jerks his chin up. "Come here."

I pace across the room, my strides so shaky, you'd swear I was wearing heels instead of flats. Alice's choice of wardrobe nearly made it impossible to validate my father's claims I'm a virgin. If it weren't for Smith suggesting that I ask Dimitri's housemaids for help, I may have still been in my room, sewing together four skimpy outfits with the hope of making one modest one.

Smith's unexpected assistance scared the crap out of me, however it also assured me I wasn't going into tonight blind. I had eyes on me—many of them—including the pair gawking at me now.

After sitting in his fat leather chair, Dimitri pushes it away from his desk. "Sit."

I want to crawl into a ball and die when my attempt to straddle his lap has the faintest of chuckles ringing in my ears. This is more horrifying than I could ever explain and has me suddenly knowledgeable about why I've only ever dated men who thought they could milk my loins of their nectar.

"Ass on my desk." When Dimitri lifts and locks his eyes with mine, the lust in them reveals my embarrassment is unwarranted. He isn't chuckling because he thinks I'm an idiot. He's pleased I am as naïve as his guests tonight hoped. "Legs opened wide."

Through quaking, breathless lungs, I do as requested, confident Dimitri is too possessive to let anyone see me in a vulnerable state. I like when he watched me climax in the alleyway many months ago, but that doesn't mean I'm open to a free for all.

After planting my backside on the edge of his desk, I part my thighs in an unladylike manner.

"More."

My thighs are stretched to the width of Dimitri's large frame when he scoots his chair back in close to his desk.

"Keep them there."

It's virtually impossible to follow his clipped command when he runs the back of his hand down my lace panties. Since I couldn't morally borrow underwear, I had no choice but to don one of the many risqué thongs Alice added to my collection. They leave nothing to the imagination, which means I feel every delicious callous on Dimitri's newly-battered hand.

"How much?" Dimitri strains his words through the jealousy

clutching his throat. I know this as his voice has the same gravelly deliverance mine had when several women approached him at the start of tonight's event. They didn't have the eyes of any of the men wanting to get to know me. They didn't care. They had their target locked, and they weren't going to stop until they had him. "How much was the highest bid you received tonight?"

Even aware he knows the answer since Smith recited each offer to him as they were received, I say, "One hundred and eighty-three thousand dollars."

My thighs press together when his low growl races lust through my womb like a wildfire. It has my knees curving inward even faster than it has his face sitting within an inch of my aching sex. "Then why aren't your panties soaked through with the scent I can smell building in your clenching cunt? Weren't you turned on knowing how much men we're willing to pay to spend one night with you?"

While fighting my hips not to gyrate toward his mouth, I shake my head. They could have offered me ten times as much, and I wouldn't have been flattered. Money shouldn't enter the equation in exchanges like this. Hell, right now, I'm not even sure love should. It's all about lust and chemistry so blistering, even if it fizzles out as quickly as it ignites, it deserves to be explored. Ignoring something this sweltering should be criminal.

When I say that to Dimitri, he runs his hand down my panties for the second time. His fingers don't make it through the carnage unscathed this time around. The wetness glistening on them is as noticeable as the fiery glint darting through his eyes. I'm soaked in an instant, and it has Dimitri paying more attention to me than he did my final suitor when he kissed my cheek goodnight. He looked seconds from killing him, although it has nothing on the urge masking his face now.

"Some of the bids tonight were the highest I've ever seen." I lose the ability to breathe when he mutters, "Yet here you are, sitting on my desk, getting wet over my briefest touch."

After switching on the lamp on his desk, he scoots in so close, nothing but his next breath is on my mind. They batter my aching sex with so much heat, my delirious head has me confusing them as excited breaths instead of angry ones. I've never been more turned on and terrified in my life.

I'm not scared of him. I'm terrified he'll never touch me like I'm silently begging him to. The amounts thrown around tonight were impressive. If my esteem was as low as my father aimed for it to be, I may have considered their offers to fund my studies. Alas, even with him wrongly believing I'm to blame for his daughter's captivity, my body yearns for only one man.

I begin to wonder if Dimitri has mindreading capabilities when he says, "You could have your choice of any man, but that isn't what you want, is it, Roxanne? You don't want a man. You want a monster, a bastard, a man who'd rather destroy you than ever have you believe you deserve more than him."

His usually icy eyes switch to the color of a bottomless ocean when I shake my head. "You're not a monster, Dimitri. You're angry and confused, and oh-so-fucking tired, but you're not a monster."

The air that whizzes out of his nose sends my senses into overdrive. "I allowed men to bid on your virginity *after* beating a man for doing the same thing."

His underhanded confession about hurting my father should dampen the intensity brewing between us. it doesn't. Not in the slightest. If anything, it doubles it. "You may have let them bid for me, but you never had any intention to let them cash in their bids." He's too possessive for that, too neurotic, but since that confession could possibly knock our exchange back a few spots, I keep my mouth shut.

It's for the best. I can barely breathe when he slips my panties to the side. When my pussy is awarded the heat of his breaths without hindrance, the dampness his fingers briefly felt moments ago jumps to saturated. His thorough inspection of my private parts should make me feel vulnerable, whereas all I'm feeling is wanted. My prospective buyers peered at me with the same hungry, wanton eyes, but not once did their gawks have the edge Dimitri's does now. He stares at me as he did in the alleyway a year ago, his watch so needy, if he can't get past his neurosis that he shouldn't touch me, I'm willing to pick up the slack on his behalf.

"Please," I beg when the tension tethering us together as if we're one becomes too much to bear. His mouth is an inch from my pussy, my orgasm is just as close to the finish line. This is the cruelest form of torture.

Panicked sexual deprivation is only the beginning of his punishment. I skate my hand toward my pussy. One flick of my aching clit will have me freefalling off the cliff. That's how crazy the tension is between us.

My hand makes it halfway to my pussy before Dimitri snatches it away. "When you touch what isn't yours, you lose fingers." The heat trekking through my veins becomes dangerous when he growls out, "If you don't believe me, ask the guest I just showed out."

The trickle of desire surging through me turns catastrophic. I hate he felt the need to intervene when his guests get overly friendly, but I also love it. I'll never make anyone feel guilty about protecting me. I've been seeking this level of protectiveness since I was three. Furthermore, his comments imply that he classes me as his. That excites me more than how dangerously close his thumb is hovering near my clit.

When nothing but needy breaths fill my ears for the next twenty seconds, I get desperate. "Please, Dimi."

My rare use of his nickname sees his eyes locking with mine. They're not the same withdrawn pair I'm used to seeing. They're still full of danger, darkness, and recklessness, but there's a yearning gleam to them that makes them unique. "Please, what?"

Desperate, I blurt out without thinking, "Touch me. Please. I'm begging you. I won't intrude on your time or seek more attention than you're willing to give. I just can't take it anymore. The tension is too much. I feel like I'm about to explode—"

My shameful beg is cut off by Dimitri sucking my clit into his mouth. When he tugs at the bundle of nerves with his teeth, I call out in an erotic scream. He gives head better than the many daydreams I've had about him doing precisely that the past five days.

While his tongue snakes out to toy with my clit, I weave my fingers through his dark locks. My frantic tugs on his hair has him eating me more expertly. He pokes his tongue inside of me, drags it up my slit, then tangles it around my clit until I chant his name on repeat. Then he does it all again just for fun.

My prediction months ago was one hundred percent accurate. His skills at giving head are out of this world. Every lick, nip, and suck doubles the fiery warmth spreading across my midsection. It burns me up as much as the tension that's raged between us the past five days.

"I fucking knew you'd taste delicious," Dimitri moans into my throbbing sex when he takes a breather to survey the damage he caused. "As did every man here tonight. They wanted to taste you, fuck you, and smear their cum over every inch of you." His dangerous aura that mesmerized me since day one beams out of him when he says, "Then there were the ones who wanted you for so much more than your virginity."

His confession has him eating me faster, more aggressively. It's a painstaking blur of bites, licks, and nips that have me riding his face like our exchange won't cost me a thing. It's silly of me to believe, but right here, right now, I don't care. He can have my soul for all I care. I'd give it to him willingly if he promised not to end our exchange until the bomb in the lower half of my stomach detonates.

"Oh, God," I pant when he drags his tongue up my slicked slit before circling it around my clit. The flicks he hits my clit with are delicious as is his tight grip on my ass. They have me freefalling so quickly, it should be embarrassing.

While shuddering and shaking in the cool evening air, Dimitri's name rips from my throat in a husky moan. The blistering sensation blasting through me lasts for several long minutes. I've never experienced anything close to this in all my life. It's better than I predicted and has me craving a second hit even with the first one still occurring.

When my orgasm finally relents its firm clutch of my senses, I'm emotionally and physically wiped. It wasn't building for days, weeks, or months. It's been gaining intensity for years. Its body-limping strength is a sure-fire proof of this.

"Fuck..." Dimitri growls in a low, shallow tone as he soaks up evidence of my arousal with two hearty licks. "You taste better than predicted, but you hit the target for speed."

The shame burning my cheeks shifts to desire when he stands from his seat so he can work his trousers down his thighs. Even with his trunks hiding the mouth-watering visual I'm dying to see, I'm confident in saying he's harder than he was when he blew his load on my chest. The sheer girth of his cock has me hopeful my taste was addictive enough to have him craving me time and time again.

The primitive part of my brain takes hold when Dimitri frees his cock from his trunks. Precum is already wetting the head of his perfect manhood, and it has my mind blank on how much pain a cock that size will cause. His penis is large, angry, and arrowing toward an area of my body that won't stop clenching in anticipation.

"Are you sure you want this, Roxanne?" Dimitri asks as he fists his cock to give it a hearty squeeze, "Because it'll hurt. Your tight little cunt is going to feel me for days once I'm finished with it."

I nod, a better response above me. I thought my earlier orgasm was as powerful as they'd get, but the image of Dimitri working his cock in and out of his fist while staring down at my drenched sex reveals I starkly underestimated their abilities. The one cresting in my womb now feels like a tsunami, growing more devastating when Dimitri loses the ability to harness his desires for the second time.

He doesn't plunge his thick cock into me like my devious mind was hoping. He falls to his knees, spread my thighs wide, then burrows his head back between my legs. "You taste too fucking good for only one sample."

After notching a single finger inside of me, he delves his tongue around his frozen digit, easing the burn his fat finger caused. He eats me for the next several minutes before adding a second finger to the mix.

I don't realize how noisy I'm being until my moans bounce off the walls of Dimitri's office. I grunt and moan on repeat while fighting the urge to tell him to stop. I don't want him to stop, but if I don't say something, I'll explode into a blubbering mess of wetness and sin even quicker than I did the first time. I hadn't considered the thought of him fingering me and giving me head at the same time. None of my college boyfriends could multitask. I either got one or the other, there was no option for both.

Seemingly linked to my inner workings, Dimitri grips my ass, thrusts my pussy off his desk, then eats the living hell out of me. I'm brought to climax by his tongue within seconds.

"Yes," Dimitri hisses into my pussy when my nails grip the top of his shoulders. As scream after scream rips through me, I ride the intensity of my second climax like its more vital than my lungs needing air to function.

I've barely merged from hysteria when Dimitri attempts to squash a third finger inside of me. Unlike his earlier penetration, this one can't enter without protest. I'm drenched from front to back, but no amount of wetness will simplify this process. It's not meant to be easy.

"You're close to taking a third finger," Dimitri mutters under his breath as he swivels the two inside of me, "But it won't be done without pain." His bedroom skills are undeniable when he continues finger-fucking me without pause while standing to his feet. "I want to hurt you, but I don't want to hurt you so much, you're out of action for days on end."

Any worries on me drying up fly out the window when he fists his cock in his other hand for the second time. He doesn't choke it to calm it down. He strokes it to bring himself to climax like he did when his jealousy got the better of him. His pumps are fast and fluid despite the fact his eyes never once leave my face. He watches me watching him come undone, his stroke quickening the more my eyes dart between his face and his impressive cock.

I moan when the heat of his spawn mingles with the fiery warmth between my legs a few seconds later. Instead of coming on my chest to intermingle our scents, he ejaculates on my pussy, so his climax slicks with mine.

As his nostrils flare to cool his dangerous body temperature, he rubs his climax around the opening of my pussy before he pushes it inside of me. Once he's confident I'm the wettest I've ever been, his cock's head overtakes the helm of our scorching exchange. He coats himself in my juices before lining up, gripping my hips, then driving home.

I won't lie. It fucking hurts—a lot.

While kicking out, I scream like I'm being murdered. This is worse than I could have comprehended. It makes me convinced I should have joined a nunnery. There was no way I would ever take a man the size of Dimitri without pain, but this goes beyond that. He's doesn't have impressive length, he's got eyewatering girth too. I'm full to the brim and doing everything I can not to cry.

As shards of pain claw through me, Dimitri drops his thumb to my clit. His dedicated attention to my achy bud lessens my pussy's vicious clutch on his cock. He circles the bundle of nerves on repeat, bringing me back from death one delightful swivel at a time. Within seconds, I've withdrawn my application to sainthood and resubmitted one to the fiery depths all orgasms come from.

It's amazing how responsive my body is to his touch. He could beat me to the point of death, however, and I bet my body would still respond positively to him. It's fucked up to consider, but the most honest I've ever been.

Only seconds later, I'm more frustrated with Dimitri's calm than terrified about additional pain. Excluding his initial thrust that pushed me to the brink of hell, his cock hasn't budged an inch. He's inside of me—very *very* deeply rooted—but he isn't rocking his hips how his delicious 'V' muscle is designed to move. He's completely still, frozen like a statue.

The worry blistering through me nosedives toward the negative when I lock my eyes with his face. He is inside me like no man has ever been, but he isn't in the room with me. He's far *far* away from here.

"Dimitri?" I gabble out on a groan when he withdraws his cock as quickly as he jabbed it inside of me.

I thought the blood smeared on his rapidly deflating cock would have his chest swelling with pride—it was clear tonight the men in his realm view virginities as a gift. They're willing to pay over a hundred thousand dollars just to secure a night with a virgin, however Dimitri's chest is filling more with anger than smugness. He once again looks set to kill, and once again, all of his fury is directed at me.

After tugging up his trousers with enough aggression the thread around his zipper pops, he says, "Get dressed and go straight to your room."

My hands instinctively move to cover my chest, suddenly vulnerable about the angsty in his tone. "Is everything okay—"

"Get dressed and go straight to your room!"

Tears almost spill down my face when his roar makes me jump out of my skin. When he spots their sudden arrival, the mask over his face is the sternest I've ever seen him. He appears as if he wants to strangle me until the light he lit in my eyes has been extinguished, or better yet, until I'm dead.

Confident I won't defy him for the second time tonight, he pivots on his heels and stalks to the door. "I'll be back to deal with you later." The way he says 'deal' confirms my earlier worry. Dimitri Petretti no longer wants to claim my virginity. He wants my life.

# 31

**Roxanne**

I brush away stupid blobs of wetness sitting high on my cheeks when the creak of a door breaks through my quiet sniffles. I'm so angry, so fucking mad, but more than anything, I'm hurt. I gave myself to Dimitri in a way I can never repeat, and what did I get for it? Another cold, hard rejection.

He made me come undone twice, marked me with his cum, then spat me out as if I was worthless the instant I fell for his tricks. God, I thought I was smart! I didn't have the best upbringing, and my parents loved drugs more than me, but I've always had a good head on my shoulders.

Well, I did. Perhaps I lost more than my integrity in the alleyway all those months ago. Maybe this is punishment for my wicked sins.

I continue my deliberation on my opposite hip when the shadow from the door moves to my side of the bed. I know its Dimitri because I can smell myself on his skin like his sudden departure from his office was too important to wash off the desecration my desperateness shrouded him in.

"Roxanne."

When he tugs on my shoulder, I stay perfectly still, my body ignoring his touch as skillfully as my mind does his snapped delivery of my name. I'm not scared of him anymore. How can I be scared when all I'm feeling is embarrassed?

"Roxanne." Dimitri's voice is louder this time—as is his shove. "I know you're not asleep."

I almost bark out that he doesn't know me well enough to know when I'm fake sleeping, but hold back the urge. I'm done playing his game as much as I'm done playing nice.

"Do you want to know how I know you're awake?"

More silence—lots and lots of silence.

"Your nipples always bud when I touch you, but when you're asleep, you instinctively roll onto your back, begging for more."

I don't know what to respond to first. His confession that he touches me when I'm sleeping or his lower, more controlled tone. I can feel how worked up he is, smell it roasting on his skin, but he's fighting to keep his anger under wraps. For why? I have no clue.

The stranglehold of emotions clutching my throat flies out the window when Dimitri tries a different tactic. "We got a solid lead from one of your contacts tonight."

I roll over, too inquisitive for my own good. "Who?"

Dimitri's smile when he calls me for being a sucker shouldn't make me hot, but it does. "Dr. Bates."

"The OBGYN?" I sound shocked. Justly so. Dr. Bates was the least creepy of the bunch. He was half the age of my other suiters and wasn't shy about his intentions. He didn't just want a virgin for the night. He wanted something more long term.

When Dimitri nods, I scoot up in the bed. "What type of lead?"

He fiddles with the cuffs on his shirt, a sign he's stressed. "His practice ordered more prescriptions, fertility drugs, and pregnancy supplements than what was needed for the number of patients he's had the past three years."

His confession appears to be a solid lead, but I'm a little lost. Smith went light on details when he explained what happened to Dimitri's wife, but he let it drop that she wasn't given any type of anesthetics, so what does a prescription scandal have to do with any of this?

When I advise Dimitri of my confusion in a way that won't drudge up bad memories for him, he shunts my horror into terrifying blackness. "Tonight's guests weren't here solely to bid for your virginity. Some are involved in the baby-farming market."

"Farming? As in, they produce babies—"

"For well-to-do clients who can't have their own," Dimitri fills in as if I'm talking slow for any other reason than confusion.

Although his see-sawing personality has me all types of baffled, I can't hold my curiosity back. "But that isn't what happened to Fien, right? You paid to keep her safe."

An unfamiliar expression hardens his features when I say his daughter's name, but he's quick to shut it down. "The incident with Fien is different than what we're investigating, but like most things in life, there are a handful of common links I can't ignore." When I remain quiet, too confused to speak, he keeps talking. "Over the past couple of days, I've been led to believe that the people who took Audrey didn't realize who she was to begin with. They didn't know she was my wife."

I twist my lips. "That kind of makes sense. They'd have to be nuts to go against a man as powerful as you."

I thought my comment would lift a thousand bricks off his shoulders. Regretfully, it seems to have had the opposite effect. "A baby farm nets a tidy profit every year, but its overhead is high. You have to feed the women, cloth and house them—"

"Let alone a woman can only give birth on average once a year. You might get a rare one who can pop out two kids in eleven months, but that's generally not recommended."

A spark darts through Dimitri's eyes before remorse strangles it. "That's why they changed tactics. The upkeep of a baby is nowhere near as expensive, especially when you have a father willing to pay any amount requested."

"About that, something has been bugging me." It's obvious Dimitri isn't familiar with two-way conversations. He doesn't know whether to be amused or annoyed by my interruption. "Why are Fien's ransoms so minute? The figures tossed around by your guests tonight were ridiculous, and then there was the money being laid down for gambling last week. You'd have to be making a killing, so why are her captives only asking for a little over a million dollars every year. If I had an endless money pit at the ready, I'd milk it for all I could."

My throat grows scratchy when Dimitri's eyes narrow into tiny slits. "Perhaps if you're still around tomorrow, you can give me your opinion on a fairer amount."

*Still around? Am I going somewhere?*

A rock-hard mask slips over Dimitri's face when he spots my unvoiced questions in my eyes. After standing from the bed, he rolls up the sleeves of his dress shirt like his night isn't close to ending before he nudges his head to the door. "Come with me."

A part of me wants to tell him to go to hell. After what he did, I don't owe him a thing, but the stonewalled expression on his face keeps my lips locked tight.

The desire to bend in two bombards me when Dimitri hands me my dressing gown. He hates it as much as Estelle. I've heard him threaten to burn it under his breath multiple times the past five days. "It's cold where we're going. I wouldn't want your lips turning blue."

Ignoring the dread in the lower half of my stomach, I slip into my dressing gown and cinch it around my waist before following Dimitri's stalk out of our room. My pace is a little slower than his. Although our tryst didn't end as I was hoping, pain is still being felt.

The atmosphere in the lower half of the compound is starkly contradicting to the party-like one I faced only hours ago. All the guests have gone—even the scantily clad ones who were hoping to occupy Dimitri's bed for the night.

A worry that Dimitri no longer needs me skitters through my veins when our descend down the stairwell is quickly chased by another decline. We're heading toward the basement—the dark and dingy basement Dimitri had Rocco order for me to stay away three times earlier tonight. He was adamant I wasn't to go anywhere near it. Now he's walking me right into the underbelly of it. It has me sick with worry.

I didn't think my life could get any worse until Dimitri swings open a door at the end of the corridor. My father isn't bound to a chair by rope, chains, or any humanitarian way to keep a captive hostage without carnage. He's nailed to the wood. If that isn't bad enough, almost every inch of his skin is covered with a range of bruises, nicks, and cuts. However, they aren't the cause for the sob racking through me. It's the low hang of his head. The purple mottling of his skin. The evidence he's dead even without seeing the bullet pierced through his skull.

When I take a stumbling step back, Dimitri grips the tops of my arms, forcing me to stay in my nightmare longer than necessary for him to get across his point. I said he wasn't a monster, that he was just tired and angry. I realize my error now. He's a cruel, vindictive man who'd rather cut out someone's heart than have it handed to him willingly.

As I'm forced to scan an image too horrifying to share, I choke through the ragged breath I scarfed down to swallow the vomit racing up my throat. I can't believe I gave myself to him, that I thought he was misunderstood. He killed my father, my flesh and blood, all because he tried to sell me just like he did.

"I hate you." I'm sobbing now, full-on crying. Tears stream down my face as my body uncontrollably shakes. "Rocco said you wouldn't kill him. He promised it would be my choice."

"Is that why you helped, Roxanne, because you thought it would see your father's life spared? Is that why you almost gave yourself to me?"

"*Almost*?" His words make me sick. "I didn't *almost* give myself to you. I *gave* myself to you. There was no almost. I was yours! I would have always been yours!"

I push him off me, hating that I ever felt an ounce of anything for him. Remorse, lust, I'm disappointed by them all.

He's a murderer.

A cheat.

He doesn't deserve to get his daughter back.

When I say that to Dimitri, he gets up in my face in an instant. He pins me to a blood-splattered wall, towering over me like he's seconds from crashing my windpipes with his bare hands. "I should kill you where you stand."

"Then do it," I snarl in his face, my fear non-existent. "Kill me like you've threatened time and time again. Drain the blood from my veins and parade my dead carcass like you are my father's so your enemies will see you as a real man." The way I spit out the last half of my sentence reveals I think he's anything but a man. "But remember, no matter what you do, and no matter what you say, one thing will never change. I'm someone's daughter. I'm someone's Fien, so when Karma responds to what you've done, you better pray she doesn't gnaw the wrong ass."

Dimitri leans into me deeper, fully stilling me. His large, team-ing-with-anger body isn't solely responsible for my frozen state, though. It's the words he screams into my face, "He cut my daughter out of my wife's stomach! He held her like she was a fucking animal. He deserved to die!"

When he shoves a freshly printed piece of paper into my face, my stomach heaves. I feel like I'm drowning like my worst nightmare is coming true. The image of my father sitting lifeless in a pool of blood is horrific, but this is ten times worse.

Not only does Dimitri have undeniable proof my father was a part of the backyard operation to remove his daughter from his wife's stomach, he has evidence I was there too.

---

*Dimitri and Roxanne's story continues in the next explosive episode of* **The Italian Cartel** *Series. It is titled Roxanne - you can find it here:*
Roxanne

If you want to hear updates on the next books in this crazy world I've created, be sure to join my social media pages.

Facebook: facebook.com/authorshandi

Instagram: instagram.com/authorshandi

Email: authorshandi@gmail.com

Reader's Group: bit.ly/ShandiBookBabes

Website: authorshandi.com

Newsletter: https://www.subscribepage.com/AuthorShandi

Isaac, Nikolai, Trey, and Enrique stories have already been released, but Rocco, Maddox, and all the other great characters of Ravenshoe/Hopeton will be getting their own stories at some point during 2020/2021.

**Subscribe to my newsletter to remain informed:**
www.subscribepage.com/AuthorShandi

*If you enjoyed this book please leave a review.*

# ACKNOWLEDGMENTS

This book was a hard one for me to write. We were in the middle of a pandemic, I found out my mother has cancer, and the entire world went to shit. Yet, here we are, at another acknowledgement page. It wouldn't have happened without the support of my readers and those who continuously prop me up every day. My husband is my number one supporter and my mother slots right in next to him. Even with the unknown keeping her thoughts occupied, she read Dimitri's first draft like she has every one of my books. She helped fix my many stuff ups (I'm infamous for them) and discussed what she thinks will happen in the next book.

Her strength the past month has been phenomenal. I hate that it takes something like cancer to truly understand how strong someone is, but it does make it undeniable. There's no one stronger than her.

I hope you enjoyed Dimitri's story, even with that cliffhanger ending. The second instalment will follow shortly.

Take care, and hug your loved ones.

Shandi xx

PS: A special shout out to my editing crew, Nicky and Kaylene at Swish Design and Editing. I can't thank my cover designer, as that is me, but I can thank Jonny James for having such a sexy face. He adds to Dimitri's dark and dangerous aura with an edge of sexiness I hope you can appreciate.

**Facebook:** facebook.com/authorshandi

**Instagram:** instagram.com/authorshandi

**Email:** authorshandi@gmail.com

**Reader's Group:** bit.ly/ShandiBookBabes

**Website:** authorshandi.com

**Newsletter:** https://www.subscribepage.com/AuthorShandi

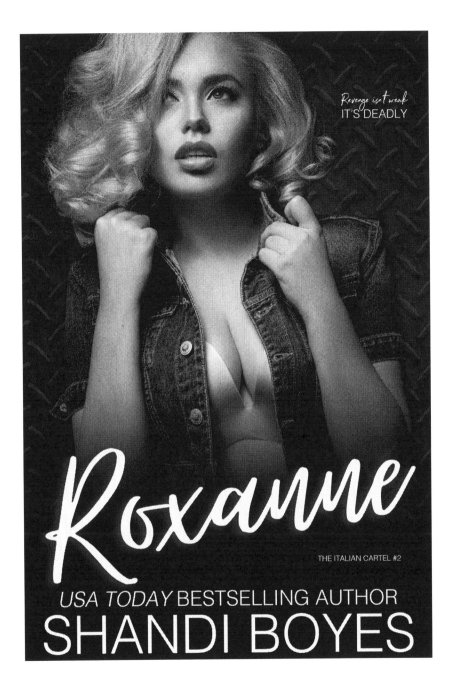

Revenge isn't weak
IT'S DEADLY

# Roxanne

THE ITALIAN CARTEL #2

USA TODAY BESTSELLING AUTHOR
# SHANDI BOYES

# 1

## ROXANNE

As Dimitri's eyes bounce between mine, I shake my head, denying the claims I see in his narrowed gaze. There's no doubt my face is visible in the image that's so zoomed in, the pixilation that should make me unrecognizable to anyone who doesn't intimately know me, but I'm not present in the physical sense. My face is being bounced off an industrial-size filing cabinet. The same filing cabinet I saw stacked behind my mother when she FaceTimed me the day after my failed meet-up to reconnect with my father.

She said she was sorry he had made me upset, and that she was determined to mend the rift between us. I told her not to worry. My father was the same cruel man he always was, so I wasn't interested in rebuilding bridges that had burned years earlier.

Our conversation barely lasted a minute, but if the anger teeming out of Dimitri is anything to go by, my last contact with my mother is more significant to him than it was to me. He's blistering mad. Our combined dispositions are enhanced beyond reproach.

"That isn't me," I hiccup through a sob.

When anger flares through his eyes, making them dark cesspools of annoyance, I realize my error. Denials won't get me anywhere. I need to prove to Dimitri I'm on his team. That's the only way I'll come out of this exchange with my life intact.

"It's me, but I wasn't there when they took Fien. You can see it's a reflection. Even a surveillance novice wouldn't be able to deny that..." My words trail off when Dimitri releases the first surveillance image from his death-tight grip to reveal a second, more terrifying one. It shows a tiny baby covered with white goop and blood being dangled mid-air by her feet. She's as still as a board, her only coloring coming from the cruel grip her captor has on her feet. He's clutching her so tightly, the blood that's supposed to pump around her feet pools in them instead. Their red hue matches the flames tattooed on the man's wrist—the same flame tattoo barely noticeable on my father's blood-smattered arm since he had it recently covered with a much bigger design.

If that isn't concerning enough, a tiny hand in the very far left of the image has an identifiable feature. It isn't a birthmark like Fien has on her stomach nor a tattoo. It's a ring—a ring that feels like it weighs a ton when Dimitri's eyes lower to take in its uniqueness firsthand. He glares at the custom jewelry piece I inherited from my grandmother, his blazing stare heating it up as effectively as his evidence makes my stomach flip.

I can't see the face of the man in the image, it's covered by a balaclava, but both his tattoo and his eyes are familiar to me. As are the hands of the woman reaching out to remove Dimitri's daughter from his clutch.

As tears flood my eyes, horrified I have any association with people capable of doing such a horrendous act, I blubber out a string of apologies. I'm sickened my parents would do something so inhumane, but I also don't want to be punished for something that wasn't my fault. They're my parents, but their actions don't lie on my shoulders.

When my apologies reach Dimitri's ears, he leans into me deeper, stealing both the words from my mouth and the air from my lungs. "They killed my wife. Your parents *killed my wife!*" He screams his last three words in my face.

"I know. I am so sorry. I had no idea they were capable of doing such an appalling act. I swear to God, I don't condone a single thing they've done. If I had any inkling they were involved, I would have told you."

"You're lying."

Tears fling off my face when I shake my head. "No. I had no clue. I swear I was in the dark as much as you." I am shocked I can talk. I'm not just stunned at the evidence he's presenting, I am also shocked we're holding this conversation in the room my father was murdered in. The anger emanating from him has vomit racing up my food pipe. It's seconds from being released. "I'm as angry as you."

Air traps in my throat when Dimitri interrupts, "Prove it."

"W-what?" I stare at him, utterly lost. How can I prove I'm as devastated as him? He killed my father. I can't display my anger as brutally as that. The person deserving of my wrath is dead. There's no one left for me to take my anger out on.

*Oh no.*

As the truth smacks into me, the door we walked through only minutes ago pops open, and a woman with reddish-blonde hair and arms scarred with track marks is thrust into the room. When my mother lands on the floor with a thud, first instincts have me wanting to race to her side. The only reason I don't is because I can't get the images Dimitri showed me out of my head. Although most of my focus was on Fien and my parents, no amount of shock could stop my eyes from drinking in the blurry person behind them. Dimitri's wife wasn't treated with any respect, so why should my mother be given any leeway?

An idealism on who our parents are supposed to be is embedded in us when we're kids. If you're lucky, your unfounded hopes might stack up. But for the most part, you'll be lucky to stumble out of childhood unscathed. Have you ever heard the saying, *Just because you can have kids doesn't mean you should?* That resonates well with my parents. I wouldn't be here if it weren't for them, but Fien would be. That, in itself, explains Dimitri's fury.

My heart tries to break out of my chest when Dimitri steps back, unpinning me from the wall. The anger radiating out of him isn't responsible for my heart's thuds, it's the angst he strikes it with when he digs his gun out of the back of his jeans and shoves it into my hand.

I could direct it at him as he did to me days ago, I could save my mother before saving myself, but for the life of me, I can't. I'm not a parent, but that doesn't mean I can't understand what Dimitri is going through. He was barely holding on last week, so I can only imagine how thin the thread is now. The images he showed me were horrific, and the pain in his eyes tells me they were just the beginning of the horrendous things he has seen.

"Please don't make me do this," I beg when he slides off the safety on his gun, so it's ready to maim. I'm shocked at how fast he moves. I am shuddering like I'm in an ice bath. The gun isn't close to stable—and neither am I. "I can make it up to you. I'll do anything you ask."

"You're already doing everything I ask." His words snap out of his mouth like venom, both vicious and maiming. They have nothing on the hate in his eyes, though.

"I'll do more—"

Dimitri whips around so fast, the waft of his quick movements blasts my face with the scent of a pricy aftershave. "More what, Roxanne? More trouble? More hurt?"

"Anything! I'll do anything you ask."

Tears roll down my cheeks unchecked when he says, "Kill the woman responsible for my wife's death. That's *all* I want you to do."

Ignoring the rapid shake of my head advising him I could never do that, he grips the scruff of my mother's shirt. His brutal strength forces her eyes from the floor. When they collide with mine, I almost become one with the wall. I don't recognize her in the slightest. She isn't close to the woman I remember. Her eyes aren't lit with life. They're shallow and lifeless, as bleak as my father's now are.

That doesn't mean I want to kill her, though.

"I can't," I whimper on a sob. "She's my mother."

"She's a kidnapper and a murderer. She deserves to die!" After dragging my mother to within an inch of my feet, Dimitri screams in her face. "Tell her what you told me." When the quick shake of her head grates on his last nerve, he backhands her so hard, my teeth feel the collision. "Tell her what you told me!"

I stare at my mother, begging for her to do as asked. If she wants to live, she must jump on cue, and even then, it may not be enough. Her death certificate was signed the instant she went against a man more powerful than she'll ever be, and no, I'm not solely referencing Dimitri.

While scratching at fresh needle marks in her arms, my mother stutters out, "We had to give them someone. W-w-we couldn't arrive empty-handed. We owed them money. *Lots* of money."

"So, instead of selling them your daughter as arranged, you convinced your husband to take my wife instead!" Even if we weren't in a small, concrete room, I'd still hear Dimitri's roar twice. That's how loud he's shouting.

"They wanted someone who could have children. They didn't care who they got. As long as she was fertile, they'd take anyone." My mother's cracked lips quiver as she locks her eyes with mine. "I just couldn't give them *my* child."

Dimitri is as unbelieving of the remorse in her tone as me. She was never overly motherly, so why would she start years after she abandoned me? "So, you gave them mine instead *after* cutting her out of my wife's stomach!"

"No." She adds to her denial of Dimitri's claim by shaking her head. "That was never the plan. They were only supposed to take your wife. T-t-they weren't supposed to take your daughter. I didn't know Ian's plan. He kept me in the dark." Against her better judgment, she slants her head to the side so she can peer at me past Dimitri's brimming-with-anger frame. "That's why I ended our call so fast that night. I heard screaming. I tried to stop him, Roxie, but I couldn't. You know what your father was like. He didn't listen to anyone, not even me."

She speaks about her husband as if his corpse isn't in the room with us, her disrespect as telling as the expression on her face. She once loved the man bound lifeless to the chair, however that was a very long time ago.

"Nothing I could have done would have changed anything. Once they realized who Audrey was, they were never going to listen to me."

I unconsciously shake my head, my body choosing its own response to the lies I see in her eyes. Audrey was eight months along. Her pregnancy was noticeable, so although she's pledging she had no part in what happened to Fien, she *is* responsible for her captivity—even more than me.

I try to make sense of the mess. "Why didn't you call the

police? Or reach out for help? You can't live with a secret like this and not expect it to eventually come out, so why not come clean when it could have done some good?"

"I couldn't." When she shuffles closer to me, Dimitri raises his hand back into the air. It stops both the scuttles of my mother's knees and my heart. A slap is almost caring compared to how he could handle her stupidity, but I'd rather not witness her torture. She may not be the woman I once remembered, but she's still my mother.

With her hands clutched a mere inch from my bare feet, she locks her eyes with mine. "I haven't seen the sun in months. I don't even know what month it is, so how could I have sought help? Why do you think I didn't call you back that night, Roxie?"

I want to say because she abandoned me like she did when I was ten, but since that would swing the pendulum in Dimitri's favor, I keep my mouth shut. My stomach won't quit flipping from the smell emitting off my father. I don't want to see my mother killed the same way. I hate what she did, but turning into a monster to kill a monster won't stop the vicious cycle. It will continue circling until everyone is extinct—even the good monsters.

My queasiness takes on an entirely new meaning when Dimitri strikes my mother for the second time. "I told you to tell the truth, not the shit you tried to spurt earlier."

"Don't!" I shout when Dimitri raises his hand for the third time. His second hit split my mother's cheek. She won't come out of a third one without irreparable damage. Although she deserves his anger, a small part of me wonders if she's telling the truth. It's minute but undeniable.

When my words don't get through to Dimitri, I use the weapon he forced on me to my advantage. I fire one shot into the roof, squealing when it takes out the light hanging above my head.

It rains shards of glass down on me and has Dimitri's face the maddest I've ever seen. "You're going to shoot at *me*, the man who lost everything so *you* could continue living *your* miserable existence? They swapped *my* wife for *you*! They made her take your place!"

He grips the barrel of his gun like it isn't scorching hot from its recent firing, but instead of yanking it out of my grasp, he uses it to pull me in front of him.

With his hands curled around mine and his front squashed to my back, I can't garner the strength to stop him from aiming his gun at the pinched skin between my mother's brows. He isn't just stronger than me, his closeness has more hold on my wickedness than my morality.

"For once, give your daughter the decency she deserves. Tell. Her. The. Truth."

The reason for the extra thump in Dimitri's pulse is exposed when the quickest gleam darts through my mother's eyes when she spots the ring I inherited from my grandmother. For the first time tonight, I feel like siding with my family will place me on the wrong team.

Family members are supposed to be your go-to support network. They usually back you up in ways strangers can't.

I'm not getting that vibe from my mother.

All I'm feeling is devastation.

I've seen her wear this look before. It was when she raced out of my grandfather's barn, stating her eldest brother had been in an accident. When Nanna and I tried to race to Uncle Mike's side to offer assistance, my mother and father held us back, declaring it was too late. He was already gone.

That was mere days before my grandfather cut my parents out of his will. He didn't care about the tension it caused at Uncle Mike's funeral. He wanted it documented that in the event of his death, every possession he owned was to go to my grandmother. When she passed, it was to come to me. My parents were to get nothing.

That's how I inherited the antique Celtic ring Dimitri glared at earlier. Anything in my grandmother's possession at the time of her death was classified as mine—including the ring she gifted my mother when she birthed her first child.

My God, how could I not have put two and two together until now? My mother inherited my ring first. She never took it off, so why was it in the wreckage of my Nanna's accident?

"You were there. You..." I can't say it. The words won't come out of my mouth. Claudia's wrongful imprisonment proves traffic accidents aren't always as they seem, but still, this is too shocking to articulate.

Dimitri doesn't face the same issues as me. He has no trouble spelling things out as he sees them. "Not only did your mother attempt to sell you when her stash got low, she killed her only sibling *and* her mother with the hope of a big payout. It will take a few days for preliminary reports to come back, but I won't be shocked to discover your grandfather didn't die of natural causes."

I shake my head, too stunned by the honesty in Dimitri's tone to make sense of it.

"Killing my nanna wouldn't help my parents. If they wanted money, they would have needed to take me out as well."

When I say that to Dimitri, he presses his lips to the shell of my ear and growls, "They didn't want money..." His pause is the worst form of torture "They needed space. Space you gave them when you moved into a one-bedroom flat in the middle of the burbs."

I'm confused as to what he means until my wide-with-terror eyes collide with my mother's. She's wearing the same smug glare she wore when Uncle Mike's lawyer informed us he forgot to change his will when he married. When he died, all his assets went to my mother. Although he wasn't a wealthy man, he lived more comfortably than my parents. They thought they had hit the motherload when their bank balance rose by six digits.

"What did she need space for?" Although I'm asking questions, I don't need Dimitri to answer me to get the gist of what's happening. It's staring me straight in the face, eating away my morals as much as drugs stole the life of the woman kneeling in front of me.

"Was it for farming?" I don't mean to plant potatoes, tomatoes, or zucchini. I'm talking about the farms Dimitri mentioned during our talk before we came to the basement, the ones I can't forget no matter how hard my twisting stomach wishes I could.

If my intuition is true, if my parents are knee-deep in the industry responsible for Fien's captivity, this is worse than them switching a product mid-sale. They're selling babies for crying out loud—stolen-from-the-womb babies.

When I spot Dimitri's nod in the corner of my eye, I want to fold in two. The only reason I don't is because I have more pressing matters to attend to. It isn't just my mother's life at stake anymore. Mine is on the chopping block too.

"You need to tell him who you work with and *that I'm not involved.*" The last half of my sentence is voiced more punchily than the first half. I'm not just desperate to save my hide, I don't want *anyone* thinking I'm associated with such a callous, cruel world, much less Dimitri.

"Tell him!" I scream when my mother's silence works me over as well as Dimitri's hand pummeled her face. "For once, protect me as you should have when I was a child. Put me first for a change!" Blinded by a rage too hot for me to think rationally, I curl my index finger around the gun Dimitri directed at her head. "Tell him! Tell him now!"

"I don't know who they are," she chokes out on a whimper, shocked I'm treating her as poorly as she treated me my entire life. "We didn't exchange names. We weren't a part of the production side. We were just... we..."

"Were a dumping site," Dimitri fills in when words allude her.

I never thought I would have a wish to kill someone, let alone the ability, but it's a close call when my mother bobs her head at Dimitri's claim. She isn't a victim like I believed during my childhood. She's as bad as my father and just as abusive, and once again, I'm done playing nice.

# 2

# DIMITRI

When I entered this room hours ago, my first thought was that I should crush Roxanne's windpipe as Smith's whispered words crushed my soul. I should destroy her as her parents destroyed me. At one stage, I even considered keeping her parents alive so they could witness me torture their child as they had mine.

None of my previous suggestions are being considered now.

Despite my intuition begging me to reconsider, I don't believe the anger blistering out of Roxanne is a ploy. Just like earlier tonight, she's prepared to slay for me by killing her own blood. If that can't convince me she's on my team, nothing will.

Audrey was taken as her replacement. She was kidnapped purely to fill the slot Roxanne's absence caused, but for the life of me, I can no longer place the blame for that on Roxanne's shoulders.

I looked away.

I fucked up.

This isn't Roxanne's fault.

In all honesty, Roxanne is so under my thumb, if she had the opportunity to switch places with Fien, she would in a heartbeat. I have no doubt about that. It isn't just men who are led by their libidos. Women are just as bad. The way Roxanne stared at me in the alleyway all those months ago is proof of this.

There's just one difference between her and women like my wife.

Some sit back and watch the shit unfold.

Others get into the nitty-gritty.

Roxanne is the latter.

The way she put her life on the line earlier tonight proves that as does the obvious twitch of her index finger. It's curled around the trigger of my gun, ready to be pulled back. She's just waiting for permission.

Permission I won't give since it would change her in an instant.

Your first kill never leaves you, and when it's your blood, it haunts you long after you've entered your grave. That's one of the reasons my father is so fucked up. He may not have killed my grandfather, but he was responsible for the bullet that pierced his brain.

I feel Roxanne's sigh more than I hear it when I lower the gun I'm forcing her to aim at her mother's head. She knows this isn't the end of her mother's punishment, she's just glad she isn't going to be her torturer.

I promised to protect Fien no matter what. Even with my emotions not knowing which way to swing, I'll keep my promise. I just need to make sure the right people are being held accountable. I won't lie, it will be a hard road, but even a man bogged down with grief knows a child can't be held responsible for their parents' actions. I've never accepted culpability for my father's crimes, and Fien will never be at fault for mine, so why the fuck am I writing a new set of rules for Roxanne? I could blame grief, but in all honesty, I've worked that excuse to death the past twenty months. It's time for me to stand on my own two feet. I'm a man. I can admit my mistakes.

For the most part.

My heart stops harmonizing its beats with Roxanne's when she sinks to the far corner of the room to suck in some much-needed breaths. Her eyes reveal she's as mad as hell and ready to kill, but they also expose she wishes the outcome of her mother's poor judgment could be anything but death.

I'd be lying if I said I don't feel the same way. I hate killing women. Their punishments usually come with an automatic clause for mercy. However, this isn't something I can let slide. Not only did Sailor organize the kidnapping of my wife, she attempted to sell her daughter before killing the only person who gave a crap about her. That, in itself, deserves a much harsher punishment than death.

After sliding on the safety on my gun to ensure my teetering moods won't cause an accidental firing, I nudge my head to the door. "Head up with Rocco and pack. We need to be at the airstrip by eight. I'll meet you there."

Hearing the words I don't speak the loudest, Roxanne strays her wide-with-fear eyes to my side of the room. "Dimi—"

"Go." I keep my tone stern, assuring she knows I'm not suggesting she leave. I'm telling her to go. "I'll only be a minute."

My reassurance that I won't torture her mother for hours on end does little to ease the heavy groove between her brows, but it does get her feet moving.

After glancing at Sailor for the quickest second, she makes a beeline for the door. Even with my pulse booming in my ears, I hear Rocco exhale when Roxanne breaks into the dimly lit corridor. He was waiting with three body bags, confident no amount of pleading would see Roxanne's family escape conviction for the second time.

Roxanne's gall ensures he will only need two.

Once the door closes with Roxanne on the other side, I devote all my attention to her mother. I want to maim, I want to kill, but more than any of that, I want to give Fien's mother the burial she deserves.

I'm not a religious man, but Audrey's family is. Until her body is returned to the ground, her soul won't rest. I'm happy to give them closure if it means they won't contest Fien's custody. They'd never win, but the less I have to worry about, the easier it will be for Fien to settle once she's returned.

"Where is Audrey buried?" My words are somewhat calm for how hot my veins feel. I'm seconds from blowing my top, but I am showing restraint, the shackle of my go-to emotion solely for Fien... and perhaps Roxanne.

When Sailor's eyes lift to mine, I realize just how fucked she is, and for once, her undoing has nothing to do with me or my crew. She's been taken by demons way worse than a man's possessiveness. Drugs fuck you over in a way no man can. She's lost to it, completely fucking gone.

"I don't know—"

"*Where* did you bury *my wife!*"

She recoils at my shouted words, but they get her talking better than my fists ever could. "I took your daughter to get checked over. When I returned, your wife was gone."

I don't know her well enough to know if she's lying or not, but I do know one thing, pretending she gives a shit about Fien won't sit well with me. She didn't care about my daughter when she was forcefully removed from her mother's stomach weeks too early. She didn't care that her daughter was emotionally abused by her husband. She cares about no one but herself. The way she treated Roxanne her entire life is proof of this.

If Audrey hadn't arrived at Slice of Salt when she did, who's to say Sailor wouldn't have gone ahead with the original plan to sell Roxanne. She said it herself, Rimi wanted anyone. That anyone could have been Roxanne, and for some reason, that annoys me more than knowing she's responsible for Audrey's death. Don't ask me why. It's fucked for me even to think this way, but I'm merely being honest—for once.

Sailor's eyes shift from her dead husband to me when I drag a chair over from the side of the room. I balance one of the chair's legs onto her ring finger before taking a seat. Her tear-choked scream is similar to the one Roxanne's suitor released earlier tonight when I removed the finger he sneakily dragged up Roxanne's arm. He thought the severity of his punishment didn't fit his crime. I believed otherwise. He'll think twice before he ever touches something he doesn't own again.

If I truly believed Sailor had more information than a standard bottom-dweller in this industry, I'd torture her for the next several hours until she spilled the beans. Since I'm aware that isn't the case, I use her open mouth to my advantage.

When I ram the barrel of my gun down her throat, it shuts her up in an instant and has her paying careful attention to everything I say. Although I don't have a lot to say, it's best for her to listen. Paying attention is the highest form of respect. Without it, there will be no possibility of me offering her any leniency.

I don't mean from death, her expiration date is well past perished. I'm merely proposing a quick, clean death compared to letting Clover have his way with her. He won't rape her, that isn't his kink, but he'll be more than happy to add additional splits to her cheeks.

"This is your last chance, Sailor." I speak slow to ensure the hammering of her heart doesn't affect her ability to hear me. "Where did you bury my wife?"

# 3

## ROXANNE

When the ricochet of a bullet being fired booms into my ears, I grip a designer dress so firmly, its pricy threads pop. I'm on the third level of Dimitri's New York compound, packing for a trip to God knows where. However, I still know the direction the noise came from. Not only did the devastating vibration tickle my toes, it also chipped away a piece of my soul like it did when my father carried Uncle Mike out of my grandparents' barn a decade ago.

I was barely ten, but the deathly swing of Uncle Mike's arm revealed he was gone. His skin was mottled like my father's. Even with my parents saying otherwise, I often wondered why he looked the way he did. He was run over by a tractor not placed into gear, but he was marked and nicked as if he had been in an underground cage fight.

Since I was so young, I never suspected my parents were involved in his accident. Only after seeing the flare dart through my mother's eyes an hour ago did reality dawn. My parents didn't witness his accident. They killed him as they most likely did my grandparents.

My grandparents would never admit it, but everyone knew Uncle Mike was their favorite. He helped without being asked, never accepted a dime for his time, and agreed with their decision not to sell their little slice of heaven in the middle of a busy metropolis. His decision had nothing to do with money. Unlike my parents, he had done well for himself. He wasn't close to wealthy, but he had a humble, happy existence. He was married and expecting his first child in the spring.

Last I heard, Aunt Melissa was residing in Arizona. Her child was born three months after my uncle's death. I don't know if my cousin is a boy or a girl. When my uncle was laid to rest, it was as if his little family no longer existed.

After dumping my dress into a suitcase open on the floor, I drag the sleeve of my dressing gown under my nose, removing the mess pooled there. The past hour has flown by in a blur. I've been packing and guzzling down vodka like the man I willingly gave my virginity to isn't in the process of torturing my mother.

Estelle always says blood doesn't make you family, but still, I expected to feel some sort of grief at the thought I'm about to be an orphan. I feel a little empty and somewhat confused, but I also feel like the purge of my emotions will be good for me.

It's a sad reality, but by Dimitri wiping my slate clean, I'll have the chance to move forward without constantly looking over my shoulder. Although I never imagined it being this bad, I've always known there was something not quite right with my parents. It wasn't just the sex and drugs, there was a handful of other things that set alarm bells off in my head. I was just too young to understand what they meant.

I don't face that same issue now. My father didn't make me watch because he wanted to embarrass me. He was grooming me to take my mother's place, preparing to sell me as he had her. That's why some of his 'friends' gawked at me like they did my mother. They knew it was only a matter of time before I'd eventually be offered up as well.

With my stomach a twisted mess of confusion, I pace to the large window in my room to drink in the tranquil setting you wouldn't expect this close to a major city. The rugged terrain with a skyscraper backdrop has me recalling the time my mother dropped me off to live with my grandparents. For years, I thrived on the fact she cared enough about me not to let my father hurt me.

It was silly of me ever to believe.

While seeking financial aid for school, I discovered my grandparents had a significant mortgage on their estate. They had lived on their little ranch for over a decade before my mother was born, so it should have been paid off years earlier.

I initially blamed bad money management for their poor credit.

Even with my head blurred with alcohol, I'm not so stupid now.

"How fast can Smith look up transactions from closed bank accounts?"

Rocco cranks his neck to face me. He's been stationed at the corner of my room for the past hour. His unusual quiet has been off-putting, but considering the circumstances, it's also understandable.

Just as Rocco's lips move to speak, Smith's unique timber vibrates my ears. "About as quick as I can make a girl come. Why? What do you need?"

My eyes don't shoot around my room as they did hours ago, seeking the direction his voice came from. They hone straight in on the tiny camera in the far corner of the elaborate space. The lens appears to be a fault in the distressed wooden frame of a priceless piece of artwork above Dimitri's desk. Only those in the know are aware it's a state-of-the-art surveillance instrument. Smith disclosed not only can he see and hear me in every room, so can Dimitri. At the time, the thought intrigued me. Now it makes me worried. I don't want Dimitri to think I'm seeking excuses for my parents. I'm just trying to occupy my time before I go as crazy as drugs have made my mother.

While pacing closer to Dimitri's desk, I ask Smith, "My grand-parents' accounts, can you see if there were any irregularities in their transactions?"

"Such as?"

My eyes rocket to Rocco when he answers Smith's question on my behalf, "She wants to know if her grandparents paid to keep her safe." As the thump of a keyboard being punished booms out of a hidden speaker above my head, Rocco pushes off the wall he's had his shoulder propped against the past hour. "Are you sure you want to go down this rabbit warren, Roxie? Knowing the reason for someone's fuck-ups don't make them any easier to swallow."

"I know that. I just..." I've got nothing but a heap of tension in my stomach and watering eyes. "What if it wasn't her fault? What if my father forced her like she said? He had a hold over her like Dimi..."

When my words are gobbled up by the shame raining down on me, Rocco takes up their slack. "Like Dimitri does you?"

I nod, too confused to continue acting like I'm fine. I held a gun to my mother's head in the room where my father was killed. I almost fired at her. If that isn't proof I'm already deep down the rabbit hole, nothing will convince you.

After watching me brush away a tear sitting high on my cheek, Rocco locks his murky green eyes with mine. They're still brim-ming with cheekiness, but there's a smart, noble gleam to them as well. "Even with taking out all the shit that happened when you were a kid, knowing what you know now, do you think your parents were or would have been upstanding, moral citizens?"

It should take me longer than two seconds to reach my decision. However, it doesn't. My parents have always been awful human beings, and that was before I discovered just how polluted their morals have become.

When I shake my head, air whizzes out of Rocco's nose. "Exactly! Don't get me wrong, I'm glad your parents couldn't resist the urge, I kinda like having you around, but if they weren't born—"

"Fien would still be here."

Confusion twists in my stomach when Rocco shakes his head. "This isn't just about Fien, Roxie. It's about you, and me, and a man who can't escape the demons of his past no matter how fast he runs." Acting as if his words don't have my heart racing a million miles an hour, he bridges the gap between us with two big strides. "No matter how fucked it is, we can't change the past... but we can stop it happening to someone else." After gripping my shoulders to lessen my unstable sways, he adds, "Your parents didn't just hit this scene once in desperation. They were shrouded in it. First, your aunt and uncle, then you and your grandparents before they moved onto Audrey and Fien. They weren't going to stop until someone stopped them. It sucks that the person has to be Dimitri, but trust me when I say it's better than it being you."

Even though I agree with him—I can see me forgiving Dimitri way sooner than I'd ever forgive myself—but I'm more confused than relieved. "What does my aunt have to do with this?"

Rocco curses under his breath before he sinks back to his makeshift station at the side of the room. No words escape his mouth for the next several seconds, but I see the truth in his remorseful gaze. Audrey wasn't the first pregnant woman my parents took. Even every day, decent Americans know criminals test the waters in their own backyard before playing with the big hitters.

"Hey, come on now, Roxie, breathe," Rocco says when the air in my lungs no longer feels adequate. It feels as if I'm drowning like I am being pulled into the abyss of my horrible life. My parents killed my family. All of them are dead, and I would have been next if it weren't for the man currently torturing my mother.

How fucked is that to even consider?

I can't comprehend it.

I also can't breathe.

When a high-pitch wheeze I'm certain didn't come from me breaks through the thud of my pulse in my ears, so does Rocco's clipped tone. "I'm just offering her comfort, dickwad. If you have a problem with me touching her, you're gonna need to tell me in person."

Rocco stops rubbing one of my arms in a nurturing manner, so he can give a one-finger salute to the camera in the corner of the room. With how tight my chest is, his shit-stirring grin shouldn't be comforting, but since it's full of mirth, it is. It allows my lungs to suck down the tiniest slither of air that's forced back out when a person bursts through the door on my left.

As Dimitri's narrowed gaze bounces between Rocco and me, his nostrils flare like his lungs are screaming as loudly as mine. He seems torn between wanting to punish me for accepting Rocco's comfort and taking me back to the dungeon responsible for making me an orphan.

He loses the ability to drive me to Hell's gates when I see the blood smattered on the collar of his dress shirt. It's so fresh, its putrid scent is stronger than the pricy aftershave he wears. It nose-dives my hysteria in an instant and has me on the brink of a break-down even quicker than that.

When a scream rips through me like a shard of glass, nicking my heart into hundreds of tiny pieces, I can't deny it's from me this time around. I hate what my parents did and agree they should be punished, but I still can't wrap my head around the fact it occurred without more fight.

I should have fought harder.

I should have pleaded for mercy.

And I should have done both those things long before my parents crossed paths with Dimitri's wife.

"I'm sorry," I force out through the despair clutching my throat. "For what they did. For choosing me over your wife. I'm so fucking sorry. They should have taken me. They should have hurt me. It's my fault. Everything happening to your daughter is my fault."

Dimitri appears shocked my regret centers around his daughter instead of my parents, but it has nothing on the surprise that hammers me when he replies, "You can be angry about what they did, you can hate them for how they treated you, but you are *not* to apologize for them. Do you understand me, Roxanne? You aren't to blame for a single thing they did."

Tears sting my eyes when I blubber out, "Fien would be here if it weren't for me."

I feel like he slaps me as hard as he did my mother when he shouts, "Fien would be here if I hadn't looked away. *I* fucked up. *I* made a mistake. This isn't on you."

I want to believe him, but I can't. "You said—"

"I made a mistake," he repeats, more forcefully. "And I'm trying to learn from it."

I'm so stunned by his grab of the culpability batten, I don't realize Rocco has left the room until I'm guided past the wall his brooding frame has been holding up the past hour.

As Dimitri walks me to the window I was peering out of earlier, the hammering of his heart is as audible as mine. I think it's because he noticed the half-empty bottle of vodka on his desk but am proven wrong when I notice a change to the scenic backdrop of his compound. The same city skyscrapers sparkle in the distance, and the same twelve SUVs line the cobbled driveway, however the lead SUV's taillights bounce red hues off locks not quite as vibrant as my hair's natural coloring, but undeniably similar.

After watching my mother be guided into the back seat of one of Dimitri's fleet cars, I raise my eyes to Dimitri's. I bombard him with an array of questions without a single word escaping my lips. I'm too stunned to talk, shocked my mother walked to her awaiting chariot instead of being slid into the back seat in a body bag. She's the reason Dimitri's wife is dead. There's only one punishment for that.

Seemingly wired to my inner monologue, Dimitri says, "She hurt you first. That means only you can sentence her." He drags the back of his finger down my wet cheek to gather up the tears there before adding, "I don't see you having the ability to make a rational decision tonight, so we'll wait."

The way he says 'we' makes me unsure which way is up. It was possessive and hot like I'm no longer his enemy.

Although I'm loving his changeup, something still doesn't make sense. "My father—"

"Was given a choice." Dimitri's interruption reveals he's still sitting on the edge of a very steep cliff. He's as confused as me, although not as emotional. "He either confessed to everything or took the easy way out. Although it was obvious he didn't give a crap about you, he couldn't shut down his feelings for your mother as easily. He thought he'd protect her by—"

"Taking the easy way out," I interrupt.

I hardly knew my father. Not even when I lived under the same roof as him did I understand him. He was different than my friends' fathers, and the older I became, the more I noticed that wasn't a good thing, but his love for my mother was undeniable. He became a monster to save her, and it's that monster that's slowly killing her.

Furthermore, the bullet entry point wound I've been endeavoring to wash out of my head the past hour with vodka was at an odd angle. It would have taken Dimitri distorting his wrist to replicate its oddness, but why would he bother faking his death? He's never hidden the fact he's a killer, so why would he start now?

Mistaking my quiet as deliberation on his honesty, Dimitri mutters, "If you don't believe me, Smith can show you footage."

Some may say I'm foolish to believe him, however, I do. "I believe you." Pretending the roaring buzz between us is from remorse instead of euphoria, I ask, "Where are they taking my mother?"

I feel cold when he breaks away from my side so he can commence undressing. It's been a long night in general, but he must be even more tired, considering he didn't sleep a wink last night. "To a rehabilitation center."

His reply comforts me in a way I can't explain. If he were planning to kill her, he wouldn't put steps in place to make her a better person. He would have let her go and waited for drugs to do what I'm not sure I am capable of. As I said earlier, my parents are horrible people, but at the end of the day, I still wouldn't be here without them.

After placing his cufflinks into a dish on his desk, Dimitri pivots around to face me. "If it turns out what she said is untrue, her ruling will be taken out of your hands, do you understand?"

Even with my intuition dying to drill him on what she said, I nod my head instead. He looks as burned out as I feel. The lies my mother told with the hope of saving her hide isn't a conversation for today. I don't think there will ever be an appropriate day, but despite that, this question can't wait. "Did she tell you where Audrey's body is located?"

I'm not anticipating for him to answer me, he's not a fan of two-way interrogations, so you can imagine my shock when he shakes his head.

Willing to risk punishment for the greater good, I ask, "Do you believe she's at my grandparents' farm?"

My heart pains for him when he shrugs. "I don't know." His voice is the lowest it's ever been as are his shoulders. "We'll travel there in the morning. For now, I need sleep."

I nod, agreeing with him. He looks as tired as hell.

My head bob switches to a shake when he asks, "Have you showered?"

"No. Rocco stayed with me." My eyes widen when I realized my stupidity. "We didn't do anything. He stood by the door."

His cocky trademark half-smirk makes me hot all over. I'm too tipsy to determine if it's a good or bad heat. "I know. Smith isn't the only one with eyes and ears in this room."

*Talking about Smith, he never got back to me about my earlier question.*

I mentally book myself in for a scan to check for bugs when Dimitri reads my mind for the second time tonight. "Your queries into your grandparents' estate will have to wait. Until I know the full extent of what's happening, I instructed Smith not to give you half-ass assumptions."

Should my stomach gurgle at his confession or weaken its knot? If it were straight-up good, Smith would have given me an immediate answer. The fact it's in the unknown has me unsure which direction my mood should swing. I hate the murkiness of the unknown. Take now, for example, should I slide into the sheets Dimitri is folding down like he should be rewarded for issuing mercy to my underserving mother or take a stand about him torturing her? I know what my libido would prefer, but my morals should be an entirely different story, shouldn't they?

Needing time to deliberate on my wavering personalities, I wait for Dimitri to hop into bed before I hook my thumb to the bathroom. "I'm going to take a quick shower."

I barely pivot halfway around when Dimitri's deep timbre stops me. "No. No showering. You smell like me. If you wash that off, I'll have no choice but to replace it." Fighting the urge not to sprint to the bathroom, I crank my neck back to face him. His stare slicks my panties with moisture, but it also has my knees knocking together in a non-sexual way. "You don't want that, Roxanne. Not only are you drunk, I had three body bags to fill tonight. I didn't even manage one. Now is *not* the time to test my patience."

Hearing nothing but honesty in his tone, I slip between the sheets, roll onto my side, then inconspicuously wiggle to his half of the mattress until the heat of his torso warms my back. I'm not close enough to be accused of spooning, however I do feel his battering breaths hitting the back of my neck for the next several minutes. He's as unhinged as me, and the irrefutable proof has me acting recklessly.

"Why do we sleep in the same bed every night? Your compound has heaps of rooms, but we always share the same one." I could pretend his low, shallow breaths are because he's sleeping, but I'm done playing stupid. "Is it because you want to protect me like you do Fien?" When his big inhale forces contact between us, my heart sinks into my stomach. "If you're here because you think I need saving, you're wrong."

"Stop it."

His warning growl does little to lessen the intensity of the fire brewing in my gut. Not even half a bottle of vodka could douse it, so I don't see anything working. "My father didn't hurt me. Well, not physically, so if you're thinking I'm your penance to get Fien back sooner, you're wrong."

"I'm not going to ask you again, Roxanne. Stop. It!"

I can't stop. Once my lips get flapping, there's no reeling them back in. "Most people assume I have daddy issues, and you'd be the best person to unkink them, but that isn't why I'm here."

"For fuck's sake, will you shut up!"

"I don't need saving. I was doing fine on my own. I was a little lonely and somewhat unsure what I was going to do next, but—"

"Goddammit, Roxanne." In less than a second, I'm pulled onto my back, pinned on the mattress by Dimitri's large frame, and incredibly turned on. "You're not here because I want to save you with the hope a good deed will free my daughter. You're in my bed because I want to do the exact opposite. I want to devour you. Fuck you. Possess you so bad, the next time you have a gun pressed to your mother's head, you won't think about pulling the trigger, you'll do it. I want to mark every inch of you until the thoughts of what Rimi would have done to you if Audrey hadn't taken your place leave my head. Then I want to punish you some more for making me doubt who he should have taken."

His dangerous eyes dance between mine when he asks, "Do you have any idea the guilt associated with how you make me feel? The angst of wondering why I'm glad they took my wife instead of you. You were a fucking stranger, a goth standing on the corner undeserving of my time, but every single time I've prayed to go back and switch you with Audrey, I prayed just as quickly for that prayer not to be answered. She was carrying my daughter, my flesh and blood, yet I still couldn't put her first." It feels like my heart is torn out of my chest cavity when he adds, "So the next time you feel the need to ask why we sleep in the same bed, perhaps first consider the fact even someone as heartless as me can recognize that he doesn't deserve to get his daughter back, so he has no reason to save anyone, let alone someone who doesn't need saving."

With his jaw tight and words spoken he can never take back, he springs up from the bed without so much of a strain on his face before he stalks to the door.

His long strides are cut in half when I gabble out, "You should have killed them, then I'd stop looking at you the way you hate, and you wouldn't feel guilty about something you can't control."

Nothing but my shocked breaths are heard when he replies, "Why do you think I held back?"

Stealing my chance to reply, he walks out the door, slamming it behind him.

# 4

## ROXANNE

My blurry eyes lift to Rocco when he joins Smith and me in the lead SUV of Dimitri's fleet of four. The brutal slam of his door adds to the thunderous thump of my head, but it has nothing on the worry that bombards me when Dimitri fails to follow his trek.

We've been waiting almost twenty minutes, ten minutes over the time Dimitri demanded for everyone to be here this morning. We're not behind schedule because of Rocco. He only left the car in search of Dimitri.

"Where is he?" I ask, put off by the silence even with my hangover relishing it. Smith isn't much of a talker, but when he's paired up with Rocco, a girl can hardly get a word in. "I thought our flight left at eight?"

Rocco shrugs. "It does, but I don't know where he is."

I shoot my eyes to Smith. He can't brush off my inquisitiveness as easily as Rocco. He knows the insides of a monkey's butt.

When my glare becomes too much for Smith to bear, he gabbles out, "He told me he didn't want to be disturbed."

"So," I snap back with a grimace. "This isn't a standard day. It's important." From what I gathered from eavesdropping on Rocco and Smith's conversation the past forty minutes, our arrival at Hopeton this morning will be quickly followed by a trip to my family ranch. If it's the dumping ground Audrey was taken to, we'll know by the end of today.

"He only requests not to be disturbed when he needs a few hours away from the hell-hole he's been living in the past two years. If he doesn't take a breather, Roxie, he'll crack." Rocco intertwines his tattooed fingers. "This is only his second timeout since Fien was taken. The first was the night you wined and dined his guests."

"The night you took me to his office?" I'm not stupid, I can feel the nervy edge pumping out of Rocco, but I want to get my facts straight before I exert myself in a way I've never done before.

When Rocco lifts his chin, I lock my eyes with Smith's. "Find him." I hold my finger in the air when he attempts a rebuttal. "Did that sound like I was asking?"

He smiles a full-toothed grin, loving my gall. However, he doesn't give in. "If I disturb him when he asked not to be, there'll be hell to pay."

"Will it be worse than the hell he's been living in the past two years?" I don't wait for him to answer me. I can see the truth in his eyes, smell it slicking his skin. "If he cracks it, I'll take the blame. I'm the reason he's AWOL, aren't I?"

Their lack of denial stabs tiny knives into my chest. Mercifully, they don't cause me to bleed out before I see Rocco give Smith the go-ahead in the corner of my eye.

"All right," Smith breathes out as he grabs his laptop bag from the floor of the Range Rover. "But I'm denying any knowledge of this when the proverbial shit hits the fan."

Not even two seconds later, his face screws up in shock. "He's not on-site."

He isn't the only one surprised. This compound was designed to ensure Dimitri's guests have everything they could possibly want. They don't need to leave for anything, so what possible reason could Dimitri have to abscond these four walls?

Too inquisitive to listen to the warning gurgles of my stomach, I lean over to Smith and Rocco's half of the cab, so I can peer at the monitor of Smith's laptop. A state-of-the-art tracking software program reveals Dimitri's phone was last pinged in an industrial estate way too sleazy looking for a man with a lot of cash to burn.

Ignoring the pang in my chest warning me that this is a bad idea, I instruct the driver to take us to the location Smith honed in on. When he places the address into the GPS's mainframe, it advises us that Frosty Kinks is two point four miles from the airstrip we were supposed to arrive at ten minutes ago. It also highlights the services we could obtain once we arrive. They all point toward one field—the adult entertainment industry.

When the wheels on the SUV start churning over the miles, I sink back into my chair before connecting my eyes with Rocco's. "When did you last talk to him?"

He shakes his head at the accusation in my eyes, wordlessly advising me he had no clue Dimitri was at a strip club, much less the fight we had before he went there. "Last time I saw him, he was with you."

Smith raises his hands in the air like he's about to be arrested when my narrowed gaze snaps to him. "Same as Rocco. I had false admission papers to a rehab clinic to lodge. I didn't have time for snooping."

"So he went to a strip club by himself? Sure he did..."

My teeth grit when Rocco has the audacity to laugh. I don't know what the hell he thinks is funny. I'm anything but amused. "You're super cute when you are jealous, Princess P."

"Jealous? *Please.* I'm hungover and frustrated you dragged me out of bed for this." I'm such a liar. I could only be more jealous if I were green. Furthermore, I didn't sleep a wink last night. I was too busy pacing the room awaiting Dimitri's return. The only reason I stopped wearing a hole in the rug was because Rocco advised our transport was ready. I threw on clothes in under ten seconds and bolted outside, certain I was moments away from apologizing to Dimitri in person.

Alas, the only thing hearing my regrets this morning is my grumbling stomach.

Upon spotting the lie in my eyes, Rocco's grin doubles. "You still don't get it, do you?"

Too tired to lie, I shake my head.

My fast switchback to honesty doubles the smug grin on Rocco's face. "How many women do you think Dimitri slept with the week he found out Audrey was pregnant?"

"I don't want to know," I reply before I can stop myself. Just considering the many ways Fien could have been conceived has me all types of jealous. I don't need more insanity added to the mix.

Although Rocco's lips remain tightly locked, the gleam in his eyes tells me it's a number I don't want acknowledged. It makes my stomach swirl with more intensity than my wish to fall into a drunken stupor last night. I feel seconds from barfing.

Eager to test the durability of my stomach, Rocco asks, "How many women do you think he's slept with since you arrived on the scene?"

My words are barely audible through my clenched teeth. "If you say more than one, you better hope your gun isn't loaded, or I may blow someone's brains out."

I don't know whether to gleam or cry when Rocco's boisterous laugh vibrates through my chest. It doubles the thump in my head while adding to the twists of my vodka-sloshed stomach. "Chick,

chick boom! That's *exactly* what I'm talking about. You're so fucking under, even with the blood of your mommy on the cuff of his shirt, you still wanted to take his dick between your lips."

His chuckled words are like a cold, hard slap to the face. They bring me back to reality even more than the jab my heart was just hit with. "He tortured my parents."

"To save you being buried in the same ditch his wife is most likely in." As quickly as Rocco's laughter arrived, it vanishes. "Why do you think he didn't kill them?"

Although I know the answer, I'd rather he spell it out for me, so instead of nodding, I shrug instead.

"Because the man is snowballing for you. You've got him so twisted up, he doesn't know which end is up and which end is down. He's got guilt by the bucketloads, remorse that won't quit even when he works to the bone for twenty-four hours a day, and a hard-on for you that stays firm no matter how much you piss him off... but he has no clue how to deal with any of it. He thinks that by giving you an hour, he's taking an hour from Fien, so imagine how fucked-up he feels when he realizes he wants to give you more than an hour." He scoots to the edge of his seat before tapping his tattooed index finger on my knee. "He wasn't like this with his wife. He didn't beat her father because he hurt her or offer mercy to her mother to save her from being hurt. He didn't care about her enough to even ask if she'd been hurt. That should say something, and it should have you playing on the same team."

Although I agree with him, there's one part of his statement I can't fix. "I can't ease his guilt, Rocco."

He brushes off the genuine concern in my voice as if it's fake. "Yeah, you can. You've just got to stop thinking you need to save him. He doesn't need saving. And neither do you." He lets out a chuckle. Even only knowing him for days, I know it isn't his real laugh. "You can't save someone who's drowning if you don't know how to swim."

My chance to reply is lost when the driver pulls in to the curb at the front of Frosty Kinks. As the 3D imagery on Smith's computer showed, it's a seedy, low-grade establishment that would have lost clientele when they stopped accepting pennies.

Rocco throws open his door before locking his eyes with mine. "Wait here with Smith, I'll be back in a minute."

"No," I reply while shaking my head. "I can't learn to swim if I'm not willing to jump into the deep end." After scooting across the bench seat and slipping out onto the sidewalk, I shift my focus to Smith. "Call the airstrip and advise them we're on our way. Offer them an incentive to ensure our time slot is held. If snow arrives early, our fastest transport home will take days. Dimitri will never forgive himself if his first slip-up in years delays the search for Fien for days, even if the weather is to blame."

"Now she gets it," Rocco says with a smile as he slings his arm around my shoulders. "Now bring that bat to the game, so we can knock some sense into this neanderthal before he crawls into his cave for another long hibernation."

# 5

## DIMITRI

As I make my way through the dimly lit space that gets shadier for every tanked step I take, I scan my eyes over the flurry of women vying for my attention. I'm drugged-out on the good shit I usually reserve for 'guests,' too drunk to feel my legs, and I'm reasonably sure I look like a pimp since I switched out my suit for a pair of gray sweatpants and a black baseball jacket, but the women lining the walls of the back room at Frosty Kinks still look at me like I'm a god.

Although the outside of this establishment is as shoddy as hell, I'm reasonably sure I'm not the only high-end john they cater for. No one pays attention to the packaging when ordering a steak to devour. It's all about the quality. The women eyeing me with hungry, wanton gazes aren't as high-class as the ones who prance around my compounds, but they've definitely piqued the interest of my cock. He's almost at half-mast. Another line of coke should see him reluctantly joining the party.

He's pissed at me, frustrated I won't let him finish what he started two nights ago. He's not the only one annoyed, but since

I'm miles from my compound, spaced out of my brain, I'll keep that story for another day.

Right now, nothing but forgetting my pathetic life for a few hours is on my mind. I've snorted the drugs and sculled the whiskey, now I just need a plump set of lips to seal the deal.

When I spot a woman who matches the one who won't leave my fucking head, I stumble to her half of the room. The bottle I chugged down in the dusty lot has finally reached my veins, meaning it isn't just my footing that's a little unsteady, so are my words. "How much?"

She bats her fake lashes, ignorant to the fact I'm already sold on what she's selling. "For you, I'll work for free."

"How much?" I repeat, shouting. I'm not seeking a relationship, commitment, or any of those other fucked-up things women seem to think they'll get from a casual hook-up. I want my dick sucked, and I'm willing to pay for the privilege.

When the blonde spots her competition hovering close, she pushes out, "Five hundred." Her fee is much less than I expected to pay. I would have forked out five thousand if that's what she requested.

After pulling my wallet out of the pocket in my sweats, I toss a handful of hundred-dollar bills onto the floor before pivoting on my feet and making my way to the room the manager of Frosty Kinks set up especially for me. I rarely branch outside of my industry for services like this. However, his respect won't go unnoticed. His girls will give my guests a pleasing array of new faces next month.

Because the blonde had to collect her earnings from the floor, it takes her a couple of seconds to join me in a pod similar to the one I spanked Roxanne in days ago. Just recalling the heat of her skin when my palm connected with her ass has my cock rising to the occasion. I'm almost as thick as I was when I stuck my dick in her for the first time, although nowhere near as firm.

Even fucked out of my head, my words still crack out of my mouth like a whip. "Close the door."

The blonde shudders from my roar before doing as instructed. My family name doesn't have the notoriety it once had, but my reputation is well known. I don't want my desperateness to get a feisty bleach-blonde with gleaming green eyes out of my head circulated amongst my enemies. Those fuckers are already riding my ass. I can't give them more fuel.

Pissed, my next lot of demands are almost abusive. "Remove your skirt and bra but leave your panties on." I don't want her for her cunt. I want her for her lush green eyes and fuckable lips. "Once you're done, get on your knees."

Disappointment makes itself known with my gut when the removal of her skirt reveals her sheer panties. I can see her cunt through the scant material. She's a natural blonde. The knowledge will make it harder for me to pull off my ruse, but I'm so desperate to lose myself for a couple of hours, I'm willing to give it a shot.

When she lowers herself onto her knees, I pull her hair back into a low ponytail, then wrap the glossy locks around my fist. She may be about to suck my dick, but I'll maintain all the control. One blonde has already caused me to lose my cool tonight. It won't happen again.

"Slower," I demand when she tugs on the waistband of my sweatpants with too much eagerness. I want her fumbling like she doesn't know what she's doing, somewhat naïve. I want to pretend she's Roxanne for just a minute.

"That's better," I growl on a moan when she lifts her eyes to mine while sliding the elastic waistband over the bulge in my pants with painstaking slowness. Her eyes are a shade darker than

Roxanne's, but my coked-up head has a good imagination. "Take it out."

When her hands move to the waistband of my trunks, I scrub my thumb along her jaw, preparing it for the exhaustive activity it's about to undertake. This occasion has been on the backburner for months. It won't be a done-and-dusted event.

The hooker's submissiveness is hardening my cock, but it has nothing on the raging boner I get when the door of our private suite shoots open, and Roxanne steps into the sex-scented space.

## 6

# ROXANNE

Tension hisses in the air when my eyes bounce between Dimitri's naked backside propped against a sturdy desk and a virtually naked blonde on her knees in front of him. She has his erect cock in her hand, and her red-painted lips are narrowing in on the bead of precum on the top. Not even my unexpected interruption has the bitch taking her eyes off her target. Her mark is locked and loaded, and she isn't giving him up for anything.

*Like fucking hell she isn't.*

Acting as if I'm double my height and weight, I scoop up the blonde's clothes that are barely scraps of material from the floor, march across the room, then drag her away from Dimitri by the strands of her pretty little head. Her squeal at her hair being wretched out of her scalp has my heart falling from my chest, but it does little to slow me down. My anger arrived with barely a second to spare. Her mouth was a mere hair's breadth from Dimitri's cock. She was a second from tasting him how I never have.

That's unacceptable.

"Get out." I thrust her clothes into her silicon-filled chest before nudging my head to the door, my orders delivered with a vicious glare.

"Rox—"

"Don't!" My nostrils flare as my squinted gaze shifts to Dimitri. Since the blonde is still on her knees, his erection is almost gouging her eyes out, and the blood of my father is still on his neck. Now is *not* the time for him to test me. And don't get me started on how intoxicated this man is. Dimitri isn't leaning against the desk for no reason. He can barely stand, for crying out loud. Payment or not, the blonde is more fucked in the head than my mother if she thinks this is acceptable.

"You have a plane to catch." I return my eyes to the blonde staring at me with a smidge of shock and a bucketload of annoyance. "*We* have a plane to catch." My words are possessive and brimming with unwarranted jealousy. They rip the blonde's heart out of her chest as effectively as mine was removed when the horrendous thoughts bombarding me during my search of Frosty Kinks came true. Although I'm confident she only felt the weight of Dimitri's cock, who's to say that would have still been the case if my hunt was delayed by a measly two seconds.

The thought alone has me the most furious I've ever been.

"Leave before I show you what happens when you touch something you don't own."

Hearing my threat exactly how I intended, the blonde stammers out, "I didn't know he was take—"

"Go!" My roar kickstarts both her heart and her feet. She scampers up from her knees before making a dash for the door, her brisk exit faltered by Rocco entering from the other side.

He works his jaw side to side while taking in Dimitri's slouched frame. He's so far down the rabbit warren, he can barely hold up his head.

"Help me." My tone is lower than the one I used on the hooker, but Rocco acts as if it was just as stabby. He steps back with his hands held in the air and an arrogant grin on his face.

I discover the reason behind his lack of assistance when he chuckles out, "I ain't helping you while his dick is hanging out. We're tight, but we're not *that* tight."

Before I can issue a single scold bubbling in my chest, a much more dangerous situation unfolds. Dimitri hasn't noticed we have company. While his cock thickens to the point it must be painful, he scrubs the back of his fingers across my ruddy lips. "I bet your mouth tastes like candy." Only now does it dawn on me that we've never kissed. He's gone down on me, blew his load on my chest, and been inside of me like no other man ever has, but we've never kissed. "Your cunt is as sweet as candy, so I bet your lips are too."

While dropping one hand to his cock to squeeze it, he weaves the other one through my hair. It feels like time stands still when he drags my lips to within an inch of his. The man I can't stop thinking about is right here, directly in front of me, but for the life of me, I can't act on the impulses burning me alive.

I'd give anything to forget everything that has happened the past few days, but I can't. If I do that, I not only break a pledge I made to Dimitri about not taking more time than he can give me, I'll also break the promise I made to Fien in the wee hours of this morning.

Dimitri is all she has.

I can't steal the focus away from her for even one second.

With my mind made up, I tug on Dimitri's sweats as roughly as I did the blonde's hair to guide them back up his thighs.

"Don't put my cock away." As he struggles to hold back his grin, he drags his teeth over his lower lip. The strong scent of whiskey exuding from his mouth shouldn't make it seem sexy, but it does. "He's been dying for this for months. Don't leave him hanging."

I'm unsure if it's lust or anger deepening my voice when I reply, "We have company."

I assume my confession will have him falling in line. I soon discover I have a lot to learn about this man.

With two clicks of his fingers, Rocco slips out the door, closing it behind him. "Now, we don't. We have all the time and privacy we need."

Dimitri's growl when I step back doubles the damp slickness between my legs, but like many times in the past, I don't put myself first. "If we don't leave now, our flight will be rescheduled. I don't know about you, but I have a heap of questions I need answered. Answers I can only get in Erkinsvale."

That seems to sober him up a bit. "Erkinsvale?"

I nod before stepping back into the ring, gloved-up and hopeful the drugs running through his system will only last as long as our flight home. "I know you're tired, and you are probably sick to death of playing with the hand you've been dealt, but we're so close, Dimitri, the end is right there. It would be ludicrous for us to give up now."

Once again, my voice is more possessive than it should be, but then again, I don't care. So many of Dimitri's actions make sense now. The shift of the blame. His inability to give himself a single moment of reprieve. The remorse in his eyes when I stepped into this room. He's holding on by a thread, and my presence the past week made it the thinnest it's ever been.

That has to stop. I'm already responsible for him losing his daughter. I refuse to be the reason he loses everything.

"Let me help you, Dimitri. Please."

The crackling of energy that forever teems between us doubles its output when he runs his fingers across my mouth for the second time. His eyes are as bleak as my father's when he went on a bender. I'm not even sure he's entirely here, but it feels as if the world shifts beneath my feet when he dips his chin for the quickest second.

Stealing his chance to change his mind, I dart for the locked door to let Rocco back in. He has his back braced on the outer wall of the room Dimitri was found in, either disinterested in the theatrics of a strip club or more concerned about Dimitri than he's letting on.

I realize it's the latter when his eyes swing my way. He's quick to shut down the concern in them, but not quick enough for this sly fox. "Done already? I'll have to show the old guy some new tricks."

He laughs when I roll my eyes before he joins me inside the room reeking of desperation for a second chance. The humor on his face vanishes when his eyes follow mine to Dimitri. He's no longer balancing on the desk. He's slumped on the floor, out cold.

I didn't realize Dimitri's team followed us to Frosty Kinks until Rocco says, "Send Clover in." Past incidents advise me he's talking to Smith. The knowledge our every move is being monitored doesn't lessen the knot in my gut when Rocco checks Dimitri for a pulse, though. "It's weak but there. Trace back footage so we can get a better idea of what he's taken." Rocco lifts his eyes to mine. "Did he mention anything to you?"

I shake my head, too stunned to talk.

Clover barrels into the room just as Rocco rips up the sleeves of Dimitri's jacket. He's checking for track marks. How do I know this? My mother did the same thing to my father anytime he returned home from an all-night bender. "There are no needle marks to indicate he shot up, so I'd say his drug of choice was coke."

"Is this how he usually responds to drugs?" With fear clutching my throat, my words are as weak as the vein fluttering through the tattoos on Dimitri's neck.

Air whizzes out of Rocco's nose before he shakes his head. "But it's been a while since he's used." He drifts his eyes to Clover. "Help me get him up. We'll take him back to the compound so Ollie can take a look at him."

"No." Rocco responds to the snapped command in my tone. Clover acts as if I'm not in the room. "Take him to the airstrip as planned."

The strain of holding up a man as large as Dimitri is heard in Rocco's voice when he says, "If he's ODing, we can't help him thirty thousand feet in the air."

"We can't, but Ollie can. Make him come with us."

Rocco takes a minute to consider my suggestion. It adds even more tension to his face. "I know you're trying to help, Roxie—"

"This isn't about helping. It's about doing what Dimitri would want us to do. If you go back to the compound, we won't be able to fly out until tomorrow at the earliest, and that's only if forecasters are wrong. Take him to the airstrip, have Ollie meet us there. I'll pay him with my maxed-out credit card if you're worried about the fucking bill." I grit my teeth when my last four words come out with a sob. I'm panicked out of my mind for Dimitri, but I also know this is the right thing to do. "Please, Rocco. You want me in the deep end, but you're refusing to let me jump." When his eyes stray to Clover, my panic is showcased in the worst light. "Don't ask his opinion. He's paid to be here. We're not."

Although Clover *tsks* me, my scorn rolls straight off his back. He knows I'm no better than him as only days ago he heard me offer myself to Dimitri for a little bit of coin.

I don't have a tiny bead-like device in my ear like Rocco, but it's clear Smith is on my side when the strain on Rocco's face clears in an instant. "If this backfires—"

"It won't," I reply, issuing him a promise I have no right to issue. "I swear to God, everything will work out."

With his brows hanging as low as Dimitri's head, Rocco jerks up his chin before shifting half of Dimitri's lifeless weight onto Clover's shoulders. "Tell Ollie I'll pay him double if he beats us to the jet."

# 7

# DIMITRI

While swishing my tongue around my bone-dry mouth, I hesitantly open my eyes. The dream I was having was intoxicating until Roxanne was ripped from my grasp as cruelly as Fien was removed from her mother's stomach. Being thrust out of a nightmare so brutally has me feeling like death warmed over, although I'm skeptical not all the thump of my pulse is compliments to my rude awakening. My head is thumping as if I drowned in a bath of whiskey. My skin is patchy and dry, and my cock is acting as if the first half of my dream is all that matters.

I shouldn't be shocked. He doesn't give a fuck if it will riddle me with guilt for eternity. If he wants it, he's there with bells on—no matter the consequence. He's the sole reason I sought solace outside of my compound last night. If I didn't do something to calm the beast, he would have had me taking my anger out on Roxanne.

Although she's deserving of the wrath, for some fucked-up reason, I can't hurt her any more than she's already been hurt. I couldn't even pop a bullet between her mother's brows, for fuck's sake. Her eyes are too similar to Roxanne's. They seared through me until my fried brain had me confusing her for Roxanne. It's lucky in a way. If she hadn't issued her mercy, I doubt anything I could have said would have brought Roxanne out of her panic attack last night. She was drowning in filth years in the making, being suffocated by the very people who should have kept her safe.

She was Fien twenty years from now.

Ignoring the begs of my throbbing head, I raise to a half-seated position. I'm stunned when my awakening occurs without the grumbles of a needy redhead who accepts money for the privilege of occupying my bed, though it has nothing on my surprise when the familiarity of the room smacks into me. I'm not at a seedy strip club hidden away, so townies won't get busted by their preacher attending a show, nor am I at my New York compound. I'm home, in my bed, and the faintest trickle of a shower is heard in the distance.

"Smith..." My voice is swallowed by a husky cough. I'm so fucking dry you wouldn't think there's an IV line inserted in my arm.

*What the fuck?*

"Smith."

My eyes shoot to the side when Smith's grumbly tone booms through my ears. "I heard you the first time. There's no need to shout." Instead of his voice projecting from the speakers implanted throughout every room of my house, it comes from the reading nook in the corner of the large space. From his setup, anyone would swear he works out of the office in my room instead of his computerized hub.

After shutting his laptop screen, he paces around his desk. Worry is seen all over his face when he whispers, "I'll tell him."

Confident his words aren't for me, I wait for him to join me at my beside before asking the obvious. "What happened?"

"You—"

"If you're about to say I overdosed, you need to go back to the fucking drawing board and start again. I snorted a few lines of coke and drunk a little too much whiskey, but that's nowhere near enough to make me pass out for hours on end."

"Days." He angles his watch so I can see the date stamped on the top. If he isn't messing with my head, which would be very unlike him, I've been out cold for three days—three whole motherfucking days. "Although Ollie believes part of your condition was from exhaustion, blood work-ups showed you had GHB in your system. The high reading indicated whoever slipped it in your drink didn't do it to maim. They wanted you dead."

With my blood hot and my wish to kill the highest it's ever been, I rip out the IV tubing from my arm and stand from my bed. I'm mortified when I realize the tubing in my arm isn't the only one attached to my body. There's another one near my cock. Mercifully, it's taped over my manhood instead of being shoved inside of it.

After ripping off the second tubing more gently than I did the IV, I snatch a pair of gray sweatpants from the floor next to my bed, then shove my feet inside of them. "I'm going to kill the fucker who messed with me, and I'm going to do it slowly."

I stop considering the many ways I can kill a man when Smith says, "You're too late. Most of the culprits are already dead." He tosses a manilla folder onto my bed. When it bounces off the springy mattress, several glossy photographs fall out. They show Frosty Kinks was burned to the ground. Not even its trademark red Louboutin billboard remains. It's as black as ash.

My eyes float up to Smith's when he says, "When Rocco found you passed out, he asked me to trace your movements. Frosty's surveillance was shit, but I worked it for all its worth." He shuffles through the still images until he finds one of a man with a round stomach and a bald head. Although my head is still a little hazy, I think he's the bartender who served me most of the night. "That's Jake Warsaw, co-owner of Frosty's. He has no priors and isn't up to his ears in debt like most people in his field, leading us to believe this wasn't the first time he's done something like this." His groan is as loud as mine. "Clover and Rocco worked him over good, but he didn't give up any juice."

His smirk tells me he would have unearthed his mark even without the force Rocco and Clover love to utilize. I do too, but that's a story for when I'm not stunned like a mullet.

"Who paid him?"

The crunch of my teeth is heard over my growl when he tosses a second photograph onto the stack. Even with us only meeting once, I know this man very well. He wanted Roxanne so badly, he was willing to pay more than triple what his competitors were offering. He also called on the hour every hour for the twelve hours following her auction, demanding to be updated on when bids would be finalized.

"I went through reams of footage obtained since the auction. Dr. Bates spent more time in his car outside the compound than he did his hotel room the days following Roxie's auction." Smith locks his eyes with mine. For a guy who's usually as cool as ice, he looks extremely worked up. "He only left when he followed you to Frosty's."

Although jealousy is a perfect motive, I feel there's something more at play here than a man being pipped at the post. I'm just praying Rocco and Smith felt the same vibe as me, or I'll be left with more questions than answers.

After working my throat through a stern swallow, I ask, "Is Bates dead?"

For the first time in a long time, I feel lucky when Smith shakes his head. It grows tenfold when he adds words to his confirmation. "Roxie asked us to hold back on his punishment. She wants to discuss an idea with you before bringing him before the courts."

"Roxanne?" I could add to my query, but I don't need to. Smith can see my shock. He doesn't need it voiced.

"She's been running things around here." His smile is way too fucking blinding for my thumping skull. "With guidance from Rocco and me, of course."

He walks to my desk to gather up his laptop. Once he has it fired up, he shows me the many angles they've been working the past three days. The reports are so impressive, they have me worried I've been out a lot longer. Not only is Dr. Bates's office wired to the hilt with state-of-the-art equipment, he has a month's worth of work on display.

"For now, Roxie's grandparents' estate is a dead end. There were a handful of biochemicals there, but it was mainly placentas, fetal matter, and the occasional soiled mattress. No bodies were located." He sounds as disappointed as I feel. "Some good came from the search, though. We unearthed a set of records in the rubble. They date back years before Audrey was taken. I'm not sure of their significance yet, but I'm working a few angles." He waits for me to jerk up my chin before he hits me with the mother-lode. "We also found Roberto."

"Dead or alive?" I don't know why I asked my question. If he's not dead, he will soon be wishing he was. I had barely gotten over Ophelia's death when he disappeared, and his vanishing act sliced my siblings from four to nothing in an instant.

I take a step back when Smith says, "Alive." When he clicks on the keyboard of his laptop two times, an image of a much older and rounder Roberto fills the screen. If you exclude the dirty apron stretched across his midsection and his unnoteworthy strut, his identity could never be discounted. The Petretti genes are strong.

"Il Lido," I stammer out, testing the name on my lips. "I swear I've heard of that restaurant."

Smith nods before he opens up a secondary screen. It reveals that Il Lido is an Italian restaurant in New York. It's owned by none other than Mr. Isaac Holt.

My next question is barely heard since my words are ground through my clenched jaw. "Why is Roberto working as a dish hand for Isaac?"

The worry blazing through Smith's eyes tells me I won't like the answer to his question, but he gives it to me anyway.

I'm an unforgiving, malicious man, however even I have a hard time stomaching the image of my eldest brother huddled on the floor, tearing his hair out as efficiently as the tears streaming down his face tear my heart out. He's completely undone, wholly destroyed by the horrid world we were born into.

Once the footage ends, Smith brings up several news clippings on the death of a Rochdale woman. She was struck by a drunk driver, killing both her and her unborn son. Although the reports don't say Roberto is responsible, my heart knows that's the case. He was a drunk longer than he was a man.

Can you blame him? He was our father's firstborn son. He didn't just have the world on his shoulders. He had our entire legacy as I do now.

"How is he living?"

Smith gives me a halfhearted shrug. "It's not close to luxurious, but he's comfortable."

"Like CJ?"

His second shrug is nowhere near as willy-nilly as his first one. "Similar. He just works for what he has instead of his little brother handing it to him." His underhanded ribbing isn't to maim, he's just stating things as he sees them. CJ does nothing for his money. He merely waits for me to deposit a check every month. "We can fix that if you want?"

I take a moment to deliberate before shaking my head. "If Roberto stayed hidden this long, he wants to remain hidden." My brows join when an ill-timed grin crosses Smith's face. Unlike Rocco, he knows the right time to express himself. Now isn't the right time. "What?"

"Nothing." He places down his laptop and fiddles with some papers on my desk like he can't feel my scorning wrath burning a hole in the back of his head.

"Smith—"

"It's nothing, I swear." When I growl, he squawks like a canary. "Roxanne said the same thing. It's kinda cute how you two are synced like that." He steals my chance to respond to his ridiculous statement by gathering up his stuff and making a beeline for the door.

Since he believes he's seconds from safety, he gets on my last nerve. "Rocco wanted me to tell you he only kept Roxanne's sheets warm for two out of the three nights you were out cold."

Not thinking, I pick up the stapler on my desk and peg it at his head. It smacks into the drywall a mere second after his head darts past it. Although he's sprinting down the corridor like I'm hot on his tail, I hear his chuckles as if he's standing next to me. He isn't laughing loudly. His voice is being projected through the speakers above my head.

He should count his lucky stars his breathless chuckles remind me that I'm anal about security, or my next aim would have included a bullet.

After ensuring my door is closed, I grab my tablet off my desk and log into the security app Smith installed months ago. With

Smith's disclosure at the forefront of my mind, I drag the timeline back to three days ago. I still feel like shit, and my brain is pounding like drummers are going to war between my ears, but this can't wait. I haven't been out of the loop this long in years. I'd hate to think about what I've missed.

*Yeah, right.* If you believe that, you need therapy even more than me. All I care about is discounting Rocco's claim he kept Roxanne occupied the past three nights. Considering everything that's happened, it should be the last thing on my mind. Regretfully, the unknown can send the most stable man insane. Why do you think I went off the rails? Staying one step ahead of the game is exhausting, but it has nothing on the tiredness you feel when you're forever chasing your tail.

I stop the footage just as Ollie requests privacy to make sure I don't piss the bed. His demand sees Rocco dragging Roxanne to the far corner of the somber space for a chat. It's clear from the strain on their faces that their conversation isn't flirty, much less what Roxanne says next, "If that's what Dimitri would do, do that. Burn it down." Although Rocco's voice is too low for me to pick up, Roxanne keeps me in the gist. "I won't let anything happen to him. Ollie agreed to stay until he's awake, and I won't leave this room. I swear, Rocco, I won't cause any trouble." After a few seconds of deliberation, Rocco agrees to her request with the slightest lift of his chin. "Thank you."

My jaw tightens when Roxanne rubs her hand down Rocco's arm in a comforting manner, but it clears when her return to my side of the room sees Rocco requesting a minute with Smith. "Keep this place on tight lockdown. As far as anyone is concerned, Dimitri and Roxie are still in New York. We don't want any unexpected visitors." He doesn't say my father's name, but I know that's who he's referencing because nothing but disgust is seen on his face whenever he talks about my father.

They discuss protocol for a few more minutes before Rocco leaves the room. Within minutes of him doing so, Smith sets up a command station on my desk, where he stays for the next three days. Roxanne also doesn't move from this spot. She floats between the couch across from my desk and my bed during the day before spending the entire night in bed, with me, where she belongs.

It's the fight of my life not to jump out of my skin when Smith's voice suddenly booms through the speaker of my tablet. "She's real smart, you know. She organized the search of her grandparents' estate, unearthed Roberto's whereabouts, and coordinated the events for your guests Friday night all from the room you're standing in." The creak of his office chair sounds down the line a second before his snarky comment, "Imagine what she could achieve if you'd let go of the reins just a little?"

Either panicked he's about to be hit with my wrath, or confident he has no reason to fret since he smacked the nail on the head, he disconnects our feed just as the shower faucet in the bathroom switches off.

# 8

# ROXANNE

After sliding my drenched arms into my dressing gown, I twist my hair until it's held off my face by a low-riding knot, then pace to the vanity mirror. I'm still not a diva, but the gold-leaf framed mirror is housing more condensation than usual. I had the faucet at the highest setting, hopeful a good dose of scorching water would conceal the red marks my cheeks have been wearing the past three days.

I understand Dimitri is exhausted and am aware he had enough drugs in his system to kill him, but I wish he'd wake up. There's so much going on right now, I feel like my head is about to explode. Someone tried to end Dimitri's life, the brother he believes is dead isn't, and I've lost the ability to look at my grandparents' property with anything but disgust.

Although the hundreds of men who scoured every inch of the mostly unused land didn't find any bodies, there was enough evidence to expose my parents were a part of the baby-farming industry.

Just the thought they'd stoop that low makes me sick to my

stomach. The terror is holding on firmly, and there's no end in sight. I don't know how much longer I can continue like this. Good deeds are meant to be rewarded. That doesn't seem to be the case with the Cartel. The more you try to better yourself, the harder your competitors work to drag you down.

Just like me, Dimitri can't even rely on his family. Smith guards his secrets as if his life depends on them, but it doesn't take a genius to realize Dimitri's father is being as closely monitored as Dimitri's enemies. I doubt Rocco would have gone back to New York with Clover to persecute the men who drugged Dimitri if Col's whereabouts weren't being constantly scrutinized. The fact Col is far from here is the *only* reason Rocco has riled Dimitri via the speaker above his head instead of in person.

My sly grin doubles when I catch sight of it in the mirror. I shouldn't like the way Dimitri stirred every time Rocco picked on him, but I did. Only a heartless man fails to respond when teased. Dimitri isn't one of them. He's paying for my mother's rehabilitation out of his own pocket, and he didn't hold back on the purse strings, either. She's surrounded by celebrities and beginning to feel as remorseful as me.

I'm honestly unsure where we'll go from here. Sorrow can't take back all the horrendous things she's done, but with how far down the rabbit hole she is, I won't need to consider the next step for a while.

Once I have my game face back on, I make my way into the main part of the room. "Have you had any word from Rocco this afternoon? His silence is a little off-putting..." My words trail off, gobbled up by the shock roaring through me. Smith isn't seated behind Dimitri's desk. Dimitri is. He looks as dark and deadly as ever, but very much alive.

I've been accused of being a ditz a handful of times in my life. Today is the first time I'll agree with their assessment. I don't stand back and watch in awe that the man who was on his death bed only days ago is standing in front of me, appearing as strong as an ox. I race across the room as fast as my quivering legs will take me before throwing myself into his arms.

"Dimitri."

He startles from my unexpected affection, but as quickly as his shock arrives, it leaves. With his heart beating as erratically as mine, he pulls me into his chest as he did almost two weeks ago. This time, his shirt doesn't catch my tears, his tattooed chest does. I hate myself for blubbering like a baby, but boy, it feels good to finally release the hurt that's been eating me alive the past three days. I wasn't just upset someone tried to claim Dimitri's life, I was frustrated I was left alone to deal with feelings I've never handled before.

I jumped into the deep end as Rocco suggested, then I was left treading water for over seventy-two hours. Even an Olympic swimmer would struggle in those conditions. Since I was in waters way too deep, I should have drowned days ago. I probably would have if anger wasn't also keeping me afloat.

I've never wanted to hurt and comfort someone as much as I do right now. My emotions honestly don't know which way to swing. The last time they were this erratic, I fell asleep in Dimitri's arms, and he didn't speak to me for days.

I refuse to let that happen again. I don't care if he punishes me. I'd rather his punishment over another three days of painful silence.

After scrubbing my face to ensure I don't look like a total wreck, I peel my wet cheek off Dimitri's pec, then align my eyes with his. I startle when our eyes collide not even a second later. He's staring straight at me. His watch is heart-stuttering, but it's without an ounce of malice. His unusual mischievous gawk liberates me from the worry I'm about to overstep the mark. It allows me to talk freely for the first time in a long time. "I was worried you were never coming back. I thought I'd never see you again. Do you have any idea how panicked you made me?"

He's humored by my worry, but deep down inside, I also believe he appreciates it. "It'll take more than a little GHB to bring me down."

When he laughs, it's the fight of my life not to whack him in the stomach. I wouldn't hold back if I believed it was the only abuse he's endured in his life. "It's not funny. You could have been seriously hurt, then what would happen to Fien?"

That wipes the smile right off his face. He's as stunned now as he was when I threw myself in his arms. Even staying by his side twenty-four-seven the past three days doesn't have him believing I'm on his side. In his eyes, I'm still the enemy.

"I held a gun to my mother's head, then left her with you even on the belief you were going to kill her, yet you still think I'm the enemy. What can I do to prove I'm on your side, Dimitri? Sentence my mother to death for her crimes? Sell my virginity to the highest bidder? Take the place of your daughter? I'll do anything you want. Anything at all—"

My words are stopped in the most beautifully tormented way. Dimitri doesn't demand me to be quiet like he did when I went on a rant on how I'm not with him because I have daddy issues or cut me off with a cruel scorn.

He kisses me.

It isn't an all-encompassing kiss with teeth, lips, and tongues. He holds back a beat, so I have time to react to how I feel about being kissed by him. He isn't a nice man nor is he gentle, and he wants to ensure I know what I'm signing up for.

Even with his embrace being as innocent as a schoolyard peck, it sends fireworks exploding through me. It's sweet and blistering, and ten times better than I could have ever imagined.

When I moan into Dimitri's mouth, my body choosing its own response to the fiery blaze smoldering between us, he weaves his fingers through my hair like he did at Frosty Kinks before he adds a stack of wood to the fire in my gut. He explores my mouth with teasing bites, long licks, and breathy growls that have my temperature rising to a dangerous level.

I'm naked beneath my dressing gown, and Dimitri is only wearing a pair of sweatpants, but within seconds, it seems as if there are too many articles of clothing between us.

After uncinching the cord of my dressing gown, I shimmy my shoulders, aiding the static-loving material's fall to the floor. The waistband of Dimitri's pants come away just as easily.

His grunt when I circle my hand around his thick cock is desperate and loud. He wasn't lying when he said his cock has been waiting for this day for months. The heaviness of his impressive shaft is a sure-fire sign he was telling the truth, much less the sticky droplet of goodness on the tip.

I whine like a child when he pulls back a few seconds later. My fret is unfounded. He isn't ending our exchange before it truly begins, he's ensuring he is the sole investigator on if the light in my eyes changes like it did for my mother. He's keeping this exclusively between us.

He hits a button on the edge of his desk, curls my legs around his waist, then walks us across the room. His lips don't leave mine until the softness of bedding caresses my curves. After wedging his knee between my thighs that I'm trying in vain not to squeeze together, he drags his eyes up my body in a slow and dedicated sweep. When his eyes land on my face, the earth shifts beneath my feet. Just like his earlier watch, this one doesn't have an ounce of spite to it either. It's brimming with way too much yearning ever to be confused with a hatred response.

"Are you sure?"

His chivalry catches me by surprise, but it makes the nod of my head even more convincing. He could have taken what he wanted like he was raised to or tried to profit from me as my father did. Instead, he made it my choice. That makes the claws of his almost deceit nowhere near as painful to my heart.

"It will hurt, Roxanne." His comment seems to panic him more than me. "You're tiny—"

I cut him off by pulling him on top of me so I can reattach our lips. I kiss him how I've dreamed of kissing him since I saw him standing in the rain outside the alleyway. It's an urgent, hurried kiss, as impatient as the hand slithering between us to join our bodies in a way that's both personal and intimate.

"Fuck," Dimitri moans on a growl when he lines up his cock before he drives home, sheathing me with one quick thrust.

He was right. It does hurt, but it also feels right. I've always felt a little lost like I don't quite belong. I'm not experiencing that now. Fien is the cure to unlocking Dimitri's misery, but I could very well be the key to the cabinet holding the potion.

My hips jerk upward when our exchange goes further than our previous attempt. With his feet splayed to the width of his shoulders and his eyes locked on my overstuffed pussy, Dimitri circles the bundle of nerves between my legs with his thumb, bringing the pain ripping through me down from a ten to a seven.

"I need you wet for me, Roxie. If I pull out now, I'll fucking tear you. You're clutching me too tightly."

His unusual use of my nickname shocks me for a second. Not enough to stop me from hatching a wickedly intense plan, but enough to add a quiver to my voice. "Kiss me."

When his eyes lift to mine, certain he heard me wrong, the pain lowers by another notch. "What?"

"Kiss me," I repeat, smiling at the shock in his tone. "If you want me wet enough not to hurt me, kiss me."

I grunt in pain when my request causes him to notch another inch of his cock inside of me. I doubt he's all the way in, but I'm too in awe at how skillfully he kisses to worry about him never fully entering me.

Within ten seconds, I'm so caught up in our kiss, my clenched muscles relax.

Within twenty seconds, I'm kissing him as intensely as he's kissing me.

Within thirty seconds, the rock of our conjoined hips sees his cock moving in and out of me in rhythm with his explorative tongue. We're not close to fucking, but for how fast we got to this stage, I can see us reaching that peak remarkably quick.

"That's better," Dimitri says as he slants back so he can take in the sight of his cock pumping in and out of me. I don't need to peer down to know the evidence of my excitement is tinged with blood. The tangy scent in the air is evidence enough, much less Dimitri's increase in breaths. "But it could be better."

I feel excruciatingly empty when he suddenly withdraws before he requests my eyes to his. It's a void that's filled by a blinding climax when the collision of our eyes causes cum to erupt from Dimitri's cock. As my name tears from his throat, he coats my pussy with his spawn before he uses his still-erect cock to push the murky white substance inside of me.

He stuffs in two inches, pulls back out, swipes his engorged knot across my clit, then reenters with an extra inch. He continues doing this until the shudders making it seem as if I'm possessed, weakened to a shiver, and almost every inch of his impressive cock is inside of me.

As he rocks in and out of me, his speed increasing along with my moans, the ache of taking a man his size is notable. Although it's painful, it is a good ache, one I'm certain I'll crave time and time again.

"Lock your ankles around my back."

I immediately jump to his command. He's more experienced than me, and for now, I'm happy to use his skills to my advantage.

"Now, give me your eyes."

Pleasure overwhelms me when his cock throbs from the collision of our eyes. I'm being stretched beyond repair and am certain I'll be in pain for days after this, but the sensation roaring through me is unbelievable. My orgasm is coming hard and fast, but I want it right now. I'm barely grasping reality. I am too far down the rabbit hole to think about anything but my raging libido.

"More."

Dimitri spreads my thighs wider before he drives into me on repeat.

"Faster."

He grunts and hisses as he pushes me to the very brink of despair.

"Harder."

He fucks me like he's possessed. Pumping, grinding, and stroking every inch of me. His hands are swamping my tits, his pelvis is grinding into my clit, and his cock is commanding every inch of my pussy.

This is better than I could have ever imagined. Our fuck is raw and primal, but it's also brimming with emotions. We should be enemies who hate everything about each other. He hurt people I loved, killed others I didn't, and spanked me in a room full of spectators, yet, our bodies come together as if they've intimately known each other for years.

A sensation I've never experienced before gathers inside of me. It builds with every thrust of Dimitri's hips and each lively glint in his eyes. No one could accuse him of being dark and dangerous right now. There's too much light in his eyes—too much life.

When realization sinks in, a climax slams into me.

I'm responsible for the shift of color in his eyes.

*Me.*

As I grip the bedsheets in a white-knuckled hold, pleasure rolls through me unchecked. It hits me everywhere—my trembling thighs, my thrusting chest, my aching sex. It even hits my heart that's almost as full as my pussy.

Before I can put my ego in check, Dimitri withdraws, flips me over, then reenters me from behind. All I can do is scream. His change-up in position means he's more deeply seated than he was only minutes ago, and his thumb is pressing against a region of my body I'm unsure I want claimed by any man.

Within a few strokes, it dawns on me how unfamiliar I am with my body. Instead of repelling away from the thumb hovering above what I thought was a no-go zone, I'm arching up to it, wordlessly encouraging Dimitri to increase the pressure on my back entrance.

"Not yet." Dimitri moves his hand away from my puckered hole so he can spank my butt cheek instead. "You're too tight to take both my fingers and my cock." I'm already burning up everywhere from the fiery burn his hand caused to my ass, much less what he says next, "I can't wait to claim every inch of you, but we need to build you up to that. Once I've got your snug cunt customized to my dick, we'll switch to other parts of your body." His comment doesn't sound like he means tonight. He's talking days away, perhaps even weeks.

My muscles clench with greedy need, excited about the possibility of this lasting more than a night. The tight clasp of my vaginal walls around Dimitri's cock almost sets him off. The veins feeding his magnificent manhood throb as his poundings turn punishing. He fucks me with everything he has, not stopping until another blinding orgasm convinces my limbs that they're broken.

Even with my body refusing to play the game well, I ride my

orgasm out, shuddering and shivering while screaming Dimitri's name on repeat. His wondrously fat cock and multiple orgasms have created the perfect blend of pain and pleasure. I'm sore, delirious, and certain I'm on the brink of a coma, yet my body still craves more.

Defying legs that feel like Jell-O, I return to a kneeling position, roll my shoulders back, then meet Dimitri's pumps grind for grind. We go at it for several long minutes, pounding, grunting, and fucking like our intimate act isn't being shared with Dimitri's neighbors. I'm moaning loud enough for all of Hopeton to hear, but I don't care. This is too glorious for a half-assed response.

Dimitri demands my eyes to his when another orgasm creeps up on me. When he gets them, his hips still a mere second before his cock pulsates inside of me. The heat of his cum spurting out of his cock sends me spiraling again.

His name falls from my lips over and over as my orgasm zaps the last of my energy.

When I collapse into a heap, this time around, Dimitri comes with me. His large frame almost crushes me to death, but the rhythmic beat of his heart and the exhaustion overwhelming every inch of me soon lulls me to sleep.

I'm dead on my feet—figuratively.

Thank God.

# 9

# DIMITRI

My eyes lift to Smith when he has the audacity to snicker at me for the third time tonight. He isn't laughing because sleeping for seventy-two hours straight didn't stop me from catching a couple of hours of shut-eye with Roxanne after our romp. He's amused about the shock on my face.

He was as honest as a saint when he said Roxanne was smart. Not only did she keep my operation afloat when I was flat on my back, she improved it. She tidied up the books, found a discrepancy that will cost someone their life, then made a handful of tweaks to the Arabian events that will improve my profit margin by six percent if not more.

I'm fucking astonished, and my surprise has nothing to do with how well she fucks. I killed her boyfriend, taunted her father until he blew his brains out, then tortured her mother, yet instead of plotting my demise when I was at my weakest, she made me stronger.

The knowledge has my cock thickening like I'm not sitting across from key members of my crew, strategizing our next move.

Rules were broken, and although most of the rule-breakers have been brought before the court, the main players are still roaming free—most notably, Dr. Bates.

After adjusting my cock so my zipper stops biting it, I ask, "When is the good doctor expected back at the office?"

Even with him only returning from New York an hour ago, Rocco jumps into the conversation like he's kept tabs on proceedings while busting noses. "He was originally scheduled to return last Tuesday. However, Princess P piqued his interest too much for him to consider leaving."

He smirks when my teeth grit over his nickname. I don't need him to spell out who he's referencing. We've been friends for two decades, but we've been rivals even longer than that. It started with a video game every kid on our block played, and it continued long after Mario saved Princess Peach from the Mushroom Kingdom.

Rocco, along with nearly every other *Super Mario* fan, doesn't understand Bowser's character. He doesn't constantly attack the Mushroom Kingdom because he's evil. He wants to show Princess Peach she isn't a damsel in distress. She can kick ass as much as the rest of the characters. You've just got to push her buttons right.

*Kind of like Roxanne.*

My scowl switches to a smirk before I get back to business. "Now he's been told his bid was unsuccessful, did he readjust his schedule?"

I scrape my hand across my cropped beard when silence falls over the room. I didn't fully shave because even with my mouth going nowhere near Roxanne's intoxicating cunt, I can still smell it on my skin. It made showering before my meeting really fucking hard—both mentally and physically.

"We agreed to announce the failed bids within twenty-four hours of the auction, stating the winner wished to remain anonymous." The shit I'm spurting isn't unusual. Almost every man at the auction last week was married. They don't want their spouses knowing they're bidding for a virgin any more than I want to consider what would have happened if I had lost my cool a few hours earlier. I wouldn't have covered Roxanne with a bedspread before sneaking out of our room an hour ago. I would have been tossing dirt on her.

"That was the plan—"

"Was? What do you mean *was*?" I stray my eyes to Smith, the deserver of my wrath. "I gave an order. It should have been followed."

"Jesus, for a man who's blown his load more the past week than he has the past year, you've certainly got your panties in a twist. Calm down, D. We're not your enemy."

As my eyes shoot to Rocco, my nostrils flare. "If we haven't announced that the bids have ended, Roxanne's virginity is still up for sale. If her virginity is for sale, she's for sale. Point fucking blank. Can I explain it any simpler for you, Rocco?"

I balk like the bruises on his knuckles are from punching me in the gut when he replies, "That's the point. She wants her sale to remain open."

"That's what I was referencing earlier." Smith scoots closer to the table before balancing his elbows on a stack of paperwork he brings to every meeting. "Roxanne is willing to take our ruse one step further—"

"No."

"At least hear the man out, D."

"No!" I repeat more forcefully this time. "Bates didn't bid three times that of his competitors for no reason. He wants Roxanne for more than her virginity." Before Rocco can interject again, I continue talking, foiling his endeavors. "Furthermore, the ruse will no longer be effective."

I'm not peacocking that I pinched Roxanne's virginity, I am being straight-up honest. Roxanne said it herself. No one would believe our connection is fake because it's never been made up. She fooled them last week because she was innocent. It won't work this time around.

I stop considering a workaround when Smith says, "That's why she wants to go in as a patient instead of a purchase. If the farmers are picking up clients from Dr. Bates's office, we have another way of infiltrating their operation. Faking a pregnancy will delay things by a couple of weeks considering Roxanne was just auctioned as a virgin, but the hold-up will give me plenty of time to make sure we won't face any hiccups."

I want to immediately say no again, but for the life of me, I can't. Although her plan is dangerous, it's also smart. I've been chasing Rimi for over twenty months. The closest I've come to catching him was the night I stopped to help Roxanne. This type of ruse could increase the odds of finding him, but something isn't sitting right with my stomach.

This kills me to admit, but I'm not sure I can guarantee Roxanne's safety. If she had suggested this before she proved she's on my side by offering to switch places with Fien, I wouldn't have cared she was at risk. Now... now I don't know which way is up.

A collective sigh bounces around my downstairs office when I mutter, "Let me think about it." To the men who know me, that's a straight-up no. To those still out of the loop, it's a possibility. "But for now, I want eyes on Dr. Bates at all hours of the day and night. His name wasn't mentioned during interrogations..." —*by interrogations, I mean torture*— "... but that doesn't mean anything. People only keep quiet when they have something to hide." When another joint hum trickles into my ears, I stand to my feet, eager to get our meeting over. I loathe the political side of my job as much as I hate my father. "Is there anything else?"

I'm halfway out the door when Rocco's deep timbre stops me. "One last thing."

I work my jaw through a tight grind when he requests for everyone but Smith to leave. I understand his distrust. The longer Fien's captivity continues, the more certain I become that I have a rat in my crew. Furthermore, the tension on Rocco's face tells me I won't like what he has to say next.

Once only three bodies remain in my office, Rocco joins me partway to the door. "Theresa Veneto has made numerous requests to meet with you the past week. I assured her as derogatively as I could that you're not interested in anything she's selling, then she gave me this." He digs out a folded-up piece of paper from his pocket. Although the image is dated, I'm relatively sure it's the brunette who was on Isaac's arm last week.

My eyes lift from the college snapshot when Smith says, "Roxie was right. She did see Isabelle in a documentary. Well, kind of." He swivels his laptop around to face me. It has a poorly made video playing on the screen. It's amateur at best, even with Smith cleaning it up. "She thought this lady was Isabelle." He points to a brunette at the side of the footage that has an uncanny resemblance to the photograph of the woman I'm clutching. "Where in reality, this is Isabelle." He highlights a toddler just left of the woman he pointed out. "The documentary was filmed years ago, but the doco remembered the female. Her name was Felicia. She was Vladimir Popov's favorite whore."

I don't know which fact to work first, so I go for the easiest. "Was?"

Smith jerks up his chin. "Coroner said she overdosed. The head doco had a different recollection of events. He swears she was murdered."

"By Vladimir?"

Smith shrugs. "Rumors circulated that he choked her in a

jealous rage, but that never held much credit. Felicia was never seen with anyone, and strangulation isn't Vladimir's kink. He prefers—"

"Long, painful deaths," I fill in. "Unlike my father. He loves nothing more than to see the light fade from a woman's eyes."

Could that be the cause of the rift between the Petrettis and the Popovs? There's never comradery between opposing cartel groups, but things have been strained between the above-mentioned families for decades. Vladimir has the power my father wants but will never have. Like a spoiled child, instead of striving to outdo Vladimir, he set out to destroy him. His tactics the past few years have barely created a ripple in Vladimir's armor, although the same can't be said for his offspring.

Rico, Vladimir's eldest son, is a hothead, but he's got nothing on his younger brother, Nikolai. Nikolai has a massive chip on his shoulder and a beef with everyone. I'll be shocked if he makes it to his thirties. I've been tempted to order his hit numerous times, and I've never met the guy. He rubs me the wrong way. I have no clue why. It could be jealousy, but it feels more than that. His family's name might be more powerful than mine and his pockets lined with more money, but I'd rather suffer the injustice of being born into my family than have my fire-breathing father breathing down my neck for every hour of every day like Vladimir does to Nikolai.

Perhaps that's it? Maybe I feel sorry for the guy? I'm also the youngest of my family, but I don't have to knock down my siblings to reach the top rung. Their knighthood fell long before I picked up my sword.

I freeze when snippets of the clues Smith handed me slowly slot into place. "If Felicia was Vladimir's favorite whore, who's Isabelle's father?" Smith doesn't need to answer me. The truth is all over his face. "Isabelle is Vladimir's daughter, and now she's working for the Feds. How the fuck did that happen?"

Naysayers say I'm working for the Feds as well, but only you and I know that isn't true. Those fuckers work for me more than I work for them.

"Felicia died when Isabelle was a child. She was sold a couple of months later."

I shouldn't smile at Rocco's admission, but I can't help it. I often forget I'm not the only mafia kid with an asshole for a father. In a way, depending on who purchased her, Isabelle could have gotten lucky.

Seeing an array of questions in my eyes, Rocco says, "She was bought by none other than Mr. Fed himself."

"Tobias?" I query, certain Rocco is mixing up his nicknames. Most of my exchanges with Tobias occurred while Rocco was in jail, so a slip-up is understandable.

When Rocco lifts his chin, air whizzes out of my mouth. Tobias was a little shady, but he usually still followed protocol by the book. This isn't close to any legislations I've seen in the Feds' handbook for agents.

Although I'm somewhat shocked, and a smidge proud of Tobias's bend of the rules, I don't understand what any of this has to do with Theresa's request to meet with me.

When I say that to Rocco, his grin turns blinding. "Maybe it isn't just you and Roxie that have a sixth sense around each other. Perhaps we have one, too?" Smith coughs to cover his chuckle when Rocco puckers up his lips for an air kiss. "Who said Mario was chasing Princess P? He might have liked hairy Italians."

His words become as windless as Smith's chuckles when I sock him in the stomach. I understand the reason for his riling, it's how he handles things when he feels out of his element, but I've got too many theories swirling around in my head to add his antics into the mix.

"What was Theresa's response to your question?"

Rocco rubs his stomach, feigning injury while replying, "That you'll lose more than a couple of bricks of coke if you don't meet with her."

My brow cocks, shocked she had the audacity to threaten me. If my thoughts hadn't shifted to Fien after she stole from me, she'd be lying on the bottom of the ocean with Eduardo, feeding the fish.

Rocco's grin reveals he responded to Theresa's threat with the same malice tracing through my veins. "My gun got real friendly with her head, but you know bitches, they don't lay down even when they're in heat."

I take a moment to deliberate a response. Although it could be a waste of my time, discovering the reason Theresa met with my father last week should swallow the injustice. Theresa is like India. She only sniffs around when there's a carcass ready to be boned. If my family is carving it up, I want to know about it.

"Set up a meeting for the AM." Smith appears shocked about my offer, but his lips remain locked. "But warn her if she wastes my time, she'll need to clear her schedule for the remainder of her life."

Believing all is said and done, Smith grabs his paperwork and laptop off the desk and makes a beeline for the door. He doubles back when I add, "Also announce that Roxanne's auction was finalized and that her winning bidder was me." When a fretful mask slips over Rocco's face, I do my best to shut it down. "The auction was conducted under my father's branch of our entity. I could have been in attendance as a bidder. Furthermore, if you want the people Dr. Bates is working for to be tempted by the lure we're considering dangling in front of them, we need to make it as appetizing as possible. If this is personal, as we believe it is, making the mark associated with me will work in our favor." Before relief can cross Smith's features, pleased I'm considering his tactic, I continue, "*If* I go through with this, there will be no holds barred. I won't be fucked in the ass by Rimi for another two years."

"I agree with what you're saying." Rocco's words are more at ease than his facial expression. "But by going down this road, you'll place Roxie on your father's radar."

He looks torn between wanting to pat me on the back and punch me in the face when I reply, "Isn't that the point?"

# 10

# ROXANNE

I stretch out lazily, loving that a solid few hours of sleep hasn't fully unwound my tired muscles. I slept through dinner, dessert, and the midnight cap Smith forced on me every night the past three days to encourage me to sleep, but I feel refreshed. Calm, even.

It's amazing what back-to-back orgasms can do. My hang-ups from the past week have vanished, and nothing but optimism appears on the horizon. It's a nice feeling after years of worry.

"You better quit moaning before I come over and take care of them."

The bedding falls away from my naked chest when I prop myself on my elbows so I can stray my eyes in the direction the voice came from. If it were twanged with anything but an Italian accent, I'd cover up, but since I want to entice my greeter into following through with his threat, I don't bother.

"Good morning."

My eyes shift to the only window in the room, truly unsure if it's morning or not. I feel like I've been asleep for weeks but am untrusting of my delirious head.

My lips twist when not a ray of sun shines through the pleats of the drapes. It's early enough for the slightest bit of gray to mottle the sky, but it isn't close to the time I usually wake up.

A hunger unlike anything I've ever felt before smacks into me when Dimitri says, "Rosa left a club sandwich on the nightstand. You should eat. You'll need the energy."

His voice is as seductive as the lust roaring through my veins, however I can't act on it. He isn't seated behind his desk at this late hour for no reason. He's working through the files Smith and I collated while endeavoring not to make it seem as if we were holding a candlelight vigil at his bedside.

After placing on my dressing gown Rosa must have gathered from the floor, I snatch up the sandwich Dimitri mentioned before pacing to his half of the room. I won't lie, lust thickens my veins when I notice his inconspicuous watch. He stares at me through hooded eyelids, acting as if my frumpy dressing gown is made from the finest silk.

The indecent swing of my hips tapers when I notice which articles he's perusing. He has 3D printouts of my grandparents' farm spread across his desk. Smith took my knowledge of burial sites up a notch when he showed me how ground-penetrating radars and electromagnetic tests can narrow down the search area when seeking unmarked graves. It was fascinating to watch, but the circumstances for our search sucked.

Once I've swallowed down my unease, I say, "No significant increase in conductivity was found during electromagnetic testing, leading us to believe there were no bodies buried on-site."

Dimitri raises his eyes to mine, either shocked at the extent of my knowledge or turned on by the lack of disgust in my voice. He should count his lucky stars he was out cold the first three days of my internship, or he would have witnessed me heaving more than once. I have a morbid curiosity for crime shows and the scientific side of hunting for murderers, but having a personal connection with the people involved was a bitter pill to swallow.

After a quick breather, I continue updating Dimitri on our findings. "Smith organized ground-penetrating searches for a handful of smaller sites that had increased conductivity. Nothing came from it. Most were stock animals or farming equipment."

"Did they dig below the animal carcasses?"

I shake my head. I wasn't on-site during testing, but I kept a close watch on proceedings from my station in Dimitri's room with Smith. "Why would they dig deeper?"

I'm reasonably sure I won't eat for a week when Dimitri asks, "When searching for a body, what's the most obvious shape examiners seek?" Although he's asking a question, he continues talking as if he didn't. "If you don't want a body found, instead of burying it horizontally, dig a vertical gravesite. It makes the disturbance to the land less noticeable and often has conductivity results overlooked by examiners." He snickers about my whitening gills before adding, "The smart criminals might even add a dead animal on top of the corpse to ward off suspicion."

"That's disturbing."

He smiles at the gag my reply was delivered with before muttering, "It's actually smart depending on which side of the law you're on. If you were digging up a square burial site, and you stumbled upon a family pet, would you keep digging?"

"Uh, no," I force out through a gag. "And I'm reasonably sure ninety-nine percent of the population wouldn't, either."

I wish he'd quit smiling. They're making me all types of hot. "That's my point. We're not seeking an upstanding member of society, Roxanne. We want that one percent."

Considering what we're discussing, I shouldn't relish how he says 'we.' However, I do.

After standing to his feet, Dimitri says, "We need to take another look at your grandparents' farm." Ignoring the loud gurgle of my stomach that has nothing to do with hunger, he gets straight down to business. "Smith... Smith..."

Before his third call for Smith can rumble out of his mouth, I place my hand over his balled one resting on his desk. "He's probably sleeping."

My reply was meant to calm him down, not rile him up. He's more frustrated now than he was when I placed on my dressing gown. He's pissed Smith isn't at his beck and call, having no clue he'd be dead if he continued walking down the path he has the past eighty-plus hours.

"He barely slept the past three days, Dimi. He was a walking zombie." When Dimitri's eyes snap to mine, shocked at my unusual use of his nickname, I forcefully swallow the brick in my throat. "We'll get the search done, but it will have to wait until the morning. You won't find anything but raccoons at this hour."

The jest in my tone adds the slightest furl to his top lip. It's not a smile, but it isn't a scowl either.

"Have you eaten?" When he jerks up his chin, I ask, "Was it better than this?"

His eyes stray in the direction my head is nudging. After drinking in my soggy sandwich I'm sure was super fresh six hours ago, he shakes his head.

"Do you want to risk death?" The unease I see in his eyes makes me smile. "I can whip up a mean batch of pancakes... I just have a bad habit of burning them."

I can tell he wants to smile, he's just riddled with too much guilt to allow himself to be happy. I can't say I don't understand his objection. I still haven't laid my eyes on Fien, and I feel bad I'm standing across from her father instead of her.

"Come on. I'm sure your insurance will cover a kitchen fire. If not, I'm just as confident you have the dough to cover my mishaps."

My thumping heart from barging him out of his comfort zone could be to blame for my poor hearing, but I swear he grumbles, "If only money could keep you safe."

---

Two dozen burned pancakes and six salvable ones later, I prop my backside onto the counter Dimitri is seated behind before blurting out a question that hasn't stopped bugging me the past hour. "Can I see a photo of Fien?" When Dimitri's fork drops onto his plate with a clang, I talk faster. "I'm just curious if I'm picturing her right. Like you know how when you read a book, and you imagine the character one way, but when you jump onto the author's Facebook page, you realize they look completely different than you were picturing. It's like that for me with Fien." I stop for a much-needed breath before raising my eyes to Dimitri's. He's as shocked by my ramble as I am. He has been inside of me. I should no longer be nervous around him, but for some reason, I am. "I just want to know if she looks like you."

There he goes with his infamous half-smirk again. "The Petretti genes are strong."

"I'm sure they are," I say with a smile as blinding as his. "But I'm still curious. Does she have curly hair or straight? Blue eyes or brown? Dimples in her top lip like her daddy when he smiles, or did she inherit his elf ears instead?"

With the sentiment in the air thicker than lust, I'm anticipating for him to shut down my inquisitiveness with the cruelness he was raised by, so you can envision the dramatic drop of my jaw when he says, "Her eyes are blue, her hair is as straight as an arrow, and she got both my dimples and my elf ears."

Tension cracks between us when he slips off his barstool to gather something out of the drawer next to my thigh. His fridge and fire mantel aren't adorned with family snapshots and heirlooms. This is more a business premise than a home, so the last thing I anticipate for him to remove from a drawer full of cutlery is a palm-size photograph.

Upon spotting my shock, Dimitri mutters, "I have a photo in every drawer and cupboard as a reminder of why I'm here."

After a quick breather, he hands me Fien's photograph. It's the fight of my life not to coo like an imbecile. She isn't just cute, she's downright adorable. Her nose is tiny, her eyes are wide, and she has the rosiest lips I've ever seen. And Dimitri was right, she did get both his elf ears and his dimple-blemished grin.

"She's adorable." I sound like a ditz, but it's the most honest I've ever been. Seeing Fien's chubby cheeks has brought everything into perspective. It's also made me super mad. If it weren't for me, she'd be standing across from her father instead of me.

I'd hate to think what my life would be like now if my mother hadn't convinced my father to swap me with Audrey, but it's just as horrid realizing you're the cause of someone else's unhappiness. I'm not solely referencing Fien, either. My pain centers around Dimitri and Audrey as well.

"Can I be a part of the search today?"

Dimitri doesn't consider my offer for even a second. He immediately shakes his head.

"I lived there half of my life. I could see something important, stuff others may have missed."

"No, Roxanne." He snatches Fien's photograph out of my hand

before he places it back into the drawer. "Shit like that changes you."

I don't pause to consider the protectiveness in his tone. "Shit like this *has* changed me, Dimitri. I'm not the same woman I was when I walked into this house, and I won't be the same when I walk out."

He's up in my face in an instant, his clutch on my face anything but kind. "I said no."

His reply is stern and to the point, but it doesn't weaken my determination in the slightest because it isn't anger in his eyes, it's worry. "You said I could help."

"Fixing your parents' fuck-ups isn't your job."

With every ounce of my self-control lost, I shout, "It isn't yours either, but you're still doing it!"

I don't solely mean my parents. From what I've overheard the past few days before Dr. Bates was seen following Dimitri to Frosty Kinks, Dimitri's father was suspect number one. As far as I'm concerned, he still deserves to be watched. Dr. Bates isn't operating alone. Our one-on-one talk included the words 'our' and 'we' much too often to believe he's the sole operator of a baby-making franchise.

Before I can announce that to Dimitri, I'm yanked off the kitchen cabinet by my wrist, bent over the island bench I made a mess of while preparing an early breakfast, exposed by the high lift of my dressing gown, then spanked like I'm a naughty child.

I fight his first three spanks, but by the fourth, I'm nothing but putty in the hands of a madman. Just like the public punishment he issued me in a room many miles from here, his spanking offers the perfect amount of pleasure and pain. The heat racing across my backside is enough to have my back molars gritting together, but the slap of his fingertips against an area that hasn't stopped buzzing the past twelve hours is unbelievably divine.

I'm hot all over in an instant and doing everything in my power not to beg for more. I love how he towers over me. It's like he's a big brooding giant, and I'm a naughty little fairy who loves pushing his buttons.

The lust roaring through my veins doubles when Dimitri growls, "Tell me again how you're planning to walk out on me?" I thought his anger centered around my request to be a part of the search today. I had no clue it was from me mentioning an upcoming departure.

I want to answer him, to tell him I'd stay a lifetime if he'd let me, but lose the chance when his spanking hand switches to nurturing. He rubs my butt cheeks that are clenched in pain before he lowers his hand to a wetness more prominent than the pancake batter. His fingertips barely caress the aching flesh, but it feels like he's tugging at my clit with his teeth.

I discover the reason for his unusual gentleness when he says, "You're still swollen from taking me last night."

His breaths quiver as much as my thighs when I reply, "I don't care."

"You may not care, but I do." His voice is so low, I'm reasonably sure his words weren't for me.

I almost whine when he lowers my dressing gown until its hem floats above the marble floors of his kitchen, but it's gobbled up by a moan when he growls out, "Ass on the countertop. I'm about ready for a second helping of breakfast."

Not waiting for my shock to sink in, he twists me around, throws off the dishware stained with remnants of our shared breakfast, then lifts me onto the kitchen counter as if I'm weightless. A moan unlike anything I've ever heard before rolls up my chest when my backside's collision with the gleaming counter is closely chased by him lowering his head between my legs. He doesn't wait for permission, nor does he remove my dressing gown. He merely uses the slit in the static-loving material to his advantage, so he can devour his second sickly sweet meal of the day. I don't care. I'm too in awe about him lapping up the slickness his dominance caused between my legs to worry about him gaining permission to do so.

As my fingers weave through his dark locks, he slips two fingers inside of me. They enter without effort, made easy by the wetness of his hearty licks. Within a minute of his magic fingers taking control, I'm grunting, moaning, and cursing as if I'm being tortured instead of pleasured. The sensation is almost too much. I've never felt more unhinged—even more so when Dimitri lifts his eyes to mine. His stare rings the words he spoke to me days ago through my ears. *"You don't want a man. You want a monster, a bastard, a man who'd rather destroy you than ever have you believe you deserve more than him."*

This is his way of destroying me. He will spoil me so much in the bedroom, just the thought of being with another man will feel disturbing.

I don't mind. There could be worse things to be dependent on.

My parents' addictions are proof of this.

Like everything else in life, Dimitri doesn't follow the rules in the bedroom any more than he does outside of them. He licks, finger fucks, and devours me until anyone but him is far from my thoughts. He brings me to the very brink of orgasm, tonguing me and tugging at my clit until I'm writhing against his face, then he withdraws all contact.

I can't hold back my wail this time around. It roars out of me just as frantically as a husky moan when Dimitri lowers his trousers as if they're sweats. He fists his erect cock in his hand before giving it a long and slow tug. "What was our agreement, Roxanne?" He sounds angry, but I don't pay the angst in his tone any attention.

I can't fear a man I crave more than my next breath.

My eyes snap to Dimitri's when he strangles out my name as forcefully as he fists his cock. His eyes demand my focus as much as the stimulating visual bombarding me, but I'm not strong enough to listen to both my libido and my head. It's either one or the other, which has me wondering if that's why he asked his question while stroking his cock. I'm already on the back foot for most of our exchanges, but when his impressive manhood is on the table, I'm as submissive as it comes.

Evidence of this is submitted without prejudice when I mumble, "That I'm to do as you ask when you ask..." I wet my lips, hopeful a bit of moisture will ease my next set of words past the lust clutching my throat, "... for precisely how long you ask."

"And what have you been doing?" He strokes his cock faster when he spots a witty comeback in my eyes. The way a handful of pumps alters the direction of my reply reveals I'm worse than a man. I'm not being led astray by my pussy, I am being wholly controlled by it. He has me by the throat, and he's milking it for all its worth.

It's a pity for him I saw the light in his eyes change when he went down on me. He's more powerful than me, a million times richer, and undeniably more dangerous, but there's one thing we have in common that social status will never change.

He craves me as much as I do him.

"I'm doing as requested. Answering your every whim." The bangs fanned across my forehead rustle in the frantic breaths that pump out of Dimitri's nose when I lower myself onto my knees in front of him. "Even the pleas you're not willing to voice just yet."

After replacing his fist with mine, my tongue darts out to lap up the sticky bead on the end of his impressive cock. The bunching of his thigh muscles exposes he's trying to act unaffected by my switch-up, but the growl I hear rumbling in his chest weakens his endeavor. He's dreamed about me sucking his dick as often as me, if not as long.

"This changes nothing between—"

I steal his words by taking him as deeply into my throat as I can. My impatience wasn't just to stop him saying something he couldn't take back, it was also because I couldn't wait a second longer to have his beautifully thick cock between my lips. My mouth is watering at the thought of tasting his cum, and I won't mention the slick wetness between my legs.

The pain I experienced last night makes sense when my lips burn from being stretched beyond what's comfortable. His eyewatering girth and length also explain why he's lax on protection. The condoms my nanna shoved into my hand not long after my sixteenth birthday will never get close to covering him up. He's too thick. Too long. Too delicious for the threat of a little STI to stop me from devouring him.

There's also the thought of bringing a man as powerful as him to his knees. I've barely strived for a single thing in my life, but I want this more than anything. I don't want to take his power, I merely want him to share it with me for just a second.

An orgasm builds like a tornado in the lower half of my stomach when Dimitri's wish to clutch my hair sees him licking the fingers he had inside of me. He cleans them as if my juices are tastier than the breakfast we shared.

Once all the evidence of my arousal is cleared away, he rakes his fingers through my hair as if his hand is a comb before he secures it in a tight ponytail at the back of my head. I anticipate for him to steal all the control from here, so you can imagine my surprise when his grip on my hair doesn't alter the speed of my sucks. He just drinks it all in, loving that not even a strand of over-bleached hair blocks his view.

Stroke after stroke, I take him deeper. I'm greedy, so much so, every suck has the head of his cock bottoming out at the back of my throat. I gag but continue, more than happy to suffer the injustice if it keeps him moaning the way he is.

When his dick jerks several long minutes later, I swivel my tongue around the rim circling his knob, moaning when my eagerness to taste his precum produces more of the sticky substance.

"You like this, don't you? You've wanted my cock between your lips for months."

I don't deny the cockiness in his tone because everything he said is true. I wanted this even while in the room he tortured my father in.

After flattening my tongue to ensure his impressive manhood sinks to the very back of my throat, I raise my eyes to Dimitri's. His are showcasing his triumph, smug as fuck I didn't deny his claim.

"Finish me." This isn't a command. It's a beg. He's as undone as me and just as desperate. "Then, perhaps if you've shown you can follow orders, I'll let you come with us today."

Although his response has me all types of excited, it has nothing to do with him bending the rules. I love how on edge his voice is. Anyone would think this has been in his dreams as often as mine the past few weeks.

"It'll be my pleasure."

My husky words draw his balls in close to his body. He's on the brink, and the realization that I'm going to push him over the edge has me hollowing my cheeks to the point it's painful.

"Fuck, Roxie," Dimitri growls on a moan, his hips rocking. "You're such a wildcat, a dirty, filthy fucking minx." I love his use of my nickname, not to mention the dirty words that followed it. The way he loses control is as intoxicating as the taste of his mouthwatering cock. "I'm going to come down your throat, then I'll give you everything you want." His arrogant smirk should be one of his less stellar features. It isn't, especially when it's directed straight at me.

"Well, as much as you can take. I don't want to ruin your sweet little pussy before customizing it to my cock."

My moans whizz out of my nose, forced there by Dimitri's dick commanding every inch of my throat. He pumps in and out of me, burying himself deeper with every thrust. He face-fucks me until I forget this is supposed to be about getting him off. His dirty words, the taste of his scrumptious cock, and the tight grip he has on my hair has me right there with him, on the very peak of the cliff, ready to fall, but I hold back, remembering he needs this as much as me. Keeping your head above water is exhausting in general, let alone when you're dealing with all the shit Dimitri is. I doubt he's let go of the reins like this in months, if not years.

"Look at me."

My hands fly out to get a grip on Dimitri's thighs when the collision of our eyes sees him losing control. With his head thrown back and his hand holding my mouth hostage to his cock, he pumps into me two more times before the saltiness of his cum floods my tongue.

Giving head isn't supposed to have this level of fireworks associated with it. I never enjoyed doing it to my college boyfriends and usually spat out evidence of their excitement within a second of their bodies expelling it, but this time around, I suck it down as if it's liquid gold, moaning when its slipperiness soothes the burn of my throat from my hearty screams.

I've hardly mollified the blister when I'm plucked from the ground, spun around, then curled over the kitchen counter. My knees knock when the lowering of Dimitri's hand to my pussy is quickly chased by a growl. "You're still swollen. If I take you now, you'll be all types of fucked by sunrise." My knees join for any entirely different reason when he adds, "Perhaps that's the solution to your disobedience? Maybe I should hurt you so bad, the only thing you'll consider doing today is soaking in a tub for hours on end."

My worry he's reneging on his offer doesn't linger for long. His fingers are too wondrous to instigate any emotions not fueled by need. He drags them through the folds of my clenching sex before circling them around the nub dying for his attention. "You're so fucking wet for me. You are dripping like my head didn't leave your cunt the past hour."

I don't respond. I can't. He's barely touching me, and I'm on the cusp of a climax.

"You better get a heap louder than that if you want me to give you permission to come."

He doesn't need to ask me twice. I moan like I'm possessed while grinding down on his hand as if it's as ribbed as his cock.

"Please," I beg a short time later. "I need..."

"Me," Dimitri fills in like anyone else is on my mind. "Because that's all you're going to get from here on out. Me and only me. Do you hear me, Roxanne?"

Sweat rolls down my cheeks when I frantically nod. It's more submissive than when I was on my knees being fed his cock one marvelous inch at a time, but he still wants more.

"Say it."

"You," I squawk like a canary, my fantasies shattered by a reality better than any dream. "I'll only ever want you."

Dimitri pinches my clit until my every sense is being held captive by a madman. "And the walking out part? What about that?"

*He's still worried about that?*

Before I can answer my unvoiced question, Dimitri asks one of his own, "Has that left your head yet, or do I need to be more persuasive?"

I'm torn on how to answer. I want to say no, hoping I'll discover exactly how alpha he is, but I also want to come. It's blistering inside me, burning as effectively as the burn my lips endured while sucking him off.

With my libido overriding all my senses, I take the coward's route. "It's left my head—"

My pathetic show of womanhood is cut off by a gravelly, accented voice. Although it's oddly similar to the one towering over me with the command of a caveman, it sends a chill scattering through me. It isn't a good shudder. I've only heard this voice once before. It was when he instructed me to turn around so he could see my eyes while he killed me.

Hell has been left unoccupied again. Except this time, the imp isn't walking the corridors of a hospital seeking new recruits, he's visiting his son.

"Eyes to the floor." When my eyes instinctively lift to Dimitri, panicked by the fury in his gruff tone, his jaw tightens. "Eyes to the fucking floor!"

Their fast drop fills my hazy head with dizziness, but the cloud isn't thick enough to miss me watching Dimitri raise his hand in the air in threat. He's seconds from striking me, and I'm at a complete loss as to why.

With my submissiveness on display for all to see, Dimitri grunts something about how frustrating it is for him to put the help in their place before he demands me to clean up the mess I made.

Confident I won't defy him for the second time, he yanks up his trousers huddled around his ankles, then hightails it in the direction his father's voice came from.

## 11

## DIMITRI

"If that's your idea of a punishment, I'm disappointed. If the help isn't smelling of blood by the time you've showed her the ropes, you let her off easy." My father jerks his chin to the kitchen I'm in the process of forcefully removing him from. "I can smell her cunt from here." The frantic pump of his nostrils makes me want to gut him where he stands. "I guess I can understand your change-up. Even I may be tempted to offer leniency for a smell that sweet."

When he pivots back around, I grip his arm with enough force, I'm certain he'll be wearing my marks as long as Roxanne's ass. "She isn't close to repaying her debt, and I'm not willing to share her until she has." When my father's brows bow, I realize my error. By admitting I want her, his interest in Roxanne tripled in an instant. "She cooks like Ma. Even with her cunt being greedy for a pounding, I'm considering sending her to Petrettis to show them how it's done before shipping her to her buyer."

For a man his age, my father should have more wrinkles on his face than he does when he cocks his brow. "Good cooking skills are to blame for your pants being wrapped around your ankles?"

It takes everything I have not to retaliate to the mirth in his tone. "She fucked up. I wanted my dick sucked. I took advantage of the situation. Sue me."

He laughs in a way that makes my skin crawl, though it has nothing on my reaction when he says, "What can I say? You take after me with more than looks."

The Petretti genes are strong, but this is the last fucking thing I want to hear.

After guiding him into my downstairs office, I gesture to him to take a seat in the chair opposite my desk. Forever willing to test the boundaries, he opts to sit in my chair, instead. He thinks he's smart. In reality, he's an idiot. I use this office for nothing but fucking, purely because of him. He can snoop all he likes down here because he'll never find a single shred of evidence about either my operation or my daughter.

As he scans the fake business documents on my desk, he slouches low into my chair. He doesn't even try to hide his snooping. To him, this is his realm. I merely live in it.

Confident the articles aren't of interest to him, he locks his eyes with mine. "I have some very dissatisfied customers." I assume he's referencing Theresa Veneto's numerous requests to meet with me. Although she was scarce with details when Rocco organized our meeting for later today, she did hint that it was concerning an unfavorable purchase she made from the Petretti entity but am proven wrong when he nudges his head to the hall we just walked. "She created quite the kerfuffle, only for her sale to be canceled because her seller couldn't keep his dick in his pants."

"As far as the buyers are concerned, her sale was umbrellaed under your entity of our family. That means I was entitled to bid as a buyer." With my tone much too possessive for my liking, I try another tactic. "You said it yourself. Her cunt smells like candy. I wanted to see if it tasted the same."

Imagine a perverted old guy grabbing his dick while watching kids play in a playground. That will give you an idea of the sleazy look on my father's face when he asks, "Does it?"

The egotistical side of my head wants to say Roxanne's cunt is the tastiest dish I've ever sampled, but my business side shuts it down. Acting as if I can't stand Roxanne won't just favor me, it will keep her safe as well.

"If it were, do you think she'd be cooking me breakfast?"

He doesn't want to believe me, but I've given him no reason not to. "If it's that bad, ship her to the next candidate. Dr. Bates will be more than happy to wade through your slops."

The mentioned name pisses me off to no end. "As I said earlier, until her debt is paid in full, she's not going anywhere."

Not even a man as arrogant as my father could deny the ownership in my voice this time around. It has his lips begging to hitch into a smirk, but for some reason, he holds it back.

"Very well. Do with her as you wish."

He stands from my seat before buttoning the middle button of his business suit jacket. Considering the hour, I'm going to assume he's about to turn in for the night. Most of the load in this industry is done at night. It's why I rarely sleep.

"But I'll expect your check on my desk by close of business today. If she were mine to sell, I expect dividends from her sale."

I want to believe the swift end of our conversation is because money comes before anything to my father. However, my gut is advising me not to be stupid. He knows as well as I do that Roxanne's auction was only the tip of the iceberg in her earnings. If this were purely about profit, he'd milk her for all she's worth.

As confident I'll jump to his command as rapidly as Roxanne does mine, he dips his chin before exiting my office via a concealed entrance. It isn't an entrance many people know about, but it's the only clue I need as to why the scent of Roxanne's juices on my hand is being overridden by an emasculating perfume.

"Entering a man's house uninvited warrants him permission to shoot you."

The shadow I'm glaring at switches on the lamp next to the single chair she's seated in before she strays her eyes to mine. "I'm an invited guest."

I shoot Theresa a stern look, warning her I'm not in the mood for her games. "You were instructed to arrive at ten o'clock, not enter my house at an ungodly hour."

I'm tempted to gouge her eyes out when she drinks in my shirt-less form with a prolonged gawk. It's clear what she's here for, so I make it just as clear I'm not interested.

"You stole thirty thousand dollars' worth of uncut coke from me. Even if I could forget that, we'll never mess the sheets." I lock our eyes, ensuring she can see the truth in mine when I say, "I don't fuck women I plan to kill."

She smiles like her life isn't on the line. "That isn't what I hear. Supposedly, that's your thing now."

Aware of her attractiveness, she rakes her teeth over her lower lip. I won't lie, she could give half the whores in my arsenal a run for their money. She just needs to thaw out her icy insides first. Not even hard-ass men like me want to bed a heartless woman.

"I wonder if you'll change your mind when I share the information I've unearthed about your father the past month?"

My lips tuck in the corner. I should have known her early visit isn't purely about whetting her sexual appetite. If the law can't catch my father, they side with him. When they get burned, they come running to me.

"I'm done fixing my father's mistakes..." My words trail off when Theresa holds a photograph into the light. It's the same image she handed Rocco earlier this week. "The bad can turn good just as easily as the good can turn bad." I don't hold back my arrogant smirk this time around. "You should know that better than anyone."

Theresa is as corrupt as they come. The only reason she hasn't done time is because she has one of those golden pussies Clover mentioned weeks ago. It's got nothing on Roxanne's, but I can see how it could make some men do whatever she asks.

"Your father is cashing in favors he'll never repay, and here you are, acting ignorant to a Russian invasion."

My laugh echoes around my office. "A Russian invasion, my ass. The last time that happened, Vladimir—"

"Found out his wife birthed a child with your father."

I take an involuntary step back. I hate that I allowed my shock to be seen, but there was too much honesty in her tone for a nonchalant response.

Theresa soaks up my surprise as if it's whiskey, and she's an alcoholic. "This can't be the first time you've heard about illegitimate siblings, surely. I know of at least three."

She's right. My family has faced rumors about my father's infidelities for decades—baby mamas included—but this is the first time the rumblings included someone who could possibly steal my crown before I've sat on my throne.

"Male or female?" I don't know why the fuck I'm contemplating this. If he or she wants to contest my position, bring it on. I'll take them down as well as I did their predecessors. I guess a part of my curiosity can be blamed on the fact the last time the Petrettis and Popovs went to war was the year before I was born. If an extramarital affair is the cause of this, there are rules not even I can break because this time around, a coup won't just get me killed, it will take down my daughter as well.

I want to pretend I don't recognize the face of the man Theresa brings up on her phone, but unfortunately, you'd have to be dead the past decade not to know him. The Popovs are loud, proud, and Vladimir's second eldest son soaks up the attention for all it's worth.

Nikolai Popov is a media whore.

He's also four months older than me.

*Fuck it!*

After working my jaw side to side, I play it cool. "Unfounded rumors like this will get you killed quicker than theft."

Theresa paces my way, her hips extra swingy. The fact she thinks I can be led by my cock pisses me off more than her presumption I'd want to get freaky with her. "Who said it's unfounded?"

When she's within touching distance, I grip her throat with everything I have. Like the dumb fuck she is, she gets turned on by my hold instead of fearing it. That's why we played well when we did. She's as kinky as she is corrupt.

A liar would tap out within seconds, a woman seeking a cheap thrill would have tears springing down her eyes shortly after that. Only someone with nothing to fear would return my glare without the slightest bit of sheen in her eyes.

Regretfully, that someone is Theresa.

She gives it her all not to answer the screaming protests of her lungs when I loosen my grip on her throat before tossing her to the other side of my office. She loses her fight when she lands on her backside with a thud. She won't stay down. She will quietly lick her wounds before kicking me in the gut with the three-inch heels she's wearing. That's her way.

Before her pumps can get anywhere near my stomach, I mutter, "Tell me what you want before I add visible wounds to your hidden ones."

For once, she pays attention to the angst in my tone. It's for the best. I wasn't joking. I hate killing women, but I'll make an exception for her. "I want the same thing you do, Dimi. Revenge."

Even having no knowledge of the inner-workings of women whatsoever doesn't spare me from knowing who her comment refers to. Women get their panties in a real twist when their baby daddies don't come to the party for child support, much less when they deny paternity all together.

As a smirk curls my lips, I prop my backside onto my desk and fold my arms in front of my chest. I can't believe it took me this long to slot the pieces of the puzzle together. This isn't a turf war. It's a law enforcement officer learning she can't always have things her way. I only fucked her to have her looking past illegal shipments, yet she still responded to her deputy's wish to deepthroat my cock with the contempt of a scorned woman, so I can only imagine how she feels knowing her baby daddy is moving on.

"As I told you years ago, the Petrettis don't meddle with custody disputes." Before she can call me out as a liar, I add, "Unless you want Isaac Holt to go on an extended vacation, we have no business."

"His girlfriend is Russian. She has Popov blood running through her veins. How can you not be worried about this?"

I give her a look, warning her she better keep herself in check. I'm already pissed I left Roxanne hanging mid-orgasm. I don't need more annoyances heating my blood. "Because if I thought she was a threat, I would have held back her transfer the instant you forced it through the system."

Now Theresa is the one balking. If she thinks I'm so stupid not to look a little deeper into her sudden return to my state, the act I worked on her was as legitimate as the one I hit Audrey with when she stated she didn't want to date someone in my 'lifestyle.'

"You brought Isabelle here for a reason... what was it?"

Theresa strives to shut down the jealousy blazing through her eyes, but she's not quite quick enough. "She was supposed to go undercover—"

"Not fall for the mark?" Her lack of denial reveals I hit the nail on the head.

My next set of words are barely audible since they're cloaked with laughter. "I'm sorry you got thrown out on your ass, but a bruised ego isn't something I can help you with."

I'm also not eager to go against Isaac again. It isn't that I'm afraid of him. I just learned that karma can gnaw the wrong ass when you attempt to get out of a fucked-up situation in a half-assed way. CJ hasn't been the same since their rigged fight, Ophelia is dead, and Roberto's hiding out as Isaac's dish hand. Those fucked-up set of circumstances would keep the deadliest man on the straight and narrow.

My last comment holds my attention a little longer than it should. I can't be accused of fucking with karma if Isaac stirred the pot first. Alas, I've got enough on my plate, so I'm not interested in anything Theresa is selling. Wasn't years ago. Certainly am not now.

"If you want my help, you'll need to come back with over thirty thousand in uncut coke and a less bitchy attitude."

Theresa attempts to fire something back, but I'm out the door before a syllable leaves her mouth, and even quicker than that, I make my next move. "Call Mikhail. If a Russian so much as schedules a flight out of Vegas, I want to know about it."

Confident Smith is always listening, I make my way to the room I share with Roxanne, eager to award her earlier submissiveness in a way that will have her eating out of the palm of my hand even quicker than Theresa organizes a raid of Ravenshoe PD's evidence vault.

# 12

# ROXANNE

I curse at the soap as if it's my whining libido when it slips from my grip for the second time the past two minutes. It's acting as if Dimitri's threatened slap hours ago would get me off as well as his teeth tugging on my clit. I should have been scared he was acting so violent. However, all I felt was excitement.

In a weird way, it felt like he was protecting me, like his shift in personality was solely reliant on the unexpected arrival of his father. I even got that vibe from Smith when he guided me through Dimitri's residence, so I'd avoid walking down the hallway Dimitri dragged his father down only seconds earlier.

I stop seeking snippets of clarity in an insane world when the faintest hum of multiple engines warming up breaks through the madness swamping me. Before his father interrupted us, Dimitri gave me permission to attend the second search of my grandparents' ranch today. Wailing libido or not, I'm not going to miss it for anything.

After shutting off the faucet, I scrub my skin dry with a towel, twist another around my midsection, then race into the main part of my room. My pace slows to that of a snail when a gleaming device catches my eye. It isn't the prototype laptop Smith loaned me when I offered to help him keep things afloat while Dimitri recovered from having his drink spiked. Nor is it the ring I tossed at my mother when I realized she was responsible for my unexpected inheritance. It's my cell phone.

My heart launches into my throat when it suddenly commences ringing. It vibrates across the nightstand to the ringtone I set for Estelle's number, wordlessly urging me to pick it up.

I almost fall for his trick until I realize what's happening. I'm proud of how well I sucked Dimitri's cock, but even if I had sucked the marrow from his bones, I don't believe he'd award me two offerings in one day. This is a test, I'm certain of it. If I answer Estelle's call, the SUVs I hear idling at the front of his compound will leave without me. If I leave her call unanswered, I further my proof I'm on Dimitri's side.

It sucks that he needs to be constantly reassured, but it's also understandable. I heard the tone Dimitri's father used on him in the hallway. He doesn't love his son. I'm not even sure if he likes him.

With that in mind, I send a telepathic message to Estelle that I'll buzz her as soon as possible before I continue my sprint for the walk-in closet. Since my time is limited, I throw on the first dress I see. It's more suitable for a nightclub crawl than a daytime hike through overgrown fields, but I act ignorant to the fact.

Once I have on a pair of shoes and have thrown my hair into a messy bun, I hotfoot it to the door.

"Smith?" I query when my attempt to open my door is thwarted by a trusty lock.

"Smith," I try again after unsuccessfully rattling the lock three times.

It feels like I'm thrust into a mean, demoralizing game I'll never win when a churlish voice asks, "Aren't you going to answer your phone?"

I peer at the camera in the corner of the room before shaking my head. I can't testify that Dimitri is watching me, but it feels as if he is.

It dawns on me that I'm on the money when his thick Italian voice asks, "Why not? Estelle hasn't heard from you in almost two weeks. I'm sure she's getting worried."

Air whooshes out of the speakers when I say, "I'm sure she is, but I don't want to fail your test."

"Who said I'm testing you?" The way Dimitri speaks freely down the line assures me he's the only one listening in. He is close with Rocco and Smith, but I doubt even they truly know how many layers he has. "Perhaps I'm trying to stop you from getting hurt."

"You can protect me better in person than you ever could locking me away."

I'm hoping my confession will have him deliberating for a minute.

He doesn't even give it a second.

"Although I appreciate your confidence, I disagree, and that's why I'm going back on my earlier offer. You're to stay in your room until I permit you to leave. Do you understand?"

"No," I say with a brutal shake of my head. "I did as you asked. I proved I'm on your side."

I push down on the door handle for the fifth time. It fails to budge just as much as Dimitri's domineering personality.

"Dimitri!"

I bang on the door three times, confident the lack of static above my head means he's no longer listening to me but unwilling to give up. He's not being fair, and I'm about ready to call him out on it.

"You're not thinking rationally! I passed your test. I'm on your side!"

I continue screaming until the hum of a fleet of top-of-the-line SUVs stops buzzing in my ears, and the debilitating silence surrounding me stretches to days.

# 13

# DIMITRI

I glare at Rocco as if he's standing directly in front of me instead of peering at me through the camera propped above Roxanne's door. "Make her eat."

He places down Roxanne's untouched breakfast onto a side table in the hallway before asking, "And exactly how would you like me to do that, D? Ram the bacon down her throat."

"If that's the only way you can get her to fucking eat, then yeah, ram it down her throat." I lower my voice a few decibels when my roar gains me the attention of a handful of staff at Petretti's restaurant. I'm hiding out like a coward, pretending its business as usual even with it feeling anything but.

Our second search of Roxanne's grandparents' estate found bodies. No, you didn't hear me wrong. I said bodies as in multiple victims. Although preliminary findings lead us to believe the decomposition of the female bodies points to them being buried quite a few years ago, I know for a fact you can alter the decay of a corpse to make aliases more concrete.

It's a little hard to pin a murder on someone when the victim supposedly died while you were in another country. Add that knowledge to the fact several victims were in their final months of pregnancy, and Fien's ransom request arriving a week earlier than usual, for triple the amount, and you've got me with a ton of attitude I could easily take it out on the wrong person. Since I don't want that person to be Roxanne, I need to maintain distance between us.

I said her mother's verdict would be her choice, that I wouldn't kill her until she gave me permission. I don't see me keeping my word if I discover her mother buried my wife on her family ranch, then lied about it. I gave Sailor plenty of chances to come clean, so she will lose more than an ability to lie if I find out she has played me for a fool.

As if the above matters aren't enough to make my mood the sourest it's ever been, I looked into Theresa's claim my father got friendly with a Russian enemy's wife. I want to report that her claims are as bogus as my oath she gives good head, but that would make me as deceitful as her.

Nikolai isn't Vladimir Popov's son. That doesn't automatically make him a Petretti, but his markings most certainly do.

He has icy blue eyes—just like me.

He has the makings of a madman—just like me.

And he hates his father with every fiber of his being—just. Like. Me.

If traits replicated genes, our similarities would automatically make us comrades. Alas, the fact we could be related won't do Nikolai any favors. If anything, it will make matters worse. I'm not giving up my throne for anyone, much less a Russian. I'd send every member of my family to the grave before I'd ever let our sanction be run by a Russian. The Petretti name isn't what it once was, but that doesn't mean it's worthless. Honor comes in many forms. The past is just one of them.

While scrubbing at the scruffy beard I haven't trimmed in almost a week, I recall the reason for the extra heat in my veins. It has nothing to do with a hotheaded Russian and everything to do with a mixed-bred American who pushes my buttons like no one else.

Roxanne hasn't eaten in days. If she doesn't soon, there won't be anything left of her. Usually, I don't give a fuck about anyone but Fien and myself. This, however, is rubbing me the wrong way. Roxanne is tiny. Her body isn't built to withstand a weeklong hunger strike. She's already looking sick, and it has me taking drastic measures—measures I usually wouldn't hesitate to use.

"Threaten her."

Rocco's eyes snap to the camera before he shakes his head. He wouldn't be standing outside Roxanne's room unattended if I weren't desperate, so I don't know why he's acting surprised by my request.

"Do you want her to eat?"

He makes a 'duh' face before rolling his eyes like he isn't tatted to the hilt.

"Then threaten her."

"I'm not fucking threatening her, D. That shit is above my paygrade." I'm about to remind him exactly how well-off he is because of me. Sadly, I don't just recall he doesn't give a fuck about money, he reminds me that he isn't here solely for his hip pocket. "If you want to hold a woman captive *like your daughter*, you gonna need to do that shit yourself."

Stealing my chance to reply, he tosses Roxanne's breakfast into the camera before hot-footing it down the corridor. I could let his temper tantrum slide, but as I said earlier, I've got too much anger bubbling in my veins. If I don't release some of it soon, I'm going to explode.

"Smith..."

His instant reply reveals he witnessed the exchange between Rocco and me. "You know he wouldn't be so hard on you if you told him the truth."

I scoff like I don't have a dick between my legs. "If you believe that, you don't know Rocco."

Air whizzes out of his nose, but he fails to cite an objection, proving I'm right. Rocco might back down for a second or two, but the instant his head is screwed back on straight, he'd be right back up in my face causing trouble like he always does.

With that in mind, I say to Smith, "I need you to send Clover on an errand for me..."

My words trail off when a disturbance in the main part of the restaurant captures my attention. Considering we're still a few hours from the lunch rush, I'm shocked when it sounds like someone getting into a scuffle. The clientele get feisty when someone takes the last dish of risotto, but it's never had this edge of excitement attached to it before.

"I'll send you the deets. Make it quick. This is a matter of utmost importance." Smith gasps like he's insulted I insinuated he'd ever slack off, but before he can voice his annoyance, I add, "Buzz me when Clover is ready. I want to be in charge of comms."

He hums out an agreeing noise before disconnecting our feed. Just as quickly, I punch out the details on the errand I want Clover to run.

I've only just hit send on my email app when the raised voice of one of my father's goons booms into my ears, "I'm his exterminator."

I make it to the entrance of the kitchen in just enough time to see a fool make a costly mistake. Brandon James, one of Tobias's highest-ranked foot soldiers, mutters out a string of unintelligible words before he jabs the edge of his palm into Don's throat.

His maneuverer is effective, but it would have been more impressive if he disarmed Don's sidekick first. He's up in Brandon's business in an instant, aiming his gun at the crease between his blond brows as if Brandon doesn't have a direct kill lined up.

With my mitts needing to remain off Roxanne, and my every move monitored by my father, my wish to kill is the strongest it's been. I should step back and watch the carnage unfold with a smile. Regrettably, I owe Tobias a heap of favors he can never cash in, so it sees me offering leniency—just.

"Standdown." Disappointment echoes in my low tone. I don't know Brandon, but that doesn't mean I can't hate him. He and his gun-toting law enforcement friends are what's wrong with society these days. Rules make everything worse—starting at my inability to kill my father because that pathetic, insolent man is the rule-maker of my realm.

When my direct order is ignored, I get inventive. "Should I remind you what happened to the last man who ignored me? Or would you like me to show you, instead?"

Since my threat was delivered in Italian, Brandon does nothing but smile when my father's goons immediately lower their guns. After assisting a third passed-out man off the floor, they race for the safety of the parking lot.

While watching their dash for freedom, Brandon unclips the magazine from the gun he yanked out of the back of Don's pants, unloads the bullets onto the floor, places the disarmed weapon onto the hostess's podium, then wipes it clean. Although I'm impressed he's distrusting enough to remove his fingerprints from a gun the Feds would love to get their hands on, the brainless blonde manning the hostess section of the restaurant reveals why blondes are given so much shit.

She stares at the gun Brandon placed down, too feared to touch it, yet somehow turned on by the thought. Her mixed emotions have my thoughts immediately shifting to Roxanne. I want to say it's a good shift, but like anything the past few days, I couldn't be so lucky.

"Go!" My shouted word scarcely reaches the other side of the restaurant when the blonde sprints for the exit even quicker than her big, burly counterparts.

Once she's out of eyesight, I drift my eyes to Brandon. He looks smug. Shows how fucking stupid he is. "You're an idiot showing up like this unannounced. You could have gotten yourself killed."

"By whom?" He follows me into the kitchen, his strut way too haughty for my liking. I discover the reason behind his peacock walk when he jabs me with a below-the-belt hit. "By you? Or the man you're sheltering after sending every one of your siblings to their deaths?"

Fighting the urge not to slit his throat with the ladle in my hand, I spoon a helping of Malloreddus into the bowl on my left before gesturing with my head for him to sit in the chair across from me. Although my father has returned from New York, I'm not worried about him walking in on our conversation. He uses the Feds to his advantage—just like me.

With the knowledge I'm more like my father than hoped, I drag the ladle across the bottom of the saucepan as if I'm scraping out my father's insides while saying, "I don't protect my father. You're well aware of that."

Brandon dips his chin, mindful I'd kill him for anything less than an agreeing gesture. "Have you been back long?"

My lips itch to lift into a smile, but I hold back the urge. I had wondered how closely I was being monitored by the Bureau after

Tobias's death. Now I know it's more than an occasional glance. The months I spent in Italy weren't widely broadcasted. The family didn't want to risk an attack if our enemies became aware one of the main players were abroad, so we kept it on the down-low.

After setting down a bowl of Malloreddus in front of Brandon, I give him a stern look. "I flew in early last month. The Bureau is unaware of my return. I'd like to keep it that way." My tone reveals I'm not suggesting for this to happen, I am warning him it better occur.

Even being close to a second bender in under a month, my glare has the effect I'm aiming for. "Your secret is safe with me, although I have a few questions I'd like to ask."

I'm not a fan of being interrogated, especially when the questions are being asked by a federal agent, but I jerk up my chin, mindful of how these things work. The more I scratch Brandon's back, the less itchy mine will be.

Unless I get hives, which is what hits me when Brandon asks, "Were you aware CJ was participating in your father's underground fighting circuit?"

After stabbing my fork into my meal with enough aggression for his throat to work hard to swallow, I answer, "I had a feeling a few months before I discovered it the hard way." Brandon isn't the only one shocked by the honesty in my tone. I'm blown away by it as well. "CJ was a good fighter. He was also willing to do anything to get into our father's good graces, so I shouldn't have been surprised."

Once again, I'm being straight-up honest. CJ had world-class skills. He just wasn't in charge of his battles. That day, Isaac walked away with the champion's belt. If CJ hadn't given up on life, he could have claimed victory on their next bout.

Brandon gives me a sympathetic look. It makes me hate him

even more. I loathe people who feel sorry for me without having the faintest clue my biggest battle is also my most unknown. It's kind of like depression. Just because you can't see the illness eating you away doesn't mean it doesn't exist. It's there, gnawing at you for every second of every day. You've just got to be stronger than it.

My thoughts shift from the present to the past when Brandon asks, "Were you aware Isaac Holt fought under your father?"

It's the fight of his life not to scowl when I say, "Who?" I could add more authenticity to my lie, but I can't be fucked. I've hardly slept the past four days, and I don't have the energy for theatrics.

"Isaac Holt." Brandon shovels a forkful of food into his mouth like he's been on a hunger strike as long as Roxanne before he pulls a photograph out of the pocket of his swanky trousers. The shoddy pixilation from being zoomed in reveals it's an image from an FBI file, much less its markings. It has 'confidential' stamped all over it. "This was obtained at an event your father organized."

When Brandon's eyes lift to gauge my response to his inaccurate statement, I stray my eyes away, acting disinterested. "Isaac didn't fight for my father." I shrug before giving him a tidbit of information on my family's inner workings, hopeful it will see him offering leniency when I cash in a future favor. "Col wanted him to, but Isaac wasn't budging. We put steps in place to make it happen."

"We?" His one word is choked through a clump of tomato goop lodged halfway down his throat.

Just like earlier, I could sit back and watch the carnage unfold. Unfortunately, I've got enough issues keeping the Feds off my ass while waiting for the bodies at Roxanne's family ranch to be identified. I don't want another corpse added to the mix.

After pouring Brandon a glass of water, I hand it to him. He chugs down half of it before he almost chokes for the second time from me explaining, "We, as in Ophelia and me."

His fork hits the edge of his bowl with a clatter. "Your sister helped you? How *exactly*?"

Needing to hide my smirk, I dab at my lips with a stained napkin before placing the bowl I used earlier into the sink. "Our father wanted Ophelia to coerce Isaac into fighting for him—"

"So she dated him to deceive him?"

I arch my brow, wordlessly warning him he better not interrupt me again.

Confident he's got the gist of my annoyance, I say, "No. Ophelia was never with him for that. She truly loved him." I pause for a beat, shocked by my confession. That's the first time I've admitted Ophelia loved Isaac. Up until now, I always pretended it was puppy love. "Ophelia wanted a way out—"

"Of?"

My nostrils flare as my glare picks up. I fucking warned him only seconds ago what would happen if he interrupted me again and look what he goes and does. He interrupts me—again!

"Sorry." He tugs at the collar of his dress shirt before gesturing for me to continue.

I give him a few seconds to authenticate the level of my threat before continuing with my purge. "She wanted out of the family. If you think my father was cruel to his sons, you should have seen how he treated his daughters. Monster is too kind of a word." The room cools drastically fast. "We knew how desperate Col was to have Isaac fight under him. We were also aware of how good of a fighter Isaac was, so we plotted for them to meet, knowing Col would use Ophelia as a bargaining chip." I work my jaw side to side, struggling to hide the tick my confession caused. "We had no clue CJ was fighting for our father that night until it was too late. They fought. CJ lost, and Ophelia went into a blackened rage."

Eager to display our conversation won't last long, I snatch up Brandon's scarcely eaten meal and throw it into the sink. "That was the night of their accident."

Although he's disappointed his meal is ruined, Brandon's inquisitiveness is too high to discount. "Ophelia and CJ's?"

I jerk up my chin. "CJ spent weeks in the hospital before he vanished." You have no idea how hard it was for me not to add, 'to the bush' to the end of my comment. The only reason I didn't was my recollection that Brandon isn't my friend. Only a handful of people know CJ's location. My father and the Feds aren't on that list. "Ophelia was buried with only one member of her family in attendance, and I never told a soul about the ruse we attempted to pull. I'll take it to the grave." *As will you if this ever leaves this room.*

I have no reason to voice my threat. The shudder rolling up Brandon's back reveals he'll take it to his grave along with me.

Curious, I ask, "What does this have to do with anything? I get you're after Isaac, but the fight circuit you're talking about has been running for decades. The Feds are well aware of its existence. They're not disbanding it for a reason. For intel..." My words trail off when Brandon echoes my confession. "So why are you bringing up old ghosts?"

It dawns on me that my purge worked in my favor when nothing but honesty rings in Brandon's tone when he says, "I'm seeking connections between Col, Isaac, Henry, and Kirill Bobrov."

The first three names I've heard a hundred times before. The latter is fairly new in my inquiries. It has only come up a handful of times the past year or two.

Although curiosity is burning me alive, I play it cool, conscious the best secrets aren't immediately unveiled. "Vladimir will be disappointed he didn't make the cut."

"He's still there." Brandon's short response exposes he's

endeavoring to keep more than a handful of secrets hidden. "Have you heard of Kirill before?"

I hesitate, untrusting of anyone. "It's been a while..." What? I'm not so stupid to link myself with a current investigation, much less one as perverse as baby trafficking. "... but his name rings a bell. What's his kink?"

Brandon shrugs. "Your guess would be as good as mine. We have an inkling perhaps he's in the sex trafficking trade, but we're only sitting on that theory because of one reason."

Since he's being honest, I do the same. "Katie Bryne?" When he lifts his chin without hesitation, I let him see a small selection of the cards I'm holding. "I knew I had heard the name before."

I can't hold back my smile when I gesture for Brandon to join me in an office at the back of the kitchen. He's carrying a weapon, yet he's still afraid of what I might do to him in a room without a camera. He isn't any safer in the kitchen. The cameras planted throughout the restaurant are solely for looks. If it's electronic, Smith has proven it can be hacked, so there's no fucking chance we'd encourage for the hub of our entity to be placed under unwanted scrutiny.

With that in mind, I come to a dead stop just inside my office. Air whizzes out of Brandon's nose when I halt his entrance by splaying my hand across his chest. He can see the demand in my eyes without a word needing to seep from my lips. It makes me wish he wasn't so anal about following procedures. If he was a little more like his former trainer, we could have an interesting collaboration.

I wolf-whistle when he raises his shirt to show me he isn't wired. I don't give a fuck if he thinks I'm a freak. I just want him on the back foot, so he doesn't reach for his gun when I run the edge of my knife down the front of his pricy outfit. I've been caught out by this preppy boy's love of camera buttons once before. It won't happen again.

"Learned my lesson the hard way," I mutter while dumping the buttons from his business shirt and coat into a half-empty glass of whiskey on my desk. Confident they're broadcasting nothing but the grumbles of my stomach from downing one too many whiskeys last night, I take a seat behind my desk before motioning for Brandon to sit. "If word of this gets out to anyone outside of these walls, my guests will dine on freshly minced veal this evening."

After a quick swallow, Brandon nods, wordlessly sealing our deal. I won't lie. My heart beats a million miles an hour when I place the eight-digit code into the safe bolted to the floor under my desk. I hate giving the Feds anything to work with, but since hardly anyone knows of Fien's existence, I don't see them having any luck working out the combination. It's Fien's birthday followed by her name, an easy combination for me to remember but almost impossible for anyone who doesn't know me to crack. Not even my father has worked it out.

I yank out the multiple cross-references to Fien's case from the leather-bound document before placing it onto my desk. Although Katie's sale has nothing to do with my daughter's captivity, I earmarked her page. Rumors were rife years ago about a rogue Russian sanction kidnapping a local girl, so when her name showed up on a Petretti ledger years after her abduction, I took notice.

I always take notice when Russians are involved.

After pushing across a handful of catering receipts, I set the handwritten ledger down in front of Brandon. "Katie Bryne..." I drag my index finger under her name in the ledger, "... was sold to K Bobrov for three hundred and eighty-five thousand dollars." From what I've discovered the past couple of weeks before Dr.

Bates bid on Roxanne, Katie's sale was a record-breaking amount. Kirill wanted her no matter what, and he was willing to pay for the privilege.

Brandon raises his confused eyes to mine. "The date shows her sale was a little under five years ago. Katie was abducted nine years ago."

While grumbling about his inability to do the legwork himself, I slap the ledger shut, then store it back into my safe. Once it's locked away, I take a moment to deliberate whether I should give him the long answer or the short answer.

Not even five seconds into my pondering, Brandon tries to cut it short. "Tobias's arrangement is still in effect, Dimitri. You're immune from prosecution. Within reason, of course."

Air hisses out of my nose as I balance my elbows on my desk. "It's the men picking the reason that I'm wary of." That was my pleasant way of saying I don't trust him. He doesn't want to hear my unkind response. "Hypothetically speaking..." I wait for conformation to register in his eyes before continuing, "... each sanction runs their operations differently. Some prefer underage girls. Others prefer more mature ones. Then there are ones who aren't specifically looking for a whore. They want a wife, someone to raise children with, but they don't have the time to seek her in a crowd of millions, so they look to someone who can give them what they're seeking without additional training."

Brandon's blond brow pops up high on his face. "Training?"

Over the game, and too fucking tired to care about the ripple on effect my father's shady dealings could cause our family name, I answer, "On being the ideal wife. They're taught how to cook, clean, raise children, and anything else their procurer wants of them. Some take months to learn their role. Others take years." I lower my eyes to the floor to hide the gleam they forever get when Roxanne's feistiness pops into my head. "Some never learn."

My eyes return front and center when Brandon stands to his feet. His eagerness isn't shocking, but what he says next most certainly is. "IRS is planning to raid this restaurant on the eighteenth. I suggest you do some in-house cleaning before then."

Not speaking another word, he makes a beeline for the door, scarcely missing Clover's entrance. It's barely noon, but he's gloved up and ready to kill, unaware the only slaughtering he will do this afternoon is to Roxanne's ego.

# 14

# ROXANNE

I roll onto my opposite hip, saving my stomach the torture of my eyes drinking in the overloaded burger and fries taking up a majority of the nightstand. My ruse is stupid, and I'm doing more harm to myself than anyone, but for the life of me, I can't give in. I'm being held against my will and persecuted for crimes I didn't commit. A hunger-strike is the low end of the scale for how I could protest to Dimitri's unfair ruling.

I've had plenty of time to contemplate other methods, but for now, I'll continue with this one. It's the safest of the three I thought up, and the least likely to shed blood. Even with my head delusional with hunger, I'm reasonably sure my other two ploys would kill more than my anger. Dimitri doesn't handle his jealousy well. It makes him as unhinged as his distrust makes me.

My brows draw together when a frantic buzz overtakes the grumbles of my hungry stomach a few seconds later. It isn't the drone of an electronic lock opening, nor the static that comes out of the speakers a second before Smith's voice. It's foreign yet familiar like it entered my room along with the eleventh meal I've refused to eat.

Too curious for my own good, I roll onto my back, prop myself onto my elbows, then stray my eyes in the direction the buzz came from. Although the black device nestled on the serving dish a scrumptious-smelling burger is resting on doesn't appear to be a cell phone, it rings as if it is one. It vibrates and bounces across the antique wood serving tray, its shriek growing louder the longer I stare at it.

A normal captive would gobble up the first sign of life outside of these walls as if it's the key to their captivity. As I've said before, I'm nothing close to ordinary. Just like each meal has become more and more enticing the longer I refuse to eat them, this is another trick in Dimitri's vault-load of arsenal. I'm certain of it.

When the device halts ringing a few seconds later, I lock my eyes with the camera in the corner of my room, glare at it as if the only meal I'll ever agree to eat is Dimitri's balls when I rip them off with my bare teeth, then I roll back onto my side.

I've barely sucked in two body-cooling breaths when the annoying buzz starts up all over again. It rings and rings and rings until my temper gets the better of me.

Imagine a robot malfunctioning after you take to it with a baseball bat. That's the noise the little black device makes when I send it hurtling across the room. It smacks into the door that only unlocks when I'm using the bathroom before it crumbles to the floor.

Feeling somewhat victorious—and a whole heap hungry—I squash my back to the bedpost that has handcuff marks notched into the wood before curling my arms around my knees. This position makes the gnawing pangs of my stomach less noticeable. We won't mention my jealousy, though, or you'll book me in for a psych workup.

I quit contemplating sneaking into the bathroom to guzzle down stomach-filling gulps of tap water when a third buzz for the morning trickles into my ears. My eyes shoot to the remnants of the device splayed across the floor, shocked as hell it still works. It's a mangled wreck—almost as twisted as my emotions when I discover the noise isn't coming from the homemade device, it's being projected through the speakers planted throughout the room.

If that isn't shocking enough, the sweet voice that drowns out the annoying hum is downright controversial. "Roxie? Are you there?" Estelle breathes noisily out of her nose, a sign she's pissed. "If you ignore my call one more time, I'm going to scream! What's the go with you lately? Are you too good for your friends now?"

I almost reply with a resounding 'no' but lose the chance when a thick Arabian accent sounds down the line. "Less talk. More looking. I haven't got all day."

I hear Estelle shoo away Clover's snappy tone as if he doesn't kill thousands of people a year. "Don't push your luck, mister. After the way she left me high and dry the past few days, she should be grateful I took her call. I'm pissed, and it's that time of the month, so you better watch yourself."

"Estelle—"

"Oh, so you do remember my name. How kind of you." Her tone is bitchy, but I know deep down inside she's more upset than angry. "Now tell me what I'm searching for so I can get on with my day." When I balk, shocked she thinks I need something from her, she reads my mind like she always does. "Mr. Cranky Pants said he was ordered here to collect a package, and that he isn't leaving until he gets it. Considering he handed me your boss's business card, I'm assuming the mysterious package has something to do with you."

The frantic scream of my pulse drowns out her last four words.

I'm panicked out of my mind, suddenly clued on as to why Dimitri would send Clover to my apartment instead of Rocco.

This isn't an endeavor to have me seeing sense through the madness.

This is a shakedown.

"Don't do this," I beg, staring straight at the camera. I can't see Dimitri, but I know he's watching me. I can feel it in my bones. "She has nothing to do with this."

"Nothing to do with what?"

I pretend not to hear the panicked gasps following Estelle's question. "I've done as you asked. I followed your rules."

When the camera swivels to my right, I follow the direction of its gaze. Although I could pretend it's staring at anything, I know its focus is on the only bit of power I have left. Dimitri is eyeing the overloaded burger as efficiently as my hungry eyes did when Rocco delivered it, his gaze as demanding as ever even with it being projected through electronic waves.

I scarcely shake my head for half a second when the panic in Estelle's voice steals my attention. "Excuse me, I asked you to wait in the foyer."

Through my raging pulse, I hear the shuffles she takes away from an unusually quiet Clover. The slosh in the bottom of my stomach threatens to spill when the terrifying noise of Estelle's knee smudging the rim of our bathtub sounds down the line. She's backed into a corner. She has nowhere to run. Her very existence hinges on me coercing Dimitri off the ledge.

"Please, Dimitri," I beg again, my eyes watering. "She's all I have. I won't cope without her."

"Roxie..." Estelle sounds on the verge of tears. She's as rattled as me. "What's going on? I thought you were working for some old geezer who can't wipe his ass."

I want to laugh at her ability always to find humor in any situation, but I'm too petrified Dimitri will use it against me to set it free. "I am. I'm just—"

"Not following the terms she agreed upon." I hate how my body responds to hearing Dimitri's voice for the first time in days. It prickles with excitement instead of repelling in disgust. "And since she's too stubborn for her own good, I had to get inventive."

"So, you sent a member of your staff to collect her belongings?" Estelle's low tone reveals she's lost as to what's happening, but she's also curious. Even being a love-sick idiot wouldn't stop her from hearing the innuendo in Dimitri's tone. It's brimming with possessiveness and a nasty side dish of arrogance. "If you want Roxie to fall into line, you should have threatened her family..." Her voice trails off when the penny finally drops. "Oh, shit."

A second later, glass smashing against tiles sounds down the line. It launches me to my feet as quickly as Estelle's breaths batter the speakers. She's endeavoring to run even with her having no place to hide.

"Please!" I scream, panicked out of my mind. "I'll do anything you want."

Dimitri's demand is stern and to the point. "Eat!"

Tears roll down my cheeks unchecked when I nod my head. The seeded bun of the burger soaks them up when I shakily lift it to my mouth and take the biggest bite I can. I don't chew. I just bite and swallow, bite and swallow until the greasy meat sits in the bottom of my stomach along with my heart.

After wiping at the slosh drooling down my chin, I lock my eyes with the camera above my head. I'm bawling, shaking uncontrollably, and on the verge of being sick, but it feels like I hit the jackpot when Dimitri says, "Enough."

He isn't approving of my grotesque eating skills. He's telling Clover to back off, halting the horrific noises of a woman fighting for her life from sounding over the speakers. He's sparing the life of my best friend all because he was handed the last bit of power I had left.

"Go," I push out breathlessly, hopeful Estelle can still hear me.

My prayers are answered when she asks, "Where?"

I wipe at the tears streaming down my face while answering, "Anywhere. I'll find you. I promise."

"Roxie—"

"I'm fine. I promise you I'm okay. I just need you to go."

Her snivels break my heart. "Okay. I love you."

"I love you too."

I wait for the creak of the safety gate on the elevator of our building to sound down the line before locking my eyes with the camera above my head. I stare straight at the blinking contraption as if not an ounce of fear is bombarding me. I don't know if my strength stems from my determination not to have my entire world stripped out from beneath my feet or the wary churns of Estelle's motor when she cranks the ignition on her shit box. Whatever it is, it shifts my protest from peaceful to anarchy in less than a nanosecond, and even quicker than that, it sees me shredding off my clothes as brutally as Dimitri did weeks ago.

Once they sit in tatters on the floor, I growl out, "Send one of your goons to deal with me now. I dare you."

## 15

# DIMITRI

"Shut down the feed." When the eyes of over a dozen thirsty men who should know better than to look at anything they don't own stray toward my laptop screen, I scream at the top of my lungs, "Shut down the fucking feed!"

Even knowing too well yanking the cord out of my laptop won't stop the camera in Roxanne's room from broadcasting elsewhere, I rip it out before sending my laptop sailing across the room. My plan worked. I forced her to eat. Now she's upped the fucking ante.

"Tell me it's shut down, Smith."

When he hesitates, my jaw works through a hard grind. "It's not an easy fix, Dimi. You wanted the best. The best doesn't crumble for anything. Besides, the feed shouldn't be the sole focus of your concern."

After spinning away from the group of men gawking at me, annoyed I canceled the provocative show early, I ask, "What should be?"

"Rocco." Smith's simple reply shouldn't agitate me to no end, but it does. "He's heading to Roxanne's room."

"Call him back."

He laughs at me as if I'm an idiot. It's the same chuckle he hit me with when I told him about my plan to force Roxanne to eat. "He isn't wearing an earpiece."

After hitting a pompous prick with a stern finger point, warning him I'm seconds from removing his finger if he dares to tap my shoulder one more time, I ask, "Why not?"

Smith's laugh shifts to a bark. "'Cause you wanted to keep him out of the loop with your plan, that's why."

"Lose the fucking attitude, Smith. My plan worked, didn't it?"

He acts as if my threat doesn't have an ounce of sting to it. "If you consider your girl being eyeballed by men who'd happily hurt her while she's butt-naked, yeah, I'd say it was successful."

I don't know what to take my anger out on first. Roxanne's gall or Smith's fucking shitty attitude. I go for both when I snarl, "She isn't my girl."

"Then you'll have no issues with her and Rocco getting super friendly in ten... nine... eight..."

I spin around to face the procession of money-hungry gangsters so fast I make myself dizzy. "Our meeting has been postponed until next month."

They have the hide to grumble at me under their breath like I don't have the ability to sideswipe their entire existence with my pinkie finger. They did the same thing when I took an intermission in our meeting to authenticate the effectiveness of my ruse with Roxanne. I acted as maniacally back then as I do now.

"You either accept a second interlude in our proceedings, or we permanently part ways." When silence stretches across the room, I get cocky. "That's what I thought. I don't want to work with you pricks any more than you don't want to lick the soles of my shoes for an ounce of my attention. Unfortunately, you don't have a choice. You need me. It'll do you best to remember that the next time we meet."

After ensuring my father absorbed my words along with the rest of our 'family,' I race out of my office and hotfoot it up a set of stairs I've avoided like the plague the past four days.

Smith is no longer counting in my ears, but I mentally tick over two just as I stop outside Roxanne's bedroom door. I'm too worked-up to mull over the fact Rocco could be inside. I just throw open the door and step into a warzone without adequate protection.

Roxanne doesn't just hurl words when she's angry. She tosses out fists as if they are grenades. She whacks them into my back, my stomach, and attempts to collide them with my nuts before I pin her to the wall with my brooding frame.

With her fists immobilized at her sides, she uses the rest of her body to inflict her anguish. She thrashes out her legs, throws her head around, and screams like she's being murdered.

"Stop it!" I shake her hard enough that her brain rattles in her skull. This isn't just about anyone but me seeing her naked anymore. If she doesn't calm down, she will hurt herself. That's as unacceptable as her wish to starve herself to death. "I had to do something to force you to eat. You were fading to nothing."

Her words seethe out of her mouth like lava, "Don't act as if any of this was about me! You tried to destroy the only person I've ever cared about."

"Clover was ordered not to hurt her."

She calls me out as the liar I am. "He's a trained killer! That's all he knows, and you put her on his radar!"

"To protect you!" I scream back, as unhinged as her. "That's why you've been locked in your room. That's why I stayed the fuck away. I was trying to protect you."

To ensure she can't miss the angst eating me alive, I release one of her wrists from my hold before bringing her eyes to mine by a brutal grip on her face. I'm hurting her, but it has nothing on the pain that ripped through me when Smith announced the price on her head was double the ransom they requested for my wife.

"Seven point six million dollars. What do you think they'd want for that amount, Roxanne? Your virginity? A couple of kids?" I press into her deeper, stealing more than the air from her lungs. "Your fucking soul? They have my daughter, my flesh and blood, yet they're still not done fucking me in the ass. They want you, too."

Roxanne's tiptoe to insanity is showcased in the worst light when she snaps out, "Then let them have me!"

I shake her again, hopeful a good rattle of her skull will have her brain switching on. "They don't want you for the trade, Roxanne. They want to torture you for hours on end before killing you like you're a piece of meat—"

I recoil like I've been slapped when she butts in, "Just like you?"

My laugh reveals how close to the edge I am. I'm ready to jump, to freefall into hell, but there's only one reason I can't let go, and for the first time in a long time, it doesn't solely fall on Fien's shoulders.

"I'm nothing like my enemies."

I step back from Roxanne like her eyes are loaded with bullets when she comes at me with more than a mutual attraction. She hits me below the belt with a rarity in this industry. She knocks me out with straight-up honesty. "You've said time and time again that I'm responsible for your wife's death, that if she hadn't been swapped for me, your life would be ten times easier, but we both know that isn't what this is about. You didn't give a shit about Audrey. If she wasn't carrying your child, I doubt you would have paid her ransom. This is about you believing I'm only here because I feel responsible for Fien's captivity. You can't believe someone would help you out of the kindness of their own heart. You refuse to accept that not everyone is out to get you. You see everyone as your enemy... even those closest to you."

As her watering eyes bounce between mine, their wetness doubles. "The spark in the alleyway, that zap so fierce, I put my entire life on the line to seek it for a second time occurred *before* I knew you had a daughter. It was there *before* we discovered how fucked up my parents are, and *before* you realized the extent of your father's evilness. It was there from the very beginning, yet, you're still trying to deny it."

For how red-faced she is, her hand shouldn't feel like ice when she curls it around my jaw. "You've always believed you were fighting this war alone. Now, I'm willing to let you." She doesn't say she's done with me, but her facial expression most certainly does. "If you want to change that, you know where to find me."

She slips under my arm before making her way to the bathroom. Her steps are extra fast, hopeful she'll make it to safety before the tears brimming in her eyes roll down her face.

Her desire for privacy is awarded with barely a second to spare. However, her retreat to the only room in this compound without a camera has its downfalls. The space is large and covered with tiles, so every painful sob she fails to hold in bounces into the main part of our room. They're as gut-wrenching as the crunch my knuckles make when they pierce through the drywall I had Roxanne pinned against, and just as devastating as my cowardly exit of a room cloaked with hate.

# 16

## DIMITRI

My eyes drift from Roxanne nibbling on her breakfast as if she's a mouse to Rocco when he enters my downstairs office without bothering to knock. It's been four days since my exchange with Roxanne, four days since I raced Rocco to her room without realizing I couldn't beat him there without overtaking him since there's only one way in and out of my room, and four days since Roxanne has uttered a syllable to me.

She hasn't spoken to me in days.

Not when I sneak into our bed in the middle of the night.

Not when I deliver the food she's eaten with protest.

Not even when I pull her into my arms so the tears she releases every night can be absorbed by my chest.

She has said nothing, and it's fucking killing me.

I've always thought violence was the only way to voice your anger. Roxanne is showing me otherwise. Her silence is worse than any massacre I've been a part of. It's draining my veins of blood as if she ripped away a part of my soul instead of my enemies.

"Don't bother shutting it down," Rocco says on a laugh as he spins around the chair on the opposite side of my desk to straddle it backward. "Even with you making her feed private, I know you're stalking her like you had me do the months after her hospital stay."

Determined to prove I'm not the soft cock he thinks I am, I switch off the monitor Roxanne's white face is filling before slouching low into my office chair.

I should have realized Rocco wouldn't fall for my tricks. He knows me too well to lap up my bullshit excuses. "Do you really think that will cut it?" Although he's asking a question, he continues talking, stealing my chance to reply. "Hiding her away won't fix shit, Dimi. Acting as if she means nothing to you won't fix shit." He slants his head to the side before arching his brow. "Holding her when she cries won't fix shit... especially when you're the reason she's crying."

Smith's silence reveals he knew Rocco's plan to throw him into the deep end without a life jacket. If he weren't aware, he would have defended himself by now.

I've avoided Rocco's emotional jabs for the past two decades, but I can't do it anymore. "What do you suggest I do, Rocco? Feed her to the wolves?"

I'm anticipating for him to come back with the loved-up shit his mother used to excuse his father for beating her to a pulp, so you can imagine my surprise when he takes our conversation in a direction I never saw coming. "Stop taking it up the ass as if you enjoy it."

My laugh belongs to a maniac. It rolls up my chest as quickly as my fists ball, but it does little to weaken Rocco's campaign. "When we were kids, every fucking game without fail, you played the character less likely to win all because you were determined to prove Princess Peach wasn't a damsel in distress. You didn't give a fuck that you lost time and time again 'cause it wasn't about winning, it was about being the better person." He points to my door as if Roxanne is on the other side. "You finally won, but instead of giving Princess P her time to shine, you locked her away in another fucked-up kingdom."

"To protect her." My words seethe out of my mouth like venom.

Rocco scoffs at me like I'm not seconds from pressing my gun to his temple and blowing his brains out. "You're not protecting her. You are bending over and taking it up the ass like you have the past two years." His words shift to a chuckle when I dive over my desk, remove my gun from the back of my trousers, and use the barrel to smooth the crinkle between his dark brows. "You can't kill me, Dimi. Your enemies haven't ordered you to, and we both know you don't do anything until they tell you to."

Too pissed to think clearly, I flick off the safety on my gun before inching back the trigger. "I'm Dimitri fucking Petretti. I don't answer to anyone."

"Prove it," Rocco mocks, staring straight at me. "Kill me."

His suggestion both shocks and pisses me off, but I play it cool. "You're willing to die for Roxanne?"

He shakes his head, his smile picking up. "Nah, D. This has nothing to do with Roxie. You, on the other hand, this has every-thing to do with *you*. If you need to kill me to get your balls back, I'm willing. As you said, you're Dimitri fucking Petretti, so how about you start acting like it? We play to play, we kill to kill, and we—"

"Take down any fucker stupid enough to get in our way."

His smile is smug now instead of mocking. "I can't imagine what's going through your head. I assume it's some fucked-up shit, but you'll never win the war if you're not willing to fire at the opposition."

Although I agree with him, there's one thing I can't discount. "Fien—"

"Is a weakness they're exploiting because they assume you won't fight back." He frees himself from my vicious clutch before scooting to the back of his chair, bringing himself closer to me. "Roxanne is a way of showing them you're not to be messed with. Bring back the fear, Dimi. Bring back the respect." He nudges his head to the monitor I switched off when he arrived. "Bring back the woman willing to die for a little girl she's never met. If you bring those things back, Fien will soon follow. I guarantee you that."

Rocco doesn't make pledges he can't keep. Everyone he has made, he's upheld—including his promise that he'd walk away from our friendship if I married Audrey. He knew it would cause a heap of trouble, though I doubt he ever guessed it would be this bad.

That's why I sent Clover to do Audrey's ransom drop instead of Rocco. We had been out of contact for months. Something about Audrey rubbed him the wrong way. He never told me what, but it was as obvious as the sun hanging in the sky.

Taking my silence as the end of our conversation, Rocco stands to his feet, flips his chair back around, then makes a beeline to the door.

He halts opening it when I ask, "What was it about Audrey that you hated."

He cranks his neck my way. "I didn't hate her, D. She just had nothing in her eyes that proved she deserved you."

"And Roxanne does?"

His lips curl into the corner. "Fuckin' oath she does." He pivots around to face me front on. "The first time I saw her, the thoughts I had when you showed me a photo of Fien rolled through my head. Born in the wrong era, to the wrong family, but so fucking full of life, she'd survive the shittiest of circumstances."

I try to hold back my nod, but my chin bobs before I can. That's almost spot on to what I thought when I saw Roxanne with black smudges smeared on her cheeks. The beauty she tried to hide with goth clothing and black makeup captured my attention but knowing she could leap over the grief holding her down utterly sealed my devotion. She had strength I'd never seen in a woman—not even my mother.

Strength she could have again if I'm willing to loosen the reins. "Rocco..."

He takes a moment to wipe the hope from his face before answering, "Yeah."

He shouldn't have bothered. It comes back in abundance when I say, "Have Smith clear my schedule. Unless it directly corresponds with Fien, I don't want to know about it."

He hits me with a frisky wink. "It'll be my pleasure."

He isn't glamouring up because he finally has the chance to run things around here. He's had numerous opportunities to create his own sanction the past decade. It's never been of interest to him. He's just grateful we're once again on the same team. That hasn't been the case the past four days. Roxanne's silence wasn't the only one I was dealing with. Rocco had kept his distance as well.

That's done with now. Rocco is right. I can't be fucked in the ass unless I'm willing to lay down and take it. For too long, I've allowed others to write my story. This is my life and my mistakes, so I refuse to let anyone edit out the parts that need to be shared— even the brutal bits. This is my story, and I'm going to tell it how it's supposed to be told.

# 17

## ROXANNE

My steps out of the bathroom are reduced to half their natural stride when I spot an outfit splayed across the mattress I've shared with Dimitri the past four nights even with us not sharing a word between us. I've climaxed on that bed, laughed on it, and shed tears on it more times than I can count, but this is the first time I've ever had an outfit laid out on it.

It's not a fancy dress like the many in the walk-in closet, nor is it an innocent outfit. It's modest yet sexy if that's possible. The cut of the full-length leather pants assures me they'll hug my butt in all the right places. The shimmery beige material of the strapless crop top adds glitz to the ensemble while the denim jacket promises to keep me warm even if my bosoms spill over the skimpy material that's meant to cover my midsection.

With my gut twisted in confusion, I seek answers from the last person likely to give them to me. "Smith..." He has been as silent as Dimitri and Rocco the past four days, but that doesn't mean he isn't watching me. Other than my thirty-second lapse of judgment days ago, the red light in the corner of the room has continuously blinked.

My eyes snap to the other side of the room when a rough, gravelly tone says, "Smith is no longer in charge of the surveillance for this room." Dimitri doesn't need to say who's helming the watch. His eyes are very telling.

Even with my body showing signs it's missed his voice the past few days, I act as if he isn't in the room with me. I dart for the walk-in closet, eager to switch out my dressing gown with something a little cooler. The heat bouncing between Dimitri and me is too much. It's as fiery as it has always been, but since it is also fueled by anger, it is unbearable.

It is the fight of my life to hold in my scream when my race for the closet reveals it's as empty as my chest feels. All the clothes have been removed—even Dimitri's. I want to say he knows I'm a stubborn ass, so he put steps in place to force me to submit to him, but I won't give him the satisfaction.

"I need you to get dressed and come with me."

I'm torn. With a sudden knowledge that I hate enclosed spaces, I'd donate a kidney to leave these four walls, but if I give in like I did my hunger strike, how bad will my next test be? Perhaps it will be a kidney? I've faced every other injustice in my short twenty years, so why not throw organ trafficking into the mix.

Proof he's as bossy and domineering as ever is showcased in the worst light when Dimitri barks out, "What's our agreement, Roxanne?"

Over him and his stupid mind games, I march to the mattress, snatch up the leather pants as if I'll skip chaffing from wearing them sans underwear, carefully pry open my dressing gown, then stuff my feet into the opening of my pants.

Once I have them over my butt, which I'm embarrassed to say

took longer than two minutes, I snap up the skimpy strapless top Dimitri picked for me to wear before I spin around to face him.

When I nudge my head to the door, requesting privacy, he has the audacity to do his infamous half-smirk. I don't know why. The slightest peek he got of the back of my knees when I tugged the rigid leather up my legs is the *only* piece of my skin he'll ever see. *Again.* I can't do anything about our previous exchanges.

"Fine." He throws his hand into the air to display his annoyance before he pivots to face the door.

Wanting to ensure there's no chance he'll get a sneaky peek later, I face the bathroom door before removing my dressing gown. I could get dressed in the bathroom, but considering my room now has multiple cameras, it wouldn't do me any good.

After ensuring my nipples aren't showing, I slip my feet into the boots at the end of the bed, then join Dimitri by the door. Sensing my approach, he spins around to face me. I won't lie, even pissed, I relish the way he can't help but glide his eyes down my body.

His gaze is so white-hot when he suggests for me to grab my jacket, I shake my head.

A brick lodges in my throat when he says, "It's cold where you're going. I don't want your lips turning a shade of blue." However, he doesn't see my panicked response since he gathers up my jacket on my behalf.

The last time he spoke those words to me, my world was upended.

Although petrified I'm about to meet with my maker, I won't beg. I'm the one who suggested for Dimitri to give me to his enemies, so how can I act shocked by him doing exactly that?

An eerie feeling bombards me when Dimitri guides me down the staircase at the end of the hallway our room is located in. His home isn't silenced by unusual quiet. Energy is bristling in the air, and I'm reasonably sure only some of it is compliments to Dimitri's hand hovering above the unconcealed skin on the lower half of my back.

When we enter a room two spots down from Dimitri's downstairs office, the reason for the hum of chatter is exposed. There are three to four dozen men filling the space. Half are seated around a large oval-size boardroom table, and the rest are standing toward the back.

"Take a good look at this face," Dimitri says when his suffocating aura deprives the room of oxygen as effectively as his next set of words steal the air from my lungs. "I'm sure you've heard the rumors that this face is worth seven point six million dollars." He strays his eyes across the men eyeing him with as much interest as me. "I'm here to tell you this face won't earn you millions if you attempt to cash in the bounty on her head. She will cost you everything. Your life. Your wife. Not even your children will be spared. I'll destroy you and anyone associated with you. If you don't believe me, I'm more than happy to display how foolish you are."

My eyes bounce between Dimitri's narrowed gaze and his ear when the faintest trickle of a unique accent sounds in my ears. Smith is guiding Dimitri's eyes around the room as he did mine weeks ago, honing him in on his targets—which is reduced by one when Dimitri lines up his gun with a man at the back of the room and fires one shot.

The man slumps to the floor in an instant, the bullet wound between his eyes as unforgiving as Dimitri's anger when the cell phone that clatters out of his hand reveals my image on the screen. My outfit proves it was just taken, although it remains unsent in the man's outbox.

"I understand the bounty is impressive, and that you believe it's worth the risk, but is it more valuable than your family?"

My eyes don't know which direction to look when a large

screen at the side of the room commences broadcasting a raid in progress. The balaclava-clad faces conducting the raid aren't members of the FBI or local law enforcement office. Their eyes are familiar. I've seen them multiple times the past few weeks, most notably the murky green pair that executes three men kneeling in front of a large brute with a clover tattoo on his cheek.

When Clover lifts one of the deceased man's heads to face the camera, a collective hiss rolls around the room. The victims' matching bullet wounds aren't their only familiarities. If you wiped three decades off the age of the first victim's face, it would be almost identical to the one Clover is holding up.

"I have men at the front of all your houses." There's too much honesty in Dimitri's tone to discount. "Is anyone else willing to test the authenticity of my threat?"

Most of the men shake their heads. Only one is stupid enough to add words into the mix. "You need to be reasonable, Dimitri. We're only trying to support our families."

Dimitri gives the gray-haired man a look as if to say he isn't as stupid as he's implying. The bounty on my head isn't the only mine these men are drilling. They've got their hands in as many pots as Dimitri.

"I'm well aware what you need money for, Mark. It has nothing to do with that pretty little wife of yours and everything to do with the underaged girls you beat and sodomize once a week." His lack of denial exposes Dimitri is on the money. "As for the rest of you, I'm willing to negotiate more suitable terms. How does fifteen million sound?" The excitement building in the room skyrockets as high as my blood pressure when Dimitri adds, "That's the amount I'll pay when you bring me the people responsible for the bounty on Roxanne's head. If they're brought in alive, I'll double it."

"Dimitri..." I can't say more. I'm too shocked. He's put thirty million dollars on the line for my safety. That's insane. I'm not worth that much.

Before I've worked through half my shock, Dimitri instructs Smith to do a final once-over of the room. Once he's confident his offer is more enticing than that of his enemies, he grips the top of my arm and drags me out of the room. I don't think he means to hurt me. He's just too doped up on adrenaline to realize how strong his grip is. I'm feeling superhuman, and I did nothing but stand at his side with my jaw hanging open.

Halfway down the hallway, Dimitri's brittle tone snaps me out of my shock. "Take them out to the Hole. There are men out there waiting." His comment exposes he knew at least one of the men would test him. "We should arrive in around thirty minutes." During the 'we' part of his statement, his eyes drift to me. "Is everything ready?"

I discover the reason he suggested for me to take a jacket when he throws open the front door of his compound and guides me outside. Although it isn't as cold here as it was in New York, there's a brisk coolness in the air.

The goosebumps coating my skin augment when Dimitri assists me into the front passenger seat of a fierce-looking sports car. It's warm in the cabin of his sleek ride. My body just couldn't help but respond to him leaning across my frozen frame to fasten my seat belt. Even with the smell of a recently fired gun lingering in my nostrils, his scent is scrumptious. It grips my senses for the next several minutes, only relinquishing its hold when Dimitri pulls down a familiar-looking road twenty minutes later.

Although this isn't the most direct route to my grandparents' farm, it's the one people use when they want to be discreet. My mom went this way when she abandoned me, and I used this off-beat track when I snuck back home after my failed meet-up with my father. My nanna told me not to go. I thought I knew better as I do again now.

"Why are we here?"

Dimitri flashes his headlights three times before he drifts his eyes to me. "My enemies think this is friendly territory. They'd never believe I'd shelter anyone here."

"You just put up thirty million dollars to guarantee my safety. You don't need to hide me anymore."

My shock shifts to panic when Dimitri says, "I'm not hiding you, Roxanne. I'm letting you out of our agreement."

"Why? Our agreement was supposed to end once you got your daughter back." I don't know whether to scream or cry when a reason for his unusual bend of the rules smack into me. "Is this a test?"

"No." His curt reply does little to slacken the noose in my stomach, but before I can continue to interrogate him, the quickest flash in the corner of my eye steals my devotion. "Sniper," Dimitri informs like it's an everyday occurrence to have men lying in wake in overgrown fields. "There are two covering the front and back entrances and one on the main gate. They'll remain until the threat has been neutralized."

I've barely gotten over my shock when I'm smacked for the second time. This surprise doesn't come in the form of violence. It's too beautifully sweet to have an ounce of disdain attached to it. Or should I say, *she* is too beautifully sweet.

"Estelle."

I throw open Dimitri's car door before he comes to a stop. Not even the slop of a recently dug-up ground can slow me down. I race Estelle's way, my feet moving as fast as my heart.

The collision of our bodies is as brutal as the rain falling down on us when the heavens open up. Although it has nothing on the wetness that fills my eyes when it dawns on me why Estelle's hair appears as red as my natural hair coloring.

Dimitri's car is no longer rolling toward my grandparents' ranch. It's heading in the opposite direction. His eyes aren't seeking potholes in the sloshy road, though. They stare at me in the side mirror, watching me as adeptly as he did in the alleyway all those months ago. It's a beautiful stare that could only be more appealing if it weren't cloaked with darkness. It feels so final like tonight will be the last time I'll see him.

If the dip of his chin before he pulls onto the main road is anything to go by, I'm reasonably sure it will be.

# 18

# DIMITRI

Paranoia can make the sanest man feel unhinged. It eats away at you worse than low self-esteem, depression, and all that other whacked-up shit therapists toss around when seeking new patients. It sees a once-stable man freeing the only person who's ever made him feel normal, so he can become a creep who crawls into voids above seedy restaurants to spy on his enemies.

When you lose the ability to tell the difference between your rivals and your comrades, you should consider shutting up shop. But since this is me, and nothing ever comes easy for me, I've done the opposite. I opened my doors and invited my enemies inside, aware that a meal shared with a rival is often less disastrous than one shared with family.

My focus shifts back to the present when Rocco's boorish tone sounds down the earpiece lodged in my ear canal. "Clover's big ass will have you receiving company in five... four..."

The manhole I closed after crawling into a roof of a restaurant that's heydays are long behind it pops open just as Rocco hits three. The lack of concern in his tone weakens the itch of my trigger finger. If he were worried about my pop-in visitor, he wouldn't have announced his arrival only seconds before it was set to occur. He wants us to meet up. For what reason? I don't know. But I will find out. You can put your money on it.

Once my guest squeezes through the tight opening like his shoulders are the width of mine, his identity is immediately unearthed. All agents have the same putrid scent, but Brandon James is more perverse since he attempts to mask the smell with a pricy cologne.

"You need to change your aftershave. I could smell that shit long before you crawled through the vent."

I'm lying, and Brandon fucking knows it. I can feel the arrogance beaming out of him, much less see it on his face when he switches on the torch mounted to his Bureau-issued pistol. "You know I'm well within my right to shoot you, right?"

A *pfft* vibrates my lips. "If you wanted to shoot me, you would have done it the instant I turned my back to you. That's how most agents operate, isn't it?"

Incapable of denying the truth, he houses his gun onto the holster on his hip before he joins me above the hub of the restaurant I've been watching like a hawk the past hour. It isn't every day a booking is made in the name of a notorious gangster, especially in a town he has no right to be in without permission, so I don't need to mention the fact this restaurant is way below Cartel standards. It has me suspicious Theresa's claims about an alleged Russian takeover were gospel. That frustrates me even more than my enemies' belief they can arrive in my town without notice. I'd usually kill a man for less. Alas, some of Roxanne's quirks rubbed off on me—most notably her inquisitiveness.

"He's smarter than he looks," Smith mutters in my ear when Brandon asks, "Who's he meeting with?"

For all he knew, I could have been scoping potential clients for the prostitution conglomerate the Petrettis have mingled in for decades. Only someone in the know understands the boss only gets his hands dirty when the target is top grade.

Albert Sokolov may not be feared as he was once, but his murder count alone ensures his respect remains high enough if he were to be killed, it wouldn't be done by a foot soldier. He's Vladimir Popov's number two, and up until ten minutes ago, I was convinced he was here on behalf of Nikolai. Now I'm eating more than my words.

"An old Russian sanction was here a few years back, but there's been no rumblings from their barracks in almost a decade."

I smirk when Brandon cringes about the cobwebs on his jacket before replying, "He's not meeting with a fellow Russian."

Feeling generous, and a little bit lost on how to absorb what's happening today, I nudge my head to the scope of my gun, offering Brandon the chance to cream his pants. He *thinks* he has a vault-load of weapons at his disposal. He's dead fucking wrong. The guns the Feds are playing with have nothing on my arsenal of toys.

"What the fuck?" Brandon mumbles under his breath a few seconds later, expressing my exact sentiment when I discovered the reason for Albert's visit. He isn't here to stake a claim on Nikolai's birthright, he's here to schmooze Isaac Holt—the very man who ran Russians out of his town only a couple of years ago.

"Party Pooper," Rocco murmurs when Brandon's brief perusal of the room below is quickly chased by him, removing a handkerchief from his pocket so he can scrub his fingerprints from a weapon the Bureau would give anything to log into evidence. "Who the fuck carries around a snot-rag in their pocket these days? What is he? A hundred!"

I have no reason to hold in my chuckles about Rocco's witty comment when Brandon warns, "Unless you want to be stuck up here all night, or better yet, detained in a holding cell, I suggest you leave now. This place is about to be raided." The concern in his voice has me wondering which team he bats for. Right now, the odds aren't swinging in his favor. I don't have anything against gay men, I just can't understand how some of them give up the holy grail without first sampling it.

I guess I can't talk. I've never tasted a cunt as sweet as Roxanne's, and I let her walk away from me. Am I regretting my decision? Ask me again when I'm not stationed outside of her ranch every night, monitoring her every move. I might be in the right headspace then to give you an accurate answer.

After dismantling my customized M-4, I remove a single sheet of paper out of my duffle bag and thrust it into Brandon's chest. "With the government eager to do some digging on my businesses, I commenced some of my own."

I lower my eyes to the photograph of Isabelle I snapped earlier this week. With Theresa's claims of a takeover ringing in my ears and discovering multiple drawings of Isabelle in Roxanne's sketchpad, I looked a little deeper into Isabelle's connection with the Russian Mafia. It isn't pretty, and it pains me to admit, the controversy isn't coming from Isabelle. She's on my father's radar, and he's making costly mistakes to ensure both she and Isaac know it.

After a quick shake of my head to remove the negativity inside it, I ask, "Do you know who she's related to?"

When Brandon takes in Isabelle's photo, his throat works through a brutal swallow. I didn't have Smith age my photograph. I kept it simple and to the point. Even the date in the far corner remains.

My lips twist when protectiveness vibrates out of Brandon in invisible waves. He looks like he's about to blow his top, and he has everyone, including Rocco, paying careful attention to every expression that crosses his face. A man only projects this level of

fearlessness when he either wants to fuck the woman he's protecting, or he's related to her. There's no in-between.

"Ah... so you do know who she is." Even knowing Isabelle isn't
causing the ruckus in Hopeton I pretend she is, hopeful it will
have Brandon on the back foot. The more Feds I have nibbling out
of my hand, the quicker Fien will be returned. "If she is what this
is about..." I motion my head to the hole in the wall I used to line
up my target, "... we're going to have issues. This isn't Russian
territory—"

"She has nothing to do with this. I don't even know if Isaac is
aware who her father is." His mortified expression is priceless. It
makes me laugh. It isn't a hinged, sane man laugh. It shows just
how deeply I've dived down the rabbit hole the past few weeks.

With my mood now hostile, it's an effort to act unaffected by it,
but I give it my best shot, mindful Brandon and I aren't on the
same team. We weren't when his team helmed the operation that
had my daughter's whereabouts unknown for months. We won't
be when I fix the injustice of his mistakes. "Bring me everything
you have in five days. *If* I find it satisfactory, I'll share some hard
truths with you."

"And if it isn't?"

My smile should tell him everything, but just in case it doesn't,
I expose exactly what will happen to him if he double-crosses me.
With my hand shaped into a gun, and my eyes slitted, I press my
fingers to his temple and mimic the sound of me blowing his
brains out.

"Five days, Brandon. Don't keep me waiting."

I make it out of the tight opening easier than I did crawling
into it. That might have something to do with the deflation of my
ego. I stormed up here loaded and ready for carnage. I leave
without a single drop of blood being shed. Some may say it's
because I'm maturing, and with that comes greater understanding.

My testimony wouldn't be anywhere near as polite as that. I've always been a grumpy, surly bastard, but it's been worse the past few weeks. I don't know why. I'm used to people disappointing me. I just never figured Roxanne would be added to the long list.

"Boy in blue on your nine when you exit."

As I make my way through the narrow corridors of a Chinese restaurant like I own the place, I jerk up my chin, advising Rocco I understand his command. Boy in blue is his nickname for Detective Ryan Carter. He's one of the rare good ones around here.

It doesn't make us friends, though.

While breaking through the rickety back entrance of a restaurant on the outskirts of Hopeton, I put on my game face. I'm weaponed up, ready for war, and heading straight toward a man who won't take bribes no matter how hard I push him. I'd let you call me insane if I wouldn't have to kill you for it. "You know you'd get more action if you placed yourself amongst the riffraff."

Ryan smirks. It's as cool as his blue eyes. "You wouldn't believe the things I've witnessed from sitting back and watching the shit unfold."

"From what I've heard, that isn't your style. Not now, and not when your daddy took his failures out on your momma."

That changes the expression on his face in an instant. He looks seconds from killing me, the only reason he doesn't is because there was nothing but respect in my tone when I spoke. If the rumors are true, if he gunned down his father like Rocco did his, he earned my respect. It takes guts to go against the man who created you—strength I've yet to garner.

"Between me and you, he deserved it." Ryan doesn't deny my claims, assuring me he believes the same thing.

Over our pointless chit-chat, I lift my chin in farewell before making my way to the tank Rocco is camped out in. I'm halfway there when the quickest warning stops me in my tracks. "They're not the only Russians you should be watching."

I have no clue who Ryan is talking about until he inconspicuously nudges his head to my right. A novice would immediately glance in the direction he nudged. I was born for this industry, so you can be guaranteed I won't make a rookie mistake. I've only done that once. It cost me everything.

After slotting into the passenger seat of a prototype vehicle I had customized to withstand war, I instruct for Rocco to take the long route home. He doesn't ask questions. He just strays his eyes to the side mirrors as swiftly as mine, aware I only ever say that when I'm suspicious we have a tail.

We're almost at the end of the street before a vehicle parked a few spaces back from our original location pulls off the curb. From the outside, it appears to be a car an underpaid federal officer would get around in. It's basic, modest, and has tinted windows. Regretfully, the plates aren't government-issued. Smith was quick to run the tags through the system the instant Ryan pointed out I had an admirer. The modest thirty-thousand-dollar ride is straight off the lot. It was purchased with cash.

"Head for the tunnel. It can shelter a body for a couple of days." I'm not in the mood to play games. As Rocco said, we play to play, we kill to kill, and we take down any fucker stupid enough to get in our way. This fucker is in my way.

While Rocco leads our prey to his final resting place, I remove the tripod and scope from my M4. I could use the weapon stuffed down the back of my trousers, but this will be more fun. An M4 wound shows precision and skill. My gun just blows people's brains out. After the shit few weeks I've had, I need to flex a bit of muscle.

"Pull over here, then continue on."

Although disappointed he will miss most of the action, Rocco does as instructed. He's been a little quiet the past four weeks like Roxanne's silence stung his ego as much as it did mine.

Once the taillights of Rocco's ride are far enough away for our lead to continue the chase, I sink myself into the marshland on the side of the road, unfearful an alligator may be lying in wake. Even prehistoric creatures aren't stupid enough to go against a madman with an M4.

As the blue sedan rolls down the asphalt, I take aim at his front passenger side tire. I don't want the flip to kill him. I want that pleasure to be all mine.

*Pop.* His tire is taken out with a clean through-and-through, and as predicted, it causes his sedan to cartwheel. It somersaults down the isolated road before it comes to a dead stop mere feet from me.

I'm up and out of the marshland in an instant, my movements replicating those of men born for carnage. I am dripping wet, peering down my gun's barrel, and ready to execute my third foot soldier this week. The only reason I hold back desires greater than anything I've ever experienced is because the man hanging upside down in the cab of his car, aiming his gun at my head, has a highly recognizable face.

Some may say he's the real brother of Nikolai Popov.

I'm the only one who knows that's far from the truth.

If DNA chooses your enemies as it does your family, Rico Popov should be Nikolai's number one enemy. The war between the Popovs and the Perettis has been running longer than both of them have been born, and despite his last name, Nikolai is a Petretti, and I have the DNA evidence to prove it.

# 19

# DIMITRI

Rico's dark eyes lift to Rocco when he places down a set of keys for a white Range Rover on the desk separating us. Rocco isn't impressed I'm gifting one of our prized fleet to the enemy, but replacing the ride I totaled is the least I can do after all the information Rico unknowingly shared with me the past couple of hours.

It's disappointing when you learn how far your father is willing to stoop for revenge. However, it's also cathartic. My father has never given a shit about anyone but himself.

If it had the possibility of making him rich, he ran with it.

If he had to stomp on his family for it to occur, he still ran with it.

If it came with the risk of killing every single person with his blood, he still fucking ran with it.

Nothing stopped him, not a single thing, so you can imagine my surprise when I learned who his revenge centers around. He didn't bring the law into a war they don't belong in for his own

benefit. He did it for Ophelia, the only daughter he ever acknowledged as his own.

His show of chivalry was years too late, but it's better than it
not happening at all.

"I'll talk to my father." My words are as bitter as the bile in the
back of my throat. I haven't seen hide nor hair of my father since
our canceled meeting weeks ago. Usually, I'd relish the silence, but
Rico's unexpected trip to this side of the country exposes that
would be stupid for me to do. My father is making costly mistakes,
blunders that could cost him more than his empire. They may
even cause my demise. "But I should warn you, my father's interest
in Isabelle isn't the only one you should be paying attention to."

Rico arches a thick brow but remains silent. His respect sees
me offering more information than I planned to give.

"Isabelle has been spotted numerous times with Isaac Holt the
past couple of weeks." I twist around the tablet Smith uploaded a
range of long-range surveillance shots onto while watching Rico's
face to see if Isaac's name registers as familiar.

Although his jaw gains an involuntary tick, his expression
remains somewhat neutral. "I've heard of Isaac before. He's not of
interest to me." His approval is shocking. However, it has nothing
on what he says next, "If you heard any of his conversation with
Albert this afternoon, you'd know why."

It isn't what he said that shocks me. It's how he said it. It had a
protective edge to it. It could be because he believes sheltering
Isaac will keep his long-lost sister safe, but I have a feeling that's
only part of his reasoning.

"It isn't Isaac I'm warning you about. It's his baggage." The
altering of his facial features I was seeking earlier occur this time
around. I'm not surprised the shockwaves of a mafia princess's
death spread across the globe like wildfire. It's why even without
proof of life, I'd still know Fien is okay. Women in this industry are

valued as useless until they're being torn between two men. Then it's a free-for-all. Nothing is off-limits.

Deciding it isn't my place to make my sworn enemy's jobs easier, I get back to the reason Rico is surrounded by over a dozen men with body-maiming weapons. "Meet-ups without prior knowledge isn't something I take lightly."

Rico smiles as if my tone didn't have an ounce of bitterness. "We advised of our arrival. Your father suggested for it to occur in Hopeton."

I want to call him out a liar before showing him exactly what happens to men who double-cross me, but there's too much honesty in his eyes to discount. He has the eyes of Satan. They're just minus the pure evilness his father's have.

"What was the business about?" We've talked shop the past two hours, but since Rico's focus was solely on my father's trek across the country to rile Vladimir about having contact with his favorite whore's daughter, Isaac's meeting with Vladimir's number two went unmentioned.

My jaw almost cracks when Rico replies, "Nothing that concerns you." As he stands from his seat, he does up the middle button on his business jacket. "Don't get up. I'll show myself out."

He laughs like his life isn't on the line when Clover forcefully places him back into his seat. His chuckles sound fake, but the mask he's wearing is anything but when he threatens Clover with the edge of a psychotic man. He's young, but this industry has aged him as much as it has me. "If you think Dimitri is the only one who removes fingers when you touch something you shouldn't have, you need to be taught a lesson on how my family operates." He cranks his head back to face Clover. Considering he's seated, and Clover is standing, there should be more distance between them than there is. "But since this isn't my turf, I'll offer leniency. Don't expect another one."

Like the paid soldier he is, Clover continues pinching Rico's shoulder until I advise him otherwise. Several men circling us should take note of his obedience. They're getting thirsty for a bloodbath, which also means they're becoming ignorant of the rules. I'd pull them immediately into line if their disrespect didn't come with benefits. It's amazing the tales men tell when they're coked out of their minds. They are almost as perverse as a mafia man unknowingly dropping information he didn't mean to give.

"Guy's punishment was handled in-house..." I walk around my desk, then prop my backside on the edge. I'm close enough to Rico, I could kill him with barely an effort, but not quite close enough he can smell the annoyance pumping out of me. "So how do you know about it?"

Guy wouldn't be game to go against me, and a majority of the bidders had left before his punishment, so I'm eager to discover exactly who tattled about an in-house operation.

I shouldn't have bothered keeping my distance. Two towns over could smell the putrid scent excreting from my pores when Rico cocks a brow and says, "You don't really believe your sweet ole Pa traveled all the way to Vegas just to rub salt into my father's wound, do you?" Although he's asking a question, he continues talking as if he didn't. "Rumors are there's thirty-million dollars on the table over this side of the country. He only wants ten percent for a finder's fee."

If it were any other man but Rico sitting across from me, I would have taken the humor in his voice as a threat. The only reason I don't is because thirty-million dollars is chump change to him. This kills me to admit, but the Popovs are riding the high of not being saddled down with the shit my father doused our family name in decades ago. It also gives reason for Nikolai's lack of interest in his true birthright.

My voice is almost violent when I switch tactics for the third time today. "Theresa Veneto organized Isabelle's placement in Ravenshoe because she has similarities to my deceased sister." With Smith on the ball, I show Rico a side-by-side comparison of Ophelia and Isabelle. Excluding their hair, eyes, and skin tone, they don't have much in common, but I'm hoping Rico is too bogged down with revenge to notice. "Isabelle was supposed to persuade Isaac into spilling secrets. Instead—"

"She fell in love. You're not telling me anything I haven't already heard," Rico interrupts, his tone bored.

"So you know about Theresa's plan to go after Isabelle?" I'm bluffing. I haven't had contact with Theresa in weeks. I'm just assuming that will be her next move since all vindictive cows operate the same way. "We can only hope things don't end as badly for her as they did your mother."

Now I fucking have him—hook, line, and sinker—although he tries to deny it. "My mother died of an overdose."

"If you believe that, I guess you also believe your father's claims he's a king." Rico watches me with unease when I move back to my side of the desk to gather a set of documents from the drawer. They're the sworn testimonies the film documentary producer lodged with the Bureau years ago. He swore until he was blue in the face that Felicia wasn't a drug addict. "Your mother didn't have a single track-mark on her arms during filming. The documentary was filmed only months before her death." I show him stills of the footage that proves what I'm saying. "The coroner's report states—"

"Coroner? What fucking coroner? Other than moving her off the kitchen floor days after her fucking death, Vladimir wouldn't let anyone touch her." The violence in his roar exposes his agitation, but it's also proof he's looked into his mother's death before. He wouldn't do that unless he were suspicious his father wasn't telling the truth.

"Your mother was murdered, Rico, and I'm reasonably sure I know who did it." I'm once again stretching the boundaries of truth, but when you are desperate, you're desperate. I'm fucking desperate. "However, I'm not going to tell you a thing until we've reached an agreement."

"Only a fool sides with his enemy."

I brush off his anger as if it doesn't have any sting. "Not when it's for the greater good. This is for the greater good."

The fret on Rocco's face when I laid down my first set of cards weakens as I reveal my final hand. It isn't an image of the person I believe is responsible for Rico's mother's death, it's a photograph of my daughter. If her angelic eyes and face can't prove to him this is bigger than anything we could have ever imagined, nothing will.

"That's my daughter, Fien. She will be two in a little under three months, and I've not yet laid my eyes on her in person." Before he can voice one of the questions I see in his eyes, I add, "Because she was taken by the same man who killed your mother."

It's the fight of my life not to rip Fien's photograph out of Rico's grip when he lifts it off my desk, but I manage—somewhat. I've tried every angle I can the past twenty-two months. I'm running out of options. My desperation could backfire in my face, but would the blow-on effect be any worse than what I'm currently facing? I doubt it, so I'm willing to give it a shot.

After staring at Fien's chubby cheeks for a couple of seconds, Rico raises his dark eyes to me. "What do you need?"

# 20

# DIMITRI

While grumbling about the brutal crunch of his gearstick as I shift from second to first, Smith shuts down the equipment he had utilized the two and a half hours of our trip. He isn't a fan of road trips, but when it forces him away from equipment he's rarely without, he fucking hates them.

"You need to update this piece of shit. Your laptops are more valuable than the junk you're carting them around in."

Smith makes a 'duh' face while Rocco gives reason for his lack of class. "That's the idea, D. Who'd suspect a rusty van would be holding half a million dollars' worth of equipment?"

Since he has a point, I quit whining before clambering out of the driver's seat. It's early, but our visit to a maximum-security prison hasn't come without notice. Three red dots highlight my chest a mere second before I'm blinded by a megawatt spotlight.

I don't know whether to be amused or pissed when the voice of Warden Mattue crackles over the speakers of the establishment we're visiting long before visiting hours commence. I'm grateful he requested for the guards to lower their weapons, but the superiority in his tone is too haughty for my liking.

Anyone would think he's running the show around here. I know that's far from the truth. I've had a hold of things for years, and my power will only get stronger now I have Rico on-side. We'll never be classified as friends, but as long as our agreement continues serving both our objectives, it will continue without bloodshed.

I stop smirking like a pompous prick when a man who walks like he has a stick shoved up his ass greets me with a wonky smile. His lopsided grin reminds me of the one Brandon gave me when he arrived at my office on precisely day five of my threat. The information he shared about Isabelle wasn't anything Smith hadn't already unearthed, but it felt good knowing I could tell Brandon to jump, and he'd ask how high.

"Dimitri, good morning," stutters Warden Mattue. "To what do we owe the pleasure?"

Ignoring the hand he's holding out, I slant my head and arch a brow. "Do I need a reason to visit?"

He gives it his best shot to hide the quiver my tone caused his thighs. His efforts are pointless. I can smell his fear, much less taste it. "No, not at all. We're pleased to have you."

When he waves his hand across his body, inviting us in, I drift my eyes to Smith.

"One sec..." While chewing on the corner of his lower lip, he taps on a silicon keyboard stuck to the hood of his old van. In quicker than I can snap my fingers, the spotlight Rocco is shielding his eyes from with his forearm switches off, once again shrouding the parking lot into darkness. "Okay, you're good to go."

After lifting my chin in thanks, I shift my focus back to Warden Mattue. "We wouldn't want news of my visit getting out, would we?"

"Not at all," he parrots again when he hears the threat in my voice.

With Smith taking care of the cameras inside and outside of the prison we're about to visit, the only way my tour will reach my father's ear is if Warden Mattue tattles. That will end badly for him. Very *very* badly, although not quite as graphic as the punishment I handed down to a group of my father's associates when they stupidly decided to test my patience last week.

They sought vengeance for the slaughter of Mikoloff and his family six weeks ago. The insolence caused their family's downfall. They're not just dead, they are buried in unmarked graves no one will ever find, and their legacy was struck from the record.

Their punishment was so brutal, no man will be game to test me again. Everything is operating like clockwork. Roxanne is safe, my bank accounts all remain in the seven figures, and Fien's last ransom was received without the slightest delay.

All I need now is an outlet for the frustration keeping my body temperature in the scalding range the past six weeks. Whores won't come close to scratching it, so I don't bother. A bloody massacre barely skimmed off the surface, and I refuse to let another drug-fueled bender curtail my life. That only leaves one thing capable of taking the edge off, and even she isn't at my disposal right now.

With my blood already bubbling with anger, you can picture my struggle to maintain a rational head when a bitch from my past shouts my name. Theresa Veneto smiles like the badge on her hip will save her brain from being pierced with a bullet from my gun. She's dead fucking wrong. This prison is home to America's deadliest criminals, which means it's located miles from the nearest town. Many people have gotten lost out here the past six years, even Federal agents who don't know how to back the fuck up when asked.

Before I can voice my annoyance about my unexpected guest, Rocco takes up my slack. "I thought only vampires roamed the planet at dusk. Who knew witches got around, too? Do you fly above the houses to avoid collisions with your sister witches, or do you prefer the sewer network?"

While Theresa hisses at Rocco, I shift my eyes to Smith, curious to discover how Theresa's movements slipped past us without notice. We've been scrutinizing her as closely as Rico has my father the past two weeks.

When Smith shrugs, as pissed as me, I return my focus to Theresa. "Are you here to cover your tracks? Or are you hoping to lead me away from them?"

The past two weeks weren't solely gobbled up embedding Rico deeply into my father's operation. My team put both the time and the snippets of information Rico has discovered in an embarrassingly short amount of time to good use. Little threads are coming undone everywhere. It will only be a matter of time before my father's outfit is unraveled, and considering Theresa seems to be very much a part of his ensemble, she'll come undone right along with him.

Theresa's laugh agitates me to no end. "Cover what tracks, Dimi?"

Her use of my nickname pisses me off. Only my friends get to call me Dimi. She most certainly isn't one of them. "Oh, I don't know. How about putting a man away for a murder he didn't commit? Or falsifying police records to conjure up a fake victim? Then we also have the fact you left an unstable woman to defend for herself."

I don't know what's more frustrating, Theresa's cocky smirk or what she says next, "The fact your focus centers around me shows how far off the mark you are." She steps closer to me, switching out Warden Mattue's feared scent with an over-priced perfume. "I was merely upholding my end of our agreement."

"*Our* agreement?" I query, too interested in the honesty in her eyes to act nonchalant.

"You're a Petretti, aren't you?"

When she attempts to hand me a stack of papers, Smith snatches them out of her grip. I don't mind. They're official-looking documents he'll have a better chance of deciphering than me.

Seemingly believing we work for her instead of the other way around, Theresa explains, "They're transcripts of conversations I've had with your father. Their seal should prove their legitimacy, but in case they don't, I forwarded links to the original files to your email."

Smith logs into my email server before I can gesture for him to, and even quicker than that, he authenticates Theresa's claims. "Imagery is shit, but the audio is first-class. Your father approached Theresa." He listens for a couple of seconds before his brows draw together. "He didn't want Megan killed. He had her admitted for a psych workup. That kept her under lock and key for over a year."

"Why?" My question isn't for Smith. It's for Theresa, who looks way too fucking smug for my liking. "What possible benefit would my father get from keeping her alive? Why wouldn't he just kill her?"

She shrugs. "I didn't ask questions. That isn't the way I operate."

I smirk before hitting her with one-tenth of the attitude she's smacking me with. "That's right. I forgot the only time you exert any kind of normalcy is when you're flat on your back being served a healthy dose of dick. Is that why you keep showing up? Does the big gaping hole between your legs still need filling?"

Rocco's snicker annoys her, but it has nothing on the rage that fills her eyes when her body responds to the faintest touch of my finger as I drag it up her arm. She doesn't hate me, even though she really wants to.

With a huff, she folds her arms in front of her chest to hide the budding of her nipples. "I'm here to cash in the favor your father is refusing to bequeath."

I *tsk* at her, disappointed she believes I'm stupid enough to fall for the oldest trick in the book. "As I've told you before, if your favor was issued by my father, he's the only one who can grant it."

"He's refusing!" she shouts in my face.

I bite my lip to half my smile before asking, "And how is that my problem?"

I swear steam almost billows out of her ears when she stifles her scream with a growl. "Because everyone knows you clean up your father's messes. It's what you do! You've done it for years."

"For clients I deem worthy. Dried-up old hags who should have gotten out of the game years ago don't count." I catch her hand before it gets close to my face. Then I use it to bring her within an inch of my snarling lips. "You might have Isaac on the back foot with your tricks, but I don't play by those rules. When you are no longer of use in this industry, you're as good as dead."

Her minty fresh breath hits my lips when she gabbles out, "Are you threatening me?"

I drag my index finger down her white cheek before trekking it across her lips. "No, baby. If I were threatening you, you'd already be on your knees, saying your final farewell." Her cheeks will feel my nails for days when I grip her face with everything I have. "Now get the fuck out of my face before I send Clover over for a visit. He's been waiting years to mess up that pretty little face of yours."

I push her away from me, smirking when she almost loses her

footing on the loose gravel. As she straightens out her jacket like it's the only thing my grip creased, her eyes bounce between Smith, Rocco, and me. She doesn't bother with Warden Mattue because even someone as fucked in the head as her knows the only pull he has around here is getting his dick sucked by one of the female prisoners.

Did I forget to mention this prison is mixed gender? My bad.

"This won't be the last of this," Theresa warns before she makes a beeline to a Fed-issued car at the back of the lot.

She's right. This won't end until one of us is dead. You can be assured my name won't be on a headstone anytime soon. I can't make the same guarantee for Theresa.

I'm almost made out to be a liar when my silent thoughts are interrupted for the second time this morning. This time, the female's call of my name doesn't send me into a fit of rage. It sees me issuing a threat so fucking firm, Satan will hear it. "If I find out your guards' fingers got within an inch of their triggers, I'll gut you where you stand."

Warden Mattue's eyes snap to Roxanne frozen at our right for the quickest second before they jackknife back to me. He drinks in the fury the red dots highlighting Roxanne's chest caused my face before he frantically waves his hand through the air, demanding for his men to stand down.

The eagerness of his request is appreciated, but it's too late for him now. He's a dead man walking. He knows it. I know it, and so the fuck does Roxanne. My ruling six weeks ago wasn't just that she wasn't to be touched. She can't be threatened either. Lighting up her chest with a dozen assault weapons is a threat, and I refuse to let the injustice off lightly.

"Go..." When Warden Mattue steps closer to me with his hands held up in a non-defensive manner, my souring mood the past six weeks steamrolls back into me. "Go!"

I want to follow through with my threat, I want to pull his insides out of his belly button before stabbing a knife in his eye, but since Roxanne is too close not to see me as the monster I am, I maintain my cool—barely.

After watching the warden's terrified scuttle, I shift on my feet to face Roxanne. I haven't seen her in the flesh in weeks. Just like Petretti's restaurant, I kept her family's ranch without surveillance. A system can't be hacked if it doesn't exist.

I want to say Roxanne has put back on the pounds she lost during her hunger strike, that she looks well-rested and healthy. Regretfully, I can't. She looks as tired as I feel like the past six weeks were as painful for her as they were for me. Don't misconstrue. She looks good—*she will always look good*—she's just a smidge below the woman my thoughts drift to every night when I succumb to the tiredness overwhelming me.

"What are you doing here, Roxanne?"

Although my question is for Roxanne, my narrowed gaze is for Smith. This is his second slip-up today. That isn't just a new record, it's also unacceptable. He can't watch Roxanne for every hour of every day, but he *is* supposed to log her movements. The last report my eyes skimmed this morning was about the light in her bedroom being switched off a little after midnight, so how the fuck did she get here by five?

"This isn't Smith's fault." Roxanne skips across the dusty lot as if she isn't placing herself in the firing line for the second time this morning. "Infrareds have their faults." She presses a kiss to Smith's cheek before she throws her arms around Rocco's neck to hug him fiercely. "Is this new?" she asks while teasingly dragging her index finger across Rocco's pecs, lingering longer than I care to admit. "I don't recall seeing it on you before. It's cute and body-hugging. I like it."

I know what's she's doing, and I don't fucking like it. She saw my altercation with Theresa, but instead of working out why it annoyed her, she's serving the jealousy our exchange hit her with back to me one bitter pill at a time.

With my mood not knowing which way to swing, I take the easy route. "Get your ass in the van, Roxanne. Smith will take you home."

She whips around so fast, her recently colored hair slaps her in the face. "No."

"I beg your pardon?" I'm reasonably sure half the block hears me. That's how loud my roar is. "I wasn't asking."

"It wouldn't make a difference if you were. You can't boss me around anymore, Dimitri." She spits out my name as if it's trash. "You lost the chance when you abandoned me."

My jaw falls open like a fish out of water. "Abandoned you? I didn't abandon you. I set you free."

She folds her arms in front of her chest all prissy like. "In the house my uncle, aunt, and quite possibly my grandfather were murdered in, with three snipers outside the door, and shitty-ass cell reception inside it! You may as well cut off my wings."

"Where the fuck are you going?" I ask when she pulls away from me. "I'm not done with you yet."

Roxanne shrugs out of my hold before I can dig my nails into her arm. "We came here to visit my friend. Since you seem to have pull with the warden, I guess we don't have to wait for visiting hours anymore."

Her friend she nudged her head to during the first half of her comment isn't eager to join her campaign. She looks on the verge of pooping her pants. I understand her concern. I'm five seconds from killing someone. I just have no clue if that someone is Roxanne or me. I love her feistiness. It thickens my cock as quickly as it fills my mind with immoral thoughts. A girl has to have spunk to be fingered in an alleyway with a stranger watching, much less go against a man as powerful as me. But her spunk also drives me nuts. Furthermore, I wouldn't have let her out of our agreement if I knew she was going to march straight back into it.

I shouldn't be surprised. She's always there, in every frame, causing trouble.

It's one of the things I like about her the most.

When Roxanne disappears into the entrance of the prison, I jerk my head in the direction she went. "Go with her. Make sure she sees who she came here to see, then load her into my car."

"What car, D?" Rocco asks as he struggles not to laugh about the rage on my face. "Do you wanna drive your girl home from your first date in Smith's beat-up van?"

I talk through a tightened jaw. "The car Smith is going to get here A-S-A-fucking-P if he wants to keep his job."

Smith holds his hands in the air, knowing he did wrong before he puts them to good use. He will build a car if he can't get one here within the next thirty minutes.

"All right." While rubbing his hands together like he's choosing a whore for the night, Rocco takes off in the direction Roxanne just went. Her friend reluctantly follows them.

Although I'm pissed at Smith, I am too confused about my exchange with Theresa to discount it for a second longer. "Did Theresa's information sway your opinion at all?"

We only arrived here on the cusp of dawn for one reason—to unearth if Maddox is aware the woman he's serving a life sentence for isn't dead. It's obvious from what Rico and Smith have discovered the past couple of weeks that Megan is alive and well, so why the fuck is Maddox keeping his mouth shut about it? If you had an out for a lifetime sentence, would you continue serving it? I fucking wouldn't.

Smith twists his lips, a sign he's confused. "From what I heard, your father is aware Megan is alive. I'm just struggling to under-stand why."

"You're not the only one," I breathe out before I can stop myself.

When they were alive, my father chewed up and spat out his daughters as if they were tobacco, so why would he give a shit about a random woman, let alone one who's batshit crazy? He kept Megan alive for a reason, I've just got to find out why.

"While I talk with Maddox, look a little deeper into the files Theresa handed over. She said she did this for a favor, but we both know she doesn't do shit without some type of payment upfront."

Air whizzes from Smith's nose when he hums in agreement. "I'll do that as soon as I organize a car. Any particular brand?"

"Something fast and noisy..." I almost add, *just like Roxanne,* but hold back the urge. I don't need to brag. Roxanne's moans could be heard two towns over. Smith and Rocco live on the same block as me.

Smith's smirk reveals he heard my inner monologue. It's as cocky as the heat that roars through me when Roxanne can't help but watch my entrance to Wallens Ridge State Prison. She keeps her gawk on the down-low with lowered lashes, but I don't need to see her eyes to know she's watching me. I can feel it in my bones. It thickens my cock in an instant, which doubles the heat of her stare.

"Prisoner 9429 is waiting for you in my office."

I shift my eyes from Roxanne to Warden Mattue. It's a fucking hard feat, only done because I'm curious to learn how he knew which prisoner I wanted to visit. This is my first time at this estab-lishment since Rocco was an inmate.

When he catches my imprudent stare, the Warden's throat works hard to swallow. "I assumed he was who you were wanting to see, considering you've seen him once a month since his conviction."

He shows me a visitor ledger with a barely eligible D Petretti scribbled in the log once a month for the past year. It's not close to my signature, but I'm reasonably sure I know who it belongs to.

"You can wait here." When the Warden attempts a rebuttal, I slice my hand through the air. "Did I sound like I was asking permission?"

I don't watch the bob of his head. I'm too fascinated by the faintest hint of a smile under locks of red hair to pay his mundane submissiveness any attention. Even with her veins bubbling with anger, Roxanne can't help but respond to my surly personality. She seems to get off on it like she's obsessed with the thought I can protect her unlike anyone else.

It instantly proves my reason for sending her away was the most stupid idea I've ever had. As I've said before, she doesn't want a man to take care of her. She wants a bastard, a monster, a man so evil, even when he has the blood of her mother on his face, she'll still crawl onto his lap and snuggle in.

If Fien weren't on my mind, I'd show Roxanne right now that I can give her all of that and so much more. Instead, I return her steely stare for a couple more seconds before I make my way to the Warden's office.

Once again, it's a fucking hard feat.

# 21

# DIMITRI

I could never be accused of being tiny, especially when my chest is swollen with smugness, but I feel a couple of inches shorter when Maddox notices my entrance into the Warden's office. The Walsh brothers don't have the notoriety the Petrettis do, but they're well known amongst the locals. Their mixed-race background makes them a little bulkier than their counterparts, and Maddox has taken it one step further by adding a good twenty pounds of muscle to his frame during his first stint in lock-up.

He has tatted up since the last time I saw him as well. His artwork almost looks as extensive as mine. If the quality of the work is anything to go by, he got a majority of them done outside of these walls, which is interesting considering he barely had a sleeve when he was arrested at Demi's place of employment.

"If I knew it was you, I would have gotten dressed up for the occasion." Don't misconstrue his words. They were laced with so much sarcasm, they left a bad taste in my mouth, so I'd hate to experience what Maddox's throat is going through. "What the fuck are you doing here, Dimitri?"

I take his brusque attitude in my stride. "I thought we were friends. Isn't this what friends do? Visit the other while they're locked up."

He looks like he wants to spit at my feet.

The feeling is mutual.

"We ain't friends."

I smirk, grateful he walked straight into the trap I was setting. After pressing my palms on the Warden's desk, I peer him dead-set in the eyes. "That's right. We're not. You just used my contacts to line your pockets with money, and then you wonder why we're not friends."

He's got nothing. Not a single fucking thing.

"Sit down, Maddox, and for once in your fucking life, listen. If you had done that from the get-go, you wouldn't be here."

His sneer would make most men shake in their boots. It doesn't cut the mustard with me. I was raised by a man who thought a fire stoke was a tool to keep his children in line. The hotter it was, the harder he struck me with it.

Don't feel sorry for me. My father's ways ensured I don't feel pain. As you can imagine, the ability made me a coldhearted man. I'm not worried. Love and hate are on par when it comes to emotions. Both take everything you have and give nothing in return.

I'm hopeful my thoughts will change when I meet my daughter in the flesh for the first time, but it's hard to change the views of a skeptic. Audrey attempted to chip at the decay. She barely made an indent. Roxanne, on the other hand, had me acting as if I had a heart in my chest. I would have taken a thirty-million-dollar hit for her—I still would.

My thoughts snap back to the present when Maddox's chuckles ring through my ears. "He was right. You're so fucking gone."

He doesn't need to spell out the name of the man he's referencing for me to understand our conversation is no longer between us.

Maddox refers to everyone by name—except my father.

"I'm gone? Ha! I'm not the one in cahoots with the man who marked up my sister with a mangy mutt." That shuts up his chuckles in an instant. Fucking good as I was tempted to use my fists. "What did he tell you, Ox? That I ordered for her to be punished?"

His silence is extremely telling. It isn't just my father whispering in his ear, it's someone he'd pay careful attention to.

Confident I know which way to take our conversation, I ask, "What's he got on her?"

He blows off the concern in my voice as if it's fake before he takes a seat as requested earlier.

"If my father has a noose around Demi's throat, I can help."

Maddox slants his head to make sure his glare has the effect he's aiming for. "Like you did Justine?"

I growl, baring teeth. "She's alive, isn't she?"

He slams his fist down on the desk separating us. "And crying every week on the phone. You fucked her over good, D. I don't know if she'll ever come back from this."

His words are a kick to the gut, but they push our conversation in the direction I need it to go. "So, you're gonna let him do the same to Demi?" When he scoffs, I hit him with straight-up facts. "You kept my daughter's existence a secret. You didn't do that for no reason, Ox. I'm here to find out why, and I ain't leaving until I do."

His tongue peeks between his teeth when I roll back the Warden's chair, take a seat, then hook my boots onto his desk. This is the first time in my life I wish I had trod in dog shit. I'd loved nothing more than to see the Warden's face when he rocked up to his office to find a big, dirty piece of shit on his spotless desk.

With Maddox as stubborn as me, our conversation soon hits a stalemate. This kills me to admit, but I have to break the silence. I don't have time to sit around and twiddle my thumbs. I'm juggling balls, many of them. If I don't want them to fall, I need to move our exchange along.

"With Megan Shroud being alive and well, your debt has *not* been fulfilled. Since you're an inmate in a maximum-security prison, I have no choice but to transfer that debt back to its original owner."

I'm all but threatening his sister, and he knows it. "You wouldn't fucking dare."

"Try me, Maddox. I've got a heap of anger and no one to take it out on." My words aren't lies. They're as gospel as my pledge to bring Fien home.

Spit seethes between Maddox's clenched teeth. "My debt is with your father."

I shrug before shaking my head. "Not according to you. I punished your sister, that means her debt falls on me."

He's speechless, truly and utterly speechless.

"I'm willing to negotiate—"

"With what? I gave your father everything I have. I have nothing left to give." The angst in his tone is more telling than the worry on his face. I don't know what my father is holding over his head, but it's more than his sister's life.

I remove my feet from the desk before balancing my elbows on the chipped surface. "Give me information—"

"I don't know anything."

I continue talking as if he never interrupted me. "And in good faith, I'll repay the favor. Special perks, hours outside these walls…" I watch his face to gauge any response to if my offers have already been brought forward. When his expression remains neutral, I continue, "I could even organize some additional conjugal visits."

He seems conflicted. I understand why when he asks, "Can you get Demi out?"

I'm reasonably sure I know what he's asking, but I'd rather he spell it out for me, then we both know *exactly* what he's asking of me. This isn't a standard favor. It will cost him more than a couple of years in county jail. "Out of what, exactly?"

He doesn't speak a word. He doesn't need to. I can see the fear in his eyes. Smell it on his skin. His debt with my father has nothing to do with his sister and everything to do with his girl.

"If she's out, she can't come here anymore, Ox. When you are out, you're out. You can never get back in. Are you willing to face that?" He takes a moment to deliberate before jerking up his chin. The worry in his eyes should see me granting him a few more minutes to consider his options, but as I said earlier, I don't have time to waste. "All right. But I'm going to need to know *everything*."

The panic on his face recedes in an instant. "Have you got a pen and a piece of paper? You're gonna need it."

---

Smith's eyes lift to mine when I race across the dusty lot like a bat out of hell. He's working from the hood of a brand-spanking-new Mercedes Benz G class. It looks like a tank, so it suits the terrain. The same can't be said of the feisty redhead in the front passenger seat. I don't know what Rocco said to get Roxanne in my car in one piece. It must have been something good because not only is she strapped in, ready to go, she's only glaring at me with half the intensity of her earlier stare.

"Did you get that?" Just because Smith switched off

surveillance doesn't mean he didn't have eyes and ears in the room with me. Feds aren't the only ones familiar with button cameras.

Smith lifts his chin. "I'm hacking into the hospital servers now."

When Roxanne slips out of the passenger seat of the Mercedes Benz to peer at Smith's screen with Rocco and me, I don't request for the feed to be shut down like I usually would. She has said all along that the organizer of Fien's captivity is a woman, so it's only fair she watches us hone in on one.

"There." I point to a female with mousy brown hair and a skittish demeanor. Even with the footage being a couple of months old, she looks similar to the child in the images I've pursued of Megan the past few weeks.

"Is that her?" I ask when Smith zooms in.

"Give me a sec..." He takes a screenshot of her profile before he uploads it to his state-of-the-art facial recognition system. It brings up a match in under three seconds. "Bingo. We have a match."

Aware he's now tracking the right person, he traces Megan's movements back several months, dragging the timeline back to the day Maddox said she was admitted to a mental hospital for a ninety-six-hour hold. It was well over a year ago. Maddox doesn't know why she was admitted. All he knew was that my father wanted her alive no matter the cost—something about her having information he couldn't get elsewhere.

"There," Roxanne parrots a few seconds later, pointing to a reflection bouncing off the admission glass mounted to protect the staff from the crazies.

The brightness of the woman's hair reveals she's blonde, but we can't see her face.

"Do you think it's the woman you were talking to earlier?" Roxanne asks after drifting her eyes to me.

I want to say yes, it would make things a shit ton easier if

Theresa were the only villain in this story, but my gut is cautioning me to remain wary, so I shrug instead. "Can you clean up the footage?"

Smith screws up his nose. "I'd have a better chance with wired equipment. The upload speed is as slow as fuck out here."

"Then head back to the compound." I take a quick snapshot of Megan's up-to-date picture before gathering up his equipment and stuffing it into the passenger seat of his van. "Forward anything you find directly to me."

Rocco cocks a dark brow as mirth hardens his features. "Are you not heading back to the compound?"

His face appears a mix of jeering and confusion when I answer, "I've got to take Roxanne home first," before it switches to straight-up anarchy.

"I can do that for you. You don't have to go out of your way."

Needing to leave before I knock his teeth out, I grip the top of Roxanne's arm before placing her into the passenger seat of the Mercedes with less aggression than I did Smith's equipment. I'm not known for being gentle, but Smith's laptop is only worth a little over half a million dollars. Roxanne's price tag is closer to thirty—*if not priceless.*

"We need to find out what information Megan has that makes her invaluable to my father. If we can do that out without needing to travel to her, I'd much appreciate it."

The last thing I want is a cross-country adventure when solid intel of a Russian invasion just landed in my inbox. Since the information came from a man with nothing to lose, I'm paying it more attention than I did when Theresa suggested the same thing.

I stop leaning across Roxanne's body to fasten her seat belt when Smith says, "Megan could come to us."

"How?" Roxanne asks before I get the chance.

I scrub at my jaw to hide my grin when Smith's eyes lift from his prototype phone. He's never without an electronic device. "She's all-types of crazy... but not enough for a permanent placement. She could be signed out to a guardian."

My eyes snap to Roxanne's. I have no fucking clue why I'm seeking her advice. I am just relaying to you what's happening. It could be the fact that I've spent the past few weeks going through the files she compiled while I was flat on my back. Or it could be her perfume. Whatever it is, a gleam in her eyes exposes she appreciates me seeking her opinion.

While bouncing her eyes between mine, she hesitantly shrugs. "She could lead us to the people we're seeking." The fact she says 'us' messes with my head even more than all the shit Maddox just bombarded it with. "It's a risk, but if the reward could potentially exceed the danger, we have to take a chance."

Because I agree with her, I give Smith the go-ahead, but with added stipulations. "Tag her before she's released. We don't want her location falling through the cracks."

Smith's hard swallow reveals he heard the words I didn't speak, and the narrowing of Roxanne's eyes exposes she's just as telepathic. "You can't microchip her like she's a dog."

"I can't? Since when?"

The huff she does while crossing her arms under her chest is cute. I can't wait to see how she responds when I order Smith to do the same to her. Then, there'll be no more sneaking up on me. I'll know where she is at all times of the day and night.

# 22

# ROXANNE

For how pricy this car is, it has shit ventilation. I've done every-thing imaginable to lessen the intensity of Dimitri's unique scent —I've rolled down the window, cranked up the air conditioning, and removed my boots with the hope stinky socks would eradi-cate it—nothing has worked! It's still there, lingering in my nostrils as often as his infamous half-smirk has trickled into my mind the past six weeks. And don't get me started on other wondrous parts of his body, or you'll book me in for more than a lobotomy.

Ugh! Why do I continue tormenting myself like this? He killed my boyfriend, tortured my parents, then sent a killer to my best friend's apartment. I should have been glad to see the backend of him. I just wasn't.

*It's for Claudia*, I remind myself. *I agreed to a ride I didn't need for her.*

With that in mind, I pull up my big girl panties, glide up the window I've been dangerously balancing out of the past hour, then shift my focus to Dimitri. Just like the first seventy miles of our trip, he stares straight at me. It should be impossible to watch both the road and me, but he makes it look easy.

"How much pull do you have with the warden at Wallens Ridge?"

He wrings the steering wheel two times before replying, "Depends who's asking."

"Me. I'm asking." His grip on the steering wheel turns deadly. It makes his knuckles go white, but I push on, determined to have an injustice rectified. "Claudia was unfairly convicted—"

Dimitri cuts me off with a brittle laugh. "That's what all criminals say."

Even though his tone is brimming with mirth, I still narrow my eyes at him. "She *is* innocent. Her boyfriend was an abusive ass. Witness statements prove his hand was on the steering wheel when they veered off the road, yet she's still serving time. How is that fair?"

He waits a beat to absorb what I said before he asks, "Who prosecuted her case?"

Although I'm a little lost to where he's going with this, I answer, "A DA more interested in looking at her tits than compiling legitimate evidence."

I thought my description would match a thousand district attorneys. I was clearly wrong. "Luca Marco?"

After picking up my jaw from the floor, I ask, "Have you heard of him?"

When Dimitri dips his chin, the scent I've been struggling to ignore the past hour doubles. I think the full beard he doesn't usually wear is responsible for the increase of his scent. It seems capable of soaking in everything around him, and considering that everything seems to only be him, it's as intoxicating as the fact he didn't replace me with the first blonde to cross his path.

"Do you have anything on him we could use to have Claudia's

conviction overturned?" There I go again, using the infamous 'we' on him. "*I'm* willing to get *my* hands dirty."

"Although *I* appreciate the offer *you're* making..." I poke my tongue out at him, stuffing his exaggerated words down his throat with a bucket load of attitude. "It's not as simple as getting dirt on someone. His rulings are out of my jurisdiction." When confusion crosses my features, he smirks, making a mess of my panties. "Marco is Ravenshoe's DA. I don't have jurisdiction there."

"How? Why?" I shouldn't sound as appalled as I do. I'm just stunned. Ravenshoe skirts Hopeton, and from the information Estelle and I have gathered the past six weeks, they've had a stronghold on that town for decades.

Dimitri appreciates my disgust. "Don't worry, I was as shocked as you." He indicates to take a left before shifting his focus back to me. "I've considered a takeover a couple of times, but I can't bring myself to do it." The reasoning behind his decision makes sense when he adds, "Isaac threw himself into that town when Ophelia died. It's his way of coping." This isn't the first time I've heard of his sister, but it's the first time it came directly from the source.

"Would he help?"

"Isaac?" Dimitri asks through crimped lips.

"Uh-huh."

His hair that's a little overdue for a trim falls into his eyes when he shakes his head. "That bridge was burned a long time ago. Besides, we're set to become enemies even more than we already are."

Now it's my turn to be confused. "Why?"

I wish he didn't need to pause to consider if he can trust me, but I understand why he does. Trust doesn't come easy for most people, much less the son of a Cartel hierarchy. "The man I was just visiting—"

"Maddox."

Dimitri's tightened jaw reveals he's going to have a talk with Rocco about his waggling tongue the instant he returns to the compound. "Yes, Maddox advised a Russian sanction is endeavoring to set up shop in Ravenshoe."

"Shouldn't that be Isaac's problem?" I'm not being bitchy. I am genuinely curious.

"If it were anyone but this man, I wouldn't have an issue with it. Since that isn't the case, I'll be keeping a close eye on the proceedings."

Dimitri wets his lips when I ask, "Bad blood?"

"It's been stale for years but turned potent a couple of years back." He doesn't need to spell out the details for me. I know what happens when you steal from the Cartel. I saw it firsthand only a couple of months ago. "Have you ever heard of Katie Bryne?"

The name freezes me for a couple of seconds. It's a common name, but I swear I've heard it before.

When the truth smacks into me, my jaw drops. "She was abducted a few years back, right?" I give myself a mental pat on the back when Dimitri lifts his chin, then almost vomit when past conversations smack into me. "She wasn't abducted for the baby-farming trade, was she?"

I gulp down a breath like I haven't breathed the past three minutes when Dimitri shakes his head. "She was taken by Russians." I nod, suddenly recalling that. The gossip spread through the local schools like wildfire, making it mighty uncomfortable for any foreign students with a Russian accent. "However, she was sold by my father years later to a Russian."

*Oh.* That can't be good. Even a mafia novice could understand that this isn't kosher.

"Do you think Fien's abduction has anything to do with Katie?"

Dimitri's pause this time around isn't to contemplate what he's

SHANDI BOYES

going to tell me. He's deliberating as to why he has never considered this angle before.

My palms flatten on the roof of Dimitri's recently-purchased ride when he yanks it off the road. Since his phone isn't linked to the state-of-the-art Bluetooth system, he has to yank his cell phone out of his pocket to make a call. Usually, he conducts his calls in private, so you can imagine my pleasure when he hits the speaker button on his phone a mere second after dialing a frequently-called number.

Smith answers a few seconds later. "What's up?"

"Did we ever find out what caused the delay between Katie's abduction and her sale?" Dimitri's question divulges he's been looking into Katie's case a little more than a standard case. Nowhere near as much effort as I've put into his family history, but still noticeable.

Smith grunts before the whoosh of a headshake sounds out of Dimitri's phone. "We figured it was training."

"What if it wasn't? What if it was something more than that?" When Smith takes a moment to deliberate, Dimitri fills in the silence. "She was taken when she was fourteen. Underage or not, her training shouldn't have taken as long as it did."

I don't want to know what training he's referencing, nor am I going to ask him about it. Sometimes it's better to have your head stuck in the sand—kind of like mine was when news of my aunt's death reached my ears.

I thought Dimitri's reluctance to let me attend the search of my family ranch was because he was being an ass. I had no clue it was because my mother told her drug counselor there was at least one corpse buried near the home where she grew up.

Curious, I ask, "Could Katie have been placed into the baby-farming trade before being sold?"

Dimitri shakes his head. "We had considered that, but Kirill only ever purchases virgins, and he doesn't take anyone's word for it, either."

I'm glad Dimitri pulled over to make his call. It saves the leather interior of his new ride being coated in my vomit.

"Is she all right?" I hear Smith ask while Dimitri's hand circles my back in a soothing motion. I told Estelle eggs aren't supposed to smell fishy. She didn't believe me.

Dimitri's eyes flick between me and the minute bit of vomit on the edge of the road surface for several long seconds before he mutters, "She will be." After switching off the speaker feature on his phone, he squashes it against his ear. "Send Rocco to correspond with Megan's release. I need you to share the information Maddox disclosed with Rico before looking more closely at Katie's sale." His eyes float to me before he says, "We'll find Demi *after* I've ensured Roxanne has eaten."

"I've eaten," I mumble, denying the accusation in his eyes with words. "Not a lot, but enough." My last comment is barely a whisper, but Dimitri still hears them. His jaw stiffens a mere second before it works through a stern grind.

He has no right to be angry. He dumped me in a house with groceries older than dirt, and his goons weren't overly friendly when we suggested for them to get us supplies. They thought we were trying to play them. In reality, we were endeavoring not to starve to death.

When I say that to Dimitri, his face reddens to the color of my favorite crayon when I was a kid—blistering red. "Send Clover extermination orders for Roxanne's ranch." He waits for panic to make itself known with my face before he adds, "Warn him if he so much as rustles a hair on Ms. Armstead's head, the next rodent I exterminate will be him."

I don't know whether to be turned on by his threat or spooked. I love that he's protecting Estelle as fiercely as he protected me weeks ago, but not only is it after he put her life at risk, so it's a little too late to act chivalrous, his reply exposes he knows Estelle's last name. That can only mean one thing. He's been looking into her past as much as he did mine at the start of our arrangement. I don't know if that's a good thing or a bad thing. Estelle has always been the more attractive one of our duo. That's why I bring the spunk. I thought it would even things between us. I'm not so confident now, though.

I'm so deep in my pitiful thought process, I don't realize Dimitri ended his call and recommenced our trip until he asks, "When was the last time you ate?"

"Other than regurgitated slop I just threw up?" I relish his lowered lids for a second before putting him out of his misery. "I ate last night." I cringe, hating my inability to lie. "If you class three in the afternoon as nighttime."

"You last ate yesterday afternoon?" When I nod, his eyes lock with the dashboard of his swanky new ride. "It's now ten in the morning." I can't work out a single thing he says after this. It's all grumbled and spaced by a heap of swear words. They make me smile until he says more clearly, "You won't be smiling when I tan your ass for thinking this is funny."

Once again, I don't know how to respond. Should I be turned on or scared by his threat?

I lose the chance to deliberate when Dimitri pulls into the first gas station he finds. It's skanky, stinky, and looks like it hasn't been updated since the nineties. "I'd rather drink water out of a toilet bowl than eat here."

Ignoring me, he throws open his door, clambers out, then locks his eyes with mine. Not a word seeps from his lips. He doesn't need to voice his commands when his eyes can take up the slack. I either follow him inside willingly, or he'll drag me in there and tie me to my seat.

"Considering you released me from our contract..." I stop my climb out of his car to air quote my last word, "... you're a little too possessive for my liking."

The brutal closure of my door should gobble up his reply. It doesn't. I hear every painstaking word. "Uncaging a bird doesn't mean you're done with her. It can be quite the opposite, actually. What's that saying? *Set her free. If she comes back, she's yours. If she doesn't, she never was.*"

On that note, he enters the restaurant, leaving me standing in the dusty lot with my jaw hanging open and my heart in tatters.

I thought he let me go to save me from the madness. I had no clue he did it to save himself from a lunacy not even someone as strong as him can survive.

## 23

# DIMITRI

My hand stops creeping for my gun when Roxanne soundlessly begs for me not to respond to an insolent man's overfriendly approach. Things have been different between us the past hour and a half—I fucked up by speaking before thinking—but one thing hasn't changed. Roxanne's ability to look a madman in the eyes and see the good in them.

This beggar has been watching her from afar since we arrived. He doesn't want the money I tossed at his feet, nor the scraps of our meals. He wants Roxanne to dance with him, knowing having her in his arms for a second will make up for a lifetime of injustices.

I'd rather he fuck off, but Roxanne is refusing to let me send him away. She finds him endearing. Why? I have no fucking clue. He stinks, his clothes are four sizes too big, and his toes are peeking out of his shoes, yet Roxanne looks at him as if he's a man who's just a little down on his luck.

My jaw almost cracks when Roxanne holds her index finger in the air. "One dance."

"Roxanne."

The gravelly deliverance of her name snaps her eyes to mine in an instant. Even though she's panicked, she holds her ground. "It's one dance." I'm about to tell her I don't give a fuck if he was going to pay her a million dollars for thirty seconds worth of work but lose the chance when her next comment stuns me as much as my earlier one did her. "If you let me go this one last time, I promise I'll come back."

I'm too shocked to talk. This has never happened before. Usually, I go in guns blazing. I don't want to do that this time around. So instead, I let her stretch her wings.

With a smile that makes me regret every decision I've ever made, Roxanne mouths, "*Thank you,*" before she accepts the hand the man is holding out in offering.

While he whizzes her around a shoddy restaurant, I watch them like a hawk, uncaring if I look like a deranged stalker. If his hands move within an inch of an area I deem unacceptable, the guests at this establishment will be eating mutton for the next six months.

Disappointment is the first thing I feel when the man keeps his hands high on Roxanne's back for their entire dance. His unusual gallantry stays with me long after I've bundled Roxanne back into my car and recommenced our trip. It played in my mind when I stopped for gas and lingered well into the three hours it took us to arrive at my cousin's last known address. It only clears when the reason for the sparkle in his eyes finally dawns on me.

"Who did he think you were?"

Roxanne's smiles compete with the low-hanging sun. "His daughter."

She adds a giggle to her grin when my lip furls. The man would have been well into his seventies, and I'm being kind considering most homeless people age quicker than their sheltered counterparts.

"His head is a little muddled," Roxanne explains when I pull into the driveway of a standard house in the middle of the burbs. "He still thinks he's serving in Vietnam."

"You learned all that by looking in his eyes?"

She shakes her head. "It was a little more complicated than that." When I wave my hand through the air, encouraging her to reveal the secrets I see in her eyes, she says, "He had a squadron tattoo on his hand. The research I did for the one I saw at Joop revealed it was from a combat unit that was deployed to Vietnam in the early seventies. His boots, although holey, were from his infantry days, and although it was badly faded, the photograph he keeps safe in his bootstrap had the faintest red coloring on the edges. It could have been a dress, but I took a chance on it being the color of his daughter's hair." She twists to face me like it's an everyday occurrence for a two-hundred-thousand-dollar car to be parked in the driveway of a house worth half the price. "How did you know he mistook me for someone?"

Untrusting of my mouth not to make the mistake it did earlier, I hit her with a frisky wink before exiting a car that will be sold for parts by the end of the week. If you think Smith secured our ride the legitimate way, you still have a lot to learn about my operation.

"Whose house is this?" Roxanne asks after joining me on the footpath. The confusion in her tone is understandable. Not only does she comprehend the reason for my silence, Demi is blood-related. You wouldn't know it from how rundown and derelict her house is.

This property has been in the Petrettis' vault of arsenal for the past two decades. I've never seen it this derelict. The gutters are paint peeled and hanging on by a single screw, several roof shingles need replacing, and the outside looks like it hasn't been touched with a paintbrush or a lawnmower in years.

"Stay behind me."

Although peeved I didn't answer her question, Roxanne does as instructed. The removal of my gun already has her on edge, much less the faintest creep of a shadow across the front living room window.

"Demi..." We walk up the cracked, overgrown footpath slowly. The shadow was larger than Demi's svelte frame, but that doesn't necessarily mean it isn't her. We're not on good terms. The fact I let her boyfriend be put away for life means we haven't spoken in over a year. "Ox sent me."

I feel Roxanne's curiosity rising. The hand she's gripping the waistband of my trouser with is very indicating, let alone the increase in her breaths. Although only a handful of people call Maddox 'Ox,' I'm confident Roxanne has heard of him before.

Our cautious approach sends my nerves into a tailspin. I'm not used to taking things slow. Just like I fuck, I approach danger with the same fierceness—hard and fast. I can't do that this time around. I put up an impressive capital to keep Roxanne safe, so you sure as hell can guarantee I won't put her life on the line for anything.

When my knock on Demi's door goes unanswered, I scoop down to gather the pistol strapped to my ankle. Some may say I'm a fool to hand Roxanne a loaded weapon—things have been tense between us today—but I'd rather have her weaponed-up and ready to fire than be a sitting duck.

Roxanne peers at me with wide apprehensive eyes when I say, "There's no safety. Just aim and fire."

She looks as if she wants to drop my gun like it's a hot potato when I place it in her palm. Then she swallows, puts on her game face, and raises her gun like I forced her to do to her mother.

Her kick-ass fighter stance crumbles when I kick open Demi's door with my boot. It isn't my unexpected show of strength that has her knees knocking. It's the horrendous smell vaping out of Demi's house. If she thought her daddy stunk up my compound while building the courage to blow his brains out, she had no idea. This place fucking reeks.

"Stay behind me," I instruct again when Roxanne's morbid curiosity gets the best of her. She isn't moving for the window we saw the shadow creep across. She's heading for the bedroom responsible for the smell.

Although pissed at her inability to do as she's told, her mix-up saves me from making a fatal mistake. The shadow didn't belong to Demi. It was from the big black beast standing over her beaten body, protecting her with fangs bared and a vicious growl. It's her Doberman—Max.

# 24

# ROXANNE

Demi's one blue eye not hidden by a smattering of bruises across her face peeks up at me when I place down a mug of coffee in front of her. Even with the fireplace of my grandparents' ranch over stacked with wood, she's still shuddering like she's in the middle of Antarctica. Her jitters are understandable. I'm still hyped up with adrenaline, and all I did was view the man she gunned down in self-defense from a distance.

I can imagine what she's been through the past three days. It's clear from the extent of her bruises that she fought with everything she had before she resorted to the gun her boyfriend made her hide under her pillow. It was horrendous holding a gun to someone's head. I couldn't imagine firing it while they're squashed on top of you. Just the thought of crawling out from beneath a dead body sends shivers rolling through me. They have Dimitri watching me even closer than he has the past three hours.

He's been endeavoring to find out what happened to Demi without being insensitive, but with her shock too high for her cousin to break through, Dimitri has been left to handle his inquiries alone. Considering those investigations are taking place here, at my family's ranch of all places, exposes who his lead suspect is. If your relationship with your son is disgruntled enough he doubts your participation in the captivity of your only grandchild, why would he think a niece would fare a better chance, especially one who seems out of the loop on all things Cartel.

"Are you sure you don't want anything to eat?" Demi would have to be hungry. From what I picked up between keeping Estelle up to date on our unexpected guests and making sure Dimitri's crew has everything they need, it appears as if she shot her intruder three days ago. If she's been as closed off the past three days as she has the past three hours, not all the grumbles I've heard seep from her mouth have been whimpers. Some may be from her hungry tummy. "I can whip up a batch of mean pancakes. Ask Dimi, he ate them and survived."

My heart flutters in my chest when the briefest smile creeps out from behind locks of dark hair. It's only faint, but her smile reminds me that the world does spin.

"If you change your mind, my kitchen is open twenty-four-seven."

Before she can thank me for an offer she shouldn't class as friendly, a much more dangerous situation than my horrific cooking skills confronts us. A fleet of five police cruisers is blazing down the driveway. Their brutal speed kicks up as much dust as my feet when I race toward Dimitri to tell him the quickest and safest exit.

I'm not the only one moving fast. Max is on his feet in an instant, growling and barking at the procession of cars as if they're the enemy. It's weird to see him acting so violent. He's been fine with Dimitri and over a dozen of his armored goons the past three hours, so why is he acting so irritated by men sworn to protect?

"It's okay," Dimitri assures me before he quiets Max's ruckus with the swiftest lift of his hand.

Although his vicious gaze remains locked on the fleet of vehicles coming to a stop at the front of the ranch, Max licks the dribble his vicious growl instigated before he returns to his protective post by Demi's feet.

Confident he has one disaster diverted, Dimitri shifts his focus back to me. "They're not here for me." I choke on my spit when he nudges his head to Demi and says, "They are here for her."

From the corner of the room, I watch the scene unfold. The dozen or more police officers don't approach my home. They maintain their stalk from outside when a man with blondish brown hair exits the convoy from the final vehicle. Although the stranger is dressed differently than the prisoner I saw in the wee hours of this morning, I'm confident he's one and the same. Not only does he have a distinct set of tattoos, when I was ushered past the Warden's office, I watched him like a hawk when he went toe to toe with Dimitri. Excluding Rocco, I had never seen a man stupid enough to go against Dimitri.

I was fascinated by their exchange and somewhat worried. Don't misunderstand. I wasn't worried Maddox would hurt Dimitri. I was panicked how turned on I was watching Dimitri in his element. He was as bossy and domineering as he was in the parking lot, but for once, his annoyance wasn't focused on me.

"Who's Maddox to Demi?"

Dimitri doesn't need to answer my question. Maddox's dart across the room tells me everything I need to know, much less Max's blasé response to his quick approach. Furthermore, Demi responds to Maddox as if he's the only man in the room, so I won't mention the loving way Maddox cups her bruised cheeks, or you'll think I'm a creeper.

I can't help but watch. The fireworks sparking between them is out of this world. It's almost as explosive as the ones that forever bristle between Dimitri and me.

"Is there somewhere they can go... for privacy?"

I glance up at Dimitri with playful mocking beaming from my eyes, adoring the unease of his question. I didn't think he knew what awkwardness was, let alone have the ability to display it. "We don't have any sex pods here. My nanna was miles ahead of her time, but she wasn't *that* advanced."

When his lips furl at the ends, I suck in a relieved breath. Even with his smile being as ghost-like as Demi's, it's better than the downward trend his lips have been wearing the past three hours. I still have a lot of anger to work through for how we departed, and why, but seeing how he coerced Demi from her hiding spot has me seeing him in an entirely different light. His naturally engrained protectiveness already makes him a great father, not to mention his ability to nurture when required.

"Perhaps my grandparents' room would work?"

After jerking up his chin, Dimitri runs his hand down my arm in thanks, then makes his way to Demi and Maddox's side of the room. I want to continue soaking up their tear-producing display of affection but lose the chance when the heat of a gaze captures my attention.

I'm assuming Estelle has noticed my body's response to Dimitri's briefest touch, so you can picture my shock when I realize her stare isn't directed at me. She's peering past me, eyeballing the last person I ever anticipated for her to watch. She's gawking at Clover, and if the fizzle of their stares going to war is anything to go by, he's watching her just as closely.

"That's not a good idea," I warn after joining her on the couch.

The hiss zapping in the air weakens when Estelle drags her eyes to me. "What isn't a good idea?" She's been super quiet this afternoon like visiting prisoners and being surrounded by gang-

sters isn't an everyday occurrence for her. She works at an establishment owned by no other than Mr. Monroe. He's as well-known
amongst the locals of Erkinsvale as the Petrettis are to Hopeton
inhabitants, so she can't play the innocent card.

"Giving gaga eyes to a paid hitman."

Estelle rolls her eyes like I didn't hit the bullseye. "*Puh-leaze.* I
was warning him to stay away."

I wiggle my finger around her flushed cheeks. "If this is your
threatening face, what was the one I saw when you and Brayden
went to town Thanksgiving weekend?"

"Don't you dare judge me." The humor on her face weakens
the intensity of her snapped tone. "You were all, '*good riddance, I
can't stand him, how dare he treat me the way he did*' to, '*hey there,
good-looking, can I get you a cup of coffee? One clump or two?*'"

I sock her in the arm, doubling her smile. "I was trying to be
helpful."

"You were trying to take the focus off your pressing thighs."
When the truth of her statement lowers my shoulders, she jabs
her elbow into my ribs. "I can't blame you. He's fucking hot, they
all are, but..."

When she fails to find a reason for my insanity, I help a girl
out. "It's crazy to think *this* is any type of normal?"

After breathing out of her nose, she nods.

"Would it make you feel any better if I said it's not close to
being normal because it's not meant to be? There's bad and good
in every person. You've just got to find the one who makes your
flaws less obvious."

"What are you saying, Roxie? You're the concealer for Dimitri's
blemishes?"

I shake my head before I can stop myself. "He's not the one
with the marks, Estelle. I am."

Before the shock of my confession can register, the man we're talking about steals my focus from across the room. The briefest glance Dimitri awards me under hooded lashes isn't responsible for my utmost devotion. It's the tick of his jaw when he stares down at a tablet Smith shoves under his nose.

My brows spike as quickly as my heart rate when Dimitri instructs Rocco to take me to my room. He only ever does that when he's going to hurt someone I love or punish me. With his narrowed eyes locked on a group of officers mingling on the front porch, I doubt the latter is a contender. He's so worked up, Smith's tablet barely dings before he races across the room like a bullet being fired from a gun.

I sidestep Rocco just as quickly, certain the cause of Dimitri's aggression has something to do with me. The image Smith showed him was blurry from a distance, but several parts of it were distinct—the most obvious, my recently dyed flaming red hair.

"Roxie..." Don't misconstrue the annoyance in Rocco's tone. If he didn't want me to sidestep him, he wouldn't have let it happen. From what I've overheard the past couple of hours, he encouraged Dimitri to let me stretch my wings, unaware Dimitri's growth would come in the form of his possessiveness. He feels somewhat responsible for the six-week gap in whatever the fuck you consider my relationship with Dimitri to be. I assured him he has nothing to feel guilty about. He disregarded my offer on the basis I didn't know all the facts. Supposedly, the bender Dimitri went on weeks ago wasn't his lowest low. The past six weeks were.

"Dimitri!" I shout when he pole drives an officer in the middle of the group. The man he's assaulting is in uniform, his colleagues are surrounding him. I don't see him coming out of this with anything less than an extremely long rap sheet.

When the group of twenty-plus officers part to watch the charade unfold, I'm given an uninterrupted view of Dimitri clambering off the unnamed officer. He isn't satisfied he beat his face to within an inch of recognition with only a handful of swings. He's moving for the old rope swing in the front tree.

He doesn't yank it out of the tree. He merely curls the frayed end around the officer's throat before he hauls him onto his feet with inhumane strength. The dark-haired man's feet dangle an inch from the soggy ground within seconds, and his friends do nothing but stare when he clutches at the rope burning his throat.

His imminent death already looks painful, but I realize it's about to get worse when Dimitri knots the rope so that the officer is suspended mid-air without Dimitri needing to maintain his grip on the pulley. It isn't just the wet patch on the front of the man's pants responsible for my beliefs, it's the deadly gleam in Dimitri's eyes when he removes his suit jacket and commences rolling up the sleeves of his dress shirt. He's set to punish this man, his endeavor only thwarted when he spots my watch.

"Get her out of here!" he yells at Rocco, his voice unlike anything I've ever heard.

Rocco doesn't ignore his command this time around. He wraps his arm around my waist and hoists me away just as Dimitri hits the officer's ribs with a punishing left-right-left combination.

As the officer slowly asphyxiates, his eyes protrude out of his head. It has nothing on the bulge mine do when I see Smith's tablet screen head-on. The man who swore to uphold the law wasn't tempted by the bounty on my head. He put my license on a rape-play site. The address of the apartment I share with Estelle is on a website specifically designed for men to connect with women who fantasize about being raped, clear as day for all to see.

It isn't the only identification card on display either. There are several beneath me. One I recognize almost as immediately as I did mine. It's a photo identification from what appears to be

Demi's place of employment. It states she enjoys being taken unaware, and the rougher her unknown john is, the better.

Oh. My. God. Is that why Demi was assaulted? Because the man Dimitri is killing made out she fantasizes about being raped? If that's the case, what would have happened to me if Smith hadn't found his disturbing website? I don't have a dog nor a gun to keep me safe.

I only have Dimitri.

In all honesty, that's all I need. It doesn't make my anger any less violent, though. What if I weren't home when the men came looking? What if they hurt Estelle believing she was me?

As the anger inside of me evolves, I fight with everything I have. "Let me go," I seethe through clenched teeth when Rocco refuses to relinquish his grip around my waist. "I'm gonna pull his insides out of his nostrils."

"You're too late, Princess P," he informs on a laugh. "He's already met with his maker."

My eyes jackknife back in just enough time to take in the fatal flop of the officer's head. Although he's still hanging from the tree I climbed as a child, I don't believe he died from strangulation. There's too much blood oozing from the many nicks and cuts on his body for the coroner to place anything but torture down as his cause of death.

# 25

# DIMITRI

My blood is boiling hot. I'm pissed, frustrated as fuck, and reasonably sure one kill won't cut it. I want to murder Officer Daniel's entire precinct. Do you truly expect my anger to be any less? He didn't arrive with Maddox's fleet. He's been here since the start, standing mere feet from Roxanne for hours, drinking her coffee, and nibbling on the only morsel of food she had left in her cupboards. But instead of thanking her for her generosity, he put her information on a rape fantasy site. *All* her information—date of birth, height, weight, and exactly how you can sneak into her apartment via the fire escape ladder on the west side of her building. He even made out she likes being sodomized with household equipment.

Why, you ask? Because Officer Daniel Packwood works for the special victims' unit branched under Ravenshoe PD's umbrella, meaning he wouldn't just be in charge of Roxanne's case if one of the sick fucks on that site believed her kink was rape, he'd hear every sickening detail of her assault directly from the source—just like he did with Demi.

That's his kink. He isn't a rapist. He just wants to hear the fear in the woman's voice when she recalls her nightmare firsthand, then he'd go home to spank one out before climbing into bed with his wife—a rape victim and advocator for women's rights.

And you thought I was sick.

"Has the site been taken down?"

Smith waits for me to remove some of Officer Packwood's blood from my hands with the towel Clover tossed at me before jerking up his chin. "A new one will be back up by tomorrow. That's how these sites operate."

"His wife?" I question through a tight jaw.

"Had no fucking clue why her hosting server was being hit with a million views per week," Rocco answers on Smith's behalf. "She isn't in the wrong here, Dimi. There's no need to punish her, too."

Even confident he's right doesn't weaken my agitation. It will take Smith hours to comb through the website's visitors to see who screenshot Roxanne's information. That's hours he will be off Fien's case, but hours I can't refuse to give. Roxanne hasn't been to her apartment building in months, but that doesn't mean she's safe. You won't believe the lengths men go when they're on the hunt. Nothing is off-limits. If they want to find her, they will. No fear.

"Send two guys to watch out front. Officer Packwood wasn't working alone, so he'll have a visitor or two show up when he fails to arrive for duty Monday morning."

"And them?" Clover asks, peering at the officers who did nothing to help their boy in blue, too grateful it wasn't them to risk punishment by intervening.

He stops rubbing his hands together like a kid in a toyshop when I say, "They're on payroll, so they'll keep their mouths shut. If they don't..." When he spots the murderous gleam darting through my eyes, he recommences rubbing his hands. "When another site pops up, what are the chances of tracing the source of the server?"

Smith pulls a face I'd rather not see when I'm itching to kill for the second time. "Not good."

"Why not? You traced that one." This question didn't come from me. It came from Rocco, who's just as pissed as me. Men like Officer Packwood are the worst of the worst to him. If he didn't need to keep Roxanne contained in her room, I'm reasonably sure he would have joined me in punishing him.

"I followed a ping off Daniel's phone. If I hadn't, I would have never found the site he was posting to. It was buried too deeply in the dark web for standard searches."

Smith doesn't say it, but I felt his underhanded jab that he's struggling to do every task I'm assigning him on the mobile equipment he only uses when we're on the road. His hub was built on my compound for a reason. I get the best from him when he's in an area specially created for him.

With that in mind, I nudge my head to the door. "Head back to the compound. Roxanne and I will join you there shortly."

I can see on Rocco's face how badly he wants to rib me for backpedaling on the decision I made six weeks ago, but since he knows better than to annoy me when I'm fuming mad, he keeps his mouth shut. It's for the best. I'm so fucking angry right now, I can't guarantee I won't take it out on the wrong person—Roxanne and my second-in-charge included.

I'm about to head for the room I hear running water coming from when an earlier incident pops back into my head. I crank my neck to peer at Rocco so quickly, I give myself whiplash. "Why are you here? You were meant to sign Megan out."

His face whitens as his panicked eyes shift to Smith. "You didn't tell him?"

"Tell me what?" I ask when Smith shrugs, my temper short-fused.

"Fuck, douchebag. I thought you were on the ball." Rocco whacks Smith in the gut before giving him and Clover their marching orders, and then he walks away from a group of men acting as if they didn't just witness a murder. "Megan skipped bail. From what I coerced out of a medical team accepting no liability whatsoever for her misdiagnosis, it occurred a couple of weeks ago. She knocked a guard out cold. Chair straight over the fucking head." He scoots in even closer. "We're not the only ones hunting her." He glances toward the corrupt cops without moving his head. "They even brought in sniffer dogs."

"Who ordered the search?" Rocco's stern facial expression answers my question on his behalf. "So Theresa's act this morning was a ploy." I'm not seeking clarity. I'm stating a fact. "She isn't worried about Maddox—"

"Because she already knows she has that boy in check."

Since I agree with him, I don't voice annoyance about his interruption. I merely continue as if he never butted in. "She's petrified we're getting close to the truth."

Rocco whistles out an agreeing tune. "That's why we need to squeeze her a little harder."

"Or I could just kill her. Get the inevitable over and done with." My tone is as flat and bothersome as I'd feel knowing Theresa was lying in the bottom of the ocean, held down by bricks. That's how inconsequential her life is. No one would care if she were dead, not even the little boy she's trying to palm off as Isaac's.

"You could," Rocco agrees, smiling, "But you won't... because at the end of the day, you know the only time that bitch shares secrets is when she's on her back, being fed a healthy dose of your dick. Considering your girl looked set to murder when you traced your finger down her cheek this morning, I wouldn't recommend it. She's more than ready to bring the bat to the game for you, so why not have her swinging at the big hitters instead of the small fry like Theresa."

His comment switches the heat of my blood from chaos to yearning in under a second. Even with my blood pressure almost bursting my eardrums, I heard Roxanne's fight when she endeavored to free herself from Rocco's clutch. She wasn't fighting to save Officer Packwood's life. She wanted to witness the monster inside of me roar to life firsthand, to drink him in, in all his glory, and I'm about ready to grant her wish.

# 26

## ROXANNE

The soap doesn't have a chance in hell of remaining in my grip when the stern and clipped voice of Dimitri rolls across my bathroom. "Eyes to the wall."

My bathroom is tiny. It has the standard square upright shower, one vanity that's missing the cupboards beneath it, and a toilet's peach coloring shows how long ago it was installed. However, I still knew about Dimitri's arrival before he announced it. The aura that beamed out of him while he used the unnamed officer's body as a boxing bag hissed in the air, heating my skin as effectively as the boiling hot water pumping out of the showerhead.

"Don't make me ask you again, Roxanne," he growls out when my shock at his request has me desperate to peer over my shoulder.

I want to drink in the energy I've been in awe of for over a year before doubling it. I love his arrogance. It's what mesmerized me when he stood outside the alleyway watching me be fingered by a man well below my league, and it's what kept my feet grounded when Estelle used the distraction to make a break for it.

She begged me to go with her, but I couldn't. Dimitri was only on a murderous rampage because a man tried to hurt me. I can't be angry at him for that. I've been seeking this level of protection since I was a child, so it'll take more than the occasional death of a stupid man for me to give it up.

"Keep them there," Dimitri demands when my eyes finally submit to the prompts of my overworked brain.

My heart rages out of control when the steam inside my little bubble is released from Dimitri opening the glass door. After stepping into the space, which feels ten times smaller with his brooding frame taking up a majority of the tiled floor, in the corner of my eye, I watch him cup a generous serving of water in his bruised and battered hands. When he throws the water over his face, I realize what he is doing. He's cleaning himself up for me, afraid the gore and violence his life is shrouded in will scare me away.

"Goddammit, Roxanne! Do you ever do as you're told?" Dimitri grinds out with a roar when I spin around to face him.

I want to shake my head but can't. The view is too wondrous for me to move, much less garner a half-assed reply to his accurate statement. Our contrasting heights and widths are obvious when we're dressed, so you can imagine how conflicting they are when we're in a tiny space, butt naked. Add that to the fact Dimitri's muscles are strained from their earlier un-koshered workout, and you've got the ultimate recipe of lust, intrigue, and mystery.

I'm a part of this story, and I'm still dying to read what happens next.

My hands rattle when I raise them to Dimitri's face. I'm not worried he will reject me. The pulsating rod of flesh stealing my smarts assures me that won't happen. I'm simply disappointed I can't nurture him without removing the blood of another man from his face.

Shockwaves roll down my spine when Dimitri catches my hand before it gets near his face. His hold isn't painful, but it's most definitely aggressive. "You don't want to act like a lady any more than I want to pretend to be a gentleman."

As I wiggle to break free from his hold, I fight not to moan. His voice was as hot as honey, warm and inviting but so bitterly sweet, it will give me a toothache for days.

"You want a monster, a bastard." His grip on my wrist firms, along with the tightness of my womb. "You want me."

There's no point resisting what he's saying. Every word he speaks is true. So, instead, I nod. It commences an avalanche of groping hands and lust-blistering kisses. While he pins the lower half of my body to the tiled shower wall with his impressive crotch, he attacks my mouth with a blurring mix of licks, bites, and moans. It's a hurried, frantic exchange full of passionate touches, wandering hands, and moans my nanna would have killed me for only two years ago.

My noisy moans can't be helped. My pussy, tits, and ass are being lavished by Dimitri's big hands while his mouth encourages mine to defeat logic. It shouldn't be possible to be this noisy when my lungs are breathless, but somehow, I pull off the inevitable.

My head lowers to take in Dimitri biting a trail of love bites down my stomach. He licks, bites, then kisses me until his mouth is an inch from my aching sex, and I'm hoisted up the tiled wall as if I'm weightless. The small confines of the shower mean he can't kneel to devour his feast, so he brings his meal to himself, instead.

I tremble with the breath he releases when he instructs me to watch him. "I like your eyes on me..." Half of his face disappears between my splayed thighs before he does one controlled lick up my soaked slit. "Especially when I'm doing this..." He licks, tugs, and makes me come undone in an embarrassing quick eight seconds. "And even more so when you do that."

He holds nothing back for the next several minutes, not even when his accidental bump of the faucet switches the temperature of the water from roasting to freezing. The change-up is nice. I'm hot all over, so excluding my initial yelp about the rapid change in my core body temperature, I relish the refreshing change.

"Oh..." I'm close to climax again. It's building inside of me like a tsunami, encouraged by the short, powerful flicks Dimitri hits my clit with. He toys with the bundle of nerves between my legs until the moans seeping from my mouth can wake the dead. "I'm... I'm..." Fucking insane if I ever believed things between us were over. Something so explosive is indestructible. Unbreakable. *Everlasting.*

An orgasm washes through me when the possibility of forever hits me. I can't do anything but pant and scream. The intensity of my climax is insane. It rushes over me again and again and again until the feverish moans bouncing off the bathroom walls switch to a pained grunt from Dimitri's cock's sudden entrance to my clenching sex.

With one of my legs curled around his waist and the other hooked around his elbow, Dimitri drives into me on repeat. The pain of taking him for only the third time shouldn't have me close to detonation again, but it does. It builds inside of me, chasing its next release right along with Dimitri's bid to find his own.

He fucks the living hell out of me, screwing me so hard, I'm confident the spasms hitting my uterus are no longer associated with my looming period. He pounds and pounds and pounds into me until I'm screaming his name as if I am possessed.

"It feels so good. You feel so good," I grunt through the tremors overwhelming me. "Don't stop. Please don't ever stop. I'll die without this, without you."

Dimitri does the exact opposite of my moaned requests. He lowers the swings of his hips before he rests his forehead on mine. I don't mind. The change-up in speed will allow him to drink in the alteration of the light in my eyes, the transferal only he can instigate.

"Do you have any idea how many times I've dreamed about this?" he asks a few seconds later. "I blanket every inch of you as envisioned. Your entire ass fits in my palm."

As his eyes bounce between mine, they replicate the variation in color mine underwent minutes ago, except they appear more painted with anger than euphoria. I discover why when he adds, "I could have squashed you like a bug, but all I wanted to do was cocoon you until your wings were fully grown."

It feels like his cock is about to poke out of my stomach when he adds a roll to his hips. He's more deeply seated now, almost fully immersed. He isn't just ensuring I'll feel him for days, he's reminding me of exactly what I gave up six weeks ago.

"But do you know what happens when a butterfly gets her wings?"

I kiss him with everything I have, hopeful my tongue will ram his hurtful words down his throat before he can express them. I understand I stuffed up. I realize I should have fought harder. I don't need him to teach me a lesson while reminding me just how explosive we are.

Although my kiss doubles the heat bristling between us, it doesn't stop his words. "She flies away."

"I didn't."

He responds to my lie with both his cock and his eyes. He pounds into me, bringing me to the very edge of insanity before he freezes like his thighs are as lifeless as my heart felt the past six weeks. "Yes. You. Did."

Even aware I'm digging my hole deeper, I continue to fight.

"No." Water flings off my cheeks when I shake my head. "You dropped me off. You let me out of our agreement—"

Dimitri's roar shudders my heart straight out of my chest. "Because I wanted to see if you'd come back! I wanted proof you were there for me and not because you were in fear for your life."

"You had armed men on every corner, Dimi."

For how hard his hips are now thrusting, his words shouldn't be as smooth as silk. "Men you had no trouble bypassing when it suited you. Hair dye, trips to visit a state prison inmate... if you fucking wanted it, you found a way to get it."

Even with it being true, I hate everything he's saying. If I wanted his attention, I merely needed to walk out the front door any time after dusk because despite what Rocco says, I know Dimitri was outside the first twenty-eight days of my incarceration. I could feel him there, I was just too stubborn to succumb to the pressure eating me alive. Then I thought I was too late. Excluding earlier today, I hadn't sensed his presence in over two weeks.

"I was angry. You threatened my friend. You sent a murderer to her house. I wanted to get back at you." I try to hold in the truth, but just like I can't stop my tears once they start, there's no stopping my honesty, either. "I wanted you to beg me for a second chance, and to understand how pathetic I felt pinning for you when you seemed to hate me."

My confession punishes me more than Dimitri. He fucks the living hell out of me, pounding, grunting, and thrusting until my orgasm peaks, then he once again freezes like a statue.

"Don't do this. Don't punish me because I wanted to be first for a change."

My drenched hair flops against my cheeks when Dimitri forces my eyes to his. "You wanted to be first? That's the excuse you're running with?"

"It's not an excuse. Wanting to be someone's everything isn't an excuse," I reply before I realize how stupid I'm being. I got angry about him not giving me his undivided attention *after* pledging not to take more of his time than he's able to give me.

How foolish am I?

Not only am I in love with a gangster who's threatened to kill me more than once, I'm hoping he'll replicate feelings he doesn't understand.

I need my head examined.

My sigh has two meanings when Dimitri shuts off the faucet and carries me out of the bathroom. Because he's still inside of me, thick and heavy, I don't advise him fresh towels are hanging on the back of the door he left wide open as if we're the only two people in the room. It's clear he isn't done with my punishment just yet. The unrecognizable mask he's wearing is sure-fire proof of this, much less the way he dismounts me from his cock and dumps me onto my bed.

In a quick snag, flip, and lift maneuver, my ass is perched high in the air, and Dimitri's big cock pokes at my puckered hole.

"Don't fucking tempt me," he growls when my back instinctively arches, seeking firmer contact. "I don't have any lubricant, and if I find out you do, your ass won't be pounded with my cock. It will wear my handprint for days."

As warmth spreads through me, I tremble.

"I knew I'd need more than an hour to work through your kinks." As he rubs his erection against a region of my body I didn't realize had its own pulse, his hand slithers around my jittery stomach. I almost vault off my bed when he finds my clit without the stumbling hands Eddie used.

The quickest recollection of Eddie's golden eyes should cause the excitement flooding my insides to dampen. It doesn't. If anything, it makes it more perverse. I suspected Dimitri killed him because of what he had done to me. The officer's murder earlier this evening reveals that was the case. Dimitri is a monster who can fly off the hinges at any moment, but I don't believe that makes him hideously ugly. He's dark, yet undeniably beautiful. Deranged, yet somehow sane. And he can love, he just hasn't been shown how to yet.

"Let me make it up to you."

"No," Dimitri immediately answers like he knows what I'm talking about.

Considering I've orgasmed multiple times tonight, he could mistake my offer as a wish to reciprocate the favor, but I know that isn't the case. Even when he's knee-deep in filth, Dimitri's thoughts are always with his daughter.

"I can help, Dimi. Dr. Bates isn't as smart as his credentials—"

"No!" he screams with a brutal thrust of his hips.

The way he enters me should have me screaming just as loudly, but my target is locked and loaded, and I'm not giving him up for anything. "He walks around with dollar signs in his eyes—"

"For fuck's sake, Roxanne, shut up before I force you to be quiet."

His threat doesn't penetrate my mind in the slightest. "He'd be an easy man for you to fool. Force his hand, Dimitri. Show him you're not to be messed with. Gut him like you did Eddie, then do the same to your father."

I'm panting now, full-on moaning, overcome by the vicious fucking Dimitri is bombarding me with. He pounds into me so hard, my insides feel like they're being shifted to accommodate his massive dick. It's painful yet beautiful—just like him.

"You have nothing to lose and everything to gain. You've just got to show the people who have your back that you believe in them by accepting their help."

There's nothing romantic about our fuck. Dimitri takes all the control, leaving nothing in his wake until I freefall into an uprising of warmth and comfort. It's a ferociously stunning few minutes that only grows more striking when Dimitri withdraws his magnificent cock, brings it to my lips, then grunts, "Reciprocate."

A normal person would mistake his command as him wanting head.

As I've said time and time again, I'm nothing close to ordinary.

After nodding, wordlessly advising him I understand his request, I take his dick between my lips and swallow down, smug as hell I guided a man as powerful as him through the fog before his cock got anywhere near my mouth.

# 27

# ROXANNE

I grimace when the quickest hiss darts through my ears. Smith numbed the area he's inserting a micro tracker into, so I don't feel an ounce of pain. It's just realizing I'll have a foreign device in my arm for the rest of my life that has me grimacing.

Although I would have preferred not to be microchipped like a dog, I didn't have much choice. If I denied Dimitri's request, he would have reneged on the agreement we made last night. I couldn't let that happen. Our ruse is his first solid chance to get his daughter back. It should come before anything—even my freedom.

Fien is a captive because my mother begged my father to swap Dimitri's wife with me, so it's my responsibility to do everything in my power to help Dimitri get her back. I'm scared, but I'm also hopeful. It's clear Dimitri loves his daughter. Once she's back, perhaps he will realize love comes in many forms.

"Does that feel okay?"

I raise my eyes to Smith, the querier of my question. "It feels a little weird."

"The device or your head?" Rocco asks on a laugh, shocked by the slur of my words. I don't know what Smith used to numb my arm, but it has my head convinced I guzzled a fifth of vodka with my dinner.

"A teeny bit of both."

"Your dizziness will settle soon." Smith rubs an alcohol swap over the nick in my arm before he places a Band-Aid over it. "If it doesn't, I'll give you another dose. It will have you sleeping like a baby within an hour."

I want to sock him in the stomach but hold back the urge when I notice Dimitri's narrowed gaze. He looks five seconds from killing Smith, and his oxygen-depriving protectiveness doubles the wooziness bombarding me.

"Thank you."

Smith lifts his chin, acknowledging my thanks before he moves to clean up the mess he made in his makeshift hospital room. We're still at my family's ranch, conscious my booking for Dr. Bates's clinic may have eyes placed on me earlier than my appointment. The shutters are closed, a beat-up Honda is in the driveway, and Smith has numerous jammers scattered amongst the dated furniture. To anyone outside of these walls, it appears as if Dimitri is still done with me. Only those in the know are experiencing his panic firsthand.

He's been more reserved than usual today. He agrees our plan is smart, but he's still cautious he's making the wrong decision. I'll do my best to assure him otherwise between now and my appointment tomorrow morning. By remaining fearless, he'll soon realize just how much faith I have in him. He will keep me safe no matter what. I've never had more confidence in anything in my life but that.

After a lengthy debate this morning, we decided the go with the ploy Smith and I discussed while Dimitri was unconscious from a combined drug overdose and exhaustion. According to our plan, I called the private cell phone Dr. Bates scribbled across his business card when he endeavored to buy me outright, panicked out of my mind that my period was late and how Dimitri would kill me if he found out.

By staying on script, we learned that Dr. Bates is knowledgeable on parts of Dimitri's life not many people know about. His voice didn't waver in the slightest when I said Dimitri would be mad as hell if I fell pregnant at the start of our relationship like his wife did. It was as if he already knew their story. I wasn't sharing anything new with him.

After ensuring me I'd be okay, Dr. Bates offered to clear his schedule so I could immediately come in. That threw me out of the loop for a couple of seconds. I hadn't expected him to react so quickly. Although I was eager to get our ruse started—the quicker it occurs, the faster Fien will be returned—I knew Dimitri's team needed more than twenty minutes to put steps into play to ensure Dr. Bates's every move was being scrutinized.

I also perhaps needed more than a measly twenty minutes with Dimitri before his life is upended for the second time. We haven't had a moment of quiet since he agreed to my offer. It's been full steam ahead since then.

"Still nothing?" I ask after stopping at Dimitri's side. I don't know who he's been trying to call the past six hours, but the tension on his face grows more obvious the longer his calls remain unanswered. I'm confident his worry doesn't stem from his cousin. She left here earlier today with an armored fleet as impressive as the one they used to bring Maddox here for the night, but it's clear he's noticing their absence.

"He must be somewhere without cell phone service as he's never not taken my call."

As he slides his phone into the pocket of his trousers, I spot the name of the man he's endeavoring to reach on its screen. Rico. He must be new to Dimitri's sanction because it isn't a name I've heard the past several weeks.

"Ask Smith to track his cell. If it's turned on, he should be able to find it." Keen to soothe the heavy groove between his brows, I add, "Even without a trendy microchip installed in your arm, it's almost impossible to remain incognito these days."

His smirk is only half what I was hoping for, but it's better than nothing.

After a few more minutes soaking up his handsome face, I say, "I'm going to go lay down for a couple of minutes. My head is a little woozy." I peer up at him with hopeful eyes. "Would you care to join me?"

Only weeks ago, I wouldn't have been game to assume he wants to sleep with me. Now, it feels as natural as breathing. Even with his quiet taking up a majority of my focus today, I've noticed his heated gaze directed at me multiple times. He finally believes I'm on his side, and I'm more than willing to continue convincing him, especially if that can only occur while he's naked. I've always been the more daring one of my friends, and now that I've discovered just how powerful sex can make you feel, I want to flex my muscles.

Either mishearing the innuendo in my tone or too worried to sleep, Dimitri replies, "I've got a few things to take care of first. I'll join you once they're finalized." The drop of my bottom lip isn't as noticeable when he lowers his voice to ensure his next set of words is only for my ears. "Sleep naked. I don't want anything between us when I come to bed."

"Okay." Considering I only spoke one word, it shouldn't be as breathy as it is.

After squeezing his hand, wordlessly assuring him he has

nothing to worry about, I skip to my room, confident it's the perfect location to ease his panic.

---

Many, many hours later, the creak of an old set of hinges wakes me from my slumber. My head is still a little woozy, but it's more compliments to Dimitri's delicious scent than the sedative Smith gave me. He strips beside the bed like he did every night we shared the same room before he slips between the sheets.

Unlike our last night together at his compound, I don't cry into his chest when he pulls me into his arms. I moan. He's thick, warm, and he smells like me since the only shower he's had the past twenty-four hours is the one we shared.

A husky moan fills my ears when he curls my leg around his waist. For once, I'm confident it didn't come from me. Dimitri is responding to my submissiveness in a way that ensures it will occur more often from here on out. I'm naked as he requested, and his scent alone has me the wettest I've ever been.

"Grip my shoulders like your cunt does my cock. If I go too fast, dig your nails in deep." He bites my bottom lip, drags his tongue across the welt, then tastes the minty flavor of my toothpaste before he adds, "I don't want to hurt you."

"You won't."

A stretch of silence follows my promise. It's a tense, beautiful moment occupied by Dimitri slowly sinking inside of me. I fist the sheets as big, extended breaths seep from my mouth. The feeling of being stretched so wide is wondrous, but it has nothing on the sensation that overwhelms me when our eyes collide. His earlier panic has receded. Now, nothing but pleasing me is on his mind.

When shudders commence rolling through me, I freeze. I can't possibly be coming already. He's barely rocked his hips four times.

The thought he can bring me to climax so fast turns me on more than I could ever explain. It doubles the tingles in my womb and ramps up my moans to an embarrassing level.

"Come hard for me, Roxie. Coat my cock with your juices, then I can try and stuff my cock all the way in."

His tongue laps at my lips as he rocks in and out of me, prolonging my orgasm to the point I'm considering classing it as two. The wetness soaking the sheets should have me blushing. However, it doesn't. I'm drenched front to back, moaning like we're the only two people in the world and clenching around Dimitri's fat cock with every plunge he does.

We're not brutally fucking as we did last night, proving I don't need violence nor an audience to get off. The perfect rolls of his hips and the dirty words he whispers in my ear is everything I need.

It's perfect.

Mind-blowing.

Fireworks producing.

It has me stuttering out a warning I'm about to come again before the first one has fully dissipated. It's a brilliant exchange that verifies every crazy decision I've made the past nine weeks was for the best.

"I knew you'd be like this. Explosive and un-fucking-relentless." Dimitri rolls me onto my back before he curls my legs around his sweaty back. "How many times did you dream about this after that dweeb's attempt to get you off in the alleyway?"

"More times than I can count," I answer truthfully, unconcerned by his name-calling. You can't be expected to think morally when you're in a situation like this. Even the most solid principles burn when the fire is out of control. "But it's better than I could have ever comprehended. No one can predict explosions like this. They're unpredictable..." I lock my eyes with Dimitri's, meowing when I notice how clear of trouble they are, "... kind of like you."

He thrusts into me deeper, faster, and harder, turned on by my words. It's crazy, but within seconds, I feel another powerful, all-encompassing orgasm building inside of me, and I'm not the only one noticing.

As he demands the attention of my dripping sex with quick, powerful strokes, Dimitri raises his hand to one of my breasts. He pinches my nipple, growling when the sharpness of his touch sends me freefalling over the edge.

A shudder rips through me from my head to my toes as Dimitri's name leaves my throat in a grunted moan. My climax is violent. It takes everything I have and then some. I feel incapable of breathing. I'm hot everywhere and screaming oh so loudly. I can't control it. It's uncontrollable. It pummels into me over and over again like a violent ocean refusing to leave a single victim. I'd let it take me if it promised every night would be as exquisite as this one.

"There you are," Dimitri mutters against my lips, God knows how long later. I'm dazed like I zoned out for longer than a couple of minutes, the prompts of my body no longer mine. They've been relinquished to Dimitri, along with my heart.

"I love..." I freeze, fretful I'm about to make a horrendous mistake.

I don't know this man. We were strangers only months ago, but that doesn't mean I can't also love him, does it? He forced me to share information I've never wanted to give anyone, but that isn't necessarily a bad thing. I may have very well fallen in love with him that morning in the plane. He didn't judge me as I thought he would. He held me in his arms and wiped away my tears. He was there for me like no one ever was.

Whether in fear or euphoria, he makes my heart beat like no

one else can. Its patters will never be matched for anyone who isn't him.

That, in itself, is worthy of recognition.

That deserves acknowledgment.

Confident this will be by far the least stupid thing I've done, I return my eyes to Dimitri's face, gulping when I notice his watch. The speed of his pumps hasn't slackened in the slightest despite him noticing my thirty seconds of deliberation. He stares straight at me, the altering of the light in his eyes as fascinating as his infamous half-smirk when I say, "I love you, Dimitri Petretti. Your fierceness, your cockiness, I love everything about you."

# 28

## DIMITRI

Doing everything I can to weaken the knot in my gut, I pace the room. I didn't know I was walking into a trap when I offered to chauffeur Audrey to her baby shower. If I'd known, I would have put actions into place to protect her and keep our daughter safe. I would have had every eye of my team on her as they are now on Roxanne. However, no matter what I did twenty-two months ago, my panic would still be valid today.

If my enemies hadn't taken Audrey, they would have taken Roxanne, and then I wouldn't have heard the words she spoke to me as clear as day last night.

I killed her boyfriend, tortured her family, and have threatened to kill her more times than I've showed her an ounce of affection, yet, she still loves me.

She. *Loves*. Me.

The thought blows my mind. It also had cum rushing out of my cock last night like I hadn't had sex in years. I filled Roxanne to the brim before displaying exactly what her words meant to me with my body. We fucked for hours. It was glorious, the best sex

I've ever had, but it feels like a thing of the past now as I watch Roxanne prepare for her appointment with Dr. Bates.

The beat-up Honda Rocco purchased from a used-car dealer three towns over is wired to the hilt. It has a tracker, multiple microphones, and almost as many cameras as Roxanne's clothing. We have every angle covered, yet I still feel like I should call off the whole thing.

I wouldn't hesitate if Fien's ransom hadn't landed in my inbox this morning. It was short, snarky, and requesting a year's payout for only one month, proving Roxanne's chat with Dr. Bates yesterday morning has circulated amongst my enemies.

It also has me confident Roxanne is right. The instigator of Fien's captivity is a woman. I can smell bullshit from a mile out. Jealousy extends to five. The scent that streamed through my nose while reading Fien's ransom request was fucking rank. The person responsible for the hell I've lived in the past two years is a female —a dead one when I find out who she is.

"Is that everything?" I ask Roxanne when she ties up the final lace of her boots.

Alice picked a casual look for Roxanne today with a free-flowing dress, a cropped jacket, tights, and boots that are more than capable of removing a guy's nuts if he gets out of line.

I requested for her to wear the boots.

Rocco was adamant they needed to be steel caps.

Nodding, Roxanne licks her lips. She won't say she's scared because she knows I'd call off our ruse in an instant. Little threads are unraveling everywhere, so it will only be a matter of time before Fien's captives are brought to justice, but Roxanne is also mindful that every hour I'm without Fien feels like a lifetime of punishment. For some insane reason, she wants to save me from the nightmare, and her motives have nothing to do with the fact she was swapped for Audrey. She's so under my thumb, even if her parents had nothing to do with Audrey's murder, she'd still offer to place her life on the line for Fien. No fear.

That thought alone has me doing something my crew would never expect to see me do. I don't bid Roxanne farewell with a dip of my chin. I kiss her with everything I have. Teeth, lips, tongue, they all get in on the action. I pass on my appreciation for what she's doing and the words she shared last night, then I promise her loyalty won't go unnoticed.

I *will* protect her better than I did Audrey.

I *will* keep her safe.

She has my guarantee I won't let anything happen to her.

By the time I pull back, Roxanne's knees are wobbling, and Rocco is clapping. "I didn't think you had it in you, D, but I was wrong. You can *totally* make me hard."

I cut off the grab of his crotch with a stern sideways glance. I appreciate he's trying to bring down the tension in the room with a little bit of humor, but now isn't the time. I'm five seconds from throwing in the towel on an operation that could get me my daughter back. That's unacceptable even to consider. However, it's straight-up honest. I've never felt as conflicted as I do now. It feels as if I have Roxanne's life in one hand and Fien's in the other with no possibility of them both making it out of the carnage unscathed.

I've just got to try what Roxanne suggested. I have to put my faith in the people who have never given me any reason to doubt their loyalty. I won't lie. The track is bumpy, but I'm giving it my best shot.

I return Roxanne's focus to me by running my index finger down the little bump in her arm. The implant site of her tracker is still sensitive to touch, but since the tracker is the size of a grain of rice, it's barely noticeable to the human eye. "If at any time you feel something is off, signal for us to move in. Rocco will be in the pharmacy next door. Clover and a team are one block over. I've got as many men on this as possible—"

"I know, Dimi," she interrupts, smiling to assure me she got the gist of what my kiss was about. "We've got every base covered. Now we just need to get your daughter back." She wipes off her sticky lip gloss from my mouth before she pivots to face Rocco. "Ready?"

Rocco's face is well-known to our enemies, so he can't drive Roxanne to her appointment, but he will tail her two-town trip. My enemies would expect her to have a constant shadow since I'm as neurotic as I am wealthy.

"I was born ready." After gathering up a set of keys, Rocco heads for the back entrance, so he can be in his truck before Roxanne departs the main entrance, patting my shoulder on the way by. "She's got this, D. She was run over *twice*. She can handle anything."

Once Smith gives Roxanne a final rundown on each camera button in her dress, she glances my way for the quickest second, waves like her heart isn't thudding in her chest, then slips out the front door.

My brain switches from personal to business just as quickly. "Bring up the surveillance cameras in Dr. Bates's office."

One of the techies Smith brings in when he gets snowed under jumps to my command. I can't recall his name. It starts with an H, I think.

Once Dr. Bates's office is displayed on multiple screens in front of me, I shift on my feet to face Smith. "Are all communication methods hacked?"

He jerks up his chin. "We've got eyes and ears in each location and frequencies scanning remotely. Even if he uses a burner phone, we'll know exactly what he sends and who he sends it to."

"Will it give us a location?"

My jaw tightens when he shakes his head. "But that will come with time."

It's an effort not to sigh as I have no patience whatsoever. That's why our plan today is slowly killing me. We have every intention to let Roxanne be kidnapped this morning, confident the group Dr. Bates is working with will take her straight to Rimi Castro. Then we'll use the tracker in Roxanne's arm to pinpoint her location, go in hard, then come out victorious.

Sounds easy enough, but very rarely does it pan out that way. And I'm not going to mention my intuition warning me to pull back on the reins, or I'll instruct Smith to overtake the controls of Roxanne's car she's steering toward Hopeton.

We have control of everything except the one thing I want to control the most. I can slay my enemies, I can gut them until they're spineless, worthless men, but I can't seem to outrun them lately. I'm always one step behind, and more times than not, that minute gap is filled with the biggest chunk of anarchy.

It kills me to admit that. I'd give anything to change it. But I can't. That isn't the way things work in this industry. If you're not giving it to someone up the ass, you're taking it. I'm so fucking over it, but I have no choice but to play the game as it's meant to be played. I can mix up the pieces as I did by bringing Rico onto my side of the board, I can strategize to ensure the princess is protected above the king, but I can't alter the rules to suit myself. If I did, it wouldn't just be me paying the penalty. Fien would, and so would Roxanne.

With that in mind, I get back to business. "How many patients does Dr. Bates have coming in today?"

"According to his schedule, over half a dozen."

Sensing some unease in Smith's reply, I ask, "And according to you?"

He takes a moment to deliberate before locking his brown eyes with mine. "He's organized to have lunch with his wife today. They're planning to eat in Ravenshoe."

"Is that out of the ordinary for them?"

He nods. "The last time they ate together was Thanksgiving four years ago. To say things are strained would be an understatement, so why would he go out of his way to wine and dine her today?"

He has a point—regretfully. "Send someone to the restaurant he's planning to dine at. It could be a waste of resources, but I'd rather be cautious."

While he attends to that, I request the techie whose name I still can't remember to bring up the main camera in Roxanne's car, praying like fuck the last time I see her face won't be through a computer monitor.

# 29

# ROXANNE

I breathe out the nerves making me a jittery mess before making my way to the reception desk at Dr. Bates's OBGYN office for the second time this morning. The foyer is inviting with music playing softly in the background and scented candles wafting in the air, but the feeling of dread refuses to leave me. Dr. Bates was the least creepy of my suitors when I was put up for auction. He was well-spoken, dressed nicely, and excluding when he tried to un-cut Dimitri's profit by offering to pay me directly for my virginity, he seemed pleasant.

Fool me once, shame on me.

He won't fool me again.

The information Smith shared about him when we discussed a way to bring him down for drugging Dimitri had me rechewing food I had earlier eaten. He has bounced his practice state to state, had more than a dozen affairs on his wife, and is linked to the disappearance of at least three women. All were in their final weeks of pregnancy, and all of them were blonde—his seemingly preferred choice.

His knowable likes are the reason I kept my hair red. We're not here to entice him into locking me up in his playroom of kinks. We want him to pass me onto the men Dimitri believes are responsible for his daughter's captivity.

Just the thought of being in the room with such men gives me the heebie-jeebies. Fortunately, the tingles I still feel buzzing on my lips from Dimitri's awe-inspiring kiss is much more potent. It would encourage a saint to walk through Hell's gates with a smile on her face and a wish for Satan to bring everything he has to the party.

"You can go straight in, Ms. Grace," informs the receptionist when I place down the clipboard she requested me to fill in on arrival.

"Are you sure?" I scan the room brimming with patients, certain almost all of them were here before I arrived.

"Yes," she responds with a smile, drawing my focus back to her. "Dr. Bates is waiting for you."

"Okay." I sound as uneased as I feel. The overflowing waiting room would make most women feel safe. There's a weird comfort you get with numbers, but I'm not experiencing that. There is less chance of me being kidnapped since it's the middle of the day, so my chances are even lower with a heap of spectators. I hope today's charade isn't utterly pointless. "Which way?"

The receptionist hands me a gown and a small jar with a yellow lid before pointing to a hall on our right. "Bathrooms are through the second door on the left. Dr. Bates is the one just after that."

Nodding, I slowly make my way to Dr. Bates's office. I could get changed as per the receptionist's underhanded demand, but that would make the camera buttons in my dress futile. Considering it took Smith almost all night to fit them, I'd rather keep them in operation.

After breathing out my nerves, I push open the door with Dr. Bates tacked on the front. "Dr. Bates, hi." My greeting is ridiculously sweet, my role of knocked-up virgin played to perfection. "The bathrooms were occupied, so I hope you don't mind me skipping that part of my appointment." I bite on the inside of my cheek, hopeful a rush of blood from my gnaw will have Dr. Bates believing I'm blushing. "I don't feel comfortable doing *that*..." I wave my hand over the ultrasound equipment next to a bed with obvious stirrups.

He swivels around to face me, blocking the images of multiple blonde females on the screen of his computer with his wide shoulders. Since he dyes his hair, it's hard to guess his age, but if forced, I'd say mid-forties. "That's fine, Roxanne. I don't need to examine you today." As he drags his eyes over my fire-engine red hair, he stands to his feet. He's dressed more casually than he was at my auction, which is shocking considering this is his place of occupation. "Is that new?"

I sheepishly balance my chin on my chest as if I'm ashamed. "Dimitri preferred redheads."

It's the fight of my life not to seek out one of the many hidden cameras Smith advised me about this morning when Dr. Bates replies, "I have heard that." While smiling at my flushed cheeks, he gestures his hand to the examination table. "Why don't you put down your things and take a seat."

I begin to wonder if we've misjudged him when my jump to his command is quickly chased by him checking my vitals. He takes my blood pressure, checks my pulse, and flashes a light into my eyes before asking a set of personal questions, such as, when did I last have my period.

"Umm..." His question legitimately stumps me. With my last thirty-six hours spent ensuring Dimitri has made the right decision to trust me, I didn't have time to sit down and calculate a date

SHANDI BOYES

that would have me six or so weeks along. "Around eight weeks ago."

I touch his arm like I'm embarrassed to admit I had no reason to keep an eye on things like that only months ago. I'm honestly ashamed, so it's an easy act for me to pull off.

An unpleasant glint darts through Dr. Bates's eyes as he asks, "Have you had unprotected sex since your last period?"

The heat on my cheeks is real this time around. Not only is Dimitri eavesdropping on our conversation, almost every member of his team is as well. "Yes. Multiple times."

I almost choke on my last two words, stunned I've not once cited an objection to Dimitri's inability to sheath his cock with protection. I shouldn't be surprised. I barely keep a rational head when he looks at me, so I don't see me having the power to bark out a set of orders when his head is between my legs.

Dr. Bates drops his eyes to the monitor of his computer before asking, "Have you had sexual intercourse in the last twenty-four hours?" He didn't need to hide his eyes for me to sense his annoyance. I can feel it radiating out of him.

I almost nod before recalling why I left my grandparents' ranch this morning. As far as Dimitri's enemies are concerned, we're over and done with, his annoyance about my 'supposed' pregnancy the cause of our breakup. "No, I haven't."

"Great!" Dr. Bates's shouted word startles me. "So, there shouldn't be any issues with your test."

Panic and fear roll through me at the same time. "Test? I thought you didn't need to examine me today?"

You could class Dr. Bates's smile as cute if he didn't have the markings of a psychopath. "Not a physical test. A pregnancy test."

I gulp back my sigh when he stands from his chair to gather the jar the receptionist handed me five minutes ago. "You can use my private restroom." He presses his palm against a wooden panel

506

next to his desk before moving to stand in front of the doorway leading to the hall, blocking my only exit. "Then you won't have any worries about stage fright."

"I don't really need to go." When the humor on his face evaporates, I switch tactics. "But I guess there's no harm in trying."

After snatching the jar out of his hand, I make a beeline for his private washroom, ensuring the door latches shut behind me.

"I'm so sorry," I apologize to my reflection in the mirror. "I didn't think he would do a test."

My lack of knowledge can easily be excused. Up until a few weeks ago, I was a virgin. It doesn't make me naïve, but it most certainly has me on the back foot when it comes to things like babies and pregnancy tests.

"Please tell me you're not going to watch me pee."

Dimitri can't answer me. The radio frequency Smith needed to track any calls coming in and out of Dr. Bates's office means I couldn't use the fancy bead-like listening device I did when my virginity was auctioned.

Confident Dimitri is too possessive to let anyone see me in a vulnerable state, I walk to the toilet, hook up my dress, yank down my panties and tights, then pee into the jar Dr. Bates was kind enough to open for me.

With my knees shaking in disappointment, half my pee lands on my hand instead of the jar. It frustrates me, but it has nothing on how annoyed I'll be when my ruse backfires in my face in a couple of minutes. When my test comes back negative, Dr. Bates may become suspicious we're onto him. If that happens, he may shut up shop for the fifth time this decade. Then our chances of finding Fien will be even lower than they already are.

Once my hands are scrubbed clean, and the panic is washed from my face, I exit the bathroom. Dr. Bates appears as if he hasn't moved. I know that isn't the case. He not only has a pregnancy test in his hand, but there's also an outline of a cell phone in his pocket.

*Sorry, buddy. Your bank accounts aren't about to become overloaded with funds,* I mumble in my head while handing him a jar of pee.

While Dr. Bates dips the end of the pregnancy test into the jar, I conjure up an excuse to leave. "How long do these things take? Should I wait outside while you do your magic?"

Light hair falls into his eyes when he peers at me over his shoulder. "No, that isn't necessary. They only take a minute at the most."

Knowing what the results will be, I gather my belongings from the examination table before hovering near the door. My nervous bob shifts to a shake when Dr. Bates says, "Or in your case, only thirty seconds."

I feel my pupils dilate to the size of saucers when he lifts a positive pregnancy test in the air a mere second before he peers into an obvious camera in the corner of the room. Then, not even a second later, I feel someone creeping up on me.

# 30

# DIMITRI

"Get her out." I leap up from my chair, too bristling with unease to sit for a second longer. "Get her out now!"

I'm stunned I can talk. My brain is fried from taking in Roxanne's positive pregnancy test. It makes the ruse I was certain was just about to bust more authentic, but I'll be fucked if I let my enemies get another one of my children.

I also don't want Roxanne to go through what Audrey went through. I could barely stomach it when it happened to my wife. I won't handle it occurring to a woman I love.

As Rocco leaps into action, I dart my eyes between the many monitors in front of me. Roxanne appears as shocked by the results as me. She stares at the now-blue stick with her mouth hanging open and her eyes bulged. Her expression is the same shocked one Audrey wore when her test came back positive. However, she isn't being subjected to the verbal tirade I spat out upon discovering the news I was about to be a father.

Back then, I thought my world was crumbling.

Now I know it most definitely is.

Even with my wish to kill the highest it's ever been, I keep a rational head. Flying off the hinges won't help anyone right now. It won't help me, it won't help Fien, and it most certainly won't help Roxanne.

"What was that?" I point to the monitor, the quickest flurry of black darted past. It could have been the shadow of one of the many pregnant women mingling in the hallway, but it seemed wider, more deviant.

It feels like the world caves in on me when the dozen monitors surrounding me suddenly plunge into blackness. It's a total communication blackout, leaving Roxanne utterly defenseless.

"Move!"

Smith forcefully plucks one of the techies from his chair so he can take over the controls. He taps on a gel keyboard like a madman, bringing up one camera at a time. He's working as fast as he can, but to me, it isn't fast enough. My worst nightmare is coming true for the second time, except this time, I'm knee-deep in the controversy.

I agreed to Roxanne's suggestion.

I put her in danger.

Once again, nothing happening is her fault.

"Where is she?" I ask fearfully when the return of the live feed to Dr. Bates's office comes up empty. As my eyes dart from screen to screen to screen seeking the feeblest snippet of red, my blood boils. She has to be there. The cameras were down for barely twenty seconds. No one can move that fast—not even me.

"There!" shouts a blond-haired techy who's pointing to a screen on my left.

Relief engulfs me when my eyes drink in Roxanne's svelte frame and beautiful face. It doesn't linger for long. She's no longer on her feet. She's been carried down an isolated corridor in the arms of a man wearing all black, their brisk walk shadowed by Dr. Bates. She is also without clothing.

"Their taking her out the hidden entrance," I advise Rocco via the comms server I'm praying is still in function.

When my demand is followed by a painful stretch of silence, I shout, "Get him on his cell."

Smith's voice makes it seem as if his throat is being shredded with the same razor blades cutting up mine. "On it."

I rip my fingers through my hair when the buzz of Rocco's cell phone rings out of the speakers of Smith's computer over and over again. He isn't in any of the frames, he's nowhere to be found, and Roxanne's unconscious body is being thrown into the back of an unmarked van.

"Prepare to commence trace." I watch in feared awe as Smith takes hold of the reins like he was born to do it. He activates the chip in Roxanne's arm and advises Clover coordinates are on their way before he raises his eyes to mine. "Are you sure you want Clover to move in now? This was the plan, Dimi. Roxie could lead us straight to Fien."

I'm so fucking torn. It truly feels like this decision will tear me in two. If I don't move now, I could lose Roxanne. If I hold off, I could bring both her and my daughter home—but what happens if that occurs *after* Roxanne has already been hurt. What if I'm too late for the second time?

I'm convinced my enemies are wired-tapped into my inner-workings when the decision is taken out of my hands. Just as quickly as the surveillance devices shutdown in Dr. Bates's office, we lose our connection with Roxanne's tracker.

Fury boils beneath my skin as I stare at an unmoving blue dot on a map of the town I should have owned years ago. "What happened?"

Smith shrugs. Anger is written all over his face. As he strives to find answers, he punishes his keyboard. I struggle not to do the same to his face when he sinks into his chair with a groan a few seconds later. "They removed her fucking tracker."

"What do you mean?" I ask, my voice unlike anything I've ever heard before. "No one knows she was wearing a tracker, so how do you know they've removed it."

My confusion is alleviated in the worst way possible when Smith hooks his thumb to the screen of his laptop. Rocco is in the middle of the monitor. He's bleeding, red-faced, and holding up the tiniest little microchip to a security camera in the back alleyway of a Publix Supermarket chain.

I played with more than I could afford to lose, and I fucking lost—*again*.

---

**The end...**

Dimitri and Roxanne's story continues in the next explosive part of the Italian Cartel Series. Reign is available NOW!

If you want to hear updates on the next books in this crazy world I've created, be sure to join follow my social media pages:

Facebook: facebook.com/authorshandi

Instagram: instagram.com/authorshandi

Email: authorshandi@gmail.com

Reader's Group: bit.ly/ShandiBookBabes

Website: authorshandi.com

Newsletter: https://www.subscribepage.com/AuthorShandi

Rico, Asher, Isaac, Brandon, Ryan, Cormack, Enrique & Brax stories have already been released, but Grayson, Rocco, Clover, and all the other great characters of Ravenshoe/Hopeton will be getting their own stories at some point during 2020/2021.

*If you enjoyed this book please leave a review.*

# ACKNOWLEDGMENTS

To all the peeps who make this happen, a huge thank you.

To my editor, Nicki @ Swish Design and Editing, my proof-reader, Kaylene Osborn, my mom, the alpha readers, beta readers, and the people who download my books without even reading the blurb. Thank you, thank you, thank you. I truly appreciate you from the bottom of my heart.

*You rock!*

I can't do an acknowledgement page without mentioning the man who makes this all possible. To my husband, Chris. Thank you for being you, and for being my number one fan before I had written a single word.

I love you, boo.

Today, tomorrow, and forever.

Shandi xx

Facebook: facebook.com/authorshandi

Instagram: instagram.com/authorshandi

Email: authorshandi@gmail.com

Reader's Group: bit.ly/ShandiBookBabes

Website: authorshandi.com

Newsletter: https://www.subscribepage.com/AuthorShandi

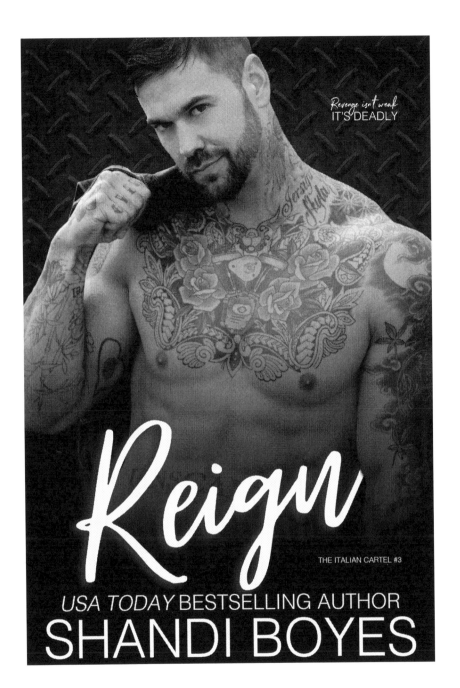

Revenge isn't weak
IT'S DEADLY

# Reign

THE ITALIAN CARTEL #3

USA TODAY BESTSELLING AUTHOR
## SHANDI BOYES

# DEDICATION

*To the voices in my head,*

*Thank you for convincing people I am not crazy.*

*Shandi xx*

# 1

## DIMITRI

Unsettled tension grips my throat as I stare at the rice-size tracking device in Rocco's hand. It's coated in as much blood as Rocco's hair, revealing the men who took Roxanne didn't just remove the device from her arm, they cut it out.

If the anxiety plaguing me is anything to go by, that's only the start of the torture they'll put her through. This is about more than money. Fien's low-ball ransoms already disclose this fact. If it were solely about the coin, as Roxanne said months ago, my daughter's ransoms would have been as extravagant as the one I placed on the table to keep Roxanne safe. They're playing me, and for once, I'm about ready to play back.

We play to play.

We kill to kill.

And we take down any fucker stupid enough to get in our way.

After licking my dry lips, I get down to business. Annoyance is bubbling under the surface of my skin. It's heard in my low tone when my snapped command leaves my mouth with a roar. "Send details of the van Roxanne was placed in to the teams located around Dr. Bates's practice. If they spot it, have them relay the information directly to me but maintain a safe distance. We don't want to spook them into doing something stupid."

The shit I'm spurting isn't anything new. This is how we planned to run our ruse. I'm merely implementing extra steps to ensure I reach Roxanne before any of the horrid thoughts in my head come true.

"Once that's done, bring up the surveillance before the blackout. I want to know the position of everyone in the clinic and a block each side of it before we were kicked in the guts." When Smith jerks up his chin, I lower my eyes to Rocco, who's peering up at the camera in the alleyway as if he can see me as clearly as I can him. "Anything?"

He reads the unease in my one word like no one else can. "I'm sorry, D, I had to take him down. He had a gun to my head and no intention of letting me leave the pharmacy once the command to move left your mouth."

He stuffs Roxanne's microchip into his pocket before dragging a man who'd weigh at least three hundred pounds into the frame. Since he's as worked up as me, he doesn't pay attention to the massive graze down one side of his skull I assume is the flesh wound of the bullet that was supposed to kill him while propping the man in front of the camera so Smith can log his face into his facial recognition software. The reason for the man's three bullet wounds to the chest makes sense when Smith gets an unhindered snapshot of his face. If Rocco had gone for a straight-up mafia kill, it would have made identification hard in this technology-dependent world.

With that in mind, I bring some old-school gangster tricks into play. Remembering where I came from and how I got here might finally have me one step ahead of my enemies. "Check his pockets.

His tats reveal he's a bottom dweller, so he may have been stupid enough to carry ID with him."

After pulling a face, disappointed he hadn't considered that, Rocco commences checking the buzz-cut man's pockets. A few seconds later, he pulls out a retro Velcro wallet. "Who the fuck carries around a tri-fold wallet these days?"

He answers his own question when he rips open the over-used Velcro with force to discover nothing but receipt after receipt after receipt. "Fuckers with no money, that's who."

My jaw has only worked through half a grind when Smith asks, "Do any of the receipts have payment details on them? Or was everything paid for with cash?" After raising his eyes to mine, he explains, "He might be lax on ID, but that doesn't mean we can't find out who he is quicker than facial recognition."

"Bing-fucking-o." After holding up a receipt for a purchase at a computer store in Ravenshoe to the camera for Smith to zoom in on, Rocco pops another bullet into the man who tried to kill him. This time, his bullet pierces his brain via a hole between his dark brows. He isn't just displaying he is pissed the wannabe gangster got a jump on him, he's sending a message. *The cartel is in town, and we want you to know it.*

"Where am I going, Smith?" Rocco asks, eager to move on to his next victim.

His hankering for a rampage hasn't been this perverse since a handful of my father's associates decided to test the authenticity of my threat. We went in hard and fast and without mercy. No one was spared.

As they won't be today, either.

"Give me a sec..." Smith punishes his keyboard as badly as I want to punish someone's face, pissed as fuck I made him work from Roxanne's family's ranch. Roxanne wasn't lying when she said the cell phone service here was shit.

My wish to kill is the highest it's ever been. It is brewing inside of me, warning that when it's finally unleashed, it will be explosive. I honestly don't know if I'll be able to control it. It has been building for years, so shouldn't it take just as long to dispel?

As the thirst for a bloodbath dries my mouth, another disturbing thought enters my mind. "How did they know Roxanne was wearing a tracker? No one knew she was wearing one. We kept it between the three of us..." My words trail off as pure rage takes their place. Although I have all my men on this case, one outsider was brought in. She left a couple of hours ago. "You fucking little snitch."

Smith appears lost to who I mean, but Rocco clicks on remarkably quick. While dragging his hand over his clipped hair, he growls out, "She's been under our nose the entire time."

"Don't remind me just how long, or I'll kill her before we get any information out of her." The roughness of my voice exposes I'm not joking. I am about to kill a friend I've known for years, and although her daughter's baby daddy isn't dead, the three consecutive life sentences he was handed down two years ago will make it seem as if she's an orphan. That messes with my head even more than wondering what's happening to Roxanne at this very moment. She's unconscious, naked, and in the back of a van with a doctor who sells babies for a living and a goon with an unrecognizable face. I could already be too late.

Rocco's deep timbre draws me from my dark thoughts. "Where am I meeting you, D? Harbortown Penitentiary or are we going directly to the source?"

My smirk tells him everything he needs to know.

"Directly to the source. I'll wait out back. Make sure the pool house is empty."

He waits for me to lift my chin in thanks before he hotfoots it to his ride, but not before laying his boot into the man now housing four of his personally selected bullets, though. He's pissed he got the jump on him. Not as much as me, but for now, I'll let it slide.

Time is critical in these matters. The verdict of me waiting until the deadline for Audrey's ransom exposes how dire things become when you leave them to chance. I took a risk my family's reputation would pull me out of the wreckage unscathed twenty-two months ago. I refuse to make the same mistake today. This entire operation falls on my shoulders. If I fail, it fails. I can't explain it any simpler than that.

"Have Rico keep a watch on my father. Until we find out exactly who has taken Roxanne, we can't assume anything. This could still be about the bounty on her head."

I know it isn't, but I'd rather be cautious, especially if it comes with less bloodshed on my side of the field. There can't be change without chaos, but can there be chaos without bloodshed? Up until a couple of weeks ago, I would have said there was no chance in hell you can't have one without the other. Now I'm not so sure.

I will protect Roxanne and Fien no matter what. I just don't want my victory to come at the ultimate price.

# 2

## DIMITRI

With traffic light and my foot heavy, I make it to a ritzy family estate in a well-to-do area within a record-breaking thirty minutes. I want to say my blood cooled a smidge during the commute, but that would be a lie. If anything, it's more heated since the tail a secondary crew had on Roxanne was lost.

The van they transported her in has been dumped and burned, and the cameras in the area aren't controlled by me. They're owned by none other than Mr. Isaac Holt, and his security personnel isn't playing friendly. Smith has attempted to reach out to Hunter numerous times the past thirty minutes. He's yet to be successful. I'm tempted to ask Isaac what his problem is, but since that could cause more issues, I'm holding back the urge—barely!

Not wanting my guest to be aware of my arrival, I park at the side gate before using the secret entrance only a handful of people know about. I'm not surprised to spot a man guarding the door with a customized M4. Only a fool goes against a man with nothing to lose halfheartedly.

The guard slumps to the floor before he knows what's hit him.

It isn't often a victim can respond to a bullet between the eyes. More times than not, they're dead before they hit the ground.

After pulling the security guard into an area he won't be seen by little eyes, I unlatch a set of keys from the waistband of his jeans, shove it into a retro-looking lock, twist, then wait for further instructions.

Smith is guiding me from above. Since this compound is wired to the hilt with surveillance, he has eyes in every room. "Target is in her office. She isn't alone. Halo is in the vicinity. Three guards are walking the hall. One is out back..." The hiss of a silencer whizzes out of the listening device in my ear a second before Smith corrects, "Pool house is clear. Rocco is on site."

As my lips curl into a smirk, I creep down the lit-up corridor like a real-life action hero. Despite my many wishes to be born to any family but the one I was, the adrenaline roaring through my veins bares reason to my birthright. Hate is strong in my bloodline, but so is vengeance. I live for this.

*Pop. Pop. Pop.*

Three guards are dead. Serves them right for standing together in an open arena. Regardless of what you've heard, there's no safety in numbers. If you want to stay alive, branch away from the group. You have a better chance of remaining hidden if the loud-mouth of the group is nowhere near you.

The faintest hum of a melody I've heard a handful of times buzzes into my ears when I lower the handle of the office door now housing the blood of three men. Their deaths were silent, but the smell of desecration is obvious. Unfortunately, it isn't solely coming from my side of the room.

Alice is standing in the corner of her home office. She has a gun butted under her quivering chin, and sweat is beading her brow. Her daughter, Lucy, sits at her left, oblivious to the fact her mother is moments away from blowing her brains out. She's immersed in a video game all kids seem to love these days.

Although shocked Alice has placed her life on the line with the very gun she bought to protect herself, it is understandable. She'd rather die via her own hands than be tortured like she was when she was seventeen. That's why Rocco is out back, waiting by the pool house. Alice's biggest fear in life is losing her daughter. Her second is being drowned like her father attempted to do when she told him she was pregnant with Lucy. Both Alice and Lucy survived his attempt to kill them. Alice's father didn't.

"I had no choice," Alice coughs out in a sputter as tears flow down her face. "They took Lucy. T-t-they wouldn't give her back until I helped them secure Roxanne. I didn't know she was *really* pregnant. I swear to God, Dimi, I had no idea."

Her blubbering response exposes holes in her defense. Roxanne let slip to her this morning that she didn't need free-flowing garments added to her wardrobe selection because her pregnancy was merely a ruse to fool Dr. Bates, so how is Alice aware Roxanne's test returned a positive result in Dr. Bates's office this morning? If all she did was inform my enemies Roxanne was wearing a tracker, she'd assume Roxanne's pregnancy was still part of our ruse.

Although pissed, news of Roxanne's positive test doesn't change anything. "Whether she's pregnant or not makes no differ-ence. You went against me—"

"F-for L-Lucy," Alice defends, her words stuttering. "Only for Lucy. I couldn't let her be a part of that lifestyle, Dimitri. I couldn't only see her through a monitor like you do..." Her words trail off as her eyes widen in fear.

Bringing Fien into this won't do her any favors because not only is she reminding me just how far I'll go to protect my daugh-ter, she's also reminding me that it's more than just Fien's life at stake now. Roxanne's is in my hands as well, and so is our unborn child's.

Too pumped with anger to stand still, I house my gun into the back of my trousers, then storm to Alice's side of the room, confident gamers these days are as ignorant as Rocco and I were anytime we played *Super Mario*.

I reach Alice before she even considers deflecting the barrel of her gun to me. She wouldn't fire at me even if I still had my gun in my hands because she knows as well as her ex-husband, it isn't an eye for an eye in this industry.

It's family for family.

Mine for hers.

Or better yet, hers for mine.

As I drag Alice toward the open French doors that lead to her patio, my anger gets the better of me. "They took my wife, they have my daughter, yet that still isn't enough for you. You want them to take everything away from me."

"No," she denies, shaking her head as she eyes the pool we're heading toward. "I was just protecting Lucy."

I've never laid my eyes on my daughter in person. That doesn't make me any less of a father, though, so I understand her objective, but I'm just too worked up with anger to absorb it. "Because your daughter's life is more valuable than mine?"

Fear leeches out of her pores before she once again shakes her head. This one is more hesitant than her earlier one.

"Then why did you do it? Why go against me knowing you could lose everything!"

As Alice's stilettos skitter across the pavers, she attempts to lodge them into the cracks, hopeful her fight to live will have me recalling the time I saved her from this exact scenario.

If my anger wasn't bubbling over, I might have, but it's too late for her now. I can't separate the past from the future any more now than I could when I was driving here. Roxanne is nowhere near as far along as Audrey was when she was taken. However, all I see when her face pops into my head is the horrific footage of Audrey going through a botched caesarian. My fucked-up head has replaced Audrey's face with Roxanne's, and it's messing with my mind even more than Lucy's frantic cries for me to stop holding her mother's head under the water in their half-a-million-dollar pool.

"Get her out of here!" I scream at Rocco a mere second before pulling Alice's head up so she can suck in the quickest breath. It isn't long enough to fill her screaming lungs with air, but it will warn her I'm not playing. I've played the game as taught the past two years. It got me nowhere, so it's time for a new set of rules.

As Lucy fights Rocco with more gusto than an eight-year-old should have, I bring Alice's drenched head to within an inch of mine. "Where are they taking her?"

"I don't kn—"

She's back under the water in an instant, gargling and screaming while her nails make a mess of my arms. She digs them in deep before dragging them to the hand wrapped around her throat. If the water doesn't suffocate her, the hold I have on her throat soon will.

With her eyes on the verge of sporting new blood vessels, I lift Alice's head for the final time. Her gasps as she struggles to fill her lungs with oxygen are barely heard over Lucy's frantic bangs on the window of her room. She's three floors above, but she thumps her fists on the glass as if breaking her window will magically save her mother.

I wish it were that easy, but sometimes, the heroes in stories need to be villains too, especially when the only person they looked up to disappointed them time and time again.

I'm waist-deep in freezing cold water, but my skin is so hot, it hisses as well as my words when I growl out, "Where. Are. They. Taking. Her."

"I..." when my hand moves for my gun, over the time waster Alice is being today, she talks faster, "... overheard them saying something about a ranch. T-t-that they had a bigger payday coming."

I instantly feel hopeful. "Roxanne's family's ranch?"

Tears mix with the saltwater coating her face when she shakes her head. "They were talking about a gala, something about a ransom drop."

When my hand raises in the air, Lucy screams my name in a mangled roar. It reminds me so much of Roxanne's endeavor to protect her mother. Even when she should have hated her, she still went in to bat for her.

"I'm telling you everything I know, Dimitri," Alice swears, her tone honest.

The truth in her eyes does little to calm me down. "You should have told me from the start. You should have warned me."

"Warned you about what?" she asks on a sob. "That your enemies were going to take Roxanne as planned *by you*? That she would be thrust into a world you should have done everything in your power to keep her away from? What was I supposed to tell you?"

I hold her under the water again, the truth of her statement too much for me to bear. Not only was this the outcome we were reaching for, I've known for years my enemies have always been one step ahead of me, so why did I expect today to be any different?

As Alice's crying comment rings in my ears on repeat, her thrashes become stiller and stiller. She's seconds from death, her fight honorable considering the circumstances. She gave all for her daughter, only to lose in front of her.

My grip on Alice's throat slackens when the frantic screams of a child in despair fills my ears. Lucy's bangs broke through the glass. She is cut up and bleeding, but her thoughts remain with her mother. "Stop, Uncle Dimitri, please stop."

Alice and I aren't related. I earned the privilege of being called Lucy's uncle when I saved her life. Now I'm taking away the only person she's ever cared about.

When Lucy's cries reach an area of my body I'm certain stopped functioning years ago, I fully uncinch my grip on Alice's throat. My unusual offer of mercy comes too late. Alice is floating in the pool. Her eyes are wide and unblinking. Her chest is still.

I killed her for doing exactly what I would have done in her situation.

I murdered her for putting her daughter first.

That makes me a fucking monster—just like my father.

# 3

## ROXANNE

As the haze making my vision murky clears, I attempt to take in the area surrounding me. I'm lying on my side, a scratchy blanket the only thing responsible for my modesty. My throat burns with every swallow I take, and my head is thumping.

I don't know where I am, but I wish I could be here without being naked. This is as awkward as it gets for me. I'm not one of those women who are comfortable in their own skin. I'd rather be found in a hessian bag than have Dimitri's crew walk in on me stark naked when they track my location.

When I roll onto my side, keen to drink in something more than the rippled steel of an outdated van, pain shreds through my stomach. I don't know much about pregnancies, but I'm reasonably sure I shouldn't be cramping like this. I feel like the goon who grabbed me from behind punched me in the stomach before doing so.

If that is the case, what's their objective for taking me?

Aren't I more valuable if I'm carrying Dimitri's child?

Pregnant. Me. I still can't believe it. We were laid-back on protection, but I still would have thought it would take more than one time to get me up the duff. I guess my life could never be accused of being easy.

The roll of my eyes stops halfway when the groan I couldn't hold back announces to my captives that I'm awake. I don't know whether to laugh or glower when the knowledge has several guns aimed at the crinkle between my sweat-beaded brows. I'm pleased they see me as a threat, but I'd rather it occur without additional harm. Being chloroformed was worse than anticipated, so I'm happy to skip extra theatrics.

"Show me those hands, girlie," croons the goon at the front.

His shoulders are as wide as Clover's, his eyes almost as deadly, his voice is just missing an Arabian accent. That means nothing, though, because I swear the first voice I heard upon awakening was twanged with an Italian accent. It wasn't laced with maturity, so I don't believe it belongs to Dimitri's father, but it did have a familiarity about it.

"Don't make me ask you again." The stranger tosses his half-smoked cigarette on the drought-affected ground, stomps it out with his boot, then moves close enough to me the bright rays of the sun stop sheltering his face. He's handsome if mass murderers are your kink. "Your plaything the past nine weeks isn't the only man around here with no patience."

After absorbing the little nugget of information he unwittingly shared, I hold my hands out in front of myself, smug as fuck about his first stumble of the day.

I can't wait for him to have many more.

With his grin as shit-eating as mine, he lowers his pistol from my head to my almost exposed chest before grunting out, "Higher."

"If I raise them any higher, I'll lose the scarce bit of coverage I have. I will spit in your face before I'll ever let that happen."

The man with a sleeve full of tattoos grin turns gleaming. "Those there are fighting words for men like me. Are you sure you want to go down that road, girlie? It won't be as pretty as your face."

*You don't scare me*, I want to say, but hold back, mindful our ruse will be more effective if I play the damsel in distress. Only someone believing they're not in real danger would act nonchalant in this situation. This isn't the movies. Not even an imbecile would remain quiet when they're being led out of a packed restaurant with a knife jabbed under their ribs.

A montage of the footage I perused before drawing sketches of the people I saw at Joops the day Dimitri's wife was kidnapped halts playing in my head when something sharp jabs into my thigh. I was so deep into my thought process on Audrey's silence when she was led away by a stranger, I didn't notice the goon removing a needle from his bag of tricks at my side and stabbing it into my leg.

"What was that..." My woozy words answer my question on his behalf. I feel like I'm floating, like more than scratchy material is moving out from beneath me when he leans into the van to lift me out. Just like when I was carried through the hidden corridors of the office building shouldering Dr. Bates's practice, I'm fully exposed.

It's not all bad. My lack of clothing uncovers elements my dazed head wouldn't have noticed. Such as the warmth of the sun when I'm carried across the gravel-crunching ground and the direction the wind is blowing. It always howls in from the ocean. Since the gusts are nowhere near as strong as the ones that roll in from Bronte's Peak, I'm confident we've headed inland.

The shadow on the man's face and the lack of warmth from the sun exposes it's still early in the day. I either slept for an eternity, or we're still close to Hopeton. If my intuition is anything to go by, I'm leaning toward the latter.

The thought makes me smile. Dimitri is closer than I realized. Perhaps he's sitting in the dark sedan I spotted near the woodlands when my eyes were wrenched to the needle sticking out of my thigh. I only got the quickest glimpse of the vehicle before my eyelids grew weary, but I'm confident it wasn't my imagination. I have a knack for taking things in much deeper than an ordinary person would. It's a disturbing trait I developed from my father's wish to embarrass me. I gawk even when I shouldn't. Mercifully, I don't see it getting me in trouble this time around.

A second after the beep of an electronic lock sounds through my ears, I'm lowered onto a cool, bumpy surface. Although this metal doesn't feel as scratchy as the rusty bottom of the van, its distinct smell assures me I've been moved from one mode of transport to another. Regretfully, it isn't an elaborate private jet. The tire jack digging into my ribs assures me of this, much less the tight confines. I've been shoved into a trunk, the bend of my legs to fit adding to the gnawing pain in my stomach.

"Get comfy, sweetheart. You're in for an all-nighter," grunts the stranger with a chuckle before he slams down the trunk, trapping me inside.

Once again, I want to get smug, but once again, the reminder that Dimitri is only one step behind stops me.

We've created a storm.

Now we just need it to rain.

Fingers crossed it doesn't turn into a flood.

# 4

## DIMITRI

"Call an ambulance!" I scream at Smith as if he's standing across from me instead of watching me via the security dome above my head.

With my earpiece bogged down by the water I'm wading through to reach Alice floating in the middle of her pool, Smith's response doesn't come out as crisp as normal. "Dimi—"

"Now!" My short reply doesn't weaken the severity of my warning. I didn't suggest for him to bring in the authorities. I told him to. That's a direct order. Ignoring it will see him on the receiving end of my wrath.

As Smith does as asked, I drag Alice's weighted body to the edge of her monstrous pool. Considering the fact my hands can circle her waist, she shouldn't feel as if she weighs a ton.

It takes all my strength to lift her onto the pool's edge, but it has nothing on the weight that slams down on me when Lucy suddenly falls at her mother's side a couple of seconds later.

She didn't escape Rocco's clutch. He freed her so he can help me fix the second injustice I made today. The first was letting

Roxanne out of my sight. "Dip her head back, you need to open up her airways."

As Lucy holds her mother's hand, crying for her to wake up, I rip open Alice's shirt and bra, cover her chest with my hands like I did almost nine years ago, then press down.

I do four compressions before Rocco uses her tilted chin to his advantage. He breathes into her mouth two times before raising his eyes to mine. "You were only supposed to scare her, D. You weren't meant to kill—."

I glare at him, cutting his scorn off halfway.

I'm riddled with guilt.

He doesn't need to make it worse.

Even confident I have nothing to answer for, the disdain in Rocco's eyes is too strong to discount. He's been angry at me many times and has wanted to rip my head off even more than that, but this is the first time he's been truly disappointed in me. "She helped them take Roxanne. She knew her pregnancy wasn't a hoax."

My confession sees me pumping Alice's chest more forcefully than needed. It can't be helped. I either take my aggression out on her chest or push her head back under the water until there's no chance she'll survive. This is the kinder of the two and only occurring because her daughter is kneeling across from me, ashen-faced and crying.

"She did it for..." I stop myself in just enough time. If anything Alice said was true, and I have a feeling it was, Lucy will already be traumatized. I don't need to add more angst to the bucketloads she has to tell her future therapists.

"Again."

Rocco barely forces half a breath into Alice's lungs when the gurgle of a woman clawing her way back from the brink of death sees him pulling back.

While Alice coughs up the water in her lungs, the sound of sirens is heard in the distance. She lives in a rich, leafy suburb that's so quiet, it's easy to distinguish the difference between a paramedic's wails and that of an unmarked police car.

"We need to go," Rocco says, stating the obvious. He rolls Alice on her side before re-tilting her head. It's clear from the rise and fall of her chest that she's breathing. She just hasn't fully come around yet—emotionally, not physically. "When she wakes up, keep her on her side, okay?" he says to Lucy. "She has lots of water in her lungs she needs to get out."

Like the brave girl she was born to be, Lucy wipes at the tears high on her cheeks before dipping her chin at Rocco's suggestion. She looks like she wants to gut me, but there's nothing but admiration in her eyes as she stares at Rocco.

"Send someone to collect her grandmother. Make sure she gets here before CPS. If she spends an hour with them, Smith, we'll have more than words."

He doesn't absorb my threat. He gets straight to work on locating Lucy's only surviving relative before updating us on how close the sirens we hear wailing in the distance are. "It's a single unit, but he isn't on payroll."

That means it can only be one man. Detective Ryan Carter.

While snagging a towel from a rack on my right to cushion Alice's head, I say, "Log a disturbance one block back. Ensure it mentions the words 'shots fired' and 'officer down.'"

Ryan can't help but be a hero. He was born to be one. Me, on the other hand, no matter what happens today, my credits won't ever include a synonym of the word. Every story needs a villain. It's just never anticipated for him to also be the leading man.

As Smith mimics the panicked voice of an officer in the middle of a furious gun battle, I shift my eyes to Lucy. It's stupid of me to do. All I can see in her big blue eyes is Fien in a couple of years. It has me convinced the carnage will never end. Whether right now or twenty years in the future, I will forever fight to keep my daughter safe. I just want the privilege of showing her how I'd go to the end of the world for her.

I also want to do the same for Roxanne. She put her life on the line for my daughter, and now she and our unborn child are at risk. I won't see her go through what Audrey did. I don't care what it takes, I will stop it before it has the chance to transpire. I'll keep her safe as I failed to do my wife. Then maybe, just maybe, the guilt I've felt the past two years will finally slacken enough I can secure an entire breath.

"I'm sorry, Luce," I whisper in a low, dull tone, the angst eating me alive too strong to discount.

My apology is barely audible, but the weight it lifts from my chest is phenomenal. It makes my steps to my car quick and buoyant like Lucy will forgive me as quickly as I'm hoping Alice will.

My lengthy strides freeze mid-pump when the faint voice of Lucy trickles into my ears not even a few seconds later. She called my name, undeserving salutation and all. It has me spinning to face her even faster than she dashes across the pavers lining the poolside to gather up her iPad she was mesmerized by when I arrived.

For the way her chubby cheeks bounce when she stops to stand in front of me, her words shouldn't be anywhere near as mature as they are. "Daddy always said it's too late to say you're sorry once you've done bad, but Mommy and I don't agree." Her lips quiver as she confesses, "She hasn't stopped crying all morning. She said it was because she was excited to see me after my sleepover. I didn't believe her. Look, she was even crying when she read me a bedtime story."

She twists her iPad around to show me a screenshot dated a

little after eight last night. It doesn't just show Alice's tear-stained face as she endeavors to put on a brave front for her daughter, it features Lucy's screen as well. Since she is holding her device far away from her face, several identifiable markers are seen behind her.

As it dawns on me what she's showing me, Lucy pushes her iPad into my hand, smiles in a way that reveals I'm still in her shit book, then she skips back to her mother's side.

I stare at her in awe for the next several minutes, stunned as fuck. If I hadn't spared her mother's life, I guarantee she wouldn't have shared this information with me. She's only doing it because she knows how this industry works. If she scratches my back, hers will never be itchy. She's a mastermind in the making, and she's only eight.

God save anyone who does her wrong when she reaches her prime.

Although the drone of a single police siren has been temporarily diverted, no amount of manipulation can alter the buzz of half a dozen. They're even howling above our heads, the big guns brought in for the sake of one of their own.

While a police helicopter circles above us, Rocco slides into the driver's seat of my car before firing up the ignition. I don't put up a protest. Not only does he drive faster and better than me, the change-up will give me time to peruse the image Lucy showed me.

"Can you see this?" I raise my voice to ensure Smith can hear me over the ruckus attempting to follow us out of Alice's gated community.

"Spikes on entry ramp 43, take Makers," Smith advises Rocco before shifting his focus to me. "I'm stripping Lucy's 'find my phone' app to trace the location the photo was taken from, but it would be quicker if you zoomed in."

My tailor-made pants slide across the leather interior of my car when Rocco takes Makers like a bat out of hell. We get airborne for a second, which increases the width of Rocco's grin.

Once our tires grip the asphalt, I get back to business. "On what?"

"Right on Lark." Smith's fingers tap out a million words a minute before he responds, "Top left. It appears to be some type of emblem. I'm certain I've seen it before."

As Rocco loses the last police cruiser tailing us by plowing through an intersection at a speed well above the designated signage, I double tap on the screen of Lucy's iPad. I don't need to angle it to ensure Smith gets a clear view of the poster in the camera hidden in my rearview mirror. I already know who it belongs to. It's a poster-size flyer of the ones I handed out the night of Ophelia's accident. The flyers Ophelia designed knowing our father would be more arrogant in front of an audience. He isn't one of those men who rain sunshine down on his family in front of others to portray the ideal husband and father. He preferred degrading us. Blood or not, if he could stand on you to make himself feel an inch taller, he would.

He still does.

With my jaw tight with annoyance, my voice is huskier than normal. "Have Clover meet us at the tunnel. We need to weapon-up before moving in." While Smith hums out an agreeing noise, I switch my eyes to Rocco. "We need to dump and burn."

He flashes me a cocky wink. "Already reported her as stolen." When I give him a look as if to ask when he had time to do that, he rubs his hands together like we're not sailing down the road at a speed well above the designated limit. "We all have our secrets, D. Even me."

If it were any day but today, I'd torture his secrets out of him. Since it isn't, they'll have to stay on the backburner. I want to finish my day strong, not burden it down with more stress.

# 5

## DIMITRI

With the eyes of a dozen bloodthirsty men on me, I say, "The warehouse we're about to storm was once a Petretti stronghold. It isn't anymore. We would be fools to walk in blind."

Even while juggling a laptop like a circus clown, Smith jumps into the conversation with no hesitation in his voice. "We heat-scanned the warehouse. Readings are coming back with the imagery of a single occupant. Height, weight, and core body temperature reveals the target is most likely female—"

"Or he'll be wishing he was by the time we're done with him," Rocco interrupts, laughing. Humor is his go-to when he's feeling overwhelmed.

"She is also breathing."

I'm reasonably sure Smith's pause is to give me time to absorb the good in what he's saying, that Roxanne is alive and well. It's appreciated, but it doesn't lessen my itch to kill. I'm fired up and ready to go, only delayed by making sure the men about to follow me to battle know what they're fighting for.

They won't come out of today with a legacy. They will only be awarded my respect.

To some, that's as worthless as a piece of paper.

To me, it's the most valuable thing I own.

Smith's next set of words gobble up the last of the laughter from Rocco's witty comment. "The fact only one occupant has been noted should concern you. This is most likely an ambush."

He brings up imagery of the terrain surrounding the warehouse. Because it's an old industrial area that pumped out as much steel as drugs in the seventies, it is swamped by similar-sized buildings.

"As per Dimitri's request..." don't misconstrue Rocco's nicely worded statement, he's beyond pissed about my 'request,' "... while he enters the main warehouse from the front entrance *like a sitting fucking duck...*" he murmurs his last five words, "... we are to search the buildings on each side of it."

Eager to get back to the operation I'm helming, I add, "Smith has deployed drones. They will jam all signals, including ours. This isn't a seek-orders mission. If you must kill or be killed, always choose the former. If we can't get information out of them, we will find a way of getting it out of their corpse."

Needing to get things moving since we lost hours waiting for Smith to work his magic, I throw open the door of the van we're camped out in before making my way to the road's edge. Since we're back a good distance from the warehouse holding one occupant, I have to shield my eyes from the low-hanging sun to take it in.

I want to say my stare-down weakens the knot in my stomach, but that would be a lie. Smith wasn't deceitful when he said this is an ambush. My enemies are waiting for me to fall, but since I refuse to continue taking it up the ass as I have the past two years,

I'm rewriting the rules. It could get me killed, but just like I'll never be a hero, I won't die a coward either.

"Let's go. The sooner we know who's in that warehouse, the better it will be for all involved." You didn't misread my tone. I'm doubtful the person holed up in the warehouse for the past two hours is Roxanne. An explosive personality like hers is felt for miles. Not even the slightest tickle is felt under my toes. My intuition is telling me I will get answers today. They just won't be answers to the questions I want answered.

After waiting for Rocco to slip into the Range Rover behind me, I slide into the driver's seat of the prototype vehicle we affectionally call The Tank. I'm not taking her for a spin because I'm afraid of a little bullet. I want to ensure if the warehouse doors are locked, I'll have no issues going through them.

With our group on radio silence, I have to hand signal for my men to move. There's an eeriness associated with our ghost-like approach. Hearing Smith's breaths in my ear has been such the norm the past two years, the ones raging in my chest sound foreign.

One by one, the vehicles following me peel off until I'm the lone soldier on a bumpy gravel road. While shifting down the gears, bringing The Tank's revs down to half of what they were, I scan my chest, anticipating the dots of a sniper's rifle to be lighting it up.

Unease melds through my veins when not a single speck is found. My chest remains clear of any visible markings when I pull The Tank up to the side of the cracked-open door, and not a dot highlights any part of my body when I make my way into the dusty space with my gun held high and my wish to kill even higher than it.

I jackknife to my left when a familiar voice says, "Has Smith always been this pedantic with protocol? Or did he become this way after we parted ways?"

My grip on my gun tightens when the pretty hazel eyes of Special Agent Ellie Gould lock with mine. She smiles like I won't kill her where she stands, unaware Smith has desired doing the same thing many times the past two years.

It isn't every day you find out your girlfriend is a federal agent, so I won't mention the fact he unearthed the truth while perusing tapes of her schmoozing with the enemy, or you might tempt me into killing her.

One less agent won't hurt anyone, except perhaps Smith. From what I've been told, you don't get over your first love. I've not yet had the chance to test the theory. That could change depending on the outcome of Ellie's resurrection. As the saying goes, 'stare at the dark so long, you'll eventually see what isn't there,' it fails to mention what you're striving not to see—a smile hidden under locks of bleached hair and a mascara-stained face. Nothing scares me, but the thought of never seeing them again is a nightmare I refuse to live.

I'll burn down this entire fucking hellhole before I ever let Rimi Castro beat me again, and I'll take Roxanne down with me because despite how many times I've told her otherwise, I want her. I want her more than anything, and I will have her. No fear.

# 6

## ROXANNE

"Out, now. This one is out of gas."

The goon with thick biceps and a bad attitude doesn't wait for me to respond, he just yanks on my arm until I fall out of the trunk of a light-colored sedan for the fourth time today. I had wondered if the churns of my stomach the past couple of hours were from hunger or fear. From the low hang of the sun, I'm confident it's a bit of both.

I understand this is part of the plan, I'm playing my part of a kidnap victim well, but I'm also worried. We've been on the road for hours. I've not been given any water or food. Even my numerous kicks on the roof of the trunk advising I needed to pee went unanswered.

This man doesn't care about me *at all*. It honestly seems as if my pregnancy is more an annoyance to him than an incentive for a big cash bonus. Every time I use it with the hope it will see him issuing leniency, he becomes more aggressive.

Take now, for example. I barely murmur about the pain tearing me in two from his brutal yank on my arm, yet he acts as if

I asked him to purchase me a box of tampons. "Quit your grumbling. I told you we were in for a long trip."

The briefest moment of reprieve smacks into me when he tosses open the front passenger door of a truck parked in the middle of a road to nowhere. He has to be working with someone because cars aren't left in the middle of the boonies waiting to be hotwired. He drives each vehicle until the gas tank hits E, then we swap rides. That reveals our trip was methodically planned. It just seems as if my being pregnant didn't factor into the equation.

"Can I please have some water?" I ask half a mile down the dusty road.

The stranger with gleaming black eyes peers at me over the bottle he's guzzling down like he hasn't had a drink in hours before he shakes his head. The brutal crossing of my arms seems to humor him as much as my stink eye.

Although pissed he finds my dehydration entertaining, I'm glad it also sees him switching things up. "All right, I'm sure I can spare a couple of drops."

His tone already has me on the back foot, let alone the way he swishes the water around his mouth before he tilts his head to my side of the cabin.

"Open up," he talks through the slop in his mouth.

He almost chokes on the water he's gargling in the back of his throat when my eagerness to get away from him has my arm getting cozy with the steel panel of the door. It isn't just tender like every other region of my body. It's also bleeding.

*What the hell?*

As my head rolls through snippets of my first drugging, my hand shoots up to caress the implant site where Smith placed my tracker. It feels like the world closes in on me when my probing fingers fail to discover anything but a wound that appears to have been inflicted hours ago.

There's no bead-size device.

No implant.

Nothing.

I'm all alone, and Dimitri isn't one step behind me.

*Fuck.*

With my plan gone to shit, my mood soon follows it, but I refuse to walk into my death without a fight. I'll give as good as I'm getting. The odds aren't in my favor. My captive has a gun, and I've got nothing but determination, but I've fought with less for longer. My entire life has been a battle I was never meant to win, yet here I am, pregnant to the man I love and willing to do anything to ensure he sees his child's every milestone.

First smile.

First word.

First step.

I want Dimitri and his daughter to witness it all.

With that in mind, I batten down the hatches and settle in. The storm we created is coming. I can smell the rain on the horizon, feel the coolness of its imminent arrival in the air. It will be a beauty. I've just got to survive its wrath. If I do that, I'll have more than a rainbow to look forward to. I'll have the entire world at my feet.

# 7

# DIMITRI

"I don't work for the Feds. I *use* them when it works in my favor."

Acting as if my tone doesn't hold half the fury it does, Ellie moves to my side of the warehouse. My entire crew is here, including Smith, so I not only have to be conscious of what I say, I can't slit Ellie's throat to stop her speaking the insolent words she's been spurting the past forty minutes.

"We're chasing the same men, Dimitri. That puts us on the same team."

I laugh in her face. Both its pitch and length reveals how agitated I am. Out of all the days the Feds could reach out for my help, they chose today. I'm running out of time. Roxanne has been gone for hours. I don't even know if she's alive anymore, but I should stop my search because a 'friend' of Ellie's needs my contacts.

"I. Don't. Work. For. The. Feds." I speak extra slow, ensuring there's no way she can miss the fury in my tone this time around. "And if I need to tell you again, not even Smith will be able to save you. Do you understand me?"

Like a woman without a wish to live, she undoes the cuffs on her belt, unlocks them with a flick of her wrist, then brings them to within an inch of my hand. "Don't make me do this, Dimitri. I don't want to force your help, but if you leave me no choice, I will. This is a matter of national security. It ranks higher than your wish for revenge."

*Wish for revenge?* That snaps my last nerve.

After signaling for Clover to put Smith in lockdown, I grip Ellie's throat with everything I have. She struggles in an instant, her hands scratching at mine as her eyes bulge. A wish to live is seen all over her face when my brutal hold lifts her feet from the ground. It's almost as bright as the gleam on Smith's face as he fights against both Rocco and Clover to get to me.

He wants to kill me. I don't blame him. I'd do the same in his situation. Alas, I'm fighting for more than my girl right now. My entire existence is on the line.

"You enter my turf, waste *my* time, then threaten to arrest me. I should have killed you before Smith laid his eyes on you, then I would have gotten away with your murder without losing a valued member of my team. Now I might have to kill you both."

For the first time this afternoon, fright registers on Ellie's face. She's fearless when it comes to dying, but she doesn't feel the same way when Smith's life is on the line with hers.

"This also isn't a wish for revenge. If you weren't fucking the enemy, you'd know that." My last sentence calms Smith down. Not a lot, but it's better than nothing. "This goes *way* deeper than that."

Certain Ellie has gotten the point, I drop her from my hold, then spin around to face Smith. He's still being held back by Rocco and Clover, and he's red-faced and real fucking angry.

"Who do you work for, Smith?"

If he says anyone but Fien, he'll leave me no choice but to take this further. We've faced these issues before. Smith came out of it with both his life and job intact. I can't guarantee he'll be as lucky this time around. My enemies are always one step in front of me for a reason. Two years ago, we placed the blame for that on Ellie's shoulders. Now I'm wondering if I made a mistake.

"Who *the fuck* do you work for, Smith?"

"Fien. I work for fucking Fien!" he shouts back, his roar as loud as mine, his anger just as palpable.

After pushing Rocco and Clover away from him as if he is double their size, he storms my way. I slice my hand in the air, warning Clover if his index finger gets within an inch of his trigger, Smith won't be the only one letting off steam this afternoon. He answered how I wanted him to, and although a heap of fury was beaming from his eyes when he said it, it was barely seen through the honesty.

Smith stops an inch from my face before he growls out, "But once she's back, I'm done. I can't deal with your shit anymore. You're doing my fucking head in."

He misses the quickest dart of panic running through my eyes I couldn't shut down because his focus is no longer on me. He's staring at Ellie, torn between offering her a hand from the ground or adding to the red welts around her neck.

He goes for neither by shaking his head in disappointment before making his way to his beloved van, punching the steel door of the warehouse on his way by.

It's obvious from the noises rocking and rolling out of his van for the next several minutes that he isn't taking his anger out on a keyboard. He's demolishing equipment worth millions of dollars because he'd rather damage the irreplaceable things he loves than the one thing he can't replace, no matter how hard he tries. He loved Ellie, so her betrayal didn't just gut him, it changed him. He hasn't been the same man since.

Although the indent his rage will cause my hip pocket should be concerning, I'm not worried. We all have our ways of blowing off steam. Mine was a bender that saw me out of action for days. Smith's will barely last an hour.

Ask any underworld figure, they'll all tell you the same thing. A loss in revenue is preferred over a loss in production. If you're not productive, you are dead. Can't put it any simpler than that.

"Give him a few minutes to cool down, then roll out. We need to get a start on scanning traffic cameras on all routes out of Hopeton. Although they could still be local, until we learn otherwise, we should assume they're going to bounce Roxanne state to state like they did Fien the first few months."

Air whizzes out of Rocco's nose as he scrubs at the cropped beard on his chin. "With the van being dumped, what are we looking for?"

The panic roaring through my veins is heard in my reply. "Anything and everything. A snippet of red hair, a pricy car rolling down a dirt road... any suspicious activity."

Rocco's chin scarcely moves an inch when a husky voice cuts him off. "They headed south a couple of hours ago. Dark blue sedan. I got a partial plate."

I want to both kill and kiss Ellie. Kill her for holding back information that would have been useful hours ago, but kiss her for finally stepping up to the plate with something useful. "How many occupants?"

"One." After standing to her feet, she dusts off the dirt on her skirt-covered backside before digging a notepad out of the breast pocket of her jacket. Seeing her in a full agent get-up is shocking. I only ever saw her in ripped denim shorts, midriff tops, and her stark blonde hair pulled up in a messy bun. She was cruisy and laid-back, the very opposite of any agent I've ever met. "Approximately six-three, two hundred and sixty pounds. Had a cross tattoo above his—"

"Left eyebrow," interrupts a voice from the right, a stern, still unhinged voice.

After clambering over several mangled pieces of a computer, Smith jumps down from his van and re-enters the warehouse. He's still pissed. His scent is very telling, much less the tight grip he has on a single piece of paper. It almost rips when he thrusts it into my chest with no intention of letting it go.

After forcefully removing it from his grasp, I ask, "Who is he?"

"A military operative from Sicily," Ellie answers on Smith's behalf. "The Bureau has been tracking him for a while. This is the first sighting we've had in years. Where did you get it?" Her last question isn't for me. It's for Smith.

Ellie chokes on her spit when Smith answers, "From your laptop."

"You hacked into my computer?" Her question is barely heard over Rocco's laugh. He loves watching couples go to war. Why do you think he's been such a thorn in my ass the past nine weeks? "That's classified information."

Smith rakes his teeth over his bottom lip in an effort to half his smile. "Then you should have changed your password."

"But that wouldn't have stopped you, would it?" Ellie responds through a tight jaw.

When she attempts to snatch the document out of my hand, I hold it out of her reach. It isn't hard considering she's a short-ass. "You can finish your lovers' squabble later. For now, tell me how you don't know who he is if this was found on your computer?"

"That's what I'd like to know."

Ellie folds her arms in front of her chest to match the snappiness of Smith's question before replying, "I don't know how it got there. This is the first time I've seen an image of him."

A scoff vibrates Smith's lips. "It was sitting in a file on your desktop, plain as day for all to see."

"That doesn't mean I placed it there," Ellie fires back, her voice as vicious as Smith's glare.

"*Puh-leaze.* You're running that excuse again? I don't know how I got there. I just woke up in his bed."

Fighting not to tear my hair out, I step between the feuding couple. "Enough."

They continue arguing until the ricochet of a gun being fired shuts their mouths as quickly as it widens their pupils.

"I said *enough*! Fuck me, you two are worse than..." I freeze, out of the loop on any couple, either famous or an everyday regular couple.

Rocco doesn't face the same dilemma. "As Roxie and you?" He backhands Clover's chest, doubling the smirk he's struggling to hold back. "It's the make-up sex. It makes couples crazy."

"Kind of like a golden pussy?" Clover questions with an arched brow.

"Exactly," Rocco answers, completely ignoring my wrathful glare warning him not to.

He doesn't ignore my second directive. The bullet that whizzes through the minute gap between his and Clover's head is as effective as the one I fired into the air. "Get your heads into the fucking game. Roxanne's life is depending on it."

As Rocco's quiet apology trickles into my ears, I shift my focus back to Smith. "What else did you find on Ellie's laptop?" I shoosh Ellie by placing the barrel of my gun against her lips. I'm sure the heat of its recent firings will sting her lips, but it's got to be better than a bullet wound between the eyes. "I don't care about anything that doesn't relate to Fien and Roxanne. Even if it has the ability to take my father down, I don't care. I just want the information that will help bring my family back."

Smith balks, as shocked by the use of the word 'family' as me, but he keeps his head in game mode. "There's information on a possible new sanction popping up in the New York region. No names were mentioned, but a quick once-over makes it clear who it's about."

"Rimi Castro?"

When Smith jerks up his chin, Ellie gabbles out, "That can't be true. I'm not working Rimi's case. I don't have any of his files."

Aware federal agents never believe anything unless it's shown to them in black and white, Smith stomps back to his van, snatches up the only bit of equipment he didn't demolish in his tirade, then returns to my side. Although he's giving proof to Ellie, he keeps the screen tilted my way, ensuring he displays whose team he's on.

"They're not my files." Ellie lifts her eyes to mine, surprising me with the amount of wetness in them. "I swear to God, this is the first time I've seen those files." When Smith scoffs, as unbelieving as me, Ellie tries another angle. "Then, I'll swear on Jonathon's life." Jonathon is her little brother. He had an even rougher start to life than Fien. She would never place him in danger, not even if it could save her life. "They're not my files. Someone placed them there."

"Why would they do that?" I'm not saying I believe her. I'm merely ensuring I flip over every stone in my endeavor to find Roxanne and Fien.

Ellie shrugs. "I don't know." She freezes before her eyes widen. "Internal affairs is investigating our unit. They think we have a leak." The color drains from her face as her eyes bounce between Smith and me. "Do you think that's why I have those files? Is someone trying to set me up?"

"Perhaps." Smith's voice is more controlled than mine.

"But we don't have time to look." I shift my eyes to Rocco and Clover. "Let's move out."

My steps halt for the second time today when Smith's hand shoots out to grip my arm. His hold isn't what frustrates me. It's the desperation in his voice. "What if these cases are linked?"

"What if they're not, and we waste another six hours preparing for an ambush that isn't a fucking ambush!"

My roar doesn't harness his objective in the slightest. "Ellie was sent here for a reason, Dimi. If you find out what that was, you'll have more chance of finding Roxie."

I drift my eyes to Rocco. Don't ask me why. I don't seem to have control of anything today, much less my emotions.

When Rocco shrugs, leaving the decision up to me, I return my eyes to Smith. He's all but begging for me to listen to him. It isn't something I often do, and in all honesty, I sometimes wonder if that's where I've gone wrong.

Smith's exhale ruffles Ellie's hair when I ask, "Who sent you here?"

She hesitates. Not long enough for me to give my crew the signal to move, but long enough to take in the plea in Smith's eyes for her to cooperate. "Theresa Veneto."

A collective hiss rolls across the warehouse.

I should have known she was involved.

"Why?"

Ellie shrugs again before her brows join. "She didn't say. She mentioned something about a Megan…"

"Shroud," Smith and I fill in when she pauses to glance down at her notepad.

With her eyes wide and her jaw unhinged, she nods. "I was to wait here until you arrived, then bring you in. I assumed you had information on her death."

"Megan Shroud died over a year ago."

SHANDI BOYES

We know that's a lie. I'm merely testing Agent Gould. If she lies, our conversation is over. If she doesn't, I truly don't know where we'll go from here.

As the confusion in her eyes grows, Ellie informs, "Megan Shroud's disappearance was ruled a homicide late this afternoon." Not asking permission, she swivels Smith's laptop around to face herself, then clicks on a file on her desktop. Since Smith is already hacked in, it makes the process remarkably quick. "See." She brings up a police report oddly similar to the one Theresa forced through the system the first time Megan was 'killed.'

"Was there a body?" Rocco asks, jumping into the conversation.

Ellie immediately shakes her head. "A significant blood pool was found, and brain matter was embedded in the carpet, but no body."

I take a moment to consider Theresa's objective. It's clear she's running the same ruse she did on Maddox, but I have no fucking clue why.

Two seconds later, a lightbulb switches on inside of my head. "Who was arrested for Megan's murder?"

"An arrest warrant for a local woman is being drawn up. Her name is..." Ellie scrolls through the information on Smith's laptop, seeking a name. The wind in my lungs expels with a grunt when she discloses, "Isabelle Brahn."

Rocco sounds as uneased as I feel when he says, "That bitch is playing at something." He lowers his voice to ensure his next set of words are only for my ears. "Theresa didn't ask Ellie to wait here for no reason. She wanted both you and your time occupied."

I jerk up my chin, agreeing with him. "But for what reason? And how did she know I'd be out looking for..." Anger burns up my words.

She didn't pick this location for no reason.

She's fucking playing me.

"I'm going to kill her."

My arm is clutched for the third time today. It isn't Smith this time around. It's Rocco. "You'll never win the game if you keep letting your opposition blind you with false razzle and dazzle."

"She's playing me."

He doesn't deny what I'm saying because he knows it's the truth. "Because she needed you distracted. Find out why, and then you'll have all the pieces you need to win." When the groove between my brows doesn't budge, he chuckles out, "You're always running a million miles an hour, Dimi. Slow down, take a breath, and look at the entire picture."

He nudges his head to Ellie and Smith during his last sentence. They're no longer going to war with words. They are working together, side by side, their natural connection making it obvious they don't just make magic between the sheets. They could be just as explosive outside of them if I'm willing to give them a chance.

"If this backfires—"

"It won't," Rocco assures, slapping me on the shoulder. "Because firecrackers don't implode with despair. They make a starry night seem bland." In a rare show of affection, he pulls me into his side and whispers, "They'll come out of this, D. They're too strong not to."

# 8

## ROXANNE

The dry throat I've been struggling to ignore the past seven or eight hours becomes unbearable when the dark-haired stranger pulls his car down a long, dusty driveway. I haven't seen a house in miles. There may have very well been ranches dotted along the many roads we traveled, but with winter arriving early, the sun commenced lowering over an hour ago. Farmers aren't a fan of burning the midnight oil, so I may have missed their ranches during our drive. Even the house we're approaching is scant on lighting. Only the flickers of a candle on a second story can be seen.

I swallow harshly when the black-haired man gleams a blinding grin. "It's not the Ritz, but compared to where you're going, it'll seem like it." He tosses a lint-riddled sweater into my chest before grunting for me to hurry up and get dressed. "If you walk in like that, you won't make it through the night untouched. Castro won't like that. He always gets first dibs."

The burn of my throat is horrendous. I've heard that name

before. It was mentioned by members of Dimitri's crew many times when they discussed the crew holding his daughter captive.

I'm grateful I am about to meet the little girl I haven't stopped thinking about since Dimitri showed me her photograph, but I'm also worried. This place is derelict and rundown. If my confines are worse than this, there's only one place I'm going. Straight to hell.

The stranger does a final glance at the shadows between my legs before he throws open the door of his truck and steps down. As he makes his way to my side of the retro-vehicle, I slip the sweater over my head, breathing easier when it falls to my knees. I'm not just grateful to have my modesty back, I am thankful for the warmth. It's a lot colder here than it was in Hopeton.

"Did this region have early snow as predicted over Thanksgiving?"

It's the fight of my life not to pout when he answers my question with a grunt. I was hoping he was as stupid as he looks. The fact he's going against a man as powerful as Dimitri reveals he's lax on smarts, he just doesn't want me to know that.

"Out." I fall out of the cabin of his truck too fast for my dead legs to keep up with when he tugs on my arm. My body isn't just sore from being motionless for hours. The press of my thighs as I've fought to hold back the screams of my bladder make it seem as if I have run a marathon.

"Can I please use the restroom?" I request from my station on the sloshy ground. "I can't hold it any longer."

"Soon." He hoists me from the ground by my arm. Although his reply wasn't what I was hoping, it's better than a straight-up no.

The reason for my unrequired deprivation of liberty is exposed when he guides me into a room on the lower level of the rundown ranch. The lights are switched off, but since my eyes have become accustomed to the dark, I can see the equipment in front of me as if it is daylight. A bed similar to the one in Dr. Bates's office sits squashed against the back wall, and an ultrasound monitor and paraphernalia is on its right.

"Get on the bed." I barely shake my head for a second when the goon rips my hair from my scalp with a brutal clutch. "I wasn't asking."

My eyes don't know which way to look when he drags me across the room by my hair—at the shadows above my head revealing there are people peering at me through the cracks in the floorboards, the shadow I hear snickering in the corner of the room, or the obvious ruckus of drunken men below me.

When I'm tossed onto the bed as if I'm weightless and tied down like a mental patient in a psychiatric hospital, I settle on the shadows dancing above my head. They're as silent as my frozen heart but somehow comforting. They wouldn't watch if this was about to be gory. Only horrible, vile people would stand by and watch someone be tortured.

A cool breeze wafts against my thighs when the man raises the waistband of the sweater, drawing my focus back to him. He bands the over-used material under my breasts before he squeezes a generous dollop of clear fluid onto the middle of my stomach.

"Lower," says a voice at the side, her tone very much feminine and unique. "If she's only a few weeks along, you need to scan just above her pubic bone."

Her knowledge of ultrasounds makes me sick.

This isn't the first time she's done something like this, guaranteed.

I stop seeking her features in the dark when the faintest movement in the corner of my eye captures my attention. With my bladder at the point of bursting, the man had no issue finding the unexpected bundle in the lower half of my stomach. I'm still a novice when it comes to all things pregnancy-related, but even someone as naïve as me has no trouble identifying the blob on the screen, even with its head appearing alien-like.

I'm so in awe at the smidge of black on the screen, I don't peer at the lady cloaking her face with darkness when she asks, "How far along?" I'm too interested in discovering the man's reply to pay the disgust in her tone any attention.

The dark-haired man twists his lips. "Not far. I'd guess around six or eight weeks."

"Good. That will make things easier." After waving her hand through the air like a regal princess, wordlessly granting the man permission to untie me, she exits the room via a hidden entrance on her left. It's just as dark in that part of the house as the room with my baby's image frozen on the screen, but the moonlight bouncing off her golden locks reveals she's as blonde as the reflection I saw in the mirror when Megan Shroud was admitted for a psych workup.

Endeavoring to keep my excitement on the down-low about the many pieces of the puzzle I've gathered today, I lower my sweater before accepting the hand the man is holding out to assist me off the sterile-looking bed.

Once my shuddering thighs are concealed by the low rise of the itchy material, I lift my eyes to the man and ask, "What will make things easier?"

I curse my inquisitiveness to hell when the man replies, "This will."

He grips the nape of my sweater, bends me in half to ensure my stomach feels the full impact of his fist, then hits me with everything he has. His punch knocks the wind right out of me. I fall back with a gasp, the pain tearing through me the worse I've ever experienced. It doubles the cramps I've been having all day and forces tears to spring into my eyes.

The only good that comes from so much pain is my body's natural instinct to curl into a ball. My new position protects my stomach from the man's boot when he kicks me over and over and over again, his onslaught only ending when the blackness seeping out of his heart overwhelms me, and my will to live gives up.

# 9

## DIMITRI

I stare at the monitor on Smith's laptop with my blood boiling and my fists balled. The shoddy live broadcast shows Roxanne lying on a dirty floor. She's curled into a ball, unmoving and unspeaking. There's no physical indication as to why she isn't moving. If it weren't for the dried streams of wetness marking her cheeks, you could believe she's sleeping. She looks peaceful, almost angelic.

"There." Rocco points to the faintest rise and fall beneath the two-sizes too large sweater Roxanne is wearing. She's breathing, but it's shallow and irregular.

"Count them out to me," Smith requests after hacking into a 911 operator's program. "By counting her breaths, we'll get an indication of her heartrate. That will tell us whether she's sleeping or not."

"She isn't sleeping," I mutter out at the same time Rocco says, "Now."

"They didn't send me this for no reason. They want me to see what they're capable of. They want me to back down." When silence falls across my office, my determination grows. "I'm not doing that this time around. I'm Dimitri-fucking-Petretti. If you mess with me, you lose your life. Can't explain it any simpler than that."

I try to breathe out the anger eating me alive. I try to keep a rational head, but before even Rocco can predict what I'm about to do, I remove the gun from the back of my trousers, flick off the safety, then squash the barrel to the teeny tiny groove between Agent Ellie Gould's brows. "Give me something."

She's been here, working side by side with us for the past couple of hours, yet she's not shared one useful snippet of information. I don't like praising the Feds, but that is as irregular as me maintaining my cool when the itch to kill is skating through my veins. The Bureau doesn't hire solely on looks. They want the smarts as well. Ellie has both, and up until today, she used them to her advantage. She not once displayed the blonde bimbo she's been faking today.

When I inch back the trigger, Ellie's lips get waggling. "I don't know anything..." Her words are gobbled up by a big swallow when even Smith hears the deceit in her tone. He was on his feet in an instant, prepared to protect her as he had promised years ago. Now he's sinking away, certain he's being played for a fool.

"Smith..." She appears hurt by his reluctance, perhaps even heartbroken. "I-I-I swear, I don't know anything."

Her pupils dilate as wide as mine when Smith flicks on the communication mic next to his makeshift terminal before he speaks a set of words I never thought I'd hear him say. "Activate extermination orders for 8324 West Mulberry Lane, Ravenshoe. Shoot to kill. No survivors needed."

"No!" Ellie cries out with a sob, fighting me with more gusto than she's shown at any stage today. "Don't do this, Smith. Please."

She's so close to collapsing, I have to grip the front of her shirt as I did her throat only hours ago. Several buttons on her silky blouse pop, but it has nothing on the scream she releases when Smith lowers the projector screen at the side of my office to display Clover and a team of three men getting ready to storm Ellie's family's beachside residence.

I'm shocked. I thought I was the only one noticing Ellie's erratic behavior this evening. I had no clue Smith, Rocco, and Clover were aware of it too. Raids like this aren't something you set up in a couple of minutes. It takes time and preparation.

"No, no, no," Ellie screams on repeat when Clover screws a silencer onto the end of his weapon before he covers his tattooed cheek with a balaclava. "You can't do this. They're not a part of this. My career isn't on them."

Smith's accent is unrecognizable when he says, "You know what to say if you want it to stop. Tell Dimitri everything you know."

Ellie drifts her drenched eyes to Smith. "As I told them, I don't know anything. We broke up before Fien was taken."

The fact she knows my daughter's name is a slap in the face, but I keep my focus on the game I'm meant to be playing, not the one I already fielded. "Told who?"

Ellie's eyes return to mine. "I don't know who they are. They wanted information about your daughter. I told them I didn't know anything." Tears topple down her cheeks when she blurts out, "That's when they told me to go to the warehouse and await further instructions."

My brows join as confusion slices the tip off my anger. "I thought Theresa ordered you there?"

Since she's so worked-up, even her breathing crackles when she tattles, "They instructed me to tell you that if you showed up."

"And the plates we've been searching for the past four hours?" My voice is as hot as the anger roaring through my veins.

Ellie chokes back a sob before disclosing, "I did see a car when

I arrived, but the tags and information on Megan's murder were patched through to my phone this morning."

I am tempted to crush her phone to death when she digs it out of her pocket to show us the messages she was sent. They're basic, but the prose is undeniable. She's being puppeteered by an outside source.

As the pieces of the puzzle slowly slot together, the truth smacks into me. "How did they get you to agree to do this? Not even an unbreakable bond could have you siding with the wrong side of the law."

Ellie doesn't need to answer my question. Her eyes tell me everything I need to know. They have the same petrified glint Roxanne's had when I used Estelle to force her to eat.

After stuffing my gun down the front of my pants, I snatch up the microphone Smith growled down a minute ago and press it to my lips. "This is a hostage situation. Exterminate the perpetrators. I repeat, *only* exterminate the perpetrators."

Clover peers at the body cam on Preacher's chest before he jerks up his chin, advising he understands my objective.

Once all four men are weaponed-up and ready to roll, they enter the Gould residence by a side entrance. The constant yap of a pair of chihuahuas exposes the perps are still in the vicinity. They don't pay Clover and his crew any attention. They're facing away from them, barking in the direction of the room Clover wordlessly instructs for his men to enter first.

The next thirty seconds is a blur of gunfire and wounded cries. The sobs aren't coming from my men. They don't murmur a peep during operations like this. They remain completely quiet, aware sneaky attacks are usually more deadly.

Within minutes of entering the premises, Clover unclips the body cam on his vest and swivels it around so I can see his face. His brows are sweaty, and his grin is massive. He is in his element.

"Perps have been exterminated. Hostages are uninjured and accounted for."

Ellie sucks in her first breath in what feels like minutes when he spins the camera around to show the remaining four members of her family bound and gagged but relatively unscathed.

"You owe me," I say before I can stop myself. "And I want payment in full, *today*."

I don't wait to see her nod because if it is slower than immediate, I'll order Clover to finish what Smith attempted to start. That's how worked up I am and how hollow my chest feels. Roxanne wasn't meant to get hurt, and although tears are usually painless, I have a feeling Roxanne isn't experiencing that tonight. She's hurting. I can feel it in my bones, and I'm going to make sure the people responsible for her pain pay with more than their lives.

I'm going to claim their souls as well.

# 10

## DIMITRI

I scrub a hand over my tired eyes when Smith and Ellie enter my office at the same time. Since Smith's shoulders are almost as wide as mine, he has to take a step back to let Ellie enter first. It's cordial for him to do and expected since Ellie has kept her word the past several hours. She's left no stone unturned as she has endeavored to repay her debt. Just like she wouldn't fall on the knife for Smith, she won't for me either, but she's convinced she doesn't need to get her hands dirty to achieve a good outcome.

"I think we have a way of unearthing Rimi's location." Smith lays a set of official-looking documents onto my desk before pressing his palms to the battered material. "Although we have no intel Roxanne is with him—"

"We both know she is," I interrupt, confident I know him well enough to know what direction he's taking.

He lifts his chin. "Ellie contacted some friends in the Bureau about an operation that's being kept under wraps. When her inquiries didn't yield any results, she contacted less-attributed colleagues."

When I shift my eyes to Ellie, she faintly smiles. She isn't comfortable with the line she's crossed, but she'll wear the injustice if it has her name smudged from my tally board sooner rather than later.

"What I said earlier about Internal Affairs investigating my department wasn't a lie. We've been under scrutiny for a couple of months now." Ellie digs through the stack of papers Smith laid out until she finds a trio of two men and one woman. "With bureaucratic tape the thickest it's ever been, IA will never say who their main suspects are, but even rookie agents can smell a rat." She waits to see if Smith smiles about the wit in her tone. When he doesn't, she gets back to business. "These were the main runners for IA's investigation. I reached out to the first two with the hope a little bit of ego-stroking would entice them into an unethical conversation." She screws up her nose. "They didn't take the bait. However..." she places down a photo of a man I'd guess to be mid-thirties with a dramatic flair, "... he loved having his ego stroked. So much so, he wanted to exchange pictures."

My lips quirk. "You went in as an admirer instead of a colleague?"

Smith doesn't look happy when she nods. "Previous exchanges with him assured me it was the right route to take."

"Was it?"

Smith nods along with Ellie this time around. "They exchanged photos. He admired Ellie's *almost* nude photograph..." he overemphasizes the word 'almost' to ensure I understand she wasn't exposed "... long enough for me to poke around on his computer. He's the nark IA is seeking." After waving his hand over the official-looking Bureau documents, he adds, "This is only a handful of stuff he's shared with the men his team is chasing."

The extra beat of my heart is heard in my question. "Is Rimi's current location amongst this?"

Disappointment smacks into me hard and fast when Smith shakes his head. "But it unveiled a way we can find out where he is."

"How?"

Ellie takes over the reins. "You're not the only one chasing Castro. A specialist team has been on his tail for months. From what I've heard, it's a joint CIA/FBI operation, which makes no sense whatsoever since Castro is a US citizen." Realizing she's getting off track, she waves her hand through the air, shooing away her inquisitiveness before starting again. "Anyhow, the lead on the case discovered Castro is after a new mark."

"Roxanne?"

"No," Smith and Ellie say in sync. "This woman."

My brows join when Ellie sets down a photograph of Isabelle Brahn. "What does Isaac's girlfriend have to do with this?"

"Nothing," Ellie says with a grin, pleased by the confusion in my tone. "Castro merely thinks she's this woman."

She hands another photograph to me. Just like Isabelle's image, I immediately recognize the blonde in the photograph. When I told Brandon James I did some digging, I wasn't lying. Not only did Smith discover he's the son of the New York governor—who I happen to have ties with—we also unearthed his first love, mindful not even the ultimate betrayal can break a connection between soulmates. Take Smith and Ellie's joint operation as an example.

"Castro wants Melody Gregg so badly, he's willing to come out of hiding to get her. He purchased tickets to an event Isabelle was set to attend as Melody this weekend." Air whizzes from Ellie's nose when she exhales deeply. "Unfortunately, the stunt was siphoned down the gurgler a couple of minutes ago."

"Why?" I don't mean to be blunt. I'm merely lost as to why

they'll build up my eagerness only to squash it like an ant a second later.

"Isabelle Brahn was just arrested," Smith informs, his tone low.

I shrug like it's no big deal. "Have a replacement brought in. Castro is like my father. He can't tell the difference between one blonde and another."

"We can't. It's too late," Ellie replies. "The lead on this case released Isabelle's image on a report she wrote up about Melody Gregg. Castro doesn't just have a name to go off on anymore, he has a face."

"She's a fucking woman not a priceless painting. Surely, you can find someone with similar features."

I know what I'm saying is wrong. I am just too filled with anguish to rope in my arrogance. This is the only solid lead we've had in hours, and it's for a function that's days away.

I can't wait days.

For every hour Roxanne is gone, her chances of survival greatly decrease. She's already been at Rimi's mercy for over twenty-four hours. I could already be too late.

Furthermore, I'm beginning to suspect her kidnapping isn't about money. Audrey's ransom landed in my inbox almost instantaneously with her kidnapping. That hasn't occurred this time around, making me believe Roxanne's captives want to drain my veins, not my bank accounts.

The best way for them to do that is to kill Roxanne.

I won't let that happen.

I'll become as vicious and relentless as my father before I'd ever let that happen.

With that in mind, I ask, "How can we get Isabelle to the event Castro will be at?"

Smith smiles as if I fell straight into the trap he set for me. "Simple. Get Isabelle out of lock-up."

I give him a look, warning him to dull down the antics before growling through clenched teeth, "She was arrested in Ravenshoe. I don't have jurisdiction there."

He completely ignores my threatening glare. "But you know the man who does."

I fall back into my chair with a laugh. It reveals how unhinged I am. "I'm not siding with Isaac."

"Why not?"

With my anger too perverse to hold back, I shout, "Because although he didn't hold a gun to my sister's head, he is the reason she's dead! If he had just forfeited the fight, Ophelia and CJ would still be here, and I wouldn't be left dealing with all my father's shit by myself."

I didn't mean to express my last sentence out loud, but I'm glad I couldn't hold back when it forces Ellie to use the non-agent side of her head. "Get Brandon to ask Isaac for help." She angles her body to face Smith. "You saw the way he protected Isabelle during her arrest. He cares for her, but—"

"He's still in love with his ex, so he'll always choose to place Isabelle into the fire over her," Smith fills in, gleaming. "Who were the arresting officers?"

They stop shuffling through papers when I mutter out, "You won't find them." I smirk at the shock on their faces before adding, "If Isabelle was my sister, and she needed someone to protect her during her arrest, you'd never find the officers responsible for it. The cartel doesn't leave evidence, and neither does the Russian mob."

Ellie gasps in a shocked breath. Smith's response is much more deviant than that. He smiles a grin I've only ever seen on his face once before. It was the night we bumped into Ellie as we exited a private jet. We were in New York to create havoc. Smith fell in love.

"What's your plan?" Smith asks, knowing me well enough to read the expression on my face as plotting.

After a few seconds of deliberation, I reply, "Brandon's father owes me a favor. Cash it in." After standing to my feet, I gather my suit jacket from the hanger in the corner of my office. "Her chariot won't be a pumpkin, and her footmen won't be knights, but we'll get Cinderella to the ball, even if I have to drag her there myself."

# 11

## ROXANNE

A grunt involuntarily leaves my parched throat when my wrist is snagged in a firm clutch, and I'm yanked off the floor I've been cowering on the past several hours. I'm sore, on the verge of weeping, but still willing to fight. Even though he knocked me down, until my legs are broken, I will get back up, bigger, stronger, and meaner than ever.

My grunt this time around is well-timed. It adds to the fury of the fist I ram into the unnamed man's face and propels me so far out of his arms, I'm halfway out the door before he knows I'm running.

I don't race for the entrance he forced me through last night, I charge for the whispered voices that encouraged me to wake up when the blackness overwhelmed me. They want me to win as much as I want them to be free. We are in this together. I've just got to find where they're hiding to ensure them I am on their side.

I make it up four stairs before my ankle is gripped and pulled out from beneath me. While breathing through the windedness my collision with the wooden stairwell caused my lungs, I kick out like a madwoman. I smash my heel into the man's face that's already dribbling blood on repeat, determined to show him I'm not as weak and pathetic as he thinks.

It takes three solid stomps on his nose for him to release my ankle from his hold, and even longer than that for me to reach the peak of the stairwell. As I gasp in much-needed air, I take a moment to gather my bearings. The pain distorting my mind has me confused as to whether I took a left or right when I exited the room that had me gleaming with happiness and sobbing with sadness in under a minute. I think it was left, but I'm truly unsure.

When the heavy stomps of the man's boots boom into my ears, I dart to the left, praying I'm heading in the right direction. If the number of voices I heard overnight are anything to go by, just the volume of women in one space should conceal me until I work out my next plan of attack. I don't stand out in a crowd. I never have.

I send a quick thanks to my Nanna when she answers my silent prayer. The room I just barged into is brimming with women. There are ethnicities from across the globe—Americans, Asians, Europeans—they have every nationality covered.

There are children too.

Many of them.

Although I'm dying to seek a toddler with chubby cheeks, elf ears, and a dimple in the top of her lip, the furious breaths of the man hot on my tail stops me. I will find Fien, I've just got to survive this madman's wrath first.

"Thank you," I mutter in shock when several women switch out my sweat-drenched sweater with the Mormon-like clothes they're wearing.

Their nighties are white, cotton, and very bland considering how attractive their faces are. I thought they'd be glammed up to the hilt, ensuring they got top dollar from interested buyers. Instead, they're dressed as if they are in a convent.

"Sit, sit," says a blonde with a heavy accent as she tugs on my arm.

Once I'm on the floor, I am surrounded by over three dozen women. The fact they want to protect me springs tears to my eyes. They're living in horrible circumstances, and I don't want to think about how they've been treated, yet here they are, still willing to help someone in need.

Despite the circumstances, it is truly a beautiful thing to witness.

I tuck my chin in close to my chest when the man enters the door I left hanging open. The reason for his delay is unearthed when I spot the cleaver in his hand. He had to get reinforcements. The thought makes me smile.

"Where is she?" he asks a group of women on my right.

They don't answer him. They keep their heads bowed and their lips shut.

It angers him further. "I won't ask again! You know what happens when you don't listen to my first order."

My heart launches into my throat when he fists the nightgown of the smallest woman in the group. He's so much taller than her, her feet dangle inches from the grubby floor when he brings her close enough to him, the brutal crunch of his hand colliding with her cheek will ring in my ears for days.

"Where. Is. She?"

When he moves the cleaver toward her left breast, I almost vault out of my spot. The only reason I don't is because the blonde next to me curls her hand over my balled one before whispering in broken English, "He won't hurt. Not allowed. Slap okay. Further..." She makes a throat-cutting gesture. "Watch."

As promised, within seconds, the brute releases the brunette from his grip before he swings his eyes across the room. I'm confident he won't spot me in a crowd, so you can imagine my surprise when he mutters out a few moments later, "There you are."

The women rally around me when he grips my hair like he did before my ultrasound to drag me out of the room. They claw him, bite him, and whack into him as if their biggest fear is losing me. They give it their all, but it still isn't enough.

Before my head can register I'm the only one left fighting, I am tossed on a bed in a sterile, uninviting room, and the man tugs at his belt as unforgivingly as he did my hair. "If you don't want to get hurt more than you already are, I suggest you remain still."

I kick out with a scream when he suddenly dives for me. It does me no good. He pins me to the mattress in an instant, my small frame no match for his height and weight. My vision blurs with unshed tears when he uses his recently removed belt to bind my hands above my head. He isn't restraining me until I calm down, nor is he planning to mark me with his scent. He wants to take something from me I'm not willing to give. He wants the very thing I will fight to the death for.

"Get off." I fight him with everything I have, hating the disgusting slither of his hand when he slips it underneath the nightgown the women dressed me in. "He will kill you just for looking at me before setting his men onto your family. You'll die a death more painful than a thousand. He won't stop until your eyes cry blood and your entire lineage is extinct."

His voice is almost too composed for a maniac. "Not if we kill him first."

I don't get time to absorb the actuality in his tone. I'm too busy recoiling about the growl he releases when he notches a finger inside of me.

"Tight," he purrs on a moan before he swivels his finger around like he's testing the durability of my vaginal walls. I'm clenched so tight, I almost dismember him when he suddenly yanks his finger back out.

He stares down at his dry index finger like he's disappointed there isn't any residue for him to inspect. I realize that is the case when he swivels his torso to a mirrored door at the side of the room. He holds the finger he had inside of me in the air before briskly shaking his head.

Even with the spectator's sigh occurring after the *doink* of a microphone being switched on, I still heard it. It was as depressing as the dread that sludges through me when she says, "Do whatever is necessary to get rid of it." She spits out 'it' as if it scorched her throat.

Confident he will do as asked, the shadow under the door clears away a mere second before the goon yanks off a sheet from a silver tray next to the bed I'm tied to. It houses an assortment of instruments that are every woman's nightmare—a hospital-grade kidney dish, long skinny clamp-type instruments, a needle filled with a murky substance, and the most concerning, a rusty coat hanger that's been flattened so only the hook at the end remains.

"W-w-what do you need that for?" I hate the stutter of my first word, but it can't be helped. The coat hanger should be the least worrying of the instruments on his tray of horror. However, it isn't. I grew up in a region of America that didn't have the funds to handle unwanted pregnancies with dignity. I heard many horror stories during my two years at college. This isn't as brutal as the backyard cesarean Audrey was forced to endure, but the result will be so much worse.

Fien survived Audrey's ordeal. My baby doesn't stand a chance, even more so when the man uses my distraction to his advantage.

He jabs the needle from the medical tray into my leg, paralyzing me from the waist down. Then, shortly after that, my vision blurs as blackness strives to overwhelm me for the second time in less than twenty-four hours.

## 12

# DIMITRI

As I tap my tattooed-covered finger on my knee, Smith's voice comes down the earpiece in my ear. "The call has been made. Agent James should be out any minute."

I'm parked in front of Ravenshoe PD, awaiting Brandon's break for freedom. If the gleaming glare Detective Ryan Carter hit me with when he noticed Rocco's illegal park is anything to go by, he knows who we're here for. He was outside the restaurant when the Russians came to town for a visit, so he'd be aware of my impromptu meeting with a Federal Agent.

I could tell him things aren't as they seemed, but where's the fun in that? Ryan isn't my friend. He wasn't when he snagged the most attractive girl in junior high and won't be when he finally discovers where she's been hiding these past few months.

The restlessness keeping my stomach empty the past fourteen years ramps up when my cell phone suddenly buzzes in my pocket. With Smith in my ear, Clover on high alert a couple of blocks over, and Rocco acting as my driver, there's only one other person who has my private number—my father.

Since he's the last person I want to speak to, I slide my phone out of my pocket and hit the 'end call' button without peering at the screen. "Have my father's calls sent straight to my voicemail. I've got eyes on him. I don't want him in my ear as well."

Smith hums out a panicked murmur before he discloses he has footage of my father nowhere near a phone.

"Live feed?"

He gags. "From the pendant on the whore you sent over to keep him occupied this afternoon. Trust me, none of his fingers are able to dial right now."

While fighting the urge not to slit Rocco's throat over his chuckle about my disgruntled expression, I swipe my thumb across the screen of my phone and hit my phone app. The area code reveals my caller is in the New York region, but the number isn't familiar.

I'm about to ask Smith to commence a trace when a text message pops up on my screen.

**Unknown number:** *Please tell me she wasn't found on the Shroud ranch. I can't stand the thought of her being buried so close to home and not knowing. I thought I'd sense her presence. We were close like that.*

Against Smith's recommendation not to engage until he completes a trace, I type out a reply.

**Dimitri:** *Who is this?*

"Someone wanting to cover her tracks since she's bouncing her signal off multiple towers," Smith growls down my earpiece just as my caller's text pops up.

**Unknown Number:** *It's India. I thought you had my number stored. Was she there, Dimi? Did you finally find her?*

"What is she talking about?" I ask anyone listening, the twisting of my stomach too perverse to ignore.

Smith breathes out a curse word a mere second before Ellie's voice comes down the line. "I'm sending you a link. It isn't pretty."

Mine and Rocco's phone buzzes in sync. My eyes don't know which section of the article to absorb first. The fact multiple bodies were found on a ranch only a hundred miles from Hopeton, that they were buried beside enough hospital supplies to fill an antenatal ward with or the headline that the body of a toddler was found in the wall of the residence.

"How old was she?"

When nothing but silence resonates out of my earpiece for the next several seconds, my panic shifts to fury. "How fucking old was she!" I scream like my lungs don't need air to function. I thought the knot in my stomach centered around Roxanne. I had no fucking clue my focus should have been on Fien.

*It should have always been on Fien.*

If I had protected her mother as I'm endeavoring to protect Roxanne, I wouldn't be here, fiddling my thumbs while maniacs run my town to the ground.

Perhaps I am as bad as my father.

Maybe this is my penance for the wrongs I've done.

My self-reflection is held back for another time when Smith discloses, "The corpse was mummified. She had been in the wall for a while."

His tone is both sorrowed and angry, but it does little to ease my agitation. "That wasn't what I asked. You know you can alter the age of a corpse. You're aware you can manipulate it to fool forensic scientists. She could be Fien. She could be my daughter."

The pain clawing my chest gets a moment of reprieve when Rocco says, "She isn't Fien, Dimi." He swivels in his seat to face me before handing me a printout of the report Ellie just forwarded. The Tank isn't just a muscle car. She's a command station on wheels. "Not only do the dates on the newspaper clippings surrounding the little girl's corpse disclose this, so does your gut. You'd know if Fien was gone, D, because you live for her. You've not done a single thing the past two years that wouldn't benefit her in some way." His grin gets smug along with his comment. "Except Roxie, but she doesn't count because she improved your chances of getting your daughter back instead of reducing it."

Before I have the chance to reply to any part of his statement, the back entrance of Ravenshoe PD pops open, and a showdown between Ravenshoe PD's finest and the Bureau's golden boy gets underway.

It's clear Ryan and Brandon have had words before. The tension in the air is thick enough to cut with a knife, although it has nothing on the unease in the cabin of The Tank.

After slicing his hand across the front of his body, wordlessly sending Brandon off, Ryan locks his eyes with the back passenger window of The Tank. I store the report of the mass grave site at Shroud Family Ranch into the slot in my door before popping open the one opposite from me, more than happy for Ryan to know who I'm schmoozing. Perhaps if he knows my pull extends all the way to the Bureau, he might accept one of the many offers I've made him the past six years.

"Game face, Dimi," Smith mutters in my ear when Brandon's gawk at my open door sees him jogging down the stairs separating us. "He's smarter than his baby face implies."

I doubt Smith's assumption when confusion congeals Brandon's face a mere second after he slides into the back seat of The Tank. He walked into an ambush, smiling. A smart man doesn't do that.

He also doesn't test the durability of the locks the jaws of life couldn't budge.

"You'd have a better chance of shooting out the bulletproof windows than getting its lock mechanisms to budge. I paid out the eye to make this thing a tank, but the quality of the product was worth its exorbitant price tag."

I hear his jaw go through a stern workover before he shifts his eyes to me. "What do you want, Dimi—"

"Information," I cut him off, eager to get things moving. My head is spinning. I don't have time for idle chit-chat.

Like a fool unaware of what happens to men who waste my time, Brandon's lips etch into a condescending smirk. "That isn't how things work. We ask you for information. If we find it beneficial, we help you. That's what being an informant entails."

"Informant?" Ignoring Smith's advice for me to take a chill pill, I spit out, "I'm *not* an informant for the FBI. They work for me, not the other way around."

It takes everything I have not to reach for my gun when Brandon replies, "That may have been how things worked with you and Tobias, but that won't fly with me."

"Reveal your hand, Dimitri," Ellie suggests, overtaking the reins from Smith. "I've never worked with Agent James, but if he's anything like the rumors I've heard, outsmarting him will work better than threatening him. He's all about brains over brawn."

After an inconspicuous nod, I shove the report Rocco gave to me into Brandon's chest. "Is this report accurate?"

The brutal bob of his Adam's apple reveals Ellie was on the money. He isn't stunned by the information he's reading on the reports, he is shocked I have them. I just wish suspicion wasn't also on his face. He doesn't realize I'm a victim of the trade he's investigating. He thinks I'm a part of it. I guess I shouldn't be surprised. My family name has been embroiled in controversy for longer than I've been born.

"Where did you get this? This hasn't even been logged with the Bureau yet."

I lower the angst in my tone before replying, "Where I got this information isn't important. I just need to know if it's true?"

He peers at me as if I have a second head before he mutters, "Yes, it's true."

"Are all the victims female?" I ball my hands together so tightly, my nails dig into my palm when I ask, "What's the average age of the women found?"

Brandon wets his dry lips before he sings like a canary. "Preliminary findings state the victims are between the ages of thirteen to late twenties."

The fact he doesn't mention the toddler found in the wall exposes he knows more than he's letting on. The knowledge he's holding back frustrates me to no end, but I do my best to maintain a rational head. "Had any of the victims recently given birth before their death?"

He shrugs. "We won't know that until the autopsies are completed."

"You would know." My voice comes out louder than intended. It even makes Rocco jump. "You'd know because she's eight months along..." I swallow the unease burning my throat before correcting, "She *was* eight months along."

With my head cloudy from the debilitating images in the report, I honestly feel like I've stepped back twenty-two months. Rocco is right, I'd know if Fien was hurt, I'm just struggling to get my logical-thinking head with the program. It's coded to see the worst in everything. Very rarely does it consider the silver lining.

Conscious our conversation may hit a stalemate, I remove the photograph of Audrey I placed into the breast pocket of my jacket, then pass it to Brandon. I hate the sympathy vote. More times than not, it makes me angrier than recalling how my enemies have played me for a fool the past two years.

I'm not feeling that sentiment today.

Brandon wears his heart on his sleeve. If I can play on it, I'll have him eating out of the palm of my hand even quicker than my daughter's upside-down grubby face stole my heart from my chest.

"I paid the ransom they requested." My jaw tightens to the point of cracking. "They didn't uphold their side of our agreement."

It dawns on me that Brandon was closer to Tobias than realized when he asks, "Was Tobias aware you paid the ransom?"

His expression remains neutral when I shake my head. "Tobias approached me a few days after the drop. He said there was a complication securing Audrey." I can't admit my wrongdoings in her ransom. If I do, guilt will eat me alive in an instant.

"I told you he's smarter than he looks," Smith says down the earpiece lodged in my ear when Brandon gabbles out, "You're not searching for Audrey. You're trying to find your child."

"Tobias was supposed to get her out. He assured me she was safe, and that it would be only a matter of time before she was returned to me." Those were the exact words Tobias spoke to me the night he called to say they were raiding the Castro compound within the hour. I begged him to wait until I got there. He said he couldn't. "Then—"

"Tobias was killed during the Castro raid?" Although Brandon sounds as if he's asking a question, I don't see it like that. He's summarizing.

After a couple of minutes of deliberation, he moves our conversation in a direction I never saw coming. "When was your daughter last seen?"

"I didn't get you out of lockup to investigate my daughter's disappearance." Although I appreciate his wish to help, the last time I got a federal agent involved in Fien's disappearance, I lost her for months on end. I won't let that happened again. "I did it so you can continue with your ruse to force Castro out of hiding."

Shock registers on Brandon's face. It's quickly swallowed by anger. "You can't use the Bureau to get revenge on Castro."

I smile an evil grin. "I'm not getting revenge on Castro. I'm going to kill him as he did my wife."

Roxanne's father may have held Fien by her feet after removing her from Audrey's stomach, but he wasn't the only man in the room. There were several of them, and I'm confident the ringleader was Rimi Castro.

"I can't legally help you with this, Dimitri."

With his resolve strong enough to know words won't crack it, I get inventive. "You'll do as I ask, or I'll release this to the hounds."

Blood drains from his face when I hand him a drafted bounty for his long-lost girlfriend, Melody Gregg. It hasn't been lodged, but all it will take is a single push of a button for her bounty to be activated. Unlike the payout on Roxanne's head, this one will be cashed in because men like Clover don't back down when they're on the hunt.

Brandon grips the single sheet of paper enough to crinkle it down the middle before he strays his eyes to mine. I had never really paid their hazel coloring any attention previously. I only switched things up today because they're filled with so much fury, they appear more green than brown. "How do I know you haven't already released this?"

"She's still alive, isn't she? Living it up in a fancy penthouse apartment in New York City with her billionaire boyfriend." I show him the video Smith and Ellie downloaded when they discovered Brandon's ruse to have Isabelle impersonate Melody at a function later this week. It doubles the blatant rage in his eyes. "Even with a wrong set of photographs attached to her file, the real Melody wasn't hard to find."

I don't mention the fact his father led a member of my New York chapter right to his ex. Vincent McGee only owed me one favor, but when you like your women young enough, you'll face consecutive life sentences if word gets out, you're a little more generous with your 'colleagues.'

Vincent's association with my family is being taken care of as we speak, but I'll have to save the details for another day since Brandon shifts our exchange from civil to prudishly fun in zero point eight seconds.

He grips the lapels of my jacket before dragging me to his side of the cabin. "If you hurt her—"

"You'll what? Kill me as I want to slay the man who murdered my wife. He cut our daughter out of her stomach, then left her to die! He treated her like fucking scum, so if I have to use your high school sweetheart as bait because your hero-complex wants to stop a war that started long before you joined the Bureau, I fucking will. I'll do anything it takes to gut Castro as he did me."

My rant started with Audrey in my thoughts, but it ended with Roxanne. I've told myself time and time again the past two hours that she was breathing in the footage I saw of her, and she looked unharmed, but my gut knows better. She's hurting. Deep down inside, there's no denying the truth.

Needing Brandon to go before I forget he isn't the man I'm chasing, I remember the reason I got him out of lockup. "Do what needs to be done to get Castro out of hiding, then leave the rest up to me." When I hear Rocco release the lock mechanisms on the door, I lean across Brandon to open his door for him. "And start here as he'll get your Honey Pot out of lockup even faster than your daddy's fancy title will."

Brandon misses my accidental slip-up. He's too busy staring at the entrance of Isaac Holt's nightclub, stunned as a mullet that I brought him here.

It takes him a handful of attempts to get his legs to follow the prompts of his brain. I assume because his knees are knocking about meeting the man who pipped him at the post but am proven wrong when he pops his head back into the cabin of The Tank. "If you do this, you'll be hunted as fiercely as you've been chasing Castro the past two years. What kind of life will that be for your daughter? Hasn't she been through enough? You're her father. You are supposed to protect her, not put her in more danger."

When he slams the door in my face, oblivious to the fact I'm seconds from removing his insides via his bellybutton, Rocco locks his eyes with mine in the rearview mirror. "We need him."

"We don't fucking need him." I want to add that I don't need anyone, but since Rocco will see straight through that lie, I keep my mouth shut.

Just like my pain is my motivation, so is my wish not to be alone. It takes courage to wage a battle by yourself, but it is even more courageous to admit you need help.

After climbing over the partition separating Rocco and me, I switch on the state-of-the-art GPS system. "Send through Rico's last known location to The Tank's mainframe." As Smith hums out an acknowledging murmur, I swing my eyes to Rocco. "It's better to fight for something than live for nothing, right?"

Rocco's smirk reveals he understands where I'm going with this, much less what he says next, "They say you should never interrupt your enemy when he's making a mistake. They don't say anything about helping them make it."

# 13

## ROXANNE

"This will only take a couple of minutes, then you can rest up."

The drugs the dark-haired goon jabbed into my thigh must be top-shelf because he almost sounded sincere while assuring me I'll only be at his mercy for a few more minutes. Even the way he folds up the nightie the women upstairs lent me is gentle. He takes his time like he isn't in the process of stripping me of the only thing I've felt a part of wholeheartedly.

My ranch was my grandparents, my bed was bought on credit, even the shoes I was wearing earlier today weren't mine. They were from Alice's vast collection of pretty things. My child is the only thing I have of any value, and it's about to be taken away from me.

I don't know where my strength comes from when I gather it to shove the man away from me, but it's surprisingly robust. My push sends him crashing into the stainless-steel trolley he dragged closer to my bedside while waiting for me to succumb to his mind-numbing concoction. It reveals that only the lower half of my body is paralyzed. My arms, although heavy, can still protect my child and me.

"Now look what you've gone and done." His earlier niceties are now a thing of the past. He's back to the maniac who held me captive for hours on end without bathroom privileges.

While gabbling out about this being the reason he isn't nice, he bends down to gather up the instruments my push knocked to the floor. Forgetting my legs are numb, I use his distraction to my advantage. I fall to the floor with a clatter, bruising both my backside and my ego.

"Seriously?" the man chokes out, laughing. "Do you truly think you can crawl to safety? We're in the middle of nowhere, it will be below freezing as soon as the sun disappears, and you have nowhere to hide. You won't last five minutes out there."

When he folds his thick arms in front of his chest, it seems as if he wants to test his theory. He doesn't shadow my snail-like creep across the filthy floor. He watches my retreat with a smirk etched on his face and his brow arched, only jumping into action when I add a frantic scream into the mix.

"Help me! Please! I'm down here!" I bang and bang and bang my fists against the tiled floor when he hooks his arm around my waist and hoists me back, then I smack them into his chest. "He's going to kill my baby! Please help me!"

I fight him with everything I have—teeth, nails, and the brutal pounds of my fists. I whack into him on repeat, my fight only lessening when the violent crack of a skull being punished sounds through my ears.

I brace, anticipating impact.

The pain never comes because the man didn't strike me.

He was hit.

"Quickly."

A flurry of red and white circles me when my savior hoists me off the bed. With the drugs in my system finally displaying their full effect, my legs aren't the only things out of action. My head is as heavy as my limbs. I can barely see through the curtain of red in front of my eyes, and I'm not going to mention the slur of my words.

"I can't..." I stop, swallow, then try again. "I can't move my legs."

"It's okay, lean on me, we only have a few steps to take," whispers a soft female voice full of sorrow and distress.

With all my weight on her shoulders, she moves us through the residence still plunged into darkness even with it being late in the afternoon. She weaves us through narrow corridors like she intimately knows the floorplan, and within seconds, I'm once again at the bottom of the stairs.

"Help me, please," my rescuer begs to the shadows my cloudy head is confusing as demons dancing in the dark. They prance above my head, all impish and fiend-like. I'm so convinced they're Satan's urchins come to collect me for my transgressions when they finally relent to my savior's pleas, I pull back, undogged on my wish to live.

"No!" I scream at them as I did the man, certain they're destined to hurt me.

"It's okay. They will help you," assures the lady still glued to my side. "I promise."

When she strays her eyes to mine, assuring I can see the pledge in them, I'm certain my life is coming to an end.

My savior isn't an angel sent from above to protect me.

She is the very thing I'm scared about the most.

She is Dimitri's wife, Audrey.

# 14

## DIMITRI

Rocco strays his eyes from Rico to me. "Do you think he'll tell her?"

His distrust is understandable. We just told a mobster the Feds are going to use his big sister as bait. If we shared the intel with anyone but Rico, worry would be the last thing we'd feel. Regretfully, Rico values his family more than his counterparts. It was risky of me to disclose my plans, but as I said days ago, as long as we continue working toward a common objective, I have no problem pretending we're on the same team.

"He wanted the man responsible for brutalizing Isabelle during her arrest. I handed them to him. It'll do him best to remember that, or we will no longer play nice."

Rocco waits for the tail lights of Rico's car to disappear out of the marina's lot before he slides into the driver's seat of The Tank. "What do you want to do about him?"

He nudges his head to the left. Agent Grayson Rogers doesn't even attempt to shield his face with the shadows of the night. He wants me to know he's watching, and I'm more than happy for him to do exactly that.

"Nothing. He isn't after me... *this time*." Rocco chuckles at the slow deliverance of my last two words. Grayson has been hot on my tail for years. I only got him off when I proved I wasn't the one who sold Katie Bryne to Kirill Bobrov. He still hangs around every now and then, but not enough for me to respond to it. We played nice when we needed to. When we didn't, our work 'relationship' ended.

"Have you heard anything from Smith?"

Rocco didn't join Rico and me in blowing off steam on the three officers who tossed Isabelle around like she was a ragdoll. He's usually all about punishing men who use their size and strength against women but keeping tabs on Roxanne's disappearance was more important to him. It's mine too. I just needed to put steps into place to ensure I'm covered when I go in hard and brutal to get her and Fien out.

My last two hours with Rico were well spent. Although the Castros were once umbrellaed under an entity strangled by rules I've been forced to follow since birth, their 'protection' became null and void a few years back. Rico didn't go into details on what transpired, but the Popovs no longer work with the Castros. They're a completely separate entity, meaning the rules no longer apply. I can take down the king of their realm without the slightest fear of retaliation.

It's a glorious day to be a gangster.

Some of the air in my swollen chest deflates when Rocco shakes his head. "Not since you grabbed your bat out of the trunk. He's working on triangulating the location the video clip was sent from, but he said he had some bureaucratic tape to get through first."

"Isaac?" My jaw is so tight, my one word sounds like an entire sentence since it was strained through my clenched teeth.

Rocco fires up the engine before he once again shakes his head. "Not even Isaac has jurisdiction in this town, and from what I've heard, he's one of Henry's favorites."

"Henry Gottle is blocking Smith's inquiries?"

"Mm-hmm," Rocco murmurs in response to the shock in my tone. "He's making Smith real fuckin' twitchy."

He isn't the only one feeling tense. "Rico just disclosed the Castros aren't umbrellaed under the Popov entity anymore, so is Henry throwing up barriers because he took them under his wing?" When Rocco shrugs, truly unsure, I try another angle. "Smith..."

Like always, he chimes in with a hum.

"What else was on Agent Moses's computer when you hacked in?"

His voice is groggy when he replies, "You mean other than porn?"

Rocco laughs. My response to Smith's gall is nowhere near as polite. For a man who just spent two hours teaching insolent men what happens when you fuck with family, my growl is almost bloodthirsty.

After catching his breath with a quick gulp, Smith discloses, "There were some files about a money-laundering syndicate on the West Coast, a couple of borderline kiddie-porn write-ups, and an old home-invasion case from two decades ago. Why? What are you looking for?"

"A link between the Gottles and the Castros," I answer without pause.

Smith's fingers give his keyboard a workout before he sighs. "Up until a couple of years ago, there wasn't a link."

"But there is now?" I ask, my interests piqued.

Air whizzes from his nose, indicating I'm very much on the money. "It isn't close to the relationship Isaac has with Henry, but there are definite benefits being shared."

That's unusual. You've got to give Henry something big to be in his favor. He now runs the city my family built from the ground up, yet we're still not shared more than common courtesies for the past decade.

"Dig deeper into the files. There's something we're missing."

"On it," Smith replies before he disconnects our connection with a clank.

Rocco gives me a couple of minutes to shake off my confusion before asking, "Back to the compound?"

I shake my head without pause for thought. "Head to Roxanne's ranch. I want to grab a couple of her things for when she's back. She'll feel more comfortable being surrounded by her belongings."

I didn't mean to say my last sentence, but I'm glad I couldn't hold back when Rocco murmurs, "She doesn't need *things*, Dimi. She just needs you."

# 15

## ROXANNE

I wake up startled and confused. I'm in a room similar to the one I escaped from yesterday afternoon, but the sky is no longer moody with a low-hanging sun and ominous clouds. Light is beaming through the cracks in the bordered-up windows, and its bright rays alert it is well past dawn.

As I cradle my thumping head, I try to recall what happened between yesterday afternoon and now. I remember my stepless dash through a rundown ranch, the scary shadows above my head, and my near coronary upon discovering Audrey is alive, but other than that, my mind is blank. I don't remember entering this room at all. It's as if a good sixteen hours of my life just up and vanished.

Was I drugged again? Is that why I feel hungover?

While I seek answers to my questions, I swish my tongue around my mouth. My throat is drier than a desert. I wish I could say the same thing about the area between my legs.

Even without my hand creeping across the bedding that's clinging to my sweat-beaded skin, I'm confident I am bleeding.

Not only did my brief movement waft a coppery scent into the air, there's also a knot in my stomach that won't come undone no matter how long I strive to avoid the obvious.

After carefully dabbing my fingers over the dampness coating my thighs, I snap my eyes shut, then raise my shaky hand to my face. I'm not a religious person, but I pray for a miracle on repeat before I gingerly open my eyes to inspect the sticky goop on my fingertips.

*No,* I inwardly scream when I noticed the blood coating my fingers. It's red, bright, and spread from the apex of my thighs to the back of my knees.

As I scoot up the mattress, needing distance from the product ripping my heart to shreds, I suck in air, forcing down the sob bubbling in my chest. Nothing can fix the tears in my eyes, though. They stream down my cheeks unchecked before they're absorbed by the nightwear drenched with cups of blood.

I'd give anything to go back to yesterday, to feel the same numbness I felt when I was aided out of the stranger's room of horrors because the pain tearing through me now is worse than anything I've ever experienced. It's so bad, a bullet could pierce through me, and I wouldn't feel it. It hurts so much. It truly feels as if I'm dying, like more than my baby is being absorbed by a dirty set of sheets. My heart is there too.

I've barely brought my gut-wrenching sobs down to a whimper when the door to my room shoots open. With how brutal he was hit late yesterday afternoon, the last person I anticipate to walk into my room is my original captor.

Even with him being struck hours ago, his walk is staggered. Audrey's hit hurt him. I shouldn't smile at the thought, but I do. He's a murderer, he doesn't deserve my sympathy. I hope he rots in hell but not before Dimitri slowly drives him there. He didn't just hurt me when he killed my baby, he took something from

Dimitri he can never return, and it will cost him more than his life.

When I say that to the goon, he has the hide to smile. "I've always believed in an heir and a spare." He rubs his hands together like he isn't wearing a thick coat, jeans, and boots. "Unfortunately for you, royals don't like tainting the bloodline with bastard children. You should ask Dimitri about it the next time you see him. *If* you ever see him again."

"Oh, I'll see him," I snap out before I can stop myself. "You can place money on it. Just like I can guarantee you're on your last breaths."

His words are like a knife to my chest when he mutters, "At least I had the chance to breathe. It's more than your bastard child will ever get."

The amount of blood I lost overnight should make me weak. It should render me incapable of moving, much less retaliating. However, now Audrey's bewildering recovery makes sense. There's nothing more frightening than a momma bear defending her cub. I only knew of my child's existence for a little over twenty-four hours, but that doesn't lessen their significance to me. He or she meant something. *They still do.*

I drag my nails down the goon's face while he attempts to silence my campaign by shoving the barrel of a gun under my ribs. The fact he needs a weapon to defend himself humors me. He is double my weight, my head only reaches his shoulders, yet he's still scared of me.

Good. He should be scared because hell hath no fury like a woman scorned.

While grunting through the pain of my palm ramming into his sternum, the goon slams his boot into my right foot, then twists. Pain shreds through me, but I keep my howl on the down-low, refusing to give him the satisfaction of knowing he hurt me again.

Once he has me wrapped up in a bear hug I can't loosen, he lowers his lips to my ear. "I couldn't work out why you had them so worried. Yeah, you're pretty, you've got a nice set of tits, an ass you could bounce a quarter off, and a tight cunt I don't see letting up for years to come, but so do a million other American women." He lowers his arm from the top of my chest to the curves of my breasts. "But now I get it. Oh, how I have seen the light. You've got spunk, charisma..." He gropes my breast for each word he speaks. "All the things his wife doesn't have." I think he's creeping his hand down my stomach to defile me some more. I have no clue he's stabbing a final nail into my heart. "It's a pity you don't have his kid anymore. You might have given her a run for her money if you had." I fall to my knees when he unexpectedly releases me. "Get yourself cleaned up. Wouldn't want you scaring the kids."

My brain tells me to stay down, but my heart demands the opposite. If Audrey is here, that means Fien is most likely here as well. My heart is breaking for both Dimitri and myself, but Fien's cute little chubby cheeks and eyes identical to her father's in every way could very well be the cure to my heartache.

With my back facing the coldblooded stranger, I peel my blood-soaked nightie off my body before replacing it with a fresh one folded at the end of my bed. My legs shudder when I slip them into the openings of a pair of panties only my nanna would think were fashionable. I'm not scared the man is watching me like a hawk. I'm horrified about the gigantic pad someone preloaded into my underwear.

Although I hate being reminded about what I've lost, the products surrounding me make sense of the cold, sterile room I awoke in. My baby wasn't the only one delivered here. The stack of maternity pads in the partially cracked-open closet is indicating enough, let alone the pediatric medical crib just outside the door.

"How many children have these women birthed?" I ask the

man when he guides me out of the room with a firm grip on my arm.

He grunts, then continues shoving me toward the stairs.

My nanna always said my mouth would get me in trouble. If it's the good kind of trouble, I don't mind. "Are you not allowed to touch the women because your blood isn't royal? Are you a bastard like the rest of us?"

That stops him in his tracks. "My blood is more regal than any of the men here."

"Yet, here you are, nothing more than a paid goon."

His slap is brutal, but it doesn't weaken my smile. Only scared men act out with violence. Take Eddie's response to my 'betrayal,' for example. Real men prove otherwise.

"There's still time, you know?"

The grunting, red-faced goon drags me up the stairs like he has no interest in anything I'm saying. It's unfortunate for him, silence is a battle only the bravest can conjure.

"For what?" he asks with his hand resting on the door that leads to the room the women are in.

I crank my neck so I can peer into his eyes. "To save yourself. Tell Dimitri where I am, and I promise he will spare your life." I curse at my inability to lie when my eyes rapidly blink during the last half of my statement.

If Dimitri doesn't kill this man for what he did to me, I'll do it myself.

"Nice try," the stranger pushes out with a huff. "If you truly think he'll come all the way out here for you, you've got rocks in your head. He will never come here for you, he will never go anywhere for you because there's only one person Dimitri Petretti cares about, and that is himself. If you don't believe me, ask her." He throws open the door, nudges his head to Audrey in the corner of the jam-packed room, then tosses me into the quiet space. "She chipped away at his arrogance for months. She barely made an indent, so what chance would you fare since you were barely in his realm for weeks."

His smirk gets cocky when my attempt to shut down the worry on my face is two seconds too late. "What's the matter, girlie? Did you think we were only watching you the past couple of weeks?" He lowers the volume of his mocking tone to ensure his next set of words are only for my ears. "I would have gotten you off in the alleyway before running you over. Would have been more fun that way."

On that note, he shoves me into the room, slams the door shut, and twists a key into the lock, leaving me as defenseless as I am shocked.

# 16

## DIMITRI

I slap my cheeks when Rocco walks into my office, waking myself up. I have a bag for Roxanne packed and sitting by the door, my guns loaded and ready to go, but I have no fucking clue which direction I should head. My intuition is leaning toward New York. That's where the gala is being held, and a tower just outside of New York was in Smith's report on the thirty-second footage we were sent of Roxanne, indicating it was triangulated in his search, but the last time Rimi made a move, he did it in my backyard. Who's to say he won't try and fuck with my head again this time around too?

"Did you sleep at all last night?"

I shake my head at Rocco's question. "You?" The weakness of his shake is more telling than the worry in his eyes. "How's Alice?"

He doesn't twist his chair around to straddle it backward like he usually does. He sinks onto it with a sigh before rolling his head around like his neck is giving him agony. "Docs say she will make a full recovery. Word is still out on Luce. She's giving her grandmother hell."

He drops his chin to his chest when I ask, "Anything I can do?"

After taking a moment to ponder my offer, he reluctantly shakes his head. "Might hold you to it once Fien and Roxie are back, though."

"So tonight?"

He smiles a grin I haven't seen on his face in years. "You're finally clicking on, D." Don't misconstrue. He isn't asking a question, he is stating a fact. "What's the plan?"

"Other than a merciless bloodbath, my head is telling me to stay put."

He twists his lips like he understands where I'm coming from. "And your gut?"

I drag my teeth over my lower lip to hide my ill-timed smile. I'm not smirking about the situation we're in, I am appreciating that Rocco trusts his intuition more than anything. It has gotten us out of some hairy situations in the past. I can only hope it will have the same effect this time around. "It was on a flight to New York five hours ago."

Rocco's grin doubles as he holds his hands out palm side up. "Then, what are we doing here?"

"I don't know," I reply, speaking the truth for the first time in forever, shocked enough about the rarity to laugh.

After chuckling along with me for the next thirty or so seconds, Rocco asks, "Can you feel her here?"

"Who?"

He gives me a look that says he knows I'm acting ignorant before he adds words into the mix. "Your girl."

He doesn't need to say Roxanne's name for me to know who he's referencing. I've never seen Fien in the flesh, so I've never experienced that stomach-tingling, nauseating, and somewhat infuriating sensation that hits me low in the stomach anytime

Roxanne is in my vicinity. I'm sure it will be there once we meet, but for now, it's an experience I've only ever felt with Roxanne.

"No, I don't feel her here," I reply, finally at the stage where I can stop denying Roxanne is my girl. She walked through Hell's gates for me. She has more than proven she's on my side, and now I will forever be on hers.

Rocco leaps up from his chair as if he isn't exhausted beyond belief. "Then, what are we doing here, D? Let's go to New York and get your girls. We play to play—"

"We kill to kill..." we say at the same time, "... and we take down any fucker stupid enough to get in our way."

After whacking me in the chest with the back of his hand, reminding me I'm not as old as my body feels, he scoops up my keys from my desk, then moves for Roxanne's bag by the door. His race down the hallway almost takes out Smith, who's coming in the opposite direction. He's balancing a laptop on his hand, the shadowing of gray under his eyes exposing his sleep was as lackluster as mine.

"You'll want to see this," Smith says after popping his head up from the screen of his first-of-its-kind laptop. When he spots Roxanne's bag in Dimitri's hand, his brows pinch. "Are we going somewhere?"

I jerk up my chin. "Can you tell me on the way?"

Nodding, he races back to his computer hub to grab chargers, another three laptops, and a gun. Rocco quirks his brow when he leans over a sleeping Ellie with his lips puckered. He almost kisses the tiny section of her forehead not covered by locks of shiny blonde hair but pulls back with barely a second to spare.

Instead of farewelling her as if the last two years never happened, Smith jots down a message on the notepad Ellie's cheek is squashed against before spinning around to face Rocco and me.

"What?" he asks, frustrated by our silence. "Old habits are hard to give up."

"It's been over two years, Smitty," Rocco says with a laugh.

Smith's eyes snap to Rocco. "Yeah, and your point?"

Rocco steps back with his hands in the air, acting as if the words cracked out of Smith's mouth were bullets. "I'm not sayin' nuffin.'"

I don't follow his lead. "She can come with us if you want?"

We don't know what we're walking toward. For all we know, having a female on our team could come with great benefits. I'm a father, but I am still clueless when it comes to things like pregnancy and birth, not to mention kids. As far as I'm aware, Ellie doesn't have any children, but with her little brother having the mind of a child, she understands them.

Smith takes a moment to consider my reply before shaking his head. "If this goes as deep as I'm thinking, I'd rather Ellie's career not be tainted by it."

"Are you sure, Smith?" Rocco questions, jumping back into the conversation. "If she gets booted from the Bureau, you'll have no reason not to be together."

His question is fair but only because he doesn't know their breakup goes deeper than Ellie's career choice.

"I'm sure." Smith's short reply reveals he doesn't want to go into details with Rocco right now. I doubt it's a conversation he wants to have in the next decade, he just won't have a choice. Rocco is like a bull in a China shop when it comes to any relationship he isn't a part of. "Do I need to organize transport, or is this another road-tripping adventure?"

The gargle the last half of his sentence arrived with reveals he's praying we're not taking the high road again. He'd rather hitch-hike to where we're going than be stuck in the back of his van with Rocco for another three hours.

"Silas is on standby," I answer, slackening the groove between Smith's brows by a smidge. "Make sure he's ready to have wheels up in an hour." Before Rocco can grill me about the delay—the private airstrip we use is only ten minutes from here—I nudge my head to a recently approved court appearance date circled on a notepad brimming with handwritten notes. "We need to make a stopover first."

With his smile huge and his hands rubbing together like a crack dealer on payday, Rocco follows me out of the compound, aware who we're visiting and more than happy to update Smith all about it.

# 17

## DIMITRI

"Where is he?" I ask no one, frustrated as fuck Agent James isn't upholding his side of our agreement.

Brandon will have no chance in hell of convincing Isabelle to unknowingly do his ruse if he doesn't support her during her arraignment for murder. It's the people who stick by you during the bad times you protect the most. If Brandon doesn't show up today, he'll be struck off Isabelle's friends' list without delay.

It would have been the same for Rocco and me when news of Fien's unkosher arrival circulated through my inner circle. He rocked up only hours later, drenching wet, furious, and ready to kill. I honestly don't know if I would have made it this far without him. Knowing your newborn daughter is being held captive by a madman is enough to make the most lucid man insane.

Rocco and Smith watch me like a hawk when I tap out a message on my phone. If I can't force Brandon to be at his 'friend's' side, I'll lose more than my cool. My agreement with Rico will be null and void as well.

**Dimitri:** *Should I follow your plan or make one of my own? If you're not here in thirty, the decision will be out of your hands.*

I don't mean minutes, I mean seconds. Brandon's apartment is only one block over. He can run here if he has no other option.

Once the screen of my phone advises my message has been read, I snap an image of the Ravenshoe Courthouse stairs then forward it to Brandon.

It feels as if not even ten seconds ticks by when I spot him racing up the stairs. I must have woken him. His hair is a mess, his face is crinkled, and I'm reasonably sure he's wearing the same suit he wore yesterday.

I'm about to slide out of the back seat of my Range Rover when Rocco grabs my arm. "Hold up. This looks like it could get interesting."

When I stray my eyes in the direction he's peering, I notice Brandon's race up the courthouse stairs has been thwarted by a blond man with wide shoulders and an arrogant mask slipped over his face.

"Who's that?"

"Agent Alex Rogers, Field Operations Supervisor for the Federal Bureau of Investigation." Smith isn't gloating. He sounds like he wants to rip off Alex's head as badly as Alex wants to tear into Brandon. "He was Brandon's supervisor."

"Was?" Rocco and I ask at the same time.

Smith lifts his chin. "Agent James was demoted last night. The FBI's golden boy isn't as shiny as he wants us to believe. His rap sheet is almost as long as mine."

"So, sweet fuck all?" Rocco asks with a laugh. "Or are you talking about the rap sheet you got expunged for sleeping with the enemy?"

Okay, perhaps he knows a little more than he let on.

Our interrogation shifts from Smith to Brandon when the crack of a fist colliding with a jaw silences a town not known for its quiet. Alex didn't hold anything back with his hit, and shockingly, Brandon takes it like a man. He gets up in Alex's face and says a few words, but he keeps his hands balled at his sides.

His response is nothing like mine would have been. I would have retaliated with more than my fists if I were in his predicament.

"Find out what that's about. If a war is about to begin, I want to know about it, especially if it involves the FBI."

"Already on it." Smith digs one of his laptops out of his satchel, then fires it up. Within seconds, he has a confidential report up on the screen.

"Who's the blonde?"

Smith double clicks on the trackpad on his laptop to zoom in on the image of a blonde in a towel. She's attractive—if you're into ball crushers. I swear I've seen her before, but I can't pinpoint where.

Smith alleviates my curiosity. "That's the infamous Regan Myers, Isaac Holt's lawyer..." *Ah, there's the connection.* "And Alex Roger's current squeeze."

I double back, certain I heard him wrong. The half grin he's wearing reveals I didn't, much less the tap of a revolver on the window next to my head. I don't know how I didn't put it together earlier. The Rogers' familiarities are almost on par with the Petrettis. There's no denying them when you drink them in at the same time.

Grayson Rogers, another one of Tobias's little minions, acts as if he doesn't have the scope of Rocco's M4 on his chest when he requests for me to roll down the window. I could drive off, but Roxanne's exasperating habit of nosy-parking has rubbed off on me. Furthermore, the last time I was in the same room as Grayson, I walked away with him owing me a favor. My assistance this time around will cost him much more than the gratitude I have no plan to cash in.

Rocco works his jaw through a thorough grind when I signal for him to lower his weapon. He has issues with law enforcement officers, most particularly, ones who are as cocky as Grayson.

After rolling down my window as requested, I say, "I'm shocked you're up. I didn't see you leave the front of the compound until well after four this morning."

I'm happy to let him know I realize he's watching me, just like I'm happy to watch his brutal swallow before he says, "Kirill—"

"Is not a part of my operation. I've told you that many times before." My interruption is snappy and to the point. I'm sick to death of having the same conversation with these people. Yes, I run drugs, and yes, my entity is part of the prostitution conglomerate but tell me one fucking cartel unit that isn't. If we weren't running it, corrupts fuckers like Ravenshoe PD would. I don't know about you, but I know who I'd rather deal with. It isn't the corrupt members of law enforcement who put away innocent men for murders they conjure on a whim.

Grayson acts as if I didn't speak. "Is the reason for Castro's resurrection." He shoves a set of documents through the crack in the window as if he's a bank robber, and I'm the teller he's demanding cash from. "He's stateside because of this."

I lower my eyes to the document to ensure he doesn't see the shock in them. From what Smith unearthed the past couple of weeks, Kirill hasn't been stateside since he purchased Katie from my father, so for him to be back, it must be for something big.

"You fucking idiot," I mutter under my breath when I realize what I'm looking at.

My father learned nothing from my grandfather's death, not a single fucking thing. I thought he squandered the massive payout he got for my mother's death on the business ventures I've tried to steer our entity away from the past eight years. I had no clue he used it to try and regain control of New York.

We built that city. The Italians, Greeks, and Albanians made it the mecca it is, but my father lost the ability to be king of that realm when he put his drug-fucked friend above our 'family.' He had no right to stake a claim, none whatsoever, and now Henry's lack of assistance the past few years makes sense.

"Consider your favor cashed in." Needing to end our conversation before I take my anger out on the wrong person, I commence sliding up my window.

Grayson blocks its climb by lodging his elbow between the tinted glass and the metal window channeling it. "That wasn't a favor. It was a warning. If you go into this with guns blazing, *as I'm reasonably sure you're planning*, you'll be up against more than Rimi Castro."

"I'm not worried."

Grayson laughs like Rocco's finger isn't itching to inch back his trigger. "Then that makes you a fucking idiot. There's more at stake here than your family's pride, Dimitri."

Something inside of me snaps. "*Pride?* You think this is about pride? Henry Gottle can have New York, he can have the entire fucking country as far as I'm concerned *when* I get my daughter back. *When* she's sleeping in the crib I built for her." I bang my chest during the last half of my statement. "And *when* I see her face for the first time in front of me instead of via a fucking monitor. That's *when* I'll let my *pride* slide. Not before. It most certainly won't happen before."

Grayson doesn't know how to reply. Nothing but silence resonates from both inside and outside of the cab for the next several long seconds. I want to say it eases my agitation. Regretfully, it doesn't. I'm more worked up now than I was when Rocco had to strain to see Roxanne's breaths to prove she was alive.

"How old is your girl?" Grayson's voice is as rough as the wiry hair on his chin.

Not interested in idle chit-chat, I signal for Preacher to go. He slots into the position of driver when Clover wants to catch up on missed sleep. He was on alert to move all night, so he's as tired as the rest of us.

"Hey, hold up." Grayson follows the Range Rover's slow creep down the road as Preacher seeks an opening in the traffic. "Do you want your girl back or not?"

"I don't need your help to do that."

Air puffs out of his mouth when he huffs out a laugh. "I wasn't offering my help. I'm *telling* you the job will be done quicker if we work together."

"I don't work with the Feds."

"Neither do I," Grayson fires back with a waggle of his brows. "Well, not when it concerns Kirill."

My lips involuntarily curl at the tips. I had wondered if my advice months ago worked. Grayson's disclosure reveals it most certainly did. "What are you proposing?"

When Preacher's eyes shift to the rearview mirror, seeking confirmation on if I want him to pull over, I shake my head. If Grayson wants to talk, he better do it quickly. We're almost on the open road.

The fact his words aren't chopped up from the clomps of his boots reveals he has maintained his fitness while undercover in Kirill's crew. "A mutual corroboration like the one you had with Tobias. Shared information on the agreement it isn't used for *any* outside influences."

My brow cocks. "A 'you scratch my back, I scratch yours' situation."

"Yeah," Grayson answers, unaware I wasn't asking a question. I was merely validating his name got him into the academy more than his academics.

"Kind of like your arrangement with Rico."

I slice my hand through the air like I'm swatting a fly, not only wordlessly demanding for Preacher to stop, responding exactly as Grayson was hoping.

"Not as dumb as I look, hey?" He smirks a smug grin before straying his eyes to Smith. "You really should be careful which back doors you sneak through. When you leave it wide open, your footprints are easy to follow."

While grumbling several curse words under his breath, Smith attacks his keyboard with the malice of a savage. I can tell the exact moment it dawns on him that Grayson isn't lying. He not only initiates a lockdown on all our devices, he commences stripping information from Grayson's cell phone. How do I know this? A photo of Katie Bryne popped up on his laptop screen within seconds of him hacking in.

"You don't need to hack into my phone to understand my objective, Dimi." Rocco doesn't take kindly to Grayson using my nickname any more than me. "I'm more than happy to share it with you. We are, after all, on the same team."

Grayson's cockiness gets smacked into the next century when Smith barks out, "Katie Byrne was sold in a private auction when she was eighteen. Her handler was an up-and-coming prodigy your father had taken under his wing. He was supposed to prepare the mark for sale. Instead, he fell in love with her. That not only saw him falling out of favor with your father, it had his supervisor at the Bureau on the back foot as well." Smith raises his eyes to

Grayson, mouths *checkmate, motherfucker*, before he hits him with the motherlode. "Tobias did everything he could to help his rookie agent out of the pickle he got himself into, but despite both his stellar reputation and the rookie's dad's high standing in the Bureau, Katie was sold, shipped to another country, and was never seen again. Boo-*fucking*-hoo."

Ouch. I forgot how nasty Smith gets when someone tries to outsmart him.

Spit flies out of Grayson's mouth when he roars, "You punk-faced motherfucker." For a man with shoulders as wide as mine, I'm shocked how far he climbs into the car. He gets close enough to Smith to knock his laptop off his lap, but nowhere near close enough to wring his neck like he really wants to.

"Enough," I say a short time later, over the theatrics.

"Enough!" I roar for the second time when my first order is ignored. Grayson can get away with bypassing my directive, but Smith and Rocco can't. "Tell me what you have. If it is of interest to me, I'll return the favor."

Grayson's blue eyes shift to mine. They're not holding an ounce of the humor they had earlier. "That isn't how things work—"

"Then, we're done."

I signal for Preacher to go. I can tell Grayson wants to let me walk. It is in his eyes, slicking his skin. Hell, it's even readable in the way he holds his jaw. He hates negotiating, especially with men like me, but it just has nothing on the rage he felt hearing how the men who were supposed to have his back didn't.

After shaking his head in a way that exposes he thinks he's making a mistake, Grayson says, "Meet with me tomorrow morning."

"I'm going out of town for a couple of days."

"I know." He arches his brow, climbs back out the window, then taps on the roof of my Range Rover, signaling for Preacher that there's an opening before he adds, "I'll send the deets through your private network... *if* it's back up and operating by then."

On that note, he hits Smith with a cocky wink, spins on his heels, then stalks away.

# 18

## ROXANNE

"Are you okay?"

I drift my eyes from the only window in a room to my questioner. I'm not surprised when I discover the kind eyes of Audrey glancing down at me. Not only has she checked up on me multiple times today, she has a very faint voice. Even if we were the only two people in a soundproof room, I'd struggle to hear her.

I don't know if her quiet stems from the other forty or so women crammed into the room with us treating her like a lecher or because her daughter isn't held in the same room as her.

From what I gathered from the women with broken English, Fien lives downstairs. I could be wrong, but I'm reasonably sure her living arrangements aren't recent. They kept saying 'no' while wiggling their fingers at Audrey. Although the rest of their sentences weren't in English, I have a feeling Audrey understood them. Anytime they guide me away from her, she cowers instead of standing up for herself.

I'm a bit disappointed her personality doesn't match her fiery hair coloring.

Redheads are usually hot-tempered. Audrey is as timid as they come.

When the worry in Audrey's eyes doubles, it dawns on me that I didn't answer her question. "Yeah. I'm okay. A little tender, but nothing I can't handle."

It seems as if a band is stretched across my mid-section, constantly tugging and pulling on my insides, but I can't help but wonder if that's because I can't sit still. I've clawed at the deadbolt on the only door in and out of this room, endeavored to pull up the hardwood floors that are stronger than they look, and have been working on the nails hammered into the window to keep it shut.

The women captive with me find my endeavor to escape amusing. I'm not sure how to respond to their smiles. I'm annoyed by their lack of assistance, but I also understand it. Perhaps they tried as hard as I did their first few days here and soon learned their efforts were a woeful waste of time. I've only been going at it for a couple of hours, and I already feel my optimism dithering.

The concern in Audrey's eyes shift to remorse before she asks, "Have you had any more bleeding?"

Her question is sincere, but it still stabs a knife into my chest. I've always believed you live the best life by leaving the past in the past. That's a little hard to do when I'm continuously reminded about what I've lost.

With words alluding me, I shake my head. Bar the initial big bleed I had overnight, I've only detected the occasional smear of blood while using the bucket in the corner of the room. The brown-tinged byproduct had me hopeful my baby stood a chance, but Audrey quickly snuffed out that flare of optimism. She wasn't cruel. She just knows how these things operate since she's been here so long.

In a way, her bluntness could be seen as a godsend. If I were still pregnant, the goon who tortured me yesterday wouldn't have left me alone today. He only has because he knows what my heart is trying to deny. I lost any chance of filling the memories Dimitri missed with Fien.

"You should eat something," Audrey whispers just as the group of women mending loose hems notice she's speaking to me. "You need to keep your strength up," she adds while slowly sinking into the corner she's been stationed at all day. "For when Dimitri comes, you need to be strong."

She glances at me as if Dimitri's sanity hinges more on me surviving this ordeal than her. Her gawk isn't callous. It's almost hopeful, which is odd considering it was her husband's unborn child they stole from me.

My focus shifts from striving to work out Audrey's peculiar personality when Fenna, the woman who hid me yesterday afternoon, runs her hand down my forearm. "Okay?" She nudges her head to Audrey. "She... no."

"Know or no?" I ask when her accented words sound more like a question than a statement.

When she peers at me lost, I try another angle. "Me and you..." I gesture my hand between us, "... are friends. We like each other."

"Like. Yes." Her smile is bright enough to make me forget the horrible things she's been through. It's too beautiful for such a dark, horrid world. "I like..."

My heart warms when she touches my chest, advising she likes me. It could have slotted into my second-most memorable moment if Dimitri had returned my declaration of love two nights ago. Since he didn't, it holds the top spot, and it may stay there when Dimitri learns the mother of his child isn't deceased as believed.

After giving my pity-party-for-one ten seconds more than it

deserves, I get back to my conversation with Fenna. "We like each other. We're friends."

"Yes. Friends," she agrees, still smiling.

"You..." I touch her chest as she did mine, "... and Audrey. Are you friends?"

She glances in the direction I pointed when I said Audrey's name before she screws up her face. "No." She wiggles her finger in the air to get across her point. If I didn't know any better, I'd swear she was a teacher in a previous life. "No like. We no like."

"You don't like Audrey?" The shock on my face can't be missed in translation.

"No. No like. Stay away." She curls her arm around my shoulders as she has many times today before she leads me away from Audrey, her steps extra slow since my foot is blown up like a balloon. "Bad woman. Stay away."

Although the women across the room continue chatting while gawking at me, I know Audrey heard Fenna's comment. She wipes at the tears sliding down her face at the speed of lightning, but I still spot them.

If she's hurt about the women spreading vicious lies about her, why isn't she defending herself? I don't believe she needs to explain herself, but she as sure as hell doesn't need to take their crap lying down.

I shouldn't fight for her, some may say she's my competition, but for the life of me, I can't hold back. If she can't defend herself, how the hell will she defend her daughter when she reaches her age. "Say something to them. Tell them you're not who they think you are."

Audrey peers at me through the strands of auburn hair not covering her eyes before she shakes her head.

"Why not? You're a victim just like them. You didn't deserve what happened to you."

I shrug out of Fenna's hold more aggressively than I meant before I move to Audrey's half of the room, whimpering through the pain of a suspected broken foot.

"I saw the video. I saw what they did to you. That wasn't right, Audrey. What they did to you was wrong." I can tell my words are breaking her heart, but I continue on, confident a mended heart will work far better than an empty one. "Help me help them. Help me stop this from happening to anyone else." I'm getting through to her. However, my final set of words all but seal the deal. "Help me introduce a little girl to her father for the very first time. If you ever loved Dimitri, you'd want that just as much as me."

I level my breathing to make sure I don't mistake her whispered word, "Okay..."

"Yes? You'll help?" The shortness of my reply can't weaken the excitement bristling in it.

"Yes." The fire I've been seeking in her eyes for the past six hours finally shines brighter than her fear when she nods her head. "I will help."

Although I want to believe she's doing this solely for her child, a small part of me knows this isn't just about Fien. She wants Dimitri to know she is brave. She wants to show him she has the charisma and spark no one believes she has. She wants to prove she's worthy of him as much as I wish I couldn't see it in her eyes. They already have a connection that binds them together for life. Now she wants the commitment that comes along with it.

## 19

# DIMITRI

Our arrival in New York doesn't occur unnoticed. No sirens, flashing lights, or armored trucks some law enforcement officers need to get their point across are seen. Just a single Maserati Quattroporte parked halfway out the hangar my private jet is crawling toward.

Our flight was scheduled to land in the middle of the night to ward off unwanted eyes. I should have realized that wouldn't fool Henry. He's been snuck up on too many times in the past to take the news the Italian Cartel is in town lying down.

From what Smith unearthed over the past twelve hours, the takeover bids Henry has faced during his thirty-year reign lost him more than revenue. It cost him the very thing I'm endeavoring not to lose—his family. There's just one difference in our stories.

Henry could see his son if Henry, Jr. would look past his twenty-nine-year absence. He doesn't understand his father gave him up to protect him, nor does he see the regrets and mistakes on Henry, Sr.'s face like I do.

He feels abandoned.

I could tell him he got lucky when it comes to cartel families but considering my father's endeavor to reclaim a kingdom he has no right to reign is the reason for his family's downfall, I doubt it would do much good.

I've just got to pray Henry, Sr. is more approachable than his son. His war is with my father, and although I bear his last name, I'm nothing like him. My daughter comes before anyone as does Roxanne.

When I hit Henry with the motherlode of information Smith's stumbled upon from returning Grayson's hack, he'll have no choice but to side with me. Gangsters don't play fair in general, but when it comes to family, just like me, Henry has no trouble laying all his cards on the table. He is fierce and impenetrable, and if I didn't believe he's governing a realm he didn't earn, I could see myself emulating him.

Alas, I can't reach the pinnacle of success without taking him down.

That alone means we will never be friends.

A smirk curls my lips when over half a dozen red dots line my chest as I commence walking down the stairs of my private jet. Henry's reputation usually sees him going without the fanfare, so I'm somewhat pleased I've rattled him enough for him to pay attention to my visit. He isn't a fan of mine, hasn't been since we bumped shoulders a mere second before I approached Isaac to fight in my father's underground fight tournament years ago. To be honest, I doubt we will ever be.

"Dimitri, to what do I owe this pleasure?" Henry's voice is a mix of accents. It's as unique as the cartel leaders who used to run this sanction. It's pitched with superiority, but there's a snippet of hesitation that reveals our industry has worn his patience thin.

He isn't the only one feeling a little overwhelmed. I feel so haggard, I often have to remind myself I'm not as old as believed.

Henry should have more wrinkles than he does. I've been chasing my tail for two years. He has notched up more than ten times that amount, so why the fuck hasn't he given up yet?

*Because his family is safe, fuckface.*

*Yours isn't.*

Not having the time nor the interest to work through the honesty of my inner monologue, I get to the point of my interstate visit. "I'm here regarding your brother, Liam Gregg, or as you knew him, Liam Gottle, the second." When Henry's jaw ticks like he's fighting not to signal for me to be taken down, I talk faster. "Rumors state my father was part of the operation to take him down—"

"It wasn't an order to take him down. His family was brutalized, and his wife and daughter were scared half to death."

I nod, agreeing with him. There's no denying the truth. I read the reports on the Gregg home invasion during our flight. The men who entered their house were paid for a standard hit. The fact Wren, Henry's sister-in-law, would spark an attraction out of them wasn't considered. Her looks changed their tactics in an instant. If it weren't for Liam, Wren would have faced more than a handful of scratches on her inner thighs and bruises to her breasts that night, and it would have occurred in front of her daughter.

The knowledge of their change-up is why my mood is so sour this morning. Roxanne has a spark men can't help but acknowledge. Her spunk is potent enough to feed the ego of a dozen men, so what will happen when they realize there's only one way to unleash her powers? Will she be attacked as Wren was but left defenseless since I'm not there to stop it?

The thought makes me sick. It honestly makes me the most unhinged I've ever been, and it's heard in my voice when I growl out, "You have every right to go after the men responsible for hurting your family, but you won't get anywhere if you continue chasing the wrong fucking sanction."

"Your father—"

"Paid more than his share to fund the *joint* operation to take you down!" My roar reveals more than half a dozen snipers are dying for Henry to make a hand signal, but I act ignorant over a two-decade-long injustice as much as I am my inability to find Roxanne and Fien without the help of my enemies. "But he felt your wrath, licked his wounds, then sat the fuck back down. He hasn't moved since, yet you're still facing the same issues you had when he wanted your throne."

My teeth grit when the last half of my sentence comes out with a jut from a gun being forcefully pressed to my head. I don't need to sling my eyes to know who has stepped up to the plate before Henry has finished swinging his bat. His big head causes enough of a shadow on Henry's face to know who he is, much less the flick of Rocco's safety switch when he returns Kwan's gamble with one of his own.

Rocco doesn't care if his retaliation will get him killed. He'd rather respond to an act of intimidation than take it up the ass like I have the past two years.

Following his lead, I say, "You're chasing the wrong crew."

Henry brushes off my statement with a wave of his hand. "Says the man too stupid to realize he's doing all the legwork of a man undeserving of his time."

"I don't work for my father." After a stern glare at Kwan, warning him we're seconds from a brutal bloodbath if he doesn't stop digging his gun into my head, I add, "Everything I've done the past two years has been for my daughter."

Henry tries to hide the shock of my confession, but the mask slips over his face too quickly for me to ignore. I've heard he isn't as hard as his fierce reputation. I would have never believed it if I hadn't seen it for myself.

"Her name is Fien. She was born here, of all places, exactly twenty-two months ago, forcefully delivered by the very man you've been sheltering for years." I hold up the first photograph taken of Fien. You could coo at how cute she is if it didn't also show a bloody and cut-open Audrey on a stained mattress in the background.

Once I'm certain Henry understands Fien's delivery was nothing close to ordinary, I show him an image taken only days earlier. Even though no fight whatsoever is seen on Audrey's face as she's led out of the back entrance of Slice of Salt, the family crest on both Rimi's ring and his neck are undeniable. "I've been paying to keep her safe ever since."

When I gesture for Smith to move forward, Henry signals for Kwan to stand down. The goon with a head the size of a watermelon hesitates for a second but eventually does as told. All good foot soldiers do. Although Kwan is like family to Henry, he's still aware of the repercussions if he ignores his direct order.

"We have information that leads us to believe Rimi's crew is relocating to the New York region." After opening up the laptop Smith hands me, I log into the event Rimi has tickets for. "He purchased tickets to this event."

"I am aware," Henry interrupts, his voice somewhat off. It isn't brimming with anger, but it is full of distrust. Can't say I blame him. I don't trust anyone, much less people with the same last name as me. "Permission was requested to attend. We have eyes on the proceedings." His eyes stray to Kwan during the last part of his comment, falling on a tattoo that looks oddly similar to the Castro family crest.

Although suspicious as to why Kwan is wearing a crest for an entity that isn't his, I continue with my endeavor to make Henry see sense through the madness, aware time isn't in my favor. "Permission I doubt you'd give if you understood the real reason Rimi is here."

I click on the only file on my desktop. Aware Henry never takes anything on faith, I had Smith install everything onto a device we don't plan to see again. Henry would hate for his fuck-up to be broadcasted to his enemies, so I'm confident Smith's prototype laptop will be destroyed by the end of tonight.

"Milo Bobrov ran down your brother and sister-in-law, but he wasn't acting alone—"

My teeth grit when Henry interrupts. "David Crombie orchestrated it. You're not telling me anything I don't already know."

He spins away from me, his steps slowing when I add, "Rimi Castro organized both the raids that terrorized your family *and* Liam and Wren's death. He's playing you for a fool." He looks like he wants to kill me, but I carry on, unfazed and unscared. I'm already living my nightmare. It can't get any worse than this. "Why do you think Kirill returned stateside after all this time? Even he has heard how much you love sucking Rimi's dick, and he wants in on the action."

For an old guy, Henry has a lot of strength in his hits. He punishes my ribs with an unrelenting left-right combination before he slams my back into my private jet's shell that feels as cold as ice.

I don't retaliate to his brutal clutch of my throat. I'm too busy laughing at the whitening of his gills when Smith plays a recording he found buried deep in the Bureau's database. It's a private conversation between David Crombie, a former associate of Rimi's, and an undercover agent, Phillipa Russell. It exposes just how long Rimi has been playing both sides of the field and exactly who he took down in the process.

After Henry releases me from his grip, too shocked to continue with his aggressive stance, I swallow down some saliva, hopeful it will ease out my next set of words. "Rimi nagged and nagged and nagged Milo to seek vengeance on Liam for the time he served in a state facility away from his family. When he finally got through to him, you thought you were safe from carnage." I shake my head like I am disappointed I'm not the only gangbanger one step behind his enemies the past decade. I'm not, but I am happy for Henry to believe I am. "You got slack. You thought it was over, then they hit you with everything they had."

"I took care of Crombie," he seethes through clenched teeth.

I nod, once again agreeing with him. Crombie was found dead in his cell within an hour of him being arrested. "But you left the main hitter out at the plate, unconcerned about your curveball."

When Henry tries to deny my claims, I hit him where it hurts. Unlike my father, it isn't his hip pocket. It's his niece, Melody Gottle, the only surviving member of the renamed Gregg family. "You did good. For years, your enemies thought she was dead. Then Crombie couldn't keep his mouth shut."

He snatches both the recent photo of Melody out of my hand along with a ransom drop the Feds are currently in the process of organizing. "Rimi doesn't even have Melody at his mercy, yet her billionaire fiancé is willing to pay one point five million dollars to ensure it never occurs."

This is what Alice meant when she said they had a big payout to collect. Rimi won't stop at one ransom. He'll continue demanding money until Melody's fiancé stops handing over the funds, then he'll kidnap her for real. Guaranteed. It's how I would handle this if it were my operation.

I think all my Christmases have come at once when Henry mutters, "If this information is legitimate, what do you want for it?"

Being owed a favor by Henry is priceless in this industry. You can't put a dollar amount on it. However, I can, because there's something I want a shit ton more than money.

I want my girls back, and right here, right now, it feels as if my wish is about to come true.

Good things take time.

Bad things bring justice.

With Henry's help, I'm about to serve Rimi Castro a little bit of both.

## 20

# ROXANNE

"Does it have any charge?" I ask Audrey while peering at the cell phone she snuck in our room in the middle of the night.

I've been dying to see what she had up her sleeve for the past sixteen-plus hours, but with the man the women call 'Maestro' popping in and out of our room all day and night, now is the first chance I've had to speak to Audrey without an audience.

The women still watch us from afar, unmoved by my speech yesterday that an army has never won a war with only one soldier. They don't trust Audrey, and nothing I say will alter their opinion about that.

I can't say I blame them. If Audrey has had access to this device the entire time, why the hell didn't she use it to seek help?

My heart drums against my ribcage when Audrey nods. Its frantic wallops double when she slips the device out of my hand, fires it up, then shoves it back into my lap. Her hands are jittery like she's panicked out of her mind we're about to be killed.

If we're caught with this device, I'm confident we will be.

After gulping down a quick breath to settle my nerves, I log into her phone. It isn't one of those state-of-the-art ones with apps and gimmicks. It's retro, funky, and only has ten percent charge remaining. *Fuck it!*

Needing to hurry, I push out a little abruptly. "Where are your contacts?"

Audrey peers at me with her big eyes out in full force but remains as quiet as a church mouse.

"So I can look up Dimitri's number," I hurry her along.

Shock blankets Audrey's usually pretty face. "You don't know it?"

Her question shouldn't jab my heart with tiny knives, but it does. I don't even know the address of the compound I was held captive in, much less Dimitri's cell phone number. We didn't have that type of relationship. It was more fired by sexual attraction than communication, but since I can't tell Dimitri's wife that, I shrug instead.

Audrey does a quick sweep of the room to ensure we're without eyes before logging into the text message section of her phone. Dimitri's texts were the only ones received by this phone, so his number is easily distinguishable.

While endeavoring to work out how I can explain to Dimitri that his wife is still alive, I try not to look too deeply into how impersonal his messages to Audrey were during their marriage. They're stern and to the point like he was communicating with a member of his staff instead of his other half.

"Type something," I grumble to myself a short time later, frustrated I'm more concerned about how Dimitri will react to discovering Audrey is alive than getting out of the situation that caused the miscarriage of my child.

My hands shake as I type out a string of text. It's more a business-like contact for Smith to decipher than an attempt to clutch to the final hours I can pretend Dimitri is mine. I'd rather do that face to face than via the phone his wife owns.

**Me:** *Tracker disabled. Ruse still in effect. Send help to this location. Battery low. Act quickly. Roxie xx*

With the tiny gray device swamped by my hands, I move to the window I was peering out of earlier today before snapping a snapshot of the landscape. Although there isn't much to go off, I'm hopeful the preparation of the crops surrounding us will give Smith some clues to work with. It was amazing what he unearthed by looking at nothing but the satellite images of my grandparents' estate. If he can do that again here, we may be found sooner rather than later.

"Jesus."

I almost die a thousand deaths when Audrey's cell phone suddenly lets out a loud alert. I have no clue how to silence it, so I clench it with everything I have, hopeful my squeeze will suffocate its squeals without damaging it.

With my pulse beeping in my neck, and my eyes wide, I stray them to the door I'm anticipating for Maestro to shoot through at any moment.

When that doesn't occur within the next six seconds, I shift my eyes back to Audrey, wipe at the sweat on my brow, then drop my eyes to the screen of her phone. My only just receding panic gets a second wind when I discover the reason for the noise. My message couldn't be delivered to Dimitri's number since it is no longer in service.

*Dammit!*

After a couple of seconds of deliberation, I conjure up a new plan of attack. Although Audrey's phone is outdated, most social media sites were around when it was invented.

With my heart in my throat, I snap another picture of the landscape, save it, gingerly find my way to the internet browser, then log into my Instagram account. Smith mentioned he liked a handful of my drawings when he hacked into my Instagram account at the start of my 'arrangement' with Dimitri. He could have been lying to ease my panic when Dimitri was drugged, but that doesn't seem like something he would do. He's pretty truthful, even to the point of being brutally honest.

A ghost-like smile creeps across my face when I tap on the notifications on my Instagram page. Excluding clients, I don't get many interactions on my posts, so I'm certain the eight likes in a row are from Smith.

After following him, I prepare to send him a message. I could put the details in a post, but Maestro unknowingly mentioned two nights ago that I've been under surveillance for a while, so I don't want to run the risk of my social media accounts being monitored.

I have an almost identical message typed out when the faintest giggle steals my attention. It didn't come from inside the room. The women and children here have no reason to smile, so I don't see them releasing a giggle of pure joy. Furthermore, this was a babyish laugh, one I'm certain came from a toddler.

With my mind focused on anything but my freedom, I scoot toward the window before peering outside. It takes scanning the overgrown grass surrounding the ranch three times before I spot the cause of the extra flutter in my neck. Fien is sniffing wild-flowers near the rickety verandah I was marched up three nights ago. Her giggles are from the petals tickling her button nose. She screws it up, tosses her head back, laughs, then goes back for another whiff.

I watch her for the next several minutes, totally mesmerized, my stalker gawk only ending when the quickest flurry of silver catches my eye in the distance. It could be anything, but consid-ering there's nothing out here but fields and fields of crops, I pay it as much attention as the goon watching Fien's every move from his station on the corner at the verandah.

He stabs out his half-smoked cigarette into the sole of his boot before he moves to the very edge of the warped wood. My heart leaves my chest with a shocked gasp when he unexpectedly falls backward a second later. He didn't trip over the debris surrounding the rundown residence. He was taken out by a kill shot to the head. The still lifelessness of his body is a sure-fire sign of this, much less the bullet wound between his eyes.

*He's coming.*

*Dimitri is here.*

*He found us.*

The beaming smile on my face vanishes a microsecond later when a second man launches for Fien. While screaming that they're being ambushed, he holds Fien in front of himself, aware the only way he'll make it out of the carnage unscathed is by using her as a shield.

While my stomach decides which way it should flip, I track his race across the verandah holding the brain matter of his confidant. When he breaks through the front screen door under a halo of bullets, I charge for the only exit door of my room. The bullets flying past Fien didn't come from Dimitri's side of the arena. They were from the flood of men surging in the direction the silver flicker came from.

My throbbing foot screams with every step I take, but I don't slow down. Dimitri is so close to getting his daughter back, I can't stomach the idea of him losing her again. I don't think he'd survive it. The thread he's been clutching the past two years is extremely thin. One more fray could completely unravel it.

It takes me crashing into the paint-peeled door with enough force to burn my eyes with tears before it finally pops open under the strain.

I don't realize Audrey is following my race down the empty corridor until she says, "This way."

She throws open the bathroom door before jackknifing to her left. When she tosses a stack of towels out of a linen cupboard, my mouth falls open more in shock than to suck in much-needed breaths. The stack of scratchy material concealed a secret entrance. It leads to a concrete stairwell that goes to the basement.

After galloping down three flights of stairs, we enter a dark and dingy space at the very bottom of the ranch, sweaty and out of breath. It's cold down here, and the set-up makes it seem as if it housed an army in the hundreds the past week.

After taking in the multiple cots set up around the damp-smelling space, Audrey drifts her wide eyes to me. "There's a hidden garage on the fence line. If they're taking Dimitri's daughter, they'll go there."

"Where are you going?" I ask in shock when she heads in the direction opposite to the one she suggested I take.

She doesn't answer me. She just disappears through the underbelly of the ranch, her speed remarkably fast for how hard her thighs are shuddering.

I duck with a squeal when a bullet suddenly whizzes past my head a second later. Maestro stumbled upon my hiding spot during his sprint for the back exit. He isn't happy, and neither am I. He has Fien shoved under his arm. Even with her crying loud enough for two blocks over to hear, he acts oblivious to the fact his clutch is hurting her.

His rough handling of a child unleashes a side of me I didn't think I'd still have—my protective mother instincts.

With a roar, I charge to Maestro and Fien's side of the room, acting as if I am able to outrun a bullet. Maestro fires at me on repeat. I don't know if any of his bullets hit their target. I said the pain of losing my baby would be greater than the deadly pierce of a bullet, so I could be hit, I just refuse to give up.

The air in my lungs leaves with a grunt when Maestro loosens his grip on Fien's waist so he can backhand me. He has run out of bullets, meaning it is now just him versus me.

I shouldn't smile at the thought, but I do.

His hit has me seeing stars, but the howl he releases when I jab my thumb into his eye before kneeing him in the balls alerts numerous balaclava-clad men to our location. They surge into the basement two at a time, their approach more authentic than any action flick I've ever seen. Although their accents are foreign, they're not Italian, making me fretful I've been caught in the middle of a turf war that has nothing to do with Dimitri.

Maestro tries to suppress their surge like he's the Hulk, raging arms and legs go in all directions, but he's outnumbered within seconds, killed even quicker than that, and Fien and I are one measly step behind him.

# 21

## DIMITRI

Sweat slips down my cheeks when I climb a rickety stairwell two steps at a time. I've killed a dozen men already this afternoon, watched another eight be slaughtered by Rocco directly in front of me, and saw Dr. Bates hung for his crimes in a practice not even chop-shop operations like the Castros could use without cringing, but I'm still thirsty for more. I don't just want every man responsible for the pained expression on Roxanne's face when she peered out of a top-story window twenty minutes ago to pay for their stupidity, I want them gutted for witnessing my daughter's happiness before me.

She was born into a world full of violence, ripped from her mother's stomach weeks too early, yet she still stops to smell the roses. She's a baby, barely a toddler, but Rocco was right, her eyes reveal she's strong enough to survive anything. I just don't want her to fight alone anymore. As I said, she's a baby. She shouldn't have faced the things she has, much less a brutal bloodbath with the intention of only taking one hostage.

I can't believe I agreed to Henry's request. I've been hunting

Rimi for years, so the thought of harnessing his punishment until the Feds are through with him has me wanting to take down Rimi's entire crew with my knife instead of my gun. It would be more painful that way, more vengeance fueled. Alas, I shook hands with the devil more than twice earlier today. Considering it got me here at a hidden compound Rimi is endeavoring to get off the ground, I'll swallow the injustice. Rimi will still be dead by the end of the day, just not until Grayson's team has drained him of information.

My heart races like it's about to go into coronary failure when I reach the landing at the top of the stairs. Although I've never handled them before, I'm reasonably sure nerves are also jittering in my stomach. Everything I've been working toward the past two years hinges on what I discover at the end of the hallway I'm creeping down. Roxanne was last seen in this location. Neither her nor Fien have been spotted since.

"Three... two... one..."

I kick down the door when Rocco reaches one, then we race inside shoulder to shoulder. My eyes go crazy while roaming over the four dozen pairs staring back at me. It's clear from the women's clothing and demure personalities that they're not a threat, not to mention them guiding Rocco and me to a bathroom partway down the hallway we just snuck down when they realize who we're seeking. Rocco showed them a picture of Roxanne he has stored in his phone—a photograph I was unaware he had until now. We will have words about it later, but for now, I'm happy to use his fondness of Roxanne to my favor.

"Fucking prick," Rocco grunts under his breath when his dip into a secret entrance sees a bullet ping off the concrete block next to his head.

A groan of a man taking his last breath rumbles up the stairwell a mere second before I pull Rocco back so I can take the lead.

The stairwell isn't wide enough for us to go in side by side, so I will enter first. The suggestion to go in heavy was my idea, so if anyone is going to helm the charge, it will be me.

The scent of death teems into my nostrils when I step over the man Rocco took down from above. It isn't the secretion of his bodily fluids responsible for the rank smell in the air, it's the indent Henry's tactical team made to Rimi's crew when he stormed the lower level of his compound. Bodies line the floor. They stretch as far as the eye can see. The number alone reveals Rimi didn't walk into his new adventure lightly. He has almost all his men on deck for this.

Even himself.

He stands at the back of the room, smirking like the bodies of his crew aren't scattered around him.

When his eyes shift my way, and his smile doubles, my anger goes so white-hot, it could cause an aneurism.

With my eyes locked on the man responsible for years of torment, I shrug off my customized M6 machine gun, yank off the balaclava I requested the men of our joint raid wear so there'd be no mistaking the enemy, then pole-drive Rimi like several members of Henry's team aren't flanking him.

I know our agreement, I'm aware Henry only disclosed Rimi's whereabouts on the agreement Rimi would walk away from the carnage for a couple of hours, but that doesn't mean I can't fuck him over. He'll be more cooperative this way. More scared. I can rough him up how Grayson can't. I can make him bleed and not face any conflict about it. The rules changed when he orchestrated the death of Henry's brother. However, they were obliviated when he cut my daughter from my wife's stomach.

As the monster inside of me roars to life, I pound Rimi's face with my fists another two times before removing my switchblade knife from its pouch on my waist.

Rimi's scream will highlight my dreams for years to come when I slice my knife across his stomach. I gut him like he gutted me all those months ago, unconfronted and without remorse. He tore my daughter out of my wife's stomach without anesthetics, not the least bit worried about how painful that would have been for her.

I bet he's regretting his decision now.

I bet he wishes he could take it all back.

It's a pity for him it is too late. I'm on a warpath, and I don't see anything slowing me down. Rage this hot can't be contained. It's uncontrollable. Brutal. Fucking all-consuming. Although it has nothing on the fervor that stops me in my tracks when my eyes lock in on a pair of gleaming green eyes in the corner of the room.

Half of Roxanne's face is hidden by the shadows of a wooden stairwell Clover and several members of my crew are stomping down. She's cradling my daughter in her arms, sheltering her eyes from the brutality she was born in with her chest while humming a melody to save Fien's ears from the slaughter as well.

As my knife falls to the ground with a clatter, so does Rimi. His head crashing into the boilermaker matches the frantic thump of my heart. Usually, I would find his attempt to hold his stomach together humorous. Today, I don't pay it an ounce of attention. My daughter is in front of me, in the flesh, breathing, and well, and she's with the woman I love.

That outranks anything in the world. Nothing could come close to the emotions bombarding me now. Not even my deceased wife stepping into the frame with a butchered stomach and an ashen face.

# 22

# ROXANNE

Dimitri blinks several times in a row, certain he's dreaming but hopeful it won't turn into a nightmare. His daughter's messy dark brown hair is fanned across my chest, her thumb is stuck in her pouty mouth, and her eyes are puffy from her sobs, but since her mother is lying on the gurney separating them, fighting for her life, he hasn't had the chance to calculate just how many similarities they have.

I escaped injury in my endeavor to reach Fien, but Audrey wasn't as lucky. She suffered multiple stab wounds to her stomach. Her injuries would be fatal if it weren't for Dimitri's last-minute decision to bring Ollie onto the battlefield with him. He's doing everything in his power to save Audrey. He has since she collapsed into Dimitri's arms thirty minutes ago.

The back of a hotwired ambulance isn't the ideal spot for a reunion, but when news broke that the CIA was on the way, Dimitri had no choice but to bundle his crew into multiple transport vehicles and leave. I hated abandoning the women who had helped me beyond what I believed imaginable for what they had been through, but the elderly man leading the charge alongside Dimitri assured me it was the right thing to do. He said the CIA had contacts he didn't and that they would ensure every woman was returned to their families. That alone made the burden easier to swallow.

It's been a crazy thirty or so minutes since then, the haze growing more when Audrey murmurs Dimitri's name in her almost unconscious state. She barely saw him for a second before the wounds to her stomach overwhelmed her, but as I've said previously, it takes a lot to snuff the aura of a man as dominating as Dimitri. Audrey can sense his presence like I did moments before he took his wrath out on the man believed to be the head of the organization who kept his daughter captive.

I could have screamed for him to stop as I did when he tackled the police officer earlier this week, I could have shown him his daughter was safe and unharmed, but something held me back. I want to say it was because he was serving justice to the man responsible for killing our baby, but that would be a lie. I wanted Dimitri to get his revenge, to end the life of the insolent man who had caused him years of pain, then hopefully, when I reveal just how far the pain extends, he will handle the news better since the ringleader has already been executed for his crimes.

As Rocco races us through sloshy fields, Dimitri's eyes bounce between Fien and me, their springiness only slowing when I pull back the locks fanning Fien's face. It exposes more of her adorable rosy cheeks and plump lips, but it also reveals she's sleeping.

I'm not surprised. Crying is exhausting. The sob I released when I woke up in a pool of my blood had me napping for hours that day.

When Dimitri scoots to the edge of his chair, his face expressing his desire to run the back of his fingers down his daughter's chubby cheek, I nod my head, encouraging him. He can't come to our side of the ambulance since Audrey's gurney is wedged between us, and although I'd love nothing more than to hand him his daughter, the weapons strapped to his chest would make that awkward. Thankfully, the impressive reach of his arms won't throw up any obstacles for him to caress his daughter for the first time.

Dimitri's hand makes it to within a hair's breadth of Fien's blooming cheek when Audrey murmurs his name again. It's a groggy, pained wail that rips my heart out of my chest as effectively as it jerks Dimitri's hand away from Fien. He isn't retreating with remorse. Audrey conjured up the strength to slip her hand into the one she mistakenly believed was for her.

Her show of strength has me hopeful her injuries aren't as life-threatening as suspected, though I'd be lying if I said I also wasn't panicked. Dimitri appears as torn now as he was when he held a gun to my head in the woodlands outside of Hopeton. I don't believe he wants to kill me. He just has no clue how to process everything happening.

He isn't the only one lost. Fien is asleep now, but I had to fight her with everything I had to get her to settle. I'm not just the stranger who pulled her out of the line of fire, I'm also the woman who held her back when she attempted to race to a man she has mistaken as family. It broke my heart seeing her outstretch her arms for Rimi. I'm certain the cracks will heal when she learns to do the same for Dimitri, but for now, it still stings.

While Fien's daddy attempts to understand what her mother is saying beneath her oxygen mask, I carefully rake my fingers through her glossy hair. Audrey's voice is so frail, I can't hear the word she's speaking, but I'm confident it's only one. Her lips make the same weak movements on repeat, only stopping when an alarm overtakes the shrill of my pulse in my ears.

She's flatlining, and we're miles from nowhere.

With tears welling in my eyes, I watch the scene unfold. Ollie commences CPR while Dimitri tilts Audrey's head back, plugs her nose, then prepares to breathe air into her lungs. If I didn't know any better, I'd swear he's done this before. Saving lives isn't something the head of a cartel gang does. They usually take them, not fight for them.

Dimitri and Ollie continue compressions until the ambulance screeches to a stop at the front of a residence I've never seen before. I assumed we were going to Dimitri's New York compound, but I guess that was stupid of me to consider. Dimitri's crew just massacred over a hundred men. More than just local authorities will be chasing them.

The doors of the ambulance are tossed open by two large men flanking a petite blonde with big blue eyes. "Theater is prepped and ready. Take her through the double doors, into the elevator, then down one floor," instructs a lady I've never met before. She's only young, perhaps a year or two older than me. Blonde, regal-looking, and seemingly aware of who I am. Not only does the sweat beading on her forehead double when she spots my watch, fine lines crease the top of her lip. "I'll take care of Roxanne and Fien, you look after Audrey."

Although I appreciate Dimitri's quick glance my way to check I'm okay with the blonde's plan, it isn't necessary. He shouldn't feel torn between his wife and me. She's the mother of his child, and I no longer am. There's no competition. Fien needs both her mother *and* her father, and I refuse for my selfishness to steal that from her.

Besides, I rarely put myself first, so there's no chance of that changing today.

"Go," I whisper to Dimitri when his exit stalls long enough for the blonde's pencil-thin brows to join together. "I'm okay."

Dimitri lifts his chin, strays his eyes to Rocco for not even a second, then hotfoots it in the direction Ollie and a group of men dressed in white coats wheeled Audrey.

"You good?" Rocco's voice is full of suspicion, cautious of the hiss I involuntarily released while stepping down from the ambulance.

Since Fien is still cuddled in my chest, I placed our combined weight onto my sore foot to ensure my step down didn't wake her.

I shouldn't have bothered being vigilant. I've barely jerked my head up half an inch to assure Rocco I'm fine when Fien is ripped from my grasp.

"Hey!"

I'd say more if Fien responded to the woman's clutch with the devastation she displayed when I pulled her away from Maestro. She doesn't repel away from the lady like she did me. She startles, peers at her wide-eyed, then nuzzles back into her chest.

"While I get Fien settled, show Roxanne to the guest bedroom so she can get cleaned up." She spins away, takes one step, then whips back around. "The *downstairs* guest bedroom. I reserved the one on the second floor for Audrey and Dimitri." After dragging her crystal blue eyes down Rocco's blood-stained body, she purrs out, "You can stay down there too if you'd like. There are enough towels on the bed for both of you."

"Oh, we're not... we aren't..." I lose the chance to get out my stuttering reply that we're not a couple when she spins back around and stalks away, taking Fien with her.

Although my focus should remain solely on Fien, I kill two birds with one stone by asking, "Will Dimitri be okay with this?" I'm battered and bruised, but I am not so far down the rabbit hole I can't continue to fight to ensure Dimitri's wishes are being met. He has only just gotten his daughter back. I don't want her palmed from person to person like she was bounced state to state the past twenty-two months.

While rubbing at a kink in his neck, Rocco shrugs. "Dimitri isn't a fan of India's, but the fact she's Audrey's best friend means he has no choice but to put up with her."

"Oh." Now the disdain on India's face makes sense. She's defending her friend from the woman who kept her husband 'occupied' during her captivity.

Bearing in mind the circumstances, she's handling Dimitri's betrayal better than I would if it had occurred to Estelle. I wouldn't offer her husband's mistress to sleep in my guest room. If she was still breathing, she'd be in the doghouse.

Mistress. Yuck. The word alone makes me sick to my stomach, much less wondering if that's how I'm now viewed.

"No." Rocco adds a finger waggle to his abrupt reply to the question in my eyes. "I have some random dude's puke on my shirt and a ton of adrenaline to work through. I'm not up for an in-depth conversation on the uprising of deceased wives." He doesn't say how he usually expels his excessive energy after a raid, but his eyes most certainly do. "So how about we get cleaned up, fill our bellies with food, then tackle the shitstorm that comes with Audrey's rebirth?"

When I nod, cowardly bowing out of a fight I know will be the shitstorm Rocco is worried about, his lips curl at the ends. "Do you want a piggyback ride, or would you like me to carry you to your room wedding-night style?" His smile grows when confusion strains my features. "I know you're hurt, Princess P, you know you're hurt, and so the fuck does Dimitri. Why do you think he was so torn up about leaving you?"

I know what he's doing. He's trying to confirm that Dimitri cares about me in some weird, warped way, but in all honesty, his question cuts me up a little. I don't want Dimitri's attention because I'm hurt, I want it because he genuinely cares about me.

"Wedding style it is," Rocco says with a snicker when nothing but silence teems between us for the next several seconds. "It'll get more of a rile out of Dimitri, and we both know how much I like stirring that fucker."

Stealing my chance to reply, Rocco scoops me into his arms, gropes my butt in a way that isn't close to being appropriate, then charges down the hall like a groom dying to see what negligee his bride is wearing under her dress.

# 23

# ROXANNE

"The faucet is as finicky as shit, but if you like your showers scald-ing, you'll be happy."

Rocco balances his drenched shoulder onto the doorjamb separating my room from the attached bathroom before running a towel over his wet head. For a woman unprepared for guests until ten minutes before we arrived, India laid out the welcome mat. My room is made up as if it's the presidential suite at a ritzy hotel, the bathroom is brimming with toiletries that took care of the gory scent bounding out of Rocco the past three hours in less than ten minutes, and we devoured a feast fit for a king.

I could almost pretend I was whisked away for a weekend of indulgence if the right man was humming in the shower the past five minutes.

Rocco hasn't let up on his endeavor to force a response out of Dimitri one bit the past three hours. He attempted to feed me strawberries dipped in chocolate, wipe away the dribble of a juicy steak from the bottom of my lip while chewing on his own, then sat so close to me, even if I wanted to forget I was only just freed from a baby-farming trade, I couldn't.

The only good that's come from his constant attention is not having the time to think about how much has changed in the past three days. I said to Dimitri I wouldn't walk away from him as the woman I once was, but even I didn't have a clue how honest my statement was.

I'm not close to the woman I used to be. I don't necessarily believe that's a bad thing. However, I'm confident walking away from Dimitri will hurt, nonetheless.

Ignoring the pain stretched from my heart to the lower half of my stomach, I maneuver out of the cross-legged position on the floor I've been huddled in the past hour, then pad to Rocco's half of the room. He watches me, forever on alert, but seemingly at a loss on which direction he should take this time around.

We haven't stumbled anywhere near the shitstorm we feel brewing on the horizon. We bunkered down instead, preferring to ride out the storm in a shelter instead of walking into it without fear as we suggested only hours ago. It's cowardly for us to do, but when you're facing a storm as brutal as this one, only a fool would pray for impact instead of doing everything possible to avoid it.

"I really wish you'd let someone take a look at your foot," Rocco says when I stop to stand in front of him. "The ice helped with the swelling, but for all we know, it could be a twisted wreck beneath the surface."

"It's fine," I assure him for the hundredth time this evening. I can barely feel its throb. Not only has the swelling settled, nothing can compare to the pain in my chest. It's as bad as it comes. "We iced and strapped it. What more could it need?"

"Oh, I don't know," Rocco answers, unaware I wasn't asking a question. "Perhaps a splint... or how about some pain medication? That might help, too."

"Truly. I'm fine. I swear to you." I run my hand down his arm, genuinely grateful for his company the past three hours but more than ready to have a few minutes of solitude. "While I shower, why don't you head down and release some of the excess energy that has you bouncing around like an Energizer Bunny."

He smiles before shaking his head. "I'm good. I like hanging out with you."

His reply warms my heart, but it does little to weaken my campaign. "I need some time to process everything." When his brows pinch as confused by the angst in my tone as me, I make out it isn't as big a deal as it is. "I need to use the bathroom... *in private.*"

"Oh..." His pupils dilate to the size of saucers before he adds a second, "Oooh," into the mix, this one longer than his first.

Even mortified, I nod my head to the humor-filled questions in his eyes. I'd rather he believe I'm about to stink up the place than continue my struggle to hold back the wetness in my eyes. Just like I don't stand out in a crowd, I'm not one of those girls who can pull off devastation without bloodshot corneas, scary suitcase-size bags under my eyes, and a heap of snot.

India's residence is gorgeous and regal—just like her—but its walls are paper-thin. Rocco and I hear her staff's incoming arrival long before they knock on the door of my room. The knowledge makes me grateful my room is in the equivalent of the basement. I'll be out of the loop with what's going on, but since that includes reuniting couples, my inquisitiveness is more than happy to face the injustice.

After tugging on a pair of gray sweatpants sans underwear and a crisp white tee from a bag one of India's staff brought down earlier, Rocco rejoins me next to the carved wooden door that leads to the bathroom. "If you need me, call out to Smith. He's always listening."

The realization that I'm being forever watched usually comforts me. Regretfully, this time around, it doesn't. It isn't that I believe Smith will tattle on me, I'd just rather our reunion occur without the awkwardness it is already going to be filled with.

In a last-ditch attempt to rile Dimitri, Rocco presses his lips to my temple. It isn't a quick half-a-second peck. His lips linger long enough for me to hear the gurgle of his stomach when nothing but heartbreak teems between us.

I appreciate what he's doing, and I love that he still has my back even with Dimitri's wife resurrecting from the grave, but I also hate it. Audrey is fighting for her life. Now is not the time to force her to glove-up for someone she never truly lost. At the end of the day, no matter what happens, she is Dimitri's wife and the mother of his child, and I am... *nobody.*

Incapable of holding back my devastation for a second longer, I briefly lean into Rocco's embrace to accept a comfort I don't deserve before I dash into the bathroom as fast as my quivering legs will take me, shutting the door behind me.

With my eyes shut and my heart in lockdown, I squash my back against the carved wood, my tears not permitted to fall until the squeak of a second set of hinges sounds through my ears. When that occurs, my sobs are devastating. I've been holding them in for days, so I expected nothing less than pure carnage when I finally permitted them to fall. They howl through me on repeat, not slowing even when the wetness flooding my cheeks becomes too much for my swiping hands to keep up with. I cry and cry and cry until the hottest water won't remove the red streaks from my cheeks, and I fall asleep on the tiled floor, alone and heartbroken.

I lost the man I love, our child, and my principles in one night. Nothing could have prepared me for this—not even falling in love with a notorious mobster so outrageously, I'd do it all again in a heartbeat just to see the light in his eyes shift for the final time.

Fien owns Dimitri's heart.

Before Audrey stepped into his path, I was responsible for its beats.

Now I don't know which way is up.

## 24

# DIMITRI

I stop peering at my bloodstained hands when the voice of a man on the brink of exhaustion rolls through my ears. Ollie is wearing smocks like a real-life doctor. They're as blood-stained as my hands, and the knowledge it is the blood of my wife curtails my mood even more than not being given an update on her condition in hours.

I'm always a little unhinged after a raid. It causes a rush of adrenaline you can't get anywhere else—adrenaline I had planned to unleash on Roxanne until the wee hours of tomorrow morning. Instead, I'm sitting in the corridor that replicates a dungeon, waiting to see if a doctor kicked out of med school can fix the hack job someone did to the mother of my child.

I still can't believe Audrey is alive. She never showed the fight she displayed tonight once during our relationship. She was the meekest woman in the room, the one who forever shied away from controversy. I never suspected she would be able to survive the ordeal she was forced through. That's why I only ever searched for her body. I was convinced she was dead.

Shows what I know. Before Roxanne, I had never experienced the gut-tingling, ball-tightening, infuriating sensation I get when she enters the realm, but you'd think I would have felt a least a little bit of Audrey's gall. She's my wife, she carried my flesh and blood in her womb, so how could I not know she was alive, fighting to come back to me?

My frustrating debate is pushed back for another day when Ollie stops to stand in front of me. He called my name multiple times, but since I was so caught up in my thoughts, I didn't acknowledge his presence.

"Sorry, what did you say?" My voice is so rough, I don't recognize it. It's brimming with agitation and a heap of the adrenaline I've yet to disperse.

While raking his fingers through his shoulder-length hair, Ollie slots into the chair next to me. Considering we're in a residence, it should be odd acknowledging there's a fully functioning operating theater in the basement. However, since it's India, a freak in her own right, I'm not half as shocked as you'd expect.

We need to bunker down for a couple of days until the heat dies down. Although I would have preferred for that to occur anywhere but here, the realization that India has a house full of servants and access to every medical field there is had me changing tactics.

Supposedly India is in favor with an oil tycoon who has a hankering for the underworld. With the right amount of money, anyone can join some crews' ranks. That shit doesn't fly with me, though. I'd gut him just on the belief he can do what I do without earning it.

You don't get to where I am by throwing money at people. It's messy, gritty, and more fucked in the head than he'd ever understand. And more times than not, it occurs without the love of a good woman.

Perhaps that's why I can't sense Audrey as I can Roxanne? Audrey and I never shared those three little words I thought I would have to torture out of a woman before she'd ever give them to me voluntarily. Not even the day we wed saw them exchanged. We swapped rings, ate cake, then I fell into bed with a couple of hookers while Audrey went back to the honeymoon suite alone.

Fuck, I was an asshole. I still am. I just don't see Roxanne taking my shit. I was coked out of my head, but I still recall the way she ripped the blonde hooker away from me by the strands of her hair. She wanted to kill her, and in all honesty, if she had a weapon, I reckon she would have.

I scrub my hand across my mouth, hiding my inappropriately timed smirk before locking my eyes with Ollie. The way he stares at me reveals he knew my thoughts were elsewhere again, not to mention his shoulder bump. He did the same thing when he confirmed what Audrey's pregnancy test said, except back then, he was consoling me instead of livening me up.

"Is she going to make it?"

An unusual patter hits my chest when Ollie dips his chin. "She isn't out of the woods just yet, but I don't see her recovery having too many issues." As he balances on the edge of his chair, air whizzes from his nose. That's a telltale sign he's nervous. "We had to remove Audrey's uterus, ovaries, and part of her spleen. She won't be able to carry any more children."

I'm not stunned by his confession. Whoever got to Audrey made it clear if she survived the second time, she would be unable to bear children. They hacked up her uterus even more than they did when removing Fien from her stomach.

"Were there any signs she had... umm..." Who the fuck made me this whimpering, blubbering imbecile? I'm Dimitri-fucking-Petretti. I do *not* stutter.

"No," Ollie says with a shake of his head, saving me from

making a fool out of myself for the second time. "Excluding the scar from when she delivered Fien, there were no indicators that she had birthed other children."

His reply pleases me greatly. I don't want Fien to have half-siblings stretched across the globe like I had growing up. She'll only have one set. The children I'll have with Roxanne.

My cocky grin slips when Ollie discloses, "She's been asking to see you."

"She's awake?" I don't know why I sound shocked. My dead ass exposes how long I've been sitting on a hard, plastic chair, not to mention the annoying tick of my watch. I've been down here for over five hours. The delay feels as if it is slowly killing me. I don't just want to discover if Fien's cheeks are as soft as they look, I want to unearth the reason Roxanne limped when I loaded her in the ambulance Smith got onsite remarkably quick. She wordlessly assured me she was fine several times during our forty-minute ride, but I don't believe her. She's too brave to make a fuss and too fucking stubborn for her own good.

"Once you have things wrapped up here, can you take a look at Roxanne for me? I think she did something to her foot."

Ollie smiles before nodding, forever happy to please me. It makes sense when you see how much he charges for his services. "I'll stay with Audrey until she's out of recovery, then hand her over to India's crew."

After slapping him on the shoulder, issuing my praise without words, I stand to my feet.

"You coming?" I ask when he remains seated. I'm almost halfway down the corridor, yet, he hasn't walked a single stride.

My throat grows scratchy when he shakes his head. "Audrey asked to speak to you alone."

He smiles a beaming grin when my cheeks whiten. I was only married for a couple of months before Audrey was kidnapped, but even I know things aren't good when a wife requests to speak to her husband in private.

"She's pretty doped up. I doubt she'll be awake for long," Ollie says with a chuckle.

Needing to leave before I switch out his smile for a fat lip, I push through the doors he broke through a couple of minutes ago, then head toward the room Audrey was wheeled into when she was on the brink of death.

I won't lie. My footing wobbles a little when I spot her through the window of her room. She's a little pale, and she has oxygen prongs stuck in her nose, but she is as beautiful as the woman whose trek to the kitchen for a glass of water saved me from making a mistake with India I could never take back.

Audrey can turn the head of any man. She just can't make my gut tingle.

"Hey, none of that," I say when the dam in her eyes breaks upon seeing me. "You're okay. I won't let anything happen to you."

I don't know who's more shocked when I pull her into my chest so my shirt can dry her tears. I was never affectionate when we were married. Before I held Roxanne in my private jet, I had never comforted anyone.

Believing I know the reason behind her tears, I assure her, "Fien is safe. She's here, sleeping. I swear to you, she is safe."

"Fien?" Audrey's words are as weak as the bounce of her eyes. She appears truly stunned. "You named her Fien?"

"Yeah." I almost laugh at the crack of my one word. I hated the name Audrey had chosen, but now I couldn't imagine calling her anything else. "It wasn't my first choice, but you loved it, and so did your mother."

I thought my confession would lessen Audrey's sobs, not double them.

Shows how much I have to learn about women.

"Do you want me to call your parents? Tell them your safe?"

I can't believe I didn't do that instead of twiddling my thumbs the past five hours. It wouldn't have taken long to advise them their daughter is alive but organizing their flights and accommodation would have gobbled up some time.

I halt searching for my phone in my pocket when Audrey shakes her head. With how many drugs Ollie is pumping into her, it should be a weak, pathetic shake. It's nothing close to that. It was as determined as the clutch she has on my shirt and as resolute as the glint in her eyes. "I'll call them later. Once *this* all settles down."

The way she says 'this' has me suspicious she isn't solely referencing Fien, herself, and me. She was pretty out of it during our drive from Rimi's compound to here, but as Roxanne has said previously, the dead could feel the electricity brewing between us, so I'm confident a near unconscious woman would have.

Audrey will never call me out on it, though. I could go down on Roxanne in front of her, and she'd act as if I were doing something as innocent as eating breakfast.

I'm about to ask Audrey how much interaction she had with Roxanne the past three days, but the briefest tap on a window stops me. That gut-tingling sensation I mentioned missing earlier smacks into me full-pelt when my eyes stray to the noise. India is on the other side of the glass. She isn't responsible for the buzz surging my pulse with adrenaline more potent than a bloodbath. It is my daughter, who's being held in her arms.

Unlike when she was nuzzled in Roxanne's chest, Fien is wide awake, peering my way. Her eyes are more cobalt blue than I realized. Her photos failed to show the almost purple ring around her dark blue eyes. They make her eyes unique, as one of a kind as she will forever be.

When I gesture for India to join us in Audrey's room, Audrey's hand shoots out to snatch my wrist. Once she has my focus, she adds a head shake to her firm clutch. "I don't want her to see me like this. It might scare her."

I curse under my breath, frustrated I hadn't thought about that. Fien witnessed enough bloodshed today to last her a lifetime. I don't want more horrific images added to the vault.

Relief engulfs Audrey's features when I say, "All right. Once you're set up in your room, I'll organize for someone to bring Fien to see you."

Audrey smiles. It isn't the blinding one she used to give when she felt Fien kick her hand. It's more subdued than happy. "Thank you."

She loosens her grip on my wrist for barely a second before she tightens it again. When she locks her eyes with mine, an unusual spark in them reveals the words she wants to speak, her mouth simply refuses to relinquish them. I don't mind. I've only heard those words from one woman before, and I'm more than happy to keep it that way.

"Get some rest. The sooner you're back on your feet, the better it will be for all involved."

I press my lips to Audrey's temple before exiting the room, my heart racing more with every step I take. I've waited for this day for months, but instead of it happening in front of the people responsible for its occurrence, it's being witnessed by two women who have always felt more like strangers to me instead of family.

"It's okay," India coos to Fien when I hold out my hands, hopeful a demure approach won't see her releasing the tears damming in her eyes. It will break my heart if she cries when I hold her for the first time. I saw how badly her tears affected Roxanne. I don't know if I'm strong enough to endure the same torture. "It's Dada, Fien. Do you want to go to your dada?"

Months of torment, years of carnage, and a lifetime of injustices are undone when my daughter reaches out for me as I'm reaching for her. It's all forgotten in an instant, but I will never forget the people responsible for this moment. No matter which side they were on, they will stay with me forever—Roxanne included.

# 25

## ROXANNE

I wake up startled and confused. My foreign location isn't the sole cause of my bewilderment. My aching backside is responsible for the majority of it. My tailbone is screaming more than my foot. Serves me right for falling asleep on a tiled floor.

I truly didn't think I'd be left alone for hours on end, so I didn't put much thought into the location of my sob-fest. Don't get me wrong, I'm grateful for the privacy, but sometimes it's nice to have a shoulder to cry on.

Dimitri's was the first one I used. It was weird to be comforted by a man who had threatened to kill me only hours earlier. However, it displayed there was more to him than his dark and dangerous outer shell. He has a heart, a big one, and now that he has his daughter back, he has the chance to show it off.

Regretfully, it seems as if I've been shunted from the festivities again.

While grumbling about the pathetic woman I'm portraying, I clamber to my feet. Dimitri has been waiting for this moment for almost two years, so why am I annoyed he wants to relish it? I'd be mortified if he didn't at least ensure Fien settled in for the night.

Once I'm on my feet, I sway like a leaf in a summer's breeze, and white spots dance in front of my eyes. The dizziness bombarding me makes the removal of the nightgown Rocco handed me hours ago a little tedious. The one I was wearing when they rescued us was grubby and dotted with Maestro's blood, so I was more than eager to change into something fresh.

After peeling down the panties with a waistband that goes past my bellybutton, I suck in a fast breath before glancing down at the monstrous pad that should have offered more cushioning during my nap than it did.

My sigh is filled with both relief and devastation when I discover the pad is empty. I'm glad that stage of my life occurred quickly, but it will take more than a lifetime for tears not to prick my eyes when I remember the ebbs and flows of the past week.

I take a few moments drinking in my naked form in the vanity mirror. Usually, this is as uncomfortable as it gets for me. I'm not experiencing the same bother today. I look like a mess. My hair is knotted, my skin is mottled with marks, and my eyes are sunken from how much I cried, but I also look mature, strong, and undogged.

I fought, and although my victory can be accredited to the many men in Dimitri's crew, some of the credit also belongs to me. If I hadn't reached Maestro when I did, he might have left with Fien before the balaclava-clad men stormed the basement. He was mere feet from the exit. I stopped him from going through it.

That makes me proud.

That makes me strong.

And it has my chin rising instead of balancing on my chest as it has the past seven hours.

After giving my thanks to the warrior glancing back at me in the mirror, I enter the shower stall, twist on the tap until steam floats around me, then step into the heavenly hot stream of water.

I've barely drowned half the heaviness plaguing me when the heavenly gruff voice of Dimitri sends my head into a tailspin. "Eyes to the wall."

Certain I'm dreaming, I don't defy him this time around. I snap my eyes shut so fast, the scent my head is fabricating almost causes a tear to roll down my cheek. He smells so good. Dark and twisted, but oh so comforting.

My knees curve inward when the brisk scrub of a hand over a bristly chin is quickly chased by a second hand sliding around my waist. Even being afraid he might disappear won't stop me from leaning into his embrace. I'm dying to feel the heat of his skin against mine, and I am willing to risk falling out of the shower like a drunken fool to get it.

After setting my skin on fire with the briefest flutters of his fingertips over my midsection, Dimitri asks, "What did Ollie say about your foot?"

"Who?" I ask, purring. My mind is so wondrous, I don't just hear and smell Dimitri, I feel him thick and heavy behind me. He's hard like the only thing we lost the past three days was time. Our connection is as bristling as it's always been.

Dimitri peers down at me, smirking when he spots my groggy expression. "If I didn't know any better, I would have sworn you raided the liquor cabinet after dinner instead of sipping on the Sprite Rocco was adamant you must have."

I've barely gotten over the shock he's been spying on me when he stuns me for the second time. He doesn't just spin me around to face him head-on, he adds a heap of sexy words to the lusty glint in his eyes.

"Hook your sore foot around my waist. I don't want to hurt

you, but I need your cunt to squeeze my cock like I squeezed the light from Rimi's eyes an hour ago."

His confession that he just killed a man should weaken the intensity brewing between us. It doesn't. Not in the slightest. He knows as well as I do that men like Rimi Castro don't stop what they're doing with a warning. They must face whatever penalty Dimitri sees fit, and whether gutted, maimed, or killed, it will occur with haste.

Furthermore, I love how fearless he is when it comes to protecting his family. The knowledge he'd go to the ends of the earth to keep his daughter safe is the ultimate turn-on. It sees me kissing him with everything I have—teeth, tongue, hands—they all get in on the act. It's a possessive kiss, both claiming and owning. It tells him everything I'm afraid to say but would give anything to change—that I am his as long as he wants me.

My head lolls to the side with a moan when Dimitri cranks my neck a couple of minutes later so he can trail his nose down the throb in my throat. Even without his growl, I'm aware my scent has changed since the last time he smelled me. It isn't tarnished with the disaster of the past thirty-six hours, it's harmonized with hope, fortified with determination, and it has the faintest hint of his daughter's shampoo.

A shudder rolls up the length of my spine when he swipes the head of his cock across my clit. I'm buzzed all over and more than ready for the next stage of our exchange to occur.

Dimitri will never let that happen, though. He needs me wet enough to take him without pain because, for some reason, even loving the knowledge he's ruined me for any other man, he doesn't want to hurt me.

He hoists me up the shower like he did in the bathroom of my childhood home, inhales deeply, then growls when the scent of my aching sex teems into his nostrils. "You have no idea how much your smell brings me back from the brink. It can be so fucking dark, so fucking devastating, but your intoxicating scent is like a light at the end of the tunnel, forever encouraging me to find my way home."

*Home*? I almost choke on the word. It's the simplest phrase, but it has the biggest impact on my heart. I thought it had shattered beyond repair hours ago. Now it feels as if it is bigger than it was when it dawned on me that Dimitri had found us.

"Lean back, Roxanne. I'm about ready for a second helping of dessert."

After gripping my ass with his big hands, Dimitri buries his face between my legs and goes to town. He sucks my clit into his mouth, drags his tongue through the folds of my sex, and repeatedly pokes it inside of me.

He eats me for the next several minutes, his pace only slowing when the shudder wreaking havoc with my body requires him to resecure his grip on my backside.

"You better get a whole heap louder than that if you want to come, Roxie. I ain't taking no prisoners today."

He shoots his eyes to mine briefly before his head once again delves back between my legs. I call out, the sensation of him expertly eating me almost too much to bear. I was crazy to think things would ever be over between us. Our connection is too explosive to harness, too dynamic. If we tried to ignore something as destructive as the tension that forever bristles between us, it would be a catastrophe. I wouldn't be its only victim. The entire race would become extinct.

"Yes, Roxanne," Dimitri growls into my pussy when I'm blind-sided by a ferocious orgasm.

His name falls from my lips over and over again as my tugs on his drenched hair turn violent. I'm screaming, shuddering, and on the verge of waking up the entire neighborhood with my begs for him not to stop.

With how crazy he makes me feel, I should be doing the exact opposite. I should beg for him to stop before getting on my knees and returning the favor, but for the life of me, I can't. The controls of my body are no longer mine to command. They've been relinquished, handed over. They're at the complete control of Dimitri, who takes what he wants, offers nothing in return, but continues to defy the dark, dangerous man he was raised to be.

He ravishes me until my orgasm stretches from one to two. It is a beautifully brutal few minutes, enhanced by the connection of our eyes when he makes his way from my throbbing, drenched sex to my face.

He licks my peaked nipples during his trek, but the hankering in my eyes exposes how badly I need his lips on mine. I want to kiss him. Possess him. Make him as wild as he makes me.

The crash of our lips is brutal. It blazes heat through me, making me grateful the water has switched from scalding to lukewarm. We kiss for several long minutes. It's an almost frantic, somewhat rough, and very much wild exchange. Hands go everywhere, and before I know it, one is guiding the head of Dimitri's impressive cock to the opening of my pussy.

"Look at me." I'm reminded just how tall he is when my elevated position means I don't have to crank my neck to look at him. Even with my head almost reaching the top of the tiles, he's right in front of me as dark and dangerous as ever.

It's the fight of my life to hold back my excitement for the third time when the collision of our eyes causes cum to erupt out of Dimitri's cock. He coats my pussy with his spawn, both inside and out, since he's too impatient to wait until he finishes coming before notching his cock inside me.

Once almost all his impressive shaft is stuffed inside of me, he darts his tongue between my lips, then kisses the living hell out of me. The pure possessiveness fueling his kiss doubles the wetness between my legs in an instant, and it has me on the brink of ecstasy even faster than that.

"That's better," Dimitri grunts with a steady rock of his hips. "Wet, screaming, and fucking relentless. The only way you should ever be seen."

He thrusts into me faster, stronger, and deeper with every pump he does. Within minutes, a familiar sensation tightens my muscles all over again. The thought of how fast he makes me come undone hazes my mind as quickly as it speeds up the rocks of his hips.

"I love the way your cunt tugs at my dick. Forever begging." He locks his eyes with mine. They have the memorable glint I'll never stop striving for. "Just like your eyes. So fucking greedy for more... but only from me. You don't want anyone but me."

After adjusting the span of my thighs, he drives into me like a madman, getting lost in the same uncontrollable ruckus over-whelming every inch of me. I saw the strong, impenetrable man he is earlier tonight, but this is the sexier version. The control he exerts in the bedroom is unbelievable. He uses every muscle in his body to please me, and even when I've been brought to climax multiple times, he continues his relentless pursuit until my legs either give out or we collapse from exhaustion.

I can see how tired he is, feel it in the weary muscles I cling to as he drives me to hysteria, but he doesn't give in. He never tires. He gives it his all until I'm quivering and convulsing like the water turned cold hours ago.

"Fuck, Roxie," Dimitri moans on a groan, his rocks unwaver-ing. "You're so fucking beautiful when you come."

The volume of my moans jumps up a couple of decibels, inspired by his praise. I've been called cute, spunky, and sexy, but beautiful is new, and I fucking love it. It has another orgasm building inside of me. This feels more threatening than my earlier one. It spreads warmth through me, thickening my veins with the adrenaline Dimitri is trying to dimmish by pounding the living hell out of me.

He drives into me so deeply it feels as if his cock is poking more than my uterus. It's painful but crazily exciting. So much so, I succumb to my next orgasm even faster than I did my first.

As my nails dig into Dimitri's shoulders, his name falls from my lips over and over again. My screams are as uncontrollable as the orgasm rolling through me. It's almost too much, too over-whelming, too fucking good for me ever to believe this isn't a dream. It won't relent. No matter how loud I scream, it won't free me from the madness. It holds on firmly, gripping me as well as Dimitri's gaze spears my heart. He's staring straight at me, increasing the shards of pleasure shredding through me so much, I have no chance of holding back the words floating over my tongue the past hour. "I love you, Dimi. I love you so fucking much."

"There it is," he replies with a grunt, his pumps picking up like they had any more to give. "Now, let's see if I can work it out of you without another set of back-to-back orgasms."

With my legs curled around his waist and his smirk increasing the likelihood he will accomplish his objective before we reach the main part of my room, Dimitri shuts down the faucet, throws open the shower door, then walks me toward the turned-down bed.

His toss onto my mattress is playful this time around. It even arrives with a little giggle, which is pushed aside for a moan when he leans over to suck a budded nipple into his mouth.

Since the cold shower water has given my skin a blue tinge, the mottling of bruises on my thighs and hips are barely noticeable when Dimitri directs his focus a couple of inches lower. I was fortunate to get good genes from my nanna. Even when it's been put through the wringer, my skin heals rather decently.

Take the scar on my forehead, for example. Since the chemical peel Dimitri organized the first night of our arrangement, I haven't needed to cover it up with my bangs. I'm almost at a point I feel comfortable growing out my bangs. That might have more to do with how Dimitri lavishes every inch of me than anything, but it feels nice to have finally reached this stage.

When Dimitri's chin rests at the apex of my sex, I assume he's about to once again devour the feast growing more pungent with every nip, lick, and bite he does, so you can imagine my utter despair when he stops a couple of inches away from what I believe is his projected target.

There's no bump in my belly—even if I were still pregnant, there wouldn't be—but Dimitri cups it as if there is before he raises his eyes to me. My brain screams at me to tell him the truth, to expose that he didn't just right Audrey and Fien's injustices tonight, but I can't. There's too much life in his eyes for me to douse, too much happiness. I'm partly responsible for the misery they've held the past twenty-two months, so I refuse to steal the light from them for the second time.

I will tell him what happened, just not tonight, not when he finally feels capable of gulping in an entire breath. Instead, I tell him the only thing that matters, and since it is straight-up honest, not even the crackling of my words can take away from its authenticity.

"I love you, Dimitri Petretti. Your fierceness, your craziness, your protectiveness. I love it all... as will your children."

# 26

# DIMITRI

I shoot Rocco a warning look, wordlessly suggesting he keep his riling comment in his mouth or risk losing some teeth. I'm not sneaking out of Roxanne's room at five in the morning because I'm ashamed we treated India's guest bedroom as if it's a brothel. I didn't unyieldingly pound my cock into Roxanne's mouth to lower her moans. I love how out of control she is in the bedroom. She forever puts everyone first, *except* when we're messing the sheets. There, nothing but chasing the next thrill is on her mind.

The same can be said for me, except I'm not seeking the quick, unenjoyable releases I sought before Roxanne stormed into my life. I want all the shit that comes before it. The flickers in her eyes, the scent of her sweat-slicked skin, her little declarations of love I had no clue I'd crave more than the drugs that regularly tracked through my veins as a teen. They thrill me even more than knowing Rimi finally got what was coming to him.

He chirped like a bird, tattled like the rat he is, yet, he's still dead. Killed by my hands under the watchful eye of Henry Gottle, the now rightful boss of all bosses. He came to the plate for me like no one else has in this industry. It earned him both my respect and my backing.

Forever willing to test my patience, Rocco ignores my unvoiced threat. "Your sneaking around is making me feel dirty." He shivers like someone just walked over his grave. "Do you mind if I borrow your shower again so I can wash off the funk? I promise to get undressed in the bathroom this time around."

I close Roxanne's door harder than intended before sliding out a key from my pocket and slotting it into the lock. I asked Rocco to come here so Roxanne wouldn't wake up alone in a foreign place, with her head still a little murky about what happened yesterday, not to make himself fucking comfortable.

I'd stay myself if I didn't want to offer Fien the same level of comfort. She didn't cry when I held her for the first time last night, but her wish to stay in my arms ended the instant India attempted to leave the room.

I'm keen to change that.

I don't want to be a hero, but I do want to be the man my daughter runs to when she's in trouble.

"Make sure Roxanne has something to eat when she wakes. She needs to recoup her energy."

I'm not bragging, Roxanne's moans could be heard two states over, I'm just—*all right, maybe I am bragging.* I'll fluff out my feathers and strut like a peacock if it gives Rocco the hint to fuck off. He played his hand. I won his chips. He isn't ready for round two.

"And stay out of her room." I thrust the key for Roxanne's room into Rocco's palm with more force than what is needed, hopeful it will get my message across. "Smith may not be watching, but he's always listening."

Like a perfectly-timed skit—or perhaps a sick fucking pervert —Smith's voice booms out of both Rocco and my cell phones not even a second later. "Fuckin' oath I am." His voice has the same springy edge Rocco and mine has.

Victory has a way of making the toughest men sound soft and the weakest men sound strong.

Once our joint laughter has settled, Smith clears the humor from his voice before adding, "When you've finished settling Fien, Ollie has been buzzing you most of the morning. I told him you didn't want to be disturbed, but he said it was important."

"Is it about Fien?" When a hum of rejection vibrates out of my cell, I ask, "Roxanne?"

"No." I can't tell if Smith's sigh is in frustration or humor. It may be a combination of both. "But she is the reason he didn't get a chance to assess Roxanne yesterday."

It takes me replaying what he said through my head three times before my brain finally clicks on. I'm so fucking high on the good shit money can't buy, I completely forgot my wife is holed up in a hospital bed downstairs, so unwell, she couldn't have any visitors last night. Not even our daughter.

"Tell Ollie I'll be down as soon as I can."

Acting ignorant to the regret in my tone, Smith replies, "On it," before he disconnects our connection.

"Don't bother," I say to Rocco when he attempts to tell me I have nothing to be regretful about.

Guilt is eating me alive, but it has nothing to do with Roxanne. She put her life on the line for a child she had never met—*my* child. I'll never feel guilty about relaying how much that meant to me, and don't get me started on the fact she loves me, or I may never leave this room.

"Just make sure she eats, okay? I'll handle the rest."

With my mood uneased, it takes me a little longer to reach Fien's room than my travels last night when I headed in the opposite direction. Once I was assured Fien was settled and safe, I practically sprinted for Roxanne's room, my race only slowing when I discovered someone had locked her door.

Rocco assured me it wasn't him, but he was determined to find out who it was.

It's fortunate the keys in this residence open *all* the locks, or my wish to join Roxanne in the shower would have been thwarted by me kicking down her door.

The guilt I was experiencing only minutes ago pummels back into me when the creak of Fien's door is gobbled up by someone singing a lullaby. I don't recognize the words since they're foreign, but their flow is oddly similar to "Hush Little Baby." It seems like the type of nursery rhyme you'd sing if a baby was upset.

My intuition is proven right when my glance into Fien's crib comes up empty. She isn't curled into the corner of the wooden crib she's a couple of months too big for, she's resting on India's chest, her breathing in sync to the gentle rocks India does in an antique rocking chair.

It takes everything I have to hold back my naturally engrained vicious tongue when India shakes her head at my silent approach. She glares at me like I have no right to look over my flesh and blood before she presses her finger to her lips.

Stupidly believing she's in control around here, she gestures for someone in the room next to Fien's to enter before she attempts to stand to her feet.

I work my jaw side to side when she shunts away my endeavor to assist her to her feet with another brisk shake of her head. It's clear she's pissed. I guarantee she isn't the only one. I basically skipped out of Roxanne's room since my mood was so carefree and light. Now I won't be able to take one fucking step without waking the entire continent.

"Can I speak with you outside." Anyone who doesn't know

India would assume she's asking a question. I don't face that issue —regretfully. She isn't asking for a quiet word. She's demanding.

I should tell her to fuck off before reminding her who's running the show around here, then I should put plans into play to change our hideout location to anywhere but here, but since India is Audrey's best friend, and Audrey will need her support when I advise her I don't believe couples need to stay together purely for their children, I hold back the urge—barely.

It's a fucking hard feat. The strain is heard in my voice when I ask, "What is this about?"

India splays her hands across her hips before arching a brow. "Seriously? You're going to act clueless as to why I've spent the last four hours comforting *your* daughter." I'm about to tell her to cut the theatrics before I do worse to her vocal cords, but she continues talking, stealing my gamble, "Your wife is in a hospital bed fighting for her life, your daughter just came out of a life-threatening ordeal, yet you spent the last four hours fucking your current side-dish whore of the month."

I try to keep a cool head. I tell myself time and time again that I don't give a fuck what India thinks, but I lose my cool when the word 'whore' rings on repeat in my ears.

Just like she did in the limousine all those months ago, India freezes like a statue when I pin her to the wall outside of Fien's room by her throat. "Who I fuck is none of your business." My words are as cold as ice, but as quiet as a wilted leaf blowing over a frozen pond. "It wasn't anytime you tried to weasel your way into my bed *after* I married your best friend, and it wasn't the many times you encouraged me to move on when you thought she was dead, so why the fuck do you care now?" I don't wait for her to answer me. I just hit her where it hurts. "Because you know Roxanne is more than a side-dish whore, and you're worried—"

"Of course, I am. Audrey is my best friend." She shouldn't be able to talk through the brutal clutch I have on her throat, but as Rocco has said previously, bitches don't stay down even when they should. "She deserves to be treated better than you're treating her, and so does Fien."

I compress her throat a little tighter, ensuring I get across my point before snarling out, "This has *nothing* to do with Fien."

I squeeze and squeeze and squeeze until her pulse is nearly nonexistent, and then I let her go.

A smart woman would shut the fuck up before licking her wounds in private.

India clearly isn't smart.

"She bludgeoned herself to secure your attention, but it still wasn't enough for you, was it? What will it take for you to pay her an ounce of attention, Dimi? Her life? Fien's?" My hands firm into tight balls during her last question. "She fought with the strength you said she'd never have, maintained it for almost two years, yet you still ignore her."

"You're lying." My short statement is an overall generalization of what she said.

I agree, Audrey is stronger, but I don't know what to think about the first half of her statement. Audrey is a meek, shy woman who'd prefer to die a painful death than face any type of angst head-on, so it seems odd for her to use brutality as a way of demanding attention. She didn't want my attention for the first few weeks of our 'courtship.' I had to show her otherwise.

India waits for our eyes to lock and hold before she shakes her head, assuring I see the truth in them. "That's why Ollie has been trying to reach you all night. Audrey's wounds were self-inflicted. She used the knife you dropped when you couldn't take your eyes off Roxanne because she knew *everything* she had strived for the past twenty-two months wasn't going to happen. You had moved on." When the honesty in her tone stumps me of a reply, she uses my unusual quiet to her advantage. "Prove her wrong, Dimi. Chase her like you did when she was the one rejecting you."

"It isn't that simple. Things have changed."

India pulls a 'duh' face. Considering the intensity of our situation, her response is ridiculous. "Yeah, they have. You have a daughter together. A family—"

"And I'm going to have a child with another woman." I almost say to a woman I love but realizing our raised voices have gained us an audience harnesses my reply. It's barely dawn, but India's home is brimming with people. Most are staff, but I don't give a fuck. I hate having my personal business aired. Why do you think I've been so quiet about Fien's birth? Most fathers shout their triumphs from the rooftop. I kept it under wraps because I knew it was the best way to keep her safe.

I plan to do the same now that she is freed. I'm not hiding her because I believe I am incapable of protecting her. I'm doing it so she can grow up without needing to prove she isn't as grubby as her surname. My father shrouded our family name with so much controversy, I can't even say it without tasting dirt.

My brows join together when India whispers, "She hasn't told you."

"Told me what?" I hate falling for her tricks, but I'm tired and overwhelmed, so my change-up can be easily excused.

After rising to her feet, India straightens out her nightwear before moving to stand in front of us. Her breath, which is awfully minty for the early hour, fans my lips when she says, "Roxanne isn't pregnant. She never was."

Now I know she is lying. I saw the test myself. From Roxanne peeing in the cup to Dr. Bates dipping the test into her urine, I saw every step—just as I did Audrey's.

"Spurting lies will get you killed," I spit out in warning. "It'll do you best to remember that."

I anticipate for India to come out swinging—she's worse than Theresa when it comes to retaliation, so you can imagine my shock when her eyes soften a mere second before she scoops my hand into hers. "The sedative Smith gave to numb the site of Roxanne's tracker had traces of the HGC hormone."

She's losing me with the technical talk. I'm a father, but I have no clue about anything related to pregnancy and hormones.

"An increase in the HCG hormone in both blood and urine usually indicates a pregnancy, but in Roxanne's case, that isn't what happened." She steps back, folds her arms in front of her chest, then adds, "If you don't believe me, ask Smith. Or better yet, the real mother of your child."

Smith's lack of interruption reveals he's listening in on our conversation, because the only time he goes quiet is when he's being proven wrong.

With my mood souring, my words get snappy. "Did the sedative you gave Roxanne have HCG in it?"

It takes Smith a couple of seconds to reply, "Yes, but the amount was small."

"Enough to make a pregnancy test positive?" When nothing but silence resonates out of my phone for the next several seconds, my last nerve is obliviated. "Smith..."

He huffs, hating that I'm listening to a single thing India has to say. He doesn't dislike her as much as Rocco, but he isn't friendly with her either. "I doubt it."

"Doubt it or *know*. Those are two entirely different things."

He punishes his keyboard long enough to notch my annoyance from a five to an eight before he replies, "Her sedative could have *possibly* resulted in a false positive."

Disappointment is the last thing I expected to feel, but it is *all* I'm feeling. I liked the idea of Roxanne being knocked up with my baby, not to mention having the chance to experience all the things I missed with Fien. Her first word, the horrendous teething India harped on about yesterday, her first steps. There are so many things I can't get back but had planned to replicate with my child with Roxanne.

I guess I'll just have to get her knocked up again.

I can't pretend I'm disappointed by the prospect.

"Where are you going?" India asks, shocked.

Smith's frustration is a thing of the past when he snickers about my reply, "To fix an injustice."

Since my steps are thumping, India has to shout to ensure I hear her scorn, "You are seriously delusional! Your mistress fakes a pregnancy, then lies about it, but instead of killing her as you would have any other woman, you encourage her lies."

She should be glad I walked away because if I was within touching distance of her, I would finish what I started only moments ago. "Roxanne didn't lie about anything. She *thought* she was pregnant. She still does." My last three words don't come out as irritable as my first couple.

I'm a prick, have always been a prick, and will forever be a prick, but I'm not looking forward to breaking Roxanne's heart when I tell her she isn't pregnant with my kid just yet. I'll make it right. It may just take a couple of attempts.

Once again, I'm not disappointed at the prospect.

India throws her hands into the air, her nostrils flaring as she gets lost in her anger. "She doesn't *think* she's pregnant. She *knows* she isn't. Audrey said she had her period the first night at the ranch."

When I jackknife back, certain she's lying, the smugness on her face is almost her undoing. I've wanted an excuse to kill her for years, and her self-righteous expression may very well be her undoing.

Clueless as to how close to death she is, India steps closer to me. "Let me guess, she didn't tell you that either, did she?"

It's weaselly for me to shake my head, but I'm too stunned to think up another response. Roxanne acted odd when I cupped her stomach last night, but I figured she was still in shock she was about to become a mother.

Now I'm not so sure.

"If you're lying..." I don't finalize my threat. I take a deep breath and exhale before letting my glare take care of it on my behalf.

"I'm not lying, Dimi," India assures, as cool as a cucumber. "And I have the means to prove it if you can't trust the word of your mistress."

Ignoring Rocco's warning glance behind India's shoulder, I lift my chin, accepting her offer. I've only just stopped being fucked in the ass by my enemies. I'm nowhere near ready for round two, so if what India is saying is true, someone is about to die. I just have no clue who it will be. Should I kill the people responsible for unearthing the truth so my reputation remains intact, or the person lying to me? Thirty seconds ago, I would have swayed toward the former. Now I have no fucking clue which way is up.

## 27

# ROXANNE

Yesterday, I awoke with exhaustive, tired muscles. Today, I woke in the same manner, except this time, it wasn't the horrid, my-world-has-been-ripped-out-from-beneath-me feeling. It was filled with euphoria, adrenaline, and a happy little buzz in the bottom of my stomach I assumed I'd never experience again.

Dimitri can be thanked for that.

Last night went above and beyond anything we've ever done. He was attentive and sweet. He truly rocked my world. I've been on cloud nine for the past two hours, and if the scent mingling in the air is anything to go by, it is onward and upward from here. We still have a lot to discuss and a heap of issues to work through, but the cloud above my head doesn't seem anywhere near as dense as it did only yesterday.

"Good morning," I breathe groggily in the direction I sense Dimitri's presence.

I like my water scalding hot, and with my mood being extra diva-like this morning, I've gone over my allotted four-minute time slot. I've also glammed myself up, hopeful silky-smooth legs and gleaming skin will add to the seductive sparkle in my eyes.

"Would you care to join me for a mid-morning shower?"

After opening the shower door, releasing the fog making my head extra woozy, I lock my eyes with Dimitri. He has his shoulder propped up on the doorjamb. Unlike when he left our room in the early hours of this morning, his jaw is tight, and the veins in his hands are bulging like he's open and closed them multiple times since we parted.

"Is everything okay?"

Concerned by his quiet, I shut down the faucet, shove my arms into my hideous Fran Drescher-inspired dressing gown Dimitri packed for me, knot the cord into place, then float to his side of the room.

Well, I really shouldn't say float. I stumble like a newborn foul, suddenly fretful by his glare. He's only stared at me like this twice before. The first time was when he had a gun held at my head, and the second time was mere minutes before he forced me to hold a gun to my mother's head.

"What did my mother do?" If it's anything close to the horrid thoughts in my head, I don't know if I can pardon her again. She killed her own flesh and blood. She should have never come back from that. The only reason she has so far is because I'm too much of a chicken to make her pay for her injustices. I agree with Dimitri, insolent people should be punished, but it's hard when the person deserving of your fury is your parent.

I stop seeking answers from Dimitri's eyes when he says, "I need you to get dressed and come with me."

The dread his words were soaked in scorches the back of my throat. It has me more worried than the anger pumping out of him. "Can we please not do this again. If you believe my mother needs to be punished, punish her. I won't hold it against you, I swear."

"Your mother isn't the issue," Dimitri replies in a cool, calculated bark.

Even with his vacillating anger wanting me to call a timeout, I can't help but ask, "Then who is?"

It feels as if more than water circles the drain when Dimitri mutters, "You are."

"Me?" I touch my chest like I'm five. "What did I do?" I swallow to soothe my dry throat before confessing to something that's been burning a hole in my heart the past sixteen-plus hours. "If this is about the mark on Fien's arm, that wasn't from me." I cringe, hating my inability to lie. "Well, it could have been me, but it wasn't on purpose. I had to get her away from Maestro before he fell on her." When confusion crosses his features, I try to settle it. "Maestro is what the women called one of the head guys in Rimi's crew. He was taken down while he had Fien clutched under his arm. I had to grab her to pull her out of the line of fire. I never meant to hurt her, Dimi. I swear to God."

My confession soothes the deep groove between his brows, but it doesn't fully eradicate it. "I still need you to come with me. I'm out of my depth, and I have no fucking clue who's holding my head beneath the surface." His voice comes out composed but with a hint of anger.

Happy he's endeavoring to curb his dominance and eager to have him forgetting the worry his comment etched his face with, I nod before making a beeline for the bag resting by the door. I selected an outfit before I entered the bathroom, but Dimitri's wavering personalities ensures I'll need a jacket. He truly is one of the hardest people to read. For all I know, my lips could be about to turn a shade of blue.

Once I've dressed under Dimitri's watchful gaze, I follow his somber walk up a glamorous staircase. I'm hopeful his dour mood is because he kept his distance while I was getting dressed, but something tells me it's much bigger than his inability to keep his hands to himself.

It's obvious he isn't in the mood for chit-chat, but my Nanna always said my inquisitiveness would get me in trouble. "Did you see Fien this morning?"

Dimitri hums out an agreeing murmur before gesturing for me to enter a corridor before him. Since it's lined with exquisite antiques, we can't walk side by side. Dimitri's shoulders are too wide for that.

"And what about Audrey? Have you seen her today?" The jealousy in my voice can't be helped. Audrey is a beautiful woman, she is also the mother of Dimitri's child, so I have a lot to be jealous about. Dimitri spent the night with me, in my bed, but he snuck out in the wee hours of this morning like he didn't want anyone to know where he was.

That stings. Not a lot, but enough to make me feel a little sick to the stomach.

I can't tell if his murmur is a yes or a no this time around. It appeared more a growl than a hum like he's more frustrated than pleased his wife was resurrected from the dead.

With his moods a little hard for me to read, this is the last thing I should say. "If you have time today, I'd like to sit down and discuss what happened at Dr. Bates's office... T-t-the pregnancy test." I bite the inside of my cheek, loathing the stutter of my words.

I wish I could keep our conversation on the back burner for months, but that would be wrong for me to do. He has a right to know what happened to our child as much as he has the right to mourn the loss with me.

A tangy copper taste fills my mouth when Dimitri replies, "We can do that now."

"Oh... okay." I follow him into a room at the end of the hallway, grateful our talk will be in private.

I barely make it two steps into the dimly lit space when I'm tempted to walk right back out of it. We're not alone as first thought. Smith and Rocco are here as is Audrey's best friend, India. Then there's a man in a white doctor's coat standing next to an identical lot of equipment that soared me too great heights four nights ago before it all came crashing down.

"What's going on?" I choke out, almost stuttering.

When my question falls on deaf ears, I shift on my feet to face Dimitri. His expression is as cold as his icy blue eyes. He knows I'm keeping something from him, but instead of asking me what it is, he's gone down his usual route.

He wants to torture the truth from me one painful memory at a time.

Although my anger is brewing, I try to keep things amicable. "Can I please speak with you alone? This is a conversation that needs to occur between us."

My neck cranks to my left when India mumbles under her breath, "So you can fill his head with more lies?"

Even having no reason to defend myself to her, I snap out, "I haven't lied."

"So, you told him you're *not* pregnant?" India asks with a raised brow and a stern glare. "He knows you're no longer carrying his child?"

"No." For one word, it shouldn't crack my voice the way it did. It was almost as fragile as my heart feels. This isn't a conversation I wanted to have with spectators. It could only be more uncomfortable if it were happening while I was naked. "But that's because I haven't had the chance." I spin back around to face Dimitri. My fast movements cause a rush of dizziness to bombard my head, but I continue on, preferring to face an interrogation head-on than cower like a coward. "I lost our baby the first night I was taken. Maestro did an ultrasound on a machine just like that—"

"*Puh-leaze.* Like a hired goon would know how to turn on a sonograph machine, much less use it."

I continue talking as if India never interrupted me, "After discovering I was around six to eight weeks along, he hit me in the stomach, then kicked me over and over again." Tears spring in my eyes just recalling what happened. "When he couldn't kill our baby with brutality, he tried another way." Big salty blobs roll down my cheeks when Dimitri cups my jaw. His hands are so large, they take up almost all my face, and the callouses on his fingers scratch my cheek when he wipes away my tears. "They had hospital-like rooms on the lower level of the ranch. There was medical equipment, pads, and a whole heap of other things I don't want to remember."

India huffs again, but I don't care. Dimitri seems to believe me, and that's all that matters.

"He was going to..." I make a hand gesture that shouldn't speak on my behalf, but it somehow does. "... but Audrey stopped him. She hit him over the head, then helped me get away."

Now I feel bad about what Dimitri and I did last night. I thought it was the start of something magical, where in reality, it was the commencement of me being his mistress. He's married, and the woman he is married to did her best to save our child. I owe her more credit than I'm giving her.

After sucking down a nerve-cleansing breath, I finish my story on a somber note, "Unfortunately, it was too late. I miscarried our baby the following morning." I step closer to Dimitri, not wanting the slightest snippet of air between us when I say, "I wanted to tell you last night, but you were riding the high of your victory. I didn't want to steal the glory from you." I stray my eyes around the room, noting the remorse on both Smith and Rocco's faces. India's is nowhere near as repentant as theirs. "I'm sorry I had to tell you like this, with an audience, but I didn't lie. I just omitted the truth for a more appropriate time."

"Please tell me you're not believing her sob story," India gabbles out when Dimitri's thumb switches from wiping away my tears to tracking the curve of my kiss-swollen lips. "I doubt she was pregnant to begin with. Who has a miscarriage and only bleeds for an hour or two?" I feel both sorry and angry when India mutters, "It doesn't work that way. I know because I've had plenty of miscarriages." She races to the doctor's side I had forgotten was in the room. "Tell them. Tell him how unlikely her story is."

The gentleman I'd guess to be mid-sixties coughs to clear his throat before saying, "It is unlikely to only bleed for a couple of hours."

"But possible?" Smith jumps in like he too knows how it feels to be put on the spot when predicting medical anomalies.

The doctor lowers his chin, his head-bob somewhat cowardice. "But possible."

After glaring at the doctor with a stare as woeful as Satan, India locks her eyes with mine, then snaps out, "Fine. If they want to believe your sob act, prove you were really pregnant."

"How can I prove it?" The hesitation in my question is understandable. I'm still new to all of this. "Maestro didn't print out memory keepsakes for me."

India steps closer to me, her hips swinging like she's on a runway instead of a warpath. "Dr. Klein can do a quick ultrasound of your uterus. If you recently lost a baby..." she air quotes her last word like she doesn't believe a single thing I said, "... he will be able to tell."

"Is that true?" Dimitri's tone is a mixture of annoyed and hopeful. I thought he was on my side, so the unease in his voice is a little off-putting.

The doctor dips his chin. This one is more headstrong than his earlier one. "Yes. Pockets inside the uterine wall can indicate if a pregnancy was recently dissolved." The way he mutters 'dissolved' makes me sick to my stomach. I didn't dissolve my pregnancy. Our child was taken away from me against my will. I didn't do anything wrong. I am not at fault. I fought with everything I had.

As I will again now. "Okay. I agree to do your sonograph."

"You don't need to do this, Roxanne."

Although I appreciate Dimitri's sudden return to the plate with a bigger bat, it comes too late. The ugly head of doubt has already been raised.

I whip around to face Dr. Klein so quickly, my hair slaps my face. "Where do you want me?"

When he places a pillow on the opposite end of the bed, I side-step him, shrug off my coat, then lay down. I don't peer at the monitor every set of eyes in the room arrow in on when he lifts my shirt and squirts gel onto my stomach. I scan Dimitri's face, knowing there's only seconds before the distrust in his eyes switches to remorse.

I hate that he needs to bring in outsiders to trust me, but I also understand it. He can't even trust family, so why did I stupidly believe I ever stood a chance?

I renege on my wish to watch Dimitri's every expression when he asks a few seconds later, "What's that?"

My eyes shoot to the monitor so fast, my head grows woozy. I scan the black and white image like a crazy woman, seeking anything similar to the jelly-bean shape blob I saw days ago.

I don't find a single thing close to a baby. I discover why when Dr. Klein says, "That's Roxanne's ovary. It's badly damaged."

"Because she miscarried?" Dimitri asks before I can.

Sprinkles of salt and pepper hair fall into Dr. Klein's eyes when he shakes his head. "No. Excluding miscarriages in the fallopian tube, they don't affect the female reproductive system. Roxanne has what we call PCOS. Polycystic ovary syndrome. It is a hormone disorder commonly found in women of reproductive age."

"Which can cause long-term infertility issues," India jumps in, her tone smug. "So not only are Roxanne's chances of becoming pregnant again extremely low, *if she was even pregnant to begin with*, she couldn't have conceived without help."

I return her glare before requesting for Dr. Klein to check the pockets he mentioned earlier, dying to hit that smug bitch where it hurts.

Dr. Klein once again clears his throat before going to work. He taps and clicks on his sonogram machine numerous times before he pushes his glasses up his nose and says matter-of-factly, "I can't see any indication Roxanne was ever pregnant."

"What?" I blurt out at the same time a collection of hisses roll across the room. "Check again. You must not be seeing things right. Maestro said I was six to eight weeks along." I lift my shirt to my bra before tugging my pants down so they're low on my hips. "You're not far enough down. He scanned right above my pubic bone."

India tells me to stop being ridiculous, Smith and Rocco back up my request for Dr. Klein to check again, and Dimitri stares at my stomach for three painfully long seconds before he pivots on his heels and races out of the room, knocking over the free-standing sonogram machine on his way out.

Both my head and my heart scream for me to go after him, but for the life of me, I can't get my legs to move. I've seen firsthand what he does to people who betray him, and considering it feels as if my life is just getting started, I don't want it ended just yet.

# 28

# DIMITRI

A roar rips from my throat when I throw my fist into the concrete pillar holding up the top story of India's residence. It sends pain shooting up my arm and down my spine, but I don't hold back. I punch and punch and punch until my fists are bloody, my heart is colliding with my ribs just as dangerously, and my wish to kill is only ramping up.

A million phrases played through my head this morning. Little snippets of all the conversations I've had the past couple of days have been on a nonstop loop. India's sworn testimony that Roxanne is playing me for a fool. Smith presenting evidence on sedatives causing false positive pregnancy tests, and just now, Roxanne's heartbreaking confession on how she was treated the first night under Rimi's care. They rolled through my head on repeat, only stopping when I hinged every belief I've ever had on a simple sonogram.

It should have cleared everything up.

Science has a way of making liars truthful and the truthful dead.

That didn't happen today. Roxanne's ultrasound raised more doubt than it gave answers. Not because I believe what Dr. Klein said but because not only has Roxanne given me no reason to doubt her, she has evidence to back up her claims. Bruises I somehow missed, nicks I brushed off as grazes because I was too busy basking in the glory of my win to make sure she had made it out of the carnage without a scratch, and the faintest bruise on her hip that looks like the imprint of a man's boot.

Roxanne has said time and time again that the person responsible for Fien's captivity was a woman. Although it's clear Rimi was the ringleader behind the organization who staged my daughter's captivity, I agree with Roxanne.

Furthermore, if Roxanne's abduction was purely about money, they wouldn't have harmed our child. Fien's captivity netted the Castro entity millions of dollars each year, so imagine how much I would have paid to guarantee the safety of two of my children, not to mention the woman I love.

The fact they forced Roxanne through every woman's worst nightmare exposes my fatal flaw.

I gloated a victory I've yet to win.

Basked in an ambiance that isn't mine to savor.

I let Roxanne down in a way I never thought possible, and I've threatened to kill her more than once.

I've said it before, and I'll say it again, I'm a fucking asshole.

That stops today.

I can't change what happened to Roxanne. I can't undo the hurt she endured, but I can ensure it won't happen again. I've just got to play the game as I've been taught, show my enemies I'm not to be messed with, and I must do it without Roxanne by my side because, as far as my enemies are concerned, the only way you can teach a bird how to fly is by pushing her out of the nest.

# 29

# ROXANNE

"It isn't as it seems. I swear to God, I have no clue what happened back there."

"It's okay," Rocco assures me, his pace lowering so he can rub my arm reassuringly. "I don't give a fuck what the Doc said. We know the truth."

I want to believe his 'we' is referring to him and Dimitri, but regretfully, the knot in my gut won't allow me to portray a brainless bimbo. He was referencing Smith, who has done everything in his power to discredit Dr. Klein's integrity for the past two hours. He combed through decades of records, sought any insurance claims that may have been settled out of court, and he even reached out to his ex-wife. All avenues were extinguished without the slightest spark being ignited. Unlike Dr. Bates, Dr. Klein's records are as clean as a whistle.

Smith said he would continue scouring for evidence. Fien is back, so he has nothing else to fill his time, but I told him not to bother. There's only one person I want to believe me, and he's been ignoring Rocco's calls as often as he would mine if I knew his cell phone number.

"Do you know how long we're planning to camp out here for?" I ask Rocco just as we reach my room.

He scrubs at the fine hairs on his chin. "First plan was for three or four days. That's about how quickly the media would move on to another story. When the public interest shifts, so do the Feds."

It sucks to agree with him, but I do.

"But things are a little muddled now." He opens my door before gesturing for me to enter before him. "No one was expecting to find Audrey alive." I'm surprised he sounds more annoyed than relieved. Although he works for Dimitri, he is also his best friend, so shouldn't he be happy he got his little family back? "Since she's not fit to fly, we could be here a little longer."

"Great."

After flopping onto the mattress, I throw a hand over my eyes. I'm not tired, I just want to hide the tears the ruffling of Dimitri and my combined scents caused my eyes.

I'm so damn emotional lately. Take my exchange with India when Dimitri raced out of the room like his ass was on fire. She called me a homewrecking whore, and I just stood there and took it. I didn't slap her. I didn't put her in her place. I just stared at her with enough fire in my eyes, the tears welling in them didn't have a chance in hell of falling.

That killed me. I wouldn't hold back my retaliation if Audrey called me that, so a stranger who doesn't know me has no right to speak to me in such a manner. Yet, I let her.

I scold myself for a couple of minutes before I roll onto my hip to face Rocco. I'm not surprised to spot his unhidden watch. He has barely taken his eyes off me since Dimitri rocketed out of the room like he had a jetpack strapped to his back. "What's the story with India? I get she's standing up for her best friend, but something about her rubs me the wrong way."

"You're not the only one," Rocco mutters under his breath before he joins me in lying on his side. He stares at me for a couple of moments, pondering on what to say before he comes right out with it. "Dimitri and India were almost a thing a couple of years ago."

I hate thinking about Dimitri with anyone but me, but as they say, curiosity killed the cat. "Almost?"

Rocco *boinks* my nose, wordlessly advising he heard the jealousy in my one word. "*Almost.* They had a handful of dates. One night, they were heading back to her apartment to... you know—"

"I get it. You don't need to spell it out for me," I interrupt, fighting the urge not to gag.

He throws his head back and laughs, says something about Princess Peach being extra cute when she's jealous, then gets back to his story. "They didn't get past a rough game of tonsil hockey when Dimitri spotted Audrey. Despite India's best efforts, Dimi wanted Audrey then and there." This hurts to hear, but I love his honesty. "She wasn't having a bit of it, though."

I balk like he jabbed a knife under my ribs. "Audrey turned Dimitri down?"

Don't mistake the shock in my tone. Audrey is beautiful, and I can imagine the number of men she had clambering for her attention, but still, I'm shocked. I couldn't turn Dimitri down when he had the blood of my father on his shirt. I don't think he could do anything that would see me rejecting him. Even now, believing he isn't on my side hasn't changed my objective. I would stupidly sign on to be his mistress if it's the only way I could be a part of his life.

"Yeah," Rocco responds with a laugh. "Then the chase pursued. I honestly didn't think she'd ever give in, then all of a sudden, she arrived on his doorstep."

My eyes pop out of my head. "Audrey went to Hopeton?"

Rocco nods. "She spent a couple of weeks there, then moved back to her hometown two weeks before she found out she was pregnant with Fien." He shrugs like he isn't cut about the gap in his friendship with Dimitri. "The rest is a little hazy for me from there. I stepped back as Dimitri stepped up."

"You came back when he needed you, Rocco." I'm not trying to weaken his guilt. I'm being straight-up honest.

"Yeah, but I can't help but wonder if things would have been different if I had hung around." He peers at nothing while muttering, "I might have noticed something fishy, or watched Audrey while Dimitri was watching you. There's more I could have done."

"And no guarantee any of them would have made any difference. Everything happens for a reason."

Rocco scoffs, then peers at me as if I'm an idiot. "You don't really believe that, do you?"

I push him on the shoulder, unappreciative of the candor in his tone. "Of course I do."

This is outrageous for me to say, but if Audrey hadn't been kidnapped, perhaps Dimitri and I would never have crossed paths. His watch wouldn't have made me climax, Eddie wouldn't have needed to retaliate to my 'deceit,' and Dimitri wouldn't have killed him for hurting me. If none of that had happened, I'd still be in the town I hate, unemployed without two nickels to rub together, and most likely looking for a cheap thrill somewhere I'd end up either dead or a drug addict like my parents.

Or worse, I could have been sold to a baby-farming syndicate.

My voice has an unusual twang to it when I ask, "Do you think Dr. Klein's diagnosis is why my mother changed her mind?"

Rocco tries to shut down his surprise at the quick change of our conversation, but he isn't quite fast enough for this little black duck. "I'm unfamiliar with girlie shit, but I'm reasonably sure you can't diagnose PCOS by looking at someone."

"You can't, but you can via an ultrasound, which I had the week before my meeting with my father." Confusion crosses his features, but he doesn't get the chance to seek clarification for it. "For years, I had horrible periods. Cramping, clots, and—"

"I get it. You don't need to spell it out for me." Rocco grins to ensure I know there's no malice in his reply. He's mortified I'm discussing my cycle with him, but he'll handle the injustice if it helps unjumble some of his confusion.

"I went to a local women's clinic. They usually just stuffed condoms in my hand and sent me on my merry way, but there was a doctor on that day who specialized in reproductive organs. He sent me for a sonogram. Since I was young and under the impression I didn't want to have kids any time in the next century, I—"

"Didn't go back for the results," Rocco fills in, clicking on. "Sounds like something you'd do. I'm beginning to wonder if you are allergic to doctors with how hard you try to avoid them." After scrambling to a half-seated position, he digs his cell phone out of his pocket. "Smith..."

I take a mental note to remember any conversations I have with Rocco are never private when Smith replies, "I'm hacking into the clinic's mainframe now. They're as lax on security as you."

Rocco laughs before replying, "If you get anything, come back to us."

My inclusion in Smith and Rocco's duo is appreciated, but I just realized how foolish I'm being. Instead of discrediting India's claims I was never pregnant, I'm feeding the hype. This won't help me convince Dimitri I was telling the truth. It could do the exact opposite.

It dawns on me that Rocco has mindreading abilities when he

says, "Although this won't aid in smoothing things over with Dimitri, it could give us a lead on the people playing him."

"He got the people playing him." I speak slowly as if he is deaf. In reality, I need time to process my words since I'm so damn confused. "Rimi is dead."

Loving the uncertainty in my voice, Rocco hits me with a frisky wink before he heads for the door. My heart is a twisted mess, but since my head is still screwed on straight, I race him for the door, slamming it before he gets close to exiting. "Tell me everything you know."

"I don't—"

I cut off his lie with a glare before adding words into the mix. "You asked me to jump. I sailed over the edge without fear. That makes me a part of this..." I wave my hand around my room as if Dimitri, Fien, and Smith are with us, "... and I don't care what Dimitri says, I'm going to be a part of it until the end."

Rocco leans so close to me, I smell what he ate for breakfast in his shallow breaths. "Some would say the curtains are already closed, Roxie. That the show is over."

I return his lean without the slightest bit of fear knocking my knees together. "And I'd say they're full of shit because even gangsters know the show isn't over until the lights go out."

I saw the light in Dimitri's eyes when he glanced down at me partway through my story, felt it heating my skin. It isn't close to being snuffed, so that not only means I need to keep fighting, I must do everything in my power to keep it lit.

I am, after all, the reason for its glow.

Rocco licks his lips before cracking them into a smile. "Are you sure you want to go down this road, Princess P? Your castle is mighty enticing, but everyone knows mushrooms grow in fungi."

I'm a little lost to what he means, but I figuratively roll up my sleeves, preparing for battle. "You shouldn't underestimate mush-rooms. They're all edible, but some you will only nip at once."

# 30

# DIMITRI

I spot Roxanne's race past the downstairs sitting room I'm using as an office before she pivots back around and charges into my room. Considering her foot is still a little bunged-up from her time under Rimi's watch, she moves quickly.

I'm not surprised. Her firecracker personality suits her hair coloring. I don't see anything slowing her down. Not even my rejection the past three days has made an indent to her fiery personality. That's why I upped the ante today.

Unlike India's numerous staff, Roxanne doesn't knock and wait for permission to enter. She steamrolls into the room at the speed of sound, her steps so fast, the smell I've fought like hell to ignore the past three days whips up around me, tightening the front of my pants even more than her beautiful face.

"Can you please tell this *lady*..." She spits out her last word like she's doubtful India's head of housekeeping is a woman. Sofia is standing outside of the door, clutching the bag I asked her to pack for Roxanne in her hand. "That I do *not* have a flight to Hopeton scheduled for tonight. She's packing my things like I'm—"

"Leaving?" She closes her mouth, pinches her brows, then nods. "You *are* leaving. That's why Sofia is packing your belongings."

My jaw tightens to the point of cracking when Roxanne steps closer to my desk. My hands itch to touch her, but I ball them at my sides instead. The past three days have been pure torture, but the threads I stupidly stopped seeking days ago are popping back up everywhere. There is almost enough of them to ruin an entire outfit, and if the person who killed my baby with Roxanne is wearing it when I hit it with my wrath, I'm all for shredding every last piece of it.

With her eyes locked on mine, seeking any deceit in them, Roxanne says, "Rocco only said this morning that we need to lay low for a couple more days."

What she's saying is true. Although pissed I didn't hold back and wait as agreed upon, the Feds aren't the only one chasing my tail. The CIA is right there with them. I'd gloat if it didn't mean I have to maintain an amicable relationship with India. She's more demanding than Audrey, and I'm not even married to her.

With the annoyance on my face believable, I use it to my advantage. "Yes, we need to lay low for a few more days. Since the men Officer Daniel was working with have been taken care of, you are no longer included in that equation."

Roxanne scoffs, huffs, then scoffs again, truly unsure how to respond. Her shock is understandable. I'm a neurotic, jealous prick when it comes to her, but to play this game right, I have to live up to the hype of my last name. Shipping Roxanne off is the next logical step. Then, not only will the woman I'm chasing lose her scent, she'll shift her focus back to her original target—my wife.

Do I feel like an absolute cunt drawing the focus of a deranged woman back to Audrey? Yes, I do. But the knot in my gut is nowhere near as tight as it is when I consider what could happen if I don't. Roxanne put her life on the line for me, she lost our child in the process. I owe her this level of protection.

Some may say Audrey deserves to be safeguarded the same way. I agree, for the most part. There's just a niggle in my gut that won't quit warning me to remain cautious when it comes to anything to do with Audrey. It feels like there's more at play here than just my marriage, and when I find out what it is, there will be hell to pay.

Once Roxanne settles her emotions, she folds her arms in front of her chest. I really wish she wouldn't. I sustained from sexual activities for almost two years, but that was my choice. This, however, is not. "We're not doing this again, Dimitri. You're not sending me away to see if I'll come back. We've done that, we moved past it, now can we please get onto the real issue here. I can help you. You've just got to let me in."

My mask almost slips when her voice cracks at the end, but I suit back up, forever ready for battle. Her departure won't be forever. If I play my cards right, she could be back in my bed, where she belongs, by the end of the week.

But, if I don't play my hand with the viciousness it deserves, I won't have any cards left to place down. They will be burned, scorched, left wilted without purpose, and they'd still make it out of the carnage better than Roxanne.

I refuse to let that happen.

I'll kill every fucking person in this godforsaken kingdom before I will ever let Roxanne be hurt like the numerous scenarios that have played out in my head over the past three days. That's how much she means to me. That's how much it is gutting me knowing I failed her.

I promised to protect her. I'm only upholding my end of our

agreement now. Some may say it is too late, but it's better than not at all.

My hostile mood is heard in my voice. "I'm not sending you away to see if you'll come back. Our agreement is over. My daughter is home, so there's no reason for you to stay anymore."

The shock on Roxanne's face switches to frustration. "You don't believe what we had was an agreement."

"I do," I reply matter-of-factly, halving the fiery glint in her eyes. "That's why you've spent the past three nights alone." *And why I've slept in my daughter's room each night because she's the only person capable of stealing your devotion, and even then, it's a struggle.* But since that isn't something I can say, I keep my mouth shut.

I should have realized she'd see straight through my ruse. She isn't just attractive, she's smart as well. "You've been with Fien?" Since she's unsure about the authenticity of her statement, it comes out sounding like a question. "Right?"

"Wrong." I lower my eyes to the paperwork in front of me, acting as if the pain in her eyes isn't affecting me. "If you want a rundown on my activities of late, perhaps I can get Smith to clip together some footage for you. Would you like it with or without sound?" I feel like a complete and utter prick when I lock my hooded eyes with hers and mutter, "I'm sure you understand how vocal some women are when they're being fed a healthy dose of dick."

Roxanne looks set to blow her top. She's red-faced, her fists are clenched, and steam is almost billowing out of her ears, but she keeps her cool—mostly. "You can order someone to pack my bags, you can march me onto a plane on the shoulder of one of your goons, but you will never be rid of me..." she tightens her arms under her chest, all sassy like, "... because I'm unforgettable."

"My wife said that once too. She soon learned otherwise. I can only hope it won't take my mistress quite as long."

That was a low blow. I know it, and so the fuck does Roxanne.
"You... you... ugh!"

On her way out, she slams the door shut so hard, it knocks a
priceless painting from the wall. I could pick it up, but it's broken
frame and shattered glass adds to my ruse that I'm done with her.
Not even a woman known for her theatrics can hold back the urge
to drink in a daily dose of drama. "Someone isn't happy. Did she
misread the fine print that discloses the Petrettis don't do
monogamy?"

Knowing Theresa will never fall for the sweet-guy act, I bring
out the asshole gene I was gifted from my father. "Or perhaps she
also doesn't appreciate walking in on her understudy giving me
head."

Air whizzes out of her thin nose as her eyes slit. "You invite me
to some Hicksville mansion on the guise you want to talk shop,
then insult me within a second of arrival. If I wanted to be treated
like scum, I would have accepted your father's many offers to
become your step-mommy."

"I like the way you said that as if you haven't had my father's
withered dick between your legs. It was very authentic." I stand
from my chair, button my suit jacket, then gesture for her to join
me for a late-afternoon drink at a crystal bar set up next to two
leather couches. "I have a business proposal for you. An easy
exchange. Shouldn't take you any longer than thirty minutes."

Theresa paces to my side of the room with her hips swinging
and her eyes brimming with hope. "Is this the real reason you
invited me here, to discuss business?"

I work the disappointment in her voice through my ears three
times before benefiting from it. "For the most part." After placing a
whiskey decanter onto a round table, I track the back of my finger
down Theresa's cheek before moving my hand to the throb in her
throat. I'm not surprised when the vein in her neck doubles its

beeps when my touch switches from gentle to dominant. She is as kinky as she is corrupt. "But I've also been recalling the fun we had before my girlfriend's pregnancy forced her to become my wife."

"You're married?" She plays the scorned victim well, but I'm not buying her act. The grip I have on her throat relayed the increase in her pulse from my confession, not to mention the cruel curve of her lips. "Is she still in the picture?"

"She is." I release her from my grip, then push her away from me with a demoralizing shove, smirking when she almost tumbles to the floor. "For now. I'm not sure how much longer I can put up with her nagging, though."

I swallow down a double whiskey faster than intended when Theresa mutters, "Perhaps if you didn't sleep around, she'd quit nagging." I feel a little dirty when she rights herself before she runs her nails across my pecs. "What do you need from me, Dimi? A public fuck? A shakedown? I could order one of my cousins to pay her a visit."

I pretend to consider her options for a couple of seconds before saying, "I need her to go away for a little while. Not permanently. Just until her voice stops ringing in my ears. I heard you might know of a place." While I shift on my feet to face her, I make sure my face is showcasing the infamous half-smirk she's obsessed with. "Somewhere like the *establishment* you sent Megan to."

"I didn't send Megan anywhere..." Her smile would have you believing you're looking at an angel. She's attractive, she just has repulsively ugly insides. "This time. My lips are sealed pertaining to other matters. I never discuss business, even when it's with the man who ordered it." She either truly believes I set Maddox up to take the fall for Megan's murder, or she's a damn good actor. It could be a combination of both.

Needing to keep my focus on a present injustice instead of an old one, I ask, "Did you at least use an alias this time around? Shroud may be a common name, but you'd have to be a complete fucking idiot to hide her in plain sight for the second time."

"Your worry is unneeded, Dimi. I know what I'm doing." Her use of my nickname for the second time already has my mood nosediving, so I won't mention my response to her hands lowering to the buckle of my belt.

I've fucked women for less information than the underhanded easter eggs she scattered throughout our brief conversation many times in my life, but that isn't the way I operate anymore. I just can't let Theresa know that right now. I need her scratching my back, then when the timing is right, I'll drag mine down hers so brutally, she won't have time to secure a final breath.

"Nuh-uh," I force out with a fake moan while scooping up her hands. "There isn't the time nor the instruments in this room to satisfy a woman as deviate as you. I need hours, *many of them.*" Her purr makes me fucking sick. "So why don't you go freshen up in preparation for a night out, and I'll come find you when it's time to go."

"Okay." She does a childish tiptoe up my chest with her fingers before she presses two fingers to my lips. "Don't keep me waiting long. Your family already has me burning the candle at both ends, my fire might burn out while waiting."

"We only work you to the bone because we know how much you love a good workout." Imagine a sick prick stroking one out on a sandy dune in the middle of the day, then you'll have an idea how sexually suggestive my voice was.

After biting Theresa's fingers, ensuring she feels the sting of my teeth, I spank her ass before guiding her out the door she entered only minutes ago. "Wear something sexy. You never know who may end up seeing you in your little number tonight." *Fingers crossed, it's a coroner.*

She yelps about my spank, purrs like a kitty at my comment, then saunters down the corridor with her hips sashaying back and forth.

I've barely scrubbed the horrid taste of her skin from my mouth when a faint voice trickles into the room from the other side. "Was that Theresa?"

Since Audrey is still weak, she more leans on the doorjamb for support than in the casual I-want-to-beat-your-face-in stance Rocco used it for earlier today. Her folded arms, though, they're new.

*Perhaps she does have more of a backbone than believed.*

I scrub the back of my hand over my mouth for the third time before answering, "Yes, it was. I invited her here to discuss business." That was the exact line I gave her when she walked in on Theresa and me fooling around in my office weeks into our 'courtship.'

No longer smiling, Audrey enters my office. "Business?"

I jerk up my chin, my ability to lie not lost by the hope in my wife's eyes that I will one day be an honorable man.

"Okay." She takes another two frail steps. "Can you tell her I said hello?"

*Hello?* She wants me to pass on a friendly greeting to the woman she saw sucking my dick.

*What the fuck?*

Roxanne would kill Theresa just for the thought.

It would be an exchange I'd pay money to see.

After ensuring my smirk is hidden, I reply, "Perhaps you can tell her yourself. She will be at the function tonight."

I don't mean to be a prick. That's a trait I only reserve for Roxanne these days. I am merely being optimistic that if I push Audrey as hard as I pushed Roxanne, she'll gain half her gall.

Then maybe she'll have enough valor to see our daughter graduate middle school.

It seems to work when Audrey mutters out snappily, "I would have to be invited first."

"You're invited," I respond like it was always my plan to have her in attendance. "I'll have Smith forward you another invitation since yours got lost."

The event is invitation only. If you don't have one, you won't make it past my security personnel. I did that not only to ensure Roxanne wasn't in the same room as the many women I've fucked, but so I could concentrate on anything but her and Fien for a couple of hours.

My businesses ran like oil through an engine while searching for Fien, but now that she's home, everything has gone to shit. My Arabian event for this month was rescheduled, a massive drug shipment is stuck in customs in Africa since my bribe was a day late, and even with Petrettis Restaurant being raided only last month, it was hit again two days ago. It is as if the universe saw I was getting slack, so they hit me with back-to-back losses to ensure I know no matter how weary I am, the Cartel never sleeps.

After tossing back a second whiskey, I place the glass down, then spin to face Audrey. "I'm about to see Fien. You can join me if you like." I don't know why I made my demand sound like it was an offer when it wasn't.

Fien has warmed to me greatly the past three days, but it would be a smoother transition if our exchanges weren't occurring with two strangers in the room with her. It's always India and me instead of Audrey and me.

Even though India drives me bat-shit crazy, I can admit her assistance this week has been a godsend. Fien has taken a real liking to her, and since India involves me in Fien's day-to-day activities, that fondness is slowly being transitioned to me. But, once again, I believe that would be an easier process if Audrey would step up to the plate to parent our child as she deserves.

"Fien is about to have dinner. I'm certain Rosa made enough for everyone."

My clutch around Audrey's waist could be classified as cruel, considering she underwent surgery only five days ago, but it makes the dismissive shake of her head less obvious.

"Here he is. Dada has arrived to eat spaghetti." India's head pops up from the clips of Fien's highchair to the entrance of the kitchen, her eyelids fluttering when she spots Audrey tucked into my side. "And he brought Mommy with him. Aren't you a lucky girl?"

I'm a hard-ass gangster in every meaning of the word, but I'd also be a lying prick if I said Fien's giggles didn't do weird things to my chest. Even with them being produced from India tickling her tummy, they're still such a rarity, I drink in every one of them as if she released them solely for me.

The scent of someone in love with their perfume smacks into me when Audrey arrives at my side of the kitchen. Her eyes are on me, but her words are for Audrey. "How are you feeling? I'm a little concerned you are already up and about."

While India guides Audrey to the other side of the garlic-and-tomato-scented space to discuss her worries in-depth, I slot onto the dining chair directly next to Fien's highchair. "What have you got there? Spaghetti. Yum." When I rub my stomach, she peers at me like I'm an idiot. Today, it doesn't make me want to go on a murderous rampage. "Can I have some?"

She watches me with a slanted head and a twinkle in her eyes for a couple of seconds before she digs her hand into a bowl of mucky redness, then slams her grubby hand into my face.

I'm not the only one laughing about the mess coating my lips.

The faintest chuckle sounds through the door I forced Audrey through only moments ago.

Roxanne's giggles do a weird thing to my chest as well, but they also make me want to go on a murderous rampage. Not just because she has to watch my interactions with my daughter from afar, but because I have to be an asshole to ensure she maintains her distance.

It feels wrong using Fien to strengthen my objection, but I don't have a choice. I'm still being fucked in the ass. My enemies are just using Roxanne against me now instead of my daughter. "How about we feed Mommy some spaghetti too?"

Fien's eyes brighten like she understood every word I said before she holds her grubby hands in the air. She claps them together while saying, "Mama."

I assume she's reaching out for Audrey. Alas, it isn't just my businesses being siphoned down the gurgler this week. Audrey is no longer in the kitchen, and India is tiptoeing across the room like she has the ability to ease both Fien's and my disappointment.

"I'm sorry, sweetie, Mama had to lie down. She was feeling dizzy," India says before she playfully chews on Fien's outstretched hands, sending her girlie shrills bouncing around the kitchen. "Yummo, that's the most delicious sauce I've ever tasted." She rubs her belly before she shifts on her feet to face me. A devious grin is stretched across her face, and her eyes are gleaming with a sparkle I've never seen before. "Do you think we should feed Dada some more spaghetti?"

Before I can object, or at the very least, request they use a fork this time around, India scoops up a handful of spaghetti in her hand, then splats it down one side of my face.

My first thought is to reach for my gun, but the clapping cheer of my daughter stops me. She isn't giggling about India's unexpected gall, she's clapping her hands while cooing 'Dada' on repeat. It's the sweetest fucking noise in the world and has me responding in a way my crew would never expect.

"Oh. My. God. That's warmer than I realized," India says on a squeal when I upend my untouched bowl of spaghetti onto her white blouse. "Tastes good, though."

Laughing, she flings half the spaghetti on her chest into my face before playfully rubbing the other half into Fien's hair. Like all toddlers, Fien loves the mess. She adds to the sticky goop flattening her already dead-straight hair before she tosses strands of pasta off her highchair, joining the food fight India instigated.

We go at it for the next several minutes, laughing, cheering, and making a mess. Before we know it, a week's worth of spaghetti is on the floor, India's sauced-coated body is being cradled in my arms, her lips are an inch from mine, and Roxanne is racing for the closest exit.

# 31

# ROXANNE

They have no connection.

No spark.

No chemistry whatsoever, so why the hell am I pacing the floor of my room like Dimitri's 'mistress' comment was accurate?

*Because it isn't the fire brewing between him and his wife you're worried about.*

Ugh! I can't believe I stood by and watched India fawn over Dimitri like a freak. They weren't kissing, but they may as well have been. The intensity between them was ferocious enough to overcook the spaghetti they were tossing around, fully aware their mutual hierarchy would mean they'd never have to clean up the mess.

My heart, on the other hand, can't be passed onto a member of Dimitri's staff. He made it the mess it is, so it's up to him to fix it.

If that's what I still want.

I truly don't know anymore. The past three days have sucked. I was called a liar by the very woman Dimitri is playing house with, had my child's life discredited by a doctor the community believes is morally ethical, and found out even if I could somehow forge a way back into Dimitri's life as weirdly encouraged by Audrey the past three days, I could never give him what he so desperately craves—his missed months with Fien.

It appears as if my mother didn't have a change of heart. She merely knew handing me over to Rimi would have cost her more than my life. Rumors are he didn't take kindly to people who deceived him.

For future reference, selling a woman incapable of breeding to a baby-farming entrepreneur isn't recommended if you're fond of breathing.

I won't lie. It hurt discovering the real reason I was spared that day. I thought my mother had finally protected me, that she had saved me from the harm my father tried to inflict on me since I was three.

Sadly, Rimi wasn't the only person she fooled.

Rocco assured me I have the means to fix the injustices she made. I just have to work out how far I want to take it. At the moment, that isn't something I can do. My head is too muddled trying to work out what the fuck is going on with Dimitri to add more shit into the mix.

Audrey swapped seats with me twice the past three days to ensure I was seated across from Dimitri at dinner. She hasn't worn the wedding ring found amongst the carnage of Rimi's crew once, and she's been nothing but genuinely kind to me.

Even with her having every right to hate me, she truly doesn't.

Dimitri, in contrast, hasn't followed her lead. He's been avoiding me like I have the plague, and it's killing me more than I care to admit.

After flopping onto my bed and throwing an arm over my eyes, I take a moment to deliberate. Perhaps I should let India's head housekeeper pack my belongings? I can't give Dimitri what he wants, so letting him go may be the nicest thing I could ever give him.

That's what I do.

I forever place everyone's needs before my own.

My inability to place myself first is the only reason I didn't replace the sauce stains on India's blouse with blood. Believe me, it was hard walking away. It took all my strength.

Do I feel like the better person? No, I don't. But at least I didn't force Fien to witness more violence than she already has in her short life.

My deliberation gets a much-needed intermission when a tiny gust of air trickles into my ears. My door isn't locked. Excluding Rocco, no one comes down here. I usually hear the clumps of his boots long before he knocks on my door. That didn't happen this time around. My greeter's steps sounded as weightless as a feather.

Curious, I prop myself onto my elbows before I stray my eyes to the door. My heart pitter-patters in my chest when I spot an envelope on the floor mere inches from the carved wooden door. It isn't overly fancy, but the gilded cardboard inside of it most certainly is.

I creep toward the envelope like it could explode at any moment. When it fails to detonate, I scoop down and gather it up, breathing easier when I notice it is minus a single smear of spaghetti sauce.

Although my inquisitiveness is demanding for me to open the envelope this very instant, a much higher, much more willful stubbornness sees me opening the door to my room instead.

"Audrey..." I call out, certain she is the owner of the red locks swishing around the corner. Her hair is beautiful and healthy since she never chemically bleached it to change its natural coloring. I often envy it when I need a moment of reprieve from Dimitri's glaring stare across the dining room table. He wanted me uncomfortable enough not to eat. I refused to give him the satisfaction. I gobbled down my meals like my stomach wasn't bulging against the zipper in my pants, begging for some room. Then, when it produced the infamous half-smirk Dimitri would give anything to remove from his face, I tackled dessert as well.

When Audrey fails to hear my shout, I re-enter my room, close the door, then rip open the envelope like a savage. If my deliverer is who I think it was, something major must be happening. I haven't had many interactions with Audrey the past three days, but everyone we've had has involved Dimitri in some way.

The twinge of rejection I've been struggling to ignore the past four days gets a boost when my eyes scan a handwritten invitation. There's no indication it was meant to be addressed to me, and its prose indicates it's for an event way above my level of sophistication, but I act ignorant.

The event at an exclusive nightclub commences two hours before I'm due to fly out.

Its timing couldn't be more perfect.

My value hasn't decreased because Dimitri no longer sees my worth. If anything, it has increased because he helped me find the strength to believe I'm worth more than nothing, and now I have the chance to expose exactly how valuable I am.

---

A smirk etches onto my mouth when Rocco takes a staggering step back. "What the fuck, Princess P? I thought I was driving you to the airport?" As he chews on the corner of his lower lip, he rakes his eyes over my body-hugging strapless top, skintight leather pants, and pumps that would make most men cream their pants just at the thought of having them curled around their sweaty hips. It killed me trying to squeeze my ballooned foot into the tiny opening of my stiletto, but I made it work, determined it added to the authenticity of my ruse. "That outfit is *not* flight appropriate. I'm not even sure it's club-worthy." I realize I hit the bullseye when he grabs his crotch, wordlessly begging for it to calm down. "It's gonna give D a heart attack."

"Good." I snatch up my denim jacket and clutch purse from a set of drawers next to the door, then bump Rocco with my hip to barge him into the corridor so I can latch the lock into place. "Because that is the *exact* look I was aiming for."

Rocco's smile has me convinced even if my plan backfires, I will survive it. It won't be an all-encompassing life full of light-altering moments with wickedly deviate spankings, but I will still be breathing. "We're not going to the airport, are we?"

I hit him with a frisky wink. "No. We're going to a special *invitation-only* event."

"Hold up, Roxie." He reduces the length of my stride by grabbing my arm. "You need an invitation for an *invitation-only* event."

The fact he assumes I don't have an invite makes it obvious the one slipped under my door four hours ago wasn't for me. It doesn't weaken my objective, though. Tonight is my last opportunity to prove to Dimitri that this war was started with lies, so it can't end until the truth is revealed.

"Where the fuck did you get that?" Rocco asks when I slide a gold-gilded slip of cardboard out of my clutch purse.

"Where I got it from doesn't matter. It's how *we* use it that counts," I reply before making a beeline for the exit like butterflies aren't fluttering a million miles an hour in my stomach.

I hear Rocco say something to Smith before he joins me at the end of the corridor. I grow panicked I misunderstood his wish to stir Dimitri at every opportunity when he snatches up my wrist before I break into the main part of India's house—the lit section.

My worry is unfounded. He isn't foiling my endeavor to show

Dimitri I'm still on his side. He's strengthening it. "Put this away before we head out. Smith isn't the only one watching."

While shoving the invitation he returned to me into my purse with enough force to crease it, I drift my eyes in the direction he nudged his head. Unlike days ago when we entered this residence, a camera sits in the corner of the spotlessly clean space. It is clear it's new because not only has the pricy wallpaper been peeled away from the wall to accommodate a set of shiny screws, the domes housing them were only invented by Smith two months ago. He showed me his drawings of their designs when Dimitri was drugged. He was hoping Dimitri would integrate them into his security system within the year. I'm glad Dimitri hasn't shunted all his teams' ideas.

"If you want Dimitri to believe you're following orders, you might want to quit smiling." Rocco licks his lips before doing another quick sweep of my body. "And you should probably change."

With my mood as sassy as the glint in his eyes, I reply, "There's no time for that."

Once I'm certain my face represents a scorned woman, I march across the foyer of India's home, struggling not to whimper at the pain in both my foot and my stomach. Forever willing to push the boundaries when it comes to Dimitri, Rocco snatches up a random set of suitcases before he shadows my walk, his demeanor as moody as mine. Even with my room being on the lower level of the compound, I still heard the words he exchanged with Dimitri when news of my departure reached his ears. He called Dimitri a heap of names, his tirade only ending when I assured him I was happy to leave.

Shame filled Rocco's face. He thought I was giving up without a fight, unaware if you have to fight another woman for your man, you've already lost him.

Tonight isn't solely about showing Dimitri what he gave up. It's baring my strengths, displaying that I may have been knocked down, but I still got back up, and that I'm not just a force to be reckoned with. Come hell or high water, I'll be your judge, jury, and executioner if you do me wrong.

Killing my unborn baby is as low as it gets. Despite what Dr. Klein says, I was pregnant with Dimitri's child, and the woman determined to hurt him killed our baby.

Now, I'm going to kill her.

I just have to find her first.

## 32

# DIMITRI

"Married?" I pull on the collar of my shirt, acting as if I'm a naughty boy for openly flirting with a taken woman, even with me doing exactly that multiple times in my early twenties. "How long ago did that happened?"

Aria, a once-in-a-blue-moon bed companion from around the time Audrey was kidnapped, fans her flushed cheeks with a napkin. The pigheaded side of my brain wants to say she's heating up because of my trademark half smirk, but the logical side won't allow it. She was petrified about how I'd respond to her turning down an unvoiced invitation to my bed. I'm not known for my appreciation of the word 'no.'

"Almost a year and a half ago." She rubs her stomach before pivoting away from the bar, exposing her protruding midsection. "We had to rush things along when we had an unexpected intruder."

"You're pregnant." I have no clue why that came out sounding as disgusted as it did. I'm just relaying to you what's happening.

"This is baby number two," Aria exposes, giggling about the shock on my face. "Quade turned one last summer." She must move quickly as her bump looks an easy seven or so months along. "Would you like to see a picture?"

She misses the shake of my head since she's rummaging through her overloaded handbag. It should have been the first indication that I could scratch her off my suspect list. She's so accustomed to packing diapers and baby wipes, even without her kid in tow, she still carries the necessary 'mommy' supplies.

After snagging my whiskey from the glistening bar, I swivel away from Aria. "Why didn't we cross mothers and wives from the guest list?"

I hear Smith's chair creak into place before he replies to my mumbled comment, "Because some of the women you bedded were wives and mothers *before* you slept with them."

I growl, wordlessly warning him to keep his attitude in check. He's as pissed as Rocco has been the past five days. Not even requesting him to send live footage of Roxanne from India's residence saw him giving me any leeway. I guess that could have something to do with the fact it was around the time Rocco was set to drive Roxanne to the airport, but that isn't the fucking point. They're not the only ones struggling. I feel like I'm drowning. I have been since Roxanne told me what happened to her.

I want to maim.

I want to kill.

But more than anything, I want Roxanne to know I took down the people responsible for her pain. When she looks at me, I want to return her stare knowing justice was served. I feel it when I tuck Fien into bed every night, but it's only at half its strength since the person responsible for giving me that joy isn't a part of the picture.

With Roxanne incapable of leaving my thoughts for even a second, I ask, "Have they arrived at the airport yet?"

I stop scrubbing the back of my hand over my eyes when Smith says, "They?"

He isn't stupid, so why the fuck is he acting as if he is?

"Roxanne and Rocco?"

Air whistles between his teeth when he struggles for a reply. "Uh... no. They haven't arrived yet."

Pretending his delay has nothing to do with him being deceitful, I ask, "How far out are they?"

"Ah..." Another pause adds another tick to my jaw. "Around forty or so minutes."

I check my watch, noting that Roxanne's flight is due to leave within the hour. "What caused the delay? They left over an hour ago..." My words fade to silence when the answer I'm seeking waltzes into my peripheral vision.

Roxanne isn't on her way to the airport. She's mingling with the women she made me forget existed. She isn't alone. Rocco is holding the purse Alice said was a perfect match for the final outfit I gifted Roxanne before I released her into the wild.

Because it would look mighty suspicious to host a party with only female invitees. Roxanne's provocative curves aren't solely being eyed by the long list of women I've fucked, she's caught the attention of men who'll take without asking, mark without permission, and fuck without fear of prosecution.

You don't fear the law when you're one of them.

"Smith..."

He coughs to clear his throat before answering, "Yeah."

Nothing but honesty rings in my tone when I mutter, "Rocco's death is on your hands."

I throw back a double shot of whiskey, slam my glass down, then make a beeline for Roxanne, signaling for the valet to bring my car around on the way.

I barely make it three steps away from the bar when I'm

bumped into by a stumbling and somewhat drunk blonde. "Dimi, I thought our get-together was a single-invitee gathering." Theresa pouts like a child before tiptoeing her fingers up my chest. "I don't mind. I just wish you would have told me." Her childish voice shreds my eardrums almost as Roxanne's narrowed glance across the room cuts me to pieces. She isn't a fan of Theresa's. She's not the only one, but since admitting that would underhand my ruse tonight, I pretend I'm not tempted to cut off Theresa's fingers when they lower from my pecs to the crotch of my trousers. "I would have packed something more enticing if I knew I had competition. These women may know how to fuck, but that isn't what you do, is it, Dimi? You completely devour."

Her scarce friendly demeanor is explained when Smith mumbles down my earpiece, "Just like you did the little concoction Preacher slipped into your drink." When my eyes stray to a camera in the corner of the room seeking answers for his riddle, he explains, "Loose lips sink big ships, but I figured you'd rather loosen hers with some Molly instead of your cock. Despite the shit you've been spurting the past three days, there's only one set of lips you want wrapped around your cock. They don't belong to Theresa."

Neither the honesty of his statement nor his unusual mix-up will strike his name out of my shit book, but what Theresa says next improves the odds of it happening within the week. While peering at a man I'll forever hate more than I will emulate, she asks, "Do you think it's weird your father spared Megan's life twice, but he wouldn't piss on you if you were on fire?"

While laughing like her scold has no sting, she stumbles forward at a rate too fast for her hazy head to keep up with. I love carnage, my ego feeds off it, so normally, I'd step back and watch her fall.

This time, I can't because not only does her next confession have me dying to keep her awake, it knocks me on my ass even quicker than the drugs Preacher slipped into her drink. "I get she's a little kooky, and you pissed him off by keeping your daughter a secret, but still, shouldn't he treat all his kin the same?"

# 33

# ROXANNE

"Ouch!" I snap my eyes to Rocco, peeved as fuck he pinched me. I'm already dealing with horrific cramps and a sweaty body that has me dying for a shower. He didn't need to up the ante. "What was that for?"

He hits me with a stern glare someone as playful as him shouldn't be able to pull off before he scrubs a hand across his wiry beard. "Believe me, you'll rather my torture than the one you're about to subject yourself to."

I act as if I have no clue what he's talking about. "Whatever do you mean?"

Fighting the urge not the pinch me again, he spits out through a tight jaw, "The headcount the green-headed monster on your shoulder *thinks* you're doing in your head."

His reply all but answers my suspicion. It also doubles the painful churns of my stomach. I had wondered if the women in the nightclub were previous 'associates' of Dimitri's. Now I know without a doubt.

I won't give you an indication of how many women are in this room, or you'll think I'm crazy when I update you on the horri-fying amount of jealousy brewing in my stomach.

When I arrived hours ago, my eyes locked with Dimitri's across the room in less than a nanosecond. The look on his face assured me he was about to have me marched out, or at the very least, do it himself, so you can imagine my shock when neither of those things occurred. He hasn't glanced my way once, much less scowled at Rocco.

I tried to use the time to my advantage. I've spoken to almost every woman in attendance without the slightest bit of disdain in my voice.

It was no easy feat.

Only one lone wolf has slipped my net. Her evasion has more to do with the fact she's hanging off Dimitri like a leach than anything else. Just watching her rub her breasts against Dimitri's arm to whisper in his ear has me wanting to heave, and I've kept my distance, so I'm not so sure I should test my tolerance up close.

My ruse to act unaffected by their closeness will end as disas-trously as it did when I wretched a hooker from Dimitri's crotch by the strands of her faultless hair. Guaranteed. I'm already on the cusp of slaughter now, and they're still fully clothed, although I don't see that being the case if the blonde has her way. She isn't just tiptoeing her fingers along Dimitri's chest anymore, she's undoing the buttons keeping his tattooed pecs hidden.

After a couple of minutes trying to talk myself out of it, I give in to the temptation burning me alive. My nanna always said I got my rebellious streak from her. I'd hate to stain her legacy by standing back and watching my man be mauled by another woman directly in front of me.

Don't misunderstand. I won't fight her for Dimitri.

I'm merely going to make him come to me.

"You're really going to do this?" Rocco asks with a laugh before he downs his drink with one big gulp then follows me across the room.

The nightclub Dimitri hired has a moody, underground sex club feel to it, it is just minus multiple sex pods and a viewing chamber for those who like to watch. High-back booths take up a majority of the space, and a handful of sunken privacy-roped areas give it a risqué, sophisticated edge.

If the women dotted throughout the space were scantily dressed like the ones who entertain Dimitri's Arabian 'guests,' I'd suspect this establishment was a high-end brothel. Since they aren't, I'll settle on calling it a dance club for well-to-do patrons.

It's the fight of my life to keep a rational head when it dawns on me that Dimitri's buttons aren't the only things the blonde's hands are caressing. She's touching him everywhere—his pecs, his arms, the buckle of his belt. If it's a part of him, she's caressing it in some way.

The fact she can touch him so freely without fear of persecution has me switching tactics in an instant, and I throw more than just my morals under the bus in the process.

"Whoa, hold up, Princess P," Rocco pushes out, half amused, half panicked when I shove him into a bean-bag type seat across from Dimitri and the unnamed blonde before nuzzling into his side. "Aren't I supposed to get a final meal before I'm sent to slaughter?"

"I'm sure I can find you something interesting to nibble on if you'll follow my lead." While mimicking the tiptoe finger walk the blonde is doing to Dimitri's chest on Rocco's, I force my gaze away from Dimitri's slit eyes to the humorous pair peering down at me. "Unless you're scared about how Dimitri will react?"

With a smile that's as evil as it is sweet, Rocco sinks deeper into the flexible material cushioning his backside before he adjusts the span of his thighs. His stance is almost an exact replica of

Dimitri's. However, his eyes are nowhere near as narrowed. "I'm not scared of Dimi, Princess P. I'm just worried you don't understand what you're signing up for."

I hook my leg loosely around his waist before pressing my lips to the shell of his ear, shuddering when the scent of his cologne filters into my nostrils. "I'm well aware. I knew in the alleyway when he watched me come, in the woods when he spared my life, and I know right now even with him ripping my heart to shreds, Dimitri Petretti doesn't play games with anyone... *except me.*"

Dimitri has an eye on every person in the room, but there's only one person he is paying attention to—me.

Good.

All is fair in love and war, and this is about as treacherous as it gets.

Pretending he doesn't want me is one thing, reminding me he's married is another, but this, allowing a woman to slobber over him directly in front of me is an entirely new kettle of fish, and I am done pretending I'm okay with it.

Even with my heart screaming at me to pull back on the reins, I match the blonde's seductive moves, tease for tease. When she presses her lips to Dimitri's ear, mine get super friendly with Rocco's. When she drags her nails across Dimitri's pecs, I scour Rocco's with mine. And when she finally succeeds in undoing the buckle on Dimitri's belt, I tug on Rocco's just as aggressively.

"Dammit, Roxie, you've got me all types of conflicted. I don't want Dimitri to slice my dick off if it gets hard at the thought of you stroking it, but if you're going to touch the hammer, I can't have you doing it while he's half-mast. That's an injustice I *cannot* allow."

I don't pay Rocco's witty-filled comment any attention. I can't. I'm too busy staring at Dimitri, shocked as hell I am seconds from sliding my hand into his number two's pants, and he's not going to do a damn thing about it.

The cropped hairs splayed across Rocco's pelvis are tickling my fingertips. I can hear the unease in the beats of Rocco's heart that we're stepping over the line, yet, Dimitri just stares.

He doesn't blink.

He doesn't move.

*He. Just. Stares.*

"Fuck you!" I shout at Dimitri while yanking my hand out of Rocco's pants like his 'hammer' scorched my fingers. "Someone in this room killed our baby! Maestro might have punched me in the stomach and kicked me over and over again, but he was acting on the orders of a *woman*. *She* told him what to do. *She* told him to do whatever it took to get rid of our child when the finger he forced inside of me came out free of carnage." I stand to my feet like I'm not sick to my stomach with disgust. "But I guess that doesn't matter to you, does it? Because the death of our baby means there's one less person for you to pretend you give a shit about."

I shrug out of Rocco's hold when he snatches my wrist. I'm not about to race over to Dimitri's side of the club to beg for his scraps like a fool. I'm going home to lick my wounds and refuel, then I'll start again on my quest to find the person responsible for the death of my child because despite what my heart believes, she isn't in this room.

The shocked sigh that collectively rolled around the no-longer thrumming space during the middle part of my confession was too loud to exclude a single patron. They were *all* horrified by my comment our baby was killed—even the blonde with her hand halfway into Dimitri's pants.

# 34

## ROXANNE

"Can you please hurry the fuck up? It's a pimped-out Range Rover. How many could you possibly have in the lot?"

The valet excuses Rocco's foul language since it was said after a pleasantry. "Surprisingly, quite a few. Tonight's guests seem to be fans of that make and model."

"It's fine," I interject, stepping between Rocco and the valet before Rocco can sock him in the nose. "My flight was scheduled to depart hours ago. I doubt there'll be another one until dawn, so there's no need to hurry."

I twist to face Rocco when a *pfft* noise vibrates his lips. "What?"

For the first time since I've known him, he lies to my face. "I didn't say anything." Mercifully, my tapping foot and my crossed arms soon call him out as the liar he is. "Dimitri didn't organize for you to fly home commercially. He's paying five thousand an hour to have a jet fueled and on the runway. Has been since Wednesday."

"Wednesday." Although it sounds like I am asking a question, I'm not. "The day of my ultrasound?"

Unsure if I'm summarizing or seeking answers, Rocco half-heartedly shrugs. His lackluster response should ease my annoyance. It doesn't. Not in the slightest. I thought Dimitri believed my claims our baby was killed. The fact he's had a private jet on standby since the day India told him otherwise proves he doesn't.

"Then I guess you better hurry," I say to the valet. "I'd hate to waste another dime of Dimitri's hard-earned money." The way I spit out 'hard-earned' exposes exactly what I think about Dimitri's family business.

They're proof money can't buy happiness. They just rent it for a few hours and pretend their life is bliss, having no clue substance should always override quality.

"Finally," Rocco breathes out with a groan when our car rolls to a stop in front of us.

The darkness swamping me doesn't seem so dense when Rocco beats the valet to my door. He holds it open for me, his smile more welcoming now than when I used him as my pawn.

His grin would have you believing we won tonight. My nanna always said sometimes you must lose an occasional battle to win the war, but I don't feel anything close to victorious right now.

"Chin up, Princess P," Rocco mutters like he heard my private thoughts. "You've got more chance of jabbing the main players in the ass if you're tailing them from behind." He winks, shuts my door, then jogs around to the driver's side door by darting around the trunk.

Without speaking another word, he slips into the driver's seat, fires up the ignition, then commences our solemn trek to a private airstrip in the middle of nowhere.

It's a somber, unsatisfying twenty minutes filled with tension and unvoiced questions. I can feel the tension radiating out of Rocco, smell the unease slicking his skin, but he remains quiet. That is as foreign as Dimitri not responding to my attempt to goad him and proves what should have dawned on me three days ago. My relationship with Dimitri was nothing but an arrangement to improve the odds of him getting his daughter back.

For some stupid reason, I'm okay with that. I never wanted to steal him from Fien, and I most certainly have no intention to do that now. I just wish I could be a part of their unit. I've always felt a little lost. I didn't experience that once while in Dimitri's realm. Even when he threatened to kill me or hurt those I love, I still felt wanted.

My watering eyes stray from the scenery whizzing by the window when Rocco shifts down the gears in the Range Rover. As stated, a gleaming state-of-the-art private jet sits halfway out of an airport hangar in a town bordering India's suburban mansion. It's fueled up and ready to go, meaning I only need to farewell Rocco with a kiss, and I'll be done with this life.

"Are you sure you don't want me to come with you?" Rocco asks before my lips have even left his cheek. "I'm not a fan of flying, but if it saves me facing Dimitri's wrath for a couple of hours, I'm all for it."

I'd laugh at his mumbled comment if I believed it held an ounce of truth to it. Dimitri would have to be jealous to respond to our horrible scam to make him jealous, and we both know that shipped sailed the instant our ruse was implemented with only the slightest hiccup.

No one was prepared for me to be actually pregnant—not even me.

With my shoulders hanging as low as my mood, I reply, "I'm only going to sleep the entire flight, so why bother?"

Stealing Rocco's chance to reply to my lie, I press a second peck to his cheek, snatch my clutch purse from the floor, then exit his stationary vehicle.

I don't look back while climbing the stairs of the private jet. I'm not a movie starlet, and this isn't a fairy tale.

When I break into the cabin that smells of wine and freshly baked cookies, a friendly voice greets me. "Good evening, Ms. Grace. We're pleased to have you aboard this evening."

"Thank you," I reply to the air stewardess, truly grateful for the sincerity in her tone. It is the nicest one I've had all week.

After removing my denim jacket, she folds it over her arm. "Can I get you something to drink? Perhaps a snack?"

"Umm..." I take a moment to consider the demands of my aching stomach before shaking my head. "I should probably take care of my sweaty body and face before eating. Is there a restroom I can freshen up in?"

Gratitude for perks I have no need to become accustomed to smack into me when the pretty brunette dips her chin. "I turned down the bedding in your suite earlier today. It's ready as requested." She steps closer to me, her eyes genuinely friendly. "While you freshen up, I'll instruct the pilot to finalize last checks. We should be in the air within the hour."

"Thank you," I reply through a yawn.

Once I have my purse dumped onto one of the dozen or more plush leather chairs lining the aisle, I head for the highly varnished door the stewardess pointed to when she mentioned my 'suite.' My steps are sluggish and slow, weighed down by exhaustion no amount of rest will cure. I honestly feel ill, like more than heartbreak is responsible for the shards of pain sluicing my veins.

The room at the back of the jet is small but fancy with silk sheets and hundreds of scatter cushions. I'm tempted to crawl into the middle of the mattress, roll into a ball, and pretend the world doesn't exist, but I need to use the facilities first. My face is covered with gunk I haven't worn since I thought black mascara and white powder would stop the uncomfortable gawks of my high school professor. It worked for almost a month, my ruse only ruined when he stumbled upon one of my erotic drawings in my school notepad.

I usually reserved my sketching for home, but Professor Lewis's constant after-school detentions saw me switching things up. I don't know what happened to him. He was constantly there, then he reported my artwork to my grandmother, and he disappeared not long after that. I didn't think much of it at the time, but now it seems a little odd.

Too curious to discount, I do a final wipe over my face before entering the main part of the cabin. "Smith..." I wait a few seconds, aware he's always listening, but also know I'm not the only person he keeps tabs on—*if* he's still keeping tabs on me. "Smith—"

"Is handling other matters right now."

With my heart beeping in my neck, I shift on my feet to face the voice that froze my heart. Since his Italian accent was heavier than I've heard it before, I assumed it belonged to Dimitri's father. If the dangerous pump of Dimitri's nostrils is anything to go by, I'm kind of wishing it was still him. Dimitri is bristling with anger, and once again, all his focus is on me.

I hate myself for running. I pledged on the way here that the rod in my back won't bend for anyone. But that doesn't count when the man you love is looking at you like he wants to kill you.

Besides, I'm not running from him. I am running away from what he represents. More than once he hurt me, yet all I want to do is smooth the groove between his brows with my lips.

That makes me as unhinged as Dimitri's growl when he slams the door shut before I get close to darting through it, then crowds me against it. I'm scared shitless, but for some stupid reason, I relish his big brooding frame looming over me. If he didn't care, he wouldn't be here. If he were done with me, he wouldn't have needed to check that Rocco drove away after dropping me off.

As I consider the possibilities of what his arrival means, my heart picks up speed. Will he beg me to stay? Will he tell me he's sorry? Will he introduce me to his daughter instead of pretending he hasn't noticed me watching their connection from afar?

The possibilities are endless, I just never considered this one.

With his big hand cupping the little pouch in the lower half of my stomach from eating too many carbs the past week, and his lips squashed against my ear, he whispers five words more important than any, "I cared. I still do."

35
_____

# DIMITRI

Every step I take away from the private jet feels like a knife is being stabbed into my chest. My words shattered Roxanne, she broke down in front of me, yet I still walked away.

I don't have a choice. I can't be who she needs me to be and protect her at the same time. She craves a monster, a bastard, a man who'd rather destroy her than have her ever believe she deserves better than him, but I need to be more than that.

I need to be the lowest of the low, the scum on the bottom of a seedy one-star motel shower stall, the man my father raised me to be. I need to rain terror down on those who have done me wrong and resurrect the innocent I burned along the way.

And I need to start with her.

Megan's eyes are as red-rimmed as Roxanne's. They're puffy like she's been crying, but not a touch of moisture is seen on her cheeks. She's scared she is about to meet with her maker but considering that couldn't occur until I broke her out of a mental hospital alters her perspective on things. She isn't close to being free, her wings are fully clipped, but it's better than being dead.

It's the same with Theresa. As much as I want her to be the villain of my story, that isn't a title I can give her just yet. She shared information with me tonight I couldn't have gotten elsewhere. Undeniable evidence that will have Roxanne returned to my bed even quicker than I'm hoping.

That alone will spare Theresa of my fury. It isn't a lifetime guarantee, but bearing in mind the many ways I had planned to kill her when her overzealous hands had Roxanne acting out, she should count her lucky stars. If she hadn't spilled a vault load of my father's secrets the past four hours, she would have been wearing concrete boots by now, and Rocco would be guzzling down saltwater right along with her. That's how much my blood boiled watching Roxanne and Rocco get cozy and how tenacious my itch to kill was.

It's just fortunate for them both, my wish to return Roxanne to her rightful spot at my side was greater than my urge to slit their throats.

It was a fucking hard feat—one I'm still struggling to maintain.

After sliding into the back of a prototype vehicle, I signal for the driver to go. We have a long trip ahead of us, and I want it done before Fien wakes. Since that's usually right at dawn, I better get a wiggle on.

"Do you recognize any of these people?" I remove a stack of licenses Smith printed when the drugs tracing through Theresa's veins couldn't stop the waggle of her tongue before twisting them to face Megan. "Whether in your family or outside of it."

I can't believe I'm playing into Theresa's suggestion Megan and I are related. The Petretti genes are strong, and Megan looks nothing like me. Her hair is mousy, her teeth are chipped and crooked, and her eyes are hazel. And don't get me started on the fact she's batshit crazy, or we'll be here all night.

I'm fucked in the head, but I'm not mentally challenged.

"I won't hurt these people, Megan. I just want answers." I'm such a fucking liar. If any of the thoughts running through my head are true, all these men are dead, then I'll move for their families like Clover is hunting Maestro's now. He broke the rules when he touched Roxanne, and now his entire existence will pay the price of his stupidity. I wasn't lying when I said I'd remove a man's legacy if he hurt Roxanne. I don't play games when it comes to people I love.

I work my jaw side to side to loosen its grip when Megan asks, "Are you from the hotel?" Her voice is as weak as the fragile mouse she's portraying, exposing I need to play on her insecurities. If she's a damsel in distress, I need to pretend I'm a hero. It's like good cop, bad cop, everyone has their role.

I unbutton my jacket before sinking into my seat, hopeful a blasé response will show Megan I mean her no harm. I don't even have a gun on my hip. It's stuffed down the back of my trousers, but that's not the point. "I don't own any hotels, but why would you ask that? Are you having trouble with some people at your hotel? I can help you with it if you'd like."

She licks her cracked lips before twisting them so they match her screwed-up nose. "They're okay. They are just *really* annoying." The woman seated across from me would have to be mid-twenties at least, but she speaks as if she hasn't reached her teen years yet, furthering my proof she isn't a Petretti. Even when it could fuck her sideways, Ophelia was fierce.

After scooting to the edge of her seat, Megan drops her eyes to the stack of licenses. "Can I look through them?"

"Sure." I smile at her like she asked to suck my dick before handing over the pile of papers. It is stupid of me to do. She's more scared now than she was when Preacher snuck her out of a mental facility with a hessian bag pulled over her head and his hand clamped around her mouth. From what I heard from Smith, more than Preacher's hand is suffering bite wounds.

I join Megan in balancing on the end of my seat when she says, "The staff asks about him all the time. I don't like talking about him." When she swivels on the spot, it dawns on me that the heat on her cheeks has nothing to do with the heat pumping out of the vents. "Nick, though... I talk about him all the time. Have you seen him lately?" She stops, huffs, then folds her arms in front of her chest. "He wasn't with *her*, was he? I tried to fix his mistake. I gave her the drink like the man said. It didn't work. *She* still had her baby."

Her jump in and out of personalities gives me whiplash, but I attempt to maintain the momentum of our conversation. "What man, Megan?" I've shown her over a dozen images. She needs to narrow down the list of suspects for me.

She appears more innocent than insane when she brings her father's identification card to the front of the stack. Carlyle Shroud looks like a cruel, villainous man incapable of raising a rat, much less a daughter whose mother died before she reached womanhood.

"Your father gave you something to hurt a woman?" I sound like a fucking moron, but mercifully, it seems to be a language Megan understands.

"Not my daddy, silly." She laughs like I'm hilarious. "He is who the men in the white coats at the hotel asked about all the time."

"The hotel you just left?" I ask, finally clueing on to what she means. She has confused the mental hospital she was admitted in the past week with the Ritz Carlton. It makes sense when you see the conditions she grew up in. A pigsty would be glamorous compared to her family ranch.

While nodding, Megan pulls a second photo out of the stack like she isn't about to unlock the treasure chest I've been hoarding the past almost two years. "He gave me the medication." She holds up an outdated photo of Rimi Castro in front of me—the once ringleader of the baby-farming syndicate who kidnapped my wife, held my daughter captive, and killed my unborn child. He's dead, so I can't get the answers I need from him. Megan, though, she's very much alive and very much on my radar.

"How long ago did you meet with Rimi?"

She takes a moment to contemplate. Her delay reveals she isn't as stupid as she wants me to believe. She's playing an act. I'm confident of that.

Don't get me wrong, she's fucking mental, but she could be a genius if her evil was harnessed the right way.

Once she's confident she has me on tenterhooks, she answers, "Last week."

"You saw Rimi last week?" I rush out before I can stop myself. I'm supposed to be portraying a cool and collected cartel leader, not a dweeb who comes after only two pumps.

Megan smiles, loving the shock in my tone. Since it places her on my team, I let the mocking gleam that arrived with her grin slide. "Yes. His home isn't too far from here." Just like earlier when she spoke about Nick, her expression perks up as she asks, "Do you think he'd like to see me again?" As quickly as her excitement bristled, it slips off her face with a groan. "*She* won't be there again, will she? I don't like her. She's mean."

"A woman was with Rimi when you visited him?"

She mistakes the shock in my tone as devious. "They're not like that. They don't do the things Nick does with *her*." She looks like she vomited a little in her mouth. "Rimi's *friend* sleeps in her own room." I feel as if our conversation is about to veer off course when she curls her hand over her basically flat stomach, but am proven wrong when she mutters, "Her baby is really cute. My baby will be cute, too. When she's born."

The full extent of her mental illness is showcased in the worst light when she coos to her 'baby' how she will see her daddy soon. She doesn't just have a brief conversation and move on.

She's so far down the rabbit hole, she doesn't blink when my 'imaginary friend' jumps into our conversation. "I told you." Smith's voice is a mix of remorseful and fretful. "Certifiably fucking insane."

I nod, agreeing with him. "But she could be onto something. Roxanne said the women at Rimi's ranch shared the same room. What if the woman Megan mentioned had her own room because she was a part of Rimi's team? She could be the woman we're seeking."

Although every member of Castro's team was taken down in the massive blood bath last week, over four dozen 'survivors' were registered in the CIA's recovery file. The women were an integral part of the baby-farming operation, but both Henry and I agreed they played no part in Fien's captivity nor his brother's family's downfall, so they shouldn't be held accountable.

"There's one person who can give you answers to the questions you're seeking, Dimitri. She's sitting right in front of you." Smith's tone is neither malice nor mocking. It is straight-up honest.

With my deadly insides hidden by a smile, I return my focus back to Megan. She's watching me, not the least bit confronted by the viciousness of my returned stare. "Did you have your own room at Rimi's farm, too, Megan? Or did you share a room with Rimi?" I scoff like I'm disappointed her innocent act is for show. "I wonder what Nick will think about you shacking up with another man."

"I didn't share a room with Rimi." She looks genuinely unwell. "My daddy told me what would happen if I shared a bed with a man who wasn't my husband. He'd sew my eyes shut like he did my mother when she let *him* sleep in their bed."

My eyes rocket in the direction she nudged her head, gasping like a man without a cock when I realize who she's referencing. The focus is no longer on Rimi's debunked crew. It has shifted to my father.

"Smi—"

"Cross-referencing any connection between Megan's mother and your father now." He sounds as shocked as me. I'm stunned, truly and wholly scandalized. My father fucked around long before my mother died, but that doesn't mean what I think it does, does it? Megan can't be my sister—surely.

"Furthermore..." Megan waits for my eyes to return to her flaming-with-anger face before she continues, "Rimi doesn't live on a farm." She talks about him as if he isn't dead. "He has a big house my mother would have loved. It has hundreds of rooms, a picture theater, and a special hospital in the basement. That's where the ladies have their babies. Rimi said I could have my baby there if I want." My thudding heart almost drowns out her next lot of words. "I can prove I had my own room. His house is close to here." She peers around like she's gathering her bearings. "Well, it was closer to the airport than here. Can we go back there?"

"Jesus fucking Christ," Smith murmurs out loud, matching my sentiments to a T. "Show her the photos I sent to your phone."

With my mind shut down, autopilot mode kicks in. I dig my phone out of my pocket, then fire it up. My thumb hovers over the message app when Megan grunts, "That's her, the woman who lives with Rimi. How did you get her photograph?" The absolute disdain hardening her features softens when she spots Fien on my screensaver. "Aww, now it makes sense. I told you her daughter is cute. I'd put her photo on my phone too... *if I had one.*"

My itch to kill turns catastrophic when the final piece of the puzzle slots into place. My screensaver is an image of Fien I snapped the first time I saw her in the flesh. Because Audrey clutched my hand most of the drive from Rimi's compound to India's house, Fien isn't cradled in Roxanne's arms. She's being held by India.

It doesn't take me even a second to do the math. India is in every scene even more than Roxanne. She has been in every single frame—even the ones before Fien was conceived. That fucking bitch orchestrated my daughter's captivity because I chose her roommate over her, and I'm going to kill her for it.

# 36

## ROXANNE

I request the driver of my cab to pull over two houses back from India's country estate. Even with my gut warning me that this is a bad idea, I can't help but test the strength of the boundaries Dimitri lodged between us.

He could have let me leave thinking he didn't care about me. He could have walked away without telling me our baby meant something to him. He didn't.

That deserves recognition.

That deserves acknowledgment.

"Are you sure you're okay?" asks the driver when my hunt for bills in the bottom of my clutch has me grunting in pain. "You don't look real good."

Up until twenty minutes ago, I didn't know a broken heart could cause physical pain. I'm in as much pain now as I was when Maestro punched me in the stomach. It has me sweating up a storm and has my cab driver convinced I'm up to no good.

He was already suspicious when I said I would have to direct him to my location by taking a detour past a club that looks as shady as hell when it's minus its ritzy guests.

"Perhaps I could take you to the hospital?"

I lock my eyes with the kind pair glancing at me in the rearview mirror. "I'm fine. I think I ate something bad. It will pass soon." *I hope.*

He doesn't believe me, but I'm beyond caring.

After tossing a bundle of bills over the seat, I crank open my door and peel out of the cab. It's almost winter, so the chills racking my body should be from the cold. Regretfully, they aren't. I'm both burning up and shuddering like I am in an ice bath.

The unusual duo hitting me doesn't slow me down, though. Once I've ensured the cab driver has left, I cross the road, then head toward the back entrance I spotted Rocco sneaking out of many times the past week.

The secret passage could be lit up with surveillance, but I'm okay with that if it's being viewed by the man I'm endeavoring to spark a reaction out of. I still don't know Dimitri's cell phone number, and Smith is being as ignorant as my body begs for me to slow down.

Once the sweat beading my top lip has been wiped away, I push open the heavily weighted door in the far righthand corner of India's home. It takes everything I have to get the rusty hinges to budge, and even then, I have to squeeze through the gap since it barely opened a few inches.

"Smith..." I keep my voice low, hopeful my unexpected return doesn't startle the lady of the house. India isn't a fan of mine. I can't say I blame her. Audrey is more approving of my 'relationship' with her husband than her best friend. I can't help but wonder if that's because she's scarred from her ordeal. There's a pain in her eyes when she peers at Dimitri. It just seems more regretful than sad. "Smith..."

I get an answer this time around.

It isn't who I'm hoping, but mercifully, it also isn't India.

"Audrey, are you okay?" My last three words come out in a hurry when she stumbles forward at a rate too fast for me to catch her. She lands on her knees with a thump, her skidder exposing the cause of her fumbling state. Her wrists have been slashed. "Oh God, what did you do?"

I drag her into the open, positive if my screams don't reach Smith's ears, he will spot me on one of the many cameras Rocco pointed out late last night. "Help! Somebody, please help!" As I rip my shirt to make bandages for Audrey's gushing wounds, I choke out, "It's okay. You'll be okay. I promise."

My pledge should slacken the worry in her eyes not double it. The color drains from her face as quickly as it oozes out of her wounds. She looks truly panicked she's about to die, which is odd considering she attempted suicide.

"Finally," I push out with a relieved breath when the patter of footsteps racing my way sounds through my ears. "Call an ambulance while I lay her flat. If I raise her arms above her head, it should lower her blood loss." I've just got to pray she hasn't sliced an artery. If she has, help may not get here in time.

After removing my jacket, I place it under Audrey's head, then raise her arms as high as I can. It helps to lower the amount of blood gushing from her wounds, but she is still on death's door.

"Help me compress her wounds." When nothing but silence is heard for the next several seconds, my mood gets snappy. "Quick!" The shortness of my demand doesn't weaken the intensity of it. I'm beyond annoyed the person I hear creeping up on me isn't assisting me in making Audrey stable. "I get it's scary and that there's a lot of blood, but Audrey will die if you don't help me."

When a snicker overtakes the thud of the pulse in my ears, I crank my neck in the direction it came from. India is standing at the bottom of the stairwell that leads to the main part of her residence. Her hand is clamped over her mouth, and her eyes are fixed on the fading pulse in Audrey's neck.

"If you don't want your best friend to die, you need to help me... *now!*"

Unease melds through my veins when she remains standing at the foot of the stairs. She took charge last week when Audrey's injuries were much worse than this, so why is she acting like she's terrified of a little bit of blood?

When Audrey gargles out my name, my eyes jackknife back to her so quickly, my head gets a rush of dizziness. Her lips feebly move as she fights to warn me about the imminent danger I'm in, but not a sound seeps from her lips. She isn't just sinking into the blackness calling her name, someone hacked up her tongue as poorly as they did her wrists.

"Who did this to you, Audrey? Who hurt you?"

While searching her pockets for her phone, hopeful as fuck she has Dimitri's new number stored in her contacts, the shadow above my head doubles in size.

I duck with barely a second to spare, sending the vase India was attempting to knock me out with into the brick wall Audrey's forehead collided with when she stumbled to her knees.

As my sluggish head struggles to click on to what is happening, Audrey finally voices the name she was trying to get out earlier. "Fien."

Fien is not my child, but I love her father enough to wish she was, so I'll do everything in my power to protect her from the deranged woman attempting to kill her mother.

With a roar, I charge for India like Dimitri did Officer Daniel almost two weeks ago. My shove juts her so fiercely, a butcher's knife stained with blood falls from her back pocket. I snatch it up before racing up the stairwell as if my stomach isn't screaming with every pump of my legs. My plan could be a woeful waste of time, India could finish what she started with Audrey since I'm no longer in the room, but my intuition is telling me this is the right thing to do. India wants Audrey's death to look like a suicide. She can't do that without the weapon I'm clutching.

When I reach the top of the stairs on the third floor, I scan my eyes over the dozens of doors branching off the corridor. They're all identical, and there are far too many to search every one of them.

"Fien?" I call her name on repeat, unsure which room is hers. I only got to watch her connection with her father from afar. I was never invited into her inner circle. It wasn't just Dimitri shunting me from the festivities, it was India as well.

Now I understand why.

"Fien, honey, where are you?"

My heart races a million miles an hour when Fien sheepishly peers at me from behind a carved wooden door partway down the corridor. Her eyes are sleepy, and her beloved teddy is closer to the floor than her chest.

"Hey, baby," I say, optimistic she won't just recall how I ripped her out of Maestro's arms when he succumbed to a bullet. I helped her meet her father for the first time. Fingers crossed that gives me some additional brownie points. "Do you want to go see Dada? I'm sure he's dying to see you. I can take you to him."

The closer I pad to Fien, the more wetness fills her eyes. Even being raised in hell wouldn't see her eager to run into my arms. I have a bloody knife in my hand, and I'm sweating profusely. I very much look like an ax murderer.

After tossing the knife to the floor, I scrub a hand across my face, then hold out my arms. "That's it, Fien," I say on a sob when she moves out from behind her door enough I can see all of her adorable face. "I won't hurt you. I swear. We're just going to go see Dada."

I think I have her convinced.

I think she's on my side.

Then the mat is pulled out from beneath my feet.

While crying for her Mama, Fien sidesteps me with the agility of an up-and-coming state championship quarterback. She races to India at the other end of the corridor, smirking smugly about the devastation on my face.

How did she get past me? I haven't spent a lot of time here, but since I was lonely, and I pace the halls when I'm feeling that way, I know her floorplan intimately. There's no other entrance to the third floor except the stairwell I just climbed. Unless...

My mouth pops open when the truth smacks into me.

*India's home has a secret stairwell like the ranch Fien was held captive at.*

"You... you..." Come on mouth, put this bitch in her place. "You killed my baby!"

I snatch up the knife I threw down before holding it out in front of myself. Fien will most likely never forgive the murderous look on my face, but I'll do my best to erase it from her memories when I take down the conniving, two-faced bitch she has confused with her mother.

"Why did you do that to my baby? What harm could it have ever done to you? Dimitri was *never* yours. He didn't even sleep with you, so why do you think you have a claim to any children he has?"

Like the heartless snake she is, India says matter-of-factly, "My family's royal lineage hasn't been tainted in centuries, and I refuse to let it start with me."

"What?" Nothing she said makes any sense. Fien isn't her

child, so how could my child with Dimitri 'taint' her family's legacy.

It takes a little longer for the truth to smack into me this time around. The delay is understandable. This is as unkosher as it gets.

"You're Fien's mother." Since I'm not asking a question, it doesn't sound like one. "How? Dimitri went to Audrey's ultrasound. He watched Fien's brutal birth... more than once." The truth pummeling into me makes the pain in my stomach ten times worse. "You can't have children. That's how you knew about miscarriages and fibroids." I can barely breathe through the madness swamping me when disturbing thought after disturbing thought enters my mind. "Audrey was your surrogate. That's why Fien doesn't respond to her like she does you because she knows Audrey isn't her mother." When she doesn't attempt to deny my claims, my words get extra snappy. "You kept her from her father this entire time. Why would you do that, India? What did Dimitri ever do to you?"

Any chance of getting answers out of her is hit out of the park when the thud of someone climbing the stairwell two stairs at a time booms into my ears.

Dimitri races our way, his speed as brutal as the lies that fall from India's mouth when he reaches the landing. "Thank God you're here, Dimi. Roxanne killed Audrey before she turned the knife onto Fien." She sucks in breaths like she's on the verge of a panic attack before continuing with a sob, "I made it to Fien with barely a second to spare, but I'm scared, Dimi. She tried to kill your daughter. She tried to kill Fien."

"No..." The pain shredding through me becomes too much to bear. It sees me dropping the knife so I can cradle my aching stomach that's begging for me to bend in two. "I didn't hurt Fien. I'd never hurt her. *Argh*..."

I'm unsure if my gargled scream is from the intense sharpness hitting my lower stomach or from India using Dimitri's distraction to her advantage. She snatches up the knife wedged between us as quickly as Dimitri yanks his gun out of his trousers.

Instead of directing it at me, the supposed perpetrator, Dimitri aims his gun at the pleat between India's blonde brows, unimpressed she has the sharp side of the knife pressed against Fien's throat. "You will never make it out of here alive. I will gut you where you fucking stand if a droplet of blood beads on her neck!"

India is either an idiot, or she doesn't fear death. "One nick of her artery *will* kill her." Her voice is unlike anything I've ever heard. "You know this, Dimitri. We're miles from the closest hospital. Help will *never* get here in time."

When she pierces the blade in deep enough to make Fien sob for her daddy, I fall to my knees, both pained by the devastation on Fien's little face and the pain buckling my legs out from beneath me.

"Do you want your daughter to die!" India screams when my topple diverts Dimitri's eyes to me for the quickest second. "Is *she* more important than your flesh and blood?" Spit seethes from her mouth when she hisses out 'she.'

I shake my head at the same time Dimitri mumbles, "No."

I'm not only agreeing that I'll never be more important than Fien, I'm trying to relay to Dimitri that India won't do as she's threatening. She might be a callous, cold-hearted bitch, but that doesn't mean she will kill her daughter. I just can't get my mouth to work. I'm in too much pain to speak. I'm barely conscious, so I can't be expected to talk.

"Then, put down your gun, step away from the banister, and let me leave." Dimitri firms his grip instead of weakening it. It frustrates India to no end. "Do it or I'll kill your daughter like I did the bastard child you were going to have with *her*."

When she jerks her head to me during the last part of her statement, something inside of me cracks. I'm on my knees, confident I'm on the verge of death, but I somehow manage to charge for India.

I stumble more than I sprint, but my fumbling movements are all that is needed for India to take her eyes off the prize for just a second. When she drops her knife to my stomach, preparing to maim me as she did Audrey, Dimitri snatches Fien from her arms, cradles her into his chest, then falls back while firing.

*Bang. Bang. Bang,* booms into my ears.

One bullet thrusts India into the wall with a pained yelp, the other pierces through the drywall next to my head, and the last one shreds through the pain that's been crippling me the past five days. It tears through my stomach, stunning me that it isn't as painful as anticipated.

That could have more to do with the fact the man I love shot me.

He. *Shot.* Me.

"No!" Dimitri falls to my side as quickly as he screams for Smith on repeat. "Stay with me, Roxanne... Smith!"

As I peer up at the ceiling, I gargle on the blood bubbling in my windpipe. Death is more peaceful than I predicted. It isn't filled with gore and horror. It's quiet and surreal, somewhat warm, or is that the blood seeping into my clothes?

"I swear to God, Roxanne, if you don't fight, I'll tan your fucking ass. By the time I'm done with you, your ass will be bleeding more than a little bullet wound."

I shouldn't laugh, the pain it causes is horrific, but it can't be helped. Just like Estelle searches for humor in every situation, Dimitri seeks darkness.

As my breaths shiver in the coolness enveloping me, I reach out to touch Dimitri's face, startling when my briefest touch smears his cheek with blood. I must be bleeding a lot because my hands were nowhere near my stomach before I moved them.

"What the fuck were you doing here, Roxanne? You were meant to stay away. That's the only way I could guarantee your safety," Dimitri mutters as he pushes on my stomach so painfully, I cry out. "I've got to hurt you, baby. If I don't hurt you, you'll die. You don't want to die, do you? You're too fucking strong to die now... Roxanne... Roxie... Rox..."

Dimitri slaps me two times—hard. He isn't meaning to hurt me. He's merely doing everything in his power to force my head out of the black cloud it's sinking into. "Fuck, Smith, hurry. We're losing her."

The absolute pain in his voice almost drags me out of the dark. I fight with everything I have, but the pull is too strong. I'm sinking into the abyss faster than my woozy head can keep up with. I barely get 'I love you' out before the blackness swamping me takes over the reins. Still, I swear somewhere between my float from reality to a much darker realm, Dimitri responds, "As do I, Roxanne. As do I."

37

# DIMITRI

"How the fuck does a woman with a bullet wound get out of your city without you knowing about it?"

Henry doesn't get the chance to reply. My fist breaks through the drywall behind his head long before a syllable leaves his lips. I'm pissed, peeved as fuck, and since the person responsible for the anguish eating me alive isn't in my reign, I'm taking it out on the wrong person.

"She tried to kill my daughter and wife..." It feels like the final strand of the thread I'm clutching unravels when I force out, "I don't even know if she succeeded with Roxanne yet."

She's fighting—*my fucking God is she fighting*—but it's touch and go. The medics lost her twice during her transport to the hospital. If it weren't for Rocco and me holding our guns to their heads, they would have given up on her. They said she was clinically dead, that she was in cessation.

I didn't give a fuck what they called it, I wanted them to give her a chance to show she's stronger than her tiny frame and ageless face portrays. I wanted them to give her a chance to prove them wrong because if she can't do that, I'm dead too.

It was the jarring of *my* arm when I adjusted my fall to ensure Fien wouldn't get hurt that caused me to misfire. *My* bullet pierced through Roxanne's stomach, so if anyone is going to pay restitution for my error, it will be me.

Assuming my silence stems from believing he is incompetent, Henry says, "I have men combing every inch of my city looking for India. If she's still here, they'll find her."

The confidence in his comment should offer me some sort of comfort.

It doesn't.

Not in the slightest.

"What if she's already left?"

"Then we will find out where she's going and beat her there," Henry immediately fires back like he already considered the possibility our search for India will be longer than I'm hoping.

I rake my fingers through my hair, knowing it won't be as easy as it sounds, but hopeful I've been put through enough to ease Karma's nasty bite. India is smart, she has plenty of money at her disposal, and convincing-enough looks to make men disregard her hideous insides. She's a foreign version of Theresa.

"I have *all* my men on this, Dimi. The Albanians, the Italians, hell, even the Russians are looking for her. It might take longer than you're hoping, but we will find her... eventually." Henry squeezes my shoulder before stepping closer. His relaxed facial expression reveals why he was a good candidate for the boss of all bosses. He keeps politics out of the equation, and to him, it truly is family first of all.

He couldn't be more different than my father if he tried.

"But for now, your focus needs to be elsewhere."

When he motions his head to the flappy doors they wheeled

Roxanne through hours ago, I crank my neck back so fast, my muscles scream in protest. It's horrible for me to sigh in disappointment when my eyes lock with Audrey's across the room. The guilt is still horrendous, the angst won't quit, but I'd be a liar if I said I weren't praying for her to switch places with Roxanne.

*What the fuck is wrong with me?*

Audrey is the mother of my child, my wife, yet I still can't put her first.

*Because you don't love her,* screams a voice inside my head. *You never have, and you never will.*

Realizing what I need to do, I return my focus to Henry. I don't get one of the million words in my head out. He just squeezes my shoulder for the second time, wordlessly assures me he has everything under control, then leaves the Intensive Care Unit waiting room.

I'm not surprised when the number of people in the room remains the same after his departure. He has a reputation that doesn't require muscle. The fact he felt the need to bring backup to our impromptu meeting last week shouldn't make me smile, especially under the circumstances, but it does.

The boss of all bosses title isn't a handed-down legacy. It's earned through hard work and mutual respect—the very things my family's name was once founded on, and the very things I intend to return to it as soon as possible.

I just have to get a feisty redhead with gleaming green eyes out of the woods first because family comes first of all. Roxanne doesn't have the blood nor the Petretti title, but she has something more valuable than both those things.

She has my heart.

She stole it when she stood across from me with black, chunky smears rolling down her cheeks, earned it when she put her life on the line for a child she had never met, then secured it for life when she did it all again without the slightest bit of hesitation.

She went to the ends of the earth for me, and I'll do the same for her. She won't have to ask for a single thing. I will give her the world, and I might even occasionally smile while doing it.

I'm a cold, calculated killer, but Roxanne not only gives me purpose, she makes me want to be a better man. Since that will also make me a better father, I'm sure the weakening of my reputation will be worth the sacrifice.

I've faced worse things in my life, and look how well they've turned out for me.

# 38

# ROXANNE

It takes me a few seconds to work out where I am. I can feel the thud of Dimitri's pulse even with no part of his body whatsoever touching me, hear Rocco's laugh, smell the slightest hint of Estelle's perfume, and the annoying thump of Smith tapping away on a laptop matches the mariachi beat in my head.

The thought of him always working forces a smile onto my dry, blistering lips. Smith wouldn't be Smith without a laptop balancing on his hand, just like I wouldn't be me without Dimitri's dark, mysterious aura igniting my senses.

While blinking to lubricate my eyes, I attempt to sit a little straighter. I'm already in a half-seated position, but since a pillow is wedged between my bed and the mattress, I'm not comfortable. I'm actually more uncomfortable than sore.

I barely move my hand an inch when a warm one slips over it. "Stay still. You'll pull your stitches if you move too much."

*Stitches?*

The figure that moves to stand in front of me is hazy, but I know who he is. A million droplets of rain couldn't hide his eyes from me, so I doubt a healthy dose of sedatives could.

Perhaps that's why I feel so spaced out?

Maybe I'm drugged up on the good stuff Dimitri reserves for his 'special guests.'

After swishing my tongue around my mouth to loosen up my words, I ask, "Where am I? And exactly how much did I drink to get here?"

Rocco breaks the news since the concern on Dimitri, Smith, and Estelle's faces steal their ability to talk. "You're in the hospital. Dimitri shot you." His last two words come out with a groan, compliments of Dimitri's fist landing in his stomach.

Always willing to push the boundaries when it comes to Dimitri, Rocco laughs before asking, "Was I supposed to keep that a secret? My bad."

I half groan, half laugh, the humor in Rocco's voice too strong for the bland white walls and antiseptic smell surrounding me to discount. I've awoken in a room like this before. Thankfully, this time around, I'm not alone.

"It was for the best," Smith says, not only jumping into the conversation but between Dimitri and Rocco before they come to blows. "Your appendix was a mess. When it ruptured, the infection spread to your abdomen. The sepsis was severe. In a way, it was lucky Dimitri shot you. It forced your stubborn ass to the hospital and allowed the doctors to treat the infection before it became life-threatening."

He's joking, right?

He honestly doesn't want me to believe being shot saved my life.

Actually, come to think of it, it sounds about right. I'm nothing close to ordinary, so why wouldn't a bullet be my savior?

As memories of what had me admitted slowly roll into my

head, my heart dives down low. So deep, I feel its thuds in my toes when I ask, "Is Audrey okay?"

"She's alive," Dimitri answers calmly. "Thanks to you."

"Did she..." I don't want to finish my sentence. I've given Dimitri enough reasons to hate me. I don't want more added to the stack. My parents hurt his wife. They treated his daughter like scum, so I really don't want to tell him everything isn't as it seems.

Dimitri scoops up my hand in his in an almost-nurturing manner. *Almost.* He still has a little bit to go in regard to being gentle. I don't mind. I like him rough and ready. His dominance is one of his most alluring features. "She told me everything."

"*Everything?*" I shouldn't be interrogating him. I'm neither his wife nor the mother of his child, but I can't help myself. The connection between us has always been explosive, and even with me being laid up in a hospital bed, it is the most blistering it's ever been. It has me thinking I can do no wrong and more than willing to risk punishment just to see how far my newfound abilities extend.

My heart sinks even lower than my toes when Dimitri signals for us to be left alone. Rocco and Smith are his closest confidants, so for him to want privacy from them means this must be big. It honestly makes me feel ill, like more than my life is on the line right now.

Dimitri waits for Estelle to press her lips to my temple and join the boys outside before he says way too casually, "Audrey told me everything. How India forced her to come to Hopeton to gather semen samples. The surrogacy. India's last-minute change of heart when she held on longer than expected after Fien's birth, and how you tried to save her even knowing she could one day be your competition." His gaze clings to my face as the slightest smirk curves his lips. "She even told me how India tried to kill her when she confessed to pouring a mixture of tomato soup, baby oil, and corn starch over your nightgown when you passed out so Maestro would believe you had miscarried."

What is he saying?

I don't understand what he means.

Dimitri doesn't laugh, joke, or glower at the shocked mask slipped over my face. He merely clears it away with the quickest brush of his fingers. It's a callous yet gentle touch that makes my heart rate soar as much as his murmured comment, "You didn't miscarry, Roxanne."

If he's about to say I didn't miscarry because I was never pregnant, he can stop right now. I saw our baby, clear as day, directly in front of me. I'm not skilled at pregnancy, and I've never trained to be a sonographer, but I know what I saw. Deep down in my heart, I know that the little black blob on the screen was our baby.

It looked almost identical to the jellybean on the strip of images Dimitri dangles in front of me. "Does this look familiar?"

I clamp my hand over my mouth to hold back my sob before nodding. "Is that..."

I can't talk through the frantic throbbing of my pulse. It's thumping out a crazy tune, stunned by the date and name on the ultrasound images in Dimitri's hand. If the date on Smith's watch is anything to go by, my scan was yesterday. Nine days after I was freed from the hell that killed our baby, and four days after learning Fien's true paternity.

It takes me a couple of seconds to talk, but when I do, my voice is so full of hope, I may very well die if I don't hear the answer I want. "Is that *our* baby?"

There's no chance in hell I can hold back my sob when Dimitri smirks, then nods. His response is almost too surreal, too calm, too fucking outrageous ever to believe it's true.

How is he not freaking out?

Why isn't he fuming mad?

I trapped him exactly how India tried and failed. Shouldn't that make him angry?

I take a mental note to have Smith scan me for mindreading devices when Dimitri mutters, "You can't snare a man in the trap he set, Roxanne." There's no trace of emotion in his voice when he says, "You can congratulate him on his victory, then hope like hell your stroke of his ego gives you a couple of months of freedom before he traps you again." He bites on my lower lip, slides his tongue across his teeth marks to soothe the sting, then presses his curved mouth to my ear. "The future belongs to those unscared to make it theirs. My future is with you, Roxanne, and whether you agree or not, yours is with me."

His comment should fill me with dread. It should make me panicked. I'm in love with a mass murderer who'd rather slay me than see me with any man who isn't him, but that isn't close to what I am feeling.

He killed my boyfriend, tortured my parents, and has threatened to kill me more than once, but I love him, and at the end of the day, that's all that matters.

# DIMITRI

## Four Months Later...

A tap sounds at my office door before Roxanne's head pops through the gap. "Hey, Smith said you wanted to see me."

I gesture for her to enter, loving that even walking past dozens of women paid to cater to our 'guests' every whim hasn't dampened the sparkle in her eyes I re-lit when I told her our baby had survived both the carnage of her captivity and his mother being shot in the stomach without the slightest scratch. She knows whores are a part of this industry, but she also accepts that I have no interest in them.

The latter is responsible for her blasé response.

No fear.

Even with my son growing in her stomach, and my daughter on her hip, Roxanne doesn't hesitate to put the women who step over the line she deems unacceptable into place.

If you touch what is hers, expect to pay for your stupidity with your life.

Same goes for me.

I won't just kill you, though. Your entire family will be extinct. Your father, your brothers, hell, I'll even kill your second cousin if you do my family wrong because family comes first of all.

If you don't believe me, ask Maestro's family. You'll have to find them first. Trust me when I say that won't be easy. The Italian Cartel doesn't leave bodies because corpses can talk. Take the toddler in the wall at the Shroud family ranch as an example.

Is Megan related to me? Unfortunately, yes. Is she my sister? Hell-to-the-fucking-no. Our connection is a consequence of the fucked-up world my father raised me in. Babies, made-to-order wives, underage whores, if you could make money from it, my family dabbled in it in some way.

That's all done and dusted now. My father is dead, killed in a way too deserving for him, but without a single ounce of remorse felt. Most people believed he died in a joint FBI/Ravenshoe PD operation, only I know that isn't the case.

I'm not a fan of dark, hidden crevices until it conjures up a way to take down the man responsible for my family's utmost turmoil.

Fathers are supposed to protect their children.

They're supposed to save them from harm.

My father did no such thing.

If he had the chance to profit from it, he ran for it, but shacking up the only surviving member of his family with a vindictive bitch who couldn't give her husband's actual royal lineage an heir was a new low for him. Mafia blood is royal, it has been around for centuries, but it isn't something you auction off to the highest bidder without expecting to pay for your stupidity with your life.

I hate what Smith unearthed about the agreement between India and my father after Agent Brandon James left his briefcase unattended within days of my crews' return to Hopeton. It made a mockery out of my family name even more than it was already facing, but it gave me plenty of motivation to kill my father without fear of punishment. Rules not even someone as high as my father could break were shattered, leaving me no other option but to re-invent the game.

The Petretti name still isn't what it once was, but it's getting stronger every day.

Smith makes it stronger.

Rocco makes it stronger.

And having it attached to Roxanne's name completely blows it out of the fucking water.

Yeah, you heard me right. Roxanne isn't just knocked up with my kid, all five-foot-four inches of her is also my wife. Audrey was more than happy to sign divorce papers without a claim to the child most people still believe is hers or my fortune. She was so grateful her life was spared for the part she played in India's ruse to forge an unbreakable unity of our family bloodlines, she would have signed anything I placed in front of her.

Do I still wish she were dead? Yes, for the most part. The only reason I didn't siphon the blood from her veins was because Roxanne asked me not to. She wanted her alive, and although Audrey technically hurt me before Roxanne, so the decision was out of Roxanne's hands, if it weren't for Audrey suddenly growing a conscience, Maestro would have killed my son. He may have even killed my now-wife.

That alone saw me offering leniency I don't usually give.

That alone also saw Audrey shipped back to her country of origin with the promise if she ever steps foot in my country again, all mercies will be null and void. She will be dead—as will India when I find her.

She's still hiding. I can't say I don't understand her objective.

Her death won't be quick like my father's and Rimi's. I'll torture her for hours on end, perhaps even days. I would have said months if that wouldn't force me away from my family for longer than necessary.

Despite no one knowing of their existence, Roxanne and Fien haven't left my sight for a second over the past four months. Whether on a computer monitor, via my phone, or in the flesh, I have eyes on them no matter where they are. I'm not ashamed of my overprotectiveness. If anything, it makes me proud. My girls will want for nothing, and my son will be raised completely different than I was. He won't just be a contender for the boss of all bosses when he's my age, he will be *the* boss, point blank, and I'll guide his steps the entire way.

As will his mother.

Roxanne isn't scared of this lifestyle. She fucking loves it. Not as much as she does me, but I didn't lie when I said she doesn't want to be a lady any more than she wants me to be a gentleman. I killed her boyfriend, tortured her parents, yet she still takes my dick between her lips with a ghost-like smile on her mouth every single time without fail.

The same smile is curling her lips now. It makes the transfer of her ass from my extended crotch to my desk a real fucking hard feat. It's only done without anarchy because the high rise of her skirt awards me the slightest peek of her scant panties and the treasure they're hiding.

Alice spoiled Roxanne when she entered my realm with nothing but the clothes on her back and a hideous dressing gown tossed over her arm. Now she spoils her with remorse as well.

Alice is alive, breathing, and has sworn multiple times the past four months that Lucy will eventually forgive me. Fien is helping bring her around, so I'm sure it won't be too much longer until she reverts to calling me 'Uncle' again.

As the light in Roxanne's eyes shifts from sated to ravenous, she parts her thighs. Not wide enough for me to get my head between them, but wide enough to reveal she knows the reason she's been seconded to my office. Her fearlessness nearly killed her, but it's one of the things I love about her the most.

That doesn't mean I'll let her off easy, though.

"What was our agreement, Roxanne?"

I don't free my hardened cock from my trousers and stroke it to weaken the fire burning in her eyes. I do it for the exact opposite reason. I love her spark, her charisma, her spunk that is so fucking potent, a bullet couldn't dampen it. Just knowing I can unleash it with only a few strokes has me stroking my cock a little faster.

I run my thumb down the vein feeding the monster dick the alteration of light in my wife's eyes always causes before sliding it over the tip, collecting the bead of precum pooling there.

When Roxanne shudders, I realize I have her right where I need her. "What was our agreement, Roxanne?" I ask this question more sternly than I did the first time, strangled through both the brutal clutch I have on my cock and the grip Roxanne has had on my balls since the day I saw her with black smudges under her eyes and chunky, wedged boots on her feet.

With her teeth gnawing on her bottom lip, Roxanne slowly raises her eyes from my cock, rocking in and out of my fist to my face. Her eyes are fucking fascinating. They have cum racing from my sack to the crest of my cock like my pleasure can come before hers.

That will never happen, but I fucking love that she can convince my cock otherwise.

I lessen the severity of my pumps when Roxanne purrs out, "That I'm to do as you ask, when you ask, for *exactly* how long you ask."

Her last five words come out with a quiver when I grip the

back of her neck with my spare hand so I can drag her delectable lips to within an inch of mine. As predicted, they taste like candy. They're the sweetest thing I've ever sampled. I crave them *almost* as often as I crave her cunt. "And what did you do tonight?"

"I did as you asked." Her minty fresh breath mingles with the whiskey bounding from mine when she murmurs, "I read our daughter a bedtime story..." I'm not surprised she calls Fien 'ours.' She is ours. Has been since Roxanne put her life on the line to free her from captivity, will be until the day we say our final farewell. "Then raked my fingers through her hair until she fell asleep in her big girl bed, then I came downstairs for an alcohol-free nightcap with some friends."

"Friends, eh? Who *exactly* were these friends?"

I know her answer.

I don't like her fucking answer.

And once I've shown her exactly how displeased I am that she took a detour on the way to my office tonight with my cock, I'll teach Rocco the same lesson with my fists.

I'm still pissed about how cozy he and Roxanne got four months ago. He shouldn't test my patience. I've killed men just for looking at Roxanne in the wrong manner, and I'll do it again because family comes first of all, and to me, Roxanne is the very definition of the word.

No fear.

---

**The end...**

The next explosive part of the Italian Cartel Series is Mafia Ties (Novella).

If you want to hear updates on the next books in this crazy world I've created, be sure to follow my social media pages:

Facebook: facebook.com/authorshandi

Instagram: instagram.com/authorshandi

Email: authorshandi@gmail.com

Reader's Group: bit.ly/ShandiBookBabes

Website: authorshandi.com

Newsletter: https://www.subscribepage.com/AuthorShandi

Rico, Asher, Isaac, Brandon, Ryan, Cormack, Enrique & Brax stories have already been released, but Grayson, Rocco, Clover, and all the other great characters of Ravenshoe/Hopeton will be getting their own stories at some point during 2021.

*If you enjoyed this book please leave a review.*

# ALSO BY SHANDI BOYES

### Perception Series

Saving Noah (Noah & Emily)

Fighting Jacob (Jacob & Lola)

Taming Nick (Nick & Jenni)

Redeeming Slater (Slater and Kylie)

Saving Emily (Noah & Emily - Novella)

Wrapped Up with Rise Up (Perception Novella - should be read after the Bound Series)

### Enigma

Enigma (Isaac & Isabelle #1)

Unraveling an Enigma (Isaac & Isabelle #2)

Enigma The Mystery Unmasked (Isaac & Isabelle #3)

Enigma: The Final Chapter (Isaac & Isabelle #4)

Beneath The Secrets (Hugo & Ava #1)

Beneath The Sheets(Hugo & Ava #2)

Spy Thy Neighbor (Hunter & Paige) **Standalone**

The Opposite Effect (Brax & Clara) **Standalone**

I Married a Mob Boss(Rico & Blaire) **Standalone**

Second Shot(Hawke & Gemma) **Standalone**

The Way We Are(Ryan & Savannah #1)

The Way We Were(Ryan & Savannah #2)

Sugar and Spice (Cormack & Harlow) **Standalone**

Lady In Waiting (Regan & Alex #1)

Man in Queue (Regan & Alex #2)

Couple on Hold(Regan & Alex #3)

Enigma: The Wedding (Isaac and Isabelle)

Silent Vigilante (Brandon and Melody #1)

Hushed Guardian (Brandon & Melody #2)

Quiet Protector (Brandon & Melody #3)

**Bound Series**

Chains (Marcus & Cleo #1)

Links(Marcus & Cleo #2)

Bound(Marcus & Cleo #3)

Restrain(Marcus & Cleo #4)

Psycho (Dexter & ??)

**Russian Mob Chronicles**

Nikolai: A Mafia Prince Romance (Nikolai & Justine #1)

Nikolai: Taking Back What's Mine (Nikolai & Justine #2)

Nikolai: What's Left of Me(Nikolai & Justine #3)

Nikolai: Mine to Protect(Nikolai & Justine #4)

Asher: My Russian Revenge (Asher & Zariah)

Nikolai: Through the Devil's Eyes(Nikolai & Justine #5)

Trey (Trey & K)

K: A Trey Sequel

## The Italian Cartel

Dimitri

Roxanne

Reign

Mafia Ties (Novella)

Maddox

Demi

Ox

Rocco

Clover

Smith

CJ

## RomCom Standalones

Just Playin' (Elvis & Willow)

Ain't Happenin' (Lorenzo & Skylar)

The Drop Zone (Colby & Jamie)

Very Unlikely (Brand New Couple)

## Short Stories

Christmas Trio (Wesley, Andrew & Mallory -- short story)

Falling For A Stranger (Short Story)

## Coming Soon

Skitzo

Made in the USA
Middletown, DE
29 April 2022

65005778R00433